Archie's
BiG
Book

VOLUME 6: HIGH SCHOOL YEARBOOK

Publisher / Co-CEO: Jon Goldwater

Co-President / Editor-In-Chief: Victor Gorelick

Co-President: Mike Pellerito

Co-President: Alex Segura

Chief Creative Officer: Roberto Aguirre-Sacasa

Chief Operating Officer: William Mooar

Chief Financial Officer: Robert Wintle

Director of Book Sales & Operations: Jonathan Betancourt

Production Manager: Stephen Oswald

Art Director: Vincent Lovallo

Lead Designer: Kari McLachlan

Associate Editor: Carlos Antunes

Editor: Jamie Lee Rotante

Co-CEO: Nancy Silberkleit

Published by Archie Comic Publications, Inc. 629 Fifth Avenue, Suite 100, Pelham, NY 10803-1242

ISBN: 978-1-68255-853-9

WRITTEN BY

Batton Lash, Alex Simmons, George Gladir,
Mike Pellowski & Scott Cunningham

ART BY

Bill Galvan, Dan Parent, Tim Kennedy, Rex Lindsey, Stan Goldberg,
Bob Smith, Rich Koslowski, Rudy Lapick, Ken Selig, Jon D'Agostino,
John Lowe, Jack Morelli, Bill Yoshida, Vickie Williams,
Glenn Whitmore, Barry Grossman & Digikore Studios

COVER ART BY Bill Galvan, Rex Lindsey & Rosario "Tito" Peña

Archie's BiG

TABLE OF CONTENTS

CHAPTER ONE   FRESHMAN YEAR

CHAPTER TWO   CLASH OF THE NEW KIDS

CHAPTER THREE   MORE HIGH SHOOL HIJINKS

Archie's BiG

INTRODUCTION

Archie Andrews and his pals 'n' gals have been teens for over 75 years—that's a whole lot of high school hijinks! This collection will take a look at a few key moments from their tenure at Riverdale High, even exploring their humble beginnings at their long-standing educational institution!

First, Archie and his friends have forever been stuck in the latter portion of high school, but now the story of how the gang all met up is told!

See the beginning of the eternal love triangle, the introduction of Mr. Weatherbee as principal of Riverdale High, the formation of Moose and Midge's relationship (and Reggie's subsequent schemes to split them up) and other Archie staples.

Then, meet the new kids! When the doors of a nearby high school shutter, Riverdale High is teeming with new students and faculty—but how will Archie and the gang react to this influx of new faces and, more importantly, new personalities?

In addition to that, enjoy some more miscellaneous fun in the hallowed halls of Riverdale High and get a glimpse into the lives of its faculty and staff.

Turn the page to begin your lesson—and don't be late for class!

CHAPTER ONE

Freshman Year

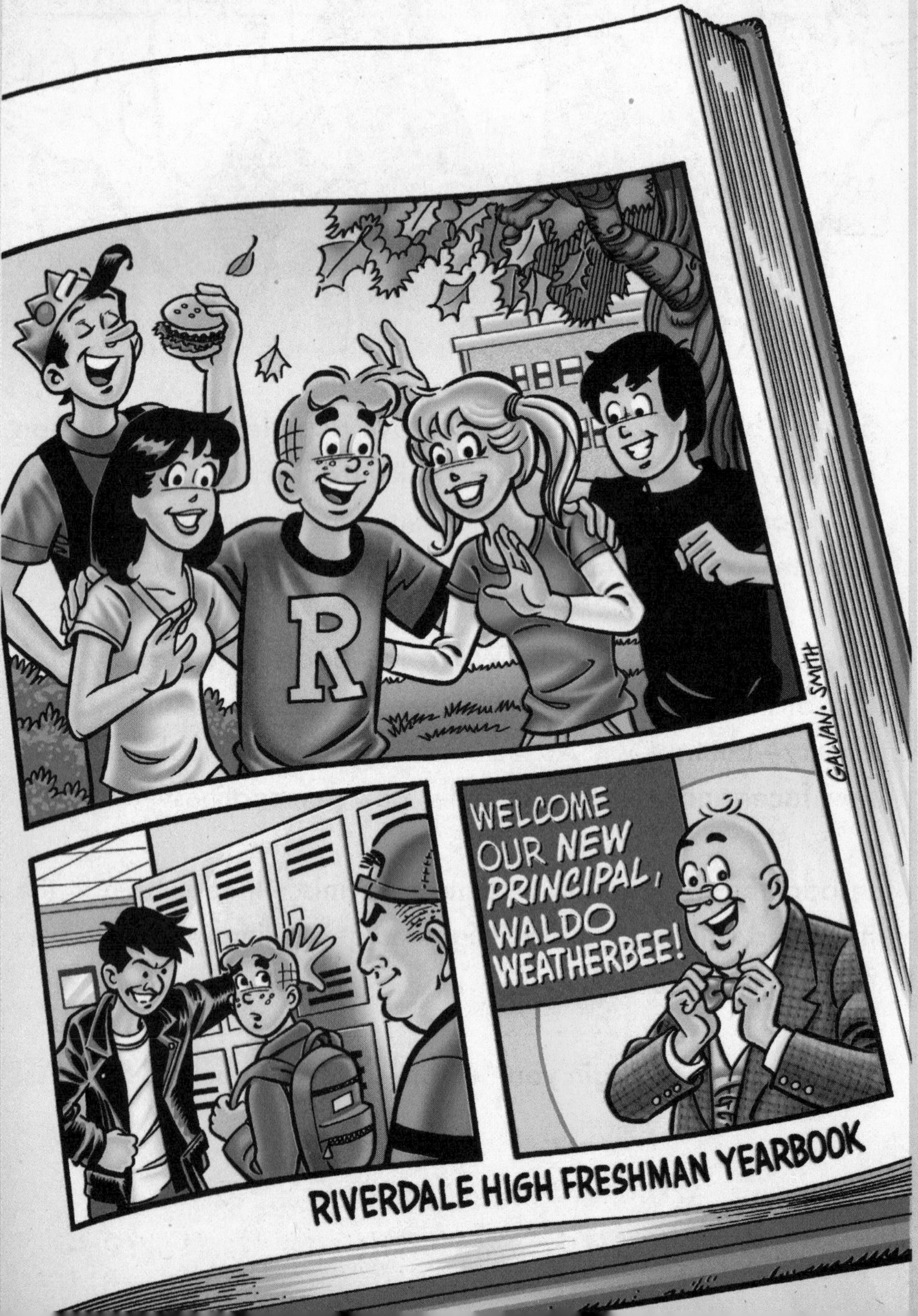
GALVAN · SMITH
WELCOME OUR NEW PRINCIPAL, WALDO WEATHERBEE!
RIVERDALE HIGH FRESHMAN YEARBOOK

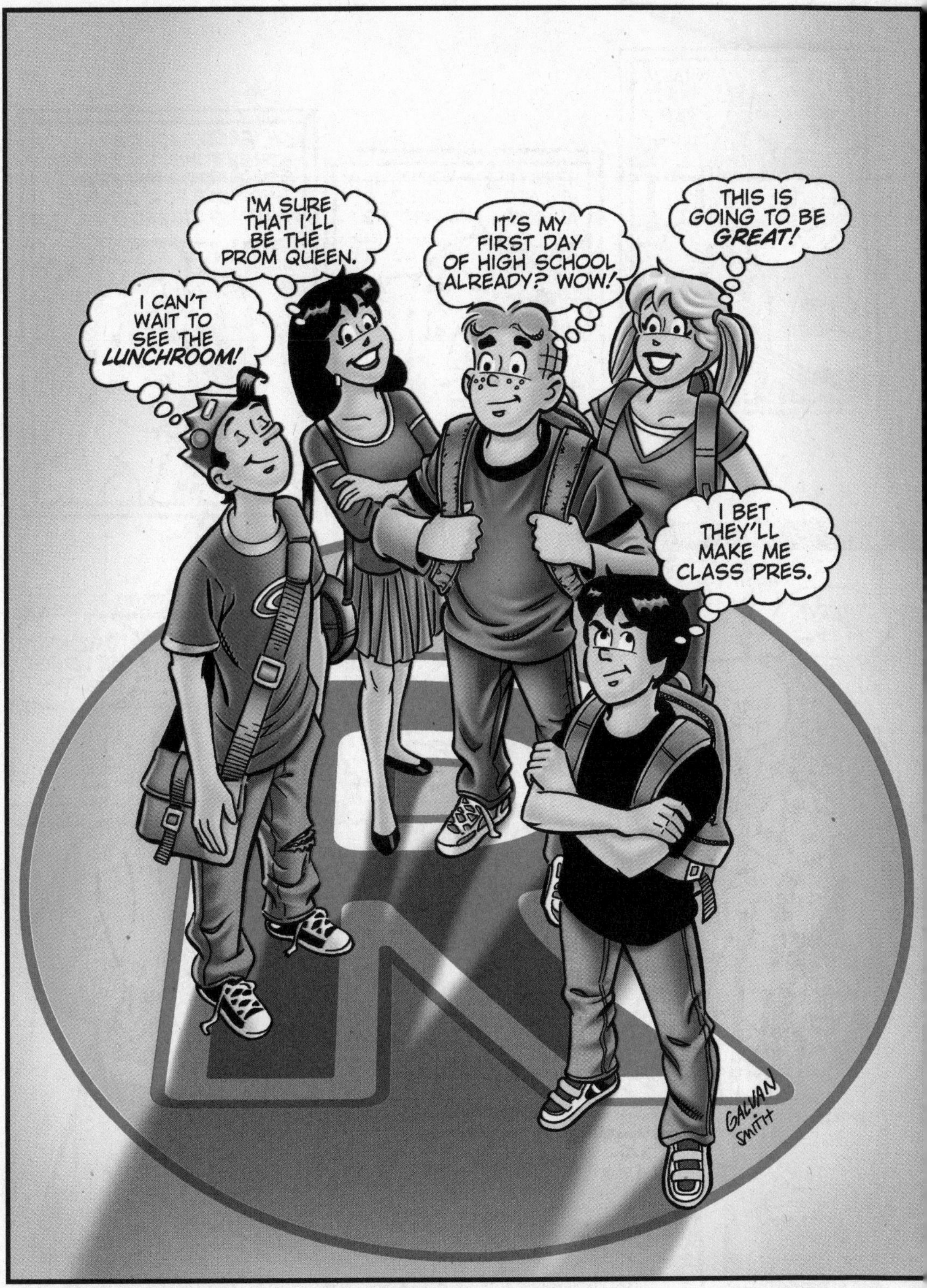
I CAN'T WAIT TO SEE THE LUNCHROOM!
I'M SURE THAT I'LL BE THE PROM QUEEN.
IT'S MY FIRST DAY OF HIGH SCHOOL ALREADY? WOW!
THIS IS GOING TO BE GREAT!
I BET THEY'LL MAKE ME CLASS PRES.
GALVAN SMITH

FRESHMAN YEAR PART 1

SCRIPT: BATTON LASH   PENCILS: BILL GALVAN

INKS: BOB SMITH   LETTERS: JACK MORELLI   COLORS: GLENN WHITMORE

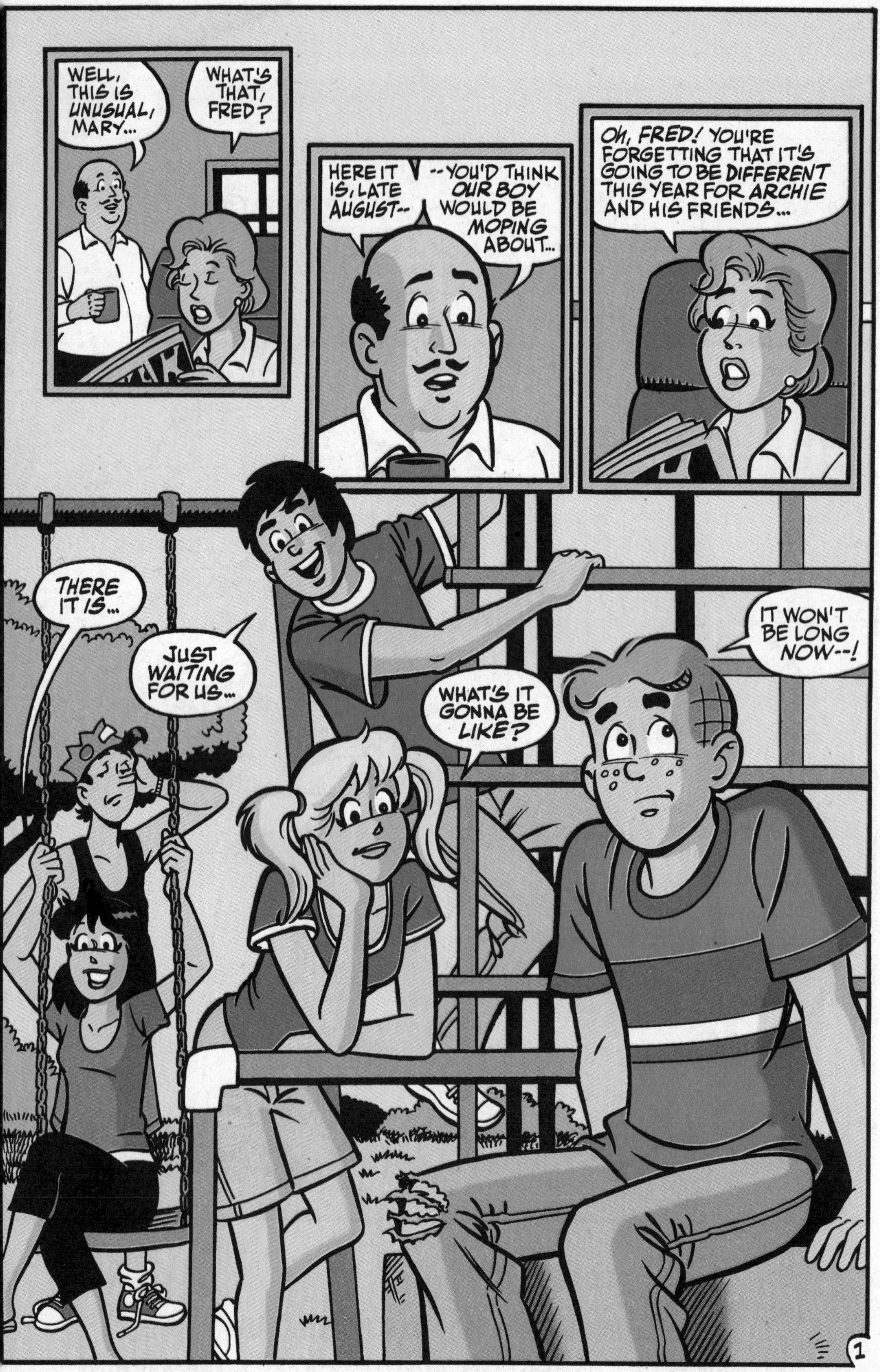

WELL, THIS IS UNUSUAL, MARY...
WHAT'S THAT, FRED?
HERE IT IS, LATE AUGUST--
--YOU'D THINK OUR BOY WOULD BE MOPING ABOUT...
Oh, FRED! YOU'RE FORGETTING THAT IT'S GOING TO BE DIFFERENT THIS YEAR FOR ARCHIE AND HIS FRIENDS...
THERE IT IS...
JUST WAITING FOR US...
WHAT'S IT GONNA BE LIKE?
IT WON'T BE LONG NOW--!
1

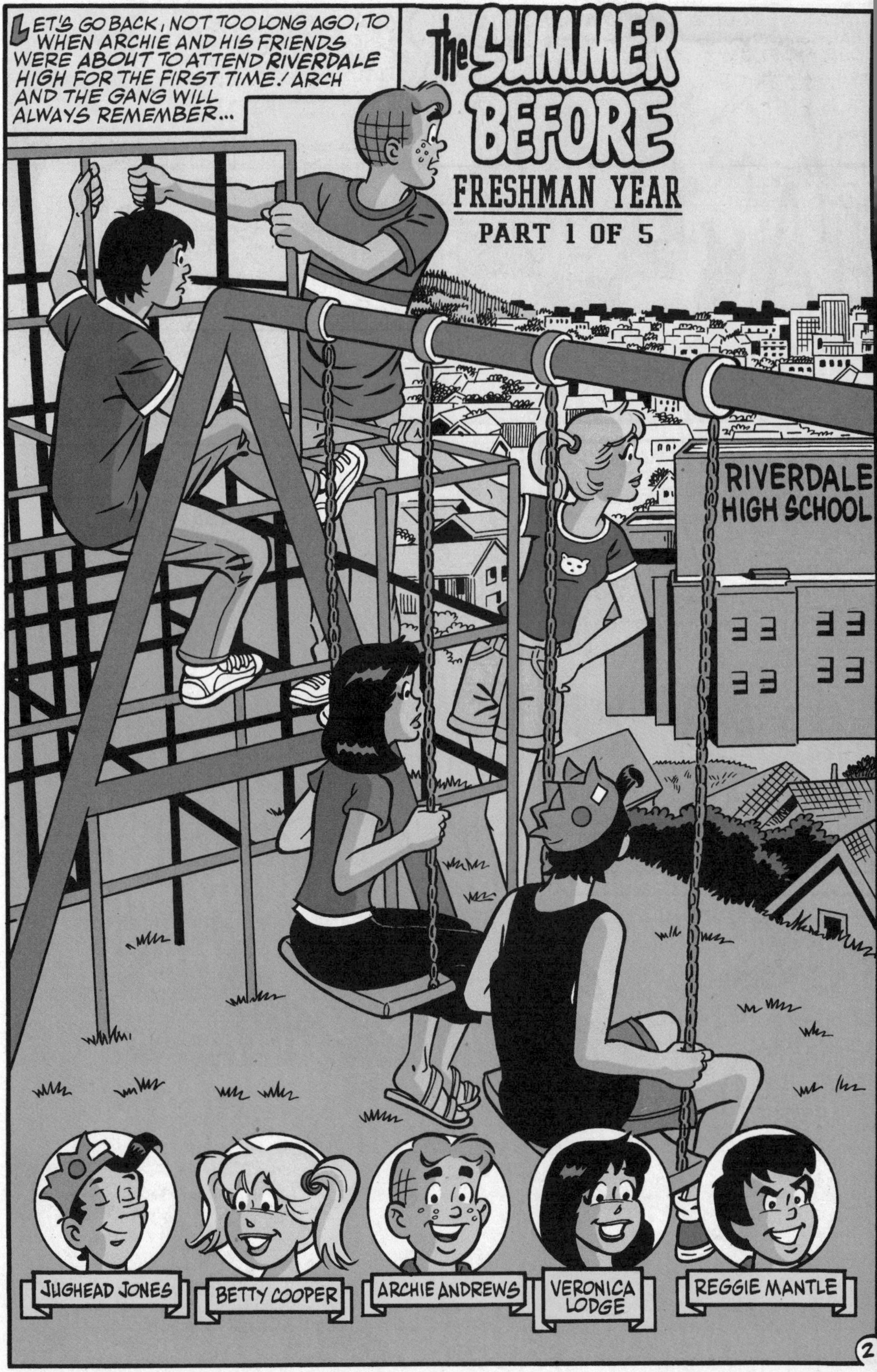
LET'S GO BACK, NOT TOO LONG AGO, TO WHEN ARCHIE AND HIS FRIENDS WERE ABOUT TO ATTEND RIVERDALE HIGH FOR THE FIRST TIME! ARCH AND THE GANG WILL ALWAYS REMEMBER...
The SUMMER BEFORE
FRESHMAN YEAR
PART 1 OF 5
RIVERDALE HIGH SCHOOL
JUGHEAD JONES
BETTY COOPER
ARCHIE ANDREWS
VERONICA LODGE
REGGIE MANTLE
2

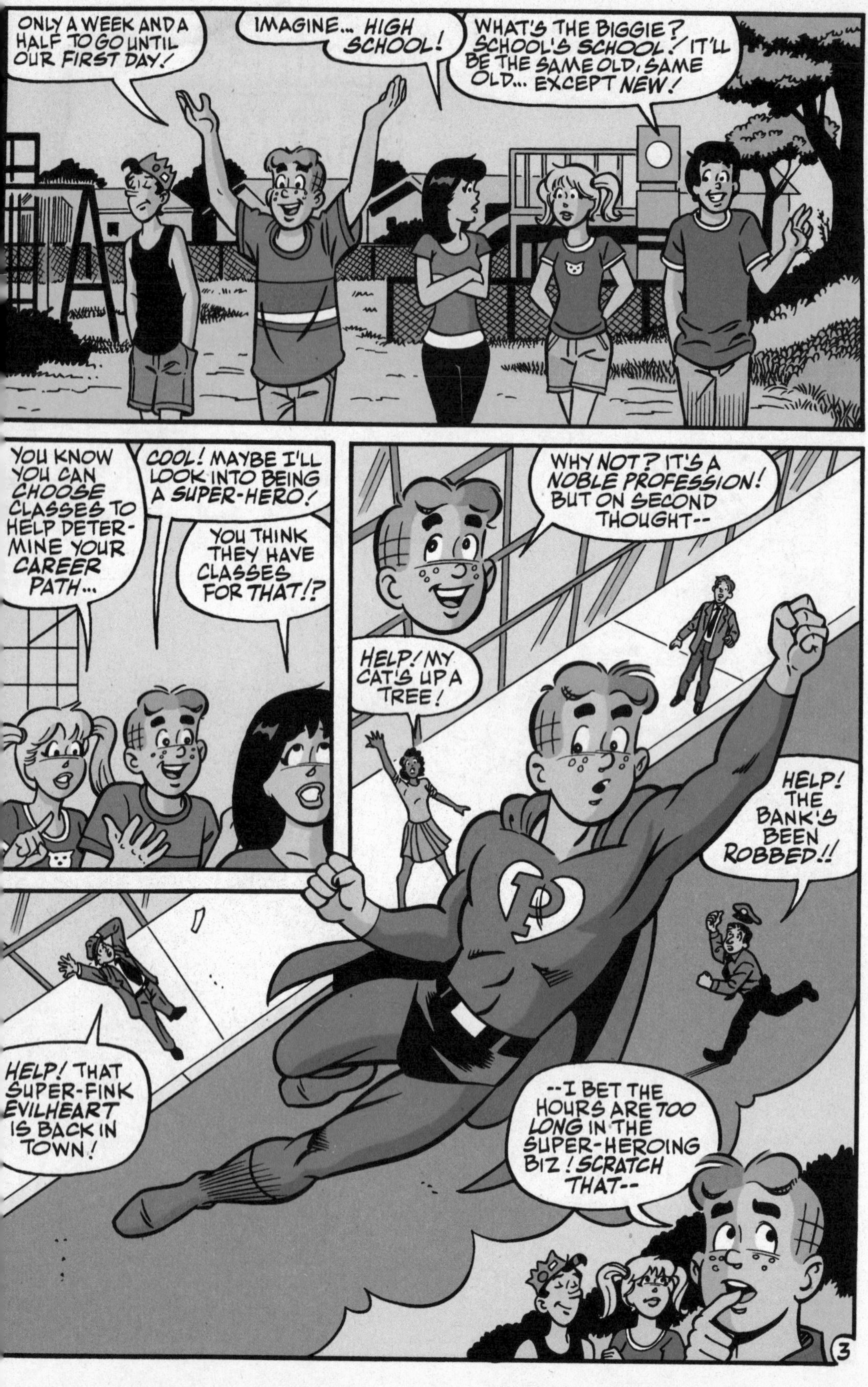

ONLY A WEEK AND A HALF TO GO UNTIL OUR FIRST DAY!
IMAGINE... HIGH SCHOOL!
WHAT'S THE BIGGIE? SCHOOL'S SCHOOL! IT'LL BE THE SAME OLD, SAME OLD... EXCEPT NEW!
YOU KNOW YOU CAN CHOOSE CLASSES TO HELP DETERMINE YOUR CAREER PATH...
COOL! MAYBE I'LL LOOK INTO BEING A SUPER-HERO!
YOU THINK THEY HAVE CLASSES FOR THAT!?
WHY NOT? IT'S A NOBLE PROFESSION! BUT ON SECOND THOUGHT--
HELP! MY CAT'S UP A TREE!
HELP! THE BANK'S BEEN ROBBED!!
HELP! THAT SUPER-FINK EVILHEART IS BACK IN TOWN!
--I BET THE HOURS ARE TOO LONG IN THE SUPER-HEROING BIZ! SCRATCH THAT--

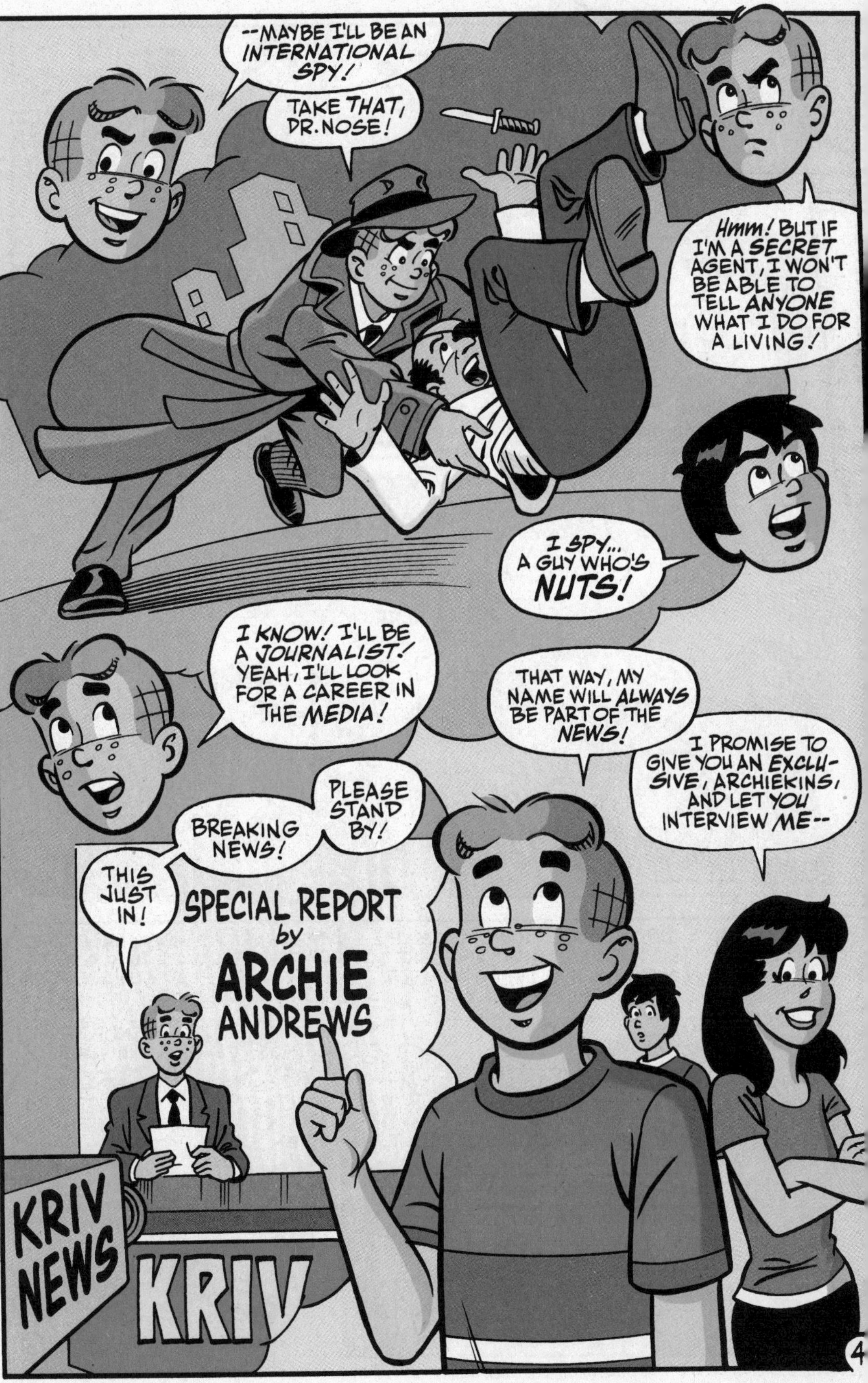
--MAYBE I'LL BE AN INTERNATIONAL SPY!
TAKE THAT, DR. NOSE!
Hmm! BUT IF I'M A SECRET AGENT, I WON'T BE ABLE TO TELL ANYONE WHAT I DO FOR A LIVING!
I SPY... A GUY WHO'S NUTS!
I KNOW! I'LL BE A JOURNALIST! YEAH, I'LL LOOK FOR A CAREER IN THE MEDIA!
THAT WAY, MY NAME WILL ALWAYS BE PART OF THE NEWS!
I PROMISE TO GIVE YOU AN EXCLU-SIVE, ARCHIEKINS, AND LET YOU INTERVIEW ME--
PLEASE STAND BY!
BREAKING NEWS!
THIS JUST IN!
SPECIAL REPORT by ARCHIE ANDREWS
KRIV NEWS
KRIV

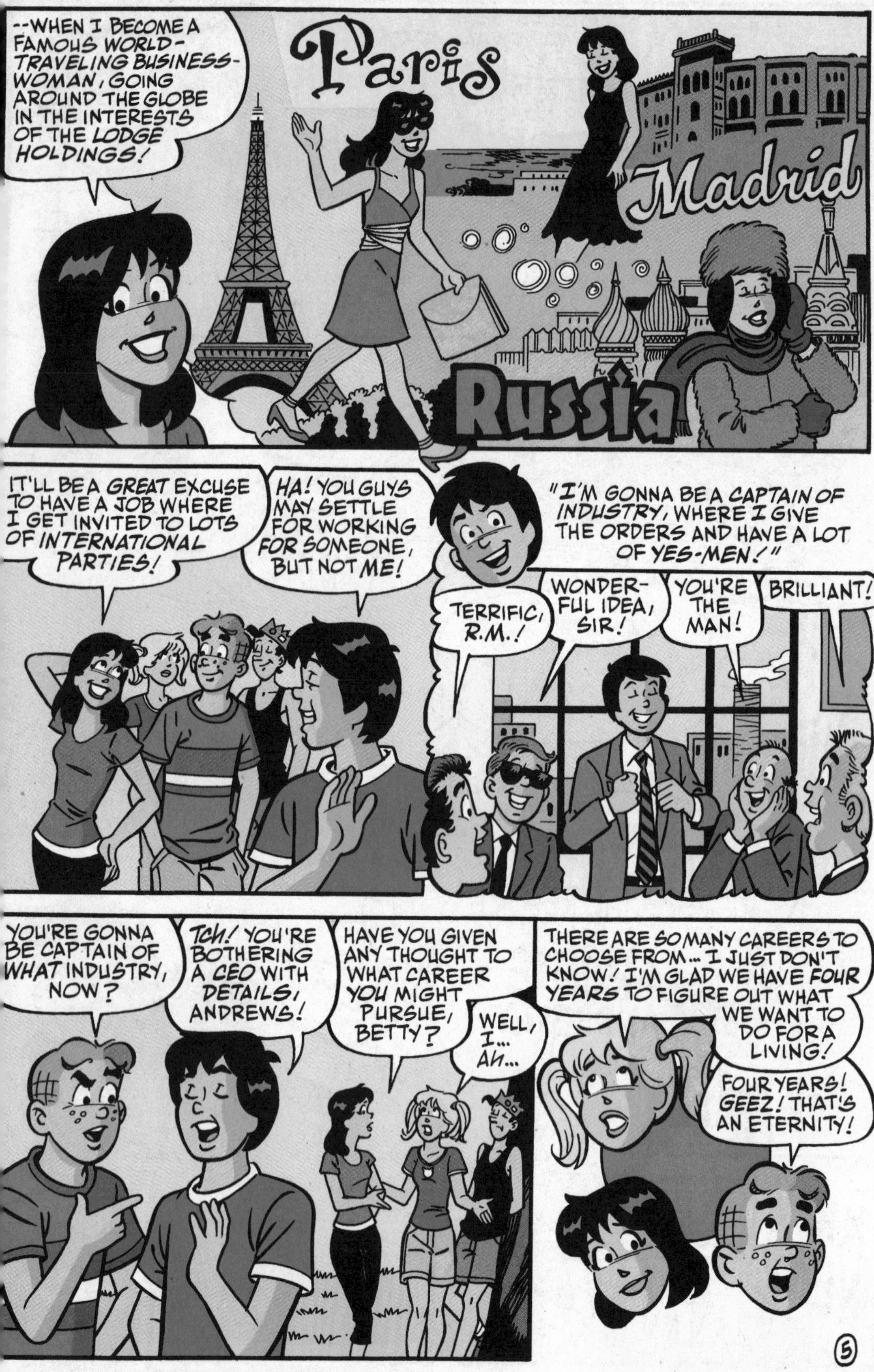
--WHEN I BECOME A FAMOUS WORLD-TRAVELING BUSINESS-WOMAN, GOING AROUND THE GLOBE IN THE INTERESTS OF THE LODGE HOLDINGS!
Paris
Madrid
Russia
IT'LL BE A GREAT EXCUSE TO HAVE A JOB WHERE I GET INVITED TO LOTS OF INTERNATIONAL PARTIES!
HA! YOU GUYS MAY SETTLE FOR WORKING FOR SOMEONE, BUT NOT ME!
"I'M GONNA BE A CAPTAIN OF INDUSTRY, WHERE I GIVE THE ORDERS AND HAVE A LOT OF YES-MEN!"
TERRIFIC, R.M.!
WONDER-FUL IDEA, SIR!
YOU'RE THE MAN!
BRILLIANT!
YOU'RE GONNA BE CAPTAIN OF WHAT INDUSTRY, NOW?
TCH! YOU'RE BOTHERING A CEO WITH DETAILS, ANDREWS!
HAVE YOU GIVEN ANY THOUGHT TO WHAT CAREER YOU MIGHT PURSUE, BETTY?
WELL, I... AH...
THERE ARE SO MANY CAREERS TO CHOOSE FROM... I JUST DON'T KNOW! I'M GLAD WE HAVE FOUR YEARS TO FIGURE OUT WHAT WE WANT TO DO FOR A LIVING!
FOUR YEARS! GEEZ! THAT'S AN ETERNITY!

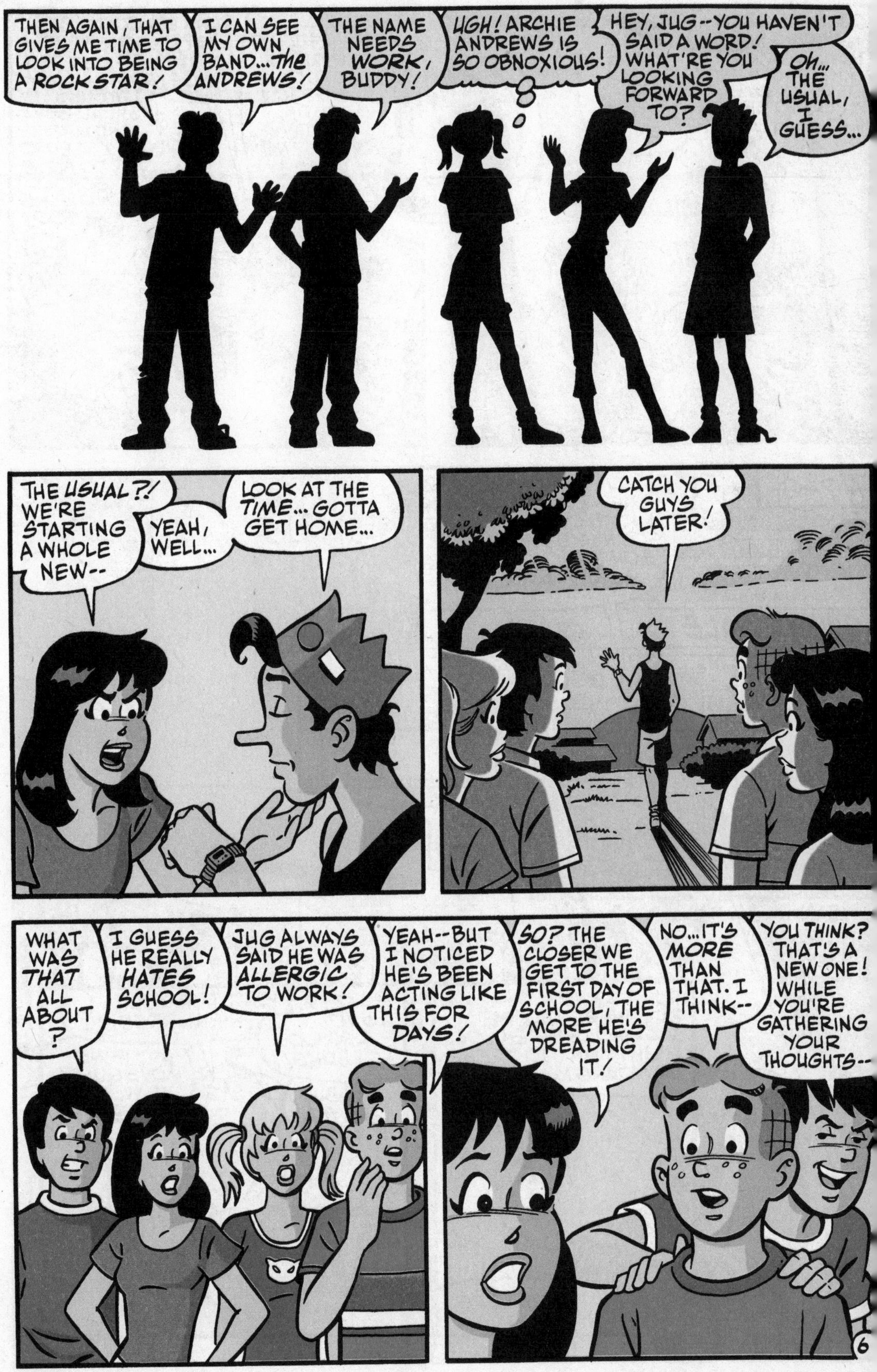
THEN AGAIN, THAT GIVES ME TIME TO LOOK INTO BEING A ROCK STAR!
I CAN SEE MY OWN BAND... The ANDREWS!
THE NAME NEEDS WORK, BUDDY!
UGH! ARCHIE ANDREWS IS SO OBNOXIOUS!
HEY, JUG--YOU HAVEN'T SAID A WORD! WHAT'RE YOU LOOKING FORWARD TO?
Oh... THE USUAL, I GUESS...
THE USUAL?! WE'RE STARTING A WHOLE NEW--
YEAH, WELL...
LOOK AT THE TIME... GOTTA GET HOME...
CATCH YOU GUYS LATER!
WHAT WAS THAT ALL ABOUT?
I GUESS HE REALLY HATES SCHOOL!
JUG ALWAYS SAID HE WAS ALLERGIC TO WORK!
YEAH--BUT I NOTICED HE'S BEEN ACTING LIKE THIS FOR DAYS!
SO? THE CLOSER WE GET TO THE FIRST DAY OF SCHOOL, THE MORE HE'S DREADING IT!
NO... IT'S MORE THAN THAT. I THINK--
YOU THINK? THAT'S A NEW ONE! WHILE YOU'RE GATHERING YOUR THOUGHTS--

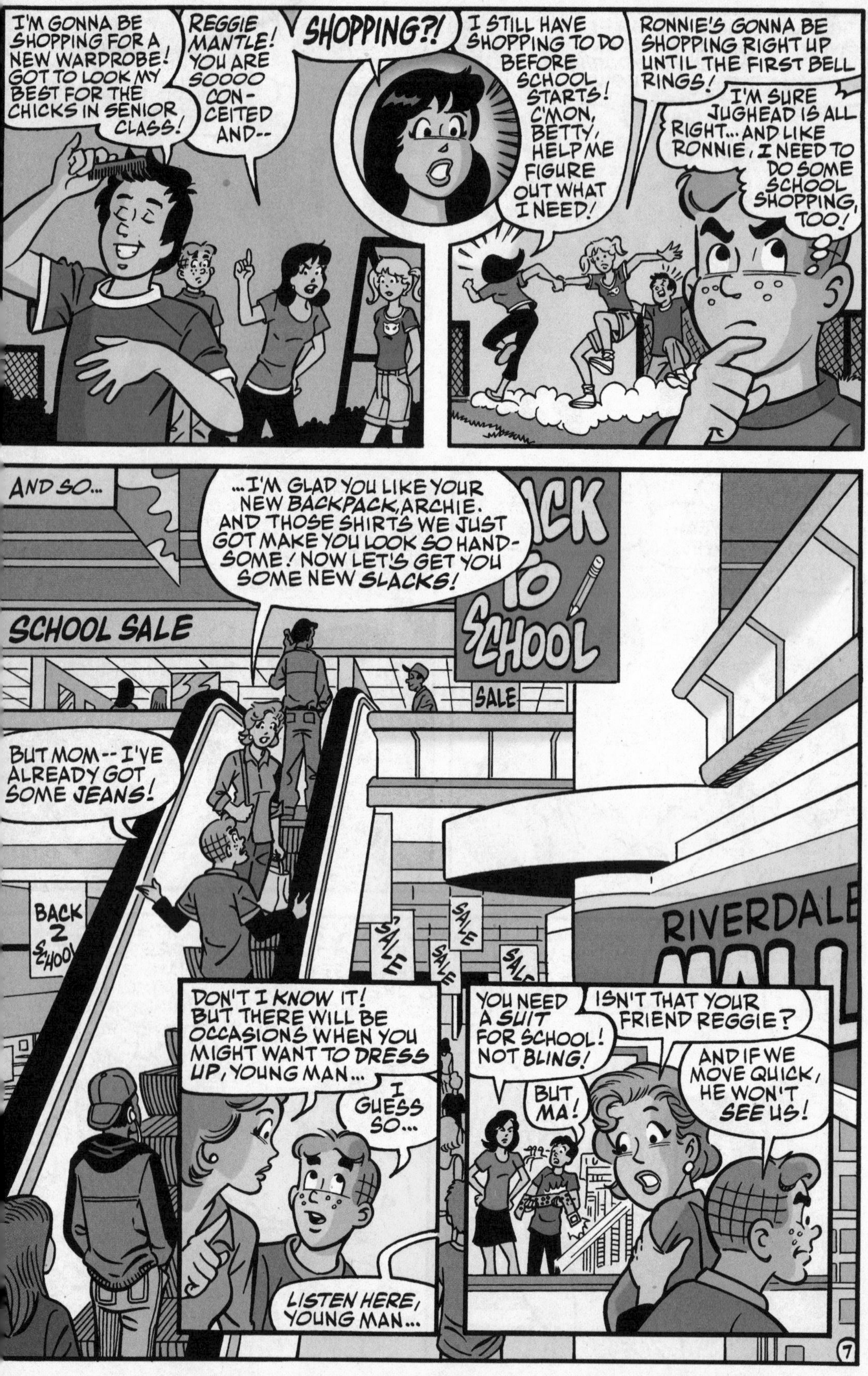
I'M GONNA BE SHOPPING FOR A NEW WARDROBE! GOT TO LOOK MY BEST FOR THE CHICKS IN SENIOR CLASS!
REGGIE MANTLE! YOU ARE SOOOO CON-CEITED AND--
SHOPPING?!
I STILL HAVE SHOPPING TO DO BEFORE SCHOOL STARTS! C'MON, BETTY, HELP ME FIGURE OUT WHAT I NEED!
RONNIE'S GONNA BE SHOPPING RIGHT UP UNTIL THE FIRST BELL RINGS!
I'M SURE JUGHEAD IS ALL RIGHT... AND LIKE RONNIE, I NEED TO DO SOME SCHOOL SHOPPING, TOO!
AND SO...
...I'M GLAD YOU LIKE YOUR NEW BACKPACK, ARCHIE. AND THOSE SHIRTS WE JUST GOT MAKE YOU LOOK SO HAND-SOME! NOW LET'S GET YOU SOME NEW SLACKS!
SCHOOL SALE
ACK TO SCHOOL
SALE
BUT MOM -- I'VE ALREADY GOT SOME JEANS!
BACK 2 SCHOOL
SALE
SALE
SALE
SALE
RIVERDALE
DON'T I KNOW IT! BUT THERE WILL BE OCCASIONS WHEN YOU MIGHT WANT TO DRESS UP, YOUNG MAN...
I GUESS SO...
LISTEN HERE, YOUNG MAN...
YOU NEED A SUIT FOR SCHOOL! NOT BLING!
BUT MA!
ISN'T THAT YOUR FRIEND REGGIE?
AND IF WE MOVE QUICK, HE WON'T SEE US!
7

SOON...

...NOW THAT WE'VE GOT SNEAKERS, LET'S GO TO THE STATIONERY STORE-- THEY'RE HAVING A SALE ON *NOTEBOOK PAPER!*

YEAH, CAN'T HAVE ENOUGH NOTEBOOK PAPER! *WHEW--!* SCHOOL HASN'T EVEN STARTED YET AND I'M ALREADY *EXHAUSTED!*

SORRY! THE STORE'S CLOSED FOR NOW!

BUT I SEE SOMEONE SHOPPING IN THERE!

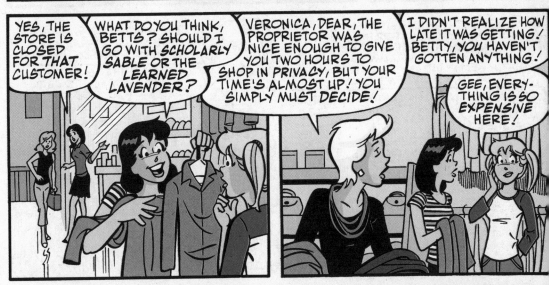

YES, THE STORE IS CLOSED FOR *THAT* CUSTOMER!

WHAT DO YOU THINK, *BETTS?* SHOULD I GO WITH *SCHOLARLY SABLE* OR THE *LEARNED LAVENDER?*

VERONICA, DEAR, THE PROPRIETOR WAS NICE ENOUGH TO GIVE YOU TWO HOURS TO SHOP IN PRIVACY, BUT YOUR TIME'S ALMOST UP! YOU SIMPLY MUST *DECIDE!*

I DIDN'T REALIZE HOW LATE IT WAS GETTING! BETTY, *YOU* HAVEN'T GOTTEN ANYTHING!

GEE, EVERY-THING IS SO EXPENSIVE HERE!

OH, DON'T WORRY! I'LL *CHARGE* IT! MOTHER SAID IT'S OKAY TO *TREAT* MY BEST FRIEND!

THANKS JUST THE SAME, RONNIE... BUT IT'S GETTING *LATE--!*

I HAVE TO MEET UP WITH MY MOM! SEE YOU LATER! 'BYE, MRS. LODGE!

SO LONG, BETTY!

RONNIE, DEAR, WHAT ABOUT *THIS* TOP? IT'S THE ONLY ONE LEFT IN *VALEDICTORIAN VIOLET!*

8

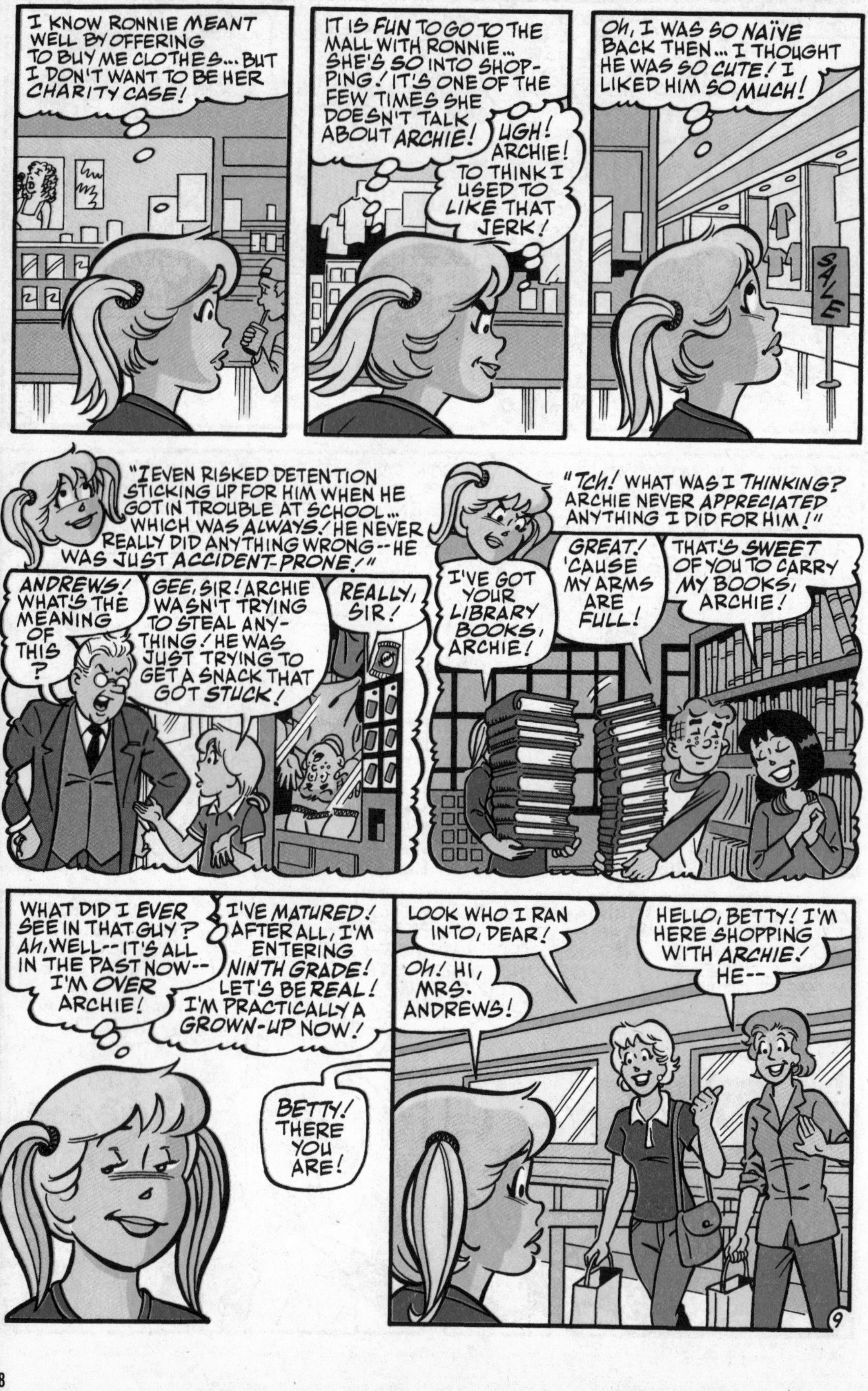
I KNOW RONNIE MEANT WELL BY OFFERING TO BUY ME CLOTHES... BUT I DON'T WANT TO BE HER CHARITY CASE!
IT IS FUN TO GO TO THE MALL WITH RONNIE... SHE'S SO INTO SHOPPING! IT'S ONE OF THE FEW TIMES SHE DOESN'T TALK ABOUT ARCHIE!
UGH! ARCHIE! TO THINK I USED TO LIKE THAT JERK!
OH, I WAS SO NAÏVE BACK THEN... I THOUGHT HE WAS SO CUTE! I LIKED HIM SO MUCH!
SALE
"I EVEN RISKED DETENTION STICKING UP FOR HIM WHEN HE GOT IN TROUBLE AT SCHOOL... WHICH WAS ALWAYS! HE NEVER REALLY DID ANYTHING WRONG -- HE WAS JUST ACCIDENT-PRONE!"
ANDREWS! WHAT'S THE MEANING OF THIS?
GEE, SIR! ARCHIE WASN'T TRYING TO STEAL ANYTHING! HE WAS JUST TRYING TO GET A SNACK THAT GOT STUCK!
REALLY, SIR!
"TCH! WHAT WAS I THINKING? ARCHIE NEVER APPRECIATED ANYTHING I DID FOR HIM!"
I'VE GOT YOUR LIBRARY BOOKS, ARCHIE!
GREAT! 'CAUSE MY ARMS ARE FULL!
THAT'S SWEET OF YOU TO CARRY MY BOOKS, ARCHIE!
WHAT DID I EVER SEE IN THAT GUY? AH, WELL-- IT'S ALL IN THE PAST NOW-- I'M OVER ARCHIE!
I'VE MATURED! AFTER ALL, I'M ENTERING NINTH GRADE! LET'S BE REAL! I'M PRACTICALLY A GROWN-UP NOW!
BETTY! THERE YOU ARE!
LOOK WHO I RAN INTO, DEAR!
OH! HI, MRS. ANDREWS!
HELLO, BETTY! I'M HERE SHOPPING WITH ARCHIE! HE--
9

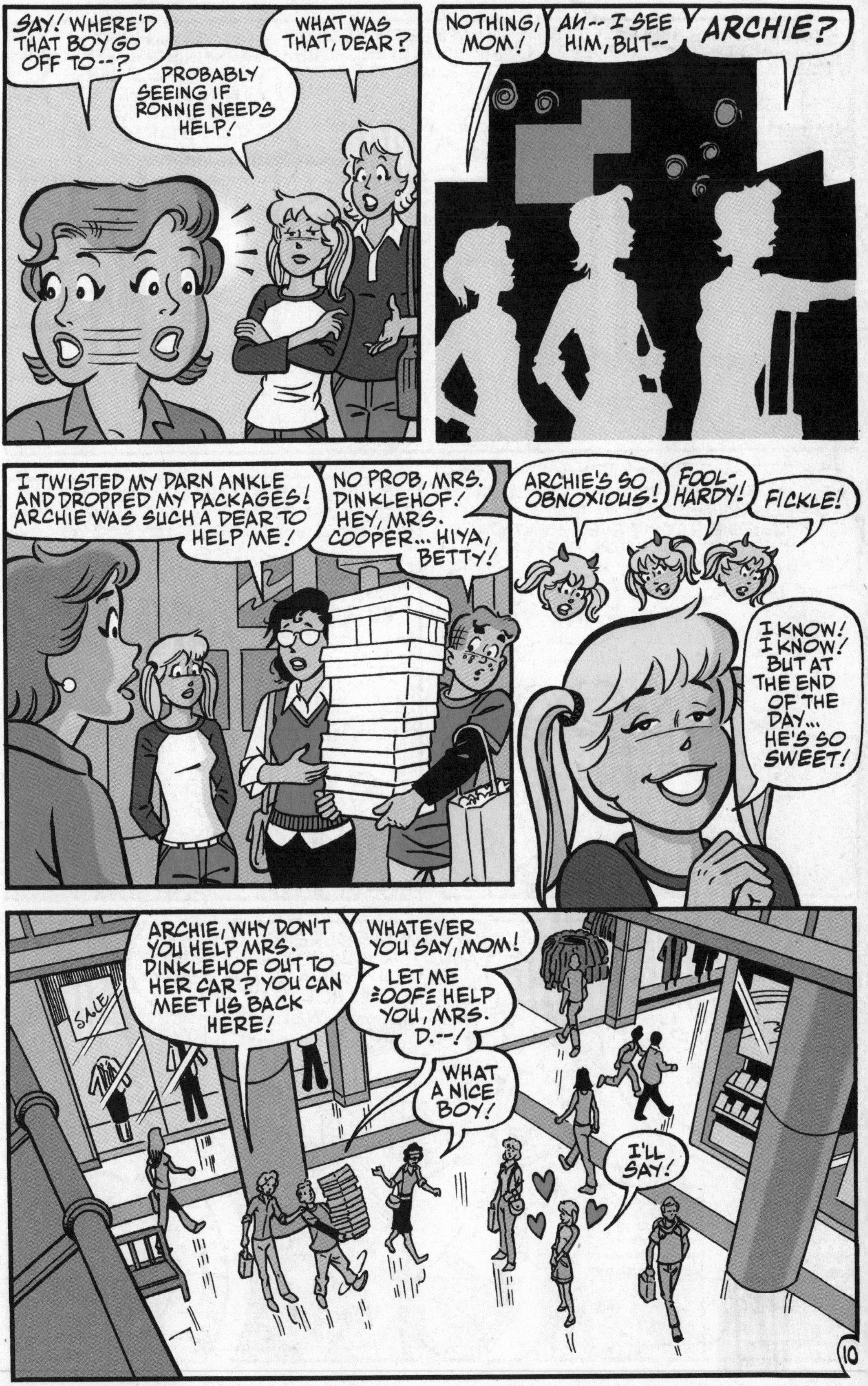
SAY! WHERE'D THAT BOY GO OFF TO--?
PROBABLY SEEING IF RONNIE NEEDS HELP!
WHAT WAS THAT, DEAR?
NOTHING, MOM!
AH-- I SEE HIM, BUT--
ARCHIE?
I TWISTED MY DARN ANKLE AND DROPPED MY PACKAGES! ARCHIE WAS SUCH A DEAR TO HELP ME!
NO PROB, MRS. DINKLEHOF! HEY, MRS. COOPER... HIYA, BETTY!
ARCHIE'S SO OBNOXIOUS!
FOOL-HARDY!
FICKLE!
I KNOW! I KNOW! BUT AT THE END OF THE DAY... HE'S SO SWEET!
ARCHIE, WHY DON'T YOU HELP MRS. DINKLEHOF OUT TO HER CAR? YOU CAN MEET US BACK HERE!
WHATEVER YOU SAY, MOM!
LET ME OOF HELP YOU, MRS. D.--!
WHAT A NICE BOY!
I'LL SAY!
SALE
10

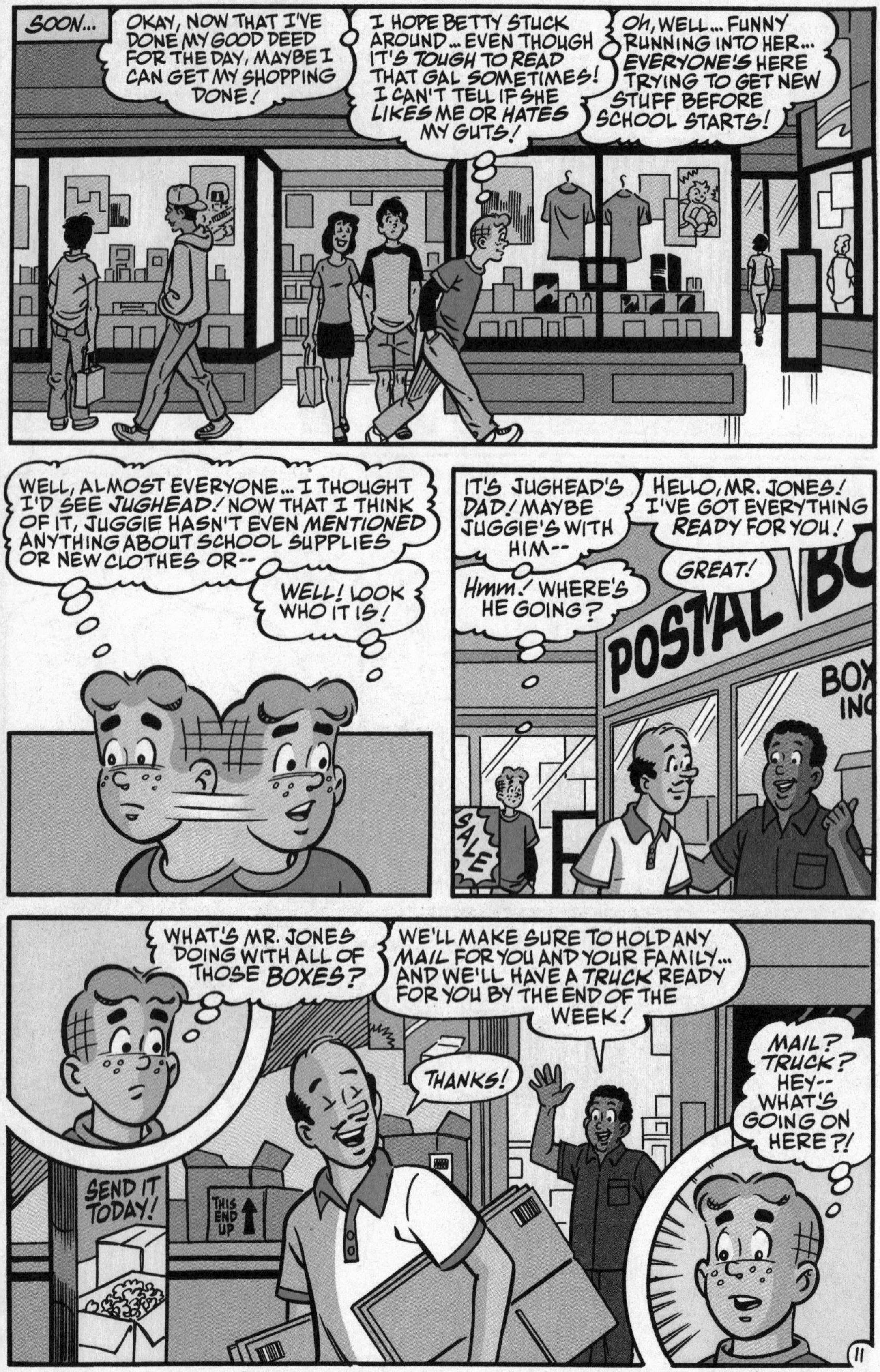
SOON...
OKAY, NOW THAT I'VE DONE MY GOOD DEED FOR THE DAY, MAYBE I CAN GET MY SHOPPING DONE!
I HOPE BETTY STUCK AROUND... EVEN THOUGH IT'S TOUGH TO READ THAT GAL SOMETIMES! I CAN'T TELL IF SHE LIKES ME OR HATES MY GUTS!
Oh, WELL... FUNNY RUNNING INTO HER... EVERYONE'S HERE TRYING TO GET NEW STUFF BEFORE SCHOOL STARTS!
WELL, ALMOST EVERYONE... I THOUGHT I'D SEE JUGHEAD! NOW THAT I THINK OF IT, JUGGIE HASN'T EVEN MENTIONED ANYTHING ABOUT SCHOOL SUPPLIES OR NEW CLOTHES OR--
WELL! LOOK WHO IT IS!
IT'S JUGHEAD'S DAD! MAYBE JUGGIE'S WITH HIM--
HELLO, MR. JONES! I'VE GOT EVERYTHING READY FOR YOU!
GREAT!
Hmm! WHERE'S HE GOING?
POSTAL BO
BOX INC
SALE
WHAT'S MR. JONES DOING WITH ALL OF THOSE BOXES?
WE'LL MAKE SURE TO HOLD ANY MAIL FOR YOU AND YOUR FAMILY... AND WE'LL HAVE A TRUCK READY FOR YOU BY THE END OF THE WEEK!
THANKS!
MAIL? TRUCK? HEY-- WHAT'S GOING ON HERE?!
SEND IT TODAY!
THIS END UP
11

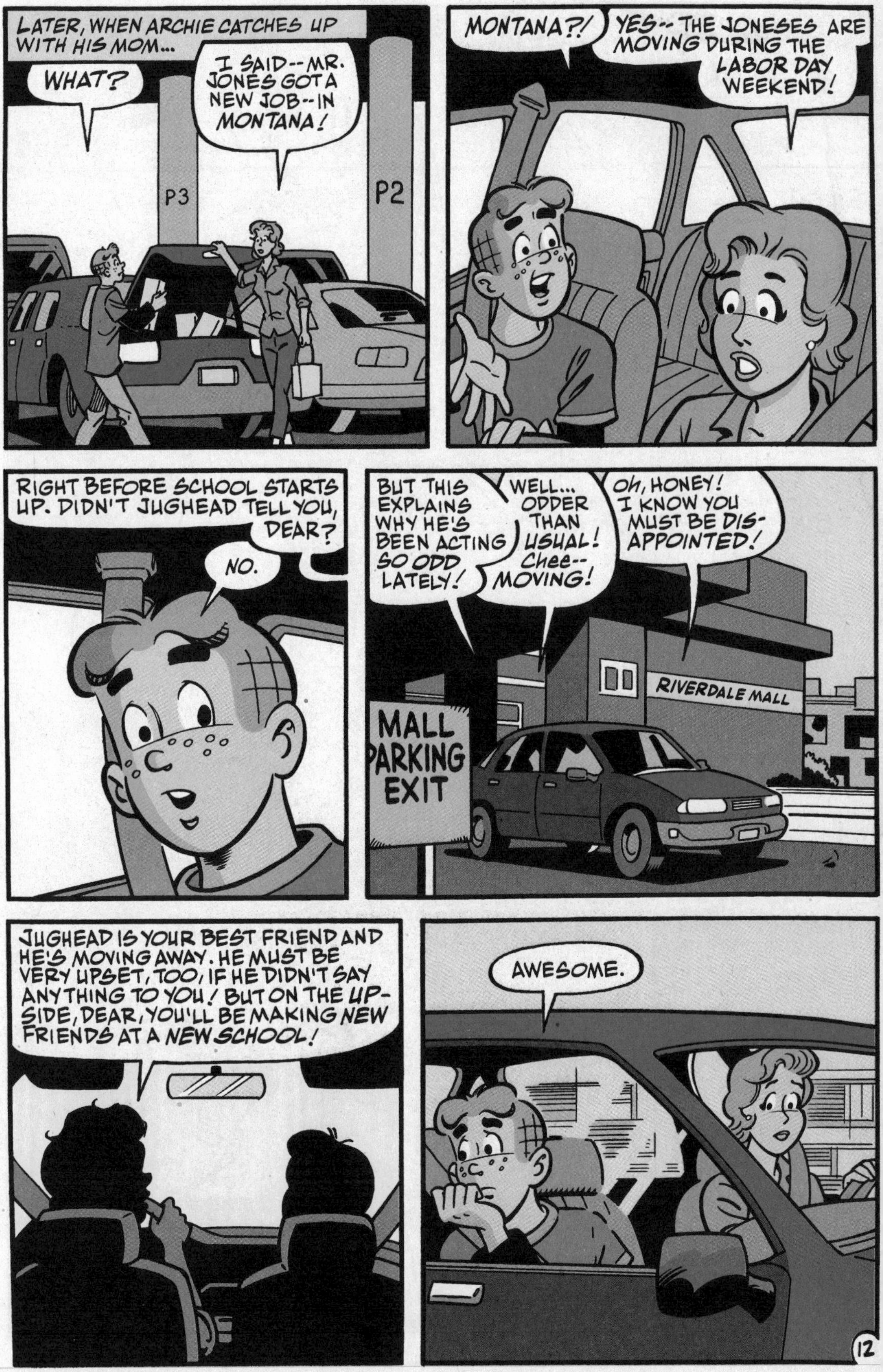
LATER, WHEN ARCHIE CATCHES UP WITH HIS MOM...
WHAT?
I SAID--MR. JONES GOT A NEW JOB--IN MONTANA!
P3
P2
MONTANA?!
YES-- THE JONESES ARE MOVING DURING THE LABOR DAY WEEKEND!
RIGHT BEFORE SCHOOL STARTS UP. DIDN'T JUGHEAD TELL YOU, DEAR?
NO.
BUT THIS EXPLAINS WHY HE'S BEEN ACTING SO ODD LATELY!
WELL... ODDER THAN USUAL! Chee-- MOVING!
Oh, HONEY! I KNOW YOU MUST BE DISAPPOINTED!
RIVERDALE MALL
MALL PARKING EXIT
JUGHEAD IS YOUR BEST FRIEND AND HE'S MOVING AWAY. HE MUST BE VERY UPSET, TOO, IF HE DIDN'T SAY ANYTHING TO YOU! BUT ON THE UPSIDE, DEAR, YOU'LL BE MAKING NEW FRIENDS AT A NEW SCHOOL!
AWESOME.
12

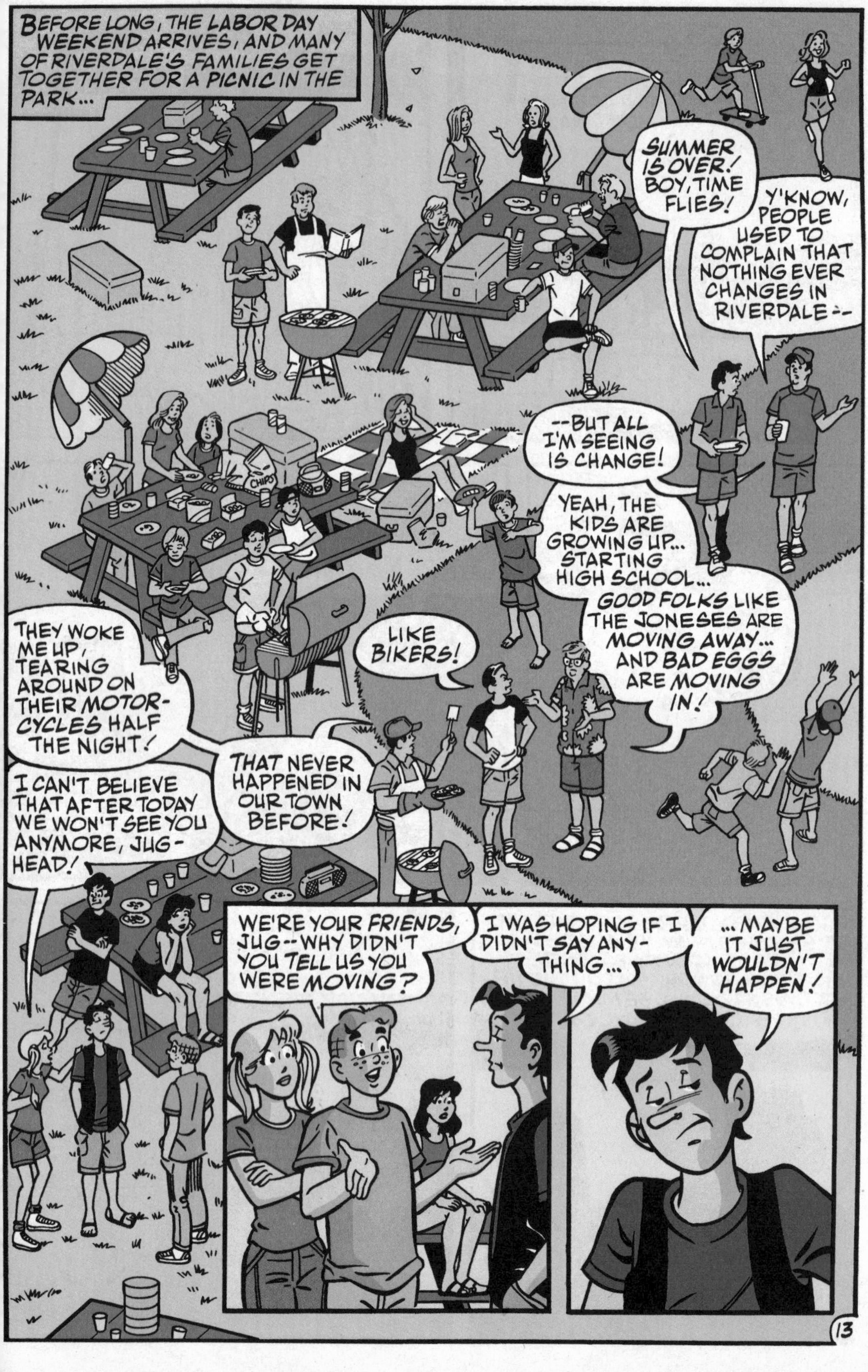
BEFORE LONG, THE LABOR DAY WEEKEND ARRIVES, AND MANY OF RIVERDALE'S FAMILIES GET TOGETHER FOR A PICNIC IN THE PARK...
SUMMER IS OVER! BOY, TIME FLIES!
Y'KNOW, PEOPLE USED TO COMPLAIN THAT NOTHING EVER CHANGES IN RIVERDALE--
--BUT ALL I'M SEEING IS CHANGE!
CHIPS
YEAH, THE KIDS ARE GROWING UP... STARTING HIGH SCHOOL...
GOOD FOLKS LIKE THE JONESES ARE MOVING AWAY... AND BAD EGGS ARE MOVING IN!
LIKE BIKERS!
THEY WOKE ME UP, TEARING AROUND ON THEIR MOTORCYCLES HALF THE NIGHT!
THAT NEVER HAPPENED IN OUR TOWN BEFORE!
I CAN'T BELIEVE THAT AFTER TODAY WE WON'T SEE YOU ANYMORE, JUGHEAD!
WE'RE YOUR FRIENDS, JUG--WHY DIDN'T YOU TELL US YOU WERE MOVING?
I WAS HOPING IF I DIDN'T SAY ANYTHING...
...MAYBE IT JUST WOULDN'T HAPPEN!
13

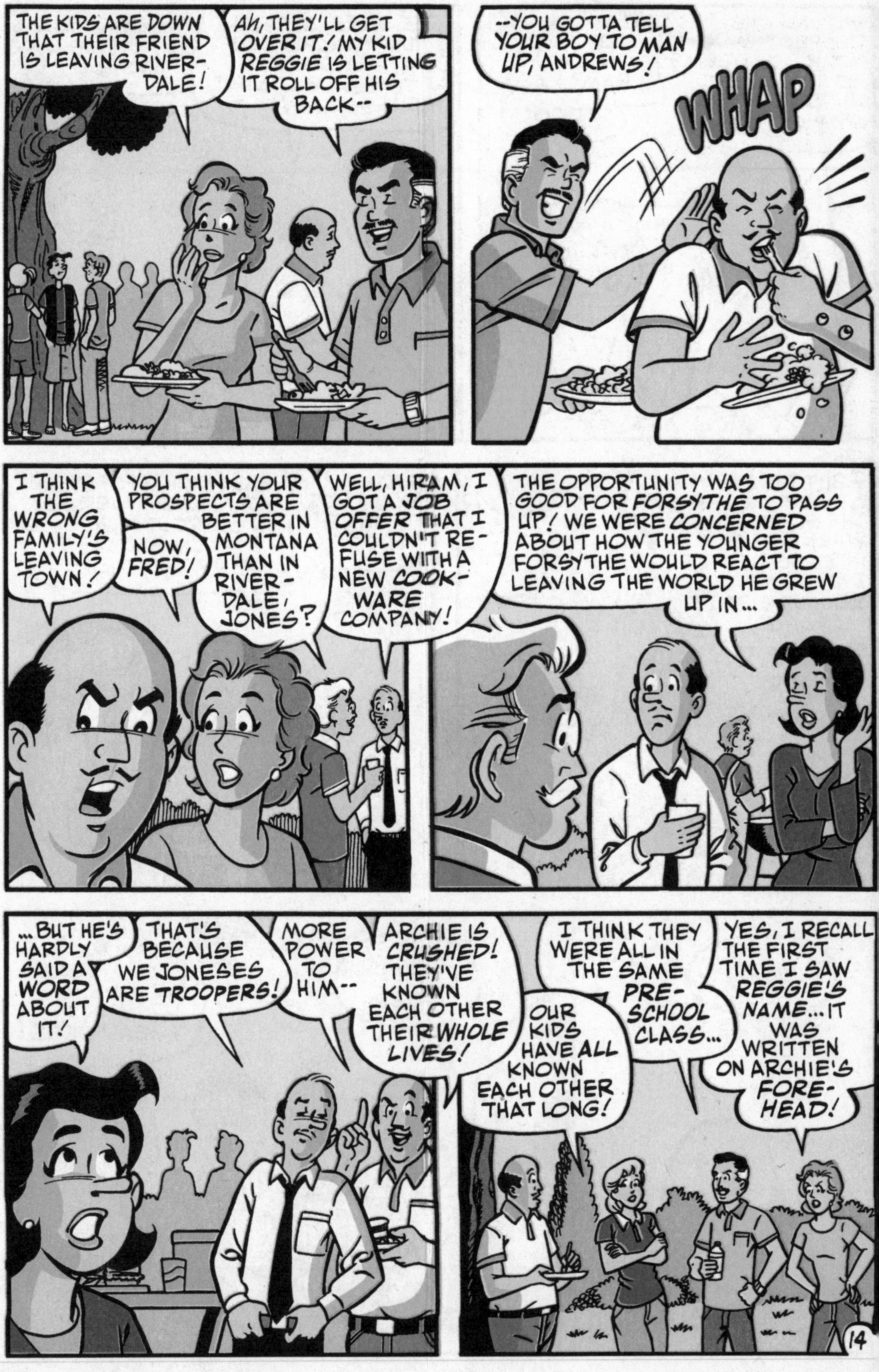
THE KIDS ARE DOWN THAT THEIR FRIEND IS LEAVING RIVERDALE!
AH, THEY'LL GET OVER IT! MY KID REGGIE IS LETTING IT ROLL OFF HIS BACK--
--YOU GOTTA TELL YOUR BOY TO MAN UP, ANDREWS!
WHAP
I THINK THE WRONG FAMILY'S LEAVING TOWN!
YOU THINK YOUR PROSPECTS ARE BETTER IN MONTANA THAN IN RIVERDALE, JONES?
NOW, FRED!
WELL, HIRAM, I GOT A JOB OFFER THAT I COULDN'T REFUSE WITH A NEW COOKWARE COMPANY!
THE OPPORTUNITY WAS TOO GOOD FOR FORSYTHE TO PASS UP! WE WERE CONCERNED ABOUT HOW THE YOUNGER FORSYTHE WOULD REACT TO LEAVING THE WORLD HE GREW UP IN...
...BUT HE'S HARDLY SAID A WORD ABOUT IT!
THAT'S BECAUSE WE JONESES ARE TROOPERS!
MORE POWER TO HIM--
ARCHIE IS CRUSHED! THEY'VE KNOWN EACH OTHER THEIR WHOLE LIVES!
OUR KIDS HAVE ALL KNOWN EACH OTHER THAT LONG!
I THINK THEY WERE ALL IN THE SAME PRE-SCHOOL CLASS...
YES, I RECALL THE FIRST TIME I SAW REGGIE'S NAME... IT WAS WRITTEN ON ARCHIE'S FOREHEAD!
14

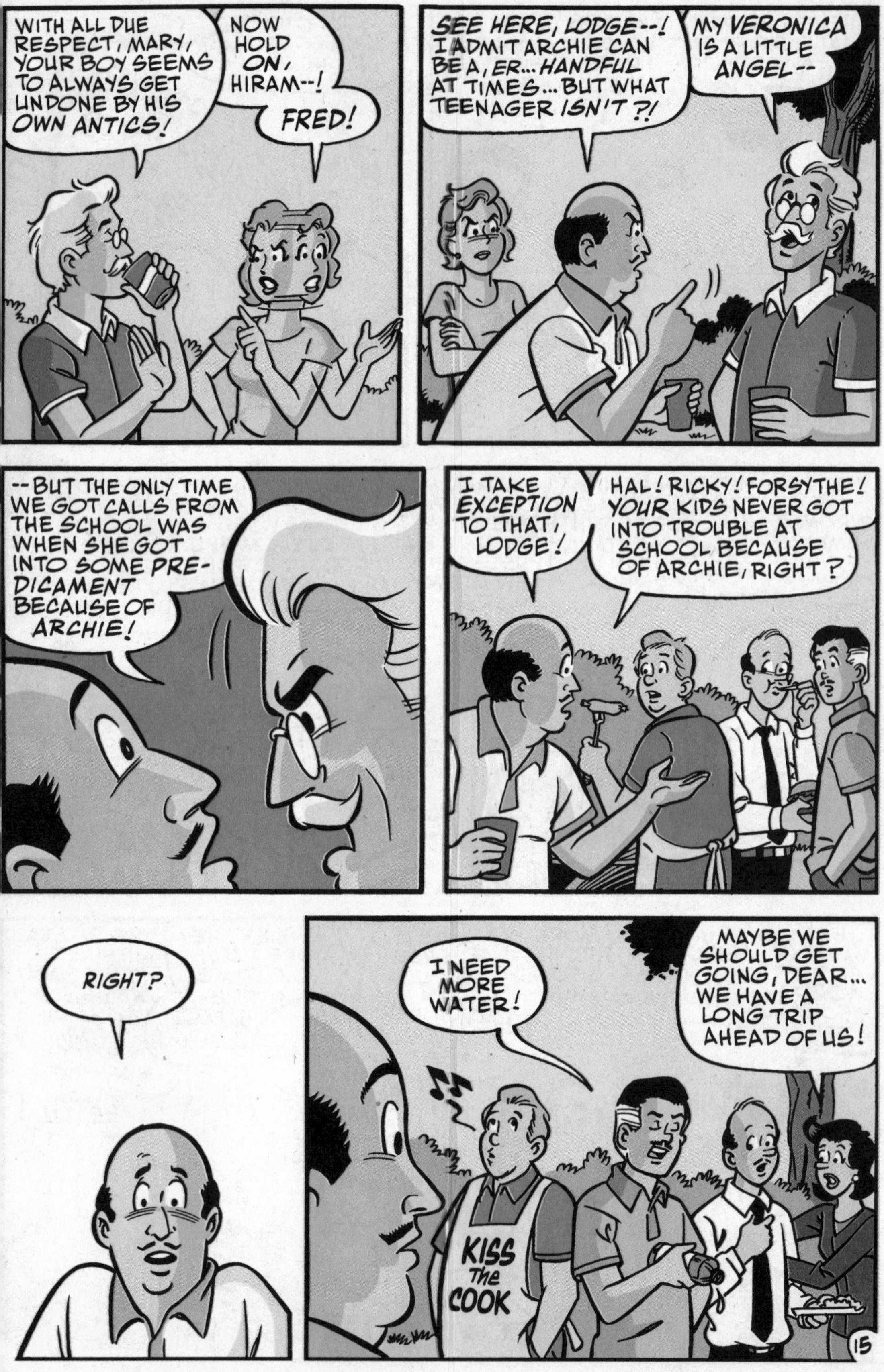
WITH ALL DUE RESPECT, MARY, YOUR BOY SEEMS TO ALWAYS GET UNDONE BY HIS OWN ANTICS!
NOW HOLD ON, HIRAM--!
FRED!
SEE HERE, LODGE--! I ADMIT ARCHIE CAN BE A, ER... HANDFUL AT TIMES... BUT WHAT TEENAGER ISN'T ?!
MY VERONICA IS A LITTLE ANGEL--
--BUT THE ONLY TIME WE GOT CALLS FROM THE SCHOOL WAS WHEN SHE GOT INTO SOME PRE-DICAMENT BECAUSE OF ARCHIE!
I TAKE EXCEPTION TO THAT, LODGE!
HAL! RICKY! FORSYTHE! YOUR KIDS NEVER GOT INTO TROUBLE AT SCHOOL BECAUSE OF ARCHIE, RIGHT?
RIGHT?
I NEED MORE WATER!
MAYBE WE SHOULD GET GOING, DEAR... WE HAVE A LONG TRIP AHEAD OF US!
KISS The COOK
15

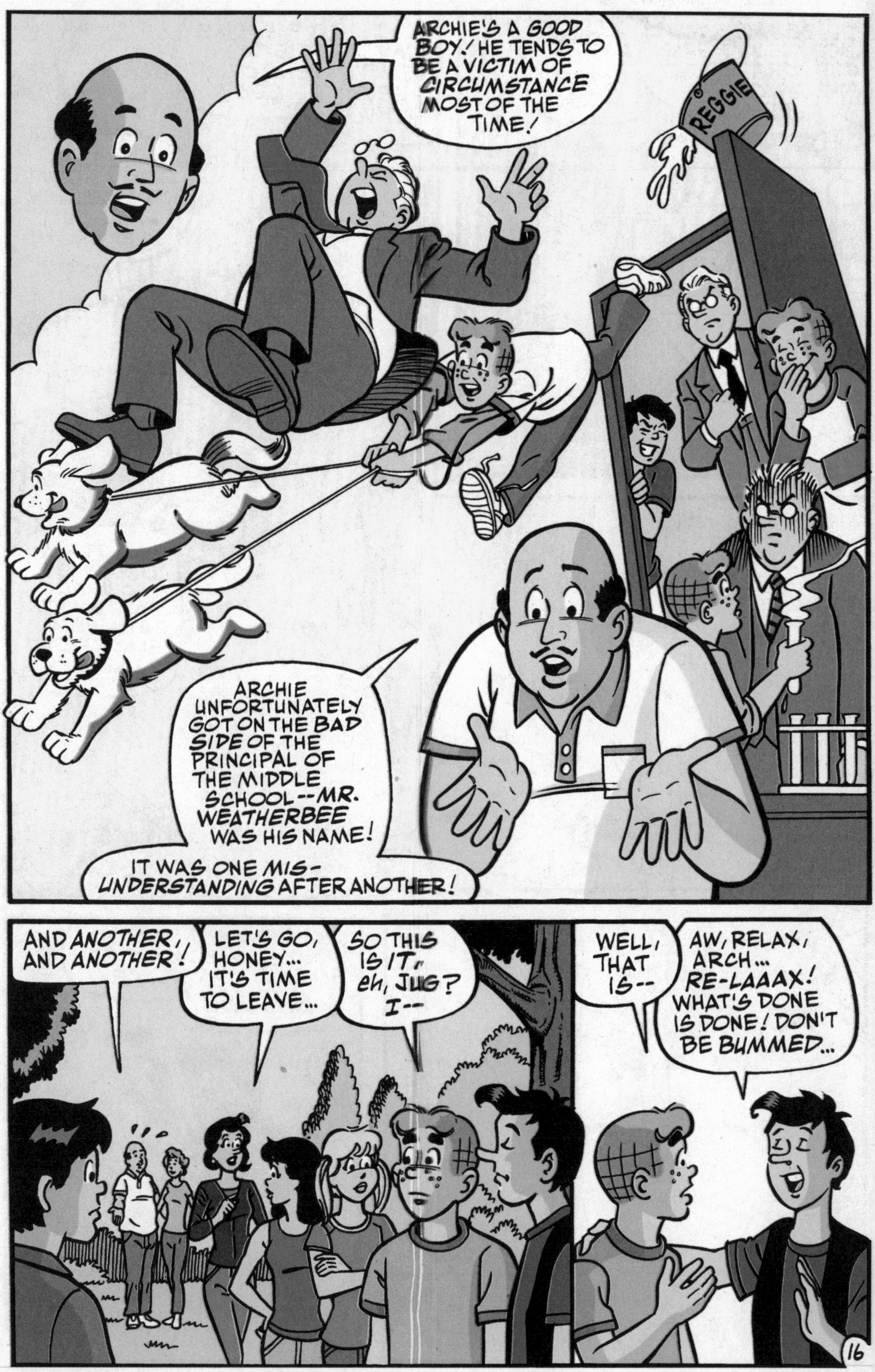
ARCHIE'S A GOOD BOY! HE TENDS TO BE A VICTIM OF CIRCUMSTANCE MOST OF THE TIME!
REGGIE
ARCHIE UNFORTUNATELY GOT ON THE BAD SIDE OF THE PRINCIPAL OF THE MIDDLE SCHOOL--MR. WEATHERBEE WAS HIS NAME!
IT WAS ONE MIS-UNDERSTANDING AFTER ANOTHER!
AND ANOTHER, AND ANOTHER!
LET'S GO, HONEY... IT'S TIME TO LEAVE...
SO THIS IS IT, eh, JUG? I--
WELL, THAT IS--
AW, RELAX, ARCH... RE-LAAAX! WHAT'S DONE IS DONE! DON'T BE BUMMED...
16

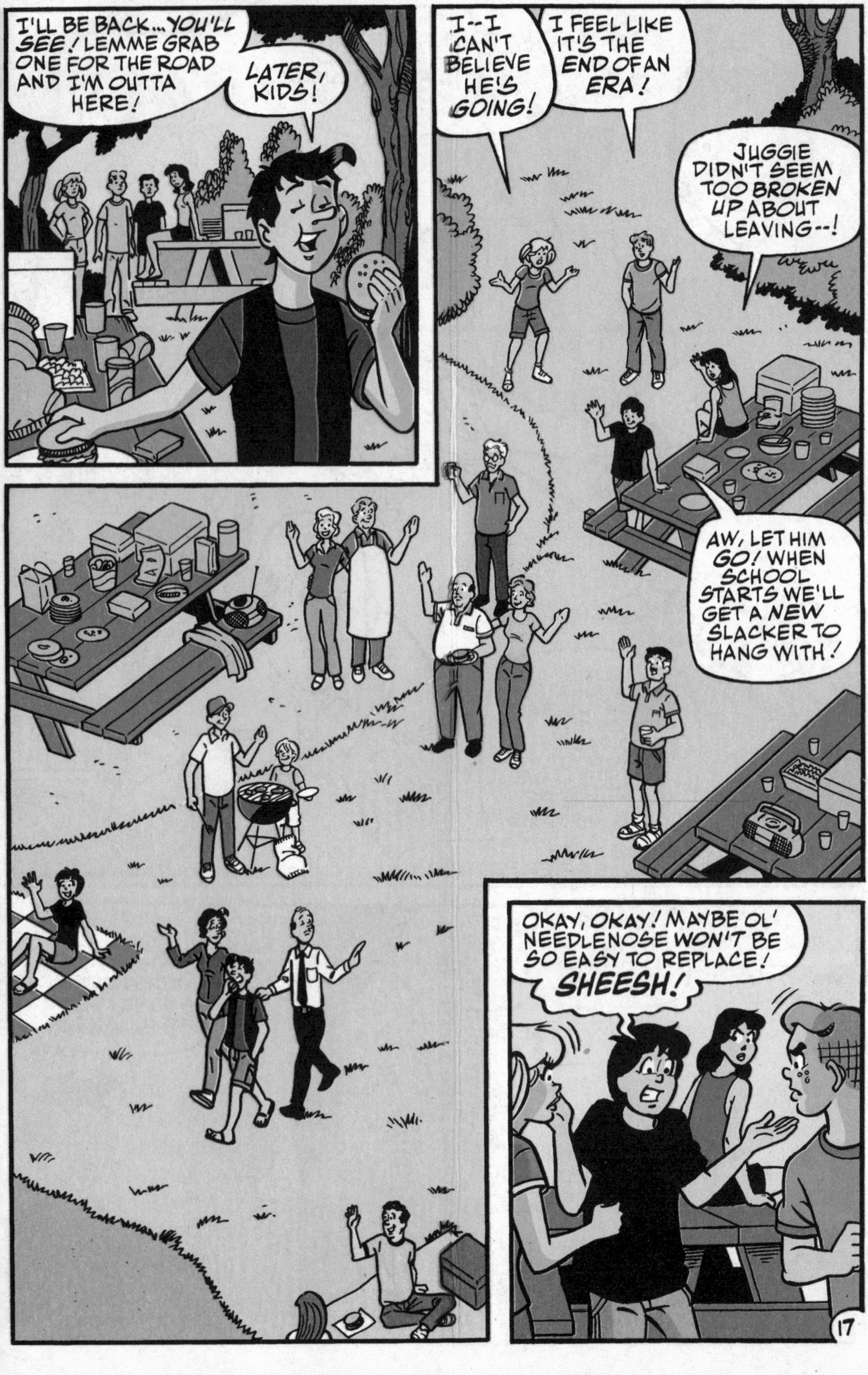
I'LL BE BACK... YOU'LL SEE! LEMME GRAB ONE FOR THE ROAD AND I'M OUTTA HERE!
LATER, KIDS!
I--I CAN'T BELIEVE HE'S GOING!
I FEEL LIKE IT'S THE END OF AN ERA!
JUGGIE DIDN'T SEEM TOO BROKEN UP ABOUT LEAVING--!
AW, LET HIM GO! WHEN SCHOOL STARTS WE'LL GET A NEW SLACKER TO HANG WITH!
OKAY, OKAY! MAYBE OL' NEEDLENOSE WON'T BE SO EASY TO REPLACE! SHEESH!
17

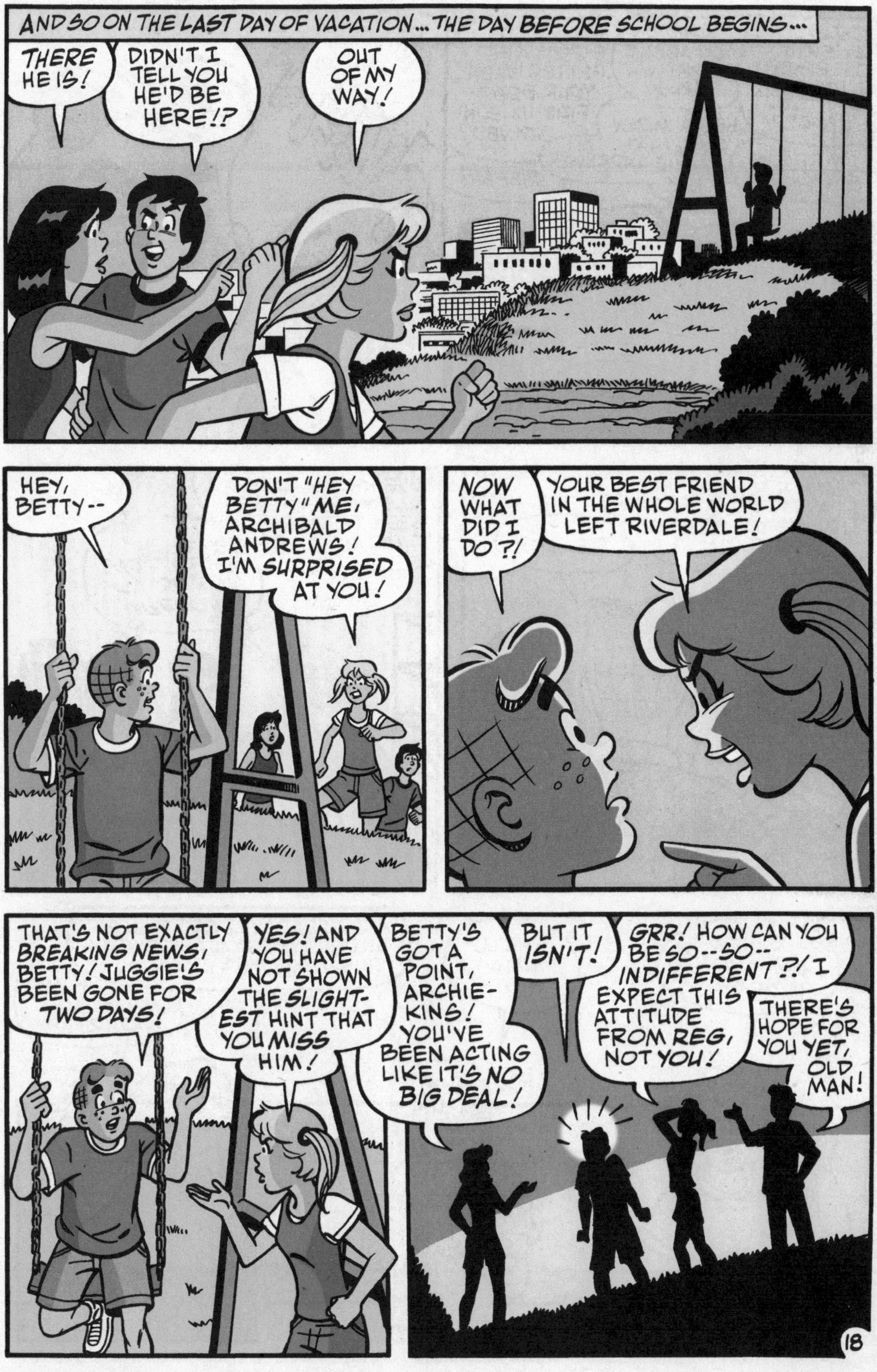
AND SO ON THE LAST DAY OF VACATION... THE DAY BEFORE SCHOOL BEGINS...
THERE HE IS!
DIDN'T I TELL YOU HE'D BE HERE!?
OUT OF MY WAY!
HEY, BETTY--
DON'T "HEY BETTY" ME, ARCHIBALD ANDREWS! I'M SURPRISED AT YOU!
NOW WHAT DID I DO?!
YOUR BEST FRIEND IN THE WHOLE WORLD LEFT RIVERDALE!
THAT'S NOT EXACTLY BREAKING NEWS, BETTY! JUGGIE'S BEEN GONE FOR TWO DAYS!
YES! AND YOU HAVE NOT SHOWN THE SLIGHT-EST HINT THAT YOU MISS HIM!
BETTY'S GOT A POINT, ARCHIE-KINS! YOU'VE BEEN ACTING LIKE IT'S NO BIG DEAL!
BUT IT ISN'T!
GRR! HOW CAN YOU BE SO--SO--INDIFFERENT?! I EXPECT THIS ATTITUDE FROM REG, NOT YOU!
THERE'S HOPE FOR YOU YET, OLD MAN!
18

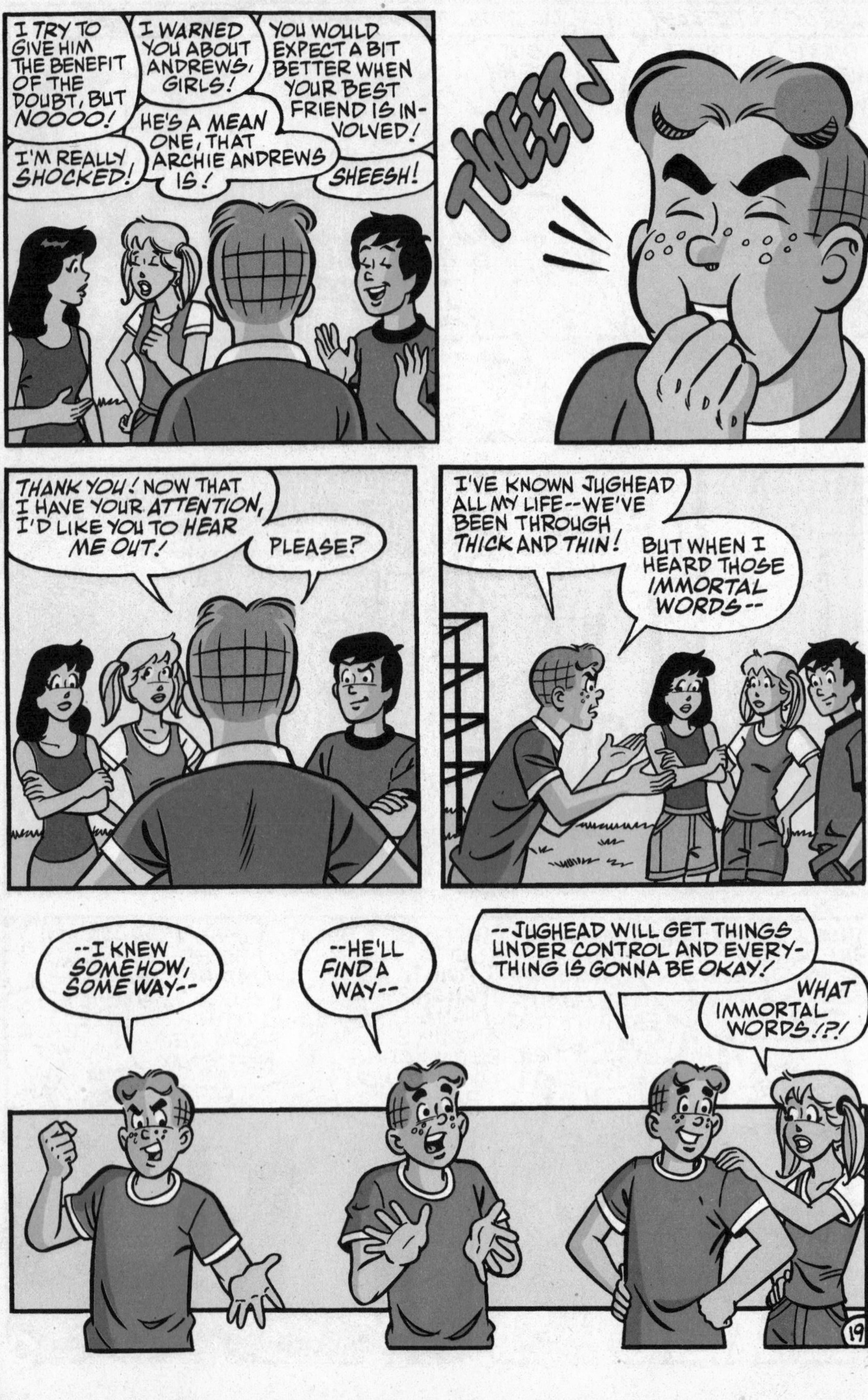
I TRY TO GIVE HIM THE BENEFIT OF THE DOUBT, BUT NOOOO!
I WARNED YOU ABOUT ANDREWS, GIRLS!
YOU WOULD EXPECT A BIT BETTER WHEN YOUR BEST FRIEND IS INVOLVED!
I'M REALLY SHOCKED!
HE'S A MEAN ONE, THAT ARCHIE ANDREWS IS!
SHEESH!
TWEET
THANK YOU! NOW THAT I HAVE YOUR ATTENTION, I'D LIKE YOU TO HEAR ME OUT!
PLEASE?
I'VE KNOWN JUGHEAD ALL MY LIFE--WE'VE BEEN THROUGH THICK AND THIN!
BUT WHEN I HEARD THOSE IMMORTAL WORDS--
--I KNEW SOMEHOW, SOMEWAY--
--HE'LL FIND A WAY--
--JUGHEAD WILL GET THINGS UNDER CONTROL AND EVERYTHING IS GONNA BE OKAY!
WHAT IMMORTAL WORDS!?!
19

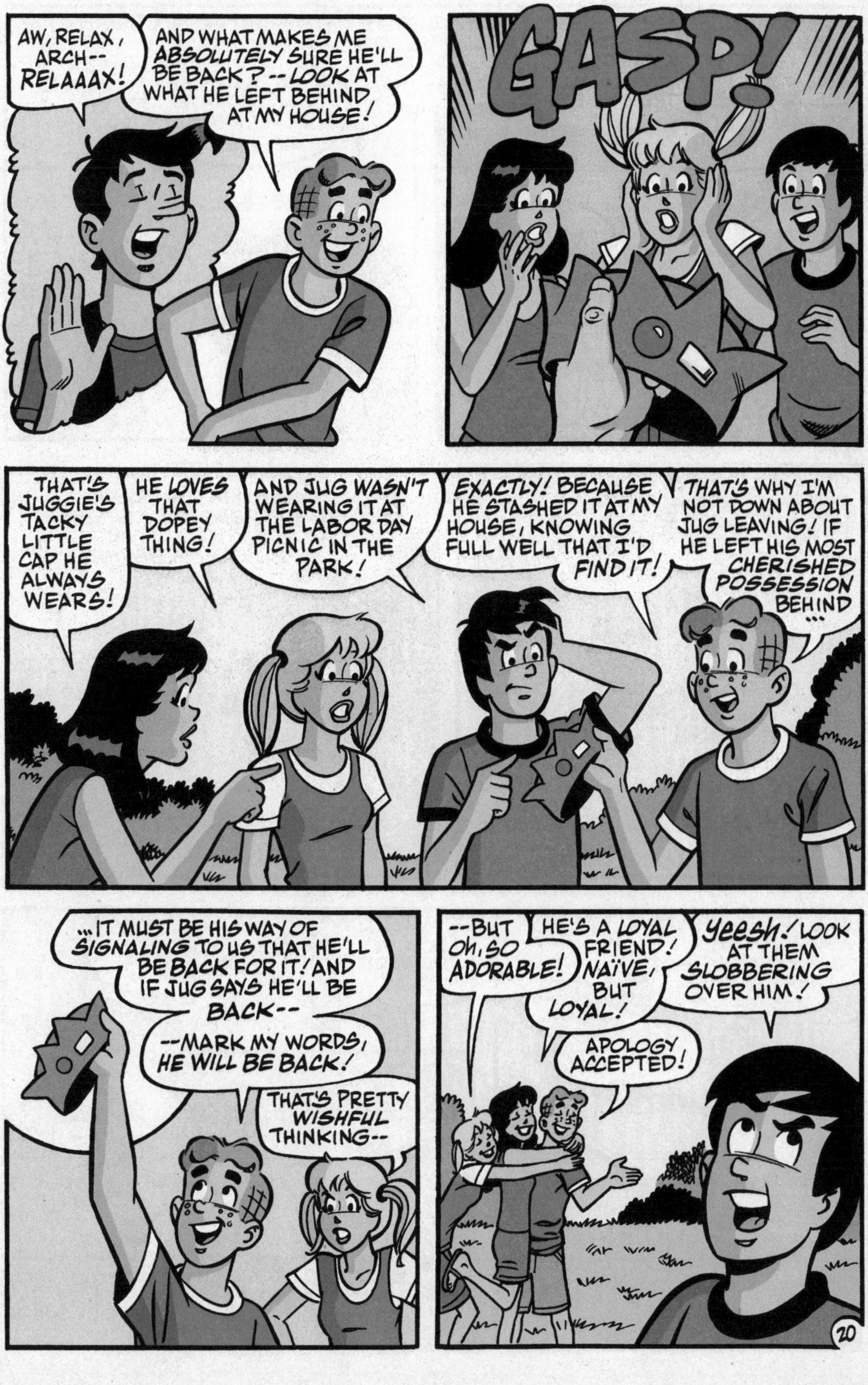
AW, RELAX, ARCH-- RELAAAX!
AND WHAT MAKES ME ABSOLUTELY SURE HE'LL BE BACK? --LOOK AT WHAT HE LEFT BEHIND AT MY HOUSE!
GASP!
THAT'S JUGGIE'S TACKY LITTLE CAP HE ALWAYS WEARS!
HE LOVES THAT DOPEY THING!
AND JUG WASN'T WEARING IT AT THE LABOR DAY PICNIC IN THE PARK!
EXACTLY! BECAUSE HE STASHED IT AT MY HOUSE, KNOWING FULL WELL THAT I'D FIND IT!
THAT'S WHY I'M NOT DOWN ABOUT JUG LEAVING! IF HE LEFT HIS MOST CHERISHED POSSESSION BEHIND ...
...IT MUST BE HIS WAY OF SIGNALING TO US THAT HE'LL BE BACK FOR IT! AND IF JUG SAYS HE'LL BE BACK--
--MARK MY WORDS, HE WILL BE BACK!
THAT'S PRETTY WISHFUL THINKING--
--BUT OH, SO ADORABLE!
HE'S A LOYAL FRIEND! NAÏVE, BUT LOYAL!
APOLOGY ACCEPTED!
YEESH! LOOK AT THEM SLOBBERING OVER HIM!
20

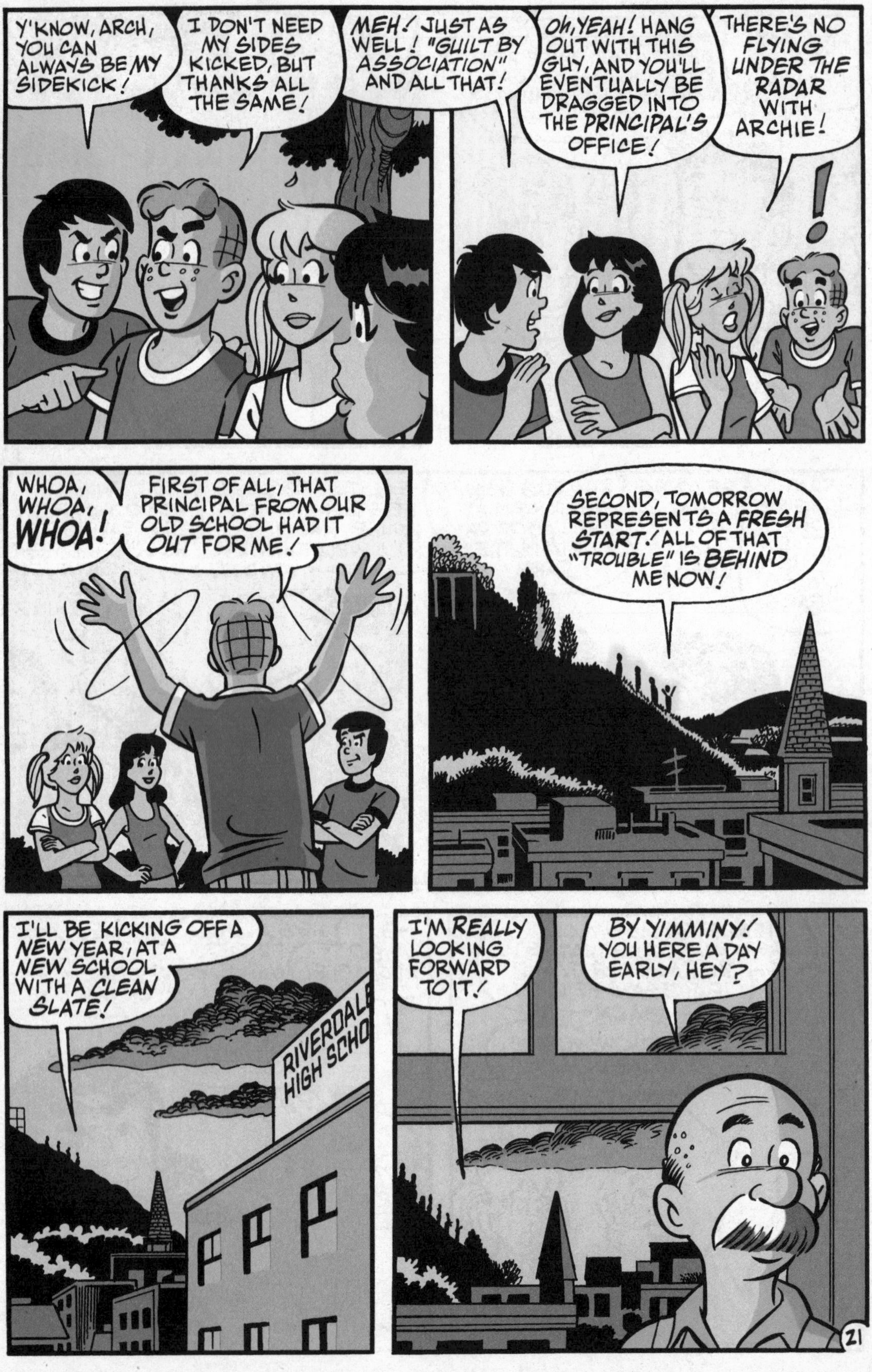
Y'KNOW, ARCH, YOU CAN ALWAYS BE MY SIDEKICK!
I DON'T NEED MY SIDES KICKED, BUT THANKS ALL THE SAME!
MEH! JUST AS WELL! "GUILT BY ASSOCIATION" AND ALL THAT!
Oh, YEAH! HANG OUT WITH THIS GUY, AND YOU'LL EVENTUALLY BE DRAGGED INTO THE PRINCIPAL'S OFFICE!
THERE'S NO FLYING UNDER THE RADAR WITH ARCHIE!
!
WHOA, WHOA, WHOA!
FIRST OF ALL, THAT PRINCIPAL FROM OUR OLD SCHOOL HAD IT OUT FOR ME!
SECOND, TOMORROW REPRESENTS A FRESH START! ALL OF THAT "TROUBLE" IS BEHIND ME NOW!
I'LL BE KICKING OFF A NEW YEAR, AT A NEW SCHOOL WITH A CLEAN SLATE!
RIVERDALE HIGH SCHO
I'M REALLY LOOKING FORWARD TO IT!
BY YIMMINY! YOU HERE A DAY EARLY, HEY?
21

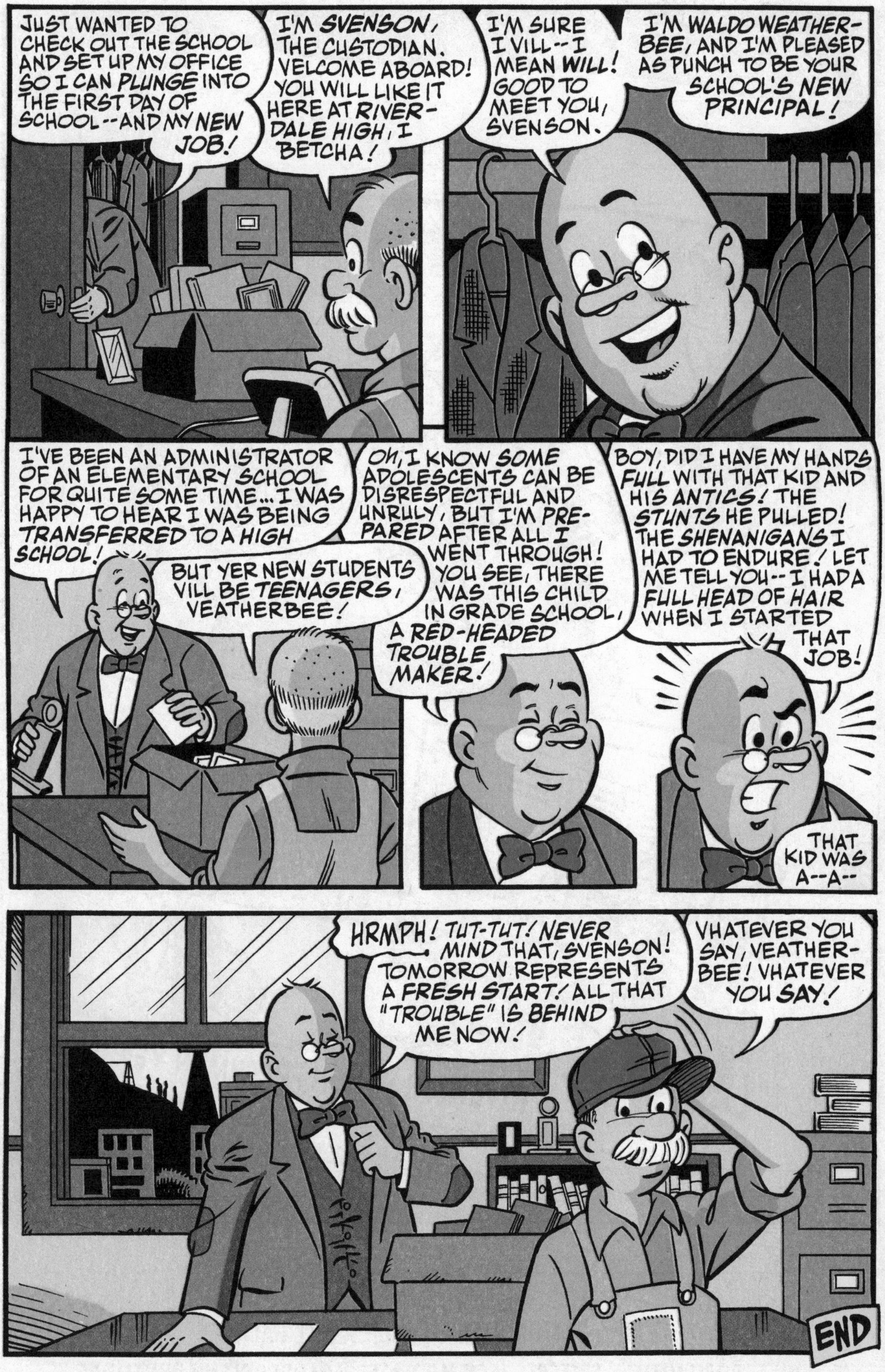
JUST WANTED TO CHECK OUT THE SCHOOL AND SET UP MY OFFICE SO I CAN PLUNGE INTO THE FIRST DAY OF SCHOOL--AND MY NEW JOB!
I'M SVENSON, THE CUSTODIAN. VELCOME ABOARD! YOU WILL LIKE IT HERE AT RIVERDALE HIGH, I BETCHA!
I'M WALDO WEATHERBEE, AND I'M PLEASED AS PUNCH TO BE YOUR SCHOOL'S NEW PRINCIPAL!
I'M SURE I VILL--I MEAN WILL! GOOD TO MEET YOU, SVENSON.
I'VE BEEN AN ADMINISTRATOR OF AN ELEMENTARY SCHOOL FOR QUITE SOME TIME... I WAS HAPPY TO HEAR I WAS BEING TRANSFERRED TO A HIGH SCHOOL!
BUT YER NEW STUDENTS VILL BE TEENAGERS, VEATHERBEE!
OH, I KNOW SOME ADOLESCENTS CAN BE DISRESPECTFUL AND UNRULY, BUT I'M PREPARED AFTER ALL I WENT THROUGH! YOU SEE, THERE WAS THIS CHILD IN GRADE SCHOOL, A RED-HEADED TROUBLE MAKER!
BOY, DID I HAVE MY HANDS FULL WITH THAT KID AND HIS ANTICS! THE STUNTS HE PULLED! THE SHENANIGANS I HAD TO ENDURE! LET ME TELL YOU--I HAD A FULL HEAD OF HAIR WHEN I STARTED THAT JOB!
THAT KID WAS A--A--
HRMPH! TUT-TUT! NEVER MIND THAT, SVENSON! TOMORROW REPRESENTS A FRESH START! ALL THAT "TROUBLE" IS BEHIND ME NOW!
VHATEVER YOU SAY, VEATHERBEE! VHATEVER YOU SAY!
END

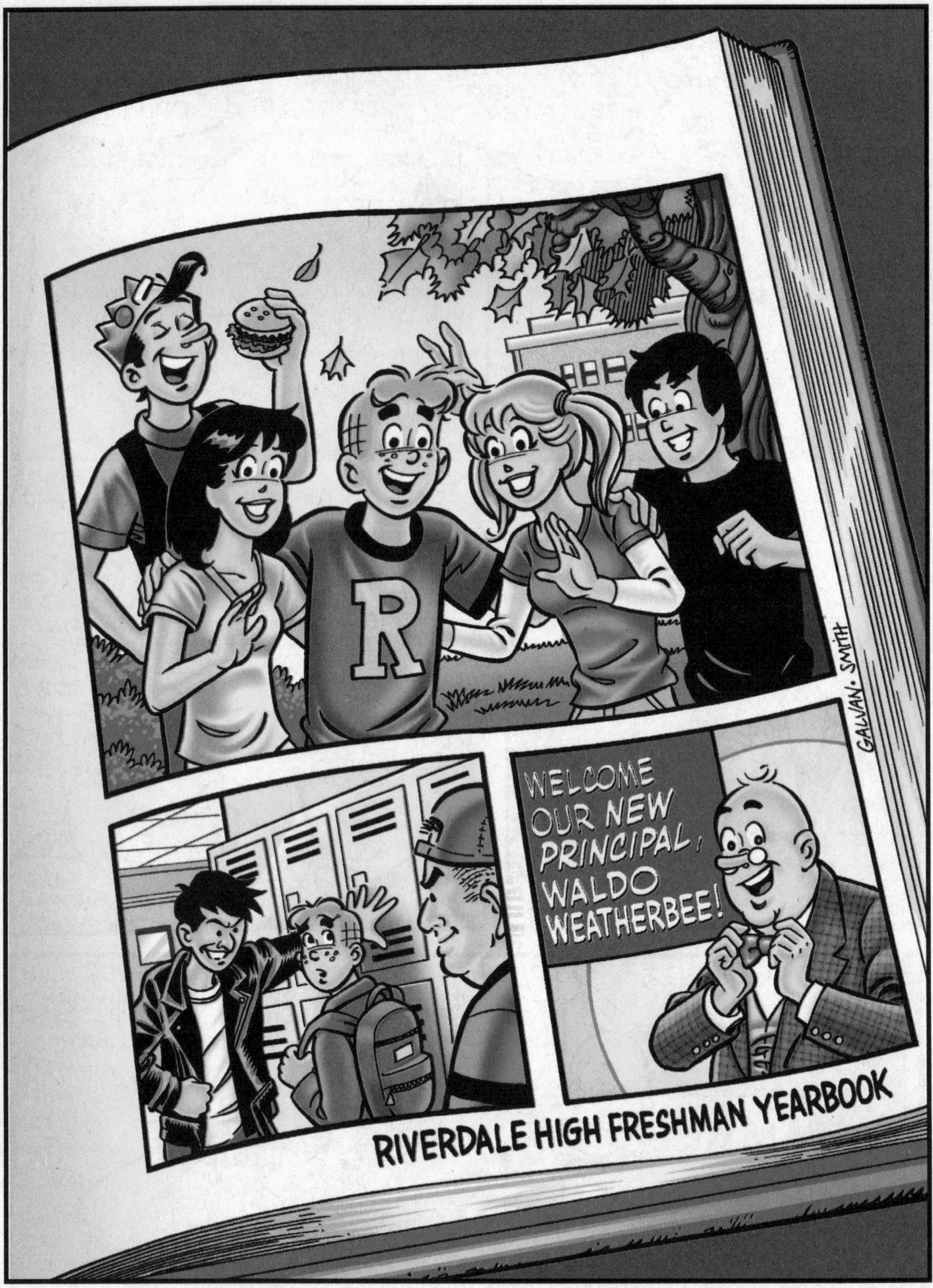
GALVAN • SMITH
WELCOME OUR NEW PRINCIPAL, WALDO WEATHERBEE!
RIVERDALE HIGH FRESHMAN YEARBOOK

FRESHMAN YEAR PART 2

SCRIPT: BATTON LASH PENCILS: BILL GALVAN

INKS: BOB SMITH LETTERS: JACK MORELLI COLORS: GLENN WHITMORE

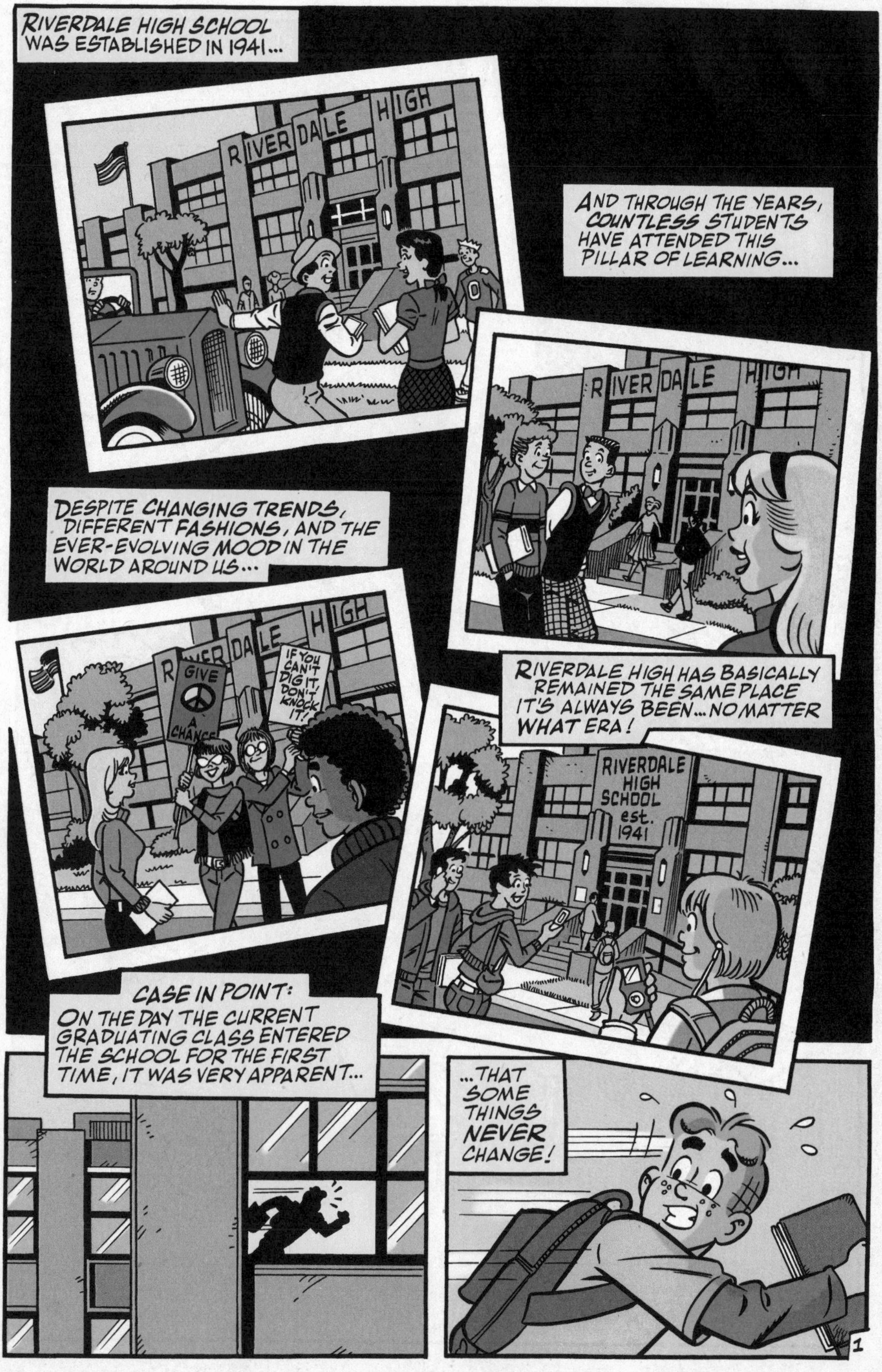
RIVERDALE HIGH SCHOOL WAS ESTABLISHED IN 1941...
RIVERDALE HIGH
AND THROUGH THE YEARS, COUNTLESS STUDENTS HAVE ATTENDED THIS PILLAR OF LEARNING...
RIVERDALE HIGH
DESPITE CHANGING TRENDS, DIFFERENT FASHIONS, AND THE EVER-EVOLVING MOOD IN THE WORLD AROUND US...
RIVERDALE HIGH
GIVE A CHANCE
IF YOU CAN'T DIG IT, DON'T KNOCK IT!
RIVERDALE HIGH HAS BASICALLY REMAINED THE SAME PLACE IT'S ALWAYS BEEN... NO MATTER WHAT ERA!
RIVERDALE HIGH SCHOOL est. 1941
CASE IN POINT: ON THE DAY THE CURRENT GRADUATING CLASS ENTERED THE SCHOOL FOR THE FIRST TIME, IT WAS VERY APPARENT...
...THAT SOME THINGS NEVER CHANGE!
1

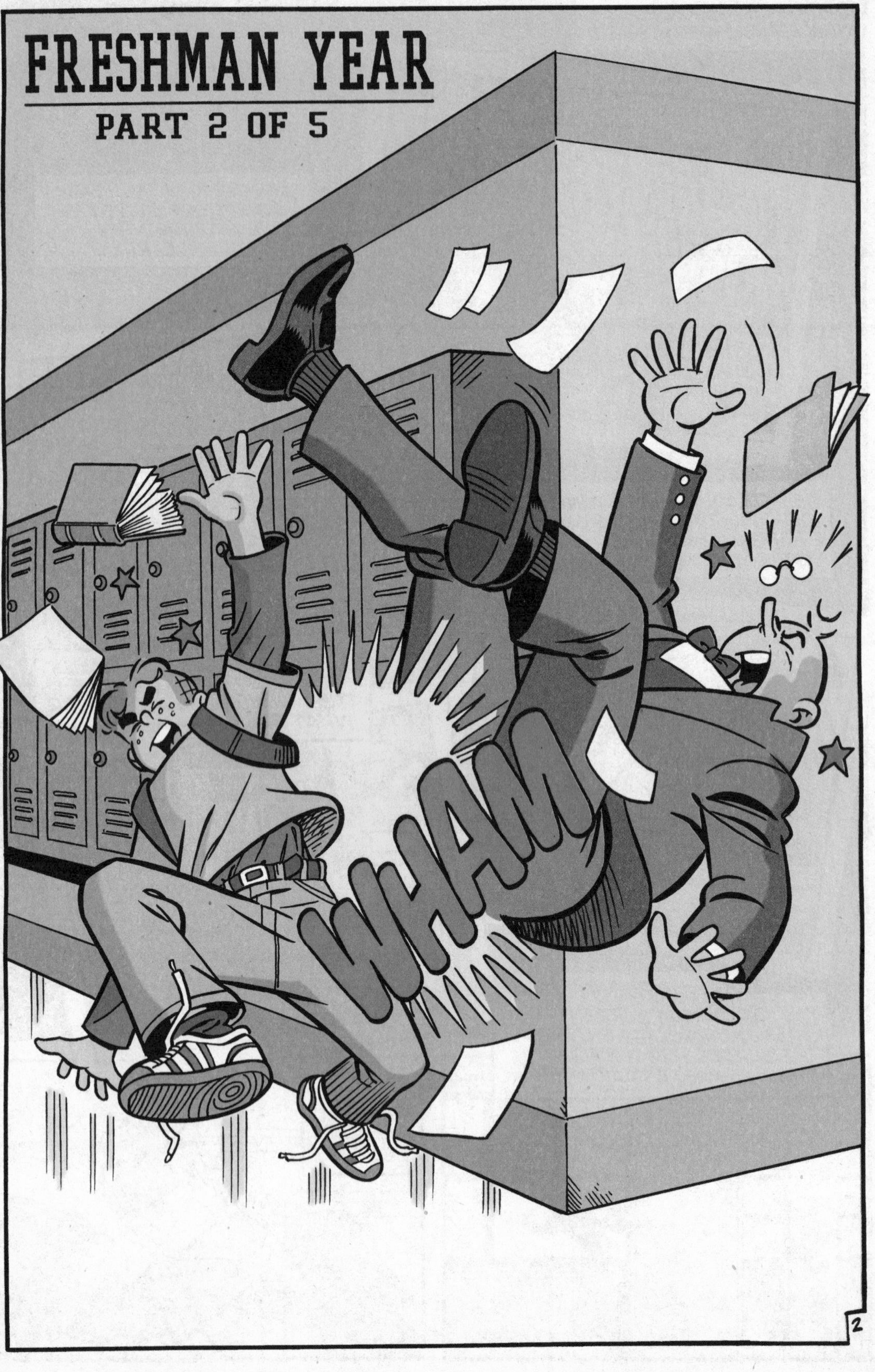
FRESHMAN YEAR
PART 2 OF 5
WHAM
2

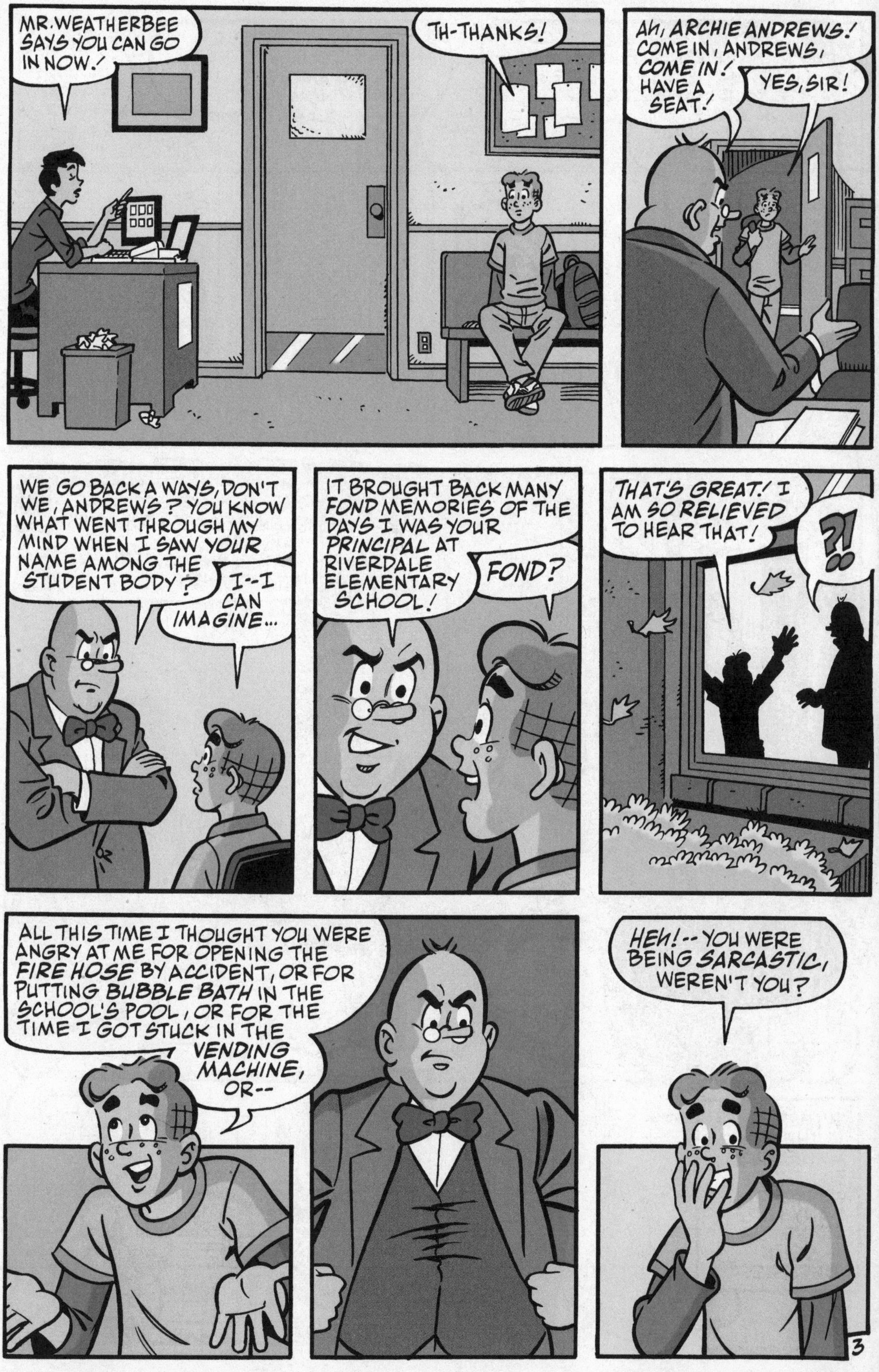
MR. WEATHERBEE SAYS YOU CAN GO IN NOW.!
TH-THANKS!
AH, ARCHIE ANDREWS! COME IN, ANDREWS, COME IN! HAVE A SEAT!
YES, SIR!
WE GO BACK A WAYS, DON'T WE, ANDREWS? YOU KNOW WHAT WENT THROUGH MY MIND WHEN I SAW YOUR NAME AMONG THE STUDENT BODY?
I--I CAN IMAGINE...
IT BROUGHT BACK MANY FOND MEMORIES OF THE DAYS I WAS YOUR PRINCIPAL AT RIVERDALE ELEMENTARY SCHOOL!
FOND?
THAT'S GREAT! I AM SO RELIEVED TO HEAR THAT!
?!
ALL THIS TIME I THOUGHT YOU WERE ANGRY AT ME FOR OPENING THE FIRE HOSE BY ACCIDENT, OR FOR PUTTING BUBBLE BATH IN THE SCHOOL'S POOL, OR FOR THE TIME I GOT STUCK IN THE VENDING MACHINE, OR--
HEH! -- YOU WERE BEING SARCASTIC, WEREN'T YOU?
3

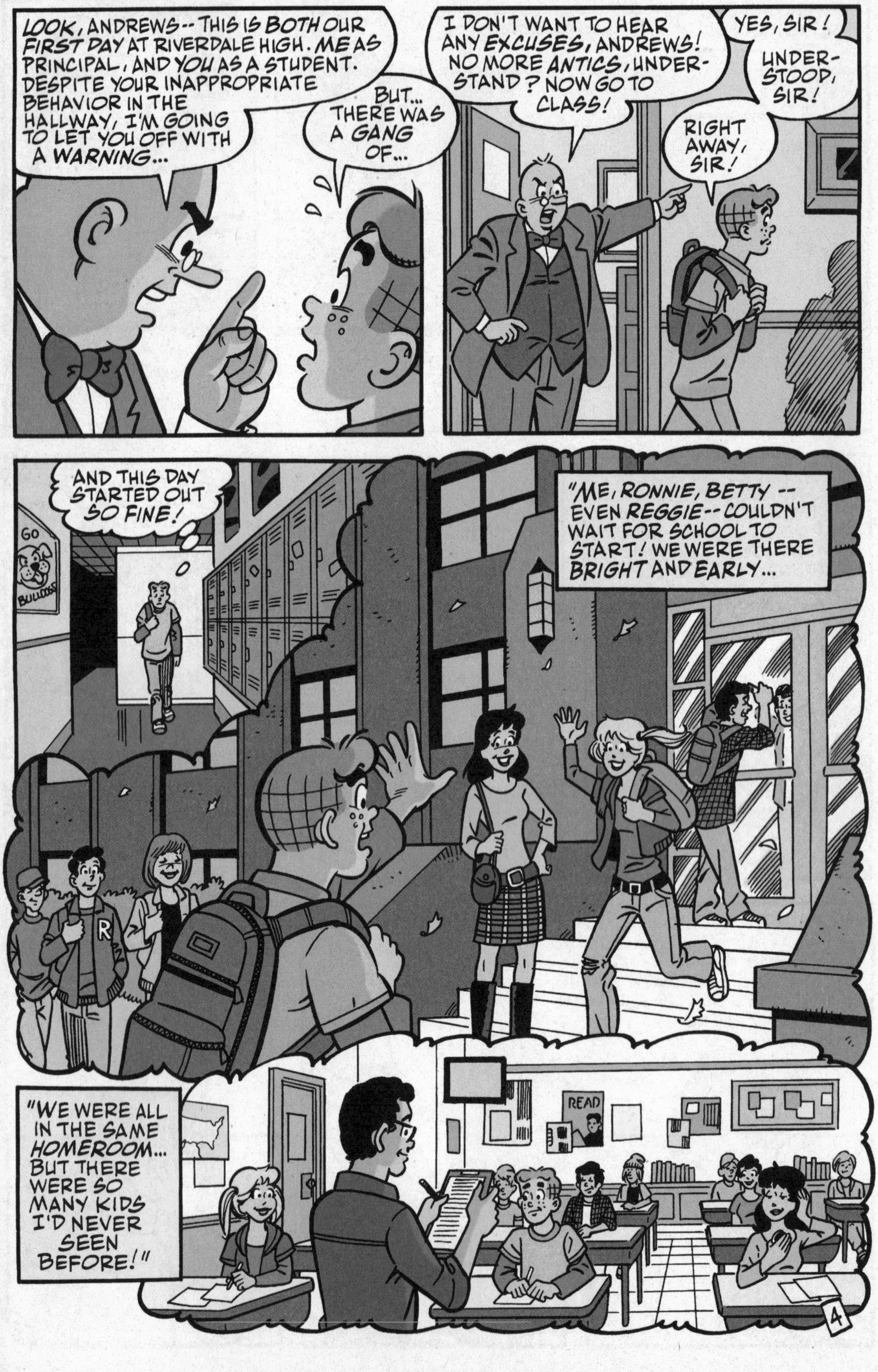
LOOK, ANDREWS -- THIS IS BOTH OUR FIRST DAY AT RIVERDALE HIGH. ME AS PRINCIPAL, AND YOU AS A STUDENT. DESPITE YOUR INAPPROPRIATE BEHAVIOR IN THE HALLWAY, I'M GOING TO LET YOU OFF WITH A WARNING...
BUT... THERE WAS A GANG OF...
I DON'T WANT TO HEAR ANY EXCUSES, ANDREWS! NO MORE ANTICS, UNDERSTAND? NOW GO TO CLASS!
YES, SIR!
UNDERSTOOD, SIR!
RIGHT AWAY, SIR!
AND THIS DAY STARTED OUT SO FINE!
"ME, RONNIE, BETTY -- EVEN REGGIE -- COULDN'T WAIT FOR SCHOOL TO START! WE WERE THERE BRIGHT AND EARLY...
GO BULLDOGS
"WE WERE ALL IN THE SAME HOMEROOM... BUT THERE WERE SO MANY KIDS I'D NEVER SEEN BEFORE!"
READ
4

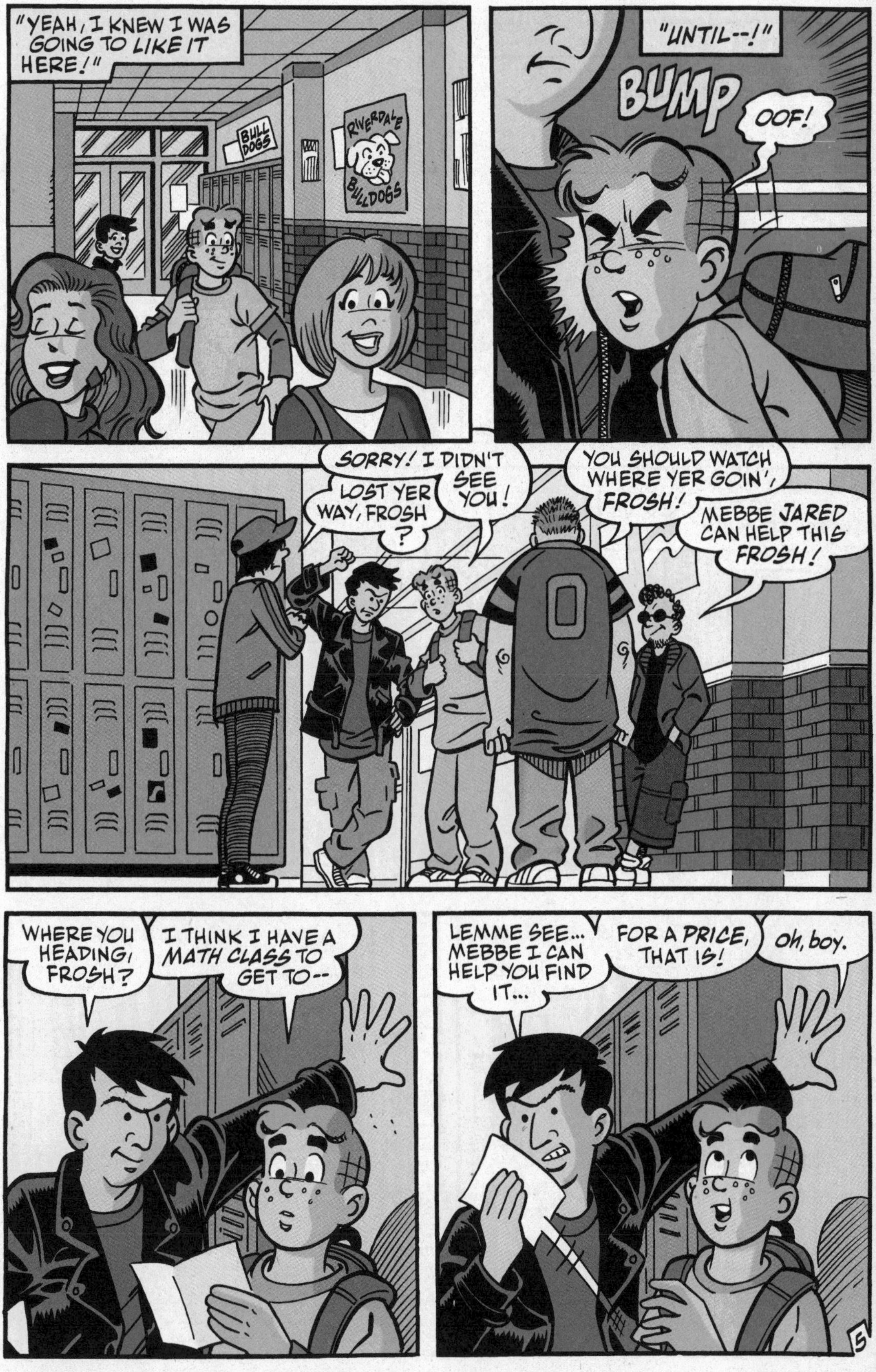
"YEAH, I KNEW I WAS GOING TO LIKE IT HERE!"
BULL DOGS
RIVERDALE BULLDOGS
"UNTIL--!"
BUMP
OOF!
SORRY! I DIDN'T SEE YOU!
LOST YER WAY, FROSH?
YOU SHOULD WATCH WHERE YER GOIN', FROSH!
MEBBE JARED CAN HELP THIS FROSH!
WHERE YOU HEADING, FROSH?
I THINK I HAVE A MATH CLASS TO GET TO--
LEMME SEE... MEBBE I CAN HELP YOU FIND IT...
FOR A PRICE, THAT IS!
oh, boy.
5

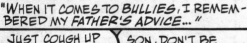

"WHEN IT COMES TO BULLIES, I REMEMBERED MY FATHER'S ADVICE..."

JUST COUGH UP SOME DOUGH-- IT'S A FROSH TAX, KID!

SON, DON'T BE AFRAID OF A BULLY! STAND UP TO HIM... HE'S NOTHING BUT A COWARD!

LET'S GO, KID!

ARE YOU GONNA DIG FOR SOME CASH, OR DO WE HAFTA DIG IT OUT FOR YOU?

HOWEVER, IF YOU'RE UNFAIRLY OUTNUMBERED, THERE IS NO SHAME IN GETTING OUT OF THERE --AND FAST!

"DAD HAD GOOD ADVICE, BUT MAYBE I SHOULD'VE WATCHED WHERE I WAS GOING--!"

BUT THAT'S ALL BEHIND ME NOW! I CAUGHT A BREAK TODAY! I'LL BE OKAY IF I JUST GO TO MY CLASSES... STEER CLEAR OF THOSE BULLIES... AND KEEP OUT OF THE PRINCIPAL'S WAY...

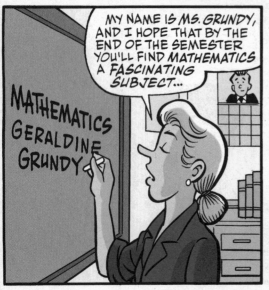

MY NAME IS MS. GRUNDY, AND I HOPE THAT BY THE END OF THE SEMESTER YOU'LL FIND MATHEMATICS A FASCINATING SUBJECT...

MATHEMATICS GERALDINE GRUNDY

...BUT THAT MIGHT BE TOO "PI" IN THE SKY ON MY PART! giggle!

PSST! CARROT TOP! WHAT HAPPENED TODAY?

MATHEMATICS GERALDINE GRUNDY

6

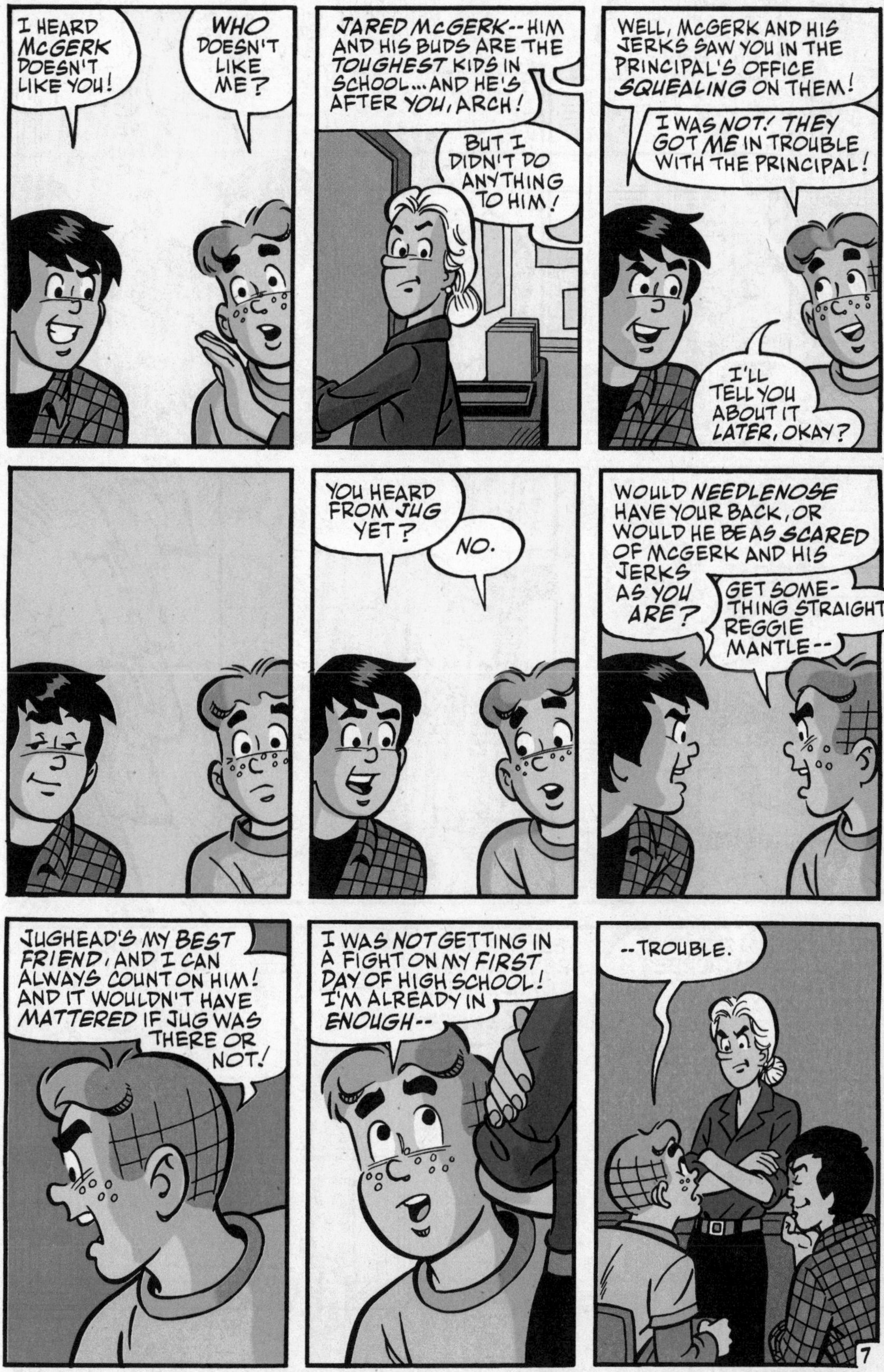
I HEARD McGERK DOESN'T LIKE YOU!
WHO DOESN'T LIKE ME?
JARED McGERK--HIM AND HIS BUDS ARE THE TOUGHEST KIDS IN SCHOOL...AND HE'S AFTER YOU, ARCH!
BUT I DIDN'T DO ANYTHING TO HIM!
WELL, McGERK AND HIS JERKS SAW YOU IN THE PRINCIPAL'S OFFICE SQUEALING ON THEM!
I WAS NOT! THEY GOT ME IN TROUBLE WITH THE PRINCIPAL!
I'LL TELL YOU ABOUT IT LATER, OKAY?
YOU HEARD FROM JUG YET?
NO.
WOULD NEEDLENOSE HAVE YOUR BACK, OR WOULD HE BE AS SCARED OF McGERK AND HIS JERKS AS YOU ARE?
GET SOME-THING STRAIGHT, REGGIE MANTLE--
JUGHEAD'S MY BEST FRIEND, AND I CAN ALWAYS COUNT ON HIM! AND IT WOULDN'T HAVE MATTERED IF JUG WAS THERE OR NOT!
I WAS NOT GETTING IN A FIGHT ON MY FIRST DAY OF HIGH SCHOOL! I'M ALREADY IN ENOUGH--
--TROUBLE.
7

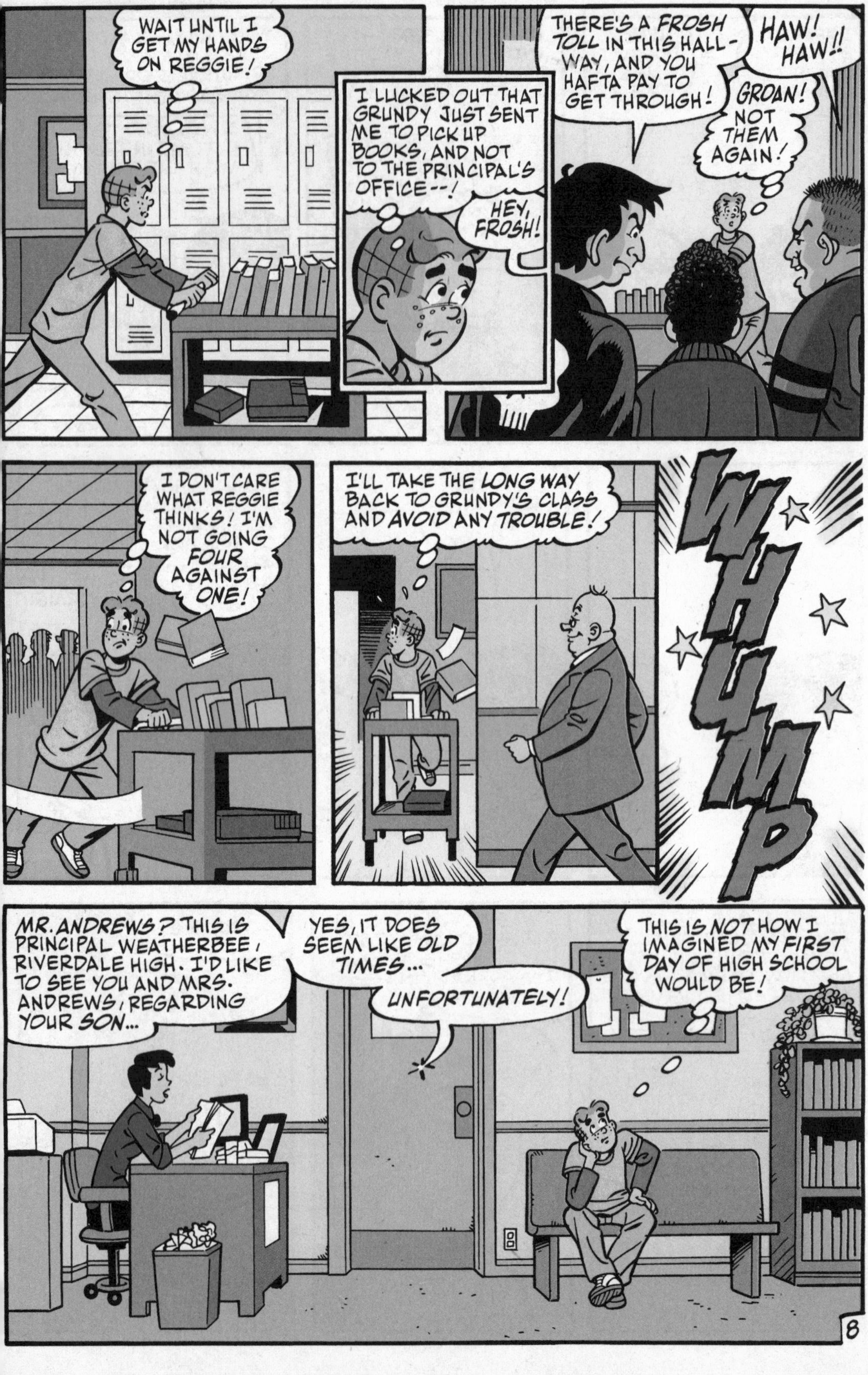
WAIT UNTIL I GET MY HANDS ON REGGIE!
I LUCKED OUT THAT GRUNDY JUST SENT ME TO PICK UP BOOKS, AND NOT TO THE PRINCIPAL'S OFFICE--!
HEY, FROSH!
THERE'S A FROSH TOLL IN THIS HALL-WAY, AND YOU HAFTA PAY TO GET THROUGH!
HAW! HAW!!
GROAN! NOT THEM AGAIN!
I DON'T CARE WHAT REGGIE THINKS! I'M NOT GOING FOUR AGAINST ONE!
I'LL TAKE THE LONG WAY BACK TO GRUNDY'S CLASS AND AVOID ANY TROUBLE!
WHUMP
MR. ANDREWS? THIS IS PRINCIPAL WEATHERBEE, RIVERDALE HIGH. I'D LIKE TO SEE YOU AND MRS. ANDREWS, REGARDING YOUR SON...
YES, IT DOES SEEM LIKE OLD TIMES...
UNFORTUNATELY!
THIS IS NOT HOW I IMAGINED MY FIRST DAY OF HIGH SCHOOL WOULD BE!
8

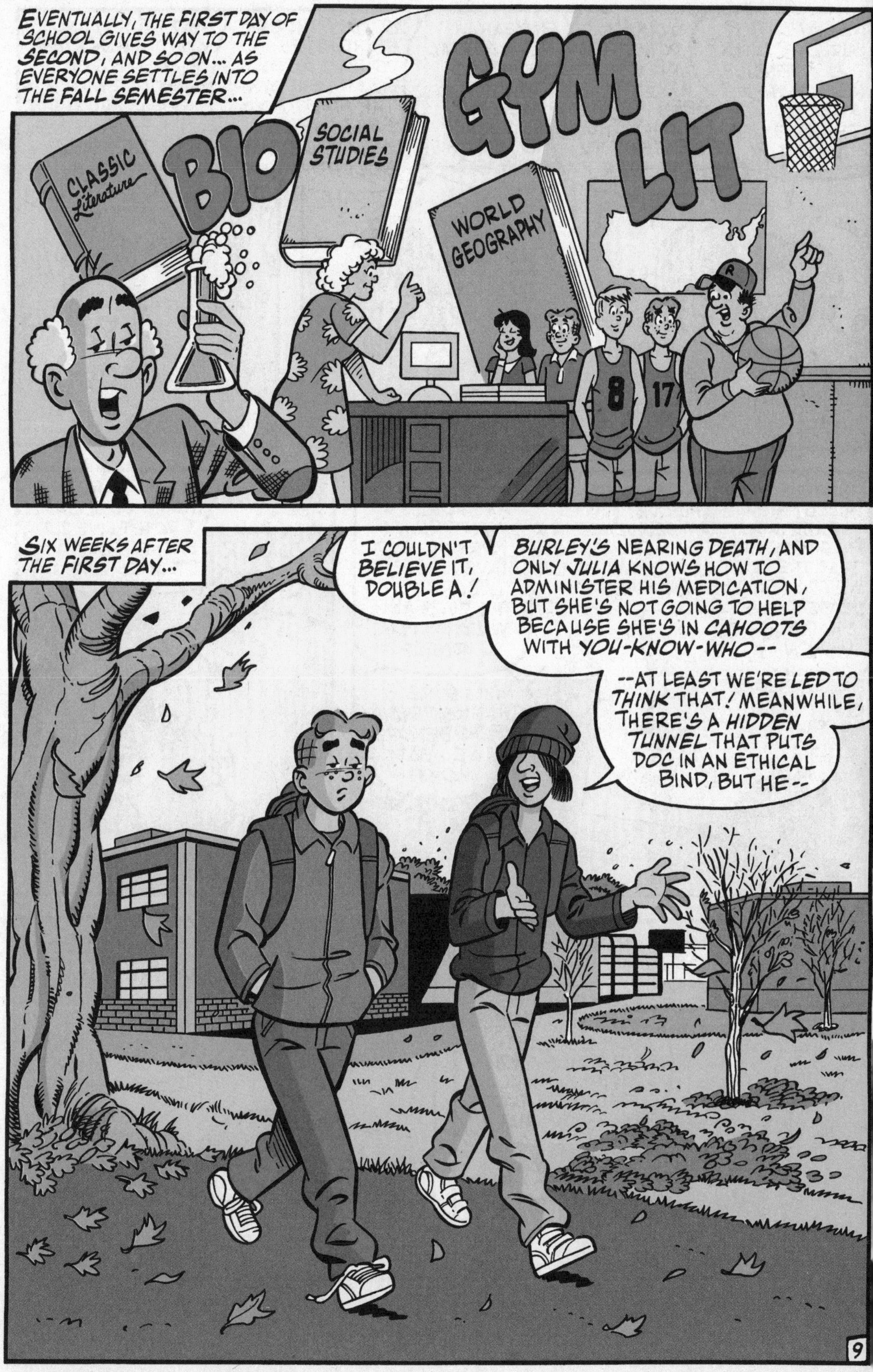
EVENTUALLY, THE FIRST DAY OF SCHOOL GIVES WAY TO THE SECOND, AND SO ON... AS EVERYONE SETTLES INTO THE FALL SEMESTER...
CLASSIC Literature
BIO
SOCIAL STUDIES
GYM
WORLD GEOGRAPHY
LIT
SIX WEEKS AFTER THE FIRST DAY...
I COULDN'T BELIEVE IT, DOUBLE A!
BURLEY'S NEARING DEATH, AND ONLY JULIA KNOWS HOW TO ADMINISTER HIS MEDICATION, BUT SHE'S NOT GOING TO HELP BECAUSE SHE'S IN CAHOOTS WITH YOU-KNOW-WHO--
--AT LEAST WE'RE LED TO THINK THAT! MEANWHILE, THERE'S A HIDDEN TUNNEL THAT PUTS DOC IN AN ETHICAL BIND, BUT HE--
9

NEAR DEATH? BURLEY? JULIA? DOC? PENCIL-NECK, WHO ARE YOU TALKING ABOUT?!

"LOSS"! DON'T TELL ME YOU HAVEN'T SEEN IT YET! IT'S LIKE THE GREATEST TV SHOW EVER!

OH, YEAH... IT'S A SERIAL, RIGHT? I THINK I MISSED TOO MUCH TO WATCH NOW, SO--

TOTALLY UNDER-STANDABLE, DOUBLE A! BUT I CAN LEND YOU THE FIRST FIVE SEASONS ON DVD! PROBLEM SOLVED!

THAT WON'T BE--

HEY! NO WORRIES, BRO! YOU CAN WATCH IT FROM THE BEGINNING, THEN WE CAN TALK ABOUT IT!

THERE WAS A HUGE "EASTER EGG" IN LAST NIGHT'S EPISODE! IT WAS IMPLIED IN A DREAM SEQUENCE IN A FLASH FORWARD FROM SEASON FOUR THAT THE PILOT OF THE PLANE WHO WE ONLY SAW IN A FLASHBACK IN SEASON ONE HAD A VISION--

I CAN'T SAY ANYMORE! I WON'T RUIN IT FOR YOU IF YOU HAVEN'T SEEN IT! BORROW THE DVDs AND WATCH IT FOR YOURSELF!

UM... SURE-- THANKS, PENCIL-NECK. BEFORE WE HEAD HOME--

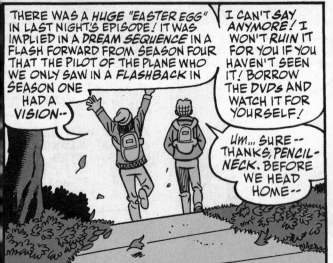

--HOW ABOUT WE GRAB A BURGER?

OOOh... BURGERS MAKE ME QUEASY! I DON'T LIVE TO EAT, DOUBLE A-- I EAT TO LIVE!

HIDE, RONNIE!

WHEW! WE ALMOST RAN INTO ANDREWS AND HIS JUGHEAD STAND-IN! I DON'T THINK IT'S WORKING OUT, THOUGH!

DON'T BE MEAN, REG! ARCHIE'S JUST BEING NICE! YOU COULD LEARN A THING OR TWO FROM HIM!

THEN LET'S GO OVER AND JOIN THEM, OKAY?

AHHH... MAYBE ANOTHER TIME! I WAS HOPING WE COULD TRY OUT A NEW PLACE TO HANG OUT!

10

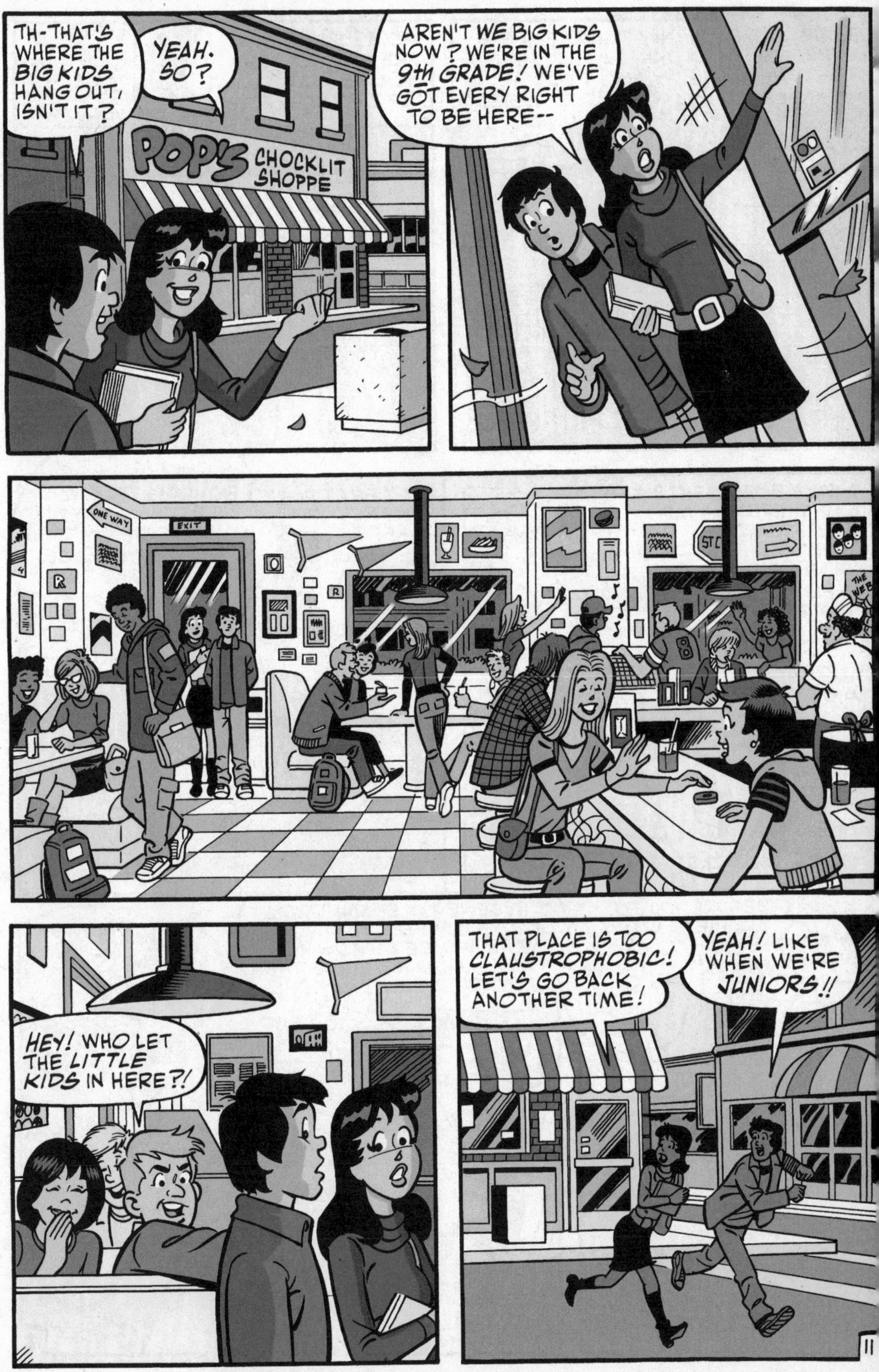
TH-THAT'S WHERE THE BIG KIDS HANG OUT, ISN'T IT?
YEAH. SO?
POP'S CHOCKLIT SHOPPE
AREN'T WE BIG KIDS NOW? WE'RE IN THE 9th GRADE! WE'VE GOT EVERY RIGHT TO BE HERE--
ONE WAY
EXIT
HEY! WHO LET THE LITTLE KIDS IN HERE?!
THAT PLACE IS TOO CLAUSTROPHOBIC! LET'S GO BACK ANOTHER TIME!
YEAH! LIKE WHEN WE'RE JUNIORS!!
11

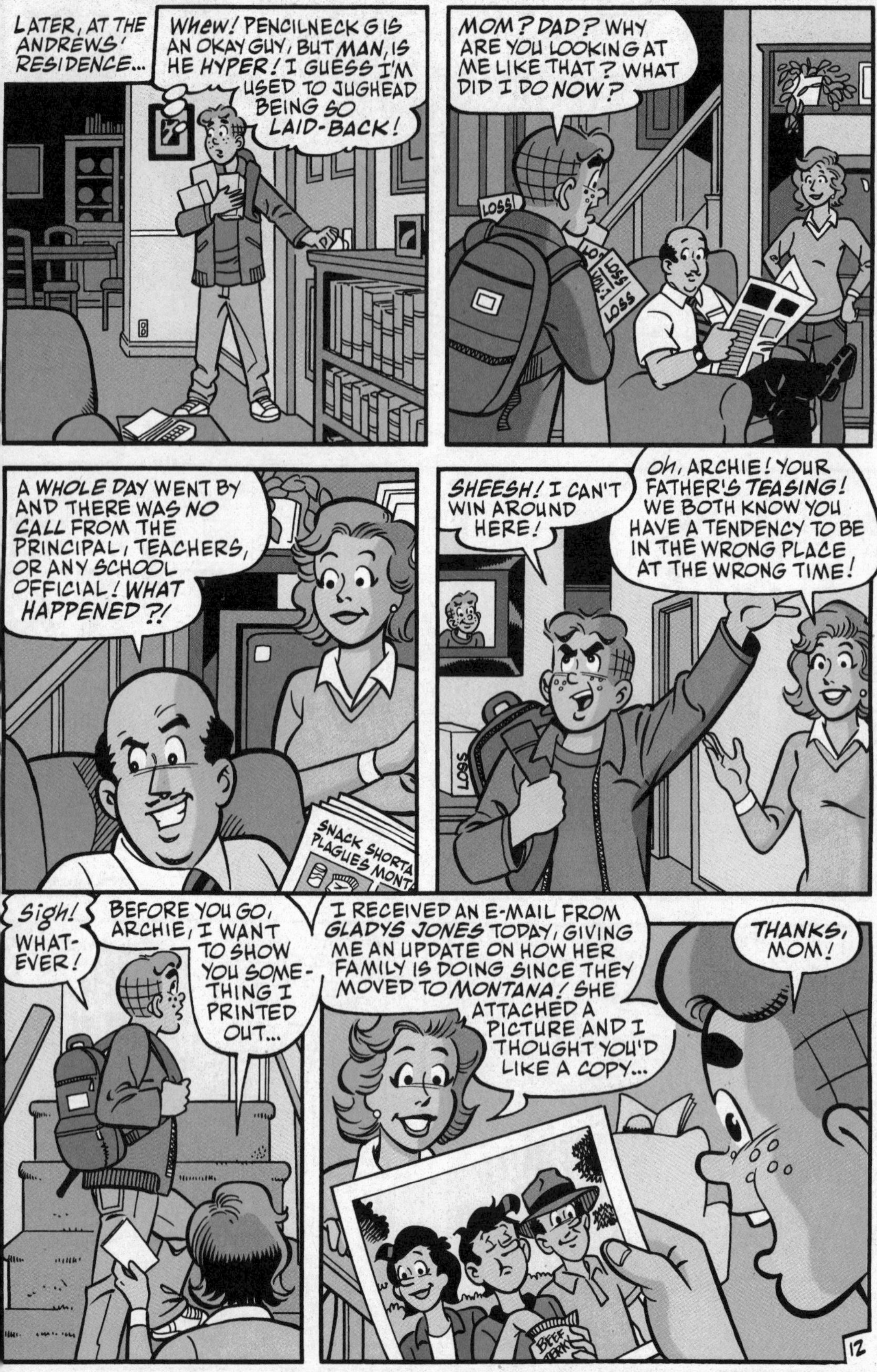
LATER, AT THE ANDREWS' RESIDENCE...
Whew! PENCILNECK G IS AN OKAY GUY, BUT MAN, IS HE HYPER! I GUESS I'M USED TO JUGHEAD BEING SO LAID-BACK!
MOM? DAD? WHY ARE YOU LOOKING AT ME LIKE THAT? WHAT DID I DO NOW?
LOSS
A WHOLE DAY WENT BY AND THERE WAS NO CALL FROM THE PRINCIPAL, TEACHERS, OR ANY SCHOOL OFFICIAL! WHAT HAPPENED?!
SNACK SHORTA PLAGUES MONT
SHEESH! I CAN'T WIN AROUND HERE!
Oh, ARCHIE! YOUR FATHER'S TEASING! WE BOTH KNOW YOU HAVE A TENDENCY TO BE IN THE WRONG PLACE AT THE WRONG TIME!
LOSS
Sigh! WHATEVER!
BEFORE YOU GO, ARCHIE, I WANT TO SHOW YOU SOMETHING I PRINTED OUT...
I RECEIVED AN E-MAIL FROM GLADYS JONES TODAY, GIVING ME AN UPDATE ON HOW HER FAMILY IS DOING SINCE THEY MOVED TO MONTANA! SHE ATTACHED A PICTURE AND I THOUGHT YOU'D LIKE A COPY...
THANKS, MOM!
BEEF JERKY
12

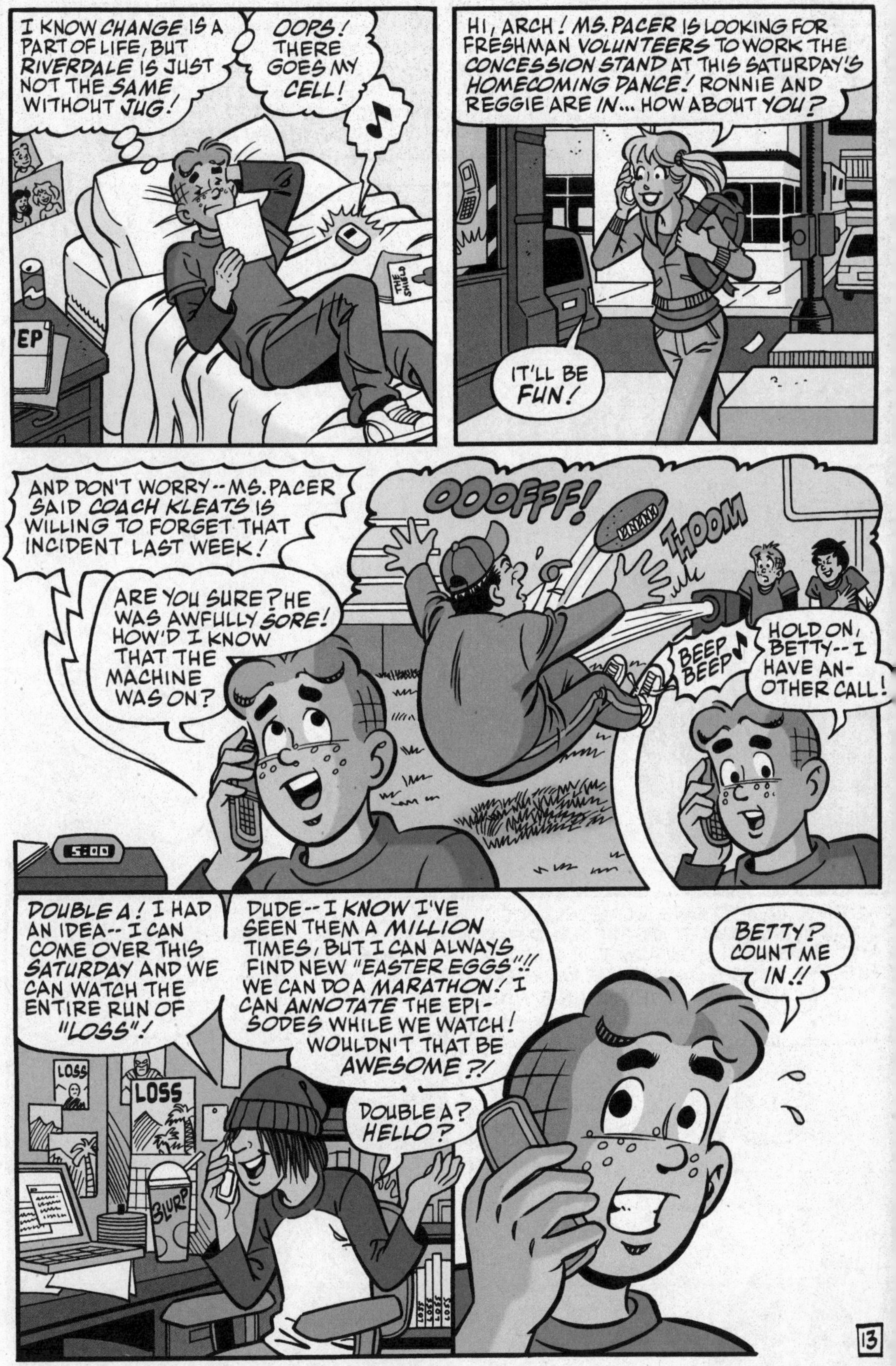
I KNOW CHANGE IS A PART OF LIFE, BUT RIVERDALE IS JUST NOT THE SAME WITHOUT JUG!
OOPS! THERE GOES MY CELL!
EP
THE SHIELD
HI, ARCH! MS. PACER IS LOOKING FOR FRESHMAN VOLUNTEERS TO WORK THE CONCESSION STAND AT THIS SATURDAY'S HOMECOMING DANCE! RONNIE AND REGGIE ARE IN... HOW ABOUT YOU?
IT'LL BE FUN!
AND DON'T WORRY--MS. PACER SAID COACH KLEATS IS WILLING TO FORGET THAT INCIDENT LAST WEEK!
OOOFFF!
THOOM
ARE YOU SURE? HE WAS AWFULLY SORE! HOW'D I KNOW THAT THE MACHINE WAS ON?
BEEP BEEP
HOLD ON, BETTY--I HAVE AN-OTHER CALL!
5:00
DOUBLE A! I HAD AN IDEA--I CAN COME OVER THIS SATURDAY AND WE CAN WATCH THE ENTIRE RUN OF "LOSS"!
DUDE--I KNOW I'VE SEEN THEM A MILLION TIMES, BUT I CAN ALWAYS FIND NEW "EASTER EGGS"!! WE CAN DO A MARATHON! I CAN ANNOTATE THE EPI-SODES WHILE WE WATCH! WOULDN'T THAT BE AWESOME?!
BETTY? COUNT ME IN!!
LOSS
LOSS
BLURP
DOUBLE A? HELLO?
13

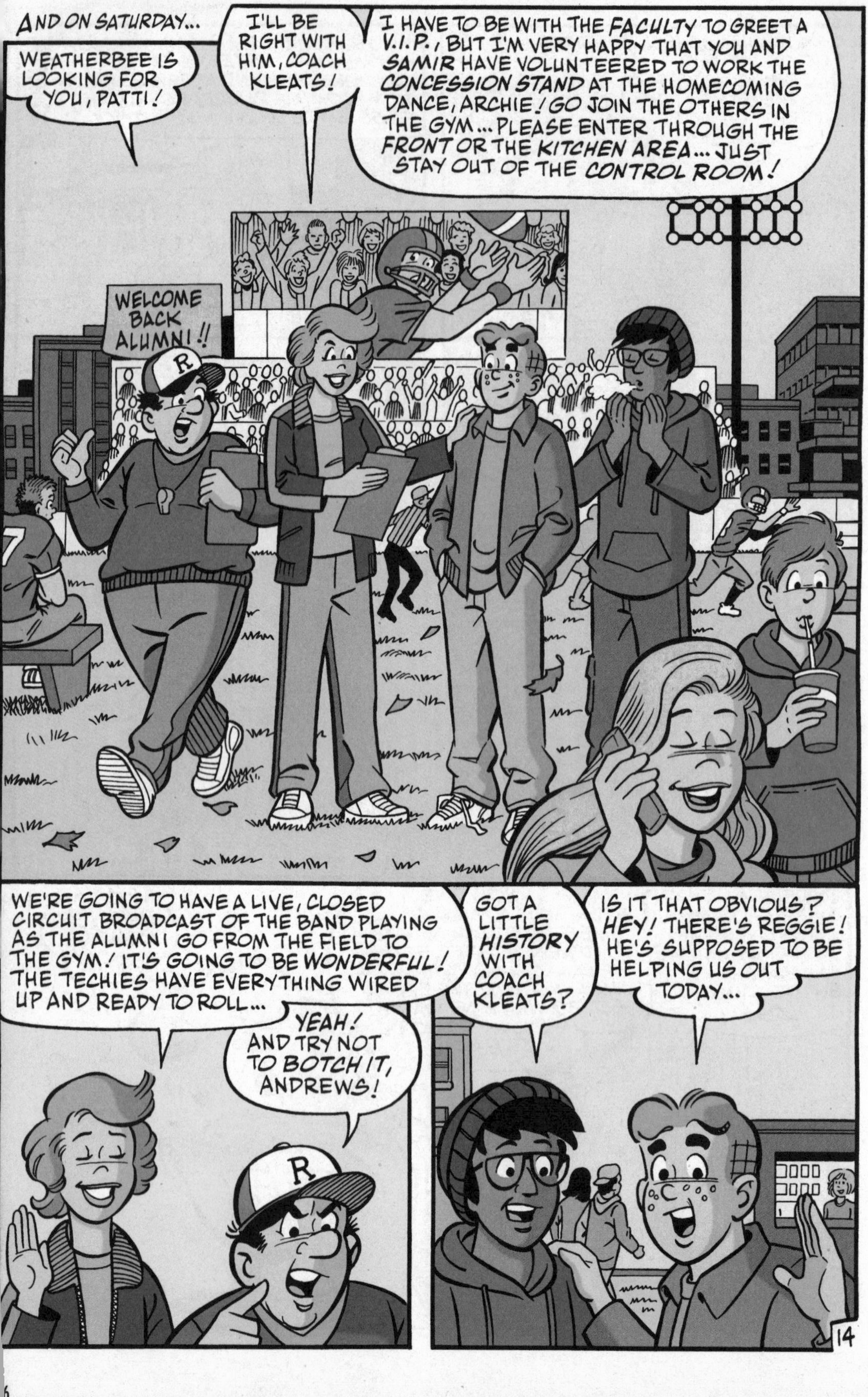
AND ON SATURDAY...
WEATHERBEE IS LOOKING FOR YOU, PATTI!
I'LL BE RIGHT WITH HIM, COACH KLEATS!
I HAVE TO BE WITH THE FACULTY TO GREET A V.I.P., BUT I'M VERY HAPPY THAT YOU AND SAMIR HAVE VOLUNTEERED TO WORK THE CONCESSION STAND AT THE HOMECOMING DANCE, ARCHIE! GO JOIN THE OTHERS IN THE GYM... PLEASE ENTER THROUGH THE FRONT OR THE KITCHEN AREA... JUST STAY OUT OF THE CONTROL ROOM!
WELCOME BACK ALUMNI!!
WE'RE GOING TO HAVE A LIVE, CLOSED CIRCUIT BROADCAST OF THE BAND PLAYING AS THE ALUMNI GO FROM THE FIELD TO THE GYM! IT'S GOING TO BE WONDERFUL! THE TECHIES HAVE EVERYTHING WIRED UP AND READY TO ROLL...
YEAH! AND TRY NOT TO BOTCH IT, ANDREWS!
GOT A LITTLE HISTORY WITH COACH KLEATS?
IS IT THAT OBVIOUS? HEY! THERE'S REGGIE! HE'S SUPPOSED TO BE HELPING US OUT TODAY...
14

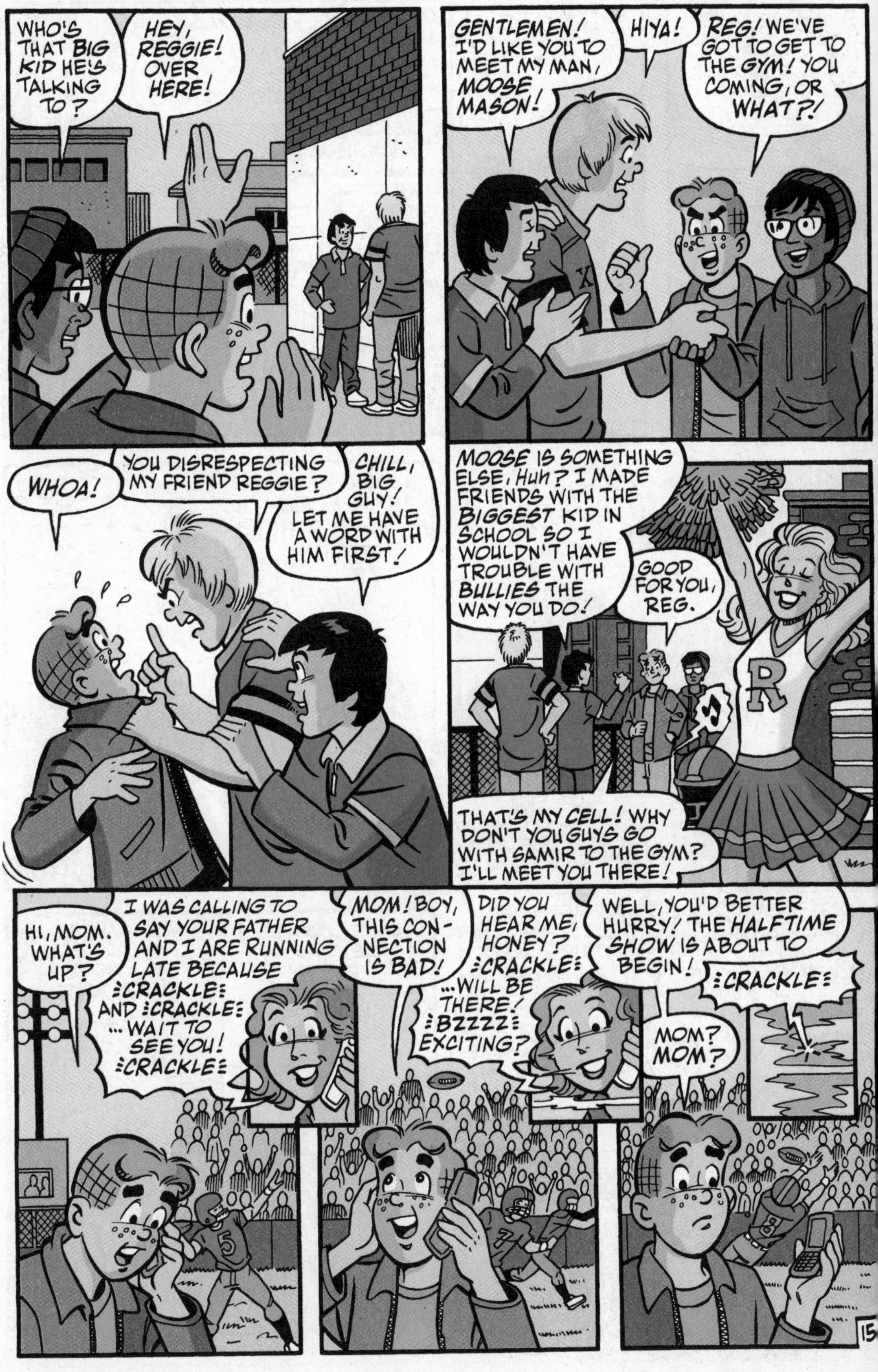
WHO'S THAT BIG KID HE'S TALKING TO?
HEY, REGGIE! OVER HERE!
GENTLEMEN! I'D LIKE YOU TO MEET MY MAN, MOOSE MASON!
HIYA!
REG! WE'VE GOT TO GET TO THE GYM! YOU COMING, OR WHAT?!
WHOA!
YOU DISRESPECTING MY FRIEND REGGIE?
CHILL, BIG GUY! LET ME HAVE A WORD WITH HIM FIRST!
MOOSE IS SOMETHING ELSE, Huh? I MADE FRIENDS WITH THE BIGGEST KID IN SCHOOL SO I WOULDN'T HAVE TROUBLE WITH BULLIES THE WAY YOU DO!
GOOD FOR YOU, REG.
THAT'S MY CELL! WHY DON'T YOU GUYS GO WITH SAMIR TO THE GYM? I'LL MEET YOU THERE!
HI, MOM. WHAT'S UP?
I WAS CALLING TO SAY YOUR FATHER AND I ARE RUNNING LATE BECAUSE ꞉CRACKLE꞉ AND ꞉CRACKLE꞉ ...WAIT TO SEE YOU! ꞉CRACKLE꞉
MOM! BOY, THIS CON-NECTION IS BAD!
DID YOU HEAR ME, HONEY? ꞉CRACKLE꞉ ...WILL BE THERE! ꞉BZZZZ꞉ EXCITING?
WELL, YOU'D BETTER HURRY! THE HALFTIME SHOW IS ABOUT TO BEGIN!
꞉CRACKLE꞉
MOM? MOM?
15

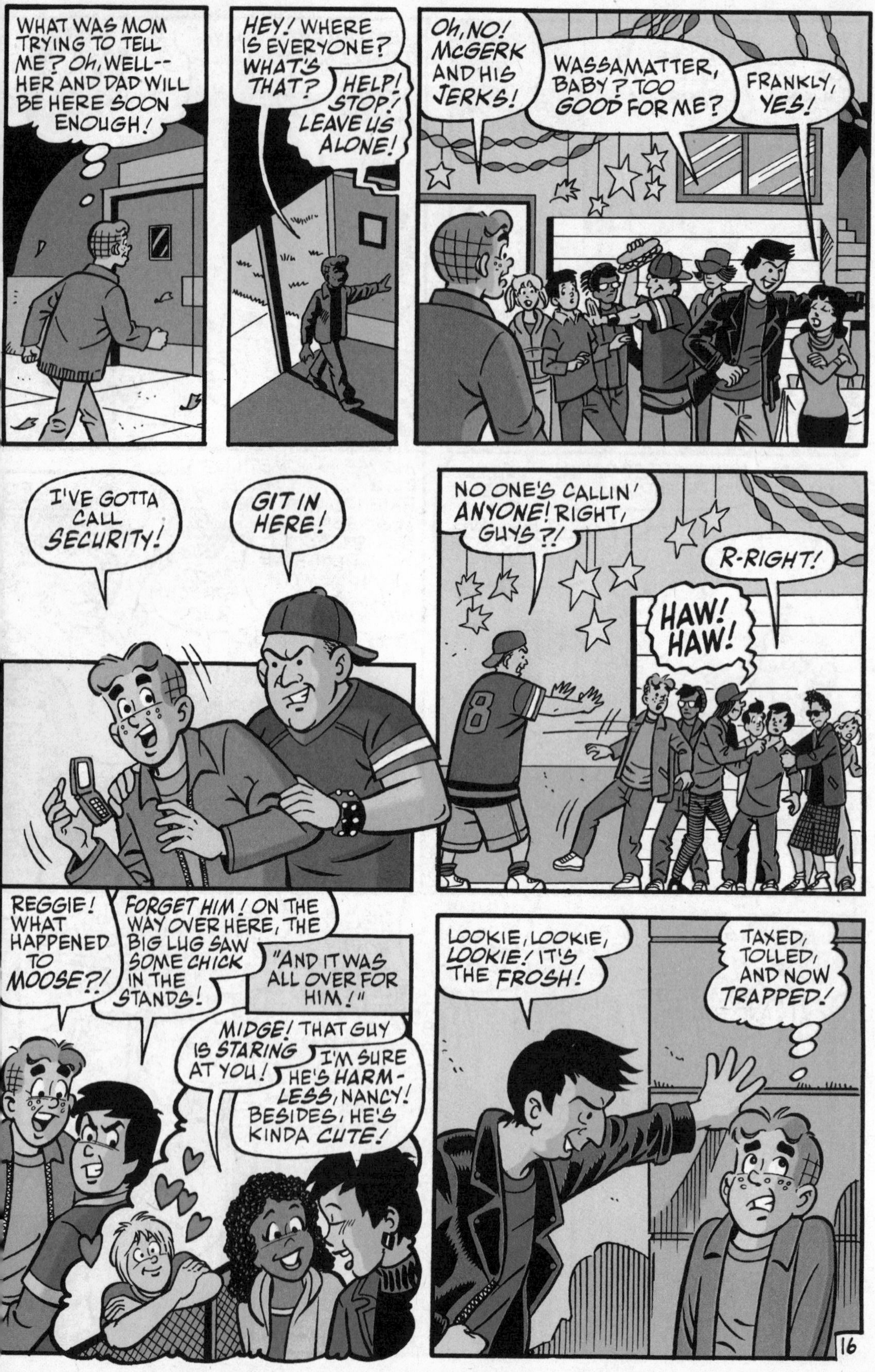
WHAT WAS MOM TRYING TO TELL ME? Oh, WELL-- HER AND DAD WILL BE HERE SOON ENOUGH!
HEY! WHERE IS EVERYONE? WHAT'S THAT?
HELP! STOP! LEAVE US ALONE!
Oh, NO! McGERK AND HIS JERKS!
WASSAMATTER, BABY? TOO GOOD FOR ME?
FRANKLY, YES!
I'VE GOTTA CALL SECURITY!
GIT IN HERE!
NO ONE'S CALLIN' ANYONE! RIGHT, GUYS?!
R-RIGHT!
HAW! HAW!
REGGIE! WHAT HAPPENED TO MOOSE?!
FORGET HIM! ON THE WAY OVER HERE, THE BIG LUG SAW SOME CHICK IN THE STANDS!
"AND IT WAS ALL OVER FOR HIM!"
MIDGE! THAT GUY IS STARING AT YOU!
I'M SURE HE'S HARMLESS, NANCY! BESIDES, HE'S KINDA CUTE!
LOOKIE, LOOKIE, LOOKIE! IT'S THE FROSH!
TAXED, TOLLED, AND NOW TRAPPED!
16

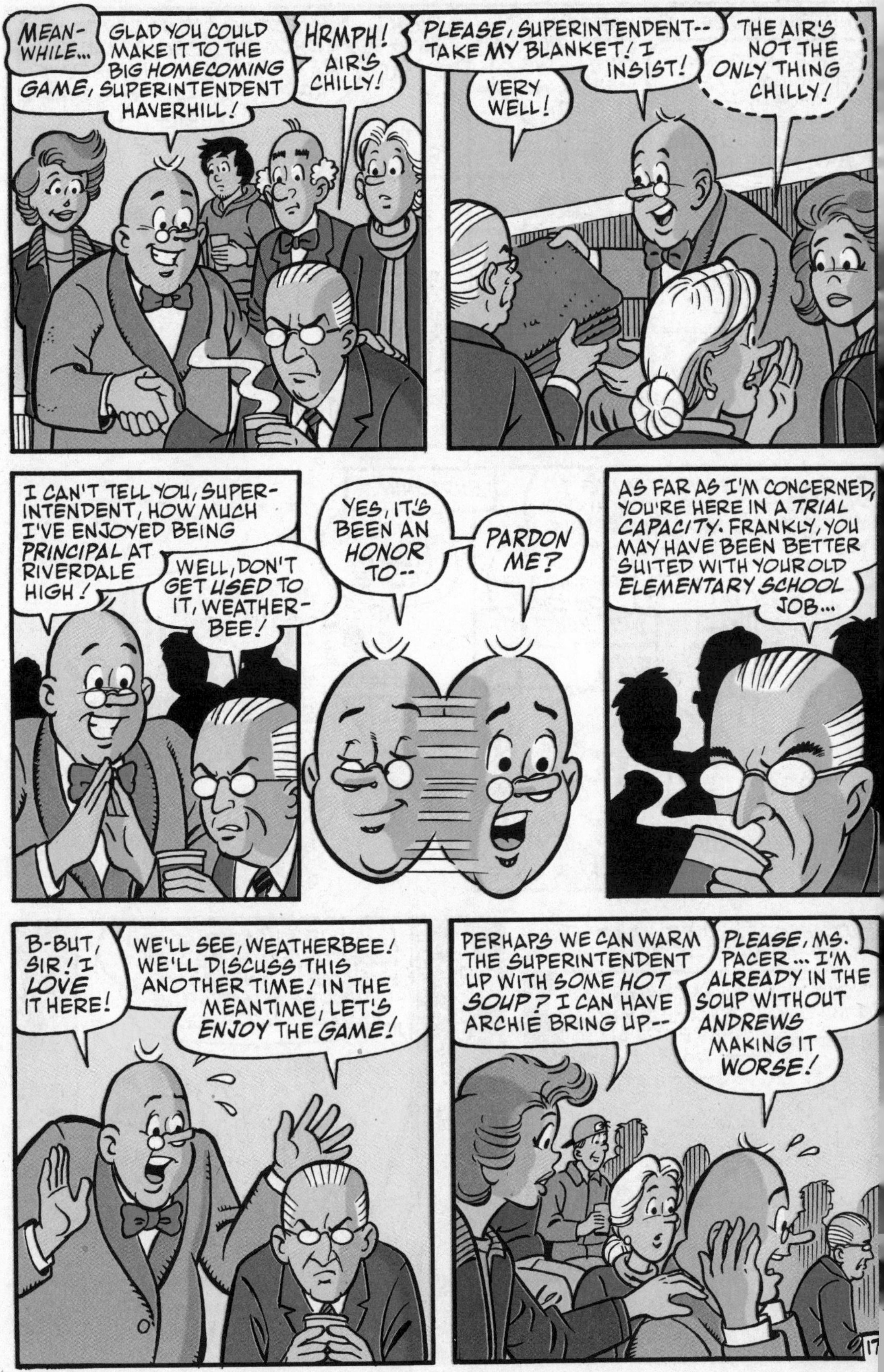
MEAN-WHILE...
GLAD YOU COULD MAKE IT TO THE BIG HOMECOMING GAME, SUPERINTENDENT HAVERHILL!
HRMPH! AIR'S CHILLY!
PLEASE, SUPERINTENDENT-- TAKE MY BLANKET! I INSIST!
VERY WELL!
THE AIR'S NOT THE ONLY THING CHILLY!
I CAN'T TELL YOU, SUPER-INTENDENT, HOW MUCH I'VE ENJOYED BEING PRINCIPAL AT RIVERDALE HIGH!
WELL, DON'T GET USED TO IT, WEATHER-BEE!
YES, IT'S BEEN AN HONOR TO--
PARDON ME?
AS FAR AS I'M CONCERNED, YOU'RE HERE IN A TRIAL CAPACITY. FRANKLY, YOU MAY HAVE BEEN BETTER SUITED WITH YOUR OLD ELEMENTARY SCHOOL JOB...
B-BUT, SIR! I LOVE IT HERE!
WE'LL SEE, WEATHERBEE! WE'LL DISCUSS THIS ANOTHER TIME! IN THE MEANTIME, LET'S ENJOY THE GAME!
PERHAPS WE CAN WARM THE SUPERINTENDENT UP WITH SOME HOT SOUP? I CAN HAVE ARCHIE BRING UP--
PLEASE, MS. PACER... I'M ALREADY IN THE SOUP WITHOUT ANDREWS MAKING IT WORSE!
17

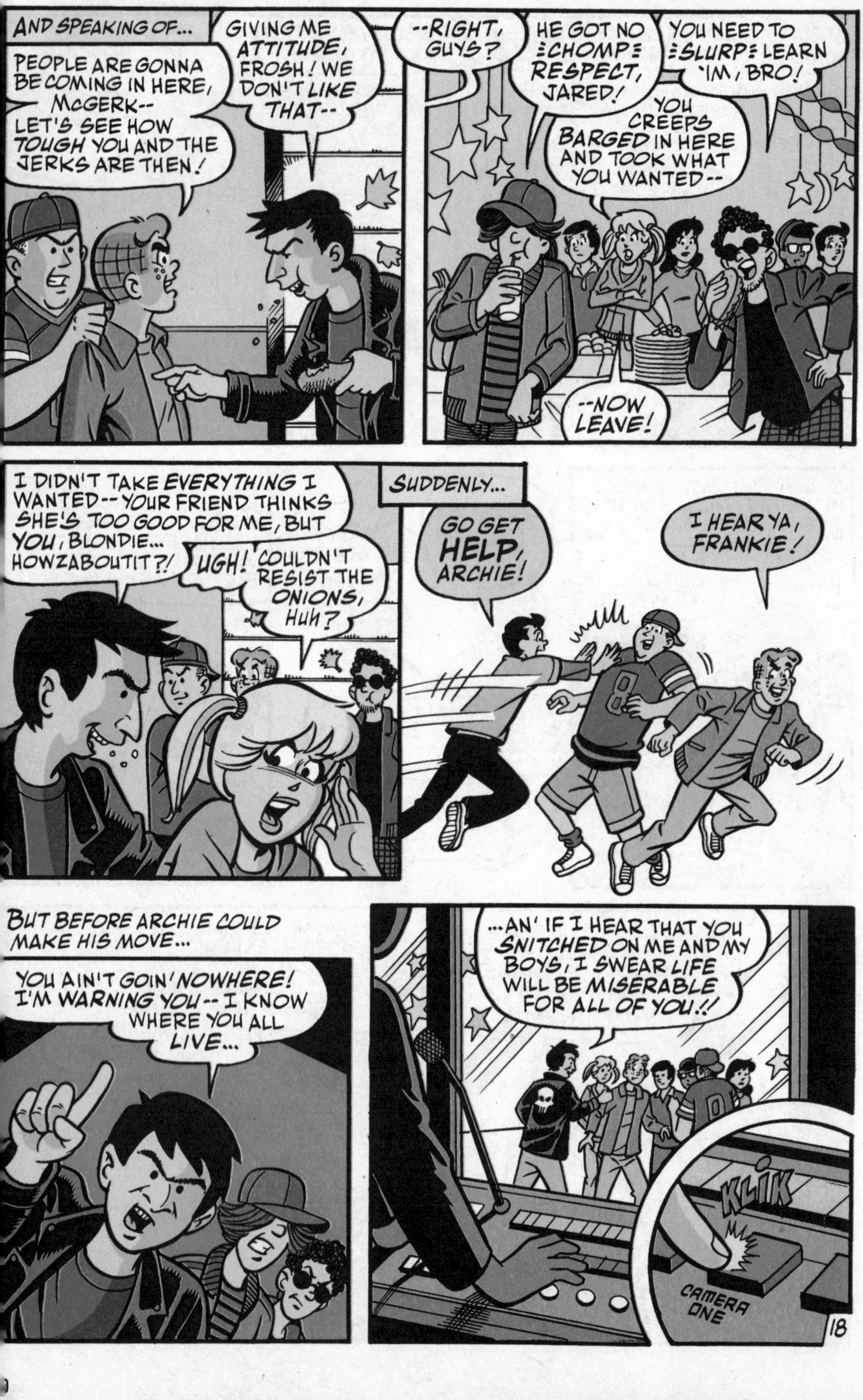
AND SPEAKING OF...
PEOPLE ARE GONNA BE COMING IN HERE, McGERK-- LET'S SEE HOW TOUGH YOU AND THE JERKS ARE THEN!
GIVING ME ATTITUDE, FROSH! WE DON'T LIKE THAT--
--RIGHT, GUYS?
HE GOT NO CHOMP RESPECT, JARED!
YOU NEED TO SLURP LEARN 'IM, BRO!
YOU CREEPS BARGED IN HERE AND TOOK WHAT YOU WANTED--
--NOW LEAVE!
I DIDN'T TAKE EVERYTHING I WANTED-- YOUR FRIEND THINKS SHE'S TOO GOOD FOR ME, BUT YOU, BLONDIE... HOWZABOUTIT?!
UGH!
COULDN'T RESIST THE ONIONS, HUH?
SUDDENLY...
GO GET HELP, ARCHIE!
I HEAR YA, FRANKIE!
BUT BEFORE ARCHIE COULD MAKE HIS MOVE...
YOU AIN'T GOIN' NOWHERE! I'M WARNING YOU-- I KNOW WHERE YOU ALL LIVE...
...AN' IF I HEAR THAT YOU SNITCHED ON ME AND MY BOYS, I SWEAR LIFE WILL BE MISERABLE FOR ALL OF YOU!!
KLIK
CAMERA ONE
18

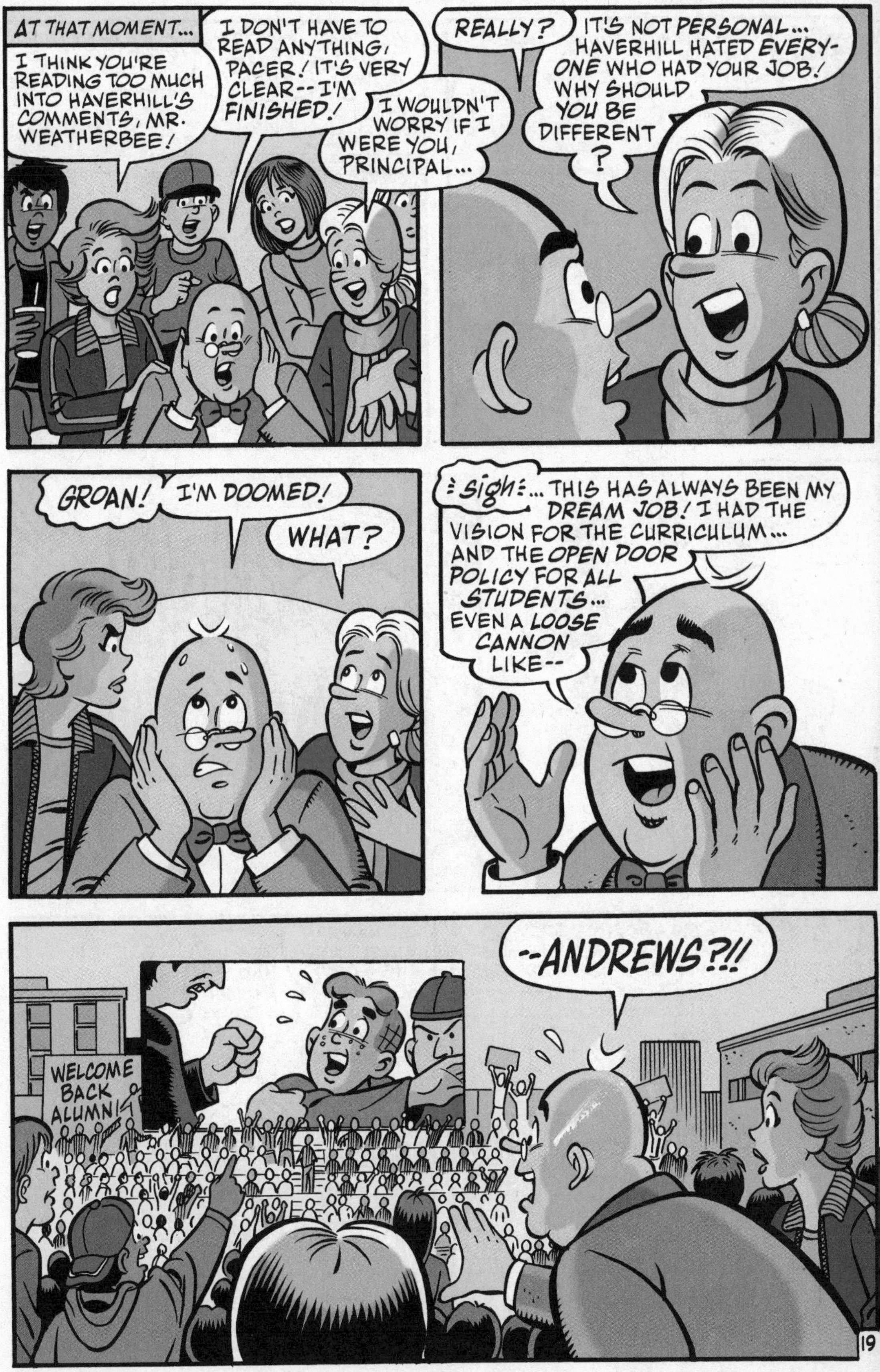
AT THAT MOMENT...
I THINK YOU'RE READING TOO MUCH INTO HAVERHILL'S COMMENTS, MR. WEATHERBEE!
I DON'T HAVE TO READ ANYTHING, PACER! IT'S VERY CLEAR -- I'M FINISHED!
I WOULDN'T WORRY IF I WERE YOU, PRINCIPAL...
REALLY?
IT'S NOT PERSONAL... HAVERHILL HATED EVERY-ONE WHO HAD YOUR JOB! WHY SHOULD YOU BE DIFFERENT?
GROAN!
I'M DOOMED!
WHAT?
:sigh:... THIS HAS ALWAYS BEEN MY DREAM JOB! I HAD THE VISION FOR THE CURRICULUM... AND THE OPEN DOOR POLICY FOR ALL STUDENTS... EVEN A LOOSE CANNON LIKE--
--ANDREWS?!!
WELCOME BACK ALUMNI!
19

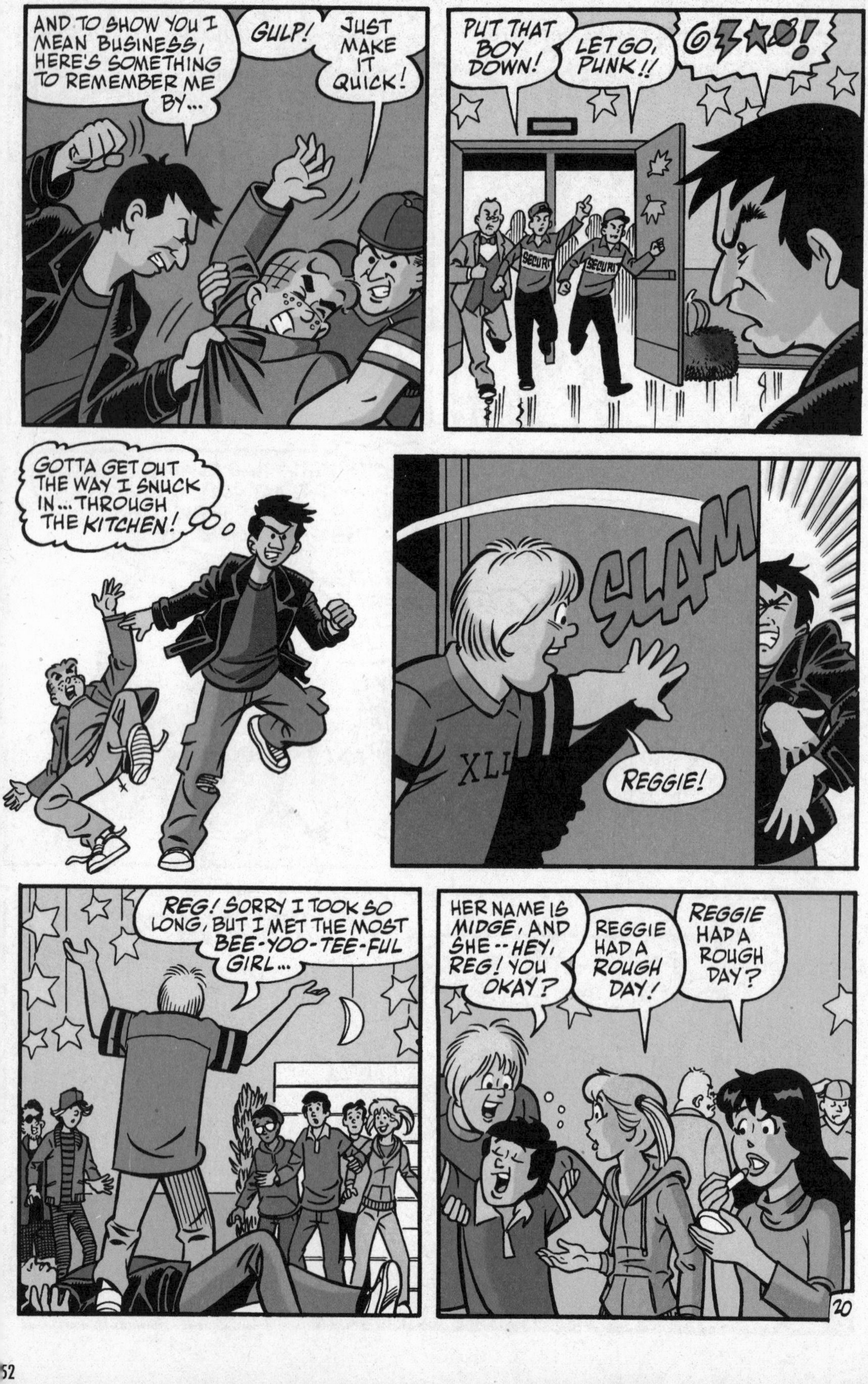
AND TO SHOW YOU I MEAN BUSINESS, HERE'S SOMETHING TO REMEMBER ME BY...
GULP!
JUST MAKE IT QUICK!
PUT THAT BOY DOWN!
LET GO, PUNK!!
SECURI
SECURI
GOTTA GET OUT THE WAY I SNUCK IN... THROUGH THE KITCHEN!
SLAM
XLI
REGGIE!
REG! SORRY I TOOK SO LONG, BUT I MET THE MOST BEE-YOO-TEE-FUL GIRL...
HER NAME IS MIDGE, AND SHE -- HEY, REG! YOU OKAY?
REGGIE HAD A ROUGH DAY!
REGGIE HAD A ROUGH DAY?
20

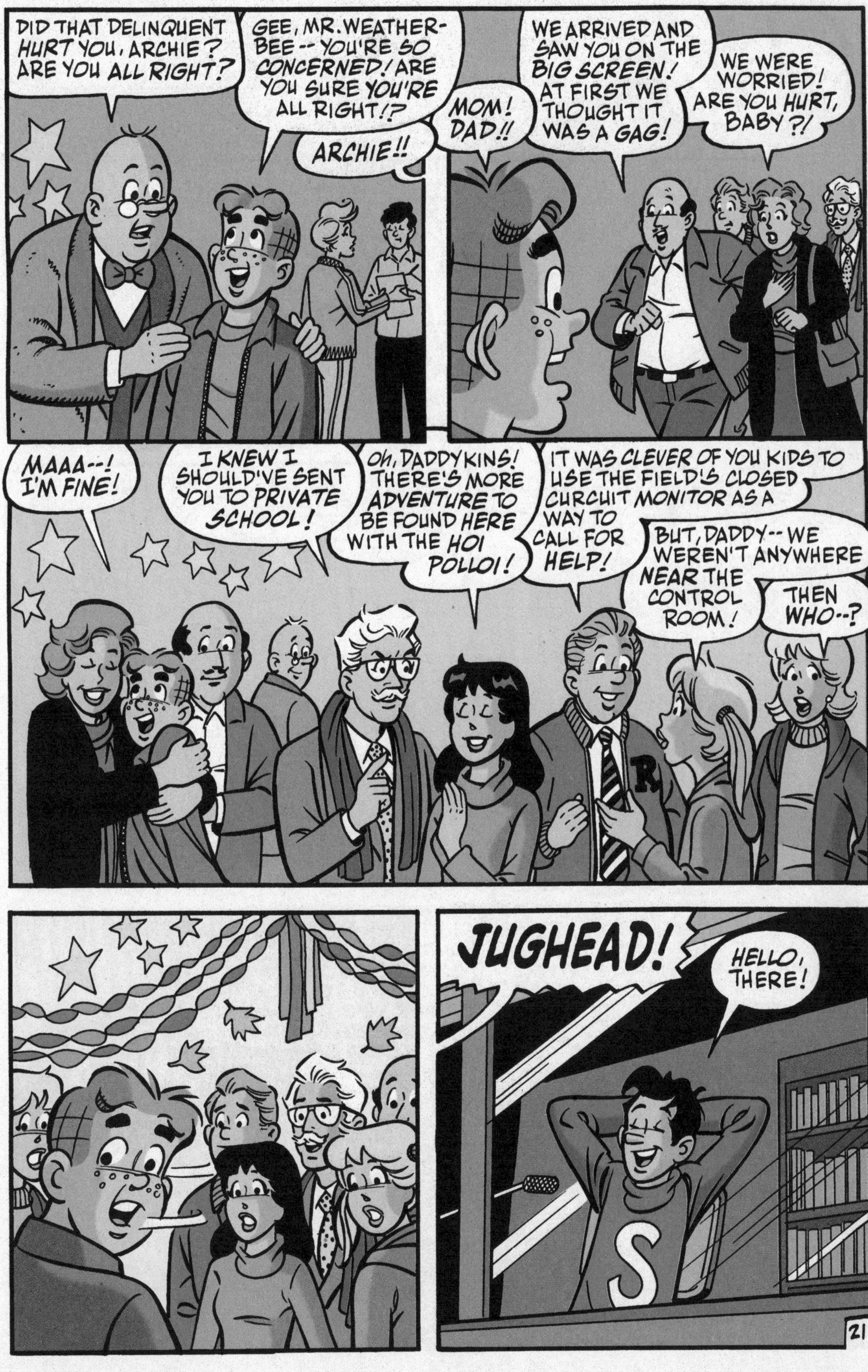
DID THAT DELINQUENT HURT YOU, ARCHIE? ARE YOU ALL RIGHT?
GEE, MR. WEATHERBEE -- YOU'RE SO CONCERNED! ARE YOU SURE YOU'RE ALL RIGHT!?
ARCHIE!!
MOM! DAD!!
WE ARRIVED AND SAW YOU ON THE BIG SCREEN! AT FIRST WE THOUGHT IT WAS A GAG!
WE WERE WORRIED! ARE YOU HURT, BABY?!
MAAA--! I'M FINE!
I KNEW I SHOULD'VE SENT YOU TO PRIVATE SCHOOL!
OH, DADDYKINS! THERE'S MORE ADVENTURE TO BE FOUND HERE WITH THE HOI POLLOI!
IT WAS CLEVER OF YOU KIDS TO USE THE FIELD'S CLOSED CURCUIT MONITOR AS A WAY TO CALL FOR HELP!
BUT, DADDY-- WE WEREN'T ANYWHERE NEAR THE CONTROL ROOM!
THEN WHO--?
JUGHEAD!
HELLO, THERE!
21

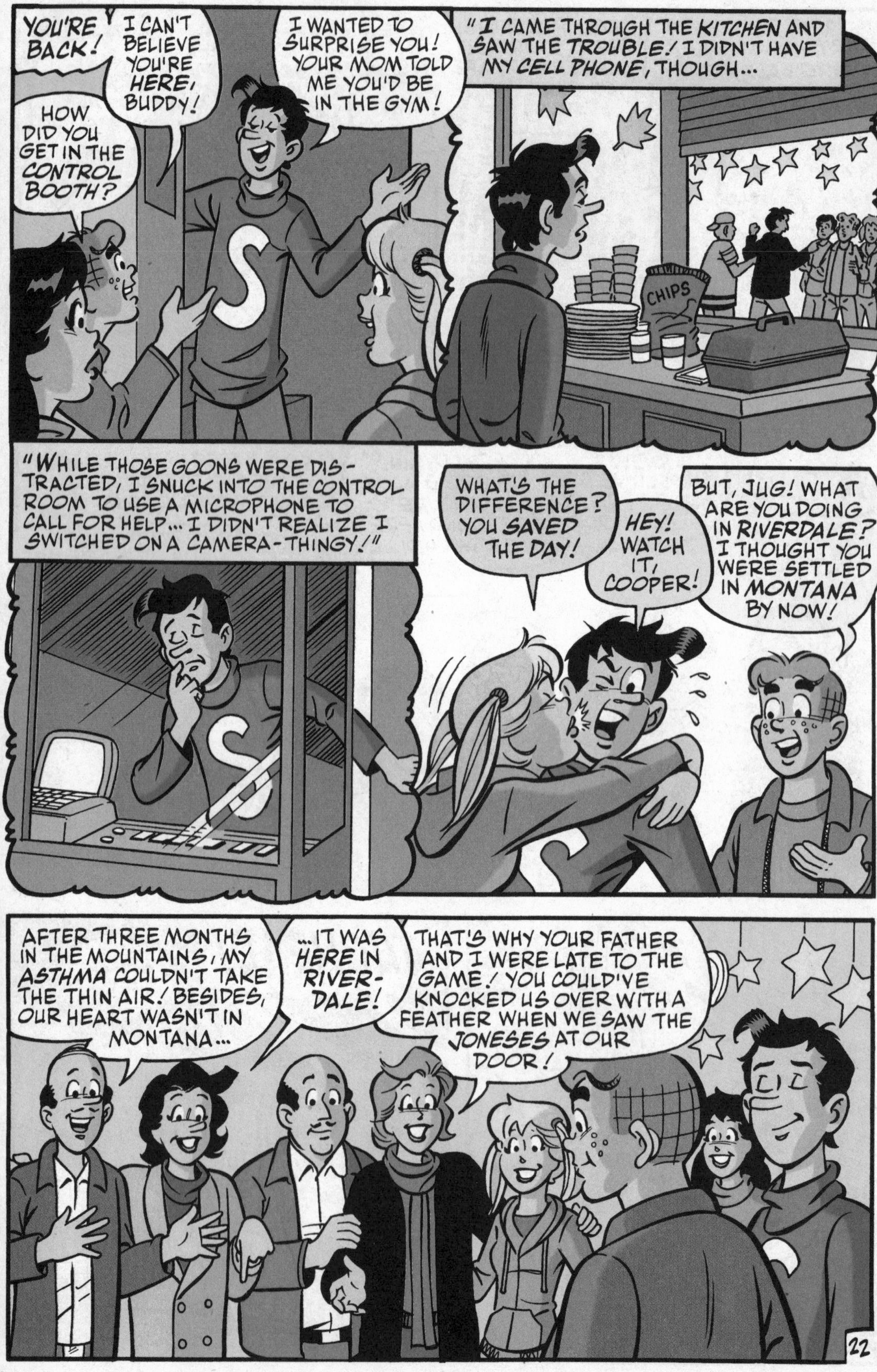
YOU'RE BACK!
I CAN'T BELIEVE YOU'RE HERE, BUDDY!
HOW DID YOU GET IN THE CONTROL BOOTH?
I WANTED TO SURPRISE YOU! YOUR MOM TOLD ME YOU'D BE IN THE GYM!
"I CAME THROUGH THE KITCHEN AND SAW THE TROUBLE! I DIDN'T HAVE MY CELL PHONE, THOUGH...
CHIPS
"WHILE THOSE GOONS WERE DISTRACTED, I SNUCK INTO THE CONTROL ROOM TO USE A MICROPHONE TO CALL FOR HELP... I DIDN'T REALIZE I SWITCHED ON A CAMERA-THINGY!"
WHAT'S THE DIFFERENCE? YOU SAVED THE DAY!
HEY! WATCH IT, COOPER!
BUT, JUG! WHAT ARE YOU DOING IN RIVERDALE? I THOUGHT YOU WERE SETTLED IN MONTANA BY NOW!
AFTER THREE MONTHS IN THE MOUNTAINS, MY ASTHMA COULDN'T TAKE THE THIN AIR! BESIDES, OUR HEART WASN'T IN MONTANA...
...IT WAS HERE IN RIVERDALE!
THAT'S WHY YOUR FATHER AND I WERE LATE TO THE GAME! YOU COULD'VE KNOCKED US OVER WITH A FEATHER WHEN WE SAW THE JONESES AT OUR DOOR!
22

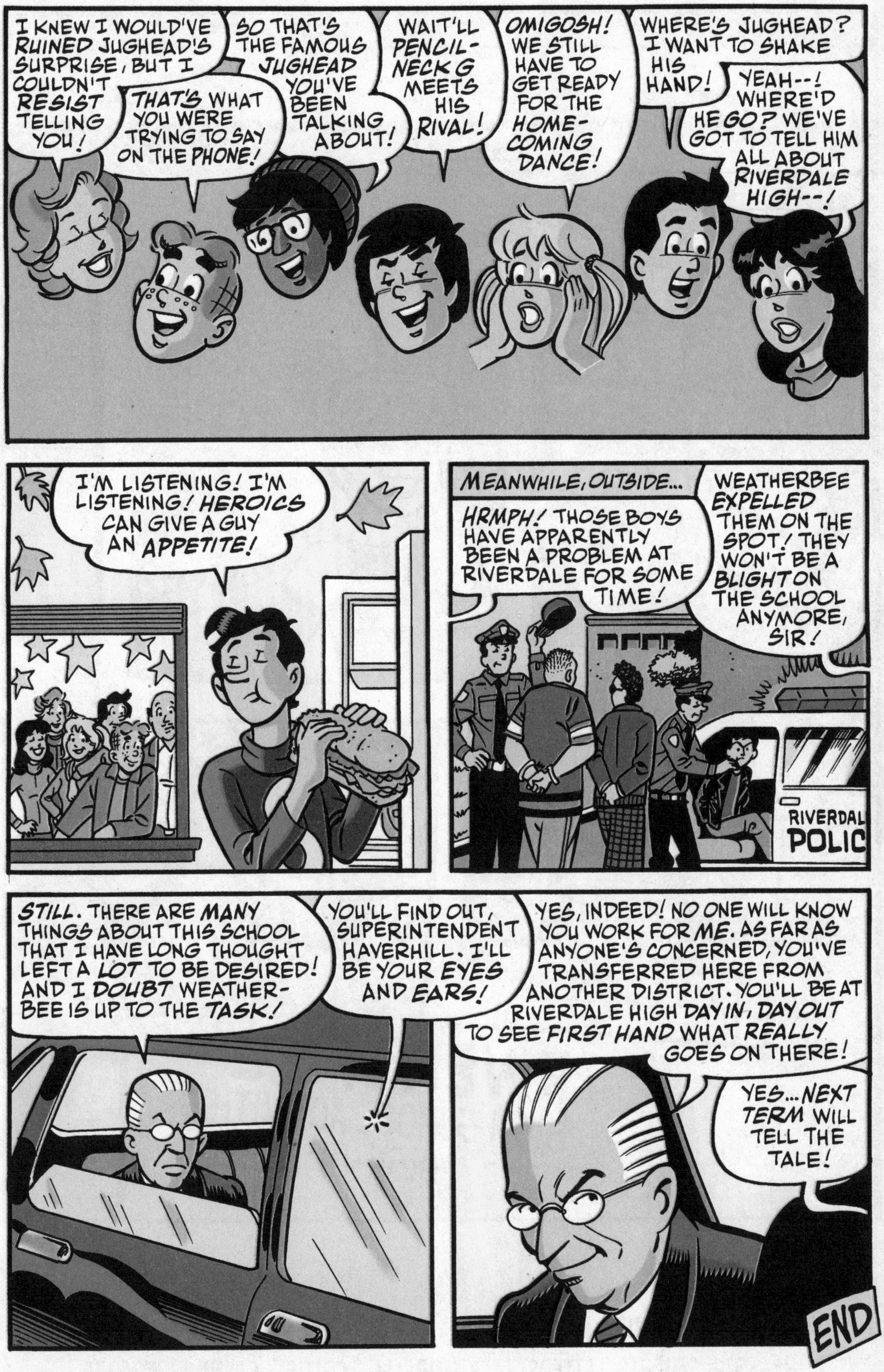
I KNEW I WOULD'VE RUINED JUGHEAD'S SURPRISE, BUT I COULDN'T RESIST TELLING YOU!
THAT'S WHAT YOU WERE TRYING TO SAY ON THE PHONE!
SO THAT'S THE FAMOUS JUGHEAD YOU'VE BEEN TALKING ABOUT!
WAIT'LL PENCIL-NECK G MEETS HIS RIVAL!
OMIGOSH! WE STILL HAVE TO GET READY FOR THE HOME-COMING DANCE!
WHERE'S JUGHEAD? I WANT TO SHAKE HIS HAND!
YEAH--! WHERE'D HE GO? WE'VE GOT TO TELL HIM ALL ABOUT RIVERDALE HIGH--!
I'M LISTENING! I'M LISTENING! HEROICS CAN GIVE A GUY AN APPETITE!
MEANWHILE, OUTSIDE...
HRMPH! THOSE BOYS HAVE APPARENTLY BEEN A PROBLEM AT RIVERDALE FOR SOME TIME!
WEATHERBEE EXPELLED THEM ON THE SPOT! THEY WON'T BE A BLIGHT ON THE SCHOOL ANYMORE, SIR!
RIVERDAL
POLIC
STILL. THERE ARE MANY THINGS ABOUT THIS SCHOOL THAT I HAVE LONG THOUGHT LEFT A LOT TO BE DESIRED! AND I DOUBT WEATHER-BEE IS UP TO THE TASK!
YOU'LL FIND OUT, SUPERINTENDENT HAVERHILL. I'LL BE YOUR EYES AND EARS!
YES, INDEED! NO ONE WILL KNOW YOU WORK FOR ME. AS FAR AS ANYONE'S CONCERNED, YOU'VE TRANSFERRED HERE FROM ANOTHER DISTRICT. YOU'LL BE AT RIVERDALE HIGH DAY IN, DAY OUT TO SEE FIRST HAND WHAT REALLY GOES ON THERE!
YES... NEXT TERM WILL TELL THE TALE!
END

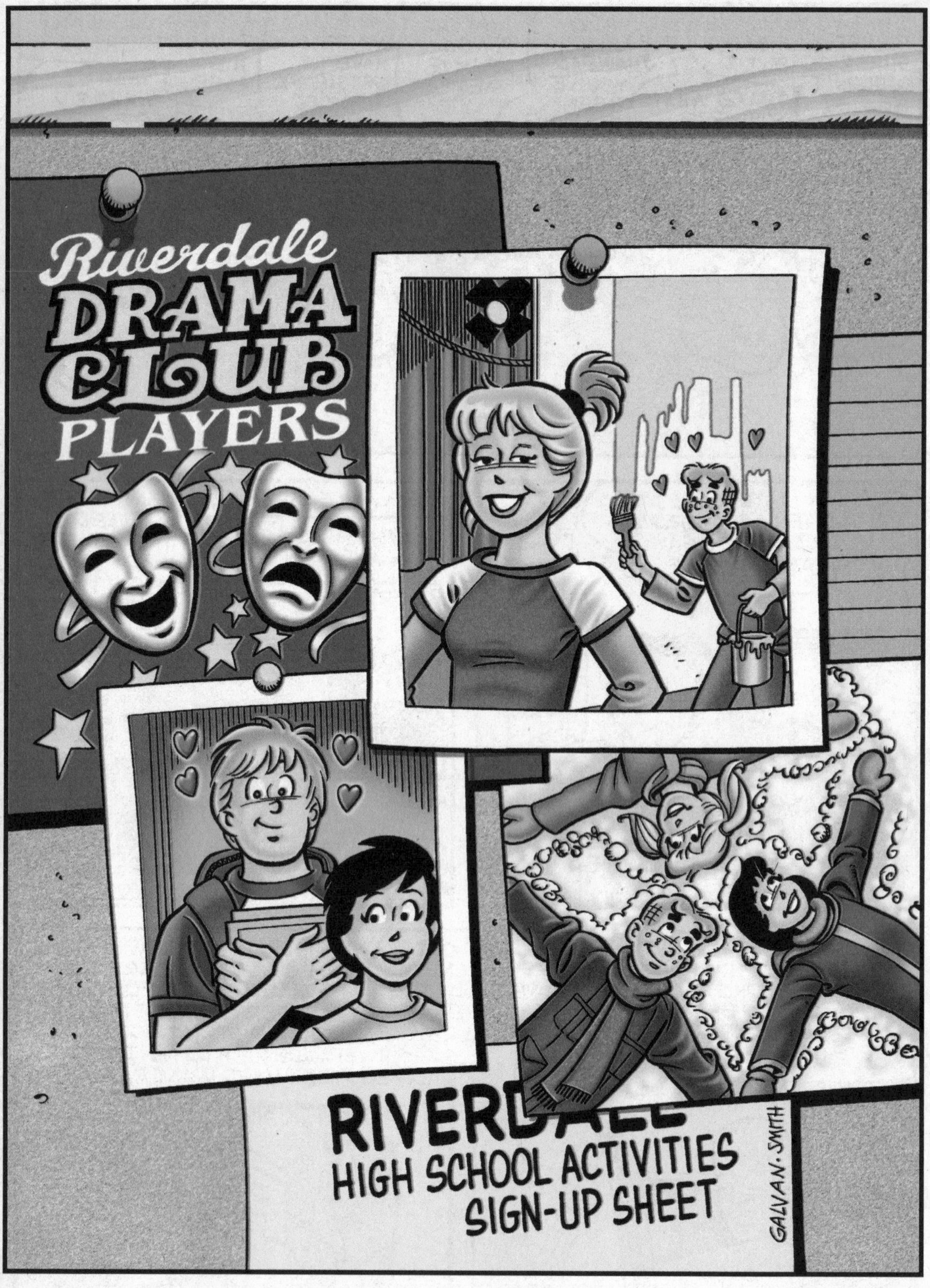

Riverdale DRAMA CLUB PLAYERS
RIVERD
HIGH SCHOOL ACTIVITIES SIGN-UP SHEET
GALVAN · SMITH

FRESHMAN YEAR PART 3

SCRIPT: BATTON LASH PENCILS: BILL GALVAN

INKS: BOB SMITH LETTERS: JACK MORELLI COLORS: GLENN WHITMORE

VROOM VROOM

RIVERDALE HAS ALWAYS BEEN A NICE PLACE TO LIVE...

...AND WE'D LIKE TO KEEP IT THAT WAY.!!

ONE WAY →

RIVERDALE SCHOOL DISTRICT

WE HAVE REVIEWED THE REPORTS OF MR. WEATHERBEE AND THE PRINCIPAL WHO PRECEEDED HIM CONCERNING YOUR *CONDUCT* AT RIVERDALE HIGH...

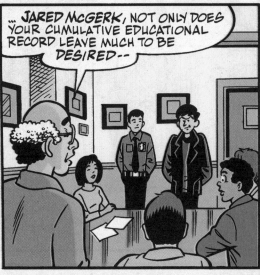

...*JARED McGERK*, NOT ONLY DOES YOUR CUMULATIVE EDUCATIONAL RECORD LEAVE MUCH TO BE *DESIRED*--

--BUT YOUR CONTINUED PRESENCE IN RIVERDALE HIGH POSES A *THREAT* TO THE OTHER STUDENTS.

THIS SCHOOL BOARD RE-JECTS YOUR APPEAL TO BEING EXPELLED. YOUR EXPULSION STANDS.

DO YOU HAVE ANYTHING TO *SAY*, YOUNG MAN?

YEAH... TELL *ANDREWS* I'LL BE IN *TOUCH*...

FRESHMAN YEAR

PART 3 OF 5

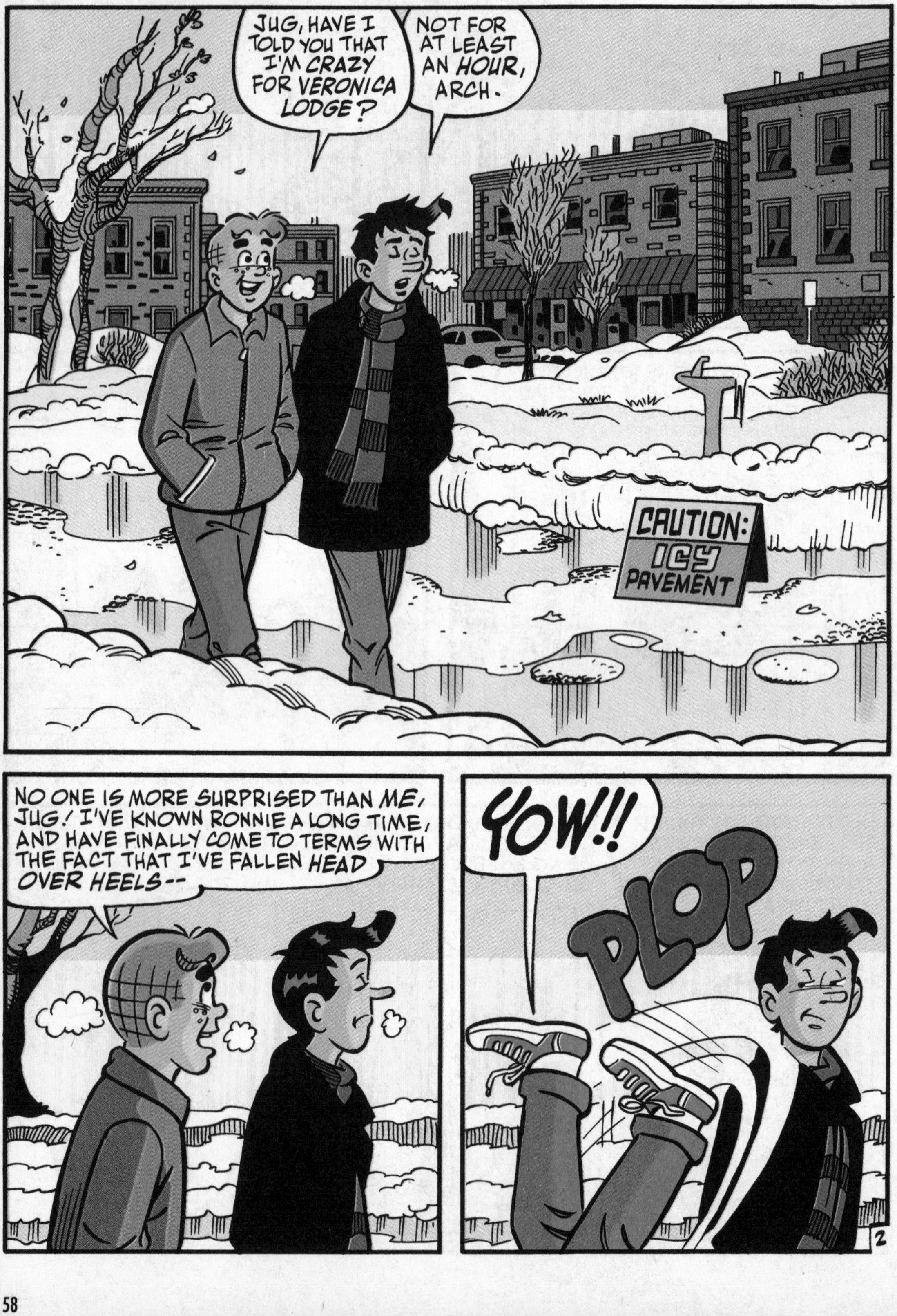
JUG, HAVE I TOLD YOU THAT I'M CRAZY FOR VERONICA LODGE?
NOT FOR AT LEAST AN HOUR, ARCH.
CAUTION: ICY PAVEMENT
NO ONE IS MORE SURPRISED THAN ME, JUG! I'VE KNOWN RONNIE A LONG TIME, AND HAVE FINALLY COME TO TERMS WITH THE FACT THAT I'VE FALLEN HEAD OVER HEELS--
YOW!!
PLOP
2

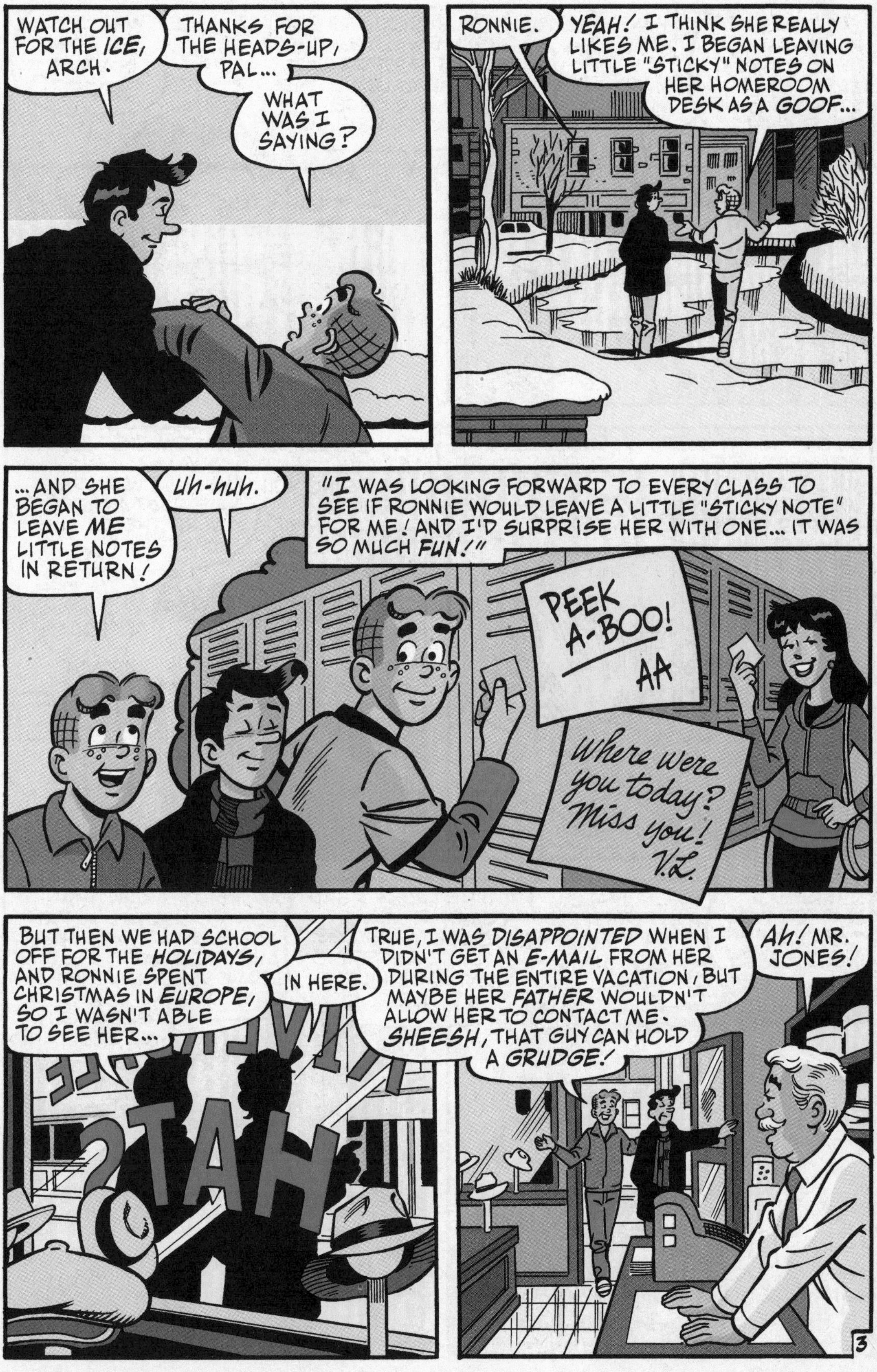
WATCH OUT FOR THE ICE, ARCH.
THANKS FOR THE HEADS-UP, PAL...
WHAT WAS I SAYING?
RONNIE.
YEAH! I THINK SHE REALLY LIKES ME. I BEGAN LEAVING LITTLE "STICKY" NOTES ON HER HOMEROOM DESK AS A GOOF...
...AND SHE BEGAN TO LEAVE ME LITTLE NOTES IN RETURN!
uh-huh.
"I WAS LOOKING FORWARD TO EVERY CLASS TO SEE IF RONNIE WOULD LEAVE A LITTLE "STICKY NOTE" FOR ME! AND I'D SURPRISE HER WITH ONE... IT WAS SO MUCH FUN!"
PEEK A-BOO! AA
Where were you today? Miss you! V.L.
BUT THEN WE HAD SCHOOL OFF FOR THE HOLIDAYS, AND RONNIE SPENT CHRISTMAS IN EUROPE, SO I WASN'T ABLE TO SEE HER...
IN HERE.
TRUE, I WAS DISAPPOINTED WHEN I DIDN'T GET AN E-MAIL FROM HER DURING THE ENTIRE VACATION, BUT MAYBE HER FATHER WOULDN'T ALLOW HER TO CONTACT ME. SHEESH, THAT GUY CAN HOLD A GRUDGE!
Ah! MR. JONES!
3

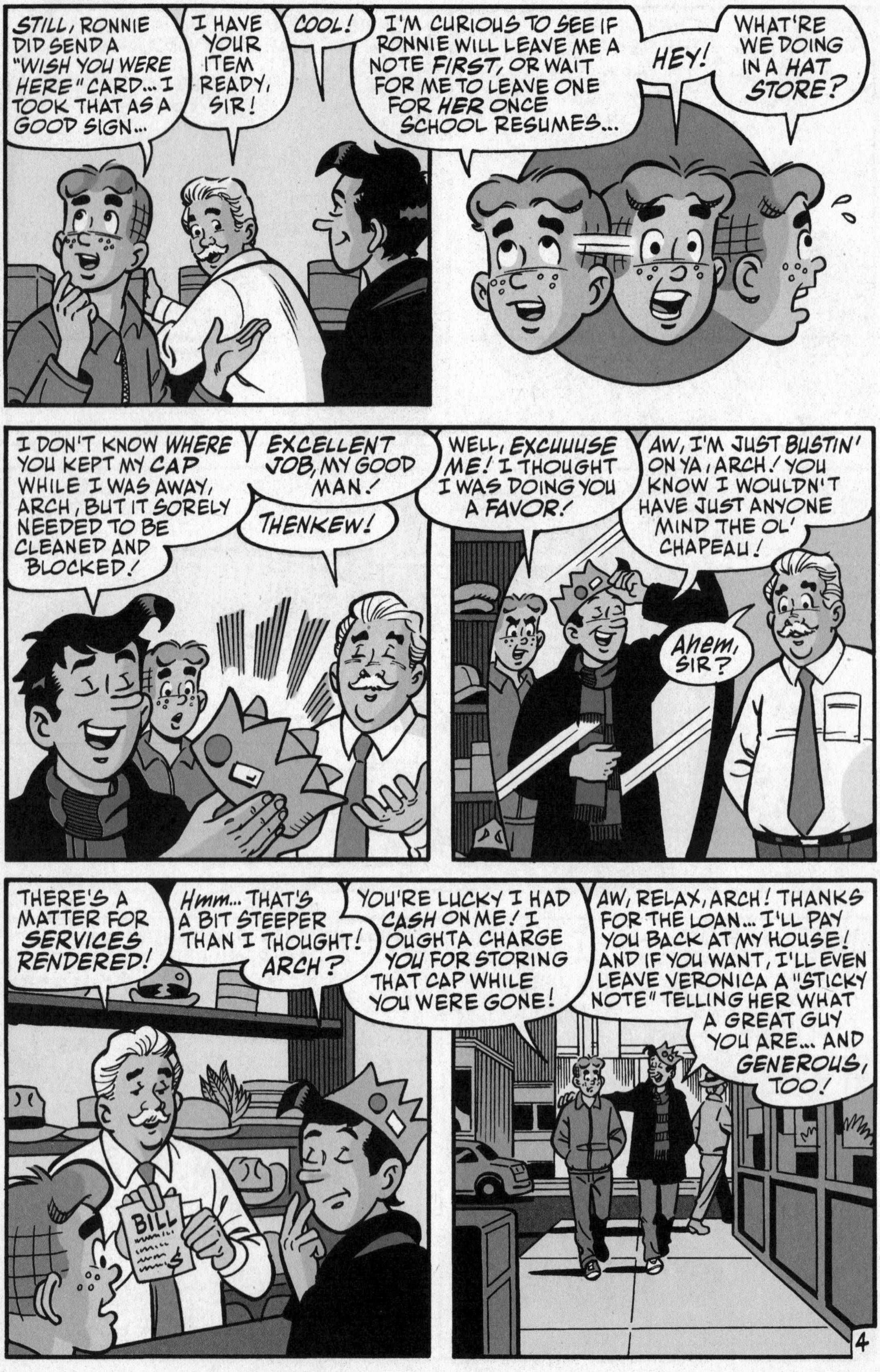
STILL, RONNIE DID SEND A "WISH YOU WERE HERE" CARD... I TOOK THAT AS A GOOD SIGN...
I HAVE YOUR ITEM READY, SIR!
COOL!
I'M CURIOUS TO SEE IF RONNIE WILL LEAVE ME A NOTE FIRST, OR WAIT FOR ME TO LEAVE ONE FOR HER ONCE SCHOOL RESUMES...
HEY!
WHAT'RE WE DOING IN A HAT STORE?
I DON'T KNOW WHERE YOU KEPT MY CAP WHILE I WAS AWAY, ARCH, BUT IT SORELY NEEDED TO BE CLEANED AND BLOCKED!
EXCELLENT JOB, MY GOOD MAN!
THENKEW!
WELL, EXCUUUSE ME! I THOUGHT I WAS DOING YOU A FAVOR!
AW, I'M JUST BUSTIN' ON YA, ARCH! YOU KNOW I WOULDN'T HAVE JUST ANYONE MIND THE OL' CHAPEAU!
Ahem, SIR?
THERE'S A MATTER FOR SERVICES RENDERED!
Hmm... THAT'S A BIT STEEPER THAN I THOUGHT! ARCH?
BILL
YOU'RE LUCKY I HAD CASH ON ME! I OUGHTA CHARGE YOU FOR STORING THAT CAP WHILE YOU WERE GONE!
AW, RELAX, ARCH! THANKS FOR THE LOAN... I'LL PAY YOU BACK AT MY HOUSE! AND IF YOU WANT, I'LL EVEN LEAVE VERONICA A "STICKY NOTE" TELLING HER WHAT A GREAT GUY YOU ARE... AND GENEROUS, TOO!
4

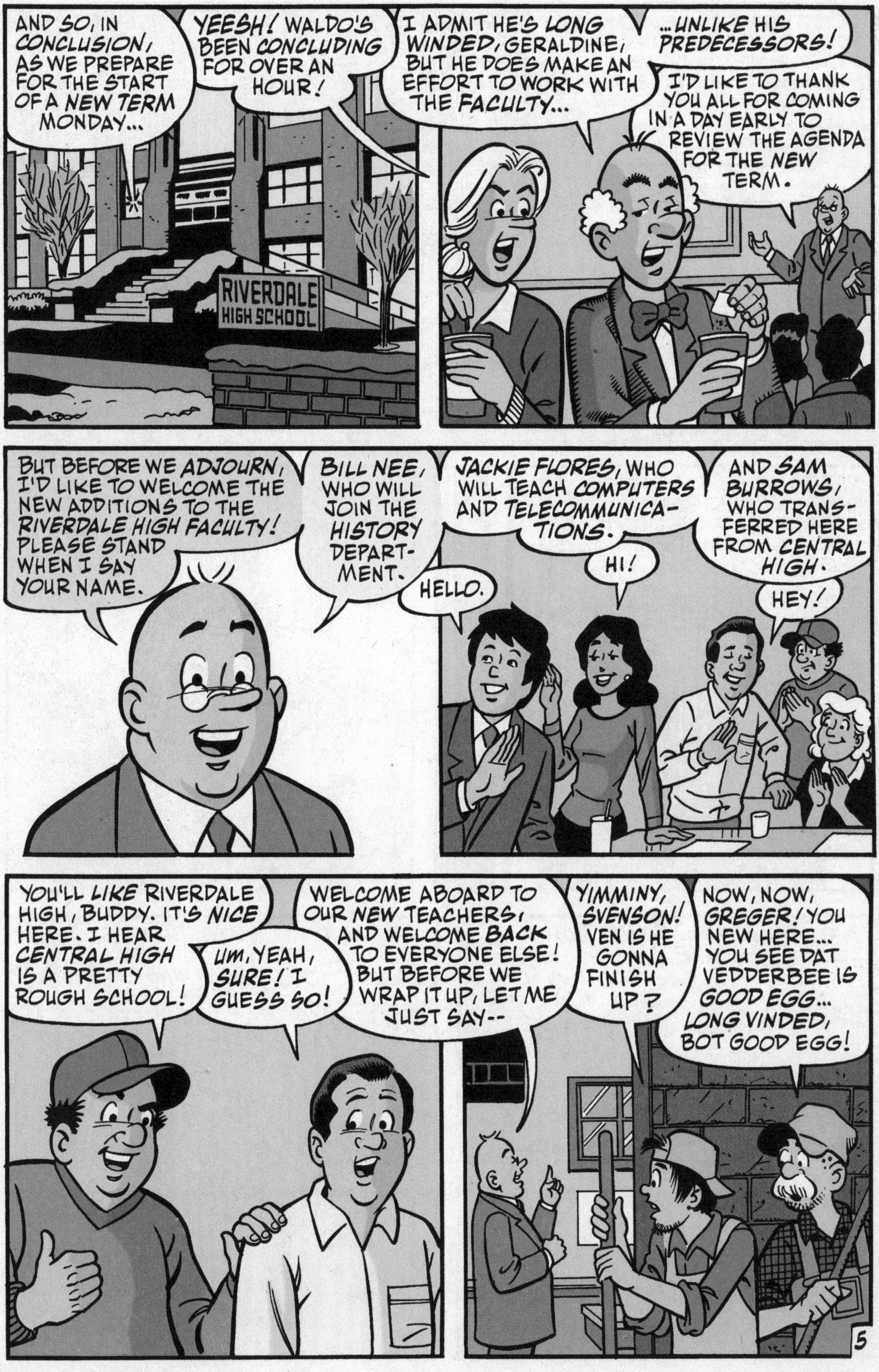
AND SO, IN CONCLUSION, AS WE PREPARE FOR THE START OF A NEW TERM MONDAY...
YEESH! WALDO'S BEEN CONCLUDING FOR OVER AN HOUR!
RIVERDALE HIGH SCHOOL
I ADMIT HE'S LONG WINDED, GERALDINE, BUT HE DOES MAKE AN EFFORT TO WORK WITH THE FACULTY...
...UNLIKE HIS PREDECESSORS!
I'D LIKE TO THANK YOU ALL FOR COMING IN A DAY EARLY TO REVIEW THE AGENDA FOR THE NEW TERM.
BUT BEFORE WE ADJOURN, I'D LIKE TO WELCOME THE NEW ADDITIONS TO THE RIVERDALE HIGH FACULTY! PLEASE STAND WHEN I SAY YOUR NAME.
BILL NEE, WHO WILL JOIN THE HISTORY DEPARTMENT.
HELLO.
JACKIE FLORES, WHO WILL TEACH COMPUTERS AND TELECOMMUNICATIONS.
HI!
AND SAM BURROWS, WHO TRANSFERRED HERE FROM CENTRAL HIGH.
HEY!
YOU'LL LIKE RIVERDALE HIGH, BUDDY. IT'S NICE HERE. I HEAR CENTRAL HIGH IS A PRETTY ROUGH SCHOOL!
UM, YEAH, SURE! I GUESS SO!
WELCOME ABOARD TO OUR NEW TEACHERS, AND WELCOME BACK TO EVERYONE ELSE! BUT BEFORE WE WRAP IT UP, LET ME JUST SAY--
YIMMINY, SVENSON! VEN IS HE GONNA FINISH UP?
NOW, NOW, GREGER! YOU NEW HERE... YOU SEE DAT VEDDERBEE IS GOOD EGG... LONG VINDED, BOT GOOD EGG!
5

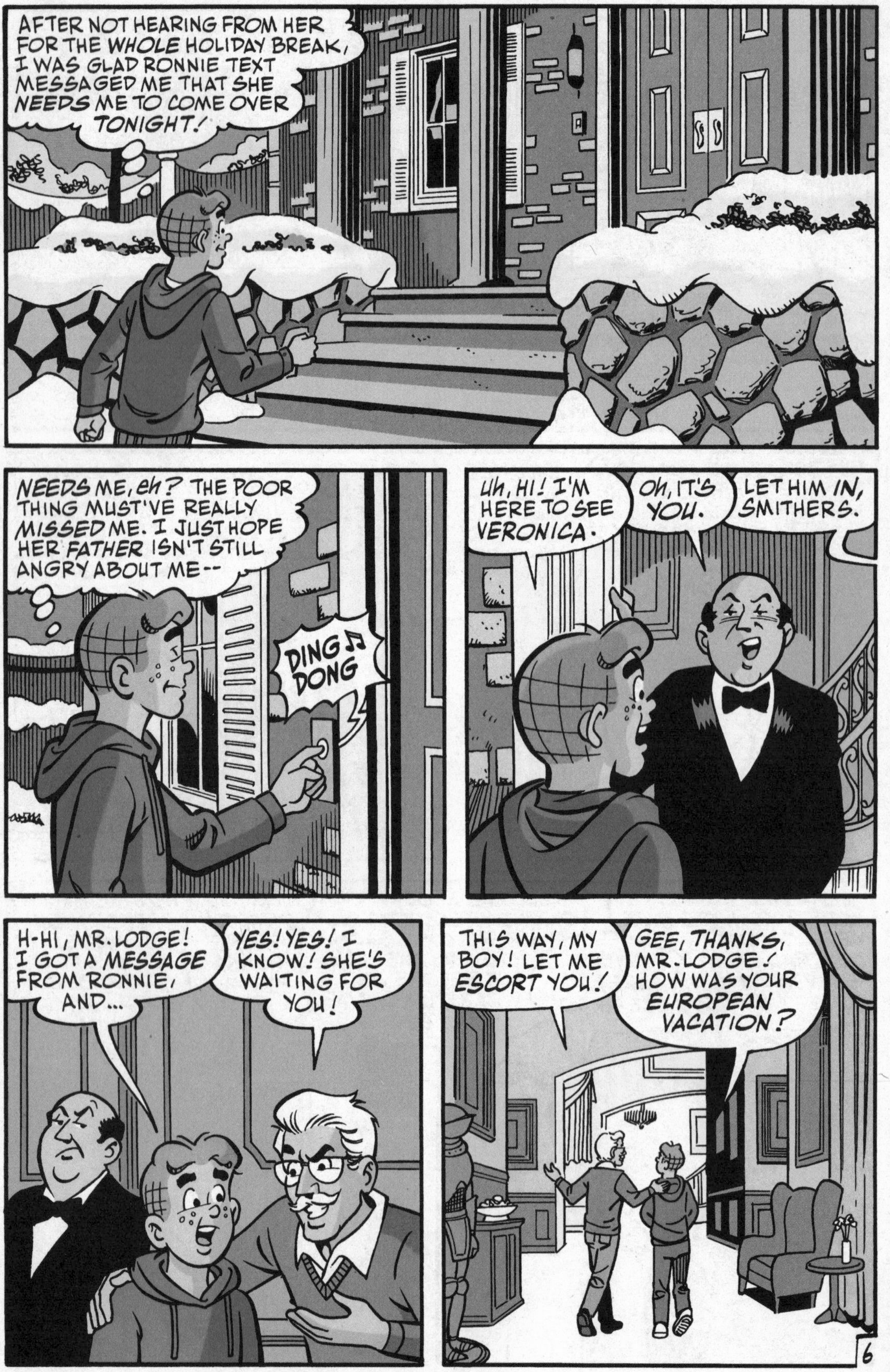
AFTER NOT HEARING FROM HER FOR THE WHOLE HOLIDAY BREAK, I WAS GLAD RONNIE TEXT MESSAGED ME THAT SHE NEEDS ME TO COME OVER TONIGHT!
NEEDS ME, eh? THE POOR THING MUST'VE REALLY MISSED ME. I JUST HOPE HER FATHER ISN'T STILL ANGRY ABOUT ME--
DING DONG
uh, HI! I'M HERE TO SEE VERONICA.
Oh, IT'S YOU.
LET HIM IN, SMITHERS.
H-HI, MR. LODGE! I GOT A MESSAGE FROM RONNIE, AND...
YES! YES! I KNOW! SHE'S WAITING FOR YOU!
THIS WAY, MY BOY! LET ME ESCORT YOU!
GEE, THANKS, MR. LODGE! HOW WAS YOUR EUROPEAN VACATION?
6

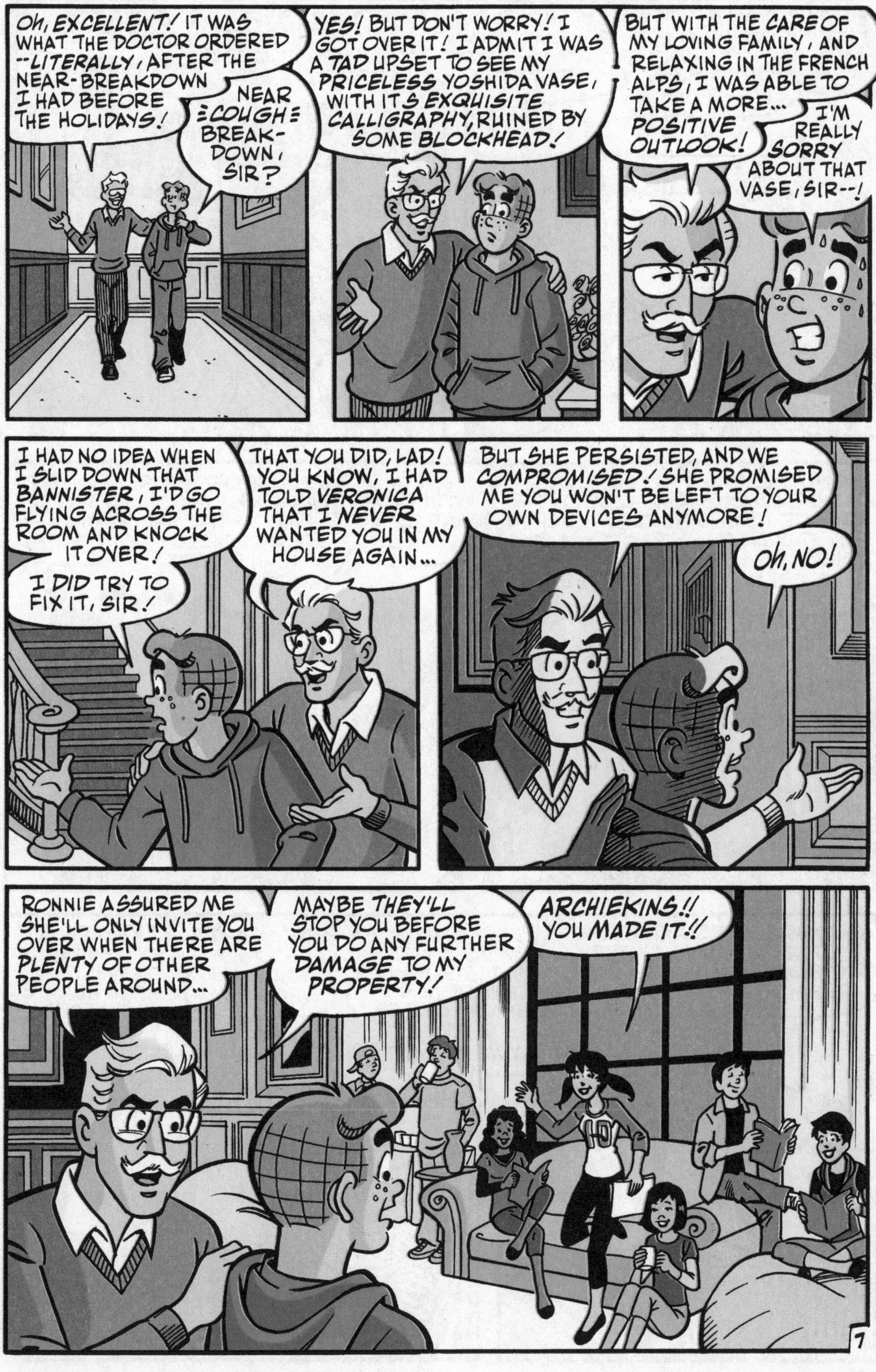
Oh, EXCELLENT! IT WAS WHAT THE DOCTOR ORDERED --LITERALLY, AFTER THE NEAR-BREAKDOWN I HAD BEFORE THE HOLIDAYS!
NEAR =COUGH= BREAK-DOWN, SIR?
YES! BUT DON'T WORRY! I GOT OVER IT! I ADMIT I WAS A TAD UPSET TO SEE MY PRICELESS YOSHIDA VASE, WITH ITS EXQUISITE CALLIGRAPHY, RUINED BY SOME BLOCKHEAD!
BUT WITH THE CARE OF MY LOVING FAMILY, AND RELAXING IN THE FRENCH ALPS, I WAS ABLE TO TAKE A MORE... POSITIVE OUTLOOK!
I'M REALLY SORRY ABOUT THAT VASE, SIR--!
I HAD NO IDEA WHEN I SLID DOWN THAT BANNISTER, I'D GO FLYING ACROSS THE ROOM AND KNOCK IT OVER!
I DID TRY TO FIX IT, SIR!
THAT YOU DID, LAD! YOU KNOW, I HAD TOLD VERONICA THAT I NEVER WANTED YOU IN MY HOUSE AGAIN...
BUT SHE PERSISTED, AND WE COMPROMISED! SHE PROMISED ME YOU WON'T BE LEFT TO YOUR OWN DEVICES ANYMORE!
Oh, NO!
RONNIE ASSURED ME SHE'LL ONLY INVITE YOU OVER WHEN THERE ARE PLENTY OF OTHER PEOPLE AROUND...
MAYBE THEY'LL STOP YOU BEFORE YOU DO ANY FURTHER DAMAGE TO MY PROPERTY!
ARCHIEKINS!! YOU MADE IT!!
7

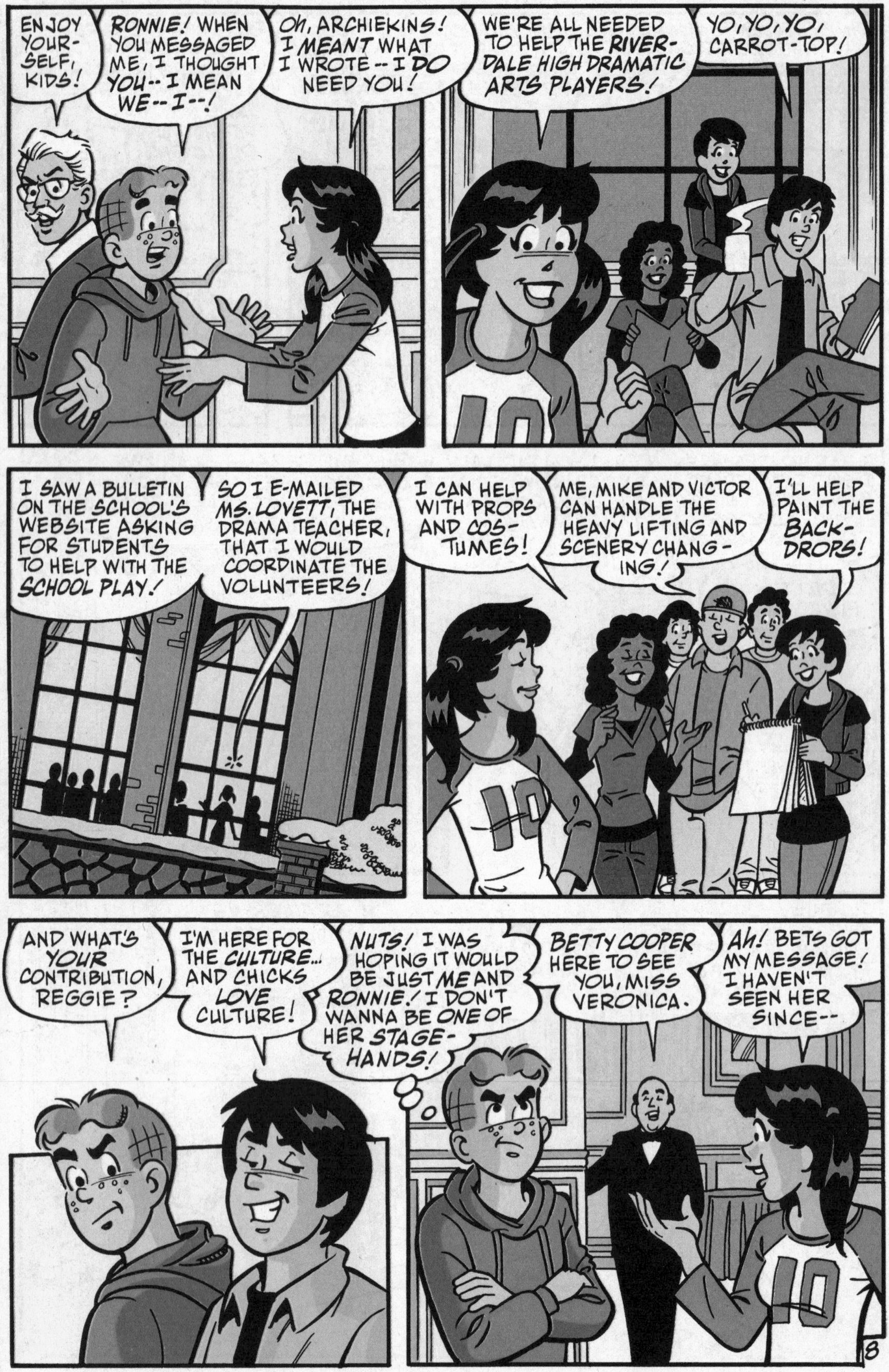
ENJOY YOUR-SELF, KIDS!
RONNIE! WHEN YOU MESSAGED ME, I THOUGHT YOU-- I MEAN WE-- I--!
Oh, ARCHIEKINS! I MEANT WHAT I WROTE -- I DO NEED YOU!
WE'RE ALL NEEDED TO HELP THE RIVER-DALE HIGH DRAMATIC ARTS PLAYERS!
YO, YO, YO, CARROT-TOP!
I SAW A BULLETIN ON THE SCHOOL'S WEBSITE ASKING FOR STUDENTS TO HELP WITH THE SCHOOL PLAY!
SO I E-MAILED MS. LOVETT, THE DRAMA TEACHER, THAT I WOULD COORDINATE THE VOLUNTEERS!
I CAN HELP WITH PROPS AND COS-TUMES!
ME, MIKE AND VICTOR CAN HANDLE THE HEAVY LIFTING AND SCENERY CHANG-ING!
I'LL HELP PAINT THE BACK-DROPS!
AND WHAT'S YOUR CONTRIBUTION, REGGIE?
I'M HERE FOR THE CULTURE... AND CHICKS LOVE CULTURE!
NUTS! I WAS HOPING IT WOULD BE JUST ME AND RONNIE! I DON'T WANNA BE ONE OF HER STAGE-HANDS!
BETTY COOPER HERE TO SEE YOU, MISS VERONICA.
Ah! BETS GOT MY MESSAGE! I HAVEN'T SEEN HER SINCE--
8

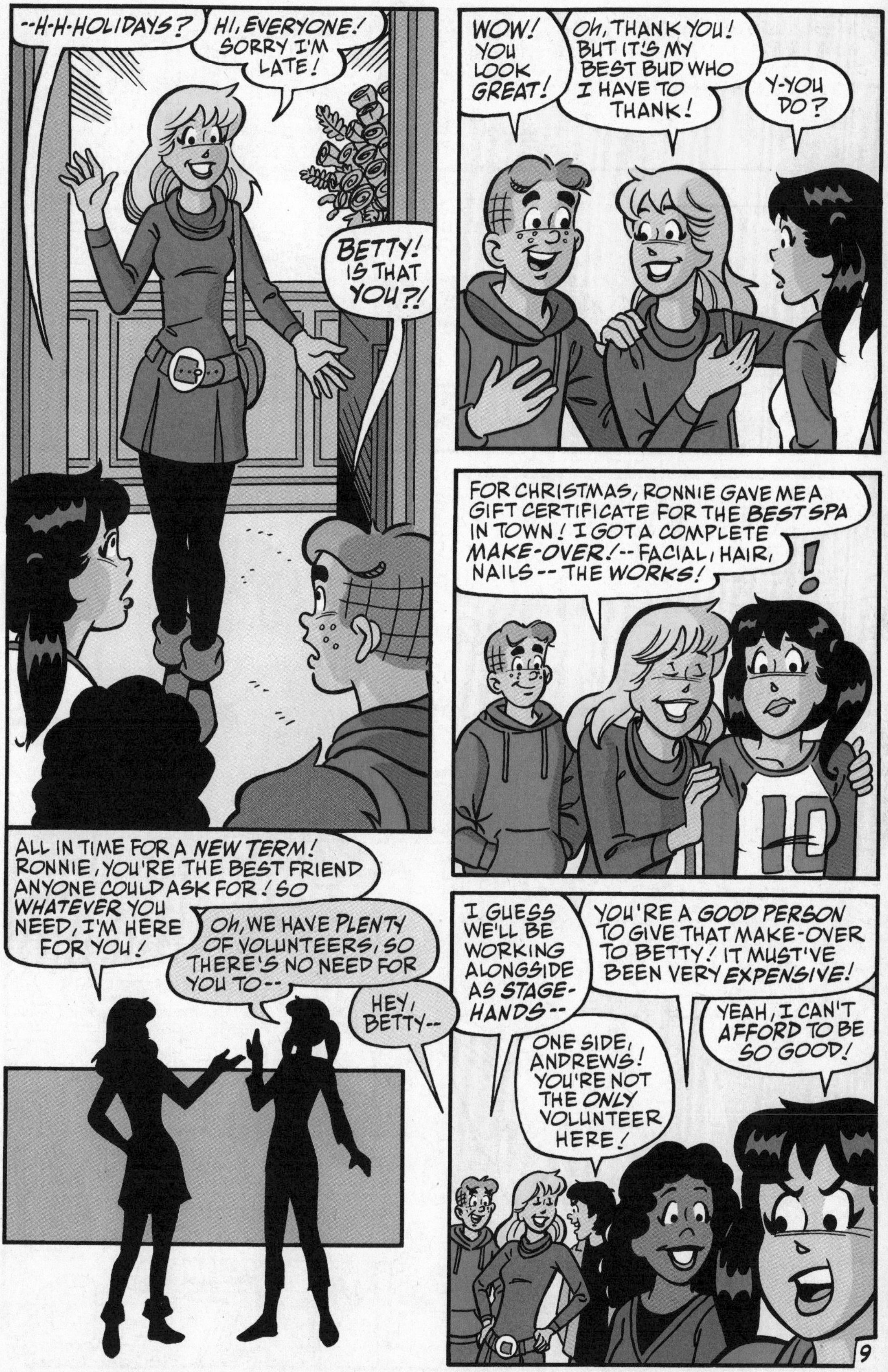
--H-H-HOLIDAYS?
HI, EVERYONE! SORRY I'M LATE!
BETTY! IS THAT YOU?!
WOW! YOU LOOK GREAT!
Oh, THANK YOU! BUT IT'S MY BEST BUD WHO I HAVE TO THANK!
Y-YOU DO?
FOR CHRISTMAS, RONNIE GAVE ME A GIFT CERTIFICATE FOR THE BEST SPA IN TOWN! I GOT A COMPLETE MAKE-OVER!-- FACIAL, HAIR, NAILS -- THE WORKS!
!
10
ALL IN TIME FOR A NEW TERM! RONNIE, YOU'RE THE BEST FRIEND ANYONE COULD ASK FOR! SO WHATEVER YOU NEED, I'M HERE FOR YOU!
Oh, WE HAVE PLENTY OF VOLUNTEERS, SO THERE'S NO NEED FOR YOU TO--
HEY, BETTY--
I GUESS WE'LL BE WORKING ALONGSIDE AS STAGE-HANDS--
YOU'RE A GOOD PERSON TO GIVE THAT MAKE-OVER TO BETTY! IT MUST'VE BEEN VERY EXPENSIVE!
YEAH, I CAN'T AFFORD TO BE SO GOOD!
ONE SIDE, ANDREWS! YOU'RE NOT THE ONLY VOLUNTEER HERE!
9

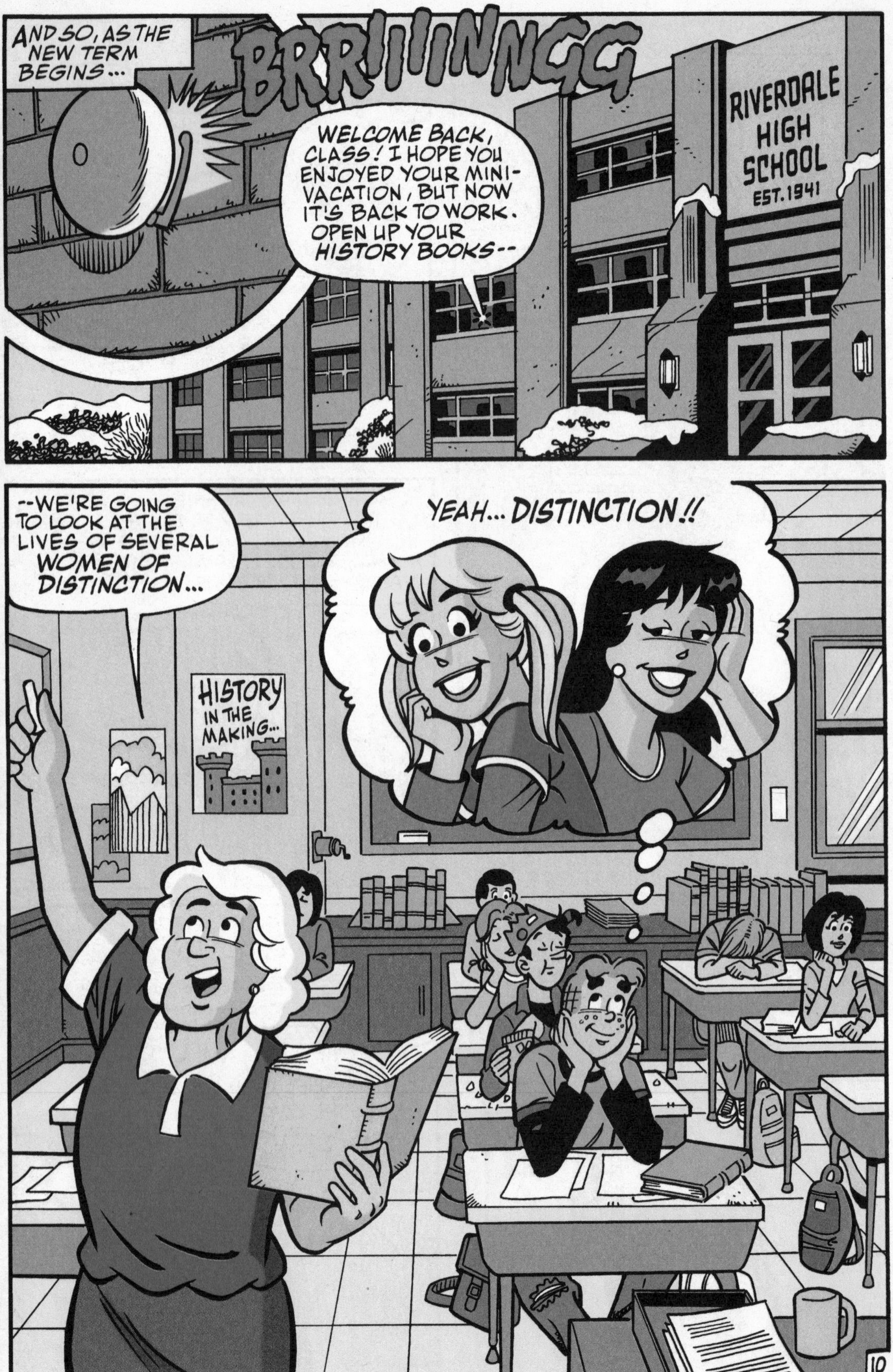
AND SO, AS THE NEW TERM BEGINS...
BRRIIIINNGG
RIVERDALE HIGH SCHOOL EST. 1941
WELCOME BACK, CLASS! I HOPE YOU ENJOYED YOUR MINI-VACATION, BUT NOW IT'S BACK TO WORK. OPEN UP YOUR HISTORY BOOKS--
--WE'RE GOING TO LOOK AT THE LIVES OF SEVERAL WOMEN OF DISTINCTION...
YEAH... DISTINCTION!!
HISTORY IN THE MAKING...
10

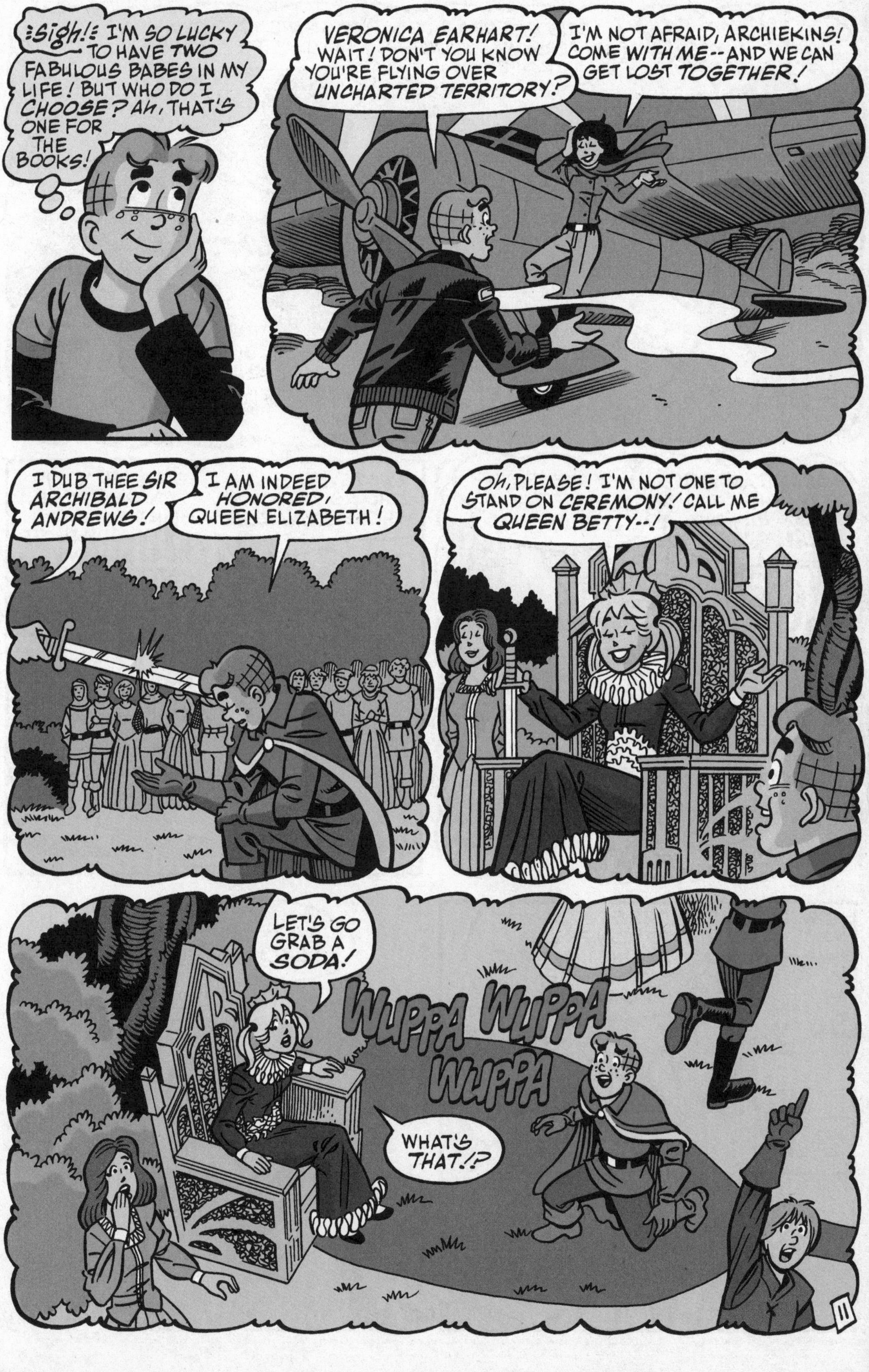
:SIGH!: I'M SO LUCKY TO HAVE TWO FABULOUS BABES IN MY LIFE! BUT WHO DO I CHOOSE? AH, THAT'S ONE FOR THE BOOKS!
VERONICA EARHART! WAIT! DON'T YOU KNOW YOU'RE FLYING OVER UNCHARTED TERRITORY?
I'M NOT AFRAID, ARCHIEKINS! COME WITH ME--AND WE CAN GET LOST TOGETHER!
I DUB THEE SIR ARCHIBALD ANDREWS!
I AM INDEED HONORED, QUEEN ELIZABETH!
OH, PLEASE! I'M NOT ONE TO STAND ON CEREMONY! CALL ME QUEEN BETTY--!
LET'S GO GRAB A SODA!
WUPPA WUPPA WUPPA
WHAT'S THAT!?
11

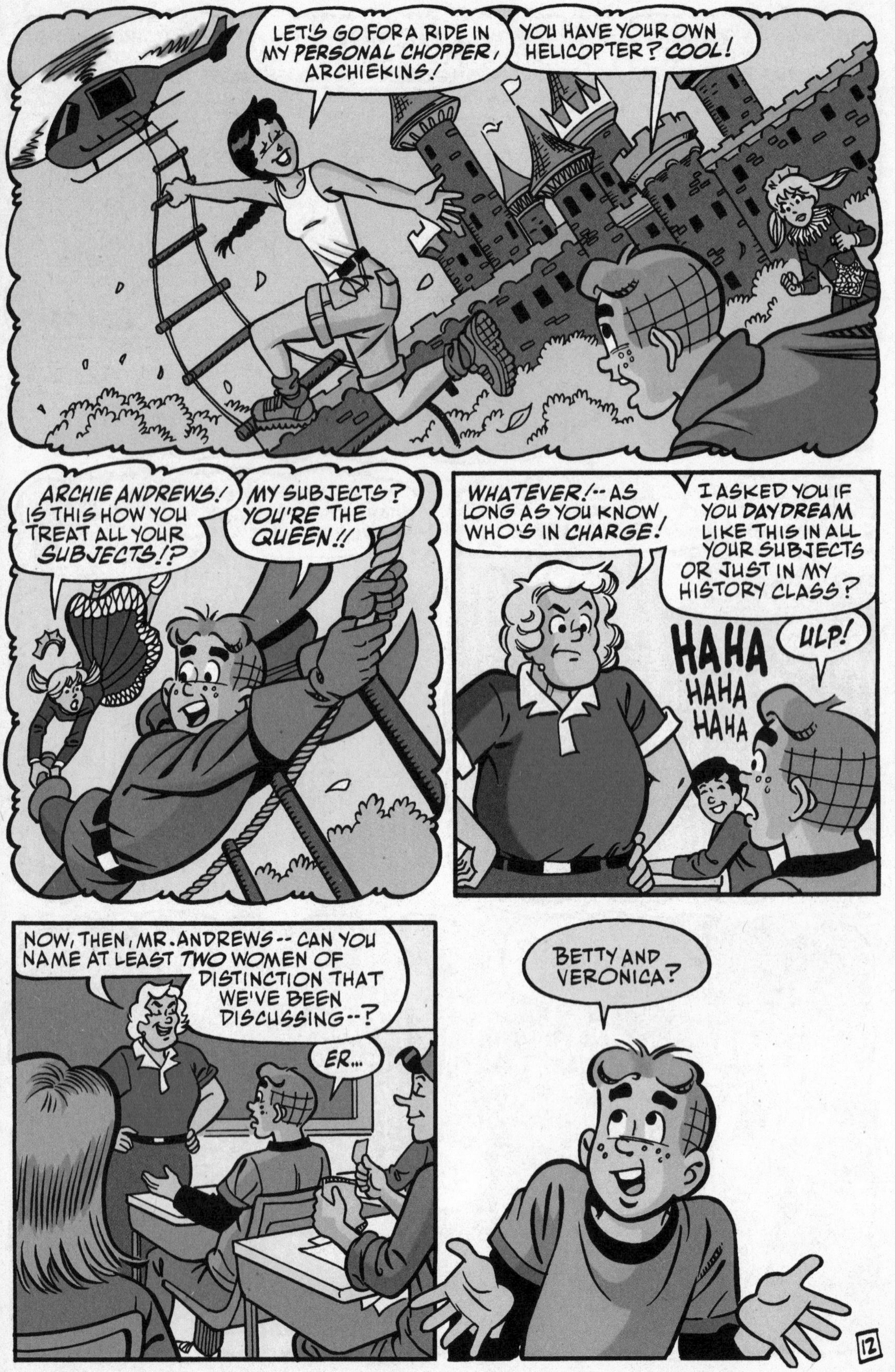
LET'S GO FOR A RIDE IN MY PERSONAL CHOPPER, ARCHIEKINS!
YOU HAVE YOUR OWN HELICOPTER? COOL!
ARCHIE ANDREWS! IS THIS HOW YOU TREAT ALL YOUR SUBJECTS!?
MY SUBJECTS? YOU'RE THE QUEEN!!
WHATEVER!-- AS LONG AS YOU KNOW WHO'S IN CHARGE!
I ASKED YOU IF YOU DAYDREAM LIKE THIS IN ALL YOUR SUBJECTS OR JUST IN MY HISTORY CLASS?
HAHA
HAHA
HAHA
ULP!
NOW, THEN, MR. ANDREWS -- CAN YOU NAME AT LEAST TWO WOMEN OF DISTINCTION THAT WE'VE BEEN DISCUSSING--?
ER...
BETTY AND VERONICA?
12

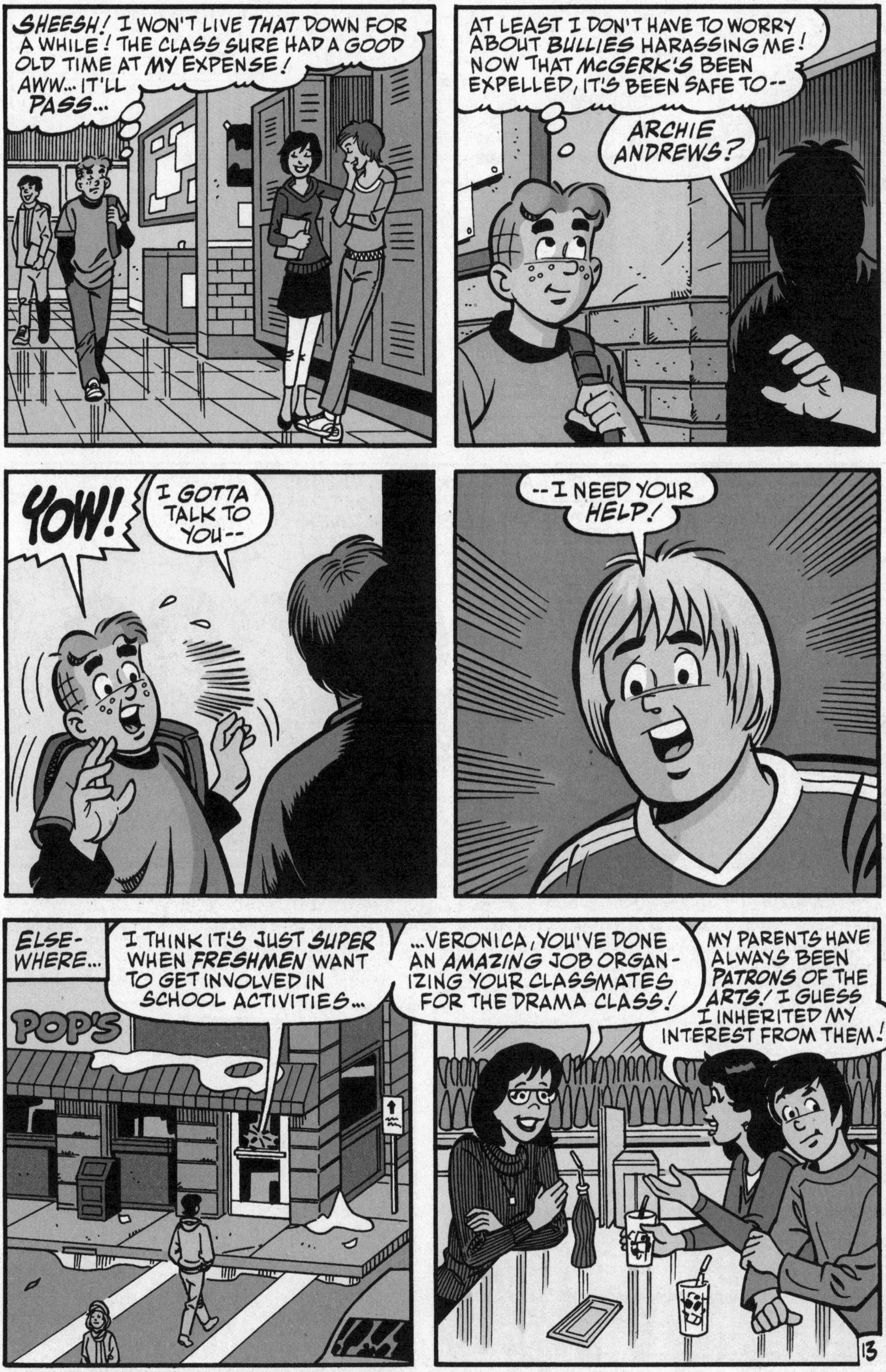
SHEESH! I WON'T LIVE THAT DOWN FOR A WHILE! THE CLASS SURE HAD A GOOD OLD TIME AT MY EXPENSE!
AWW... IT'LL PASS...
AT LEAST I DON'T HAVE TO WORRY ABOUT BULLIES HARASSING ME! NOW THAT McGERK'S BEEN EXPELLED, IT'S BEEN SAFE TO--
ARCHIE ANDREWS?
YOW!
I GOTTA TALK TO YOU--
--I NEED YOUR HELP!
ELSE-WHERE...
POP'S
I THINK IT'S JUST SUPER WHEN FRESHMEN WANT TO GET INVOLVED IN SCHOOL ACTIVITIES...
...VERONICA, YOU'VE DONE AN AMAZING JOB ORGANIZING YOUR CLASSMATES FOR THE DRAMA CLASS!
MY PARENTS HAVE ALWAYS BEEN PATRONS OF THE ARTS! I GUESS I INHERITED MY INTEREST FROM THEM!
13

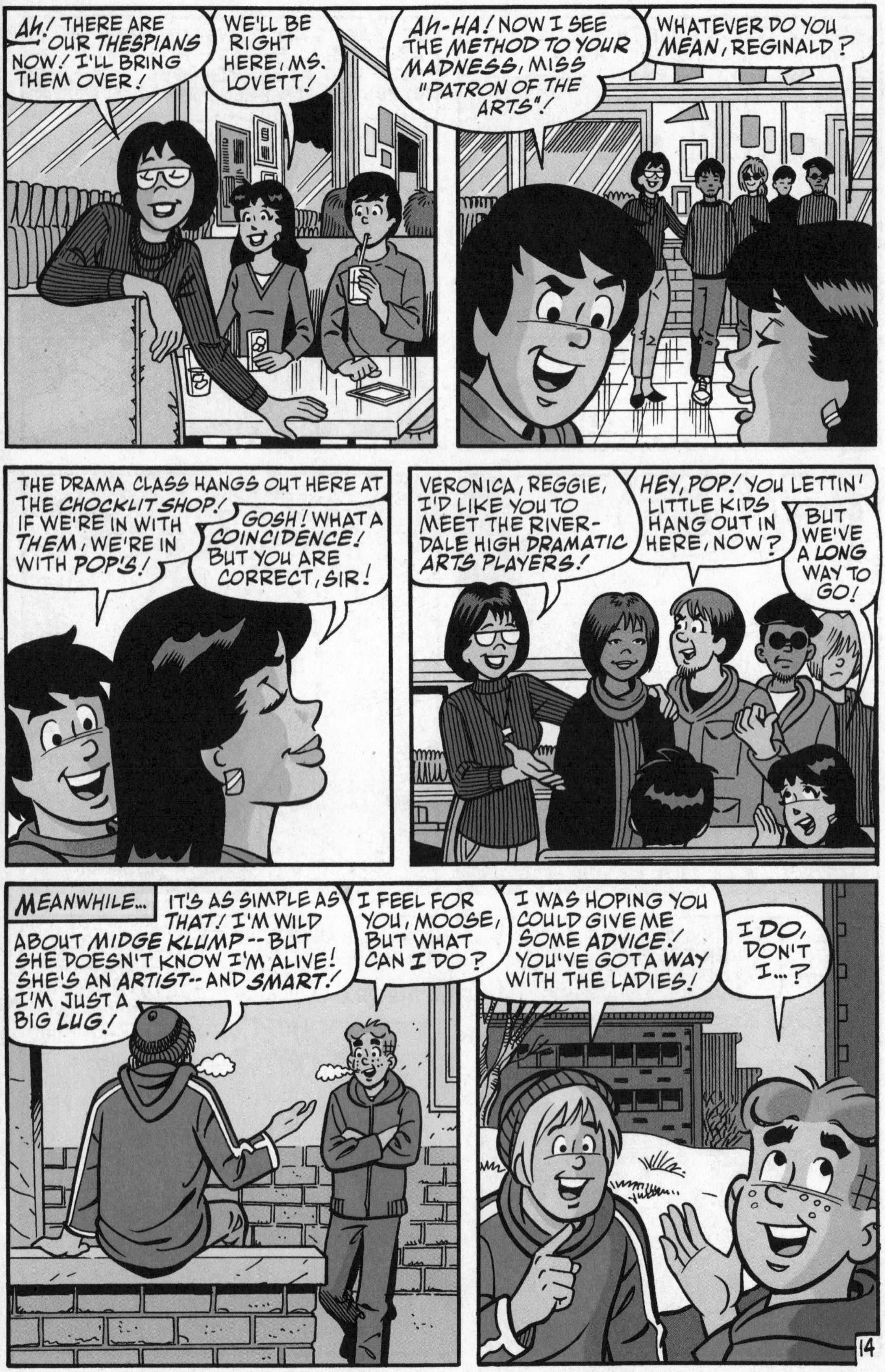
AH! THERE ARE OUR THESPIANS NOW! I'LL BRING THEM OVER!
WE'LL BE RIGHT HERE, MS. LOVETT!
AH-HA! NOW I SEE THE METHOD TO YOUR MADNESS, MISS "PATRON OF THE ARTS"!
WHATEVER DO YOU MEAN, REGINALD?
THE DRAMA CLASS HANGS OUT HERE AT THE CHOCKLIT SHOP! IF WE'RE IN WITH THEM, WE'RE IN WITH POP'S!
GOSH! WHAT A COINCIDENCE! BUT YOU ARE CORRECT, SIR!
VERONICA, REGGIE, I'D LIKE YOU TO MEET THE RIVERDALE HIGH DRAMATIC ARTS PLAYERS!
HEY, POP! YOU LETTIN' LITTLE KIDS HANG OUT IN HERE, NOW?
BUT WE'VE A LONG WAY TO GO!
MEANWHILE...
IT'S AS SIMPLE AS THAT! I'M WILD ABOUT MIDGE KLUMP -- BUT SHE DOESN'T KNOW I'M ALIVE! SHE'S AN ARTIST -- AND SMART! I'M JUST A BIG LUG!
I FEEL FOR YOU, MOOSE, BUT WHAT CAN I DO?
I WAS HOPING YOU COULD GIVE ME SOME ADVICE! YOU'VE GOT A WAY WITH THE LADIES!
I DO, DON'T I...?
14

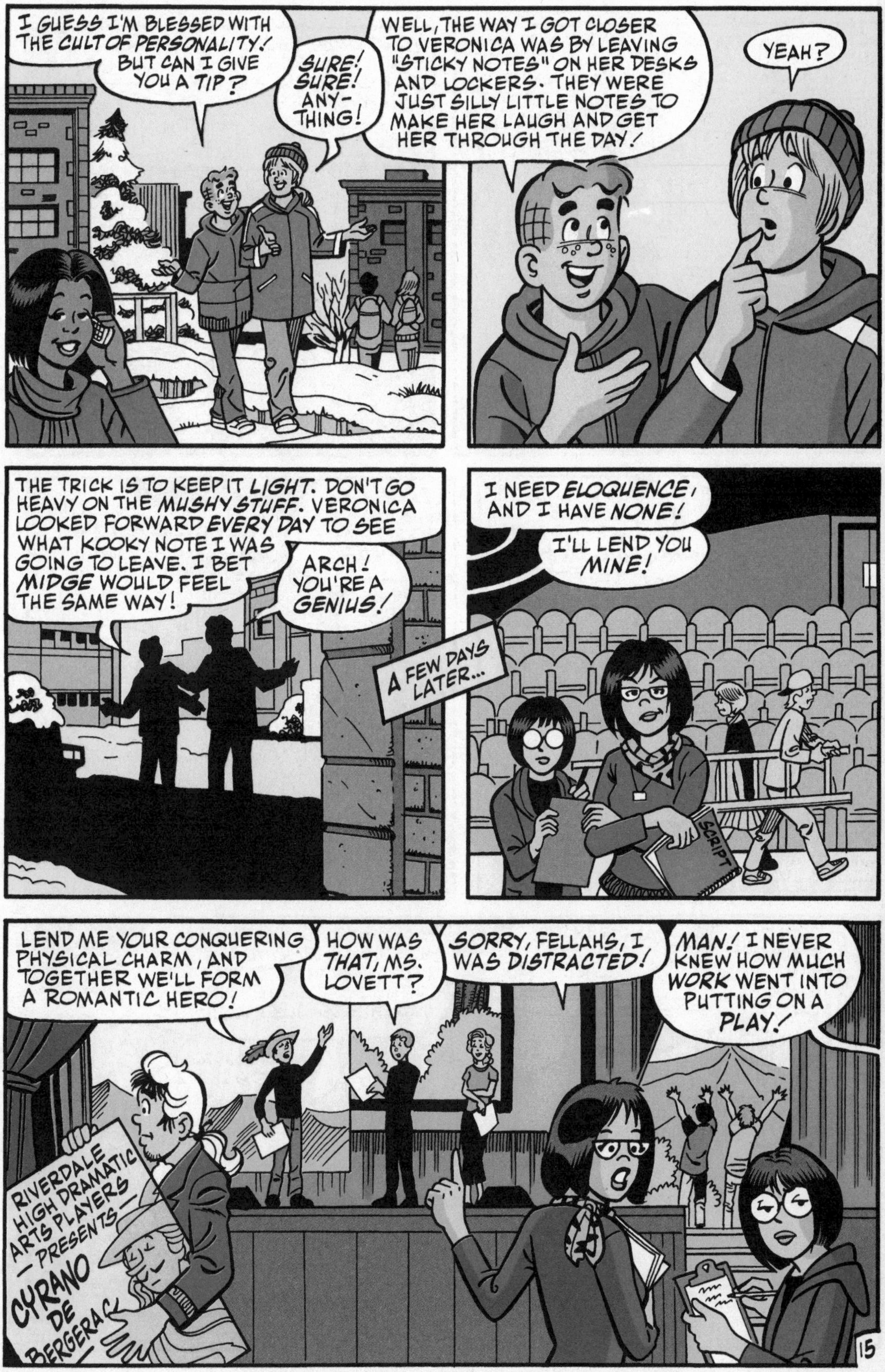
I GUESS I'M BLESSED WITH THE CULT OF PERSONALITY!
BUT CAN I GIVE YOU A TIP?
SURE! SURE! ANYTHING!
WELL, THE WAY I GOT CLOSER TO VERONICA WAS BY LEAVING "STICKY NOTES" ON HER DESKS AND LOCKERS. THEY WERE JUST SILLY LITTLE NOTES TO MAKE HER LAUGH AND GET HER THROUGH THE DAY!
YEAH?
THE TRICK IS TO KEEP IT LIGHT. DON'T GO HEAVY ON THE MUSHY STUFF. VERONICA LOOKED FORWARD EVERY DAY TO SEE WHAT KOOKY NOTE I WAS GOING TO LEAVE. I BET MIDGE WOULD FEEL THE SAME WAY!
ARCH! YOU'RE A GENIUS!
A FEW DAYS LATER...
I NEED ELOQUENCE, AND I HAVE NONE!
I'LL LEND YOU MINE!
SCRIPT
LEND ME YOUR CONQUERING PHYSICAL CHARM, AND TOGETHER WE'LL FORM A ROMANTIC HERO!
HOW WAS THAT, MS. LOVETT?
SORRY, FELLAHS, I WAS DISTRACTED!
MAN! I NEVER KNEW HOW MUCH WORK WENT INTO PUTTING ON A PLAY!
RIVERDALE HIGH DRAMATIC ARTS PLAYERS —PRESENTS— CYRANO DE BERGERAC
15

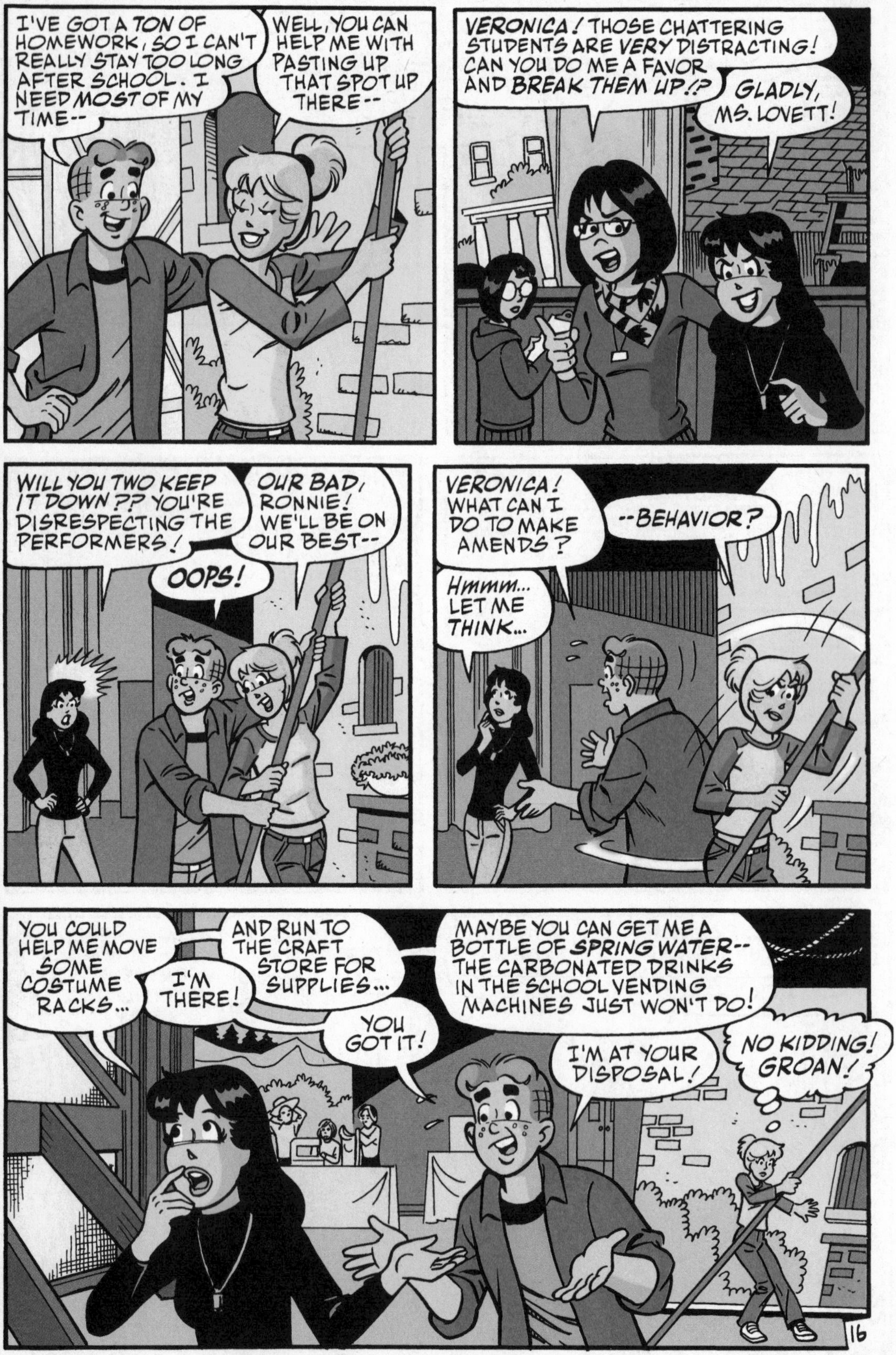
I'VE GOT A TON OF HOMEWORK, SO I CAN'T REALLY STAY TOO LONG AFTER SCHOOL. I NEED MOST OF MY TIME--
WELL, YOU CAN HELP ME WITH PASTING UP THAT SPOT UP THERE--
VERONICA! THOSE CHATTERING STUDENTS ARE VERY DISTRACTING! CAN YOU DO ME A FAVOR AND BREAK THEM UP!?
GLADLY, MS. LOVETT!
WILL YOU TWO KEEP IT DOWN?? YOU'RE DISRESPECTING THE PERFORMERS!
OUR BAD, RONNIE! WE'LL BE ON OUR BEST--
OOPS!
VERONICA! WHAT CAN I DO TO MAKE AMENDS?
--BEHAVIOR?
Hmmm... LET ME THINK...
YOU COULD HELP ME MOVE SOME COSTUME RACKS...
I'M THERE!
AND RUN TO THE CRAFT STORE FOR SUPPLIES...
YOU GOT IT!
MAYBE YOU CAN GET ME A BOTTLE OF SPRING WATER-- THE CARBONATED DRINKS IN THE SCHOOL VENDING MACHINES JUST WON'T DO!
I'M AT YOUR DISPOSAL!
NO KIDDING! GROAN!
16

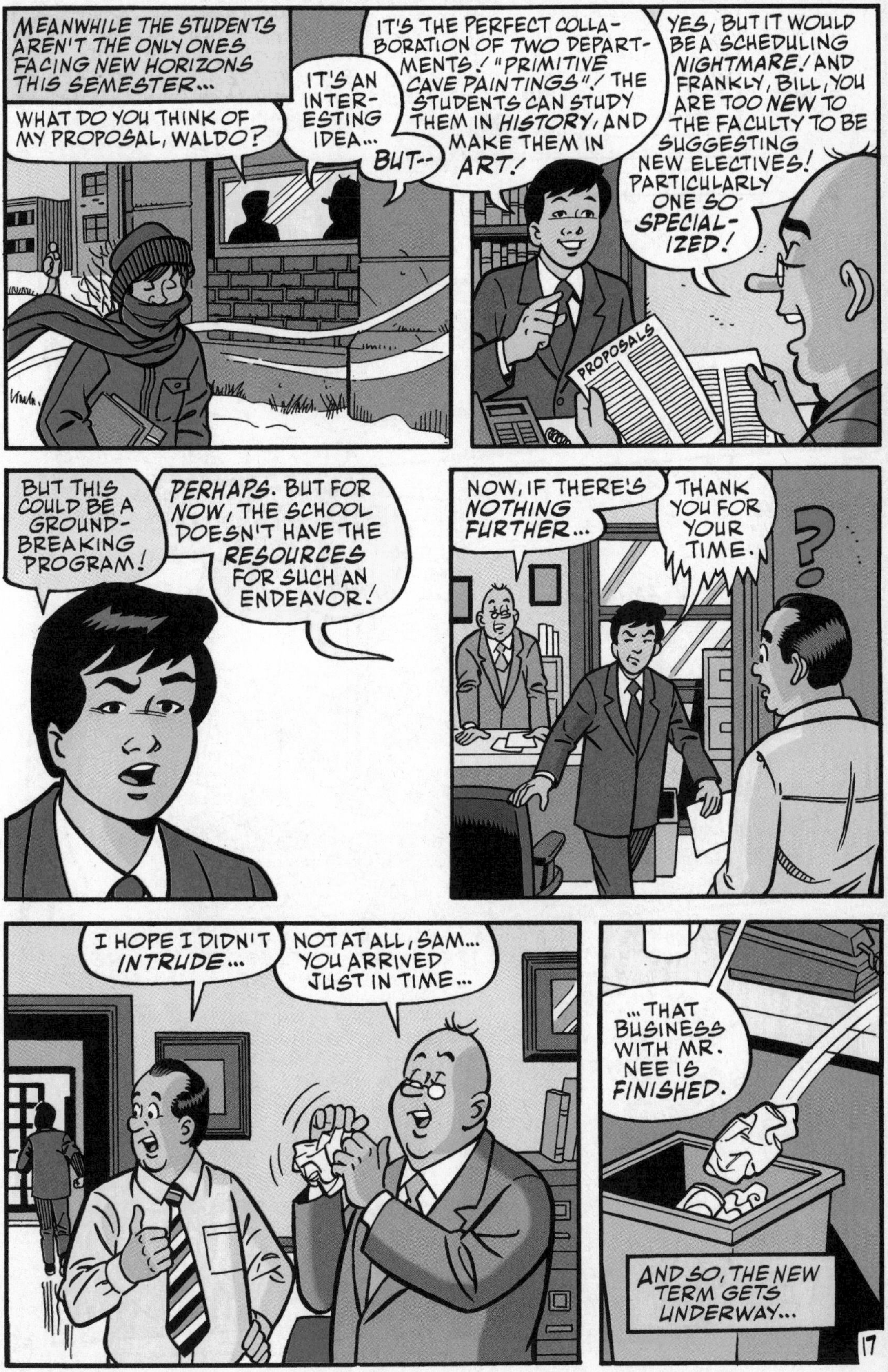
MEANWHILE THE STUDENTS AREN'T THE ONLY ONES FACING NEW HORIZONS THIS SEMESTER...
WHAT DO YOU THINK OF MY PROPOSAL, WALDO?
IT'S AN INTER-ESTING IDEA... BUT--
IT'S THE PERFECT COLLA-BORATION OF TWO DEPART-MENTS! "PRIMITIVE CAVE PAINTINGS"! THE STUDENTS CAN STUDY THEM IN HISTORY, AND MAKE THEM IN ART!
YES, BUT IT WOULD BE A SCHEDULING NIGHTMARE! AND FRANKLY, BILL, YOU ARE TOO NEW TO THE FACULTY TO BE SUGGESTING NEW ELECTIVES! PARTICULARLY ONE SO SPECIAL-IZED!
PROPOSALS
BUT THIS COULD BE A GROUND-BREAKING PROGRAM!
PERHAPS. BUT FOR NOW, THE SCHOOL DOESN'T HAVE THE RESOURCES FOR SUCH AN ENDEAVOR!
NOW, IF THERE'S NOTHING FURTHER...
THANK YOU FOR YOUR TIME.
?
I HOPE I DIDN'T INTRUDE...
NOT AT ALL, SAM... YOU ARRIVED JUST IN TIME...
...THAT BUSINESS WITH MR. NEE IS FINISHED.
AND SO, THE NEW TERM GETS UNDERWAY...
17

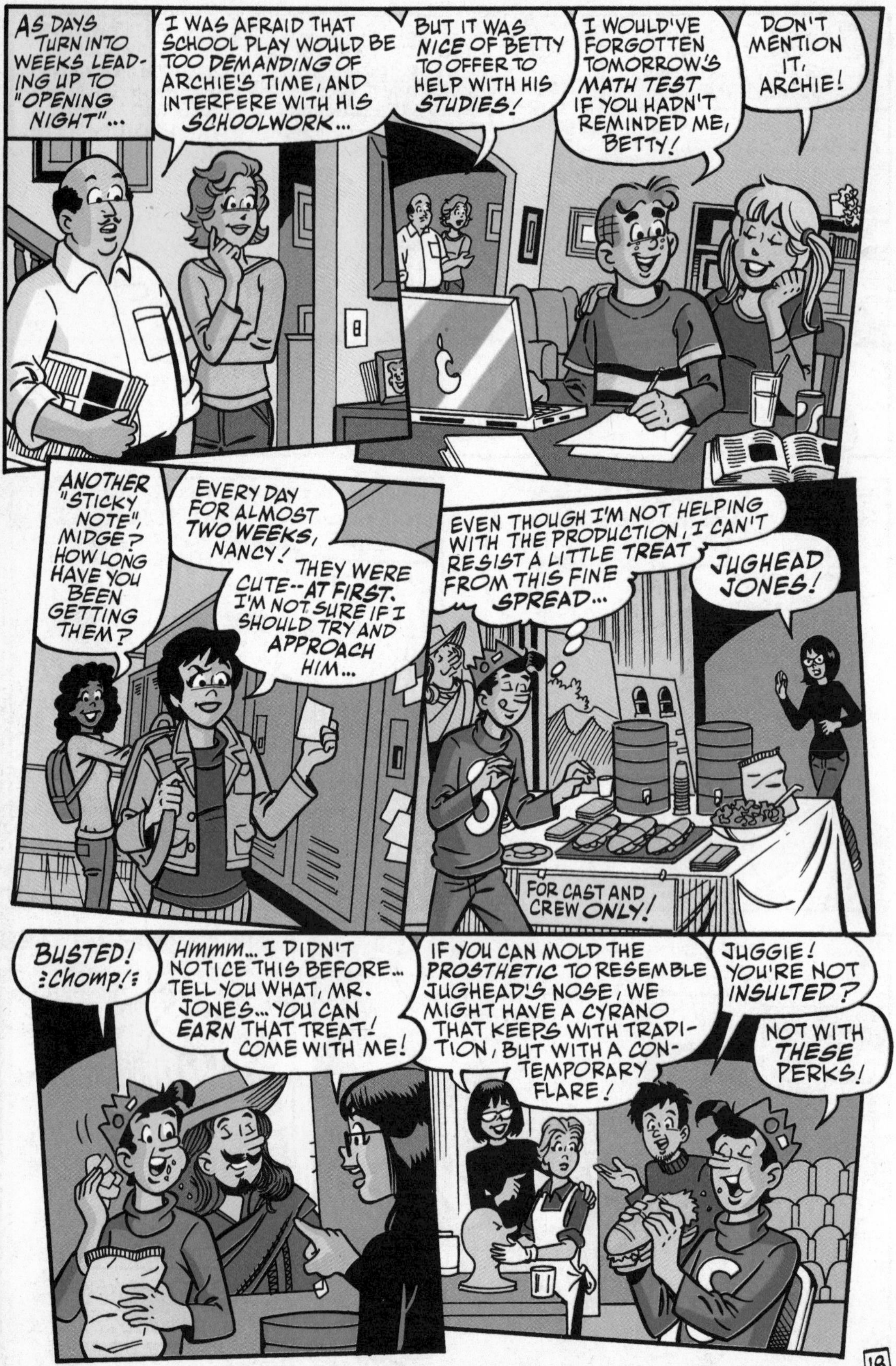
AS DAYS TURN INTO WEEKS LEADING UP TO "OPENING NIGHT"...
I WAS AFRAID THAT SCHOOL PLAY WOULD BE TOO DEMANDING OF ARCHIE'S TIME, AND INTERFERE WITH HIS SCHOOLWORK...
BUT IT WAS NICE OF BETTY TO OFFER TO HELP WITH HIS STUDIES!
I WOULD'VE FORGOTTEN TOMORROW'S MATH TEST IF YOU HADN'T REMINDED ME, BETTY!
DON'T MENTION IT, ARCHIE!
ANOTHER "STICKY NOTE", MIDGE? HOW LONG HAVE YOU BEEN GETTING THEM?
EVERY DAY FOR ALMOST TWO WEEKS, NANCY!
THEY WERE CUTE--AT FIRST. I'M NOT SURE IF I SHOULD TRY AND APPROACH HIM...
EVEN THOUGH I'M NOT HELPING WITH THE PRODUCTION, I CAN'T RESIST A LITTLE TREAT FROM THIS FINE SPREAD...
JUGHEAD JONES!
FOR CAST AND CREW ONLY!
BUSTED! :CHOMP!:
HMMM... I DIDN'T NOTICE THIS BEFORE... TELL YOU WHAT, MR. JONES... YOU CAN EARN THAT TREAT! COME WITH ME!
IF YOU CAN MOLD THE PROSTHETIC TO RESEMBLE JUGHEAD'S NOSE, WE MIGHT HAVE A CYRANO THAT KEEPS WITH TRADITION, BUT WITH A CONTEMPORARY FLARE!
JUGGIE! YOU'RE NOT INSULTED?
NOT WITH THESE PERKS!
18

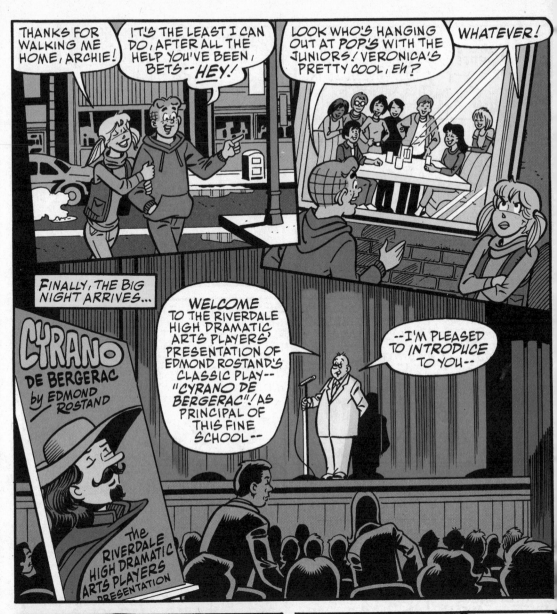

THANKS FOR WALKING ME HOME, ARCHIE!

IT'S THE LEAST I CAN DO, AFTER ALL THE HELP YOU'VE BEEN, BETS-- *HEY!*

LOOK WHO'S HANGING OUT AT POP'S WITH THE JUNIORS! VERONICA'S PRETTY *COOL*, EH?

WHATEVER!

FINALLY, THE BIG NIGHT ARRIVES...

CYRANO DE BERGERAC *by EDMOND ROSTAND*

The RIVERDALE HIGH DRAMATIC ARTS PLAYERS PRESENTATION

WELCOME TO THE RIVERDALE HIGH DRAMATIC ARTS PLAYERS' PRESENTATION OF EDMOND ROSTAND'S CLASSIC PLAY-- "CYRANO DE BERGERAC"! AS PRINCIPAL OF THIS FINE SCHOOL--

--I'M PLEASED TO *INTRODUCE* TO YOU--

--ER... THE CHAIR OF THE DRAMA DEPARTMENT... SAMANTHA LOVETT!

THANK YOU, PRINCIPAL WEATHER-BEE!

CLAP CLAP CLAP CLAP CLAP

19

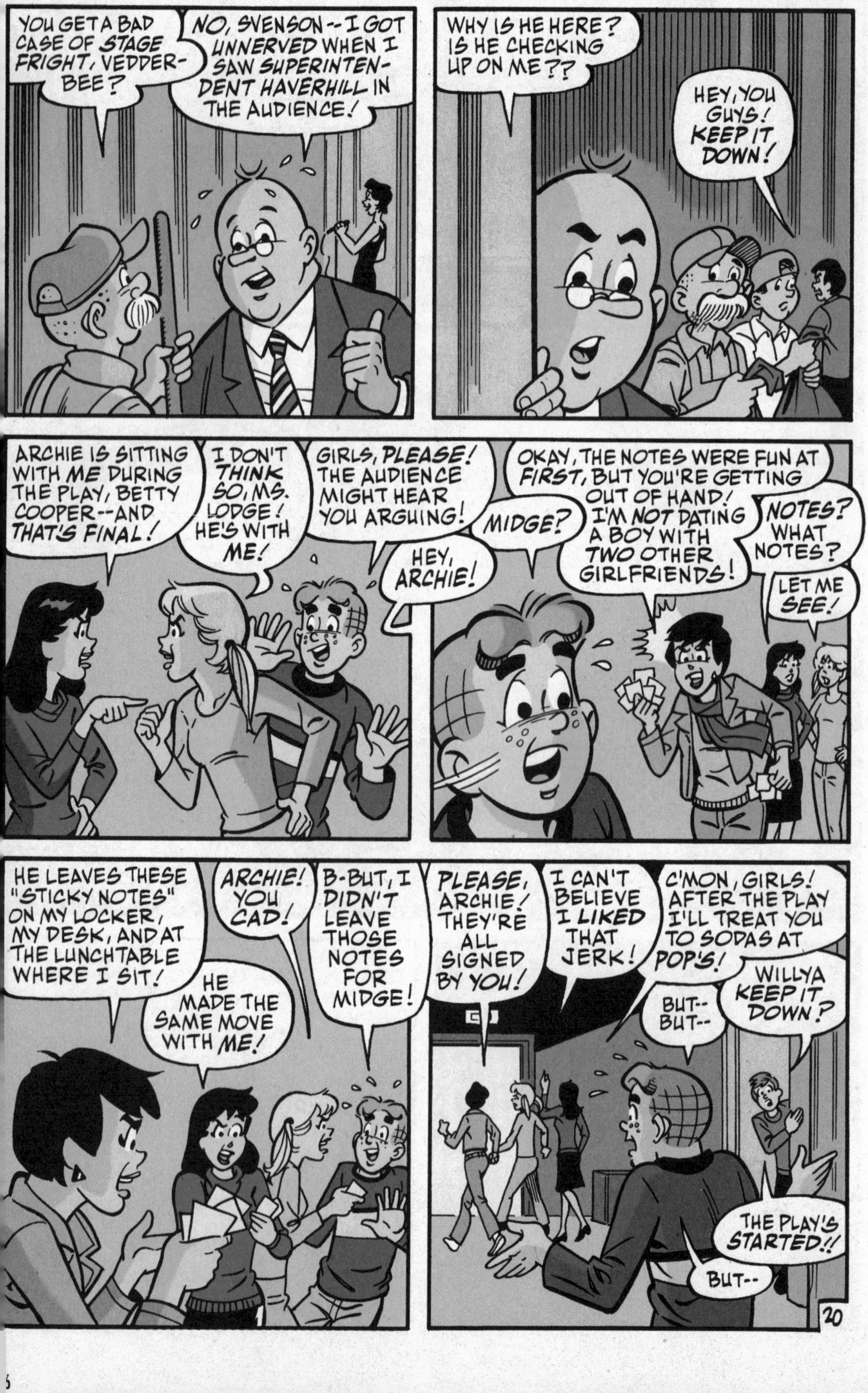
YOU GET A BAD CASE OF STAGE FRIGHT, VEDDER-BEE?
NO, SVENSON--I GOT UNNERVED WHEN I SAW SUPERINTEN-DENT HAVERHILL IN THE AUDIENCE!
WHY IS HE HERE? IS HE CHECKING UP ON ME??
HEY, YOU GUYS! KEEP IT DOWN!
ARCHIE IS SITTING WITH ME DURING THE PLAY, BETTY COOPER--AND THAT'S FINAL!
I DON'T THINK SO, MS. LODGE! HE'S WITH ME!
GIRLS, PLEASE! THE AUDIENCE MIGHT HEAR YOU ARGUING!
HEY, ARCHIE!
MIDGE?
OKAY, THE NOTES WERE FUN AT FIRST, BUT YOU'RE GETTING OUT OF HAND! I'M NOT DATING A BOY WITH TWO OTHER GIRLFRIENDS!
NOTES? WHAT NOTES?
LET ME SEE!
HE LEAVES THESE "STICKY NOTES" ON MY LOCKER, MY DESK, AND AT THE LUNCHTABLE WHERE I SIT!
HE MADE THE SAME MOVE WITH ME!
ARCHIE! YOU CAD!
B-BUT, I DIDN'T LEAVE THOSE NOTES FOR MIDGE!
PLEASE, ARCHIE! THEY'RE ALL SIGNED BY YOU!
I CAN'T BELIEVE I LIKED THAT JERK!
C'MON, GIRLS! AFTER THE PLAY I'LL TREAT YOU TO SODAS AT POP'S!
BUT-- BUT--
WILLYA KEEP IT DOWN?
THE PLAY'S STARTED!!
BUT--
20

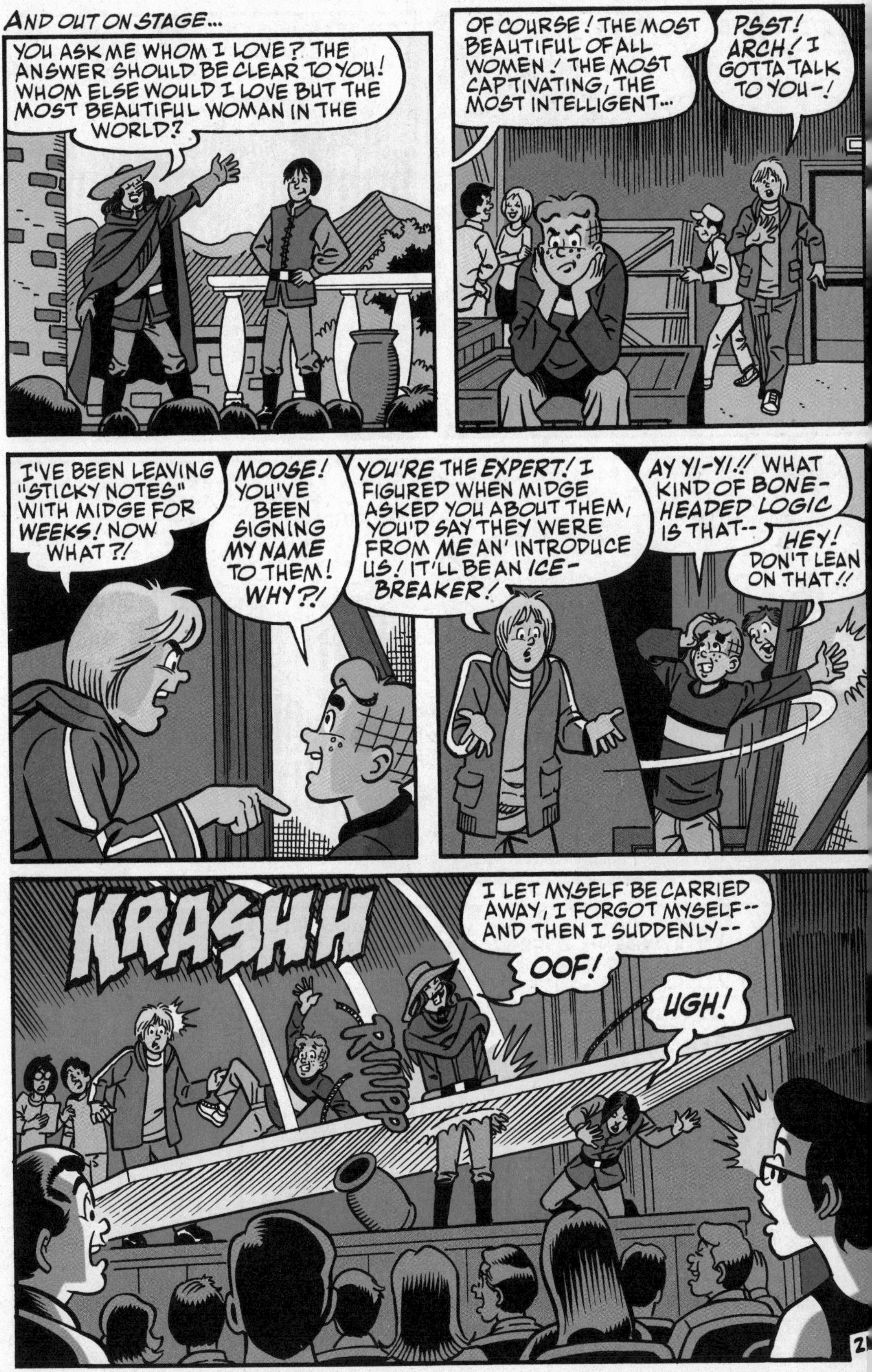
AND OUT ON STAGE...
YOU ASK ME WHOM I LOVE? THE ANSWER SHOULD BE CLEAR TO YOU! WHOM ELSE WOULD I LOVE BUT THE MOST BEAUTIFUL WOMAN IN THE WORLD?
OF COURSE! THE MOST BEAUTIFUL OF ALL WOMEN! THE MOST CAPTIVATING, THE MOST INTELLIGENT...
PSST! ARCH! I GOTTA TALK TO YOU-!
I'VE BEEN LEAVING "STICKY NOTES" WITH MIDGE FOR WEEKS! NOW WHAT?!
MOOSE! YOU'VE BEEN SIGNING MY NAME TO THEM! WHY?!
YOU'RE THE EXPERT! I FIGURED WHEN MIDGE ASKED YOU ABOUT THEM, YOU'D SAY THEY WERE FROM ME AN' INTRODUCE US! IT'LL BE AN ICE-BREAKER!
AY YI-YI!! WHAT KIND OF BONE-HEADED LOGIC IS THAT--
HEY! DON'T LEAN ON THAT!!
KRASHH
I LET MYSELF BE CARRIED AWAY, I FORGOT MYSELF-- AND THEN I SUDDENLY--
OOF!
UGH!
21

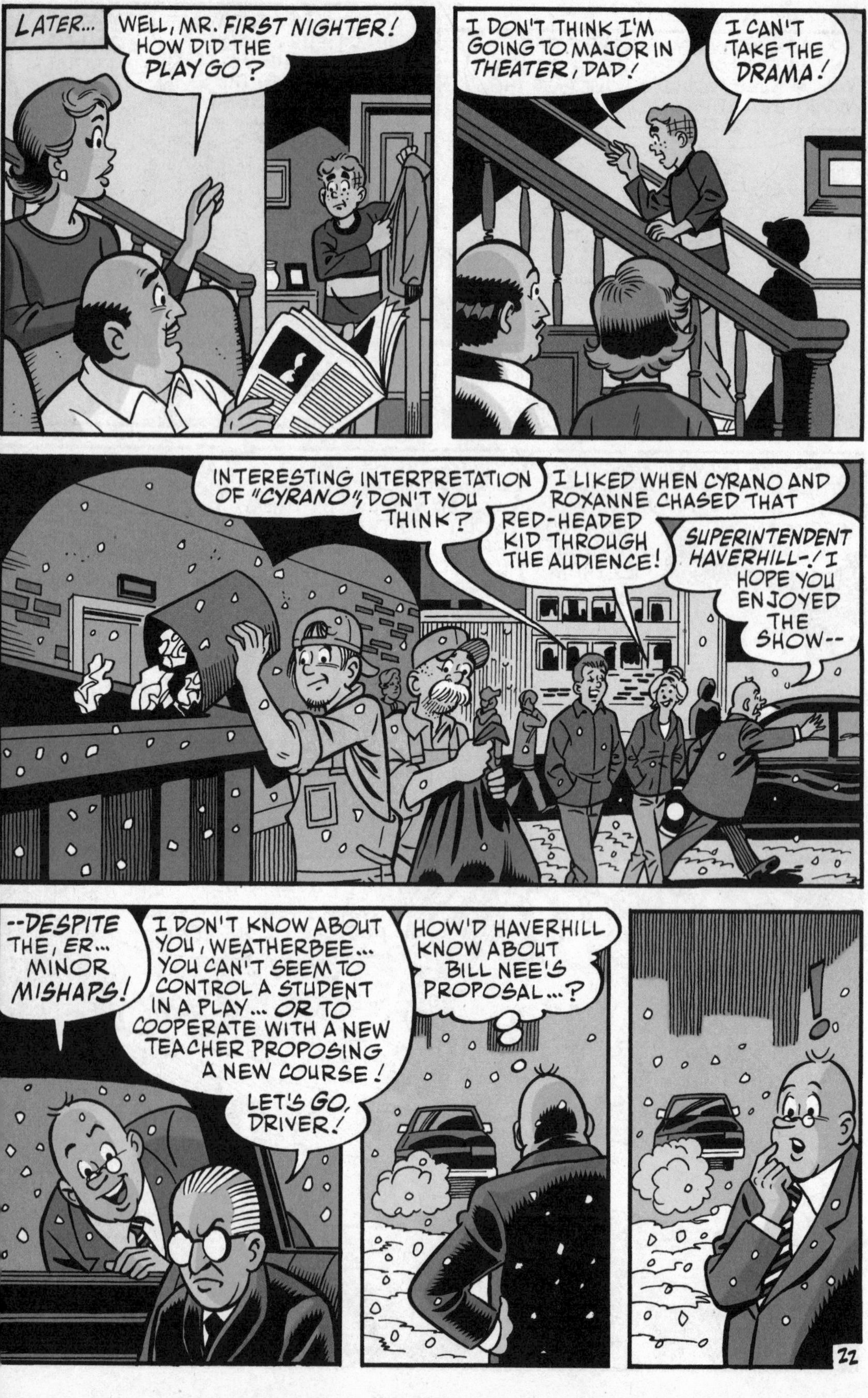
LATER...
WELL, MR. FIRST NIGHTER! HOW DID THE PLAY GO?
I DON'T THINK I'M GOING TO MAJOR IN THEATER, DAD!
I CAN'T TAKE THE DRAMA!
INTERESTING INTERPRETATION OF "CYRANO", DON'T YOU THINK?
I LIKED WHEN CYRANO AND ROXANNE CHASED THAT RED-HEADED KID THROUGH THE AUDIENCE!
SUPERINTENDENT HAVERHILL-! I HOPE YOU ENJOYED THE SHOW--
--DESPITE THE, ER... MINOR MISHAPS!
I DON'T KNOW ABOUT YOU, WEATHERBEE... YOU CAN'T SEEM TO CONTROL A STUDENT IN A PLAY... OR TO COOPERATE WITH A NEW TEACHER PROPOSING A NEW COURSE!
LET'S GO, DRIVER!
HOW'D HAVERHILL KNOW ABOUT BILL NEE'S PROPOSAL...?
!
22

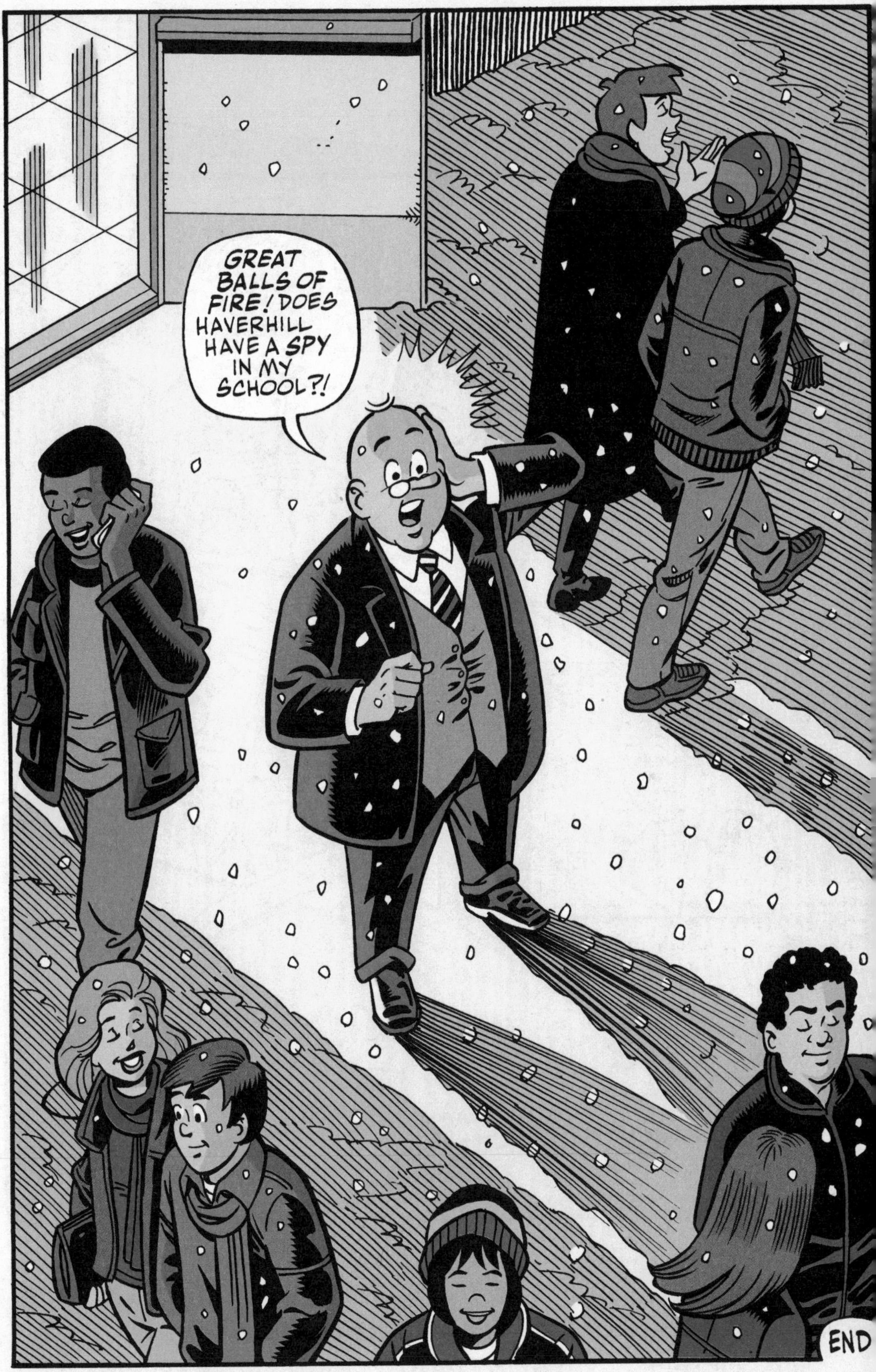
GREAT BALLS OF FIRE! DOES HAVERHILL HAVE A SPY IN MY SCHOOL?!
END

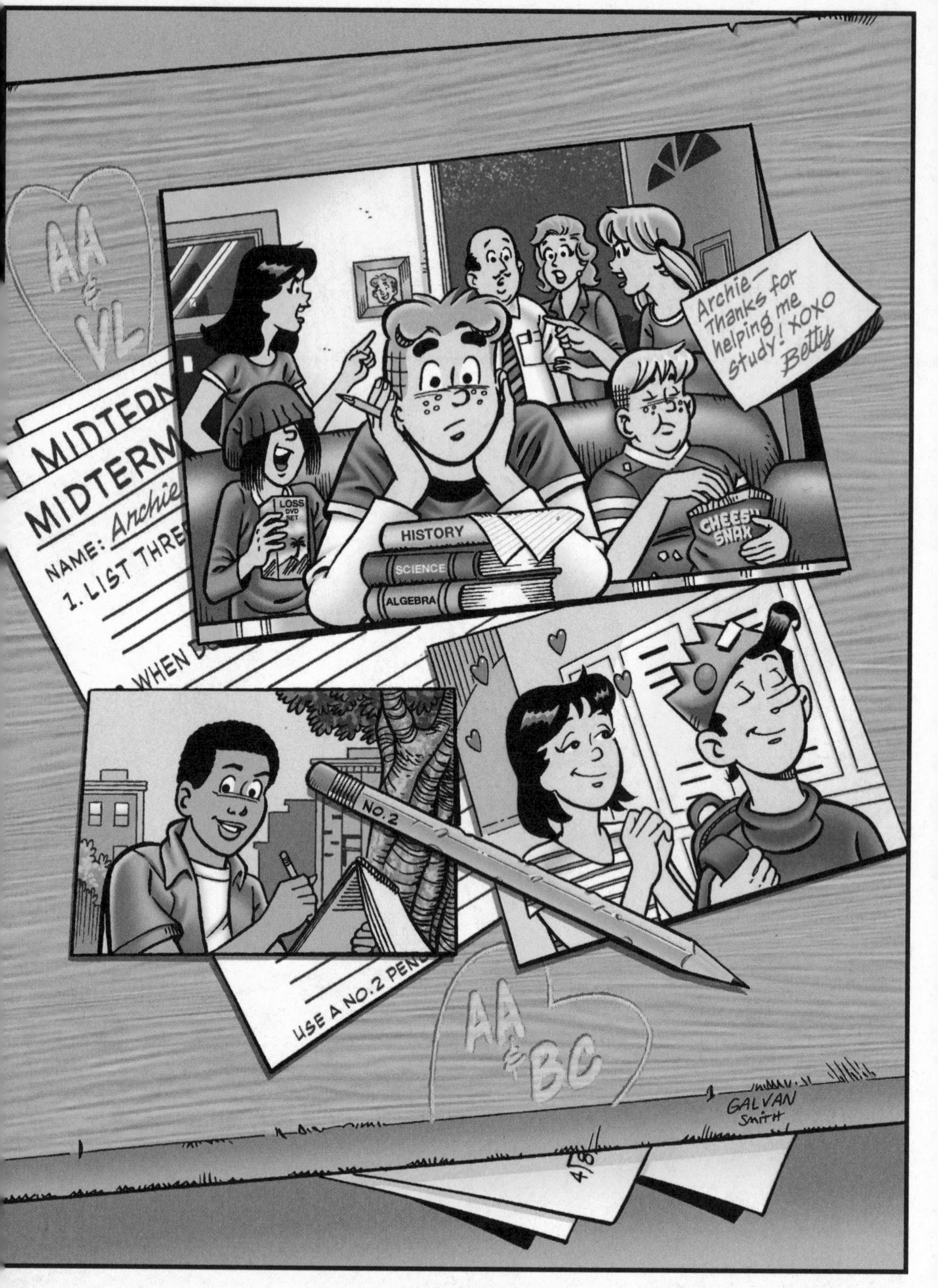

Archie— Thanks for helping me study! XOXO Betty
MIDTERM
MIDTERM
NAME: Archie
1. LIST THREE
WHEN D
USE A NO.2 PEN
HISTORY
SCIENCE
ALGEBRA
CHEESY SNAK
NO.2
AA & VL
AA & BC
GALVAN SMITH

FRESHMAN YEAR PART 4

SCRIPT: BATTON LASH PENCILS: BILL GALVAN
INKS: BOB SMITH LETTERS: JACK MORELLI COLORS: GLENN WHITMORE

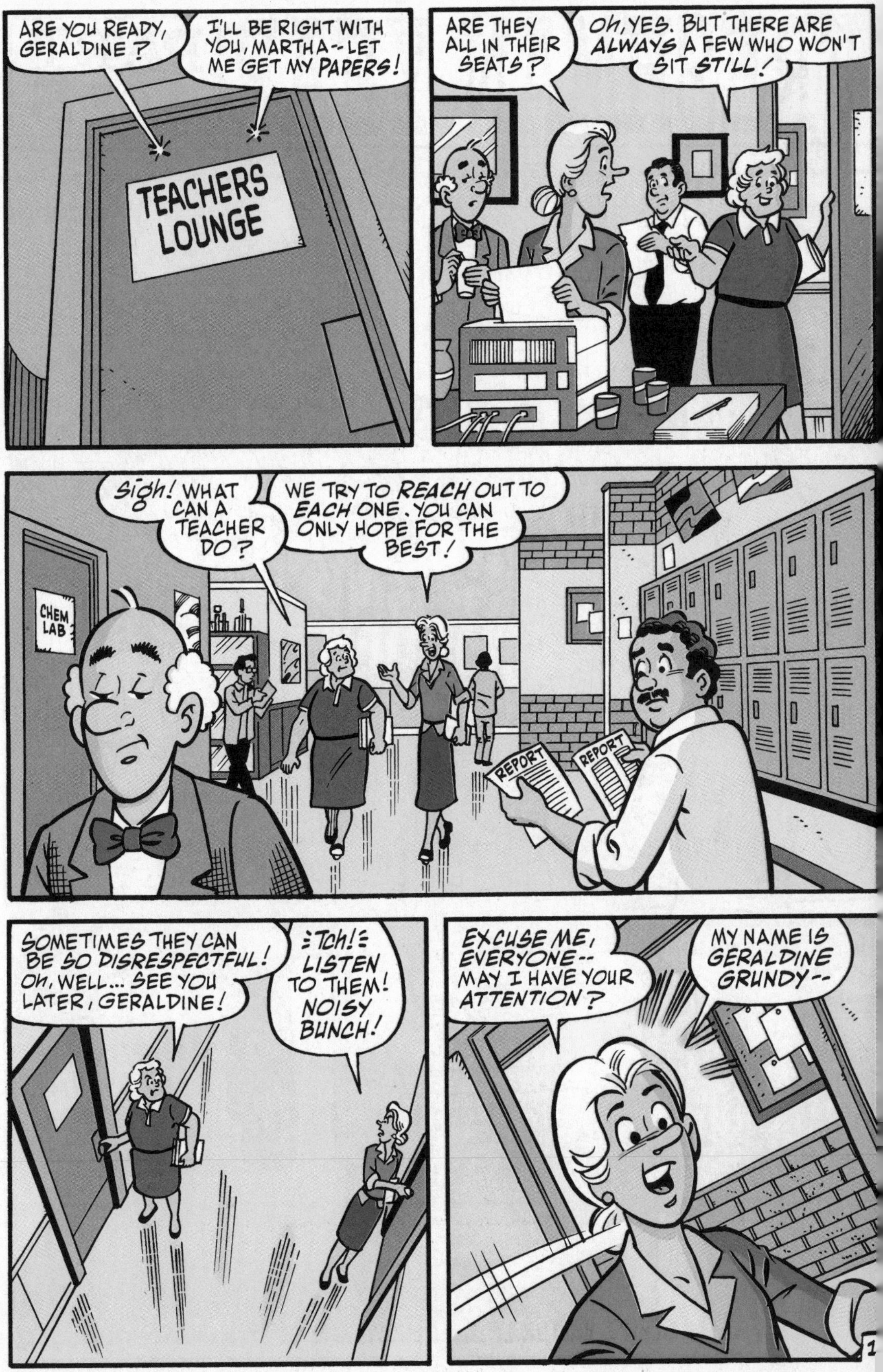
ARE YOU READY, GERALDINE?
I'LL BE RIGHT WITH YOU, MARTHA-- LET ME GET MY PAPERS!
TEACHERS LOUNGE
ARE THEY ALL IN THEIR SEATS?
Oh, YES. BUT THERE ARE ALWAYS A FEW WHO WON'T SIT STILL!
Sigh! WHAT CAN A TEACHER DO?
WE TRY TO REACH OUT TO EACH ONE. YOU CAN ONLY HOPE FOR THE BEST!
CHEM LAB
REPORT
REPORT
SOMETIMES THEY CAN BE SO DISRESPECTFUL! Oh, WELL... SEE YOU LATER, GERALDINE!
Tch! LISTEN TO THEM! NOISY BUNCH!
EXCUSE ME, EVERYONE-- MAY I HAVE YOUR ATTENTION?
MY NAME IS GERALDINE GRUNDY--
1

FRESHMAN YEAR PART 4 OF 5

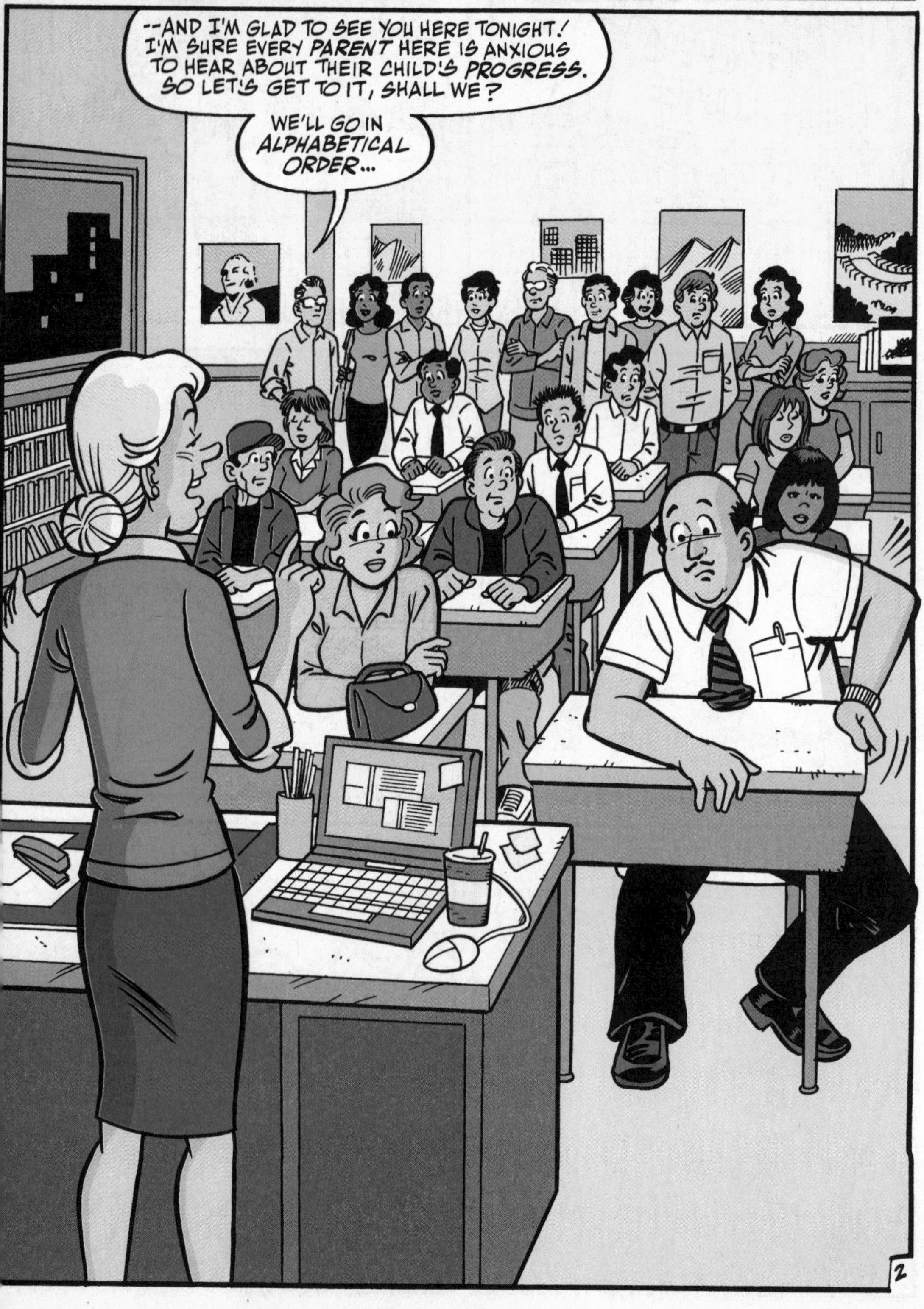
--AND I'M GLAD TO SEE YOU HERE TONIGHT! I'M SURE EVERY PARENT HERE IS ANXIOUS TO HEAR ABOUT THEIR CHILD'S PROGRESS. SO LET'S GET TO IT, SHALL WE?
WE'LL GO IN ALPHABETICAL ORDER...
2

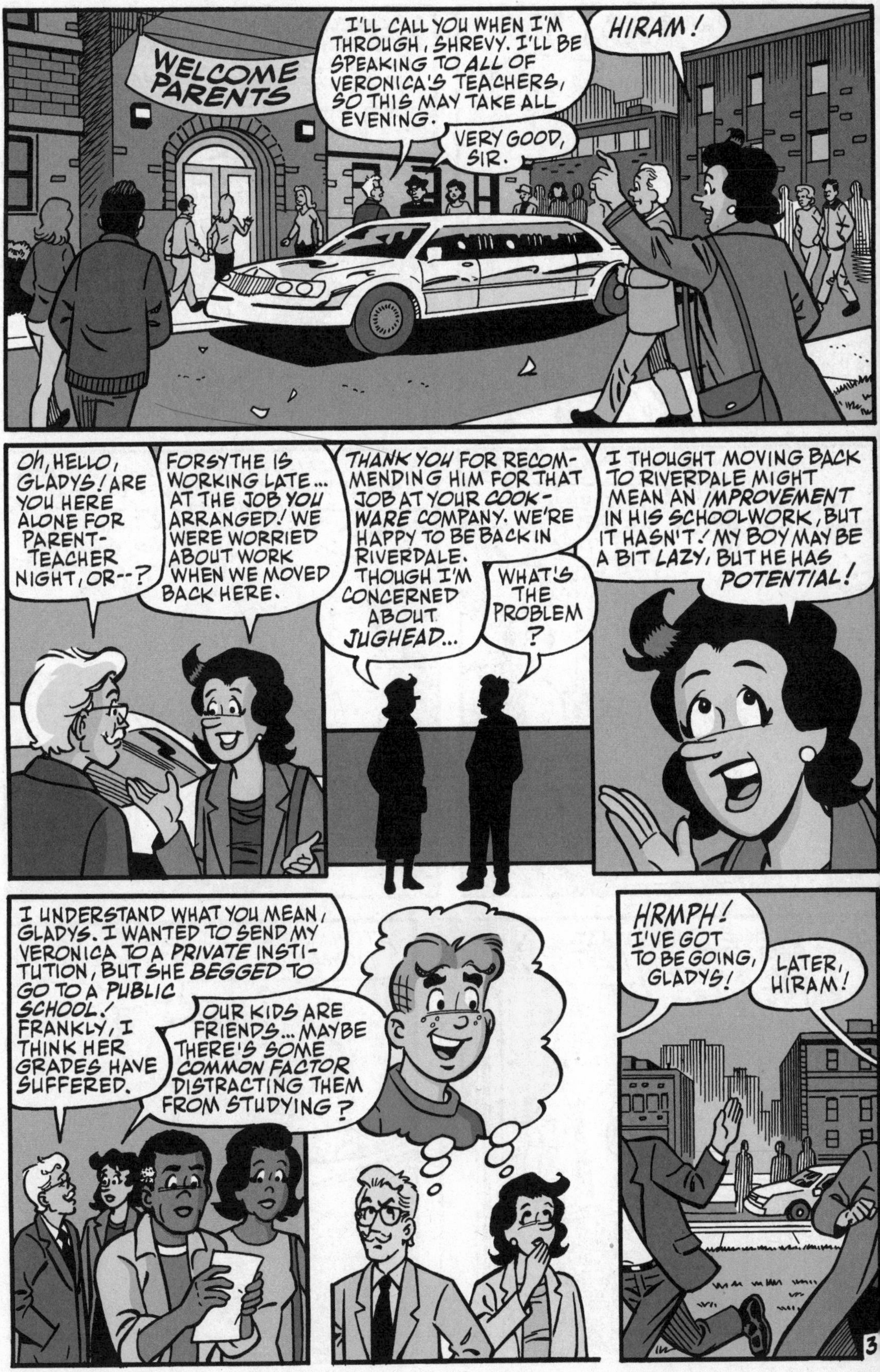
WELCOME PARENTS
I'LL CALL YOU WHEN I'M THROUGH, SHREVY. I'LL BE SPEAKING TO ALL OF VERONICA'S TEACHERS, SO THIS MAY TAKE ALL EVENING.
VERY GOOD, SIR.
HIRAM!
OH, HELLO, GLADYS! ARE YOU HERE ALONE FOR PARENT-TEACHER NIGHT, OR--?
FORSYTHE IS WORKING LATE... AT THE JOB YOU ARRANGED! WE WERE WORRIED ABOUT WORK WHEN WE MOVED BACK HERE.
THANK YOU FOR RECOMMENDING HIM FOR THAT JOB AT YOUR COOKWARE COMPANY. WE'RE HAPPY TO BE BACK IN RIVERDALE. THOUGH I'M CONCERNED ABOUT JUGHEAD...
WHAT'S THE PROBLEM?
I THOUGHT MOVING BACK TO RIVERDALE MIGHT MEAN AN IMPROVEMENT IN HIS SCHOOLWORK, BUT IT HASN'T! MY BOY MAY BE A BIT LAZY, BUT HE HAS POTENTIAL!
I UNDERSTAND WHAT YOU MEAN, GLADYS. I WANTED TO SEND MY VERONICA TO A PRIVATE INSTITUTION, BUT SHE BEGGED TO GO TO A PUBLIC SCHOOL! FRANKLY, I THINK HER GRADES HAVE SUFFERED.
OUR KIDS ARE FRIENDS... MAYBE THERE'S SOME COMMON FACTOR DISTRACTING THEM FROM STUDYING?
HRMPH! I'VE GOT TO BE GOING, GLADYS!
LATER, HIRAM!
3

... HE ALSO HAS A HABIT OF *DAYDREAMING* IN CLASS! THAT IS, WHEN HE'S NOT *TEXT MESSAGING* ONE OF HIS BUDDIES...

I SEE...

Uh-Huh.

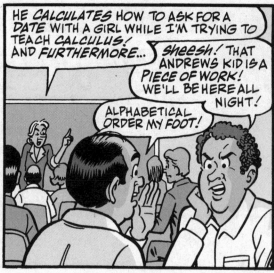

HE *CALCULATES* HOW TO ASK FOR A *DATE* WITH A GIRL WHILE I'M TRYING TO TEACH *CALCULUS!* AND *FURTHERMORE...*

Sheesh! THAT ANDREWS KID IS A *PIECE OF WORK!* WE'LL BE HERE ALL NIGHT!

ALPHABETICAL ORDER MY FOOT!

EXCUSE ME, MS. GRUNDY? WE REALIZE ARCHIE CAN BE A *HANDFUL...*

IN OTHER WORDS, WE *GET* THE IDEA...!

WE SHOULD MOVE ON TO ARCHIE'S *OTHER* INSTRUCTORS, OR WE COULD BE HERE ALL NIGHT!

FINALLY!

THANK YOU, MS. GRUNDY!

WELL, *BUCKLE* YOUR SEAT BELT, FRED... THAT WAS ONLY THE *FIRST* TEACHER...

WHAT NEXT?!

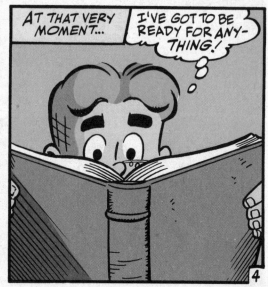

AT THAT VERY MOMENT...

I'VE GOT TO BE READY FOR ANY-THING!

4

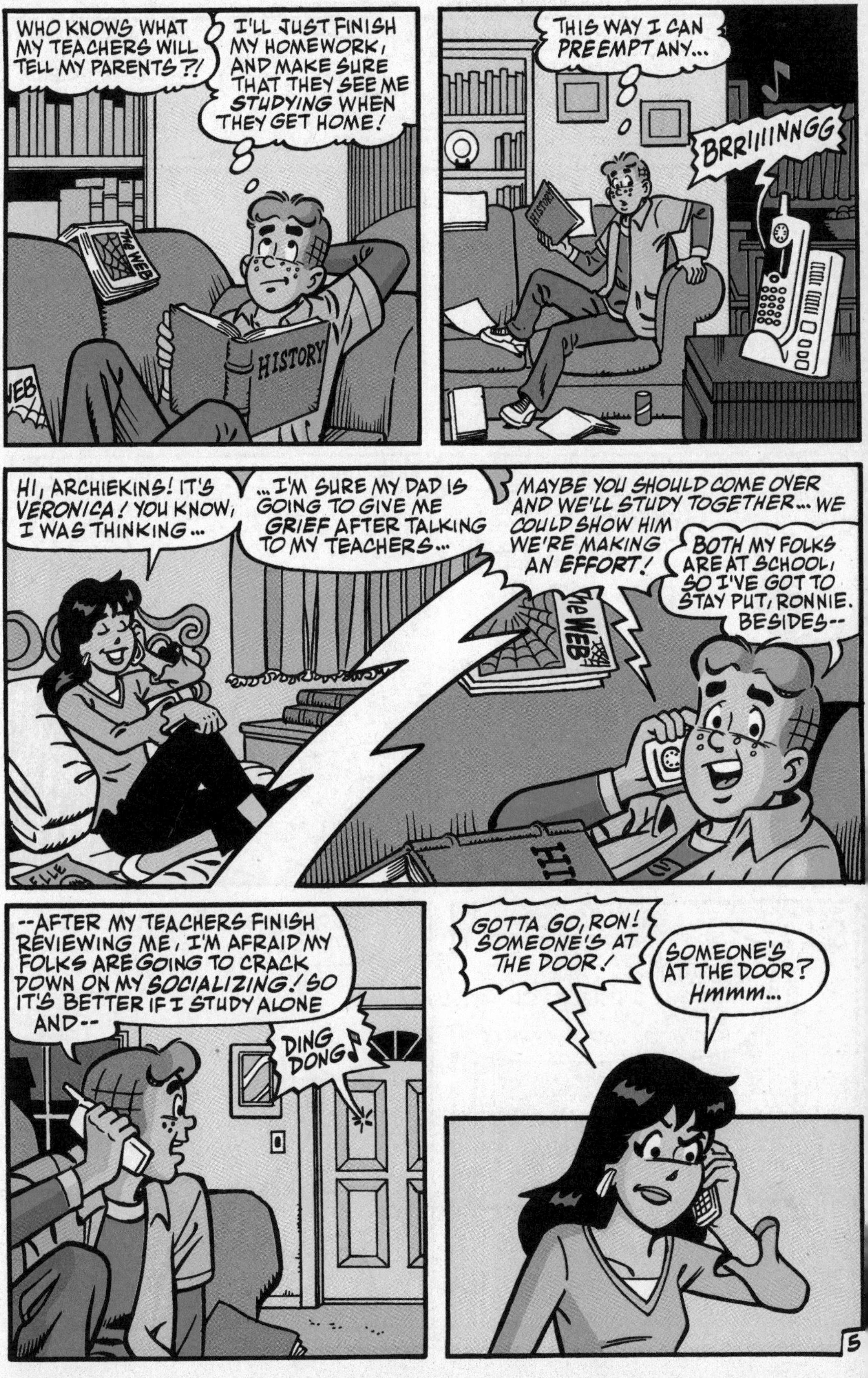
WHO KNOWS WHAT MY TEACHERS WILL TELL MY PARENTS?!
I'LL JUST FINISH MY HOMEWORK, AND MAKE SURE THAT THEY SEE ME STUDYING WHEN THEY GET HOME!
THE WEB
HISTORY
THIS WAY I CAN PREEMPT ANY...
BRR!!!!!NNGG
HISTORY
HI, ARCHIEKINS! IT'S VERONICA! YOU KNOW, I WAS THINKING...
...I'M SURE MY DAD IS GOING TO GIVE ME GRIEF AFTER TALKING TO MY TEACHERS...
MAYBE YOU SHOULD COME OVER AND WE'LL STUDY TOGETHER... WE COULD SHOW HIM WE'RE MAKING AN EFFORT!
BOTH MY FOLKS ARE AT SCHOOL, SO I'VE GOT TO STAY PUT, RONNIE. BESIDES--
THE WEB
ELLE
--AFTER MY TEACHERS FINISH REVIEWING ME, I'M AFRAID MY FOLKS ARE GOING TO CRACK DOWN ON MY SOCIALIZING! SO IT'S BETTER IF I STUDY ALONE AND--
DING DONG
GOTTA GO, RON! SOMEONE'S AT THE DOOR!
SOMEONE'S AT THE DOOR? Hmmm...
5

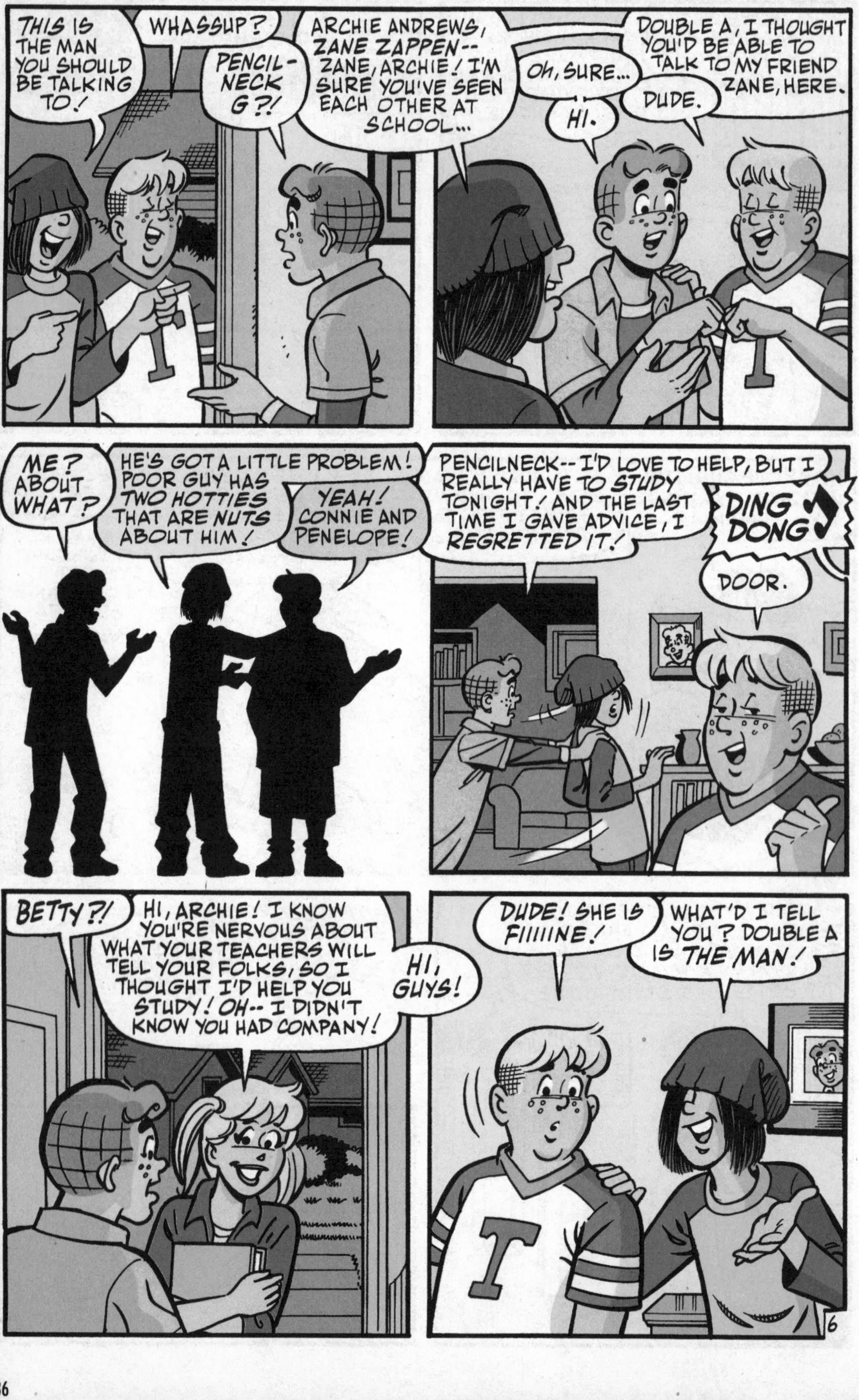
THIS IS THE MAN YOU SHOULD BE TALKING TO!
WHASSUP?
PENCIL-NECK G?!
ARCHIE ANDREWS, ZANE ZAPPEN-- ZANE, ARCHIE! I'M SURE YOU'VE SEEN EACH OTHER AT SCHOOL...
DOUBLE A, I THOUGHT YOU'D BE ABLE TO TALK TO MY FRIEND ZANE, HERE.
OH, SURE...
HI.
DUDE.
ME? ABOUT WHAT?
HE'S GOT A LITTLE PROBLEM! POOR GUY HAS TWO HOTTIES THAT ARE NUTS ABOUT HIM!
YEAH! CONNIE AND PENELOPE!
PENCILNECK-- I'D LOVE TO HELP, BUT I REALLY HAVE TO STUDY TONIGHT! AND THE LAST TIME I GAVE ADVICE, I REGRETTED IT!
DING DONG
DOOR.
BETTY?!
HI, ARCHIE! I KNOW YOU'RE NERVOUS ABOUT WHAT YOUR TEACHERS WILL TELL YOUR FOLKS, SO I THOUGHT I'D HELP YOU STUDY! OH-- I DIDN'T KNOW YOU HAD COMPANY!
HI, GUYS!
DUDE! SHE IS FIIIIINE!
WHAT'D I TELL YOU? DOUBLE A IS THE MAN!
6

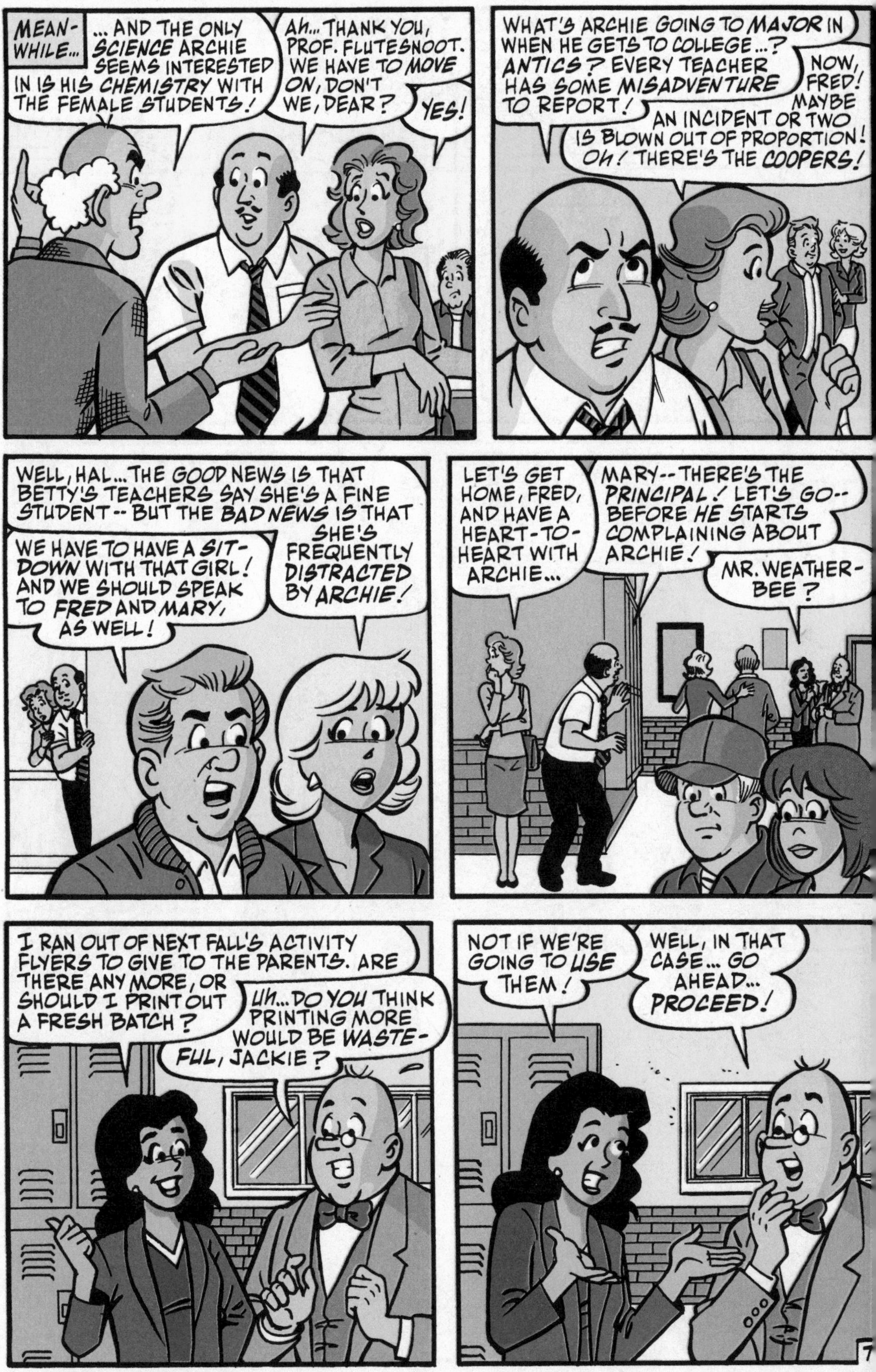
MEAN-WHILE...
... AND THE ONLY SCIENCE ARCHIE SEEMS INTERESTED IN IS HIS CHEMISTRY WITH THE FEMALE STUDENTS!
AH... THANK YOU, PROF. FLUTESNOOT. WE HAVE TO MOVE ON, DON'T WE, DEAR?
YES!
WHAT'S ARCHIE GOING TO MAJOR IN WHEN HE GETS TO COLLEGE...? ANTICS? EVERY TEACHER HAS SOME MISADVENTURE TO REPORT!
NOW, FRED! MAYBE AN INCIDENT OR TWO IS BLOWN OUT OF PROPORTION! OH! THERE'S THE COOPERS!
WELL, HAL... THE GOOD NEWS IS THAT BETTY'S TEACHERS SAY SHE'S A FINE STUDENT -- BUT THE BAD NEWS IS THAT SHE'S FREQUENTLY DISTRACTED BY ARCHIE!
WE HAVE TO HAVE A SIT-DOWN WITH THAT GIRL! AND WE SHOULD SPEAK TO FRED AND MARY, AS WELL!
LET'S GET HOME, FRED, AND HAVE A HEART-TO-HEART WITH ARCHIE...
MARY -- THERE'S THE PRINCIPAL! LET'S GO -- BEFORE HE STARTS COMPLAINING ABOUT ARCHIE!
MR. WEATHER-BEE?
I RAN OUT OF NEXT FALL'S ACTIVITY FLYERS TO GIVE TO THE PARENTS. ARE THERE ANY MORE, OR SHOULD I PRINT OUT A FRESH BATCH?
UH... DO YOU THINK PRINTING MORE WOULD BE WASTE-FUL, JACKIE?
NOT IF WE'RE GOING TO USE THEM!
WELL, IN THAT CASE... GO AHEAD... PROCEED!
7

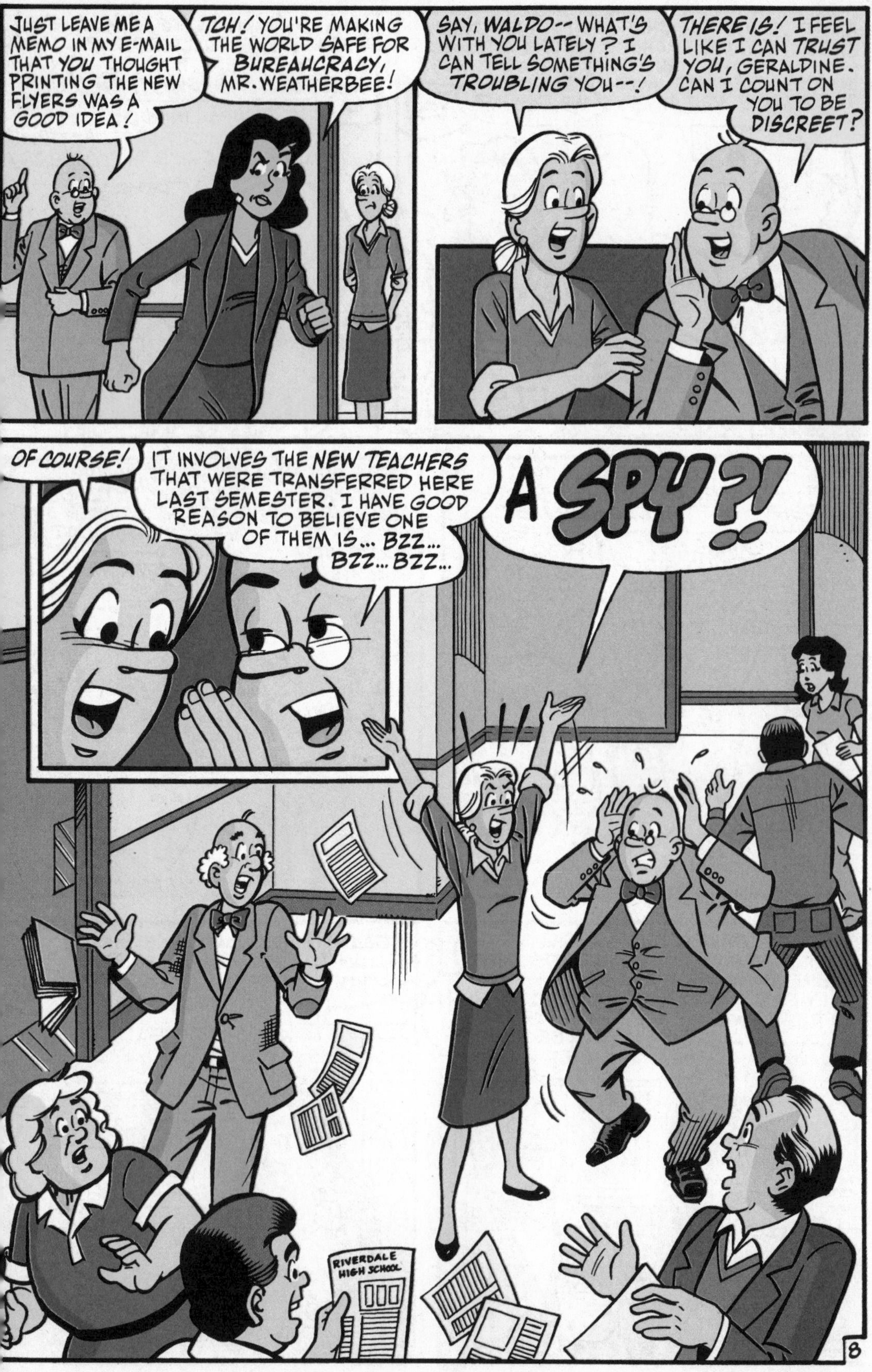
JUST LEAVE ME A MEMO IN MY E-MAIL THAT YOU THOUGHT PRINTING THE NEW FLYERS WAS A GOOD IDEA!
TCH! YOU'RE MAKING THE WORLD SAFE FOR BUREAUCRACY, MR. WEATHERBEE!
SAY, WALDO-- WHAT'S WITH YOU LATELY? I CAN TELL SOMETHING'S TROUBLING YOU--!
THERE IS! I FEEL LIKE I CAN TRUST YOU, GERALDINE. CAN I COUNT ON YOU TO BE DISCREET?
OF COURSE!
IT INVOLVES THE NEW TEACHERS THAT WERE TRANSFERRED HERE LAST SEMESTER. I HAVE GOOD REASON TO BELIEVE ONE OF THEM IS... BZZ... BZZ... BZZ...
A SPY?!
RIVERDALE HIGH SCHOOL
8

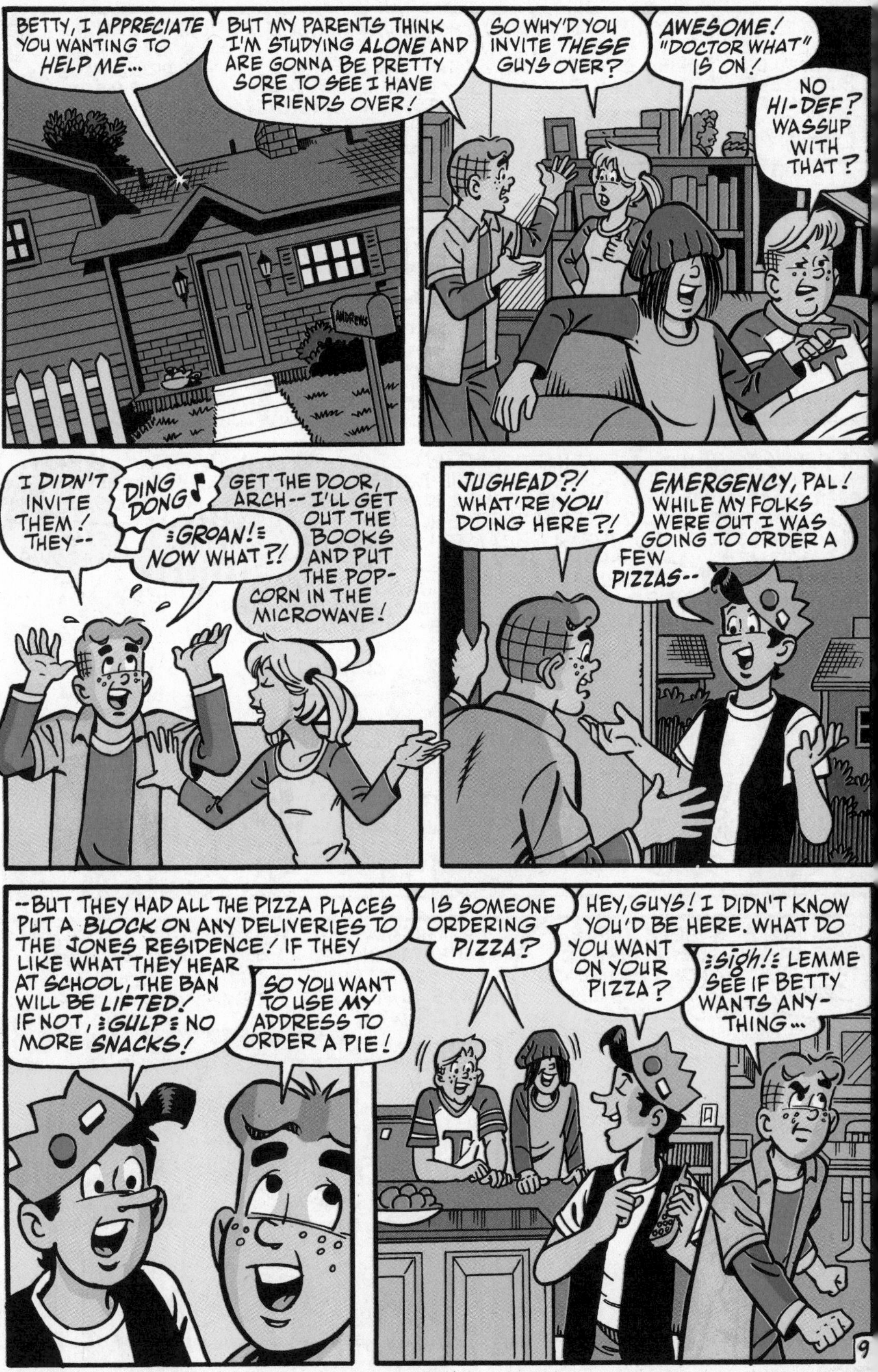
BETTY, I APPRECIATE YOU WANTING TO HELP ME...
BUT MY PARENTS THINK I'M STUDYING ALONE AND ARE GONNA BE PRETTY SORE TO SEE I HAVE FRIENDS OVER!
ANDREWS
SO WHY'D YOU INVITE THESE GUYS OVER?
AWESOME! "DOCTOR WHAT" IS ON!
NO HI-DEF? WASSUP WITH THAT?
I DIDN'T INVITE THEM! THEY--
DING DONG
GROAN! NOW WHAT?!
GET THE DOOR, ARCH-- I'LL GET OUT THE BOOKS AND PUT THE POPCORN IN THE MICROWAVE!
JUGHEAD?! WHAT'RE YOU DOING HERE?!
EMERGENCY, PAL! WHILE MY FOLKS WERE OUT I WAS GOING TO ORDER A FEW PIZZAS--
--BUT THEY HAD ALL THE PIZZA PLACES PUT A BLOCK ON ANY DELIVERIES TO THE JONES RESIDENCE! IF THEY LIKE WHAT THEY HEAR AT SCHOOL, THE BAN WILL BE LIFTED! IF NOT, GULP NO MORE SNACKS!
SO YOU WANT TO USE MY ADDRESS TO ORDER A PIE!
IS SOMEONE ORDERING PIZZA?
HEY, GUYS! I DIDN'T KNOW YOU'D BE HERE. WHAT DO YOU WANT ON YOUR PIZZA?
SIGH! LEMME SEE IF BETTY WANTS ANYTHING...
9

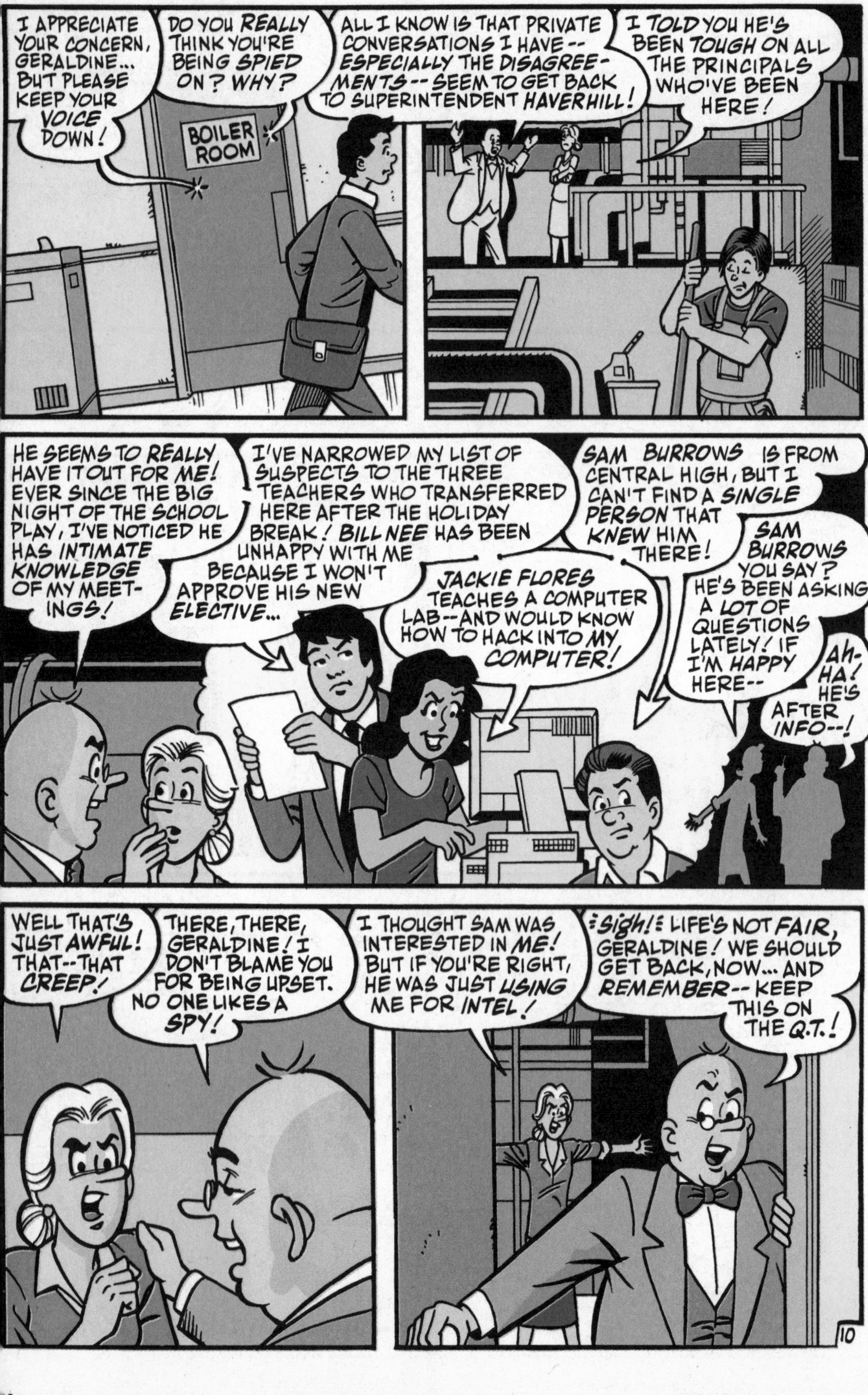
I APPRECIATE YOUR CONCERN, GERALDINE... BUT PLEASE KEEP YOUR VOICE DOWN!
DO YOU REALLY THINK YOU'RE BEING SPIED ON? WHY?
BOILER ROOM
ALL I KNOW IS THAT PRIVATE CONVERSATIONS I HAVE -- ESPECIALLY THE DISAGREE-MENTS -- SEEM TO GET BACK TO SUPERINTENDENT HAVERHILL!
I TOLD YOU HE'S BEEN TOUGH ON ALL THE PRINCIPALS WHO'VE BEEN HERE!
HE SEEMS TO REALLY HAVE IT OUT FOR ME! EVER SINCE THE BIG NIGHT OF THE SCHOOL PLAY, I'VE NOTICED HE HAS INTIMATE KNOWLEDGE OF MY MEET-INGS!
I'VE NARROWED MY LIST OF SUSPECTS TO THE THREE TEACHERS WHO TRANSFERRED HERE AFTER THE HOLIDAY BREAK! BILL NEE HAS BEEN UNHAPPY WITH ME BECAUSE I WON'T APPROVE HIS NEW ELECTIVE...
JACKIE FLORES TEACHES A COMPUTER LAB--AND WOULD KNOW HOW TO HACK INTO MY COMPUTER!
SAM BURROWS IS FROM CENTRAL HIGH, BUT I CAN'T FIND A SINGLE PERSON THAT KNEW HIM THERE!
SAM BURROWS YOU SAY? HE'S BEEN ASKING A LOT OF QUESTIONS LATELY! IF I'M HAPPY HERE--
AH-HA! HE'S AFTER INFO--!
WELL THAT'S JUST AWFUL! THAT--THAT CREEP!
THERE, THERE, GERALDINE! I DON'T BLAME YOU FOR BEING UPSET. NO ONE LIKES A SPY!
I THOUGHT SAM WAS INTERESTED IN ME! BUT IF YOU'RE RIGHT, HE WAS JUST USING ME FOR INTEL!
:SIGH!: LIFE'S NOT FAIR, GERALDINE! WE SHOULD GET BACK, NOW... AND REMEMBER-- KEEP THIS ON THE Q.T.!
10

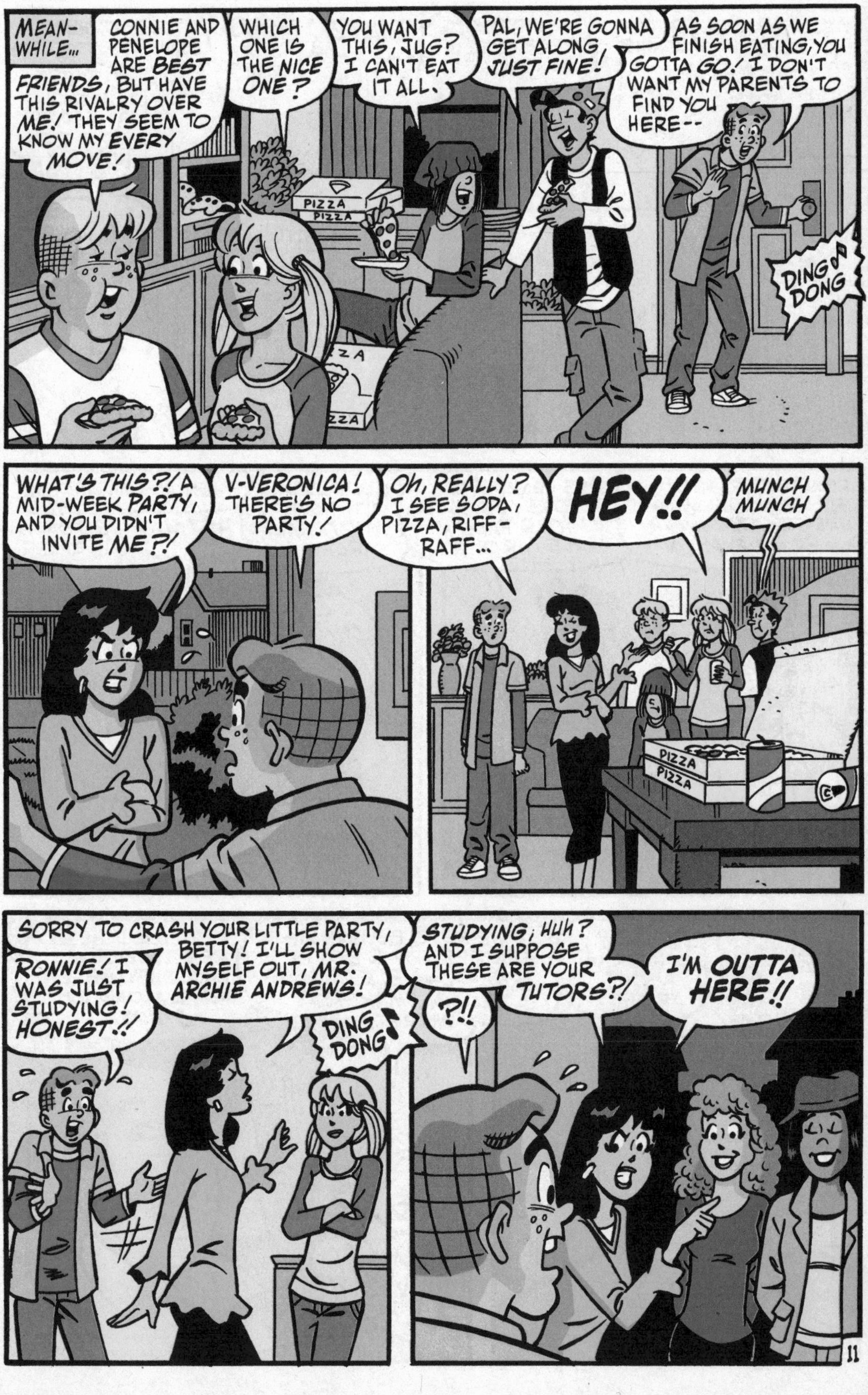
MEAN-WHILE...
CONNIE AND PENELOPE ARE BEST FRIENDS, BUT HAVE THIS RIVALRY OVER ME! THEY SEEM TO KNOW MY EVERY MOVE!
WHICH ONE IS THE NICE ONE?
YOU WANT THIS, JUG? I CAN'T EAT IT ALL.
PAL, WE'RE GONNA GET ALONG JUST FINE!
AS SOON AS WE FINISH EATING, YOU GOTTA GO! I DON'T WANT MY PARENTS TO FIND YOU HERE--
DING DONG
WHAT'S THIS?! A MID-WEEK PARTY, AND YOU DIDN'T INVITE ME?!
V-VERONICA! THERE'S NO PARTY!
Oh, REALLY? I SEE SODA, PIZZA, RIFF-RAFF...
HEY!!
MUNCH MUNCH
SORRY TO CRASH YOUR LITTLE PARTY, BETTY! I'LL SHOW MYSELF OUT, MR. ARCHIE ANDREWS!
RONNIE! I WAS JUST STUDYING! HONEST!!
DING DONG
?!!
STUDYING, Huh? AND I SUPPOSE THESE ARE YOUR TUTORS?!
I'M OUTTA HERE!!
11

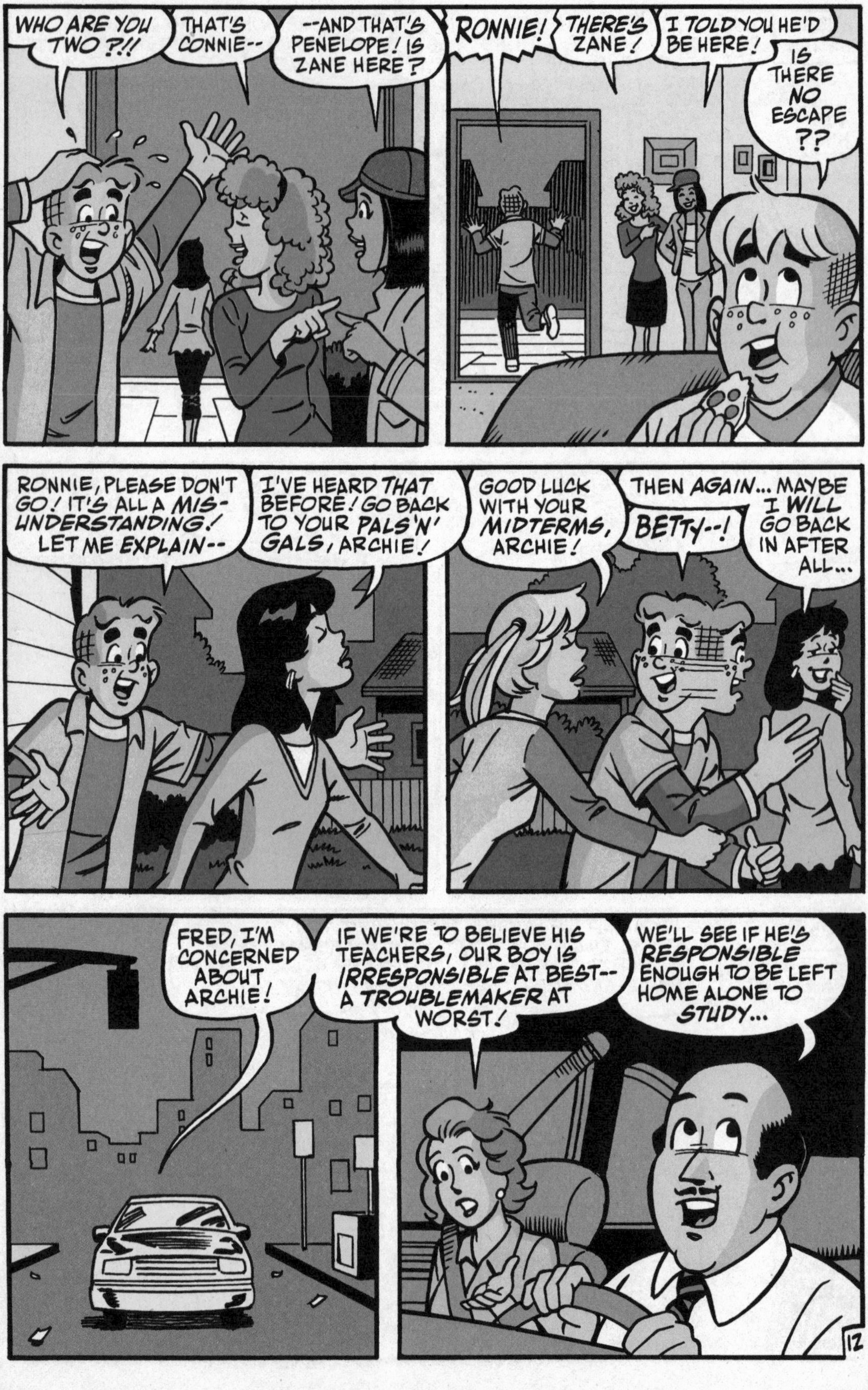
WHO ARE YOU TWO ?!!
THAT'S CONNIE--
--AND THAT'S PENELOPE! IS ZANE HERE?
RONNIE!
THERE'S ZANE!
I TOLD YOU HE'D BE HERE!
IS THERE NO ESCAPE ??
RONNIE, PLEASE DON'T GO! IT'S ALL A MIS-UNDERSTANDING! LET ME EXPLAIN--
I'VE HEARD THAT BEFORE! GO BACK TO YOUR PALS 'N' GALS, ARCHIE!
GOOD LUCK WITH YOUR MIDTERMS, ARCHIE!
BETTY--!
THEN AGAIN... MAYBE I WILL GO BACK IN AFTER ALL...
FRED, I'M CONCERNED ABOUT ARCHIE!
IF WE'RE TO BELIEVE HIS TEACHERS, OUR BOY IS IRRESPONSIBLE AT BEST-- A TROUBLEMAKER AT WORST!
WE'LL SEE IF HE'S RESPONSIBLE ENOUGH TO BE LEFT HOME ALONE TO STUDY...
12

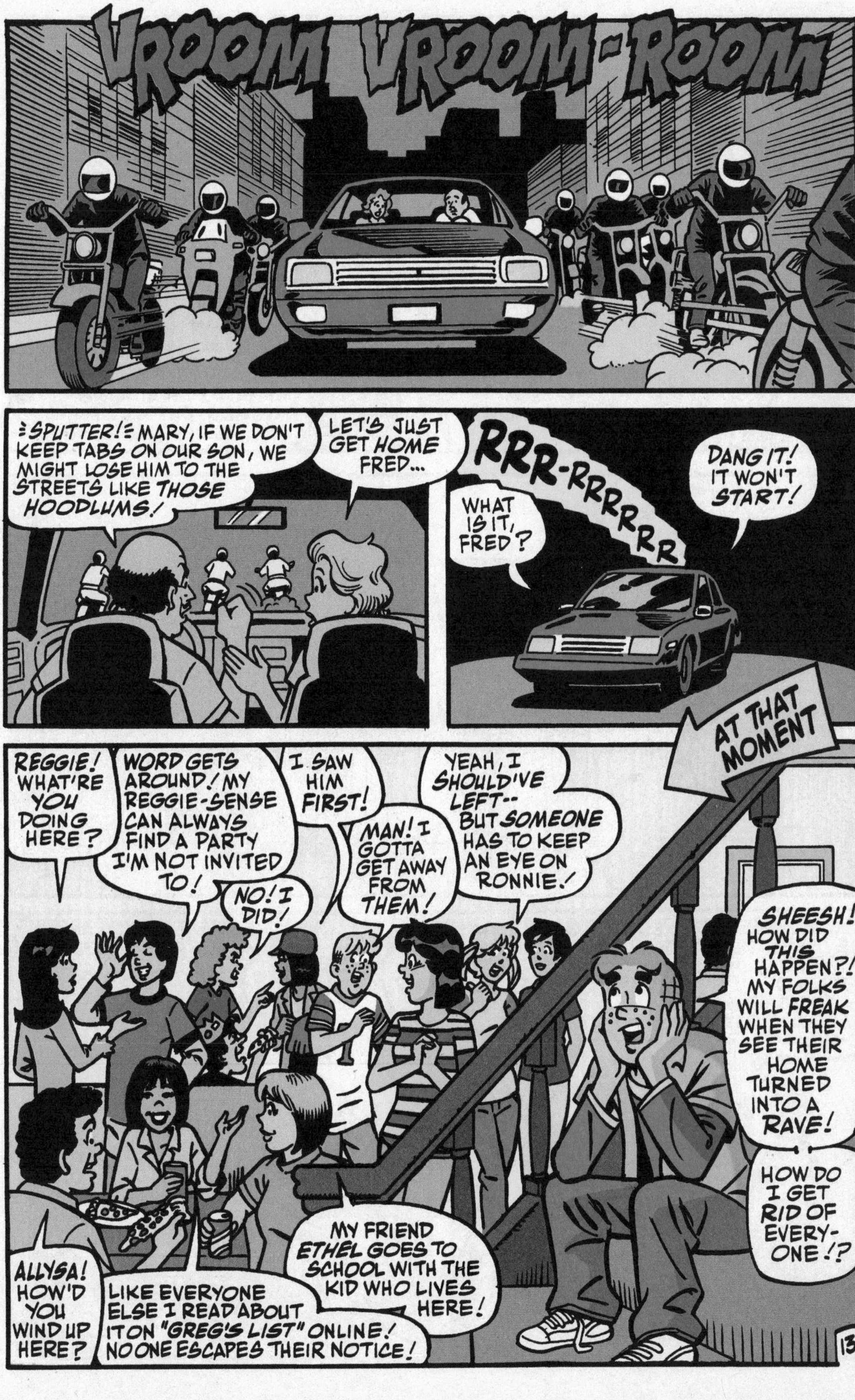
VROOM VROOM-ROOM
SPUTTER! MARY, IF WE DON'T KEEP TABS ON OUR SON, WE MIGHT LOSE HIM TO THE STREETS LIKE THOSE HOODLUMS!
LET'S JUST GET HOME FRED...
RRR-RRRRRRR
WHAT IS IT, FRED?
DANG IT! IT WON'T START!
AT THAT MOMENT
REGGIE! WHAT'RE YOU DOING HERE?
WORD GETS AROUND! MY REGGIE-SENSE CAN ALWAYS FIND A PARTY I'M NOT INVITED TO!
I SAW HIM FIRST!
NO! I DID!
MAN! I GOTTA GET AWAY FROM THEM!
YEAH, I SHOULD'VE LEFT-- BUT SOMEONE HAS TO KEEP AN EYE ON RONNIE!
SHEESH! HOW DID THIS HAPPEN?! MY FOLKS WILL FREAK WHEN THEY SEE THEIR HOME TURNED INTO A RAVE!
HOW DO I GET RID OF EVERY-ONE!?
MY FRIEND ETHEL GOES TO SCHOOL WITH THE KID WHO LIVES HERE!
ALLYSA! HOW'D YOU WIND UP HERE?
LIKE EVERYONE ELSE I READ ABOUT IT ON "GREG'S LIST" ONLINE! NO ONE ESCAPES THEIR NOTICE!
13

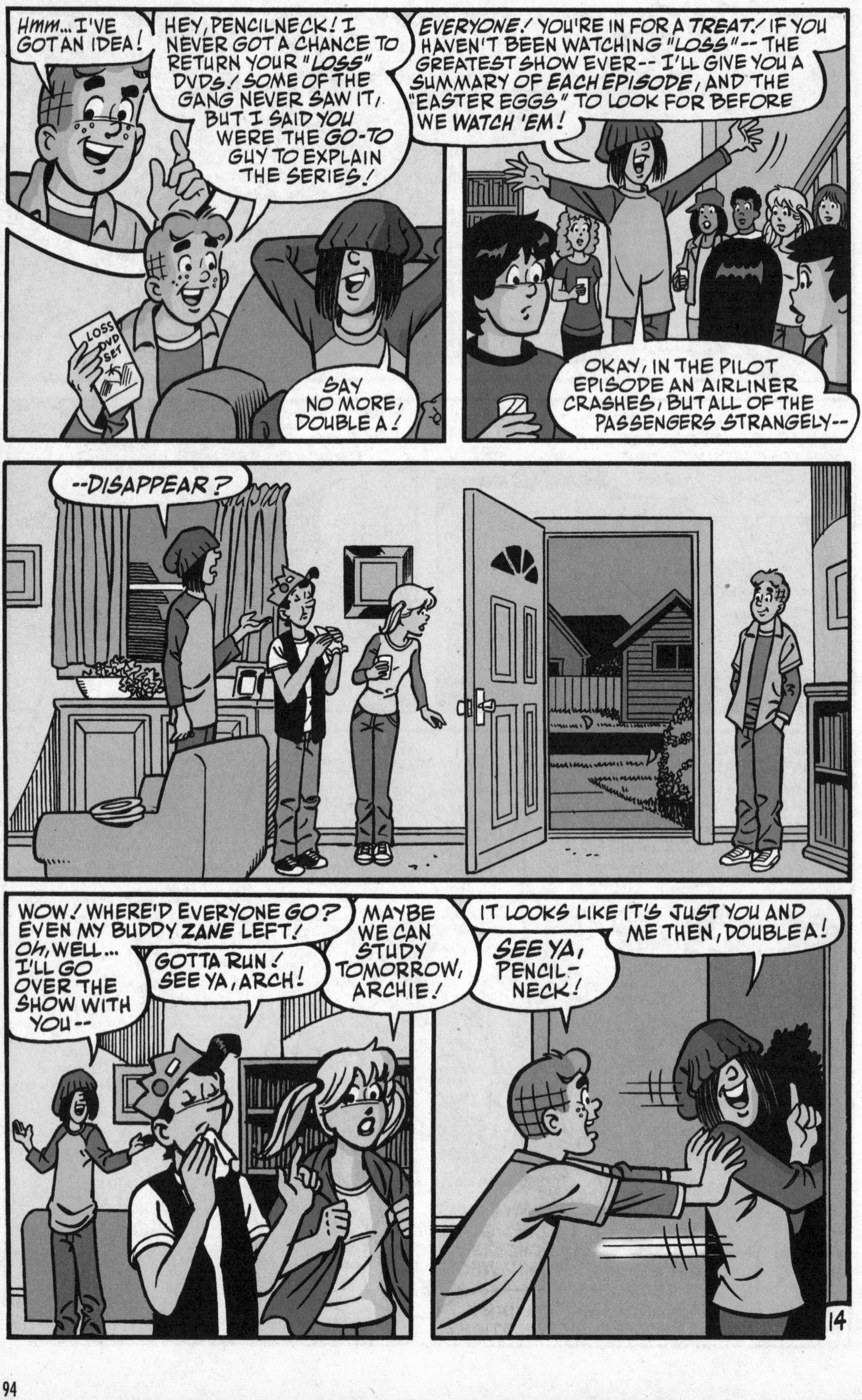
HMM... I'VE GOT AN IDEA!
HEY, PENCILNECK! I NEVER GOT A CHANCE TO RETURN YOUR "LOSS" DVDS! SOME OF THE GANG NEVER SAW IT, BUT I SAID YOU WERE THE GO-TO GUY TO EXPLAIN THE SERIES!
LOSS DVD SET
SAY NO MORE, DOUBLE A!
EVERYONE! YOU'RE IN FOR A TREAT! IF YOU HAVEN'T BEEN WATCHING "LOSS" -- THE GREATEST SHOW EVER -- I'LL GIVE YOU A SUMMARY OF EACH EPISODE, AND THE "EASTER EGGS" TO LOOK FOR BEFORE WE WATCH 'EM!
OKAY, IN THE PILOT EPISODE AN AIRLINER CRASHES, BUT ALL OF THE PASSENGERS STRANGELY--
--DISAPPEAR?
WOW! WHERE'D EVERYONE GO? EVEN MY BUDDY ZANE LEFT! OH, WELL... I'LL GO OVER THE SHOW WITH YOU --
GOTTA RUN! SEE YA, ARCH!
MAYBE WE CAN STUDY TOMORROW, ARCHIE!
IT LOOKS LIKE IT'S JUST YOU AND ME THEN, DOUBLE A!
SEE YA, PENCIL-NECK!
14

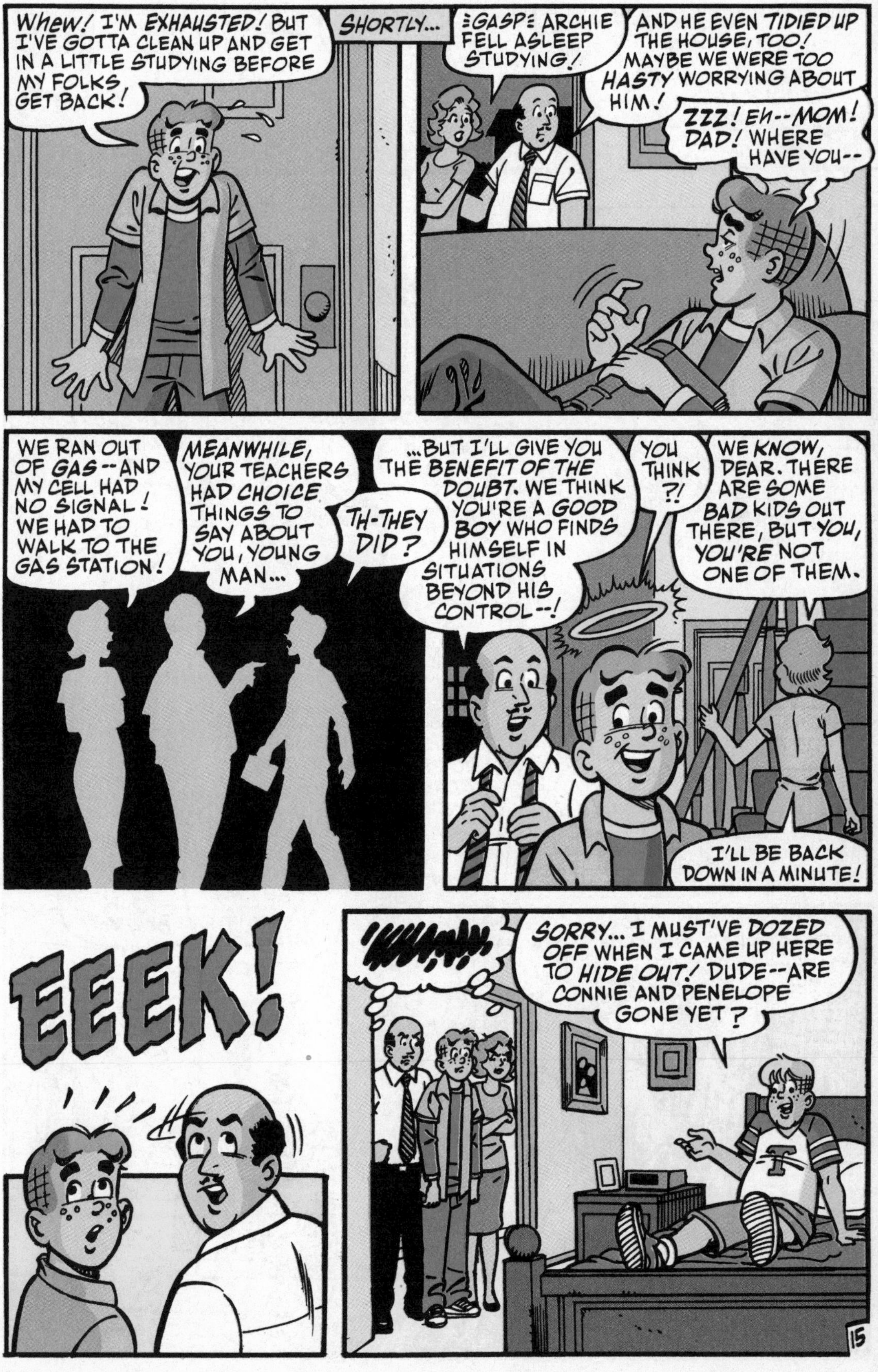
WHEW! I'M EXHAUSTED! BUT I'VE GOTTA CLEAN UP AND GET IN A LITTLE STUDYING BEFORE MY FOLKS GET BACK!
SHORTLY...
=GASP= ARCHIE FELL ASLEEP STUDYING!
AND HE EVEN TIDIED UP THE HOUSE, TOO! MAYBE WE WERE TOO HASTY WORRYING ABOUT HIM!
ZZZ! EH--MOM! DAD! WHERE HAVE YOU--
WE RAN OUT OF GAS--AND MY CELL HAD NO SIGNAL! WE HAD TO WALK TO THE GAS STATION!
MEANWHILE, YOUR TEACHERS HAD CHOICE THINGS TO SAY ABOUT YOU, YOUNG MAN...
TH-THEY DID?
...BUT I'LL GIVE YOU THE BENEFIT OF THE DOUBT. WE THINK YOU'RE A GOOD BOY WHO FINDS HIMSELF IN SITUATIONS BEYOND HIS CONTROL--!
YOU THINK ?!
WE KNOW, DEAR. THERE ARE SOME BAD KIDS OUT THERE, BUT YOU, YOU'RE NOT ONE OF THEM.
I'LL BE BACK DOWN IN A MINUTE!
EEEK!
SORRY... I MUST'VE DOZED OFF WHEN I CAME UP HERE TO HIDE OUT! DUDE--ARE CONNIE AND PENELOPE GONE YET?
15

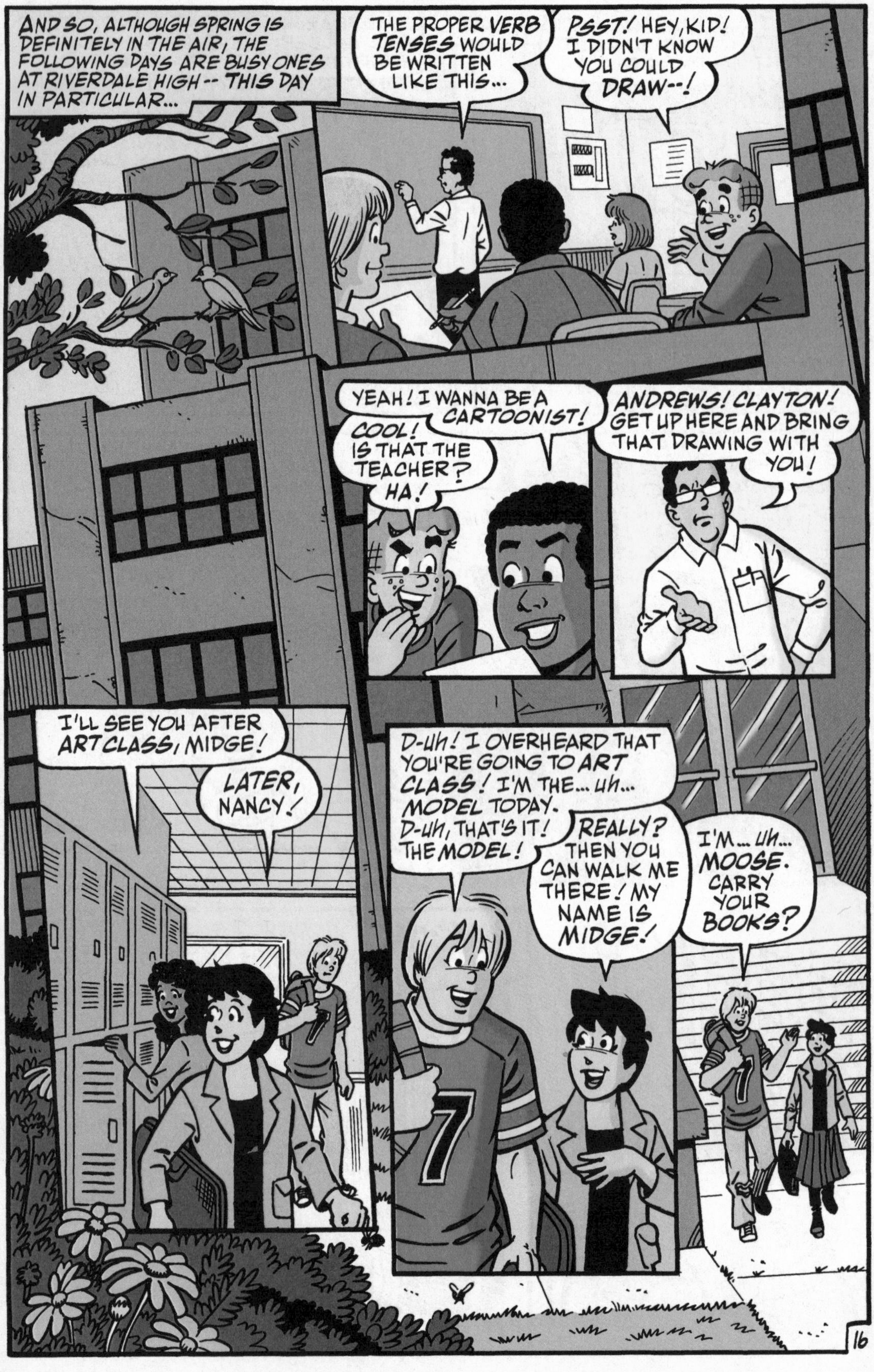
AND SO, ALTHOUGH SPRING IS DEFINITELY IN THE AIR, THE FOLLOWING DAYS ARE BUSY ONES AT RIVERDALE HIGH -- THIS DAY IN PARTICULAR...
THE PROPER VERB TENSES WOULD BE WRITTEN LIKE THIS...
PSST! HEY, KID! I DIDN'T KNOW YOU COULD DRAW--!
YEAH! I WANNA BE A CARTOONIST!
COOL! IS THAT THE TEACHER? HA!
ANDREWS! CLAYTON! GET UP HERE AND BRING THAT DRAWING WITH YOU!
I'LL SEE YOU AFTER ART CLASS, MIDGE!
LATER, NANCY!
D-uh! I OVERHEARD THAT YOU'RE GOING TO ART CLASS! I'M THE... uh... MODEL TODAY. D-uh, THAT'S IT! THE MODEL!
REALLY? THEN YOU CAN WALK ME THERE! MY NAME IS MIDGE!
I'M... uh... MOOSE. CARRY YOUR BOOKS?
16

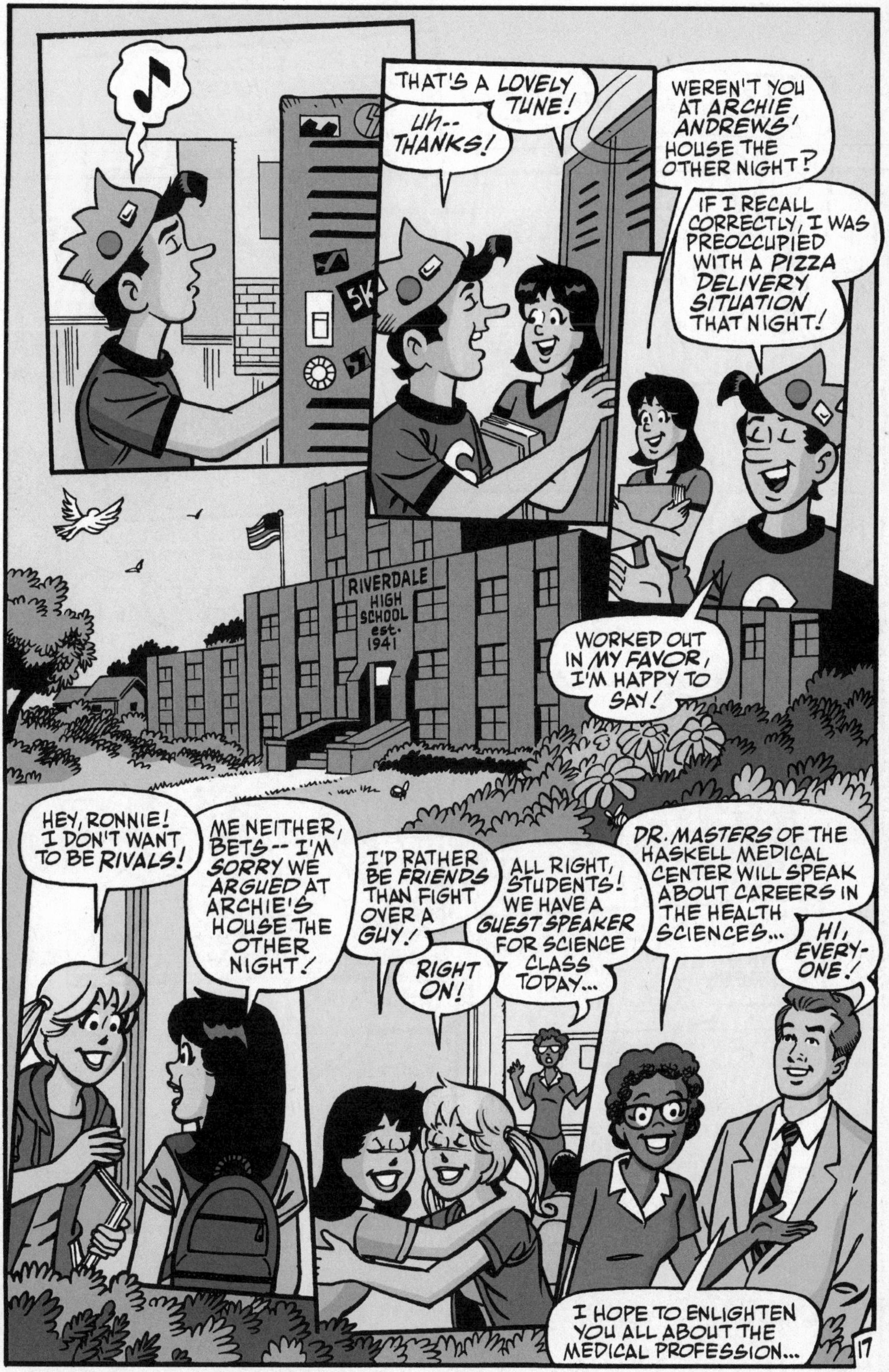
THAT'S A LOVELY TUNE!
Uh-- THANKS!
WEREN'T YOU AT ARCHIE ANDREWS' HOUSE THE OTHER NIGHT?
IF I RECALL CORRECTLY, I WAS PREOCCUPIED WITH A PIZZA DELIVERY SITUATION THAT NIGHT!
WORKED OUT IN MY FAVOR, I'M HAPPY TO SAY!
RIVERDALE HIGH SCHOOL est. 1941
HEY, RONNIE! I DON'T WANT TO BE RIVALS!
ME NEITHER, BETS -- I'M SORRY WE ARGUED AT ARCHIE'S HOUSE THE OTHER NIGHT!
I'D RATHER BE FRIENDS THAN FIGHT OVER A GUY!
RIGHT ON!
ALL RIGHT, STUDENTS! WE HAVE A GUEST SPEAKER FOR SCIENCE CLASS TODAY...
DR. MASTERS OF THE HASKELL MEDICAL CENTER WILL SPEAK ABOUT CAREERS IN THE HEALTH SCIENCES...
HI, EVERY-ONE!
I HOPE TO ENLIGHTEN YOU ALL ABOUT THE MEDICAL PROFESSION...
17

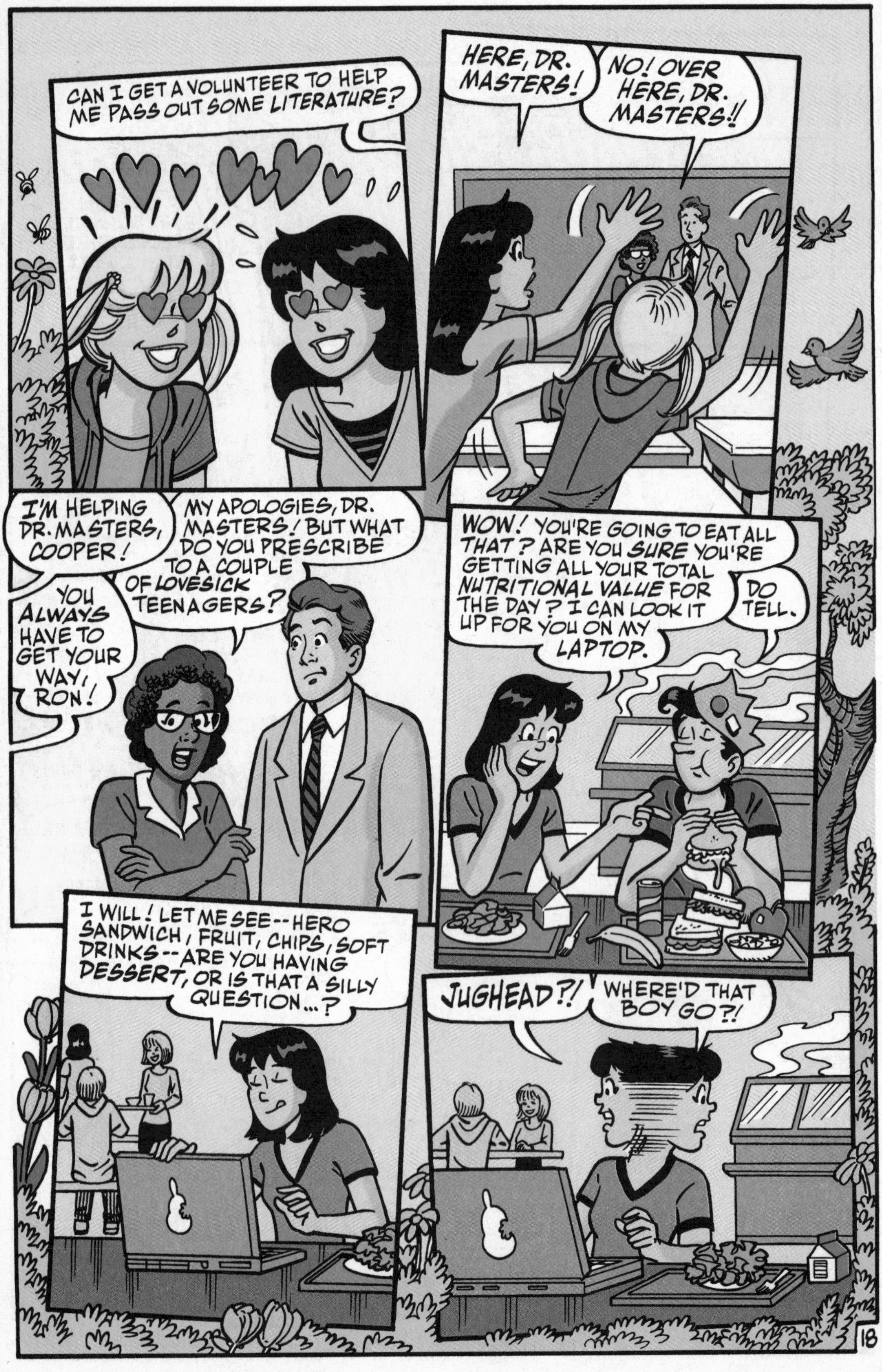
CAN I GET A VOLUNTEER TO HELP ME PASS OUT SOME LITERATURE?
HERE, DR. MASTERS!
NO! OVER HERE, DR. MASTERS!!
I'M HELPING DR. MASTERS, COOPER!
MY APOLOGIES, DR. MASTERS! BUT WHAT DO YOU PRESCRIBE TO A COUPLE OF LOVESICK TEENAGERS?
YOU ALWAYS HAVE TO GET YOUR WAY, RON!
WOW! YOU'RE GOING TO EAT ALL THAT? ARE YOU SURE YOU'RE GETTING ALL YOUR TOTAL NUTRITIONAL VALUE FOR THE DAY? I CAN LOOK IT UP FOR YOU ON MY LAPTOP.
DO TELL.
I WILL! LET ME SEE--HERO SANDWICH, FRUIT, CHIPS, SOFT DRINKS--ARE YOU HAVING DESSERT, OR IS THAT A SILLY QUESTION...?
JUGHEAD?!
WHERE'D THAT BOY GO?!
18

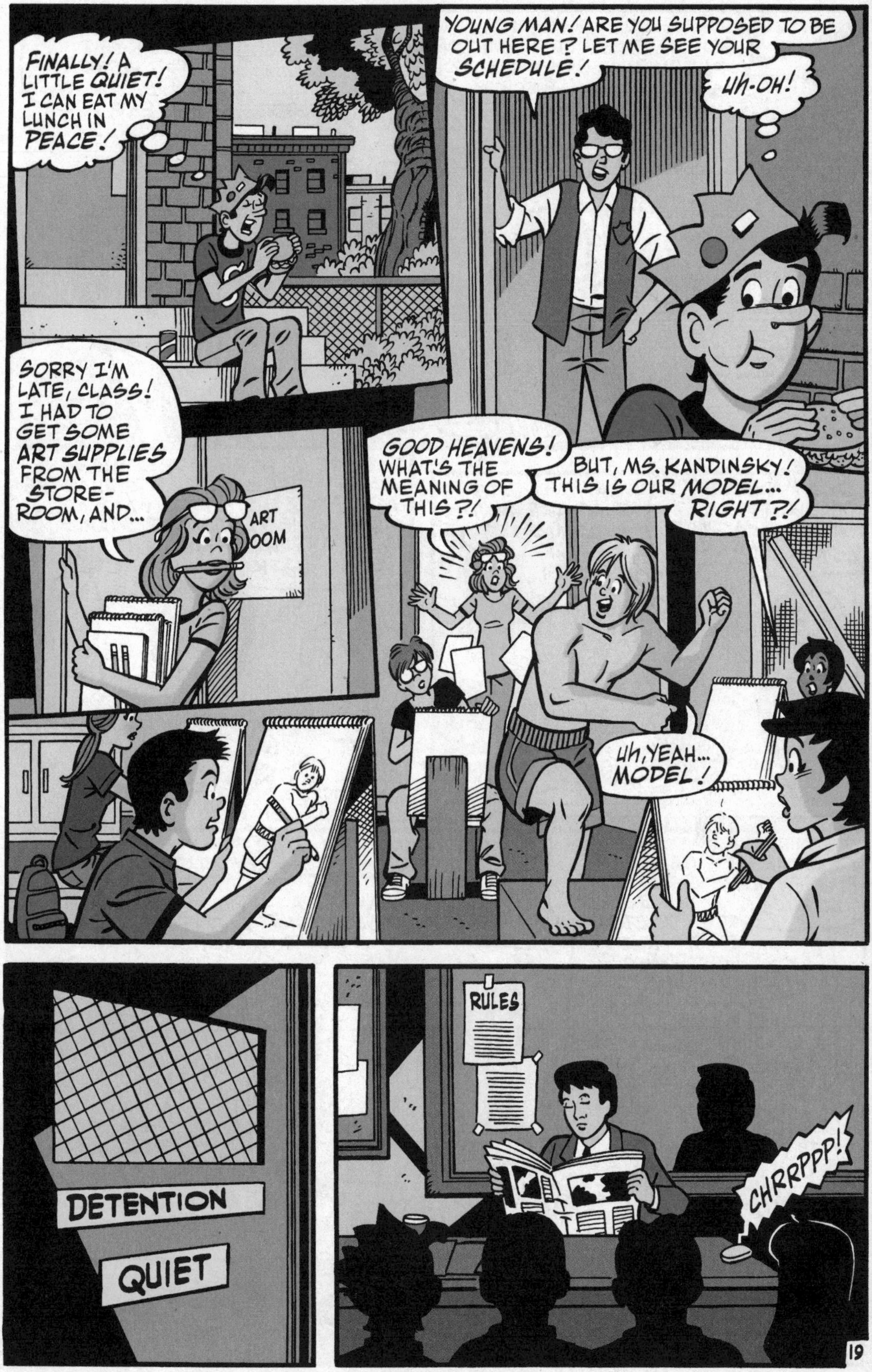
FINALLY! A LITTLE QUIET! I CAN EAT MY LUNCH IN PEACE!
YOUNG MAN! ARE YOU SUPPOSED TO BE OUT HERE? LET ME SEE YOUR SCHEDULE!
UH-OH!
SORRY I'M LATE, CLASS! I HAD TO GET SOME ART SUPPLIES FROM THE STORE-ROOM, AND...
ART
OOM
GOOD HEAVENS! WHAT'S THE MEANING OF THIS?!
BUT, MS. KANDINSKY! THIS IS OUR MODEL... RIGHT?!
UH, YEAH... MODEL!
DETENTION
QUIET
RULES
CHRRPPP!
19

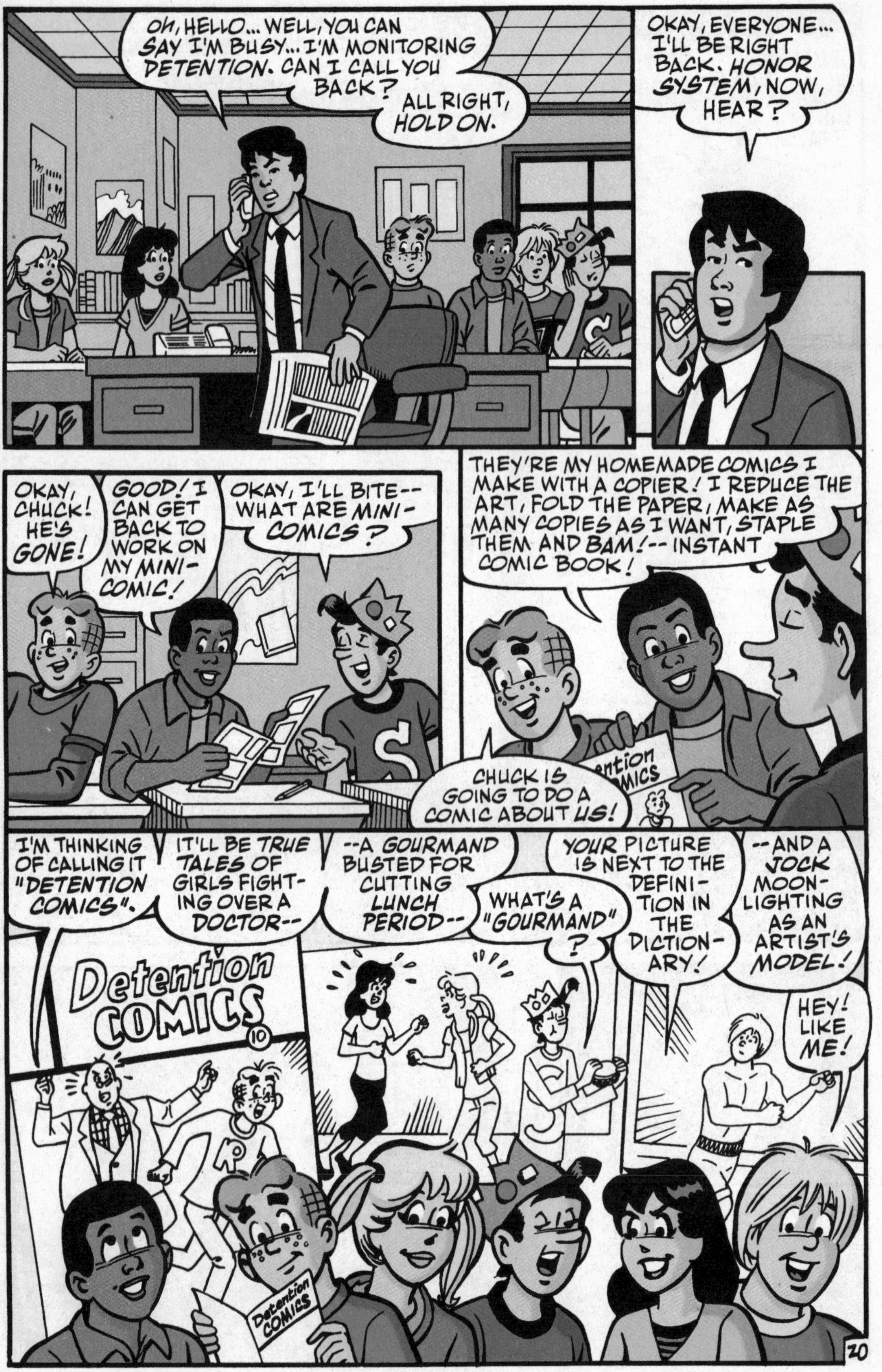
OH, HELLO... WELL, YOU CAN SAY I'M BUSY... I'M MONITORING DETENTION. CAN I CALL YOU BACK?
ALL RIGHT, HOLD ON.
OKAY, EVERYONE... I'LL BE RIGHT BACK. HONOR SYSTEM, NOW, HEAR?
OKAY, CHUCK! HE'S GONE!
GOOD! I CAN GET BACK TO WORK ON MY MINI-COMIC!
OKAY, I'LL BITE-- WHAT ARE MINI-COMICS?
THEY'RE MY HOMEMADE COMICS I MAKE WITH A COPIER! I REDUCE THE ART, FOLD THE PAPER, MAKE AS MANY COPIES AS I WANT, STAPLE THEM AND BAM!-- INSTANT COMIC BOOK!
CHUCK IS GOING TO DO A COMIC ABOUT US!
I'M THINKING OF CALLING IT "DETENTION COMICS".
IT'LL BE TRUE TALES OF GIRLS FIGHTING OVER A DOCTOR--
--A GOURMAND BUSTED FOR CUTTING LUNCH PERIOD--
WHAT'S A "GOURMAND"?
YOUR PICTURE IS NEXT TO THE DEFINITION IN THE DICTIONARY!
--AND A JOCK MOONLIGHTING AS AN ARTIST'S MODEL!
HEY! LIKE ME!
Detention COMICS
10
20

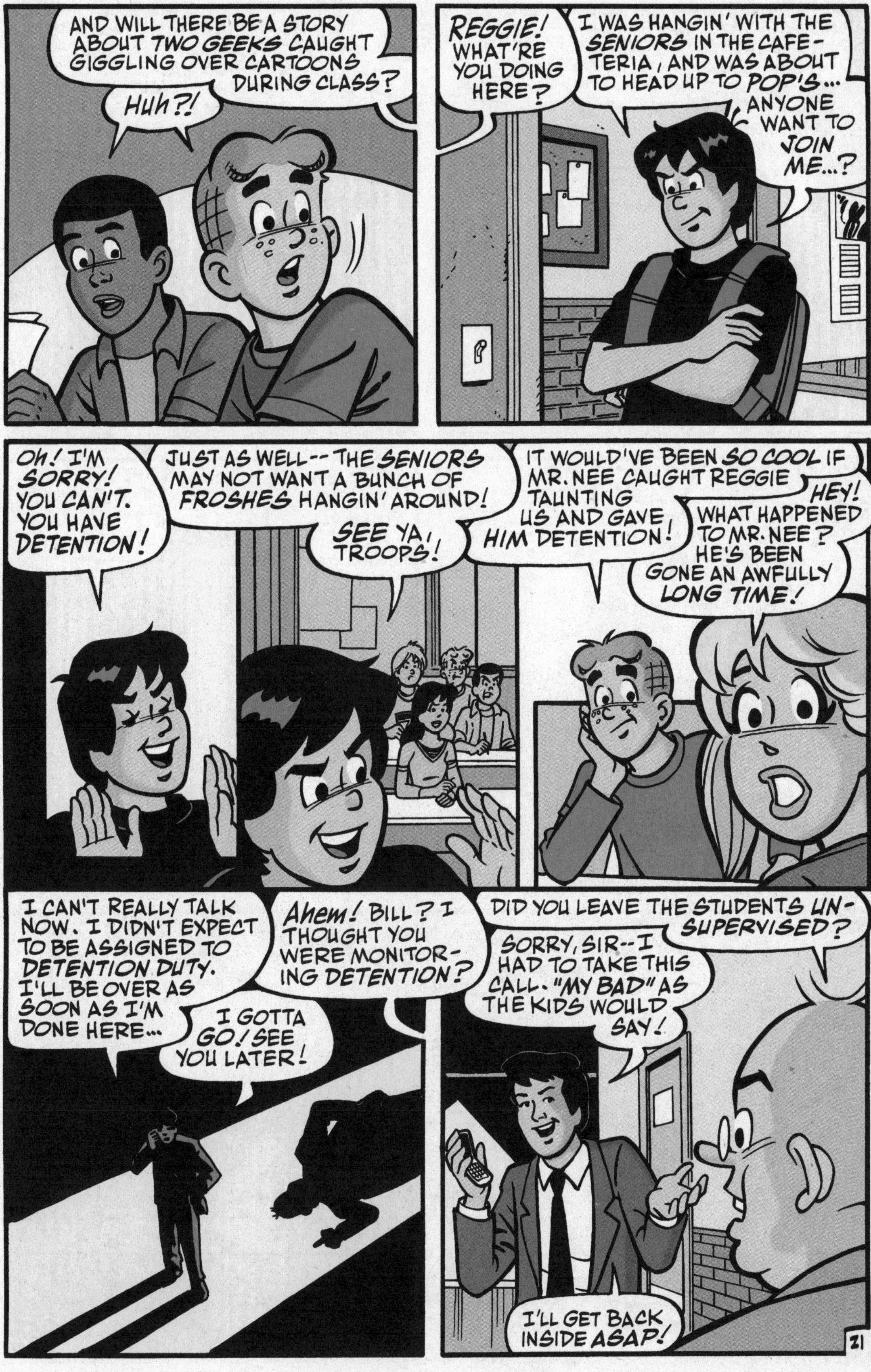
AND WILL THERE BE A STORY ABOUT TWO GEEKS CAUGHT GIGGLING OVER CARTOONS DURING CLASS?
Huh?!
REGGIE! WHAT'RE YOU DOING HERE?
I WAS HANGIN' WITH THE SENIORS IN THE CAFETERIA, AND WAS ABOUT TO HEAD UP TO POP'S... ANYONE WANT TO JOIN ME...?
Oh! I'M SORRY! YOU CAN'T. YOU HAVE DETENTION!
JUST AS WELL-- THE SENIORS MAY NOT WANT A BUNCH OF FROSHES HANGIN' AROUND!
SEE YA, TROOPS!
IT WOULD'VE BEEN SO COOL IF MR. NEE CAUGHT REGGIE TAUNTING US AND GAVE HIM DETENTION!
HEY! WHAT HAPPENED TO MR. NEE? HE'S BEEN GONE AN AWFULLY LONG TIME!
I CAN'T REALLY TALK NOW. I DIDN'T EXPECT TO BE ASSIGNED TO DETENTION DUTY. I'LL BE OVER AS SOON AS I'M DONE HERE...
I GOTTA GO! SEE YOU LATER!
Ahem! BILL? I THOUGHT YOU WERE MONITORING DETENTION?
DID YOU LEAVE THE STUDENTS UNSUPERVISED?
SORRY, SIR--I HAD TO TAKE THIS CALL. "MY BAD" AS THE KIDS WOULD SAY!
I'LL GET BACK INSIDE ASAP!
21

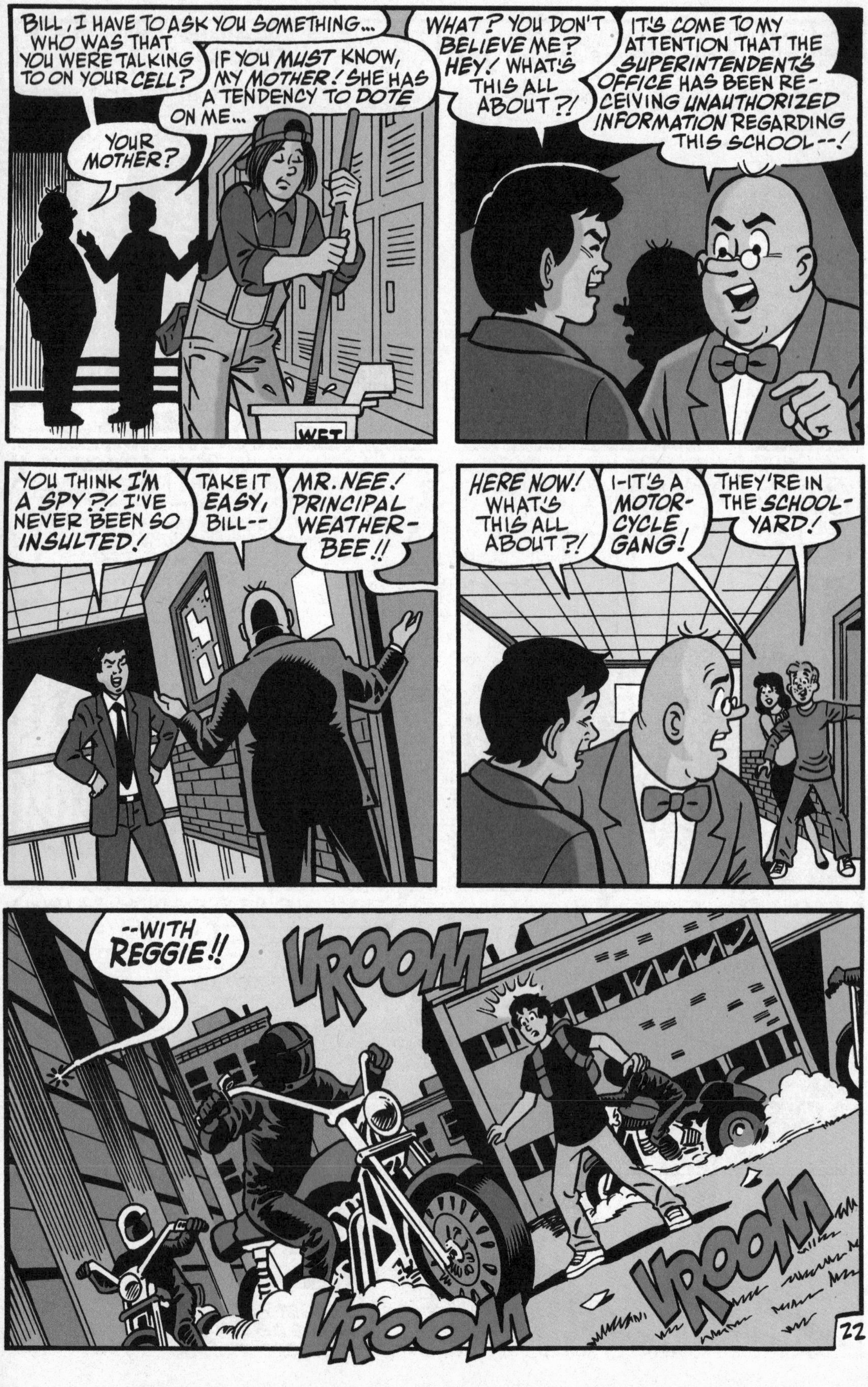
BILL, I HAVE TO ASK YOU SOMETHING... WHO WAS THAT YOU WERE TALKING TO ON YOUR CELL?
IF YOU MUST KNOW, MY MOTHER! SHE HAS A TENDENCY TO DOTE ON ME...
YOUR MOTHER?
WET
WHAT? YOU DON'T BELIEVE ME? HEY! WHAT'S THIS ALL ABOUT?!
IT'S COME TO MY ATTENTION THAT THE SUPERINTENDENT'S OFFICE HAS BEEN RE-CEIVING UNAUTHORIZED INFORMATION REGARDING THIS SCHOOL--!
YOU THINK I'M A SPY?! I'VE NEVER BEEN SO INSULTED!
TAKE IT EASY, BILL--
MR. NEE! PRINCIPAL WEATHER-BEE!!
HERE NOW! WHAT'S THIS ALL ABOUT?!
I-IT'S A MOTOR-CYCLE GANG!
THEY'RE IN THE SCHOOL-YARD!
--WITH REGGIE!!
VROOM
VROOM
VROOM
22

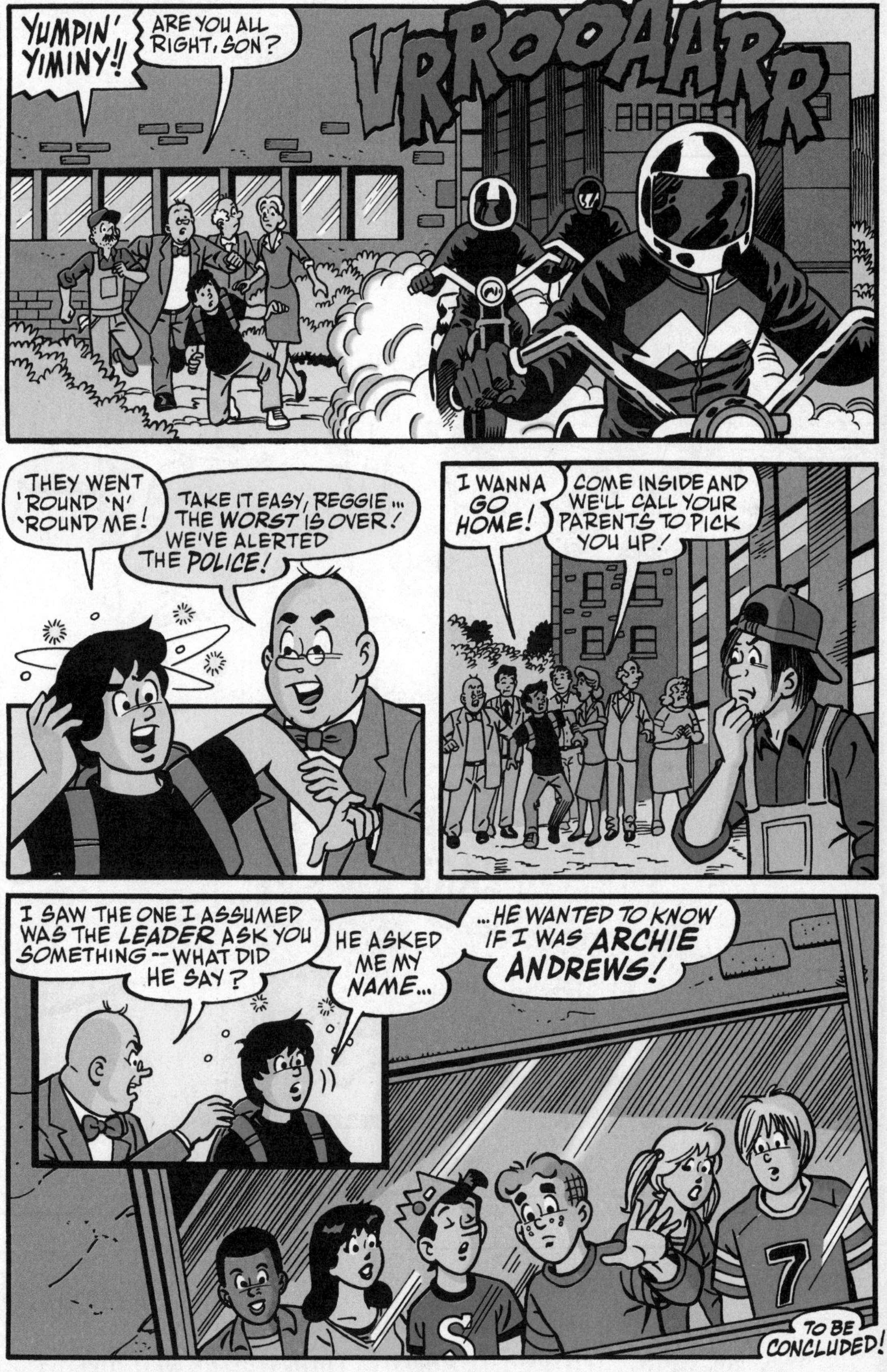
YUMPIN' YIMINY!!
ARE YOU ALL RIGHT, SON?
VRROOAARR
THEY WENT 'ROUND 'N' 'ROUND ME!
TAKE IT EASY, REGGIE... THE WORST IS OVER! WE'VE ALERTED THE POLICE!
I WANNA GO HOME!
COME INSIDE AND WE'LL CALL YOUR PARENTS TO PICK YOU UP!
I SAW THE ONE I ASSUMED WAS THE LEADER ASK YOU SOMETHING -- WHAT DID HE SAY?
HE ASKED ME MY NAME...
...HE WANTED TO KNOW IF I WAS ARCHIE ANDREWS!
7
TO BE CONCLUDED!

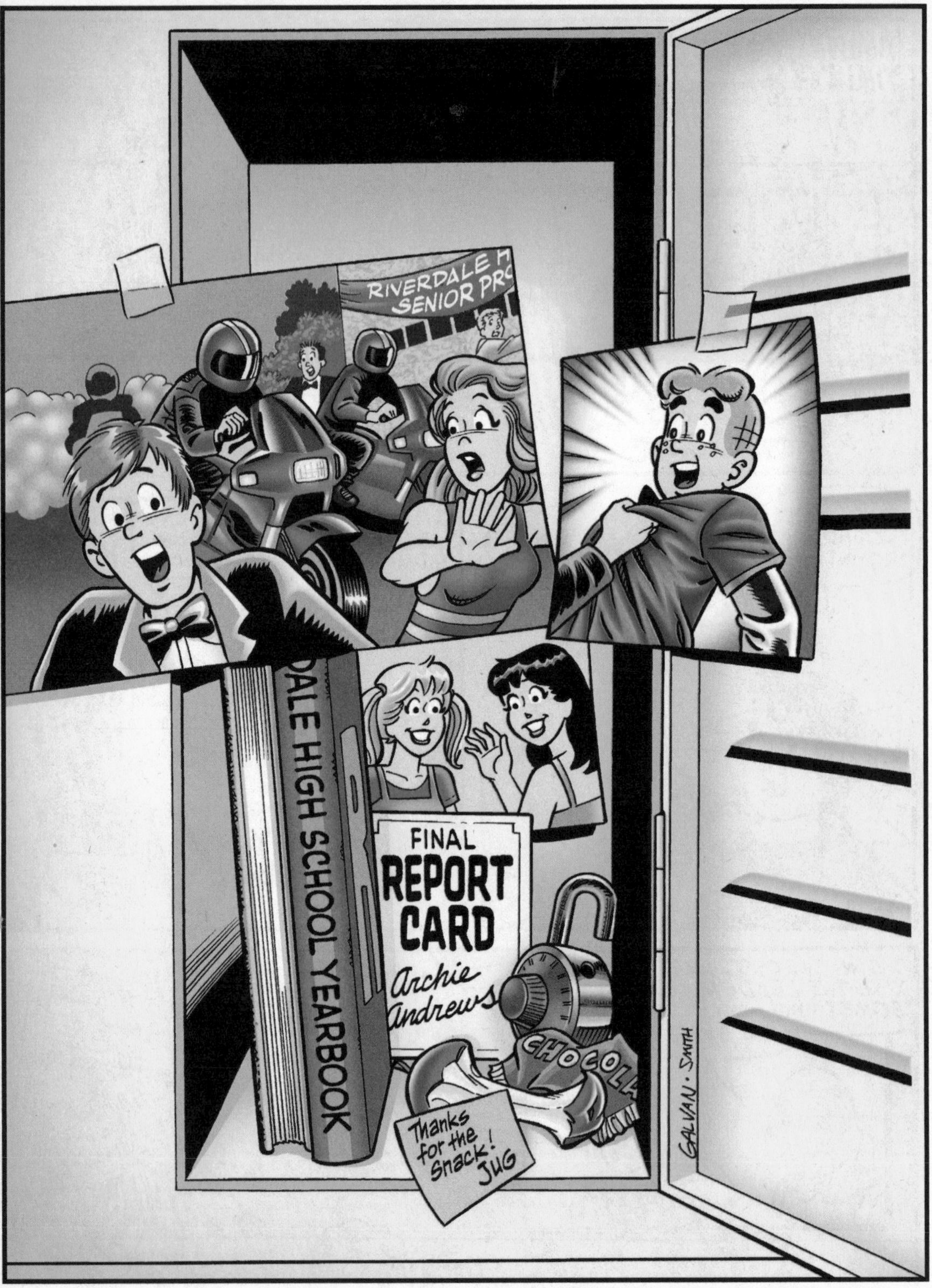
RIVERDALE H
SENIOR PRO
DALE HIGH SCHOOL YEARBOOK
FINAL
REPORT CARD
Archie Andrews
CHOCOLA
Thanks for the Snack! JUG
GALVAN • SMITH

FRESHMAN YEAR PART 5

SCRIPT: BATTON LASH PENCILS: BILL GALVAN

INKS: BOB SMITH LETTERS: JACK MORELLI COLORS: GLENN WHITMORE

FRESHMAN YEAR

PART 5 OF 5

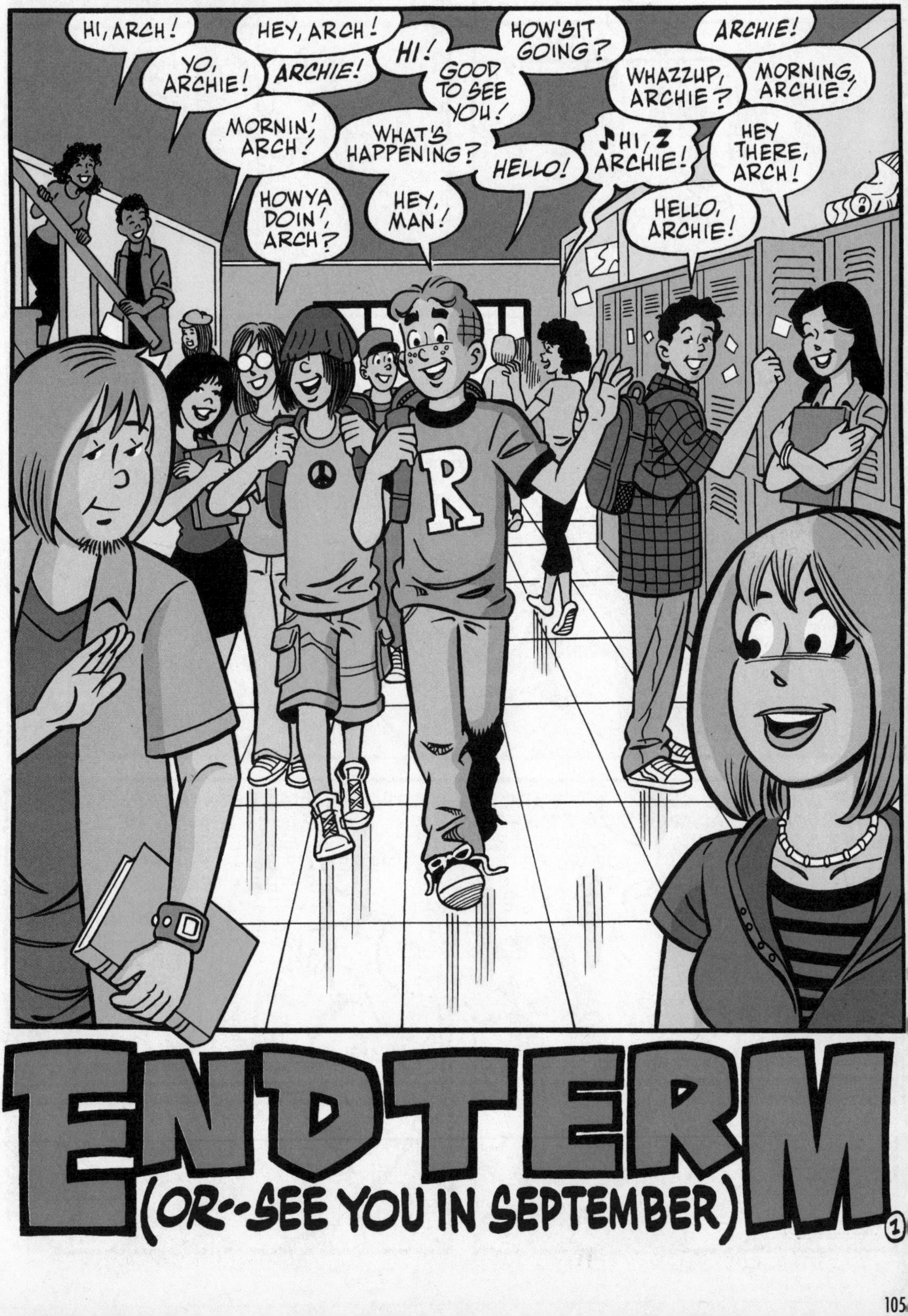
HI, ARCH!
YO, ARCHIE!
HEY, ARCH!
ARCHIE!
HI!
HOW'S IT GOING?
GOOD TO SEE YOU!
ARCHIE!
WHAZZUP, ARCHIE?
MORNING, ARCHIE!
MORNIN', ARCH!
WHAT'S HAPPENING?
HELLO!
♪HI, ARCHIE!
HEY THERE, ARCH!
HOWYA DOIN', ARCH?
HEY, MAN!
HELLO, ARCHIE!
ENDTERM
(OR--SEE YOU IN SEPTEMBER)
1

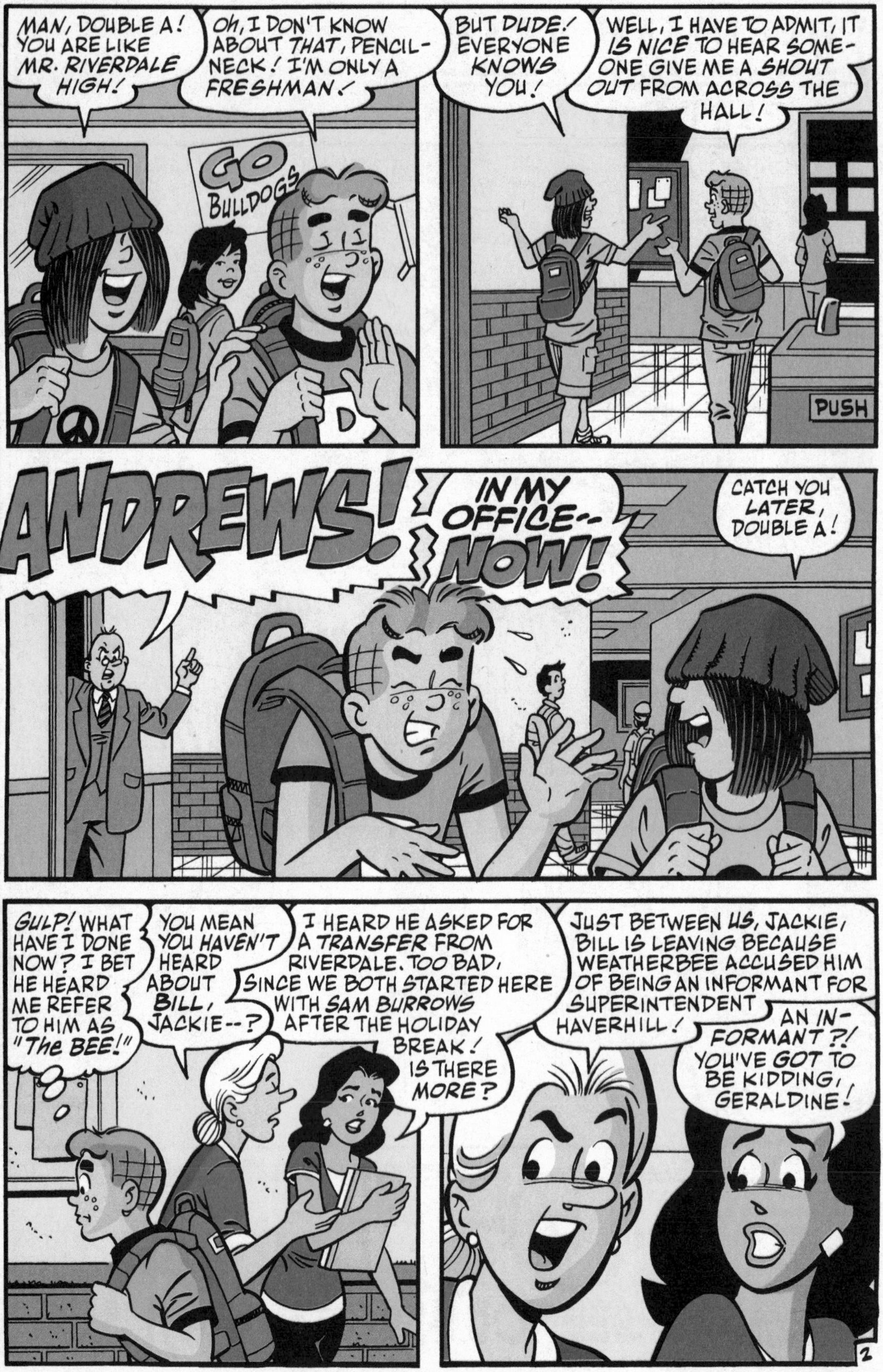
MAN, DOUBLE A! YOU ARE LIKE MR. RIVERDALE HIGH!
OH, I DON'T KNOW ABOUT THAT, PENCIL-NECK! I'M ONLY A FRESHMAN!
GO BULLDOGS
BUT DUDE! EVERYONE KNOWS YOU!
WELL, I HAVE TO ADMIT, IT IS NICE TO HEAR SOMEONE GIVE ME A SHOUT OUT FROM ACROSS THE HALL!
PUSH
ANDREWS!
IN MY OFFICE-- NOW!
CATCH YOU LATER, DOUBLE A!
GULP! WHAT HAVE I DONE NOW? I BET HE HEARD ME REFER TO HIM AS "The BEE!"
YOU MEAN YOU HAVEN'T HEARD ABOUT BILL, JACKIE--?
I HEARD HE ASKED FOR A TRANSFER FROM RIVERDALE. TOO BAD, SINCE WE BOTH STARTED HERE WITH SAM BURROWS AFTER THE HOLIDAY BREAK! IS THERE MORE?
JUST BETWEEN US, JACKIE, BILL IS LEAVING BECAUSE WEATHERBEE ACCUSED HIM OF BEING AN INFORMANT FOR SUPERINTENDENT HAVERHILL!
AN INFORMANT?! YOU'VE GOT TO BE KIDDING, GERALDINE!
2

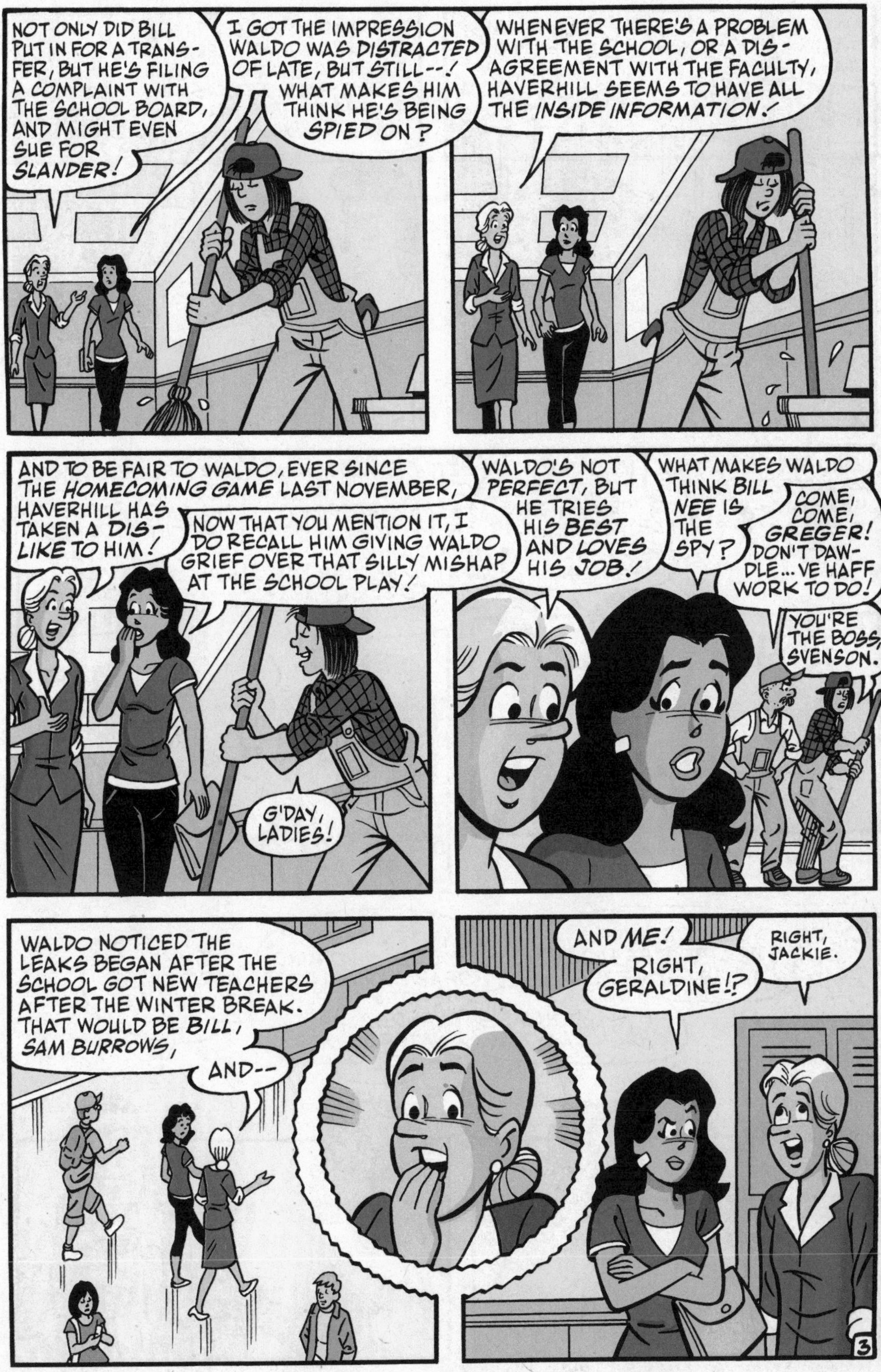
NOT ONLY DID BILL PUT IN FOR A TRANSFER, BUT HE'S FILING A COMPLAINT WITH THE SCHOOL BOARD, AND MIGHT EVEN SUE FOR SLANDER!
I GOT THE IMPRESSION WALDO WAS DISTRACTED OF LATE, BUT STILL--!
WHAT MAKES HIM THINK HE'S BEING SPIED ON?
WHENEVER THERE'S A PROBLEM WITH THE SCHOOL, OR A DISAGREEMENT WITH THE FACULTY, HAVERHILL SEEMS TO HAVE ALL THE INSIDE INFORMATION!
AND TO BE FAIR TO WALDO, EVER SINCE THE HOMECOMING GAME LAST NOVEMBER, HAVERHILL HAS TAKEN A DISLIKE TO HIM!
NOW THAT YOU MENTION IT, I DO RECALL HIM GIVING WALDO GRIEF OVER THAT SILLY MISHAP AT THE SCHOOL PLAY!
G'DAY, LADIES!
WALDO'S NOT PERFECT, BUT HE TRIES HIS BEST AND LOVES HIS JOB!
WHAT MAKES WALDO THINK BILL NEE IS THE SPY?
COME, COME, GREGER! DON'T DAWDLE... VE HAFF WORK TO DO!
YOU'RE THE BOSS, SVENSON.
WALDO NOTICED THE LEAKS BEGAN AFTER THE SCHOOL GOT NEW TEACHERS AFTER THE WINTER BREAK. THAT WOULD BE BILL, SAM BURROWS,
AND--
AND ME!
RIGHT, GERALDINE!?
RIGHT, JACKIE.
3

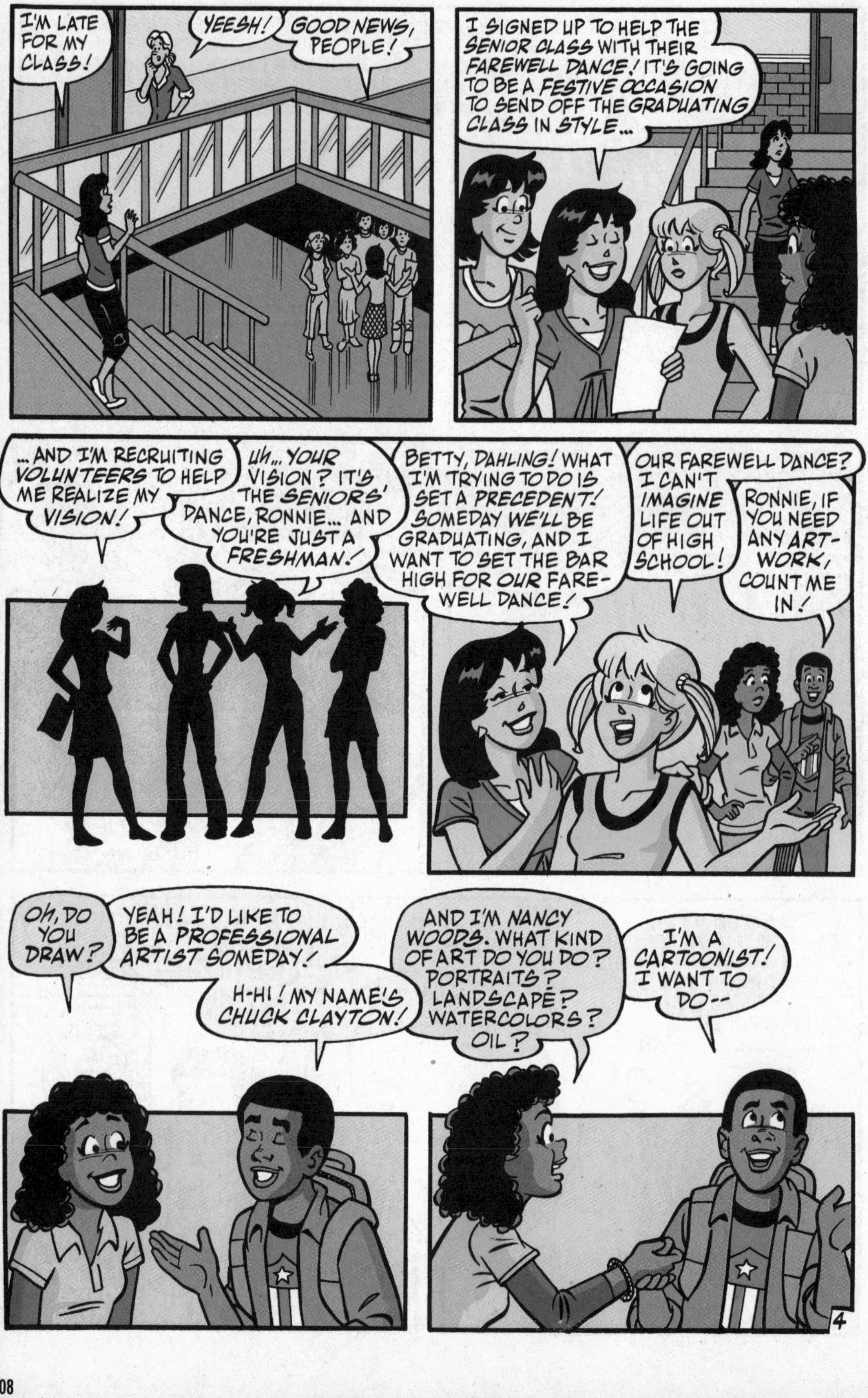

I'M LATE FOR MY CLASS!
YEESH!
GOOD NEWS, PEOPLE!
I SIGNED UP TO HELP THE SENIOR CLASS WITH THEIR FAREWELL DANCE! IT'S GOING TO BE A FESTIVE OCCASION TO SEND OFF THE GRADUATING CLASS IN STYLE...
...AND I'M RECRUITING VOLUNTEERS TO HELP ME REALIZE MY VISION!
UH... YOUR VISION? IT'S THE SENIORS' DANCE, RONNIE... AND YOU'RE JUST A FRESHMAN!
BETTY, DAHLING! WHAT I'M TRYING TO DO IS SET A PRECEDENT! SOMEDAY WE'LL BE GRADUATING, AND I WANT TO SET THE BAR HIGH FOR OUR FARE-WELL DANCE!
OUR FAREWELL DANCE? I CAN'T IMAGINE LIFE OUT OF HIGH SCHOOL!
RONNIE, IF YOU NEED ANY ART-WORK, COUNT ME IN!
OH, DO YOU DRAW?
YEAH! I'D LIKE TO BE A PROFESSIONAL ARTIST SOMEDAY!
H-HI! MY NAME'S CHUCK CLAYTON!
AND I'M NANCY WOODS. WHAT KIND OF ART DO YOU DO? PORTRAITS? LANDSCAPE? WATERCOLORS? OIL?
I'M A CARTOONIST! I WANT TO DO--
4

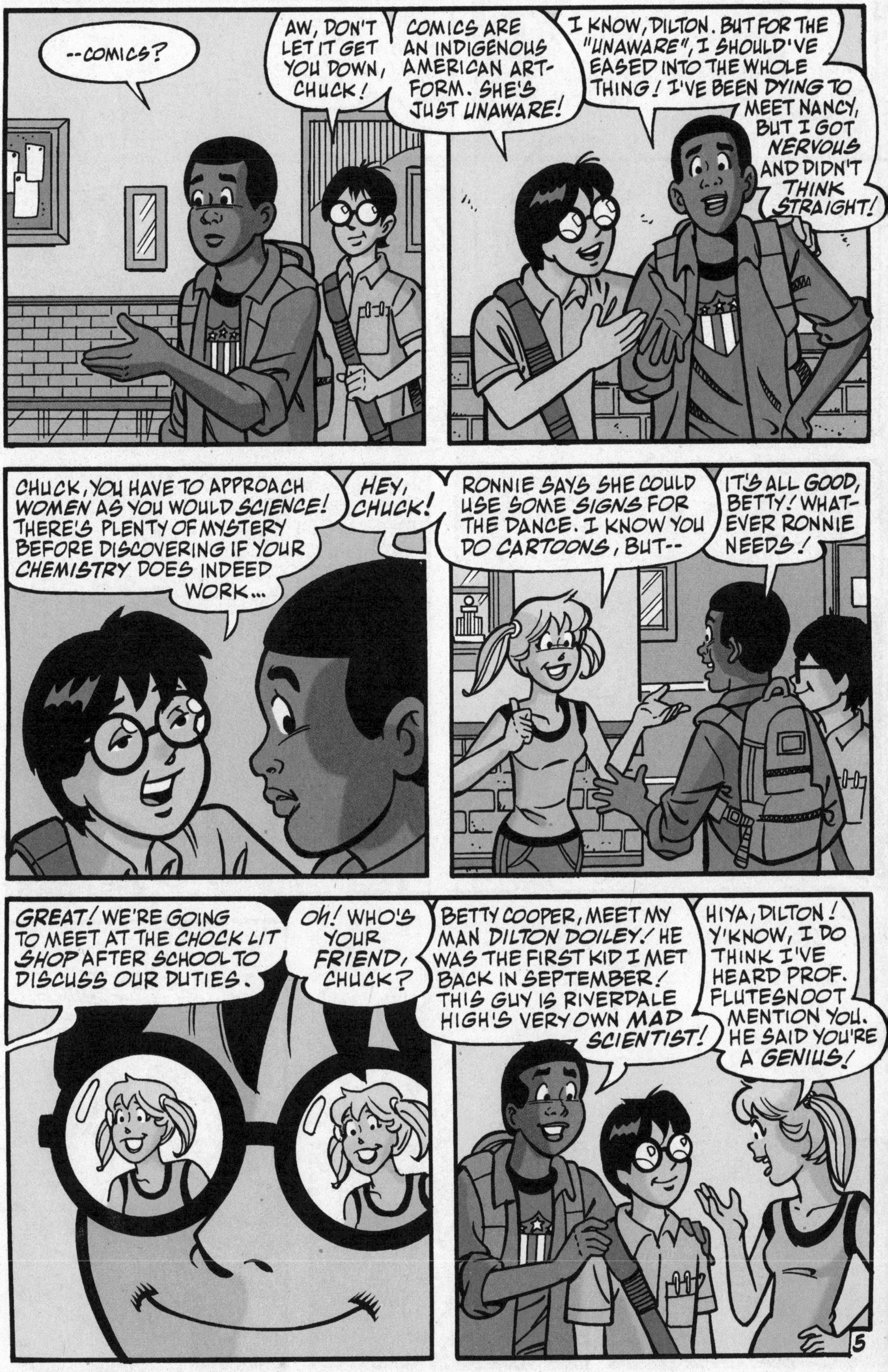
--COMICS?
AW, DON'T LET IT GET YOU DOWN, CHUCK!
COMICS ARE AN INDIGENOUS AMERICAN ART-FORM. SHE'S JUST UNAWARE!
I KNOW, DILTON. BUT FOR THE "UNAWARE", I SHOULD'VE EASED INTO THE WHOLE THING! I'VE BEEN DYING TO MEET NANCY, BUT I GOT NERVOUS AND DIDN'T THINK STRAIGHT!
CHUCK, YOU HAVE TO APPROACH WOMEN AS YOU WOULD SCIENCE! THERE'S PLENTY OF MYSTERY BEFORE DISCOVERING IF YOUR CHEMISTRY DOES INDEED WORK...
HEY, CHUCK!
RONNIE SAYS SHE COULD USE SOME SIGNS FOR THE DANCE. I KNOW YOU DO CARTOONS, BUT--
IT'S ALL GOOD, BETTY! WHAT-EVER RONNIE NEEDS!
GREAT! WE'RE GOING TO MEET AT THE CHOCK LIT SHOP AFTER SCHOOL TO DISCUSS OUR DUTIES.
Oh! WHO'S YOUR FRIEND, CHUCK?
BETTY COOPER, MEET MY MAN DILTON DOILEY! HE WAS THE FIRST KID I MET BACK IN SEPTEMBER! THIS GUY IS RIVERDALE HIGH'S VERY OWN MAD SCIENTIST!
HIYA, DILTON! Y'KNOW, I DO THINK I'VE HEARD PROF. FLUTESNOOT MENTION YOU. HE SAID YOU'RE A GENIUS!
5

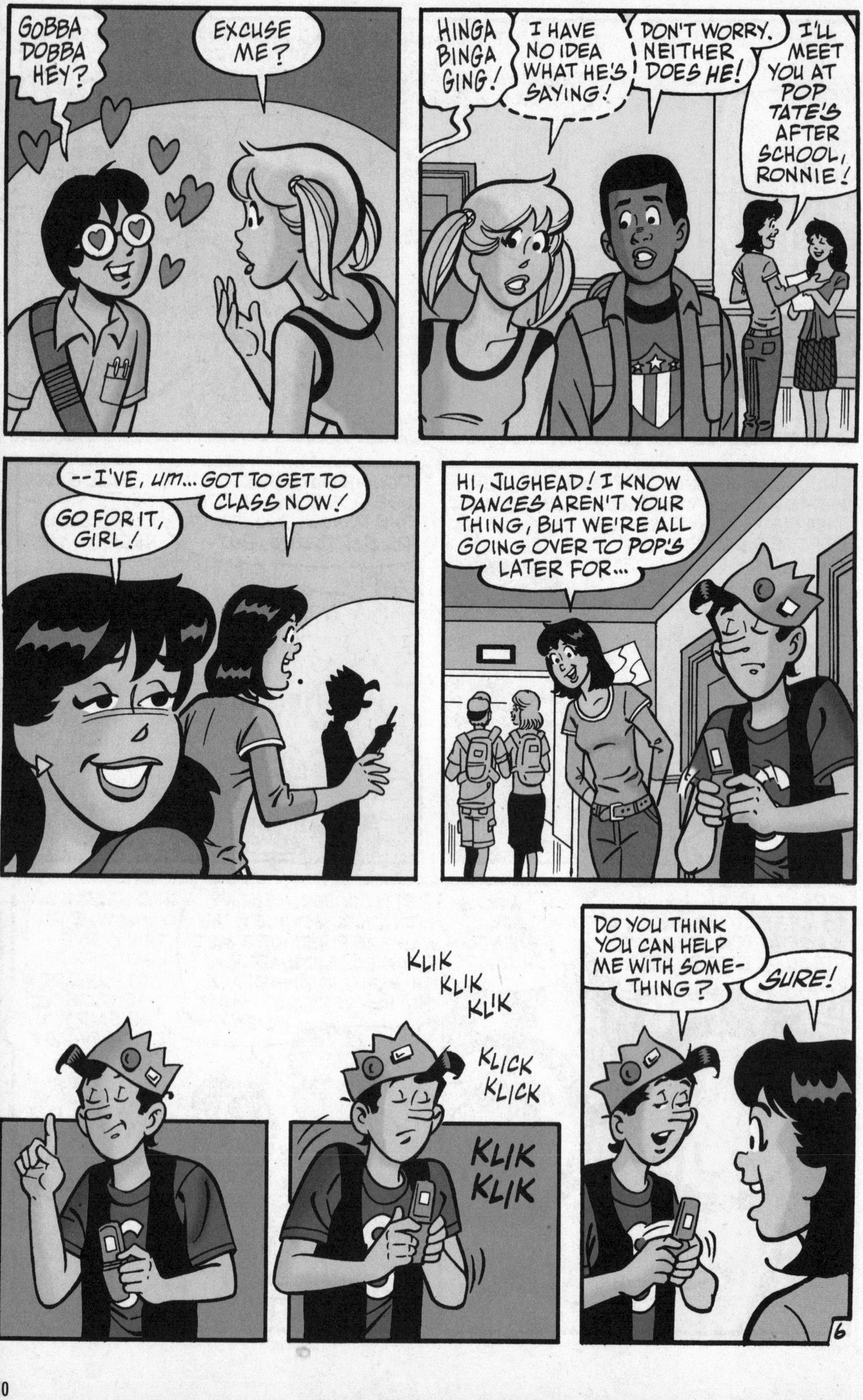
GOBBA DOBBA HEY?
EXCUSE ME?
HINGA BINGA GING!
I HAVE NO IDEA WHAT HE'S SAYING!
DON'T WORRY. NEITHER DOES HE!
I'LL MEET YOU AT POP TATE'S AFTER SCHOOL, RONNIE!
GO FOR IT, GIRL!
--I'VE, UM... GOT TO GET TO CLASS NOW!
HI, JUGHEAD! I KNOW DANCES AREN'T YOUR THING, BUT WE'RE ALL GOING OVER TO POP'S LATER FOR...
KLIK
KLIK
KLIK
KLICK
KLICK
KLIK
KLIK
DO YOU THINK YOU CAN HELP ME WITH SOME-THING?
SURE!
6

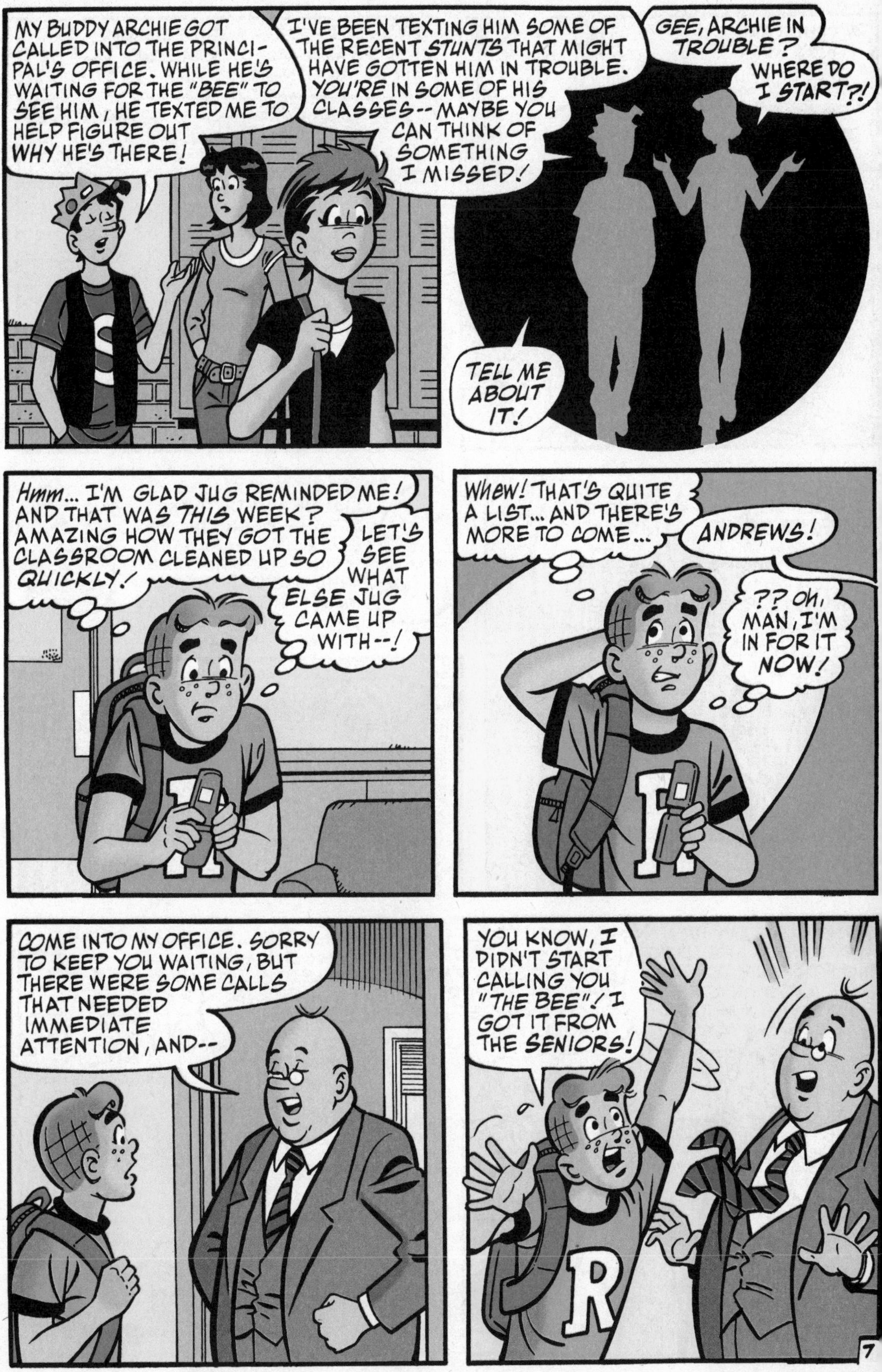
MY BUDDY ARCHIE GOT CALLED INTO THE PRINCIPAL'S OFFICE. WHILE HE'S WAITING FOR THE "BEE" TO SEE HIM, HE TEXTED ME TO HELP FIGURE OUT WHY HE'S THERE!
I'VE BEEN TEXTING HIM SOME OF THE RECENT STUNTS THAT MIGHT HAVE GOTTEN HIM IN TROUBLE. YOU'RE IN SOME OF HIS CLASSES-- MAYBE YOU CAN THINK OF SOMETHING I MISSED!
GEE, ARCHIE IN TROUBLE?
WHERE DO I START?!
TELL ME ABOUT IT!
Hmm... I'M GLAD JUG REMINDED ME! AND THAT WAS THIS WEEK? AMAZING HOW THEY GOT THE CLASSROOM CLEANED UP SO QUICKLY!
LET'S SEE WHAT ELSE JUG CAME UP WITH--!
Whew! THAT'S QUITE A LIST... AND THERE'S MORE TO COME...
ANDREWS!
?? Oh, MAN, I'M IN FOR IT NOW!
COME INTO MY OFFICE. SORRY TO KEEP YOU WAITING, BUT THERE WERE SOME CALLS THAT NEEDED IMMEDIATE ATTENTION, AND--
YOU KNOW, I DIDN'T START CALLING YOU "THE BEE"! I GOT IT FROM THE SENIORS!
7

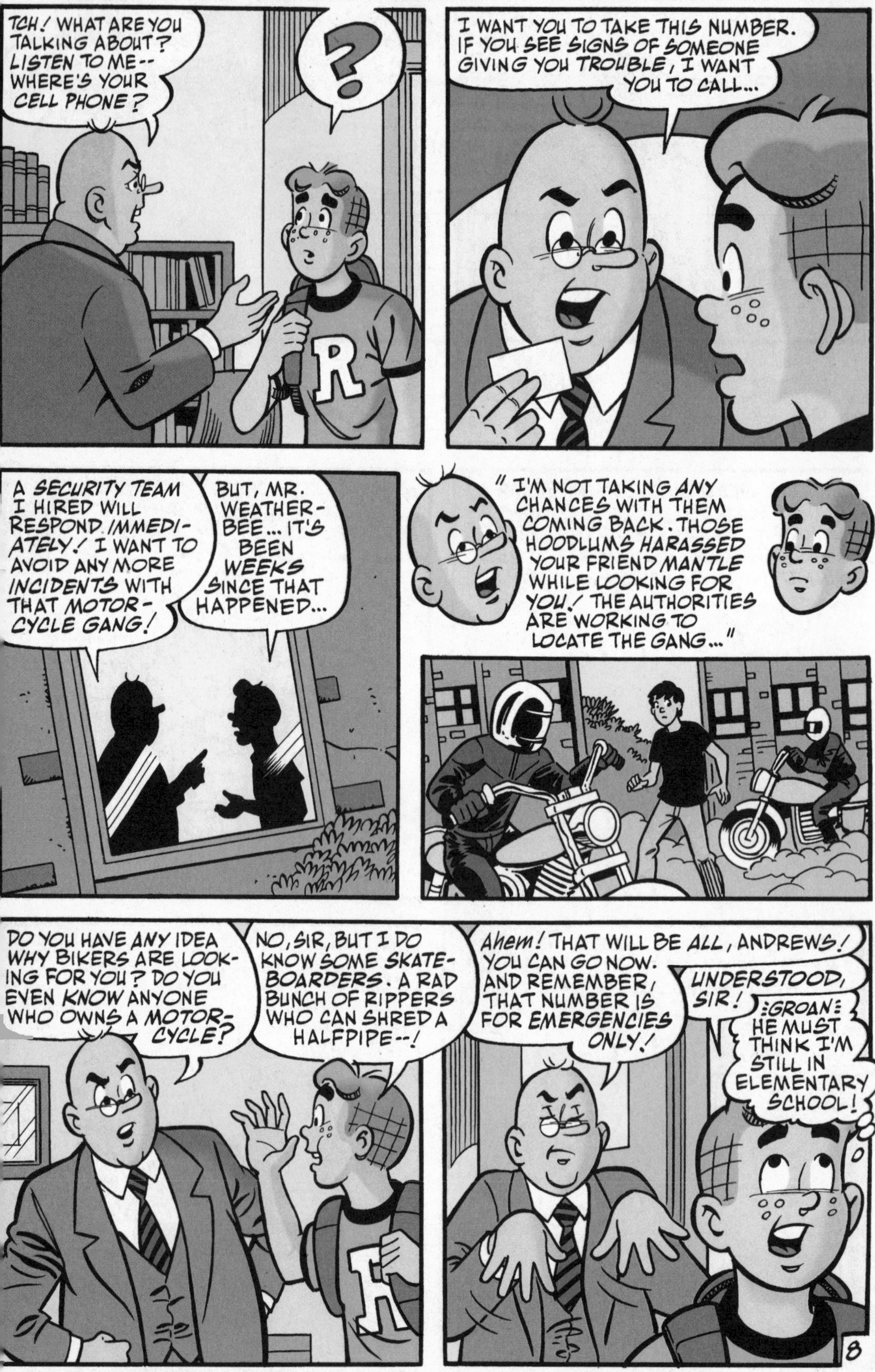
TCH! WHAT ARE YOU TALKING ABOUT? LISTEN TO ME-- WHERE'S YOUR CELL PHONE?
?
I WANT YOU TO TAKE THIS NUMBER. IF YOU SEE SIGNS OF SOMEONE GIVING YOU TROUBLE, I WANT YOU TO CALL...
A SECURITY TEAM I HIRED WILL RESPOND IMMEDIATELY! I WANT TO AVOID ANY MORE INCIDENTS WITH THAT MOTORCYCLE GANG!
BUT, MR. WEATHERBEE... IT'S BEEN WEEKS SINCE THAT HAPPENED...
"I'M NOT TAKING ANY CHANCES WITH THEM COMING BACK. THOSE HOODLUMS HARASSED YOUR FRIEND MANTLE WHILE LOOKING FOR YOU! THE AUTHORITIES ARE WORKING TO LOCATE THE GANG..."
DO YOU HAVE ANY IDEA WHY BIKERS ARE LOOKING FOR YOU? DO YOU EVEN KNOW ANYONE WHO OWNS A MOTORCYCLE?
NO, SIR, BUT I DO KNOW SOME SKATEBOARDERS. A RAD BUNCH OF RIPPERS WHO CAN SHRED A HALFPIPE--!
Ahem! THAT WILL BE ALL, ANDREWS! YOU CAN GO NOW. AND REMEMBER, THAT NUMBER IS FOR EMERGENCIES ONLY!
UNDERSTOOD, SIR!
:GROAN: HE MUST THINK I'M STILL IN ELEMENTARY SCHOOL!
8

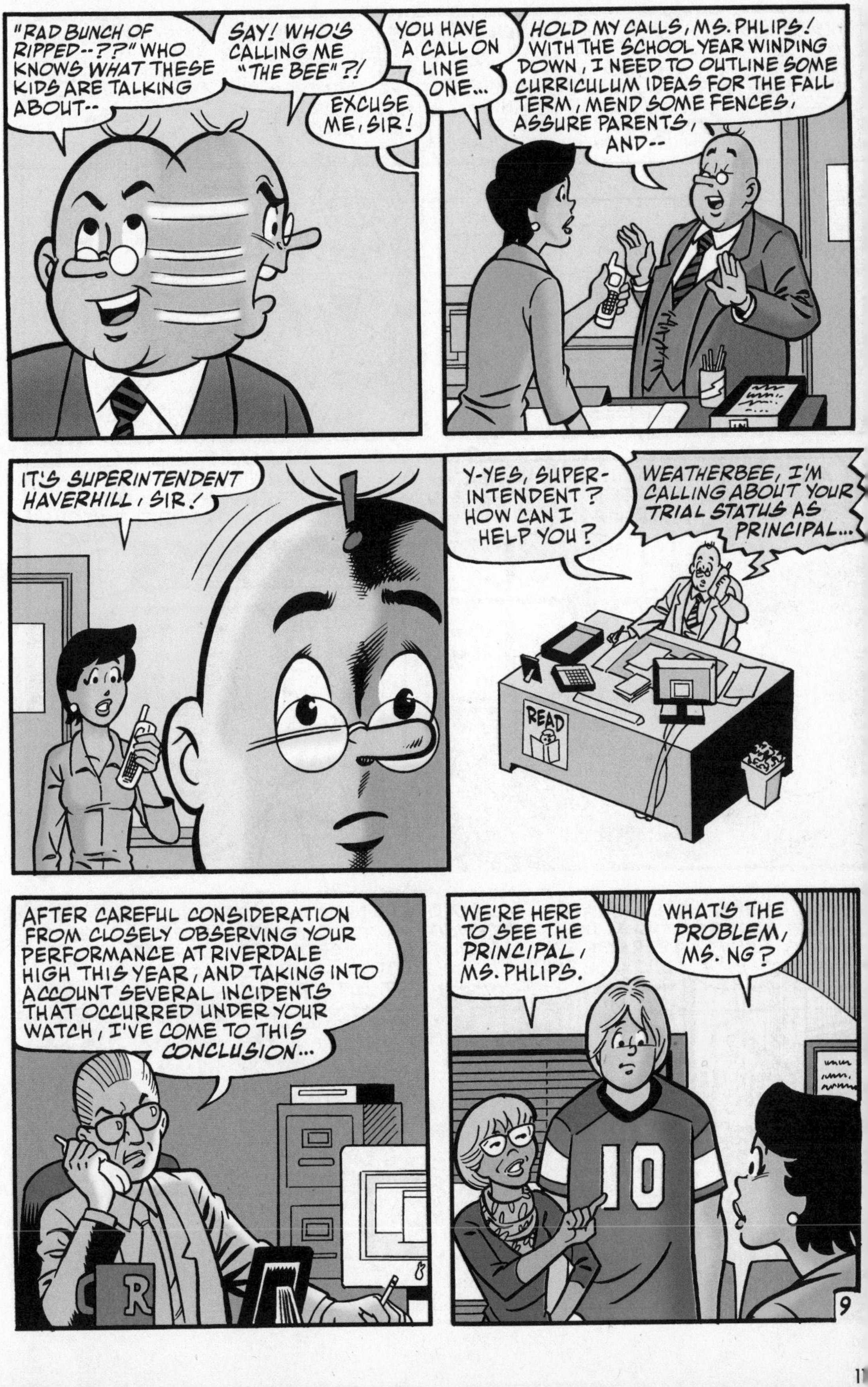
"RAD BUNCH OF RIPPED--??" WHO KNOWS WHAT THESE KIDS ARE TALKING ABOUT--
SAY! WHO'S CALLING ME "THE BEE"?!
YOU HAVE A CALL ON LINE ONE...
EXCUSE ME, SIR!
HOLD MY CALLS, MS. PHLIPS! WITH THE SCHOOL YEAR WINDING DOWN, I NEED TO OUTLINE SOME CURRICULUM IDEAS FOR THE FALL TERM, MEND SOME FENCES, ASSURE PARENTS, AND--
IT'S SUPERINTENDENT HAVERHILL, SIR!
Y-YES, SUPER-INTENDENT? HOW CAN I HELP YOU?
WEATHERBEE, I'M CALLING ABOUT YOUR TRIAL STATUS AS PRINCIPAL...
READ
AFTER CAREFUL CONSIDERATION FROM CLOSELY OBSERVING YOUR PERFORMANCE AT RIVERDALE HIGH THIS YEAR, AND TAKING INTO ACCOUNT SEVERAL INCIDENTS THAT OCCURRED UNDER YOUR WATCH, I'VE COME TO THIS CONCLUSION...
R
WE'RE HERE TO SEE THE PRINCIPAL, MS. PHLIPS.
WHAT'S THE PROBLEM, MS. NG?
10
9

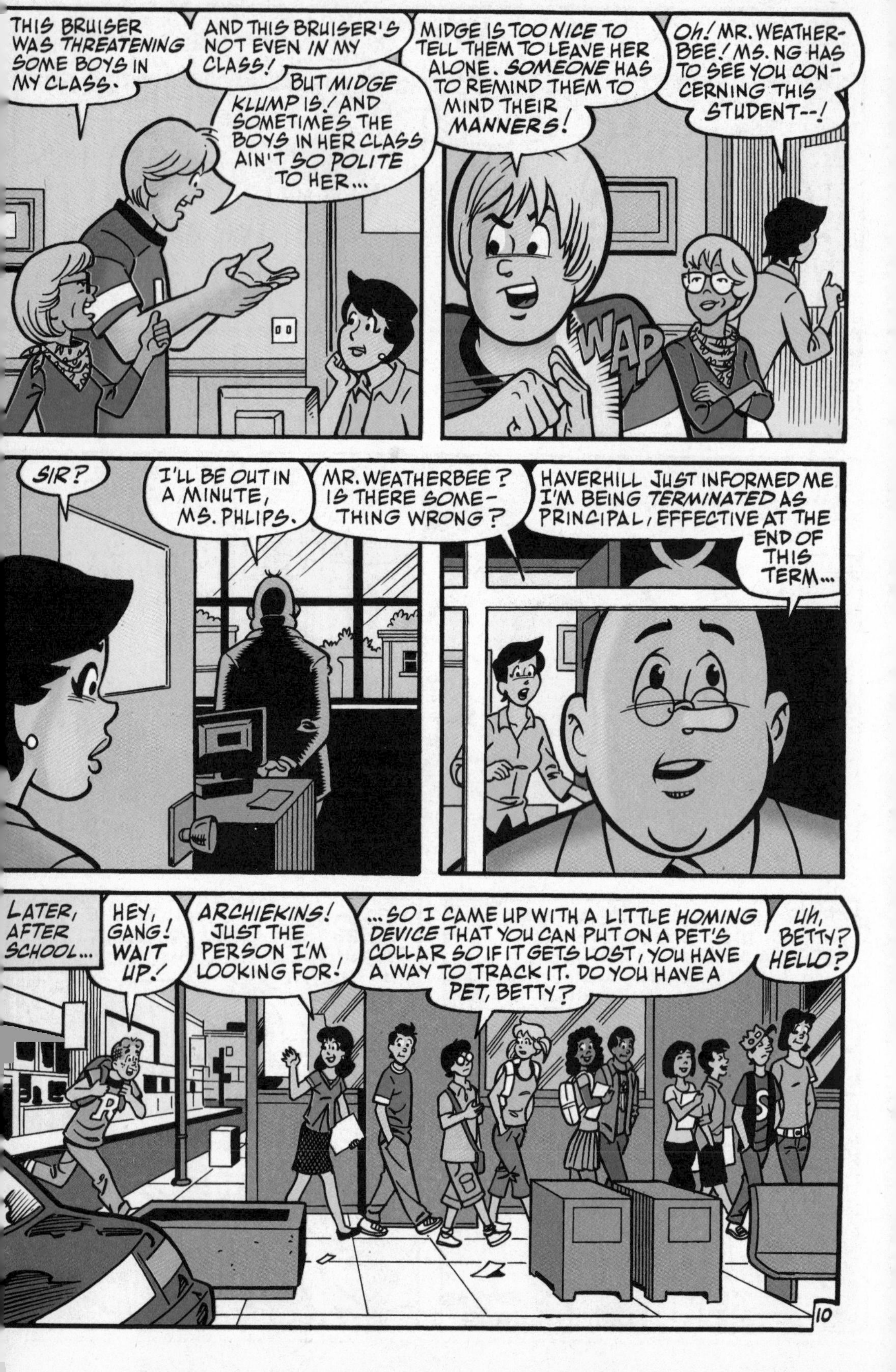
THIS BRUISER WAS THREATENING SOME BOYS IN MY CLASS.
AND THIS BRUISER'S NOT EVEN IN MY CLASS!
BUT MIDGE KLUMP IS! AND SOMETIMES THE BOYS IN HER CLASS AIN'T SO POLITE TO HER...
MIDGE IS TOO NICE TO TELL THEM TO LEAVE HER ALONE. SOMEONE HAS TO REMIND THEM TO MIND THEIR MANNERS!
WAP
Oh! MR. WEATHERBEE! MS. NG HAS TO SEE YOU CONCERNING THIS STUDENT--!
SIR?
I'LL BE OUT IN A MINUTE, MS. PHLIPS.
MR. WEATHERBEE? IS THERE SOMETHING WRONG?
HAVERHILL JUST INFORMED ME I'M BEING TERMINATED AS PRINCIPAL, EFFECTIVE AT THE END OF THIS TERM...
LATER, AFTER SCHOOL...
HEY, GANG! WAIT UP!
ARCHIEKINS! JUST THE PERSON I'M LOOKING FOR!
...SO I CAME UP WITH A LITTLE HOMING DEVICE THAT YOU CAN PUT ON A PET'S COLLAR SO IF IT GETS LOST, YOU HAVE A WAY TO TRACK IT. DO YOU HAVE A PET, BETTY?
uh, BETTY? HELLO?
10

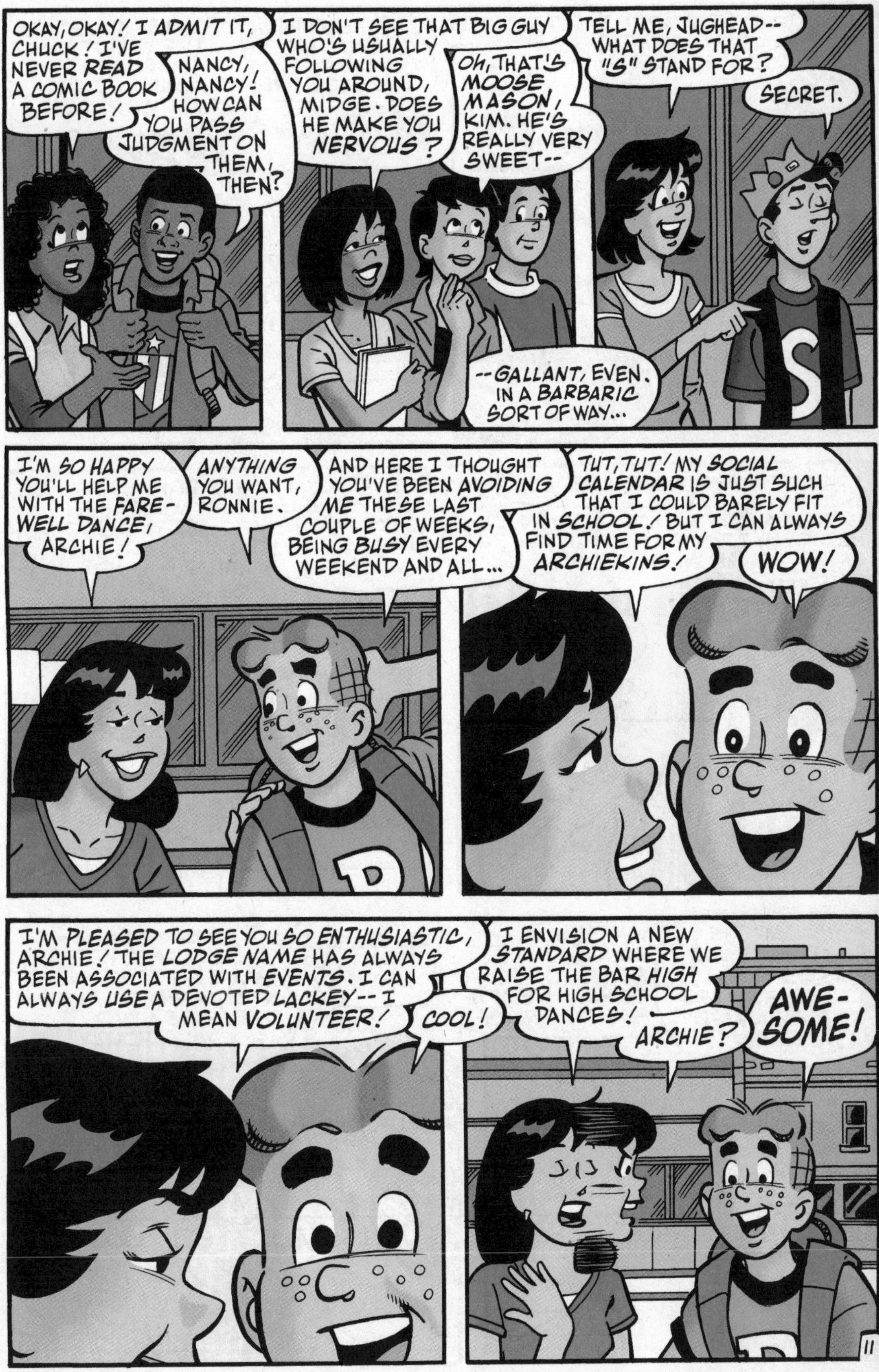
OKAY, OKAY! I ADMIT IT, CHUCK! I'VE NEVER READ A COMIC BOOK BEFORE!
NANCY, NANCY! HOW CAN YOU PASS JUDGMENT ON THEM, THEN?
I DON'T SEE THAT BIG GUY WHO'S USUALLY FOLLOWING YOU AROUND, MIDGE. DOES HE MAKE YOU NERVOUS?
OH, THAT'S MOOSE MASON, KIM. HE'S REALLY VERY SWEET--
--GALLANT, EVEN. IN A BARBARIC SORT OF WAY...
TELL ME, JUGHEAD-- WHAT DOES THAT "S" STAND FOR?
SECRET.
I'M SO HAPPY YOU'LL HELP ME WITH THE FARE-WELL DANCE, ARCHIE!
ANYTHING YOU WANT, RONNIE.
AND HERE I THOUGHT YOU'VE BEEN AVOIDING ME THESE LAST COUPLE OF WEEKS, BEING BUSY EVERY WEEKEND AND ALL...
TUT, TUT! MY SOCIAL CALENDAR IS JUST SUCH THAT I COULD BARELY FIT IN SCHOOL! BUT I CAN ALWAYS FIND TIME FOR MY ARCHIEKINS!
WOW!
I'M PLEASED TO SEE YOU SO ENTHUSIASTIC, ARCHIE! THE LODGE NAME HAS ALWAYS BEEN ASSOCIATED WITH EVENTS. I CAN ALWAYS USE A DEVOTED LACKEY-- I MEAN VOLUNTEER!
COOL!
I ENVISION A NEW STANDARD WHERE WE RAISE THE BAR HIGH FOR HIGH SCHOOL DANCES!
ARCHIE?
AWE-SOME!
11

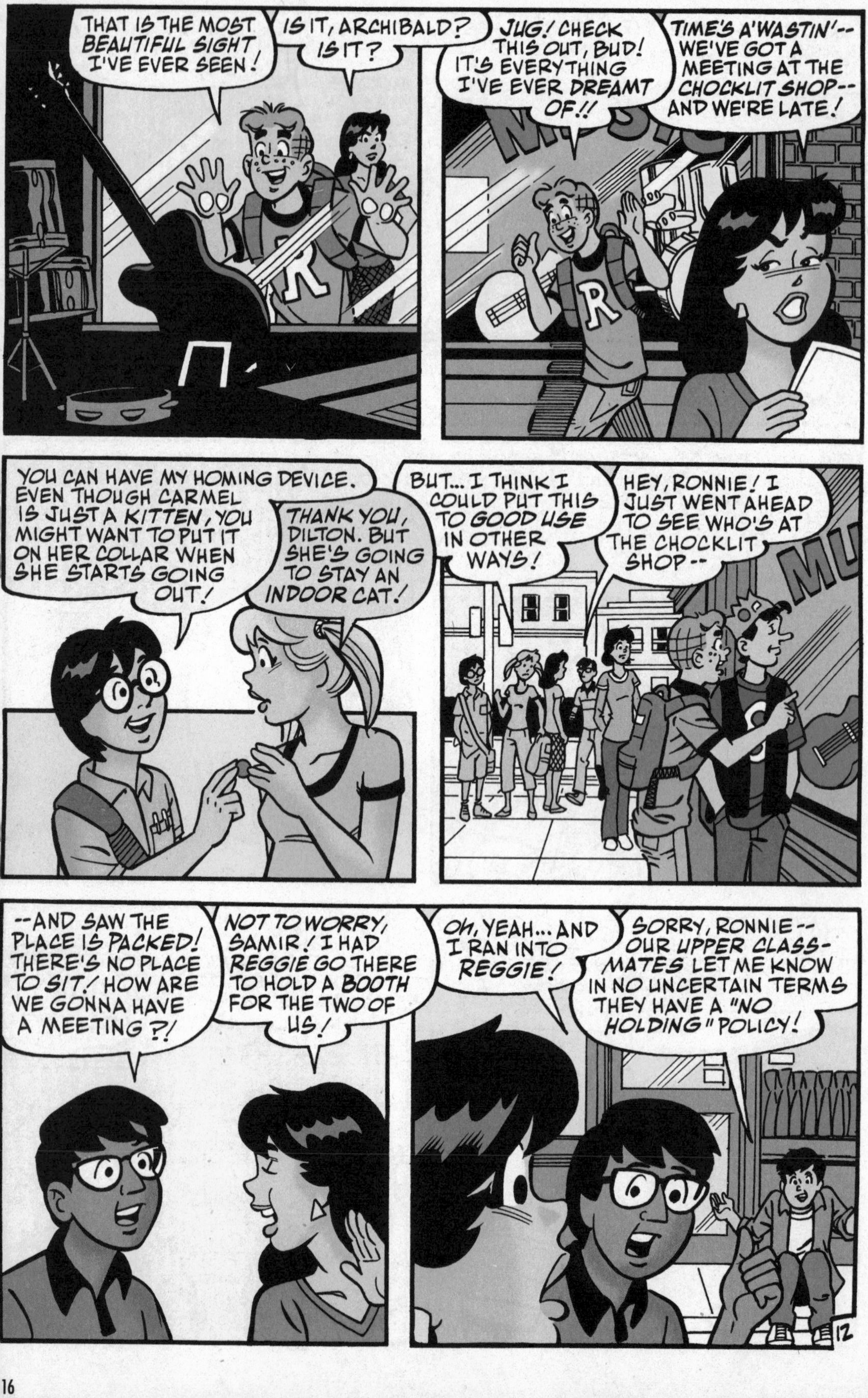
THAT IS THE MOST BEAUTIFUL SIGHT I'VE EVER SEEN!
IS IT, ARCHIBALD? IS IT?
JUG! CHECK THIS OUT, BUD! IT'S EVERYTHING I'VE EVER DREAMT OF!!
TIME'S A'WASTIN'-- WE'VE GOT A MEETING AT THE CHOCKLIT SHOP-- AND WE'RE LATE!
YOU CAN HAVE MY HOMING DEVICE. EVEN THOUGH CARMEL IS JUST A KITTEN, YOU MIGHT WANT TO PUT IT ON HER COLLAR WHEN SHE STARTS GOING OUT!
THANK YOU, DILTON. BUT SHE'S GOING TO STAY AN INDOOR CAT!
BUT... I THINK I COULD PUT THIS TO GOOD USE IN OTHER WAYS!
HEY, RONNIE! I JUST WENT AHEAD TO SEE WHO'S AT THE CHOCKLIT SHOP--
--AND SAW THE PLACE IS PACKED! THERE'S NO PLACE TO SIT! HOW ARE WE GONNA HAVE A MEETING?!
NOT TO WORRY, SAMIR! I HAD REGGIE GO THERE TO HOLD A BOOTH FOR THE TWO OF US!
OH, YEAH... AND I RAN INTO REGGIE!
SORRY, RONNIE-- OUR UPPER CLASSMATES LET ME KNOW IN NO UNCERTAIN TERMS THEY HAVE A "NO HOLDING" POLICY!
12

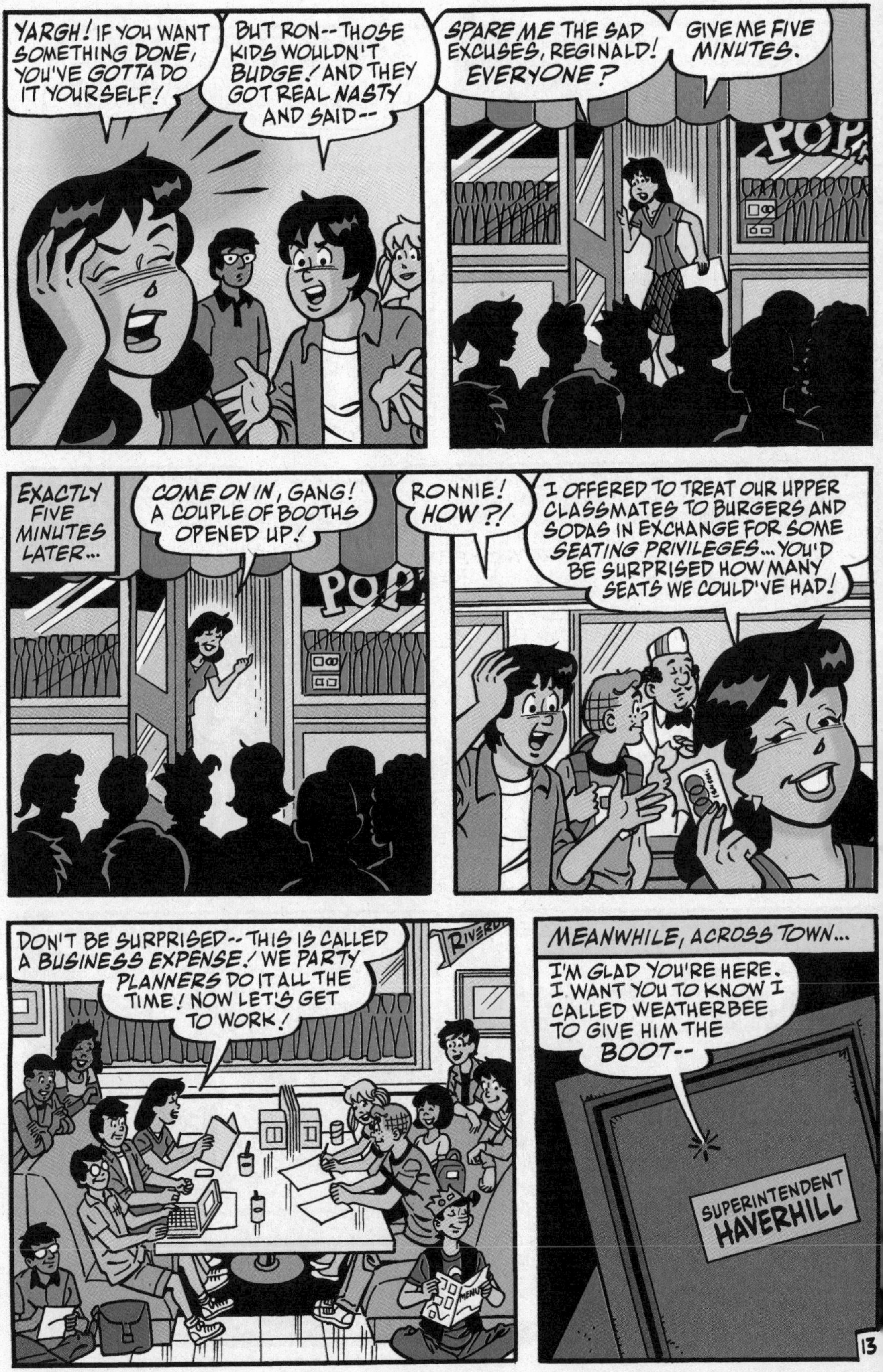
YARGH! IF YOU WANT SOMETHING DONE, YOU'VE GOTTA DO IT YOURSELF!
BUT RON-- THOSE KIDS WOULDN'T BUDGE! AND THEY GOT REAL NASTY AND SAID--
SPARE ME THE SAD EXCUSES, REGINALD! EVERYONE?
GIVE ME FIVE MINUTES.
POP
EXACTLY FIVE MINUTES LATER...
COME ON IN, GANG! A COUPLE OF BOOTHS OPENED UP!
POP
RONNIE! HOW?!
I OFFERED TO TREAT OUR UPPER CLASSMATES TO BURGERS AND SODAS IN EXCHANGE FOR SOME SEATING PRIVILEGES... YOU'D BE SURPRISED HOW MANY SEATS WE COULD'VE HAD!
DON'T BE SURPRISED-- THIS IS CALLED A BUSINESS EXPENSE! WE PARTY PLANNERS DO IT ALL THE TIME! NOW LET'S GET TO WORK!
MENU
MEANWHILE, ACROSS TOWN...
I'M GLAD YOU'RE HERE. I WANT YOU TO KNOW I CALLED WEATHERBEE TO GIVE HIM THE BOOT--
SUPERINTENDENT HAVERHILL
13

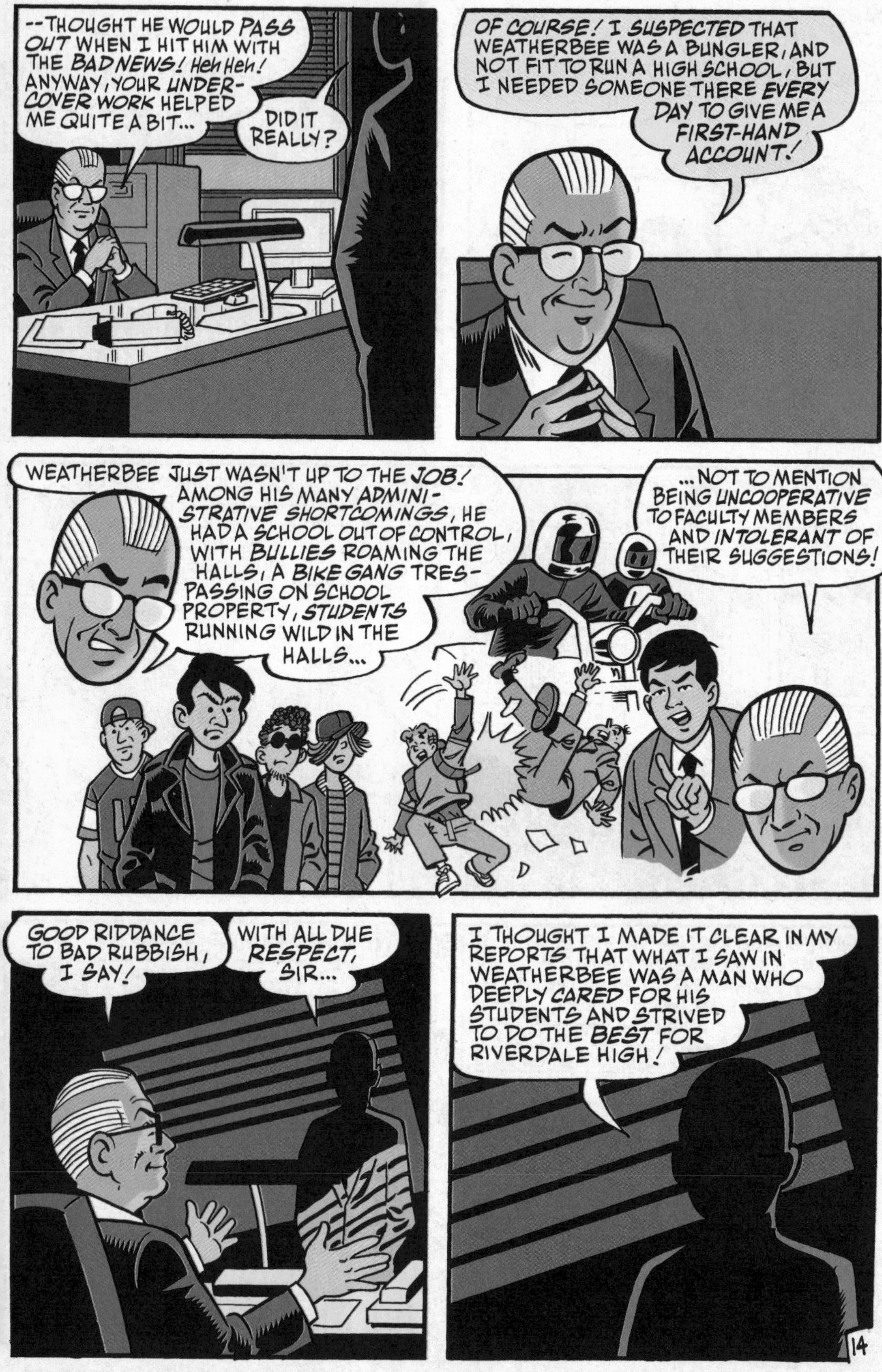
--THOUGHT HE WOULD PASS OUT WHEN I HIT HIM WITH THE BAD NEWS! Heh Heh! ANYWAY, YOUR UNDER-COVER WORK HELPED ME QUITE A BIT...
DID IT REALLY?
OF COURSE! I SUSPECTED THAT WEATHERBEE WAS A BUNGLER, AND NOT FIT TO RUN A HIGH SCHOOL, BUT I NEEDED SOMEONE THERE EVERY DAY TO GIVE ME A FIRST-HAND ACCOUNT!
WEATHERBEE JUST WASN'T UP TO THE JOB! AMONG HIS MANY ADMINI-STRATIVE SHORTCOMINGS, HE HAD A SCHOOL OUT OF CONTROL, WITH BULLIES ROAMING THE HALLS, A BIKE GANG TRES-PASSING ON SCHOOL PROPERTY, STUDENTS RUNNING WILD IN THE HALLS...
...NOT TO MENTION BEING UNCOOPERATIVE TO FACULTY MEMBERS AND INTOLERANT OF THEIR SUGGESTIONS!
GOOD RIDDANCE TO BAD RUBBISH, I SAY!
WITH ALL DUE RESPECT, SIR...
I THOUGHT I MADE IT CLEAR IN MY REPORTS THAT WHAT I SAW IN WEATHERBEE WAS A MAN WHO DEEPLY CARED FOR HIS STUDENTS AND STRIVED TO DO THE BEST FOR RIVERDALE HIGH!
14

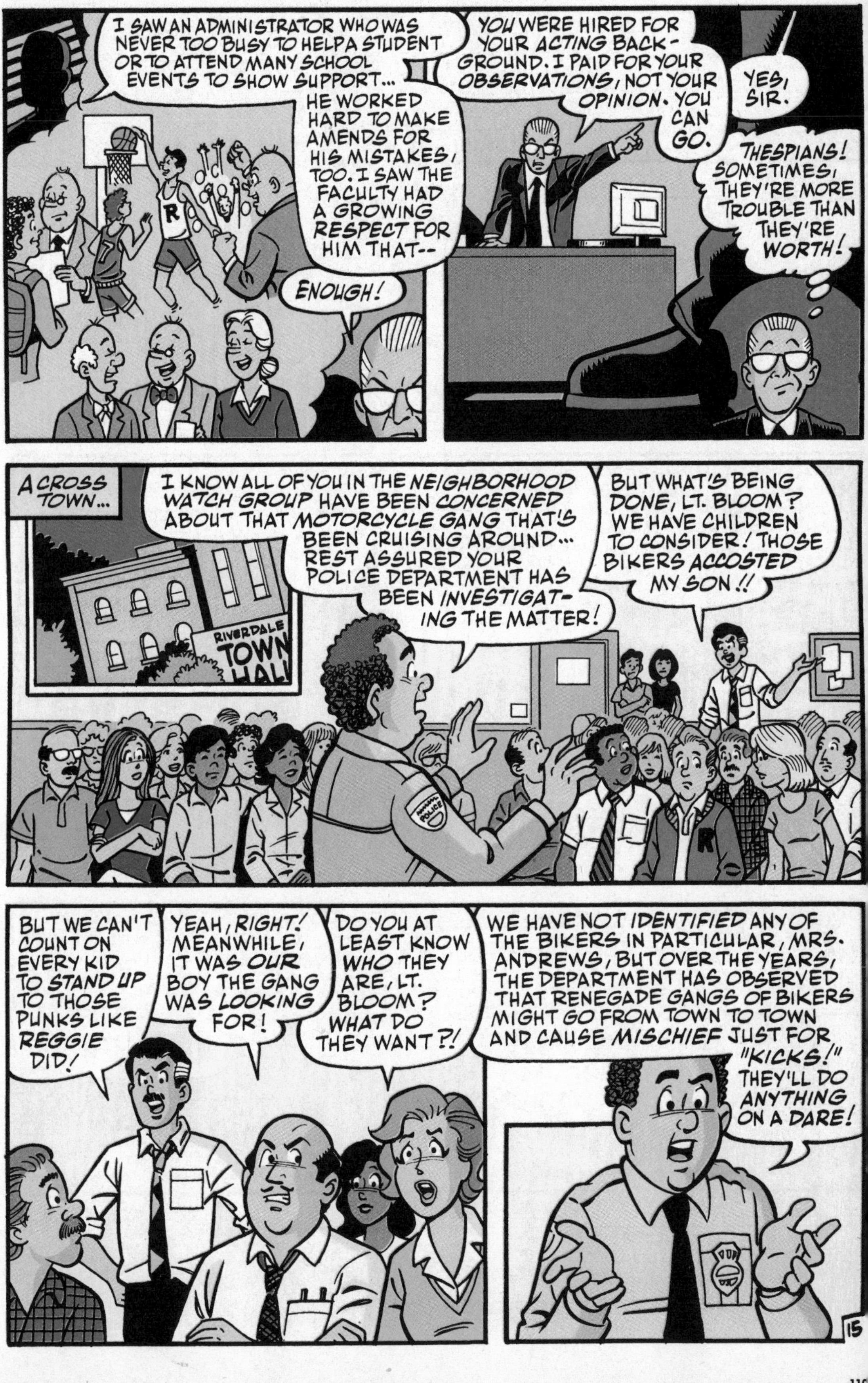
I SAW AN ADMINISTRATOR WHO WAS NEVER TOO BUSY TO HELP A STUDENT OR TO ATTEND MANY SCHOOL EVENTS TO SHOW SUPPORT...
HE WORKED HARD TO MAKE AMENDS FOR HIS MISTAKES, TOO. I SAW THE FACULTY HAD A GROWING RESPECT FOR HIM THAT--
ENOUGH!
YOU WERE HIRED FOR YOUR ACTING BACK-GROUND. I PAID FOR YOUR OBSERVATIONS, NOT YOUR OPINION. YOU CAN GO.
YES, SIR.
THESPIANS! SOMETIMES, THEY'RE MORE TROUBLE THAN THEY'RE WORTH!
ACROSS TOWN...
RIVERDALE TOWN HALL
I KNOW ALL OF YOU IN THE NEIGHBORHOOD WATCH GROUP HAVE BEEN CONCERNED ABOUT THAT MOTORCYCLE GANG THAT'S BEEN CRUISING AROUND... REST ASSURED YOUR POLICE DEPARTMENT HAS BEEN INVESTIGATING THE MATTER!
BUT WHAT'S BEING DONE, LT. BLOOM? WE HAVE CHILDREN TO CONSIDER! THOSE BIKERS ACCOSTED MY SON!!
POLICE
BUT WE CAN'T COUNT ON EVERY KID TO STAND UP TO THOSE PUNKS LIKE REGGIE DID!
YEAH, RIGHT! MEANWHILE, IT WAS OUR BOY THE GANG WAS LOOKING FOR!
DO YOU AT LEAST KNOW WHO THEY ARE, LT. BLOOM? WHAT DO THEY WANT?!
WE HAVE NOT IDENTIFIED ANY OF THE BIKERS IN PARTICULAR, MRS. ANDREWS, BUT OVER THE YEARS, THE DEPARTMENT HAS OBSERVED THAT RENEGADE GANGS OF BIKERS MIGHT GO FROM TOWN TO TOWN AND CAUSE MISCHIEF JUST FOR "KICKS!" THEY'LL DO ANYTHING ON A DARE!
15

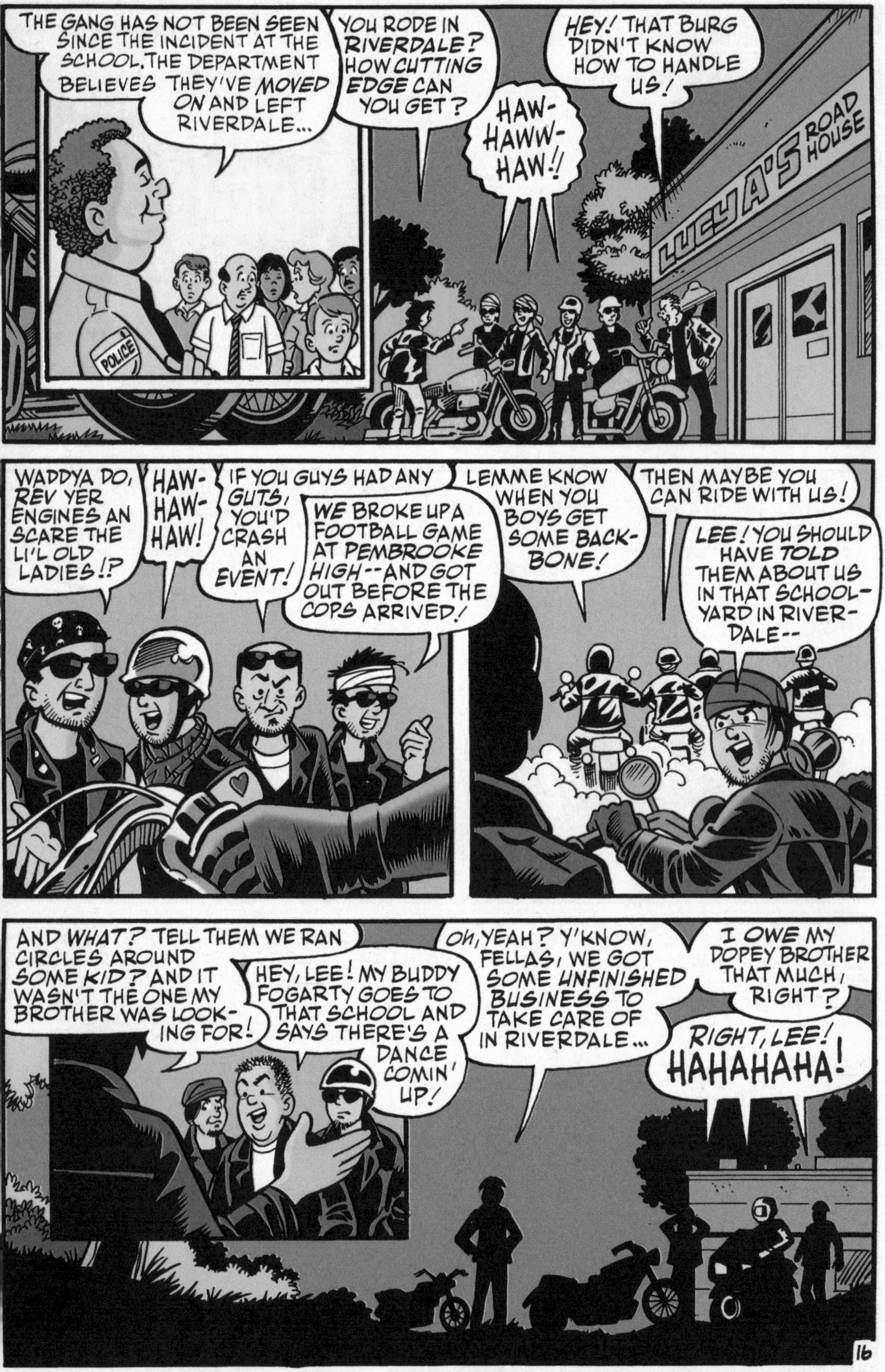
THE GANG HAS NOT BEEN SEEN SINCE THE INCIDENT AT THE SCHOOL. THE DEPARTMENT BELIEVES THEY'VE MOVED ON AND LEFT RIVERDALE...
POLICE
YOU RODE IN RIVERDALE? HOW CUTTING EDGE CAN YOU GET?
HAW-HAWW-HAW!!
HEY! THAT BURG DIDN'T KNOW HOW TO HANDLE US!
LUCY A'S ROAD HOUSE
WADDYA DO, REV YER ENGINES AN SCARE THE LI'L OLD LADIES!?
HAW-HAW-HAW!
IF YOU GUYS HAD ANY GUTS, YOU'D CRASH AN EVENT!
WE BROKE UP A FOOTBALL GAME AT PEMBROOKE HIGH--AND GOT OUT BEFORE THE COPS ARRIVED!
LEMME KNOW WHEN YOU BOYS GET SOME BACK-BONE!
THEN MAYBE YOU CAN RIDE WITH US!
LEE! YOU SHOULD HAVE TOLD THEM ABOUT US IN THAT SCHOOL-YARD IN RIVER-DALE--
AND WHAT? TELL THEM WE RAN CIRCLES AROUND SOME KID? AND IT WASN'T THE ONE MY BROTHER WAS LOOK-ING FOR!
HEY, LEE! MY BUDDY FOGARTY GOES TO THAT SCHOOL AND SAYS THERE'S A DANCE COMIN' UP!
OH, YEAH? Y'KNOW, FELLAS, WE GOT SOME UNFINISHED BUSINESS TO TAKE CARE OF IN RIVERDALE...
I OWE MY DOPEY BROTHER THAT MUCH, RIGHT?
RIGHT, LEE! HAHAHAHA!
16

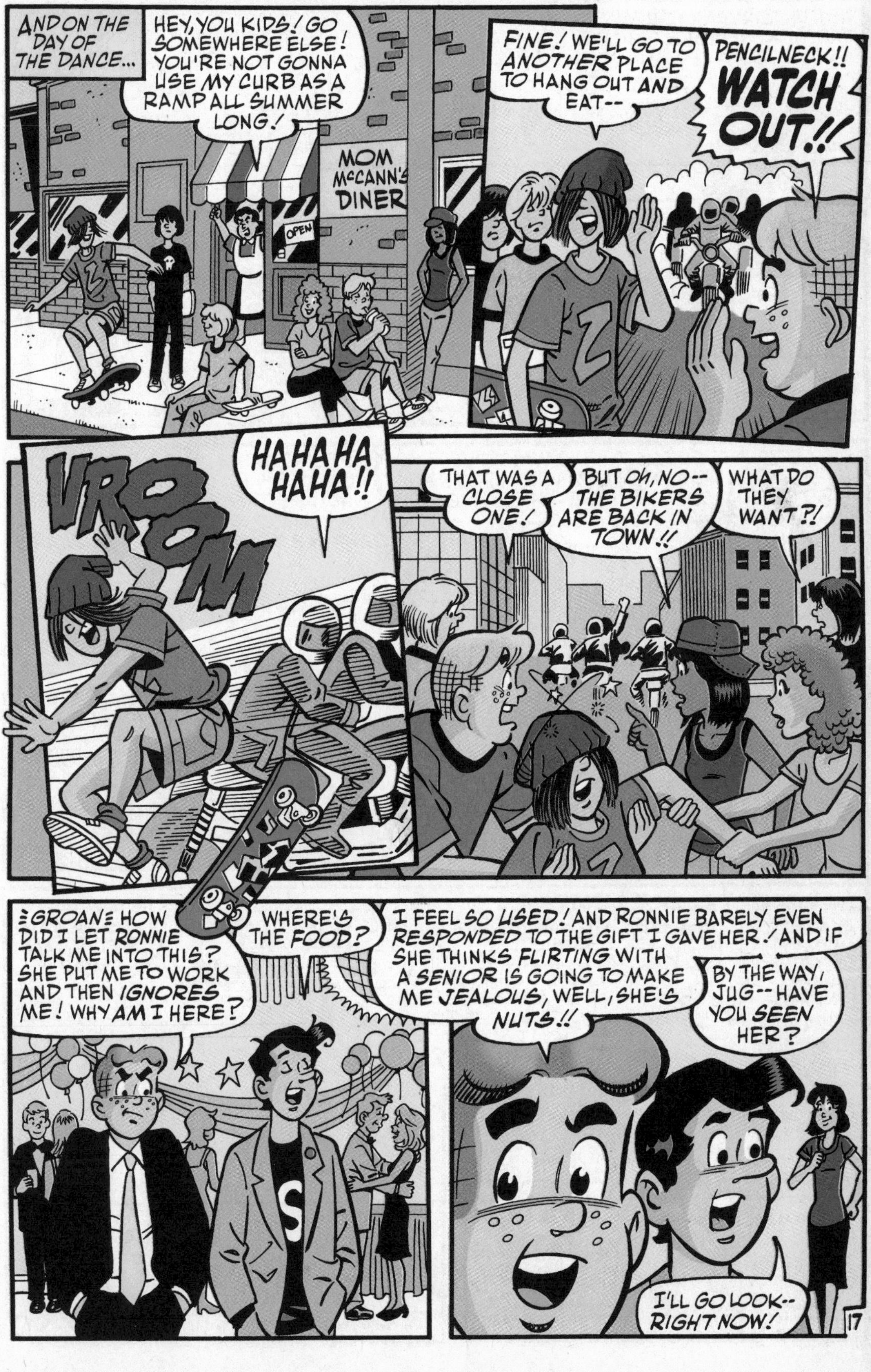

AND ON THE DAY OF THE DANCE...
HEY, YOU KIDS! GO SOMEWHERE ELSE! YOU'RE NOT GONNA USE MY CURB AS A RAMP ALL SUMMER LONG!
MOM McCANN'S DINER
OPEN
FINE! WE'LL GO TO ANOTHER PLACE TO HANG OUT AND EAT--
PENCILNECK!! WATCH OUT!!
VROOM
HAHAHA HAHA!!
THAT WAS A CLOSE ONE!
BUT OH, NO-- THE BIKERS ARE BACK IN TOWN!!
WHAT DO THEY WANT?!
GROAN HOW DID I LET RONNIE TALK ME INTO THIS? SHE PUT ME TO WORK AND THEN IGNORES ME! WHY AM I HERE?
WHERE'S THE FOOD?
I FEEL SO USED! AND RONNIE BARELY EVEN RESPONDED TO THE GIFT I GAVE HER! AND IF SHE THINKS FLIRTING WITH A SENIOR IS GOING TO MAKE ME JEALOUS, WELL, SHE'S NUTS!!
BY THE WAY, JUG-- HAVE YOU SEEN HER?
I'LL GO LOOK-- RIGHT NOW!
17

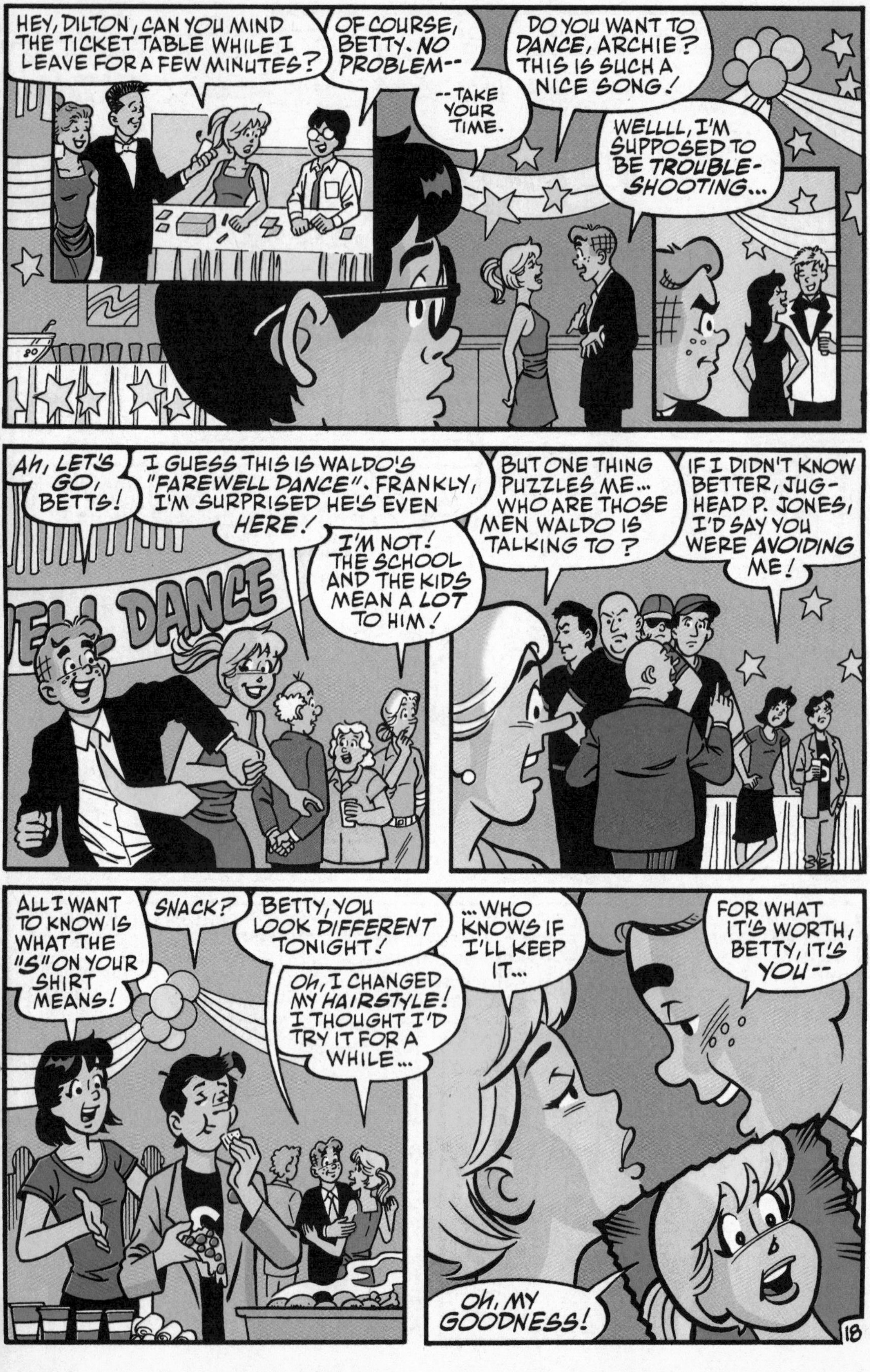
HEY, DILTON, CAN YOU MIND THE TICKET TABLE WHILE I LEAVE FOR A FEW MINUTES?
OF COURSE, BETTY. NO PROBLEM--
--TAKE YOUR TIME.
DO YOU WANT TO DANCE, ARCHIE? THIS IS SUCH A NICE SONG!
WELLLL, I'M SUPPOSED TO BE TROUBLE-SHOOTING...
Ah, LET'S GO, BETTS!
I GUESS THIS IS WALDO'S "FAREWELL DANCE". FRANKLY, I'M SURPRISED HE'S EVEN HERE!
I'M NOT! THE SCHOOL AND THE KIDS MEAN A LOT TO HIM!
WELL DANCE
BUT ONE THING PUZZLES ME... WHO ARE THOSE MEN WALDO IS TALKING TO?
IF I DIDN'T KNOW BETTER, JUG-HEAD P. JONES, I'D SAY YOU WERE AVOIDING ME!
ALL I WANT TO KNOW IS WHAT THE "S" ON YOUR SHIRT MEANS!
SNACK?
BETTY, YOU LOOK DIFFERENT TONIGHT!
Oh, I CHANGED MY HAIRSTYLE! I THOUGHT I'D TRY IT FOR A WHILE...
...WHO KNOWS IF I'LL KEEP IT...
FOR WHAT IT'S WORTH, BETTY, IT'S YOU--
Oh, MY GOODNESS!
18

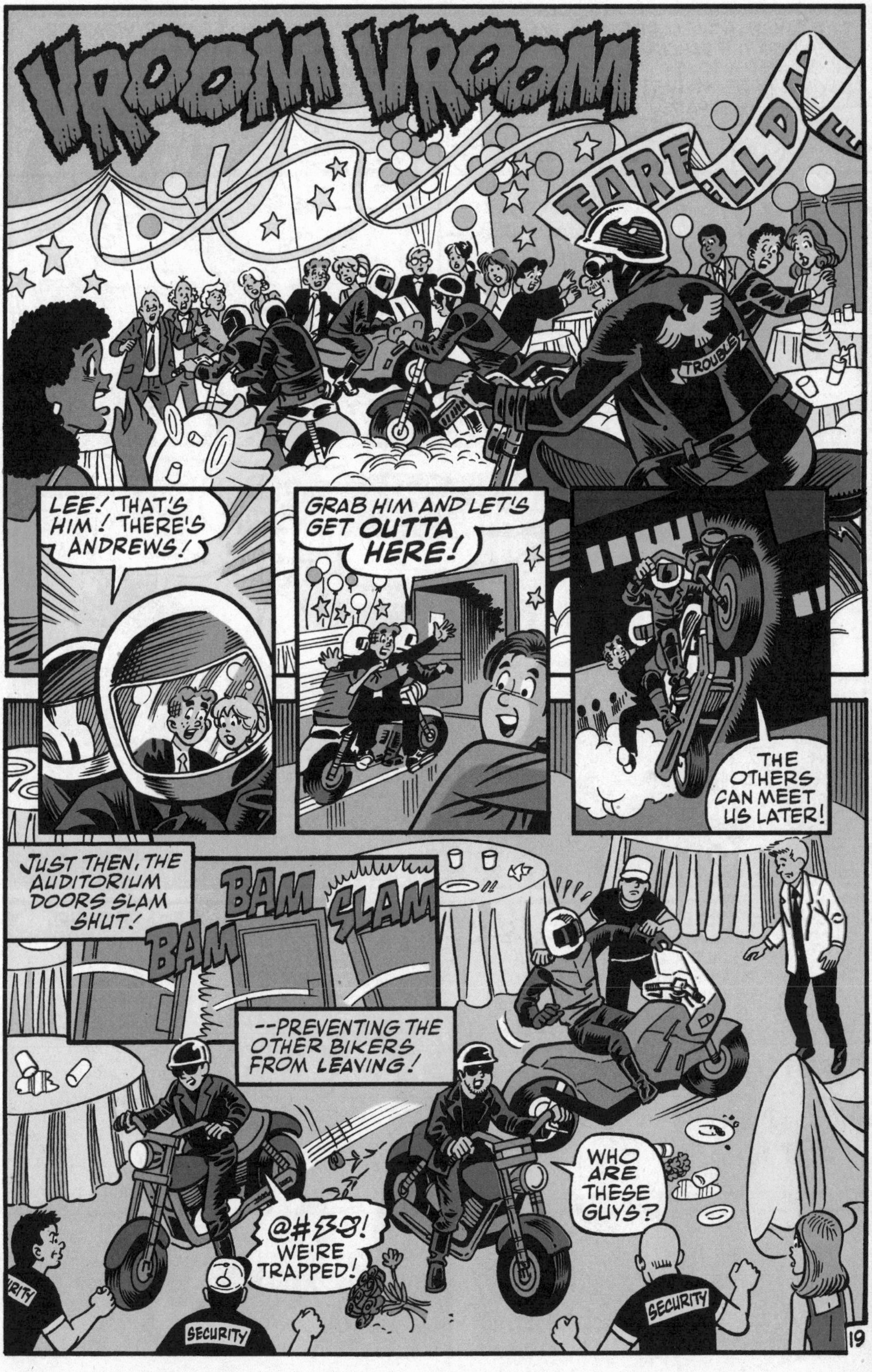
VROOM VROOM
FARE
LL D
TROUBLE
LEE! THAT'S HIM! THERE'S ANDREWS!
GRAB HIM AND LET'S GET OUTTA HERE!
THE OTHERS CAN MEET US LATER!
JUST THEN, THE AUDITORIUM DOORS SLAM SHUT!
BAM
BAM
SLAM
--PREVENTING THE OTHER BIKERS FROM LEAVING!
WHO ARE THESE GUYS?
@#$@! WE'RE TRAPPED!
SECURITY
SECURITY
19

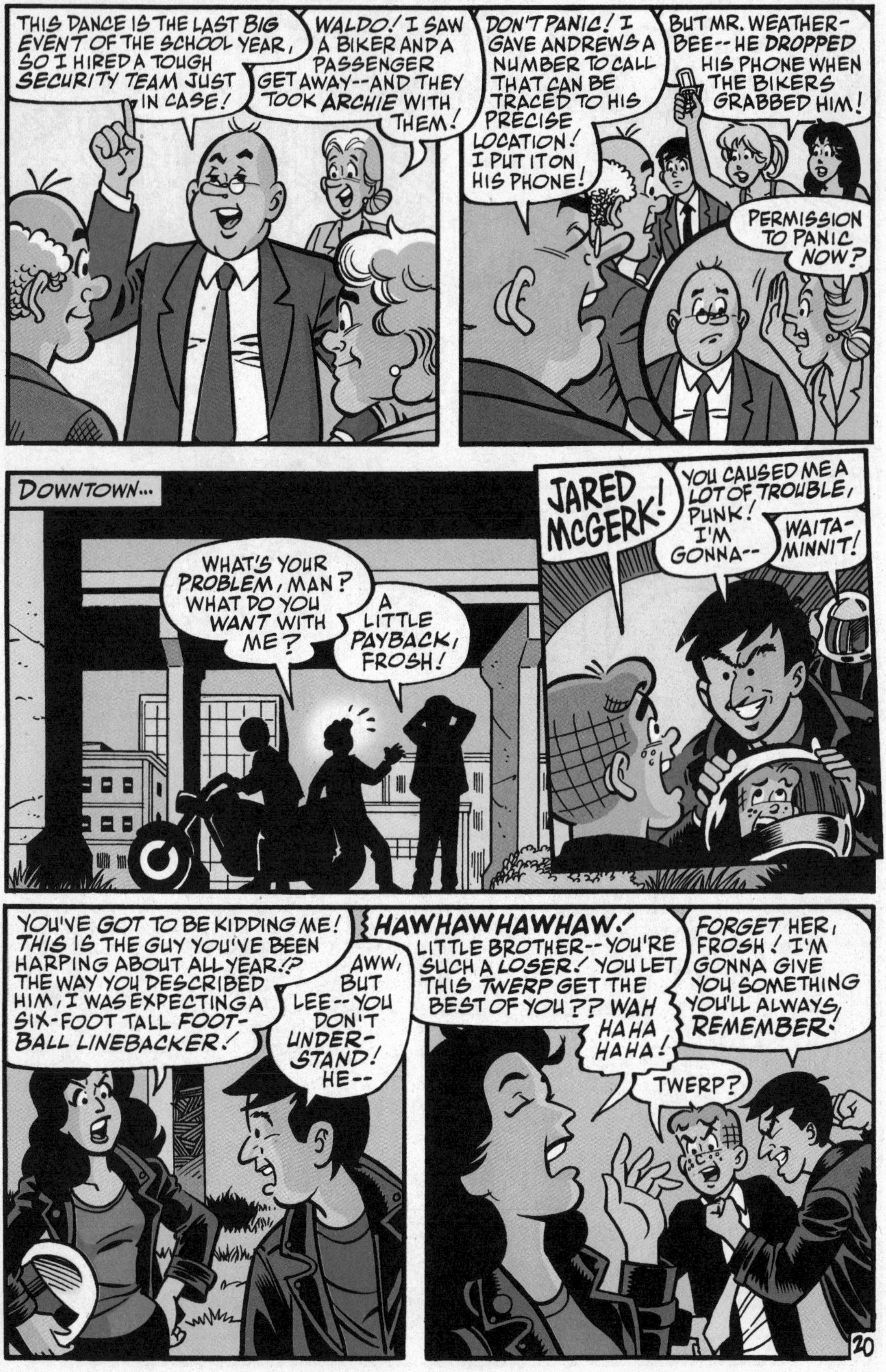
THIS DANCE IS THE LAST BIG EVENT OF THE SCHOOL YEAR, SO I HIRED A TOUGH SECURITY TEAM JUST IN CASE!
WALDO! I SAW A BIKER AND A PASSENGER GET AWAY--AND THEY TOOK ARCHIE WITH THEM!
DON'T PANIC! I GAVE ANDREWS A NUMBER TO CALL THAT CAN BE TRACED TO HIS PRECISE LOCATION! I PUT IT ON HIS PHONE!
BUT MR. WEATHERBEE-- HE DROPPED HIS PHONE WHEN THE BIKERS GRABBED HIM!
PERMISSION TO PANIC NOW?
DOWNTOWN...
WHAT'S YOUR PROBLEM, MAN? WHAT DO YOU WANT WITH ME?
A LITTLE PAYBACK, FROSH!
JARED McGERK!
YOU CAUSED ME A LOT OF TROUBLE, PUNK! I'M GONNA--
WAITA-MINNIT!
YOU'VE GOT TO BE KIDDING ME! THIS IS THE GUY YOU'VE BEEN HARPING ABOUT ALL YEAR!? THE WAY YOU DESCRIBED HIM, I WAS EXPECTING A SIX-FOOT TALL FOOTBALL LINEBACKER!
AWW, BUT LEE-- YOU DON'T UNDERSTAND! HE--
HAWHAWHAWHAW! LITTLE BROTHER-- YOU'RE SUCH A LOSER! YOU LET THIS TWERP GET THE BEST OF YOU?? WAH HAHA HAHA!
FORGET HER, FROSH! I'M GONNA GIVE YOU SOMETHING YOU'LL ALWAYS REMEMBER!
TWERP?
20

STAY AWAY FROM THAT BOY AND PUT YOUR HANDS IN THE AIR!!
WOW, OFFICER! HOW'D YOU MANAGE TO FIND ME?!
WE GOT A TIP FROM A CONCERNED CITIZEN!
PENCIL-NECK G!!
DOUBLE A! THAT BIKER ALMOST RAN ME DOWN! WHEN I SAW HER AGAIN WITH YOU, ME AND MY BROS CALLED 911 -- I WASN'T GONNA LET HER GET AWAY WITH BEING SO UNCOOL!
AND WITHIN A WEEK...
MR. HAVERHILL... WE WERE CONTACTED BY AN INDIVIDUAL YOU HIRED TO KEEP AN EYE ON PRINCIPAL WEATHERBEE DURING SCHOOL HOURS.
RIVERDALE SCHOOL DISTRICT OFFICES
WE FOUND THIS REPORT QUITE INTERESTING, SINCE IT CONTRADICTS YOUR FINDINGS, AND YOUR EX-EMPLOYEE WAS MOVED ENOUGH TO CONTACT US BECAUSE HE FELT MR. WEATHERBEE WAS NOT GETTING A "FAIR SHAKE."
AFTER READING HIS REPORT AND WITNESSING MR. WEATHERBEE'S BEHAVIOR UNDER FIRE, WE AGREE. THE BOARD OVERRULES YOUR DECISION.
NOT ONLY DOES MR. WEATHERBEE STAY AS PRINCIPAL, BUT WE'VE ALSO VOTED UNANIMOUSLY TO NOT RENEW YOUR CONTRACT AS SUPERINTENDENT, MR. HAVERHILL!
THESPIANS! MORE TROUBLE THAN THEY'RE WORTH!
WELL, HERE IT IS, WALDO! THE LAST DAY OF SCHOOL! YOU SURVIVED YOUR FIRST YEAR!
I'M JUST VERY PLEASED THAT I'LL BE HERE FOR A SECOND ONE!
RIVERDALE HIGH SCHOOL est. 1941
I JUST WISH I'D LEARNED WHO WAS THE ONE SPYING ON ME. I REGRET OFFENDING BILL NEE, JACKIE FLORES, AND SAM BURROWS BY SUSPECTING THEM, BUT THE "LEAKS" STARTED ONCE THEY TRANSFERRED HERE IN FEBRUARY!
SPEAKING OF LEAKS...
WET FLOOR
21

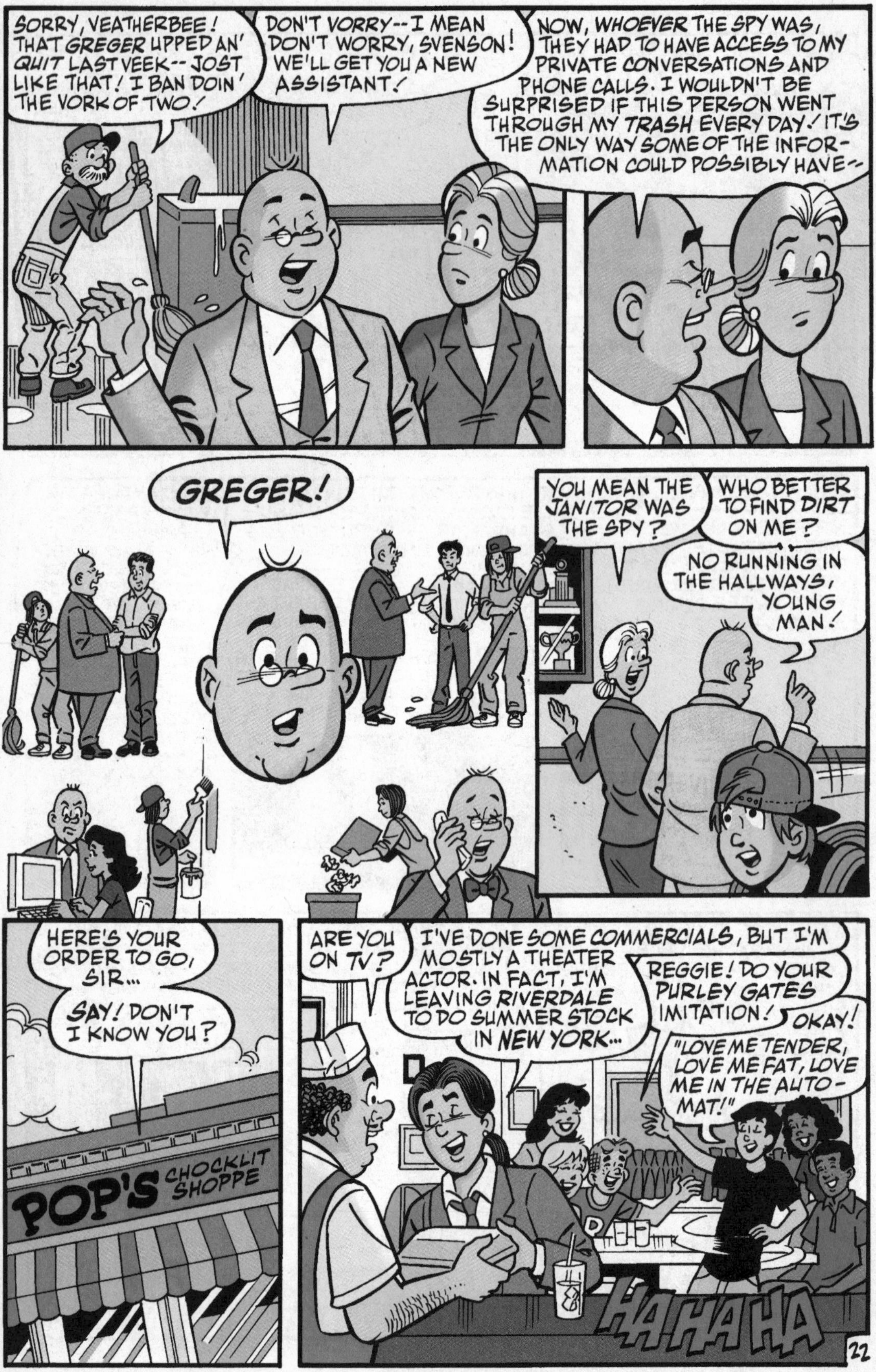
SORRY, VEATHERBEE! THAT GREGER UPPED AN' QUIT LAST VEEK-- JOST LIKE THAT! I BAN DOIN' THE VORK OF TWO!
DON'T VORRY-- I MEAN DON'T WORRY, SVENSON! WE'LL GET YOU A NEW ASSISTANT!
NOW, WHOEVER THE SPY WAS, THEY HAD TO HAVE ACCESS TO MY PRIVATE CONVERSATIONS AND PHONE CALLS. I WOULDN'T BE SURPRISED IF THIS PERSON WENT THROUGH MY TRASH EVERY DAY! IT'S THE ONLY WAY SOME OF THE INFORMATION COULD POSSIBLY HAVE--
GREGER!
YOU MEAN THE JANITOR WAS THE SPY?
WHO BETTER TO FIND DIRT ON ME?
NO RUNNING IN THE HALLWAYS, YOUNG MAN!
HERE'S YOUR ORDER TO GO, SIR...
SAY! DON'T I KNOW YOU?
POP'S CHOCKLIT SHOPPE
ARE YOU ON TV?
I'VE DONE SOME COMMERCIALS, BUT I'M MOSTLY A THEATER ACTOR. IN FACT, I'M LEAVING RIVERDALE TO DO SUMMER STOCK IN NEW YORK...
REGGIE! DO YOUR PURLEY GATES IMITATION!
OKAY!
"LOVE ME TENDER, LOVE ME FAT, LOVE ME IN THE AUTO-MAT!"
HA HA HA
22

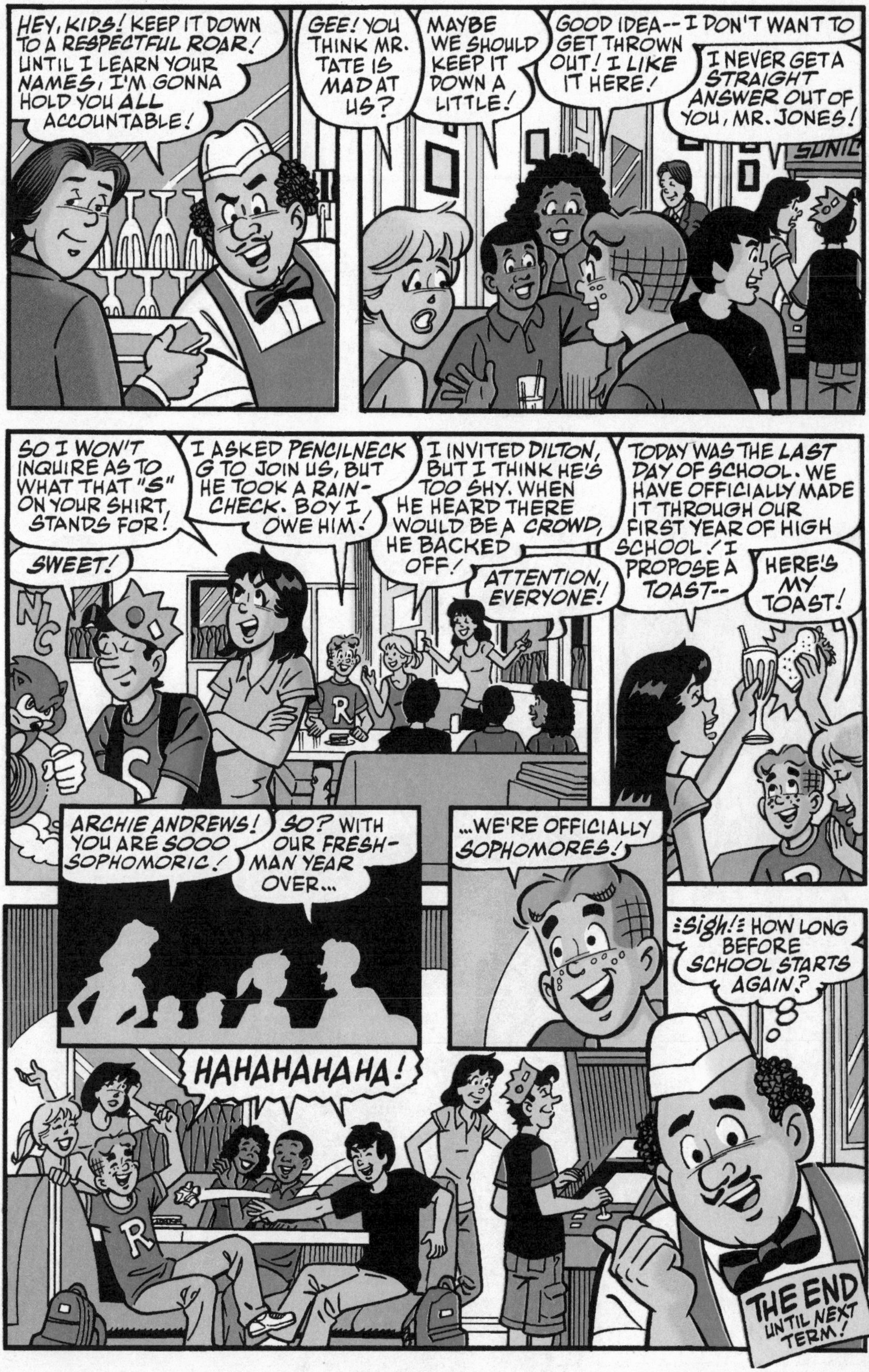
HEY, KIDS! KEEP IT DOWN TO A RESPECTFUL ROAR! UNTIL I LEARN YOUR NAMES, I'M GONNA HOLD YOU ALL ACCOUNTABLE!
GEE! YOU THINK MR. TATE IS MAD AT US?
MAYBE WE SHOULD KEEP IT DOWN A LITTLE!
GOOD IDEA-- I DON'T WANT TO GET THROWN OUT! I LIKE IT HERE!
I NEVER GET A STRAIGHT ANSWER OUT OF YOU, MR. JONES!
SO I WON'T INQUIRE AS TO WHAT THAT "S" ON YOUR SHIRT STANDS FOR!
SWEET!
I ASKED PENCILNECK G TO JOIN US, BUT HE TOOK A RAIN-CHECK. BOY I OWE HIM!
I INVITED DILTON, BUT I THINK HE'S TOO SHY. WHEN HE HEARD THERE WOULD BE A CROWD, HE BACKED OFF!
ATTENTION, EVERYONE!
TODAY WAS THE LAST DAY OF SCHOOL. WE HAVE OFFICIALLY MADE IT THROUGH OUR FIRST YEAR OF HIGH SCHOOL! I PROPOSE A TOAST--
HERE'S MY TOAST!
ARCHIE ANDREWS! YOU ARE SOOO SOPHOMORIC!
SO? WITH OUR FRESH-MAN YEAR OVER...
...WE'RE OFFICIALLY SOPHOMORES!
HAHAHAHAHA!
Sigh! HOW LONG BEFORE SCHOOL STARTS AGAIN?
THE END UNTIL NEXT TERM!

CHAPTER TWO

Clash of the New Kids

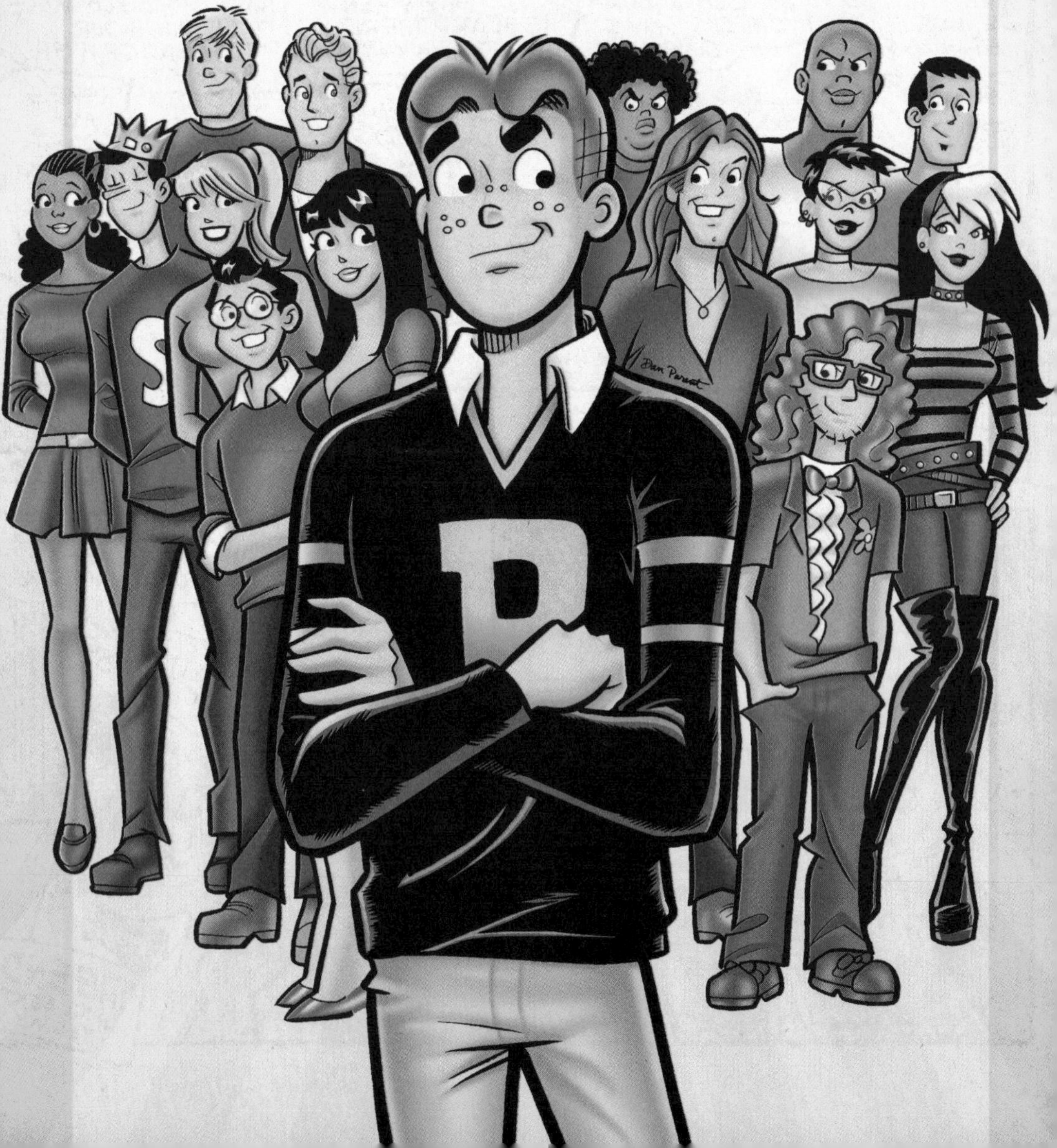
Dan Parent

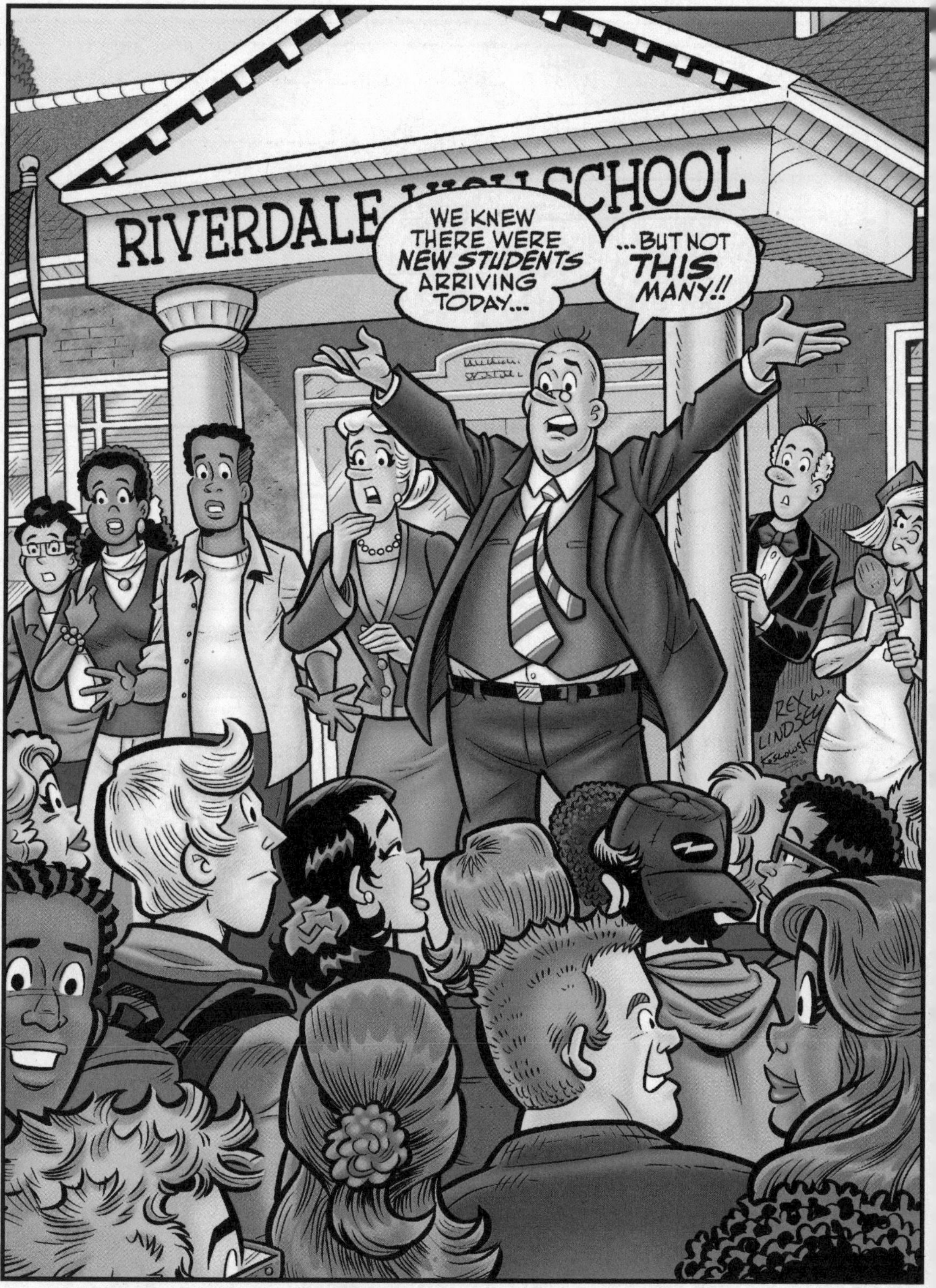
RIVERDALE SCHOOL
WE KNEW THERE WERE NEW STUDENTS ARRIVING TODAY...
...BUT NOT THIS MANY!!
REX W. LINDSEY
KOSLOWSKI

NEW KIDS OFF THE WALL - PART 1

SCRIPT: ALEX SIMMONS PENCILS: DAN PARENT

INKS: RICH KOSLOWSKI LETTERS: JACK MORELLI COLORS: DIGIKORE STUDIOS

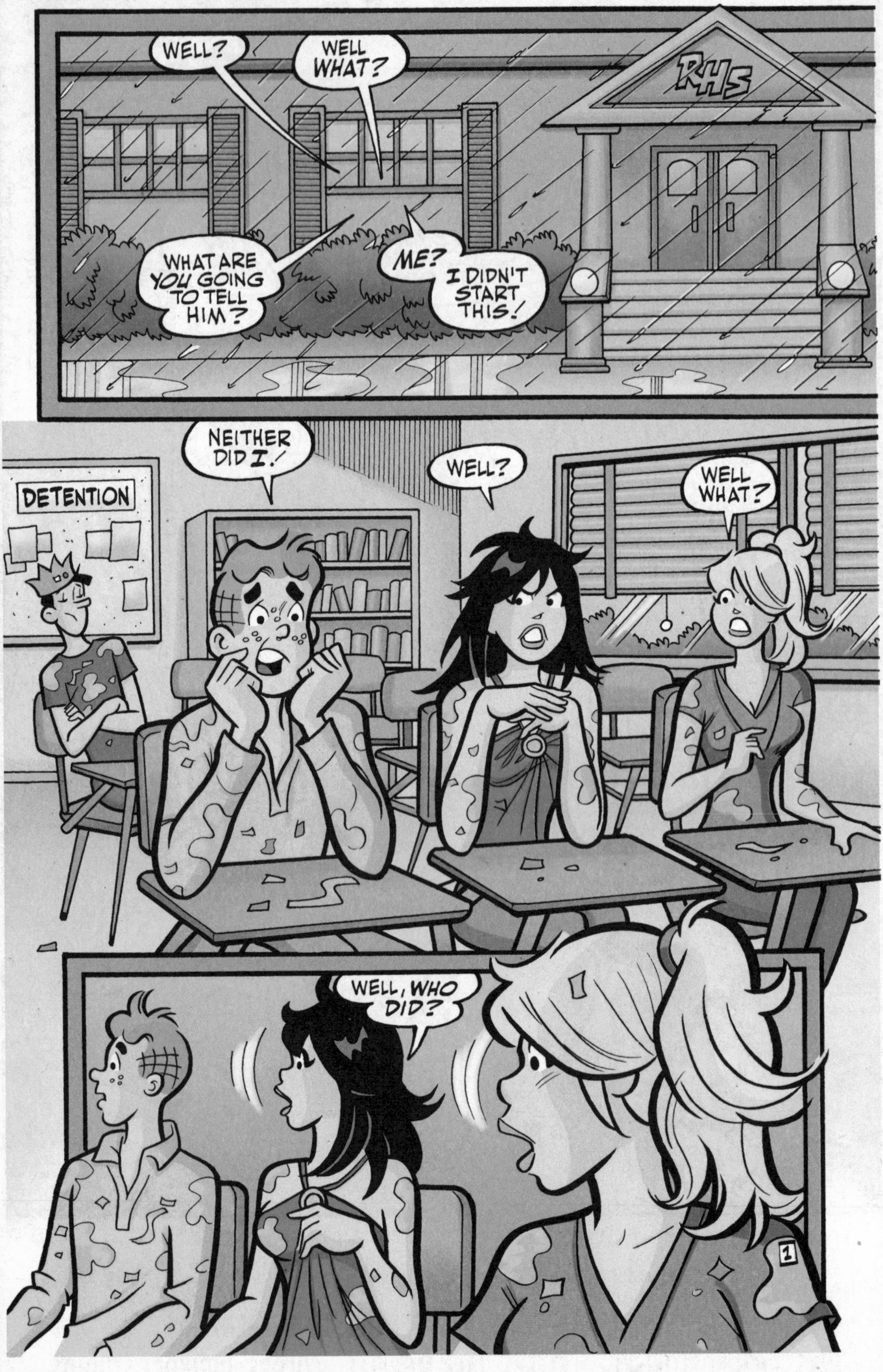
WELL?
WELL WHAT?
WHAT ARE YOU GOING TO TELL HIM?
ME? I DIDN'T START THIS!
RHS
NEITHER DID I!
WELL?
WELL WHAT?
DETENTION
WELL, WHO DID?

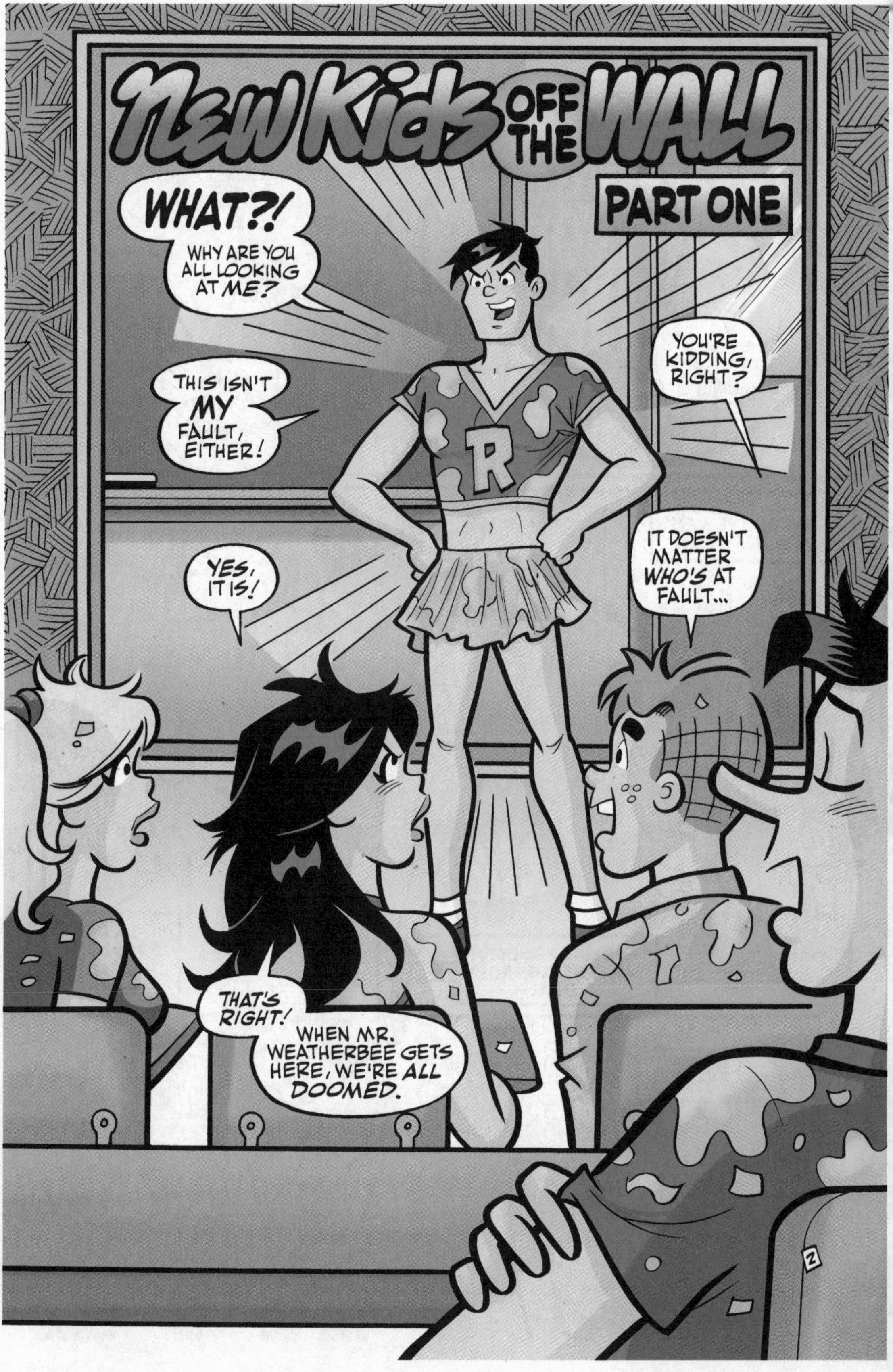

New Kids OFF THE WALL
PART ONE
WHAT?! WHY ARE YOU ALL LOOKING AT ME?
YOU'RE KIDDING, RIGHT?
THIS ISN'T MY FAULT, EITHER!
YES, IT IS!
IT DOESN'T MATTER WHO'S AT FAULT...
THAT'S RIGHT!
WHEN MR. WEATHERBEE GETS HERE, WE'RE ALL DOOMED.

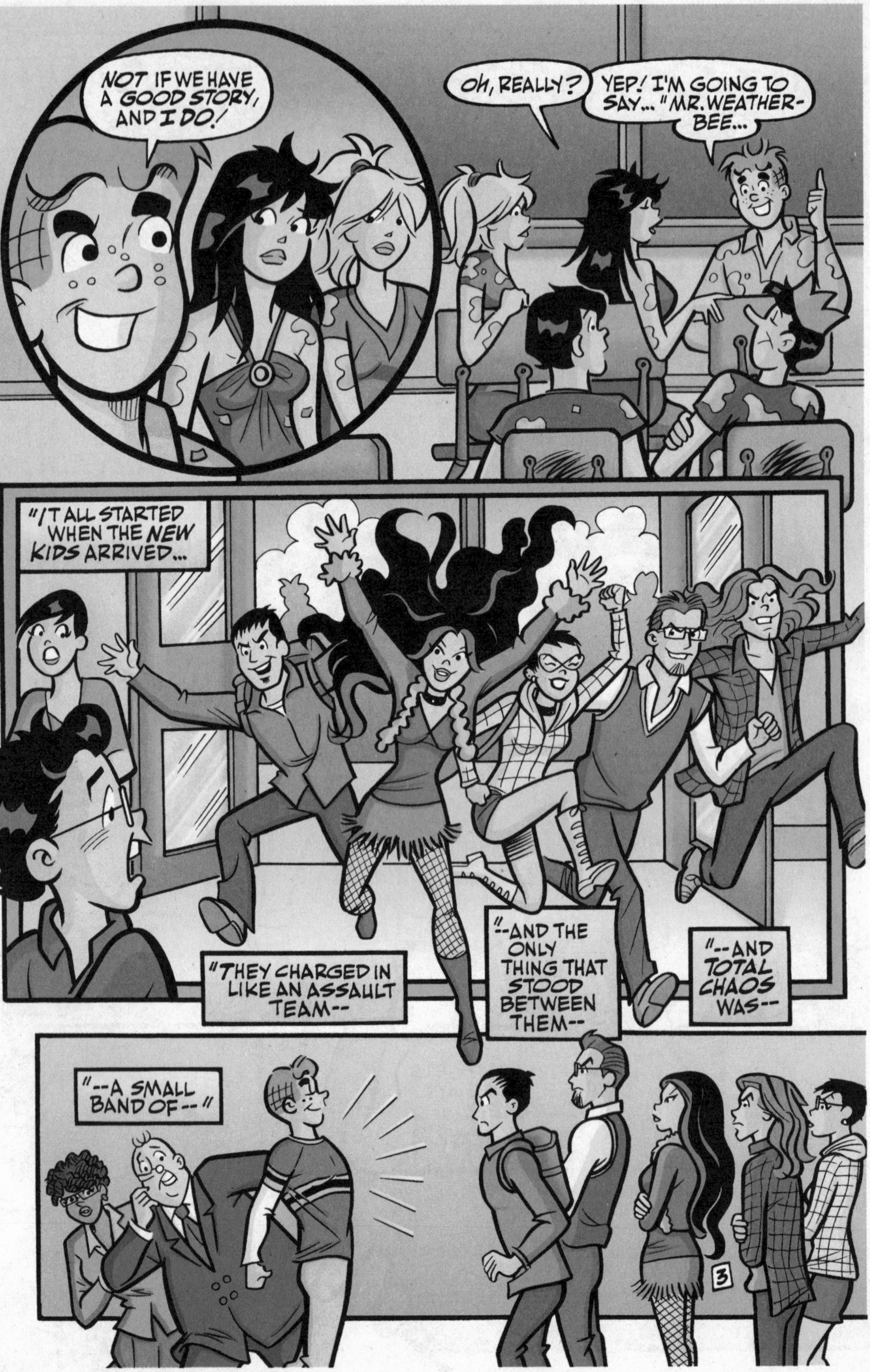

NOT IF WE HAVE A GOOD STORY, AND I DO!
Oh, REALLY?
YEP! I'M GOING TO SAY... "MR. WEATHER-BEE...
"IT ALL STARTED WHEN THE NEW KIDS ARRIVED...
"THEY CHARGED IN LIKE AN ASSAULT TEAM--
"--AND THE ONLY THING THAT STOOD BETWEEN THEM--
"--AND TOTAL CHAOS WAS--
"--A SMALL BAND OF--"
3

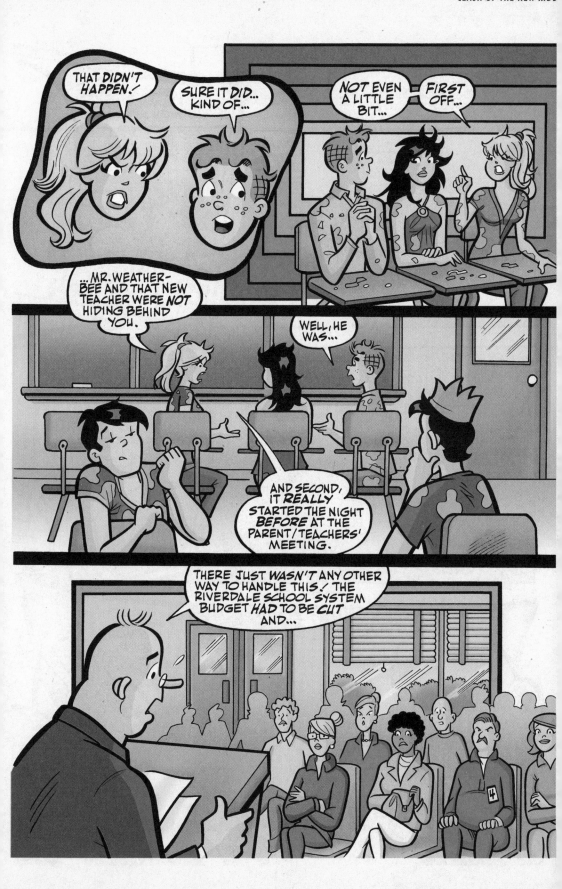

THAT DIDN'T HAPPEN!

SURE IT DID... KIND OF...

NOT EVEN A LITTLE BIT...

FIRST OFF...

...MR. WEATHER-BEE AND THAT NEW TEACHER WERE NOT HIDING BEHIND YOU.

WELL, HE WAS...

AND SECOND, IT REALLY STARTED THE NIGHT BEFORE AT THE PARENT/TEACHERS' MEETING.

THERE JUST WASN'T ANY OTHER WAY TO HANDLE THIS! THE RIVERDALE SCHOOL SYSTEM BUDGET HAD TO BE CUT AND...

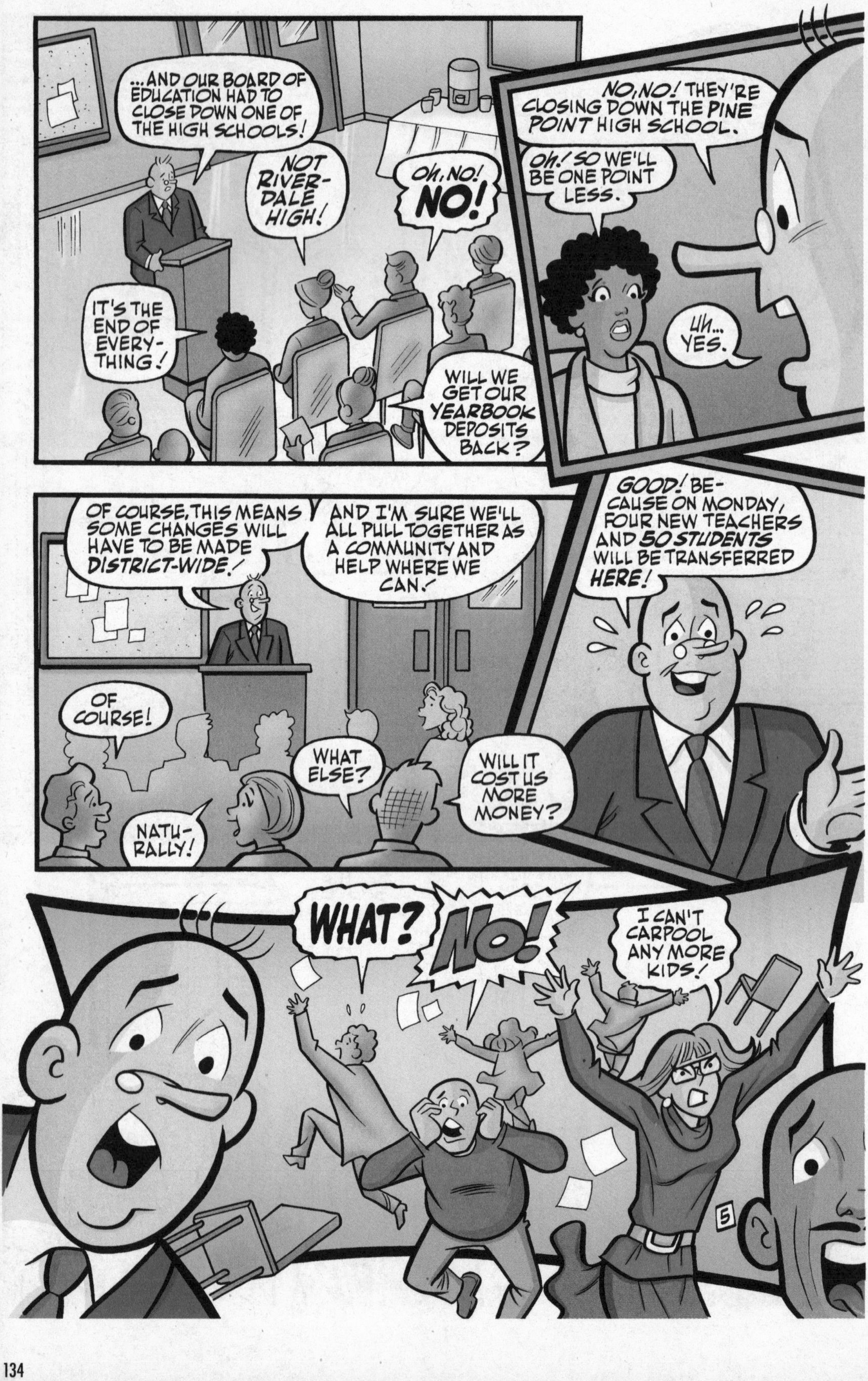
...AND OUR BOARD OF EDUCATION HAD TO CLOSE DOWN ONE OF THE HIGH SCHOOLS!
NOT RIVER-DALE HIGH!
OH, NO! NO!
IT'S THE END OF EVERY-THING!
WILL WE GET OUR YEARBOOK DEPOSITS BACK?
NO, NO! THEY'RE CLOSING DOWN THE PINE POINT HIGH SCHOOL.
OH! SO WE'LL BE ONE POINT LESS.
UH... YES.
OF COURSE, THIS MEANS SOME CHANGES WILL HAVE TO BE MADE DISTRICT-WIDE!
AND I'M SURE WE'LL ALL PULL TOGETHER AS A COMMUNITY AND HELP WHERE WE CAN!
OF COURSE!
NATU-RALLY!
WHAT ELSE?
WILL IT COST US MORE MONEY?
GOOD! BE-CAUSE ON MONDAY, FOUR NEW TEACHERS AND 50 STUDENTS WILL BE TRANSFERRED HERE!
WHAT?
NO!
I CAN'T CARPOOL ANY MORE KIDS!
5

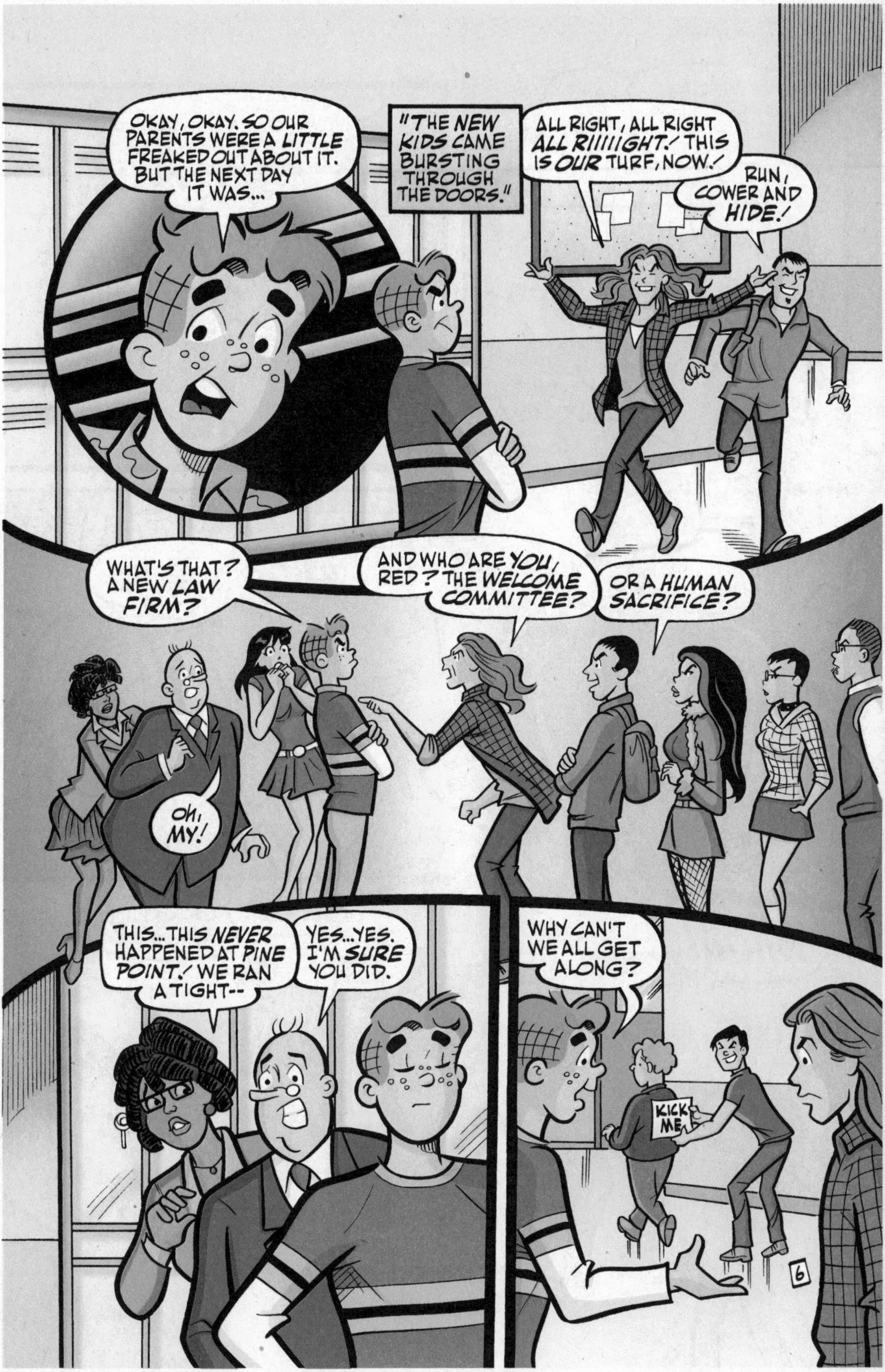
OKAY, OKAY. SO OUR PARENTS WERE A LITTLE FREAKED OUT ABOUT IT. BUT THE NEXT DAY IT WAS...
"THE NEW KIDS CAME BURSTING THROUGH THE DOORS."
ALL RIGHT, ALL RIGHT ALL RIIIIIGHT! THIS IS OUR TURF, NOW.!
RUN, COWER AND HIDE!
WHAT'S THAT? A NEW LAW FIRM?
AND WHO ARE YOU, RED? THE WELCOME COMMITTEE?
OR A HUMAN SACRIFICE?
OH, MY!
THIS...THIS NEVER HAPPENED AT PINE POINT! WE RAN A TIGHT--
YES...YES. I'M SURE YOU DID.
WHY CAN'T WE ALL GET ALONG?
KICK ME
6

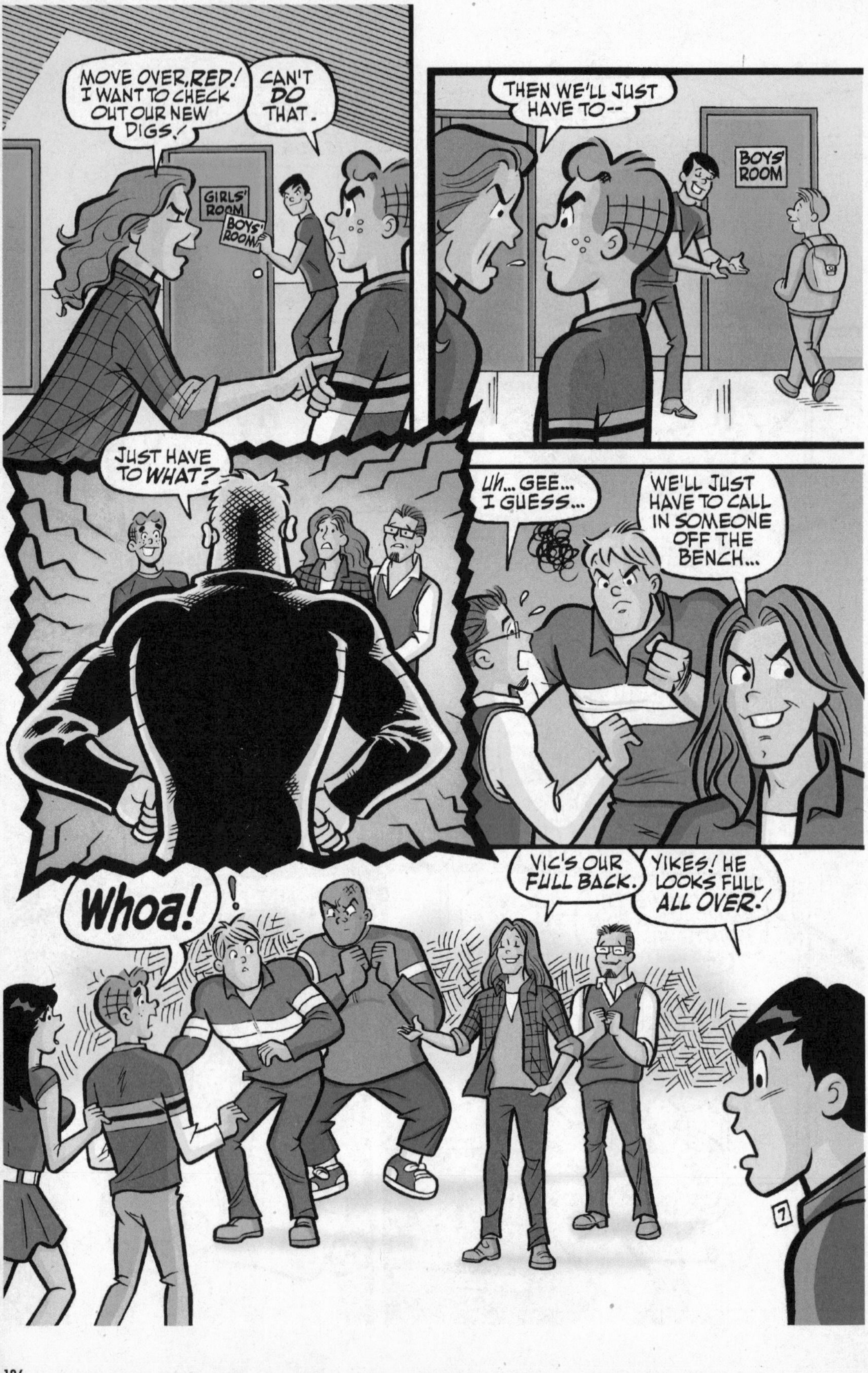
MOVE OVER, RED! I WANT TO CHECK OUT OUR NEW DIGS!
CAN'T DO THAT.
GIRLS' ROOM
BOYS' ROOM
THEN WE'LL JUST HAVE TO--
BOYS' ROOM
JUST HAVE TO WHAT?
UH... GEE... I GUESS...
WE'LL JUST HAVE TO CALL IN SOMEONE OFF THE BENCH...
Whoa!
!
VIC'S OUR FULL BACK.
YIKES! HE LOOKS FULL ALL OVER!
7

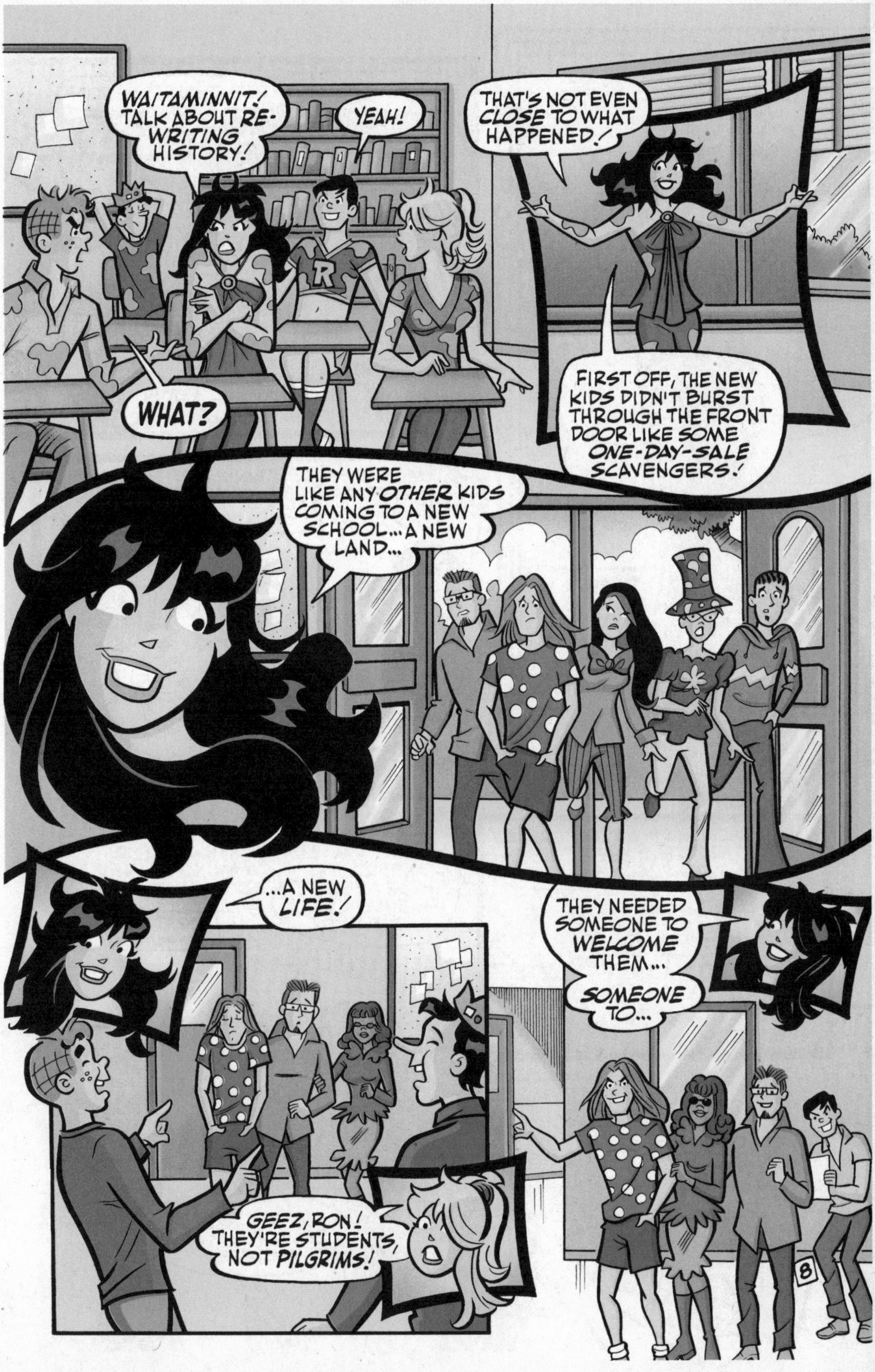
WAITAMINNIT! TALK ABOUT RE-WRITING HISTORY!
YEAH!
WHAT?
THAT'S NOT EVEN CLOSE TO WHAT HAPPENED!
FIRST OFF, THE NEW KIDS DIDN'T BURST THROUGH THE FRONT DOOR LIKE SOME ONE-DAY-SALE SCAVENGERS!
THEY WERE LIKE ANY OTHER KIDS COMING TO A NEW SCHOOL... A NEW LAND...
...A NEW LIFE!
GEEZ, RON! THEY'RE STUDENTS, NOT PILGRIMS!
THEY NEEDED SOMEONE TO WELCOME THEM...
SOMEONE TO...
8

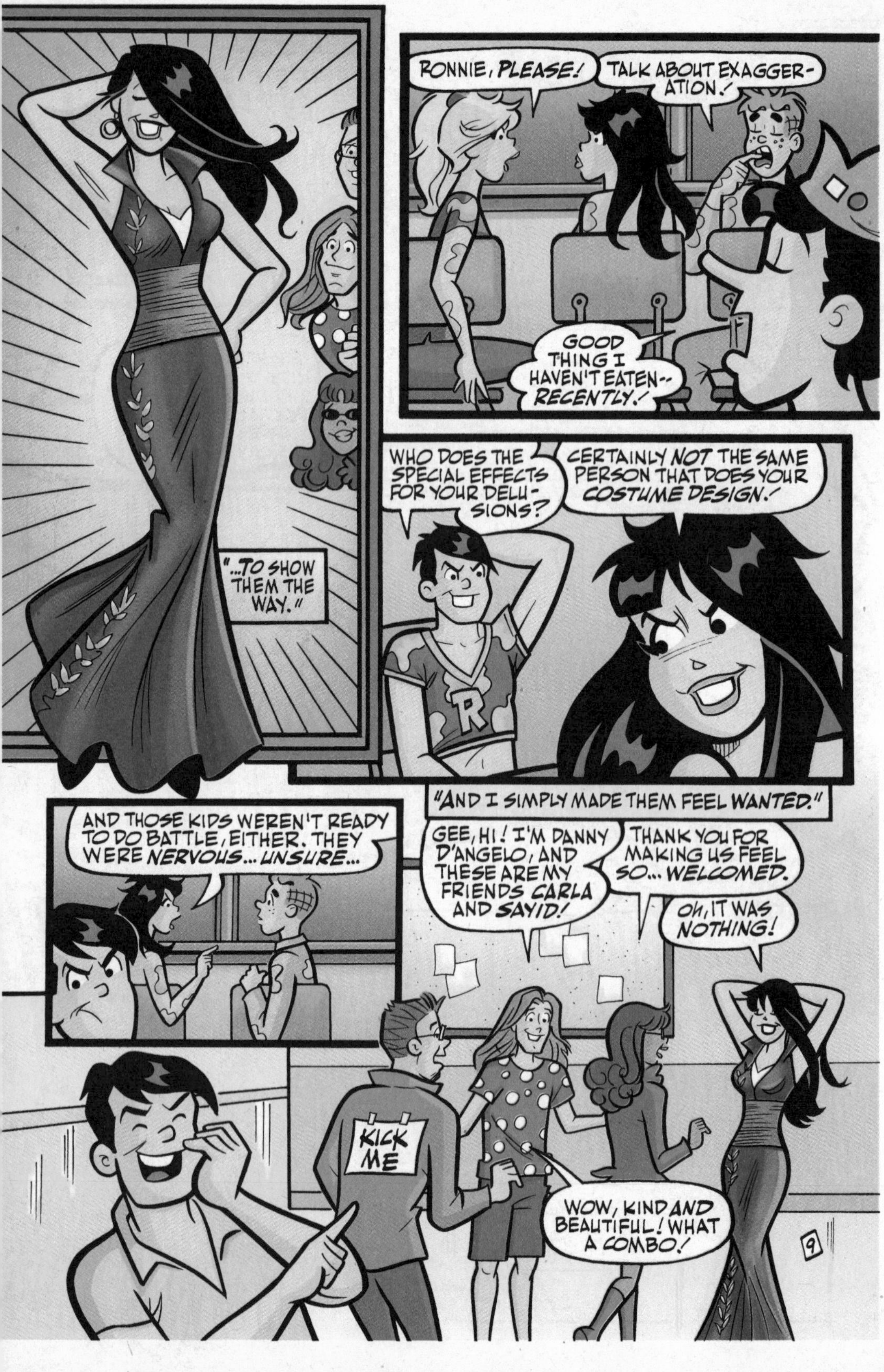
"...TO SHOW THEM THE WAY."
RONNIE, PLEASE!
TALK ABOUT EXAGGER-ATION!
GOOD THING I HAVEN'T EATEN-- RECENTLY!
WHO DOES THE SPECIAL EFFECTS FOR YOUR DELU-SIONS?
CERTAINLY NOT THE SAME PERSON THAT DOES YOUR COSTUME DESIGN!
AND THOSE KIDS WEREN'T READY TO DO BATTLE, EITHER. THEY WERE NERVOUS... UNSURE...
"AND I SIMPLY MADE THEM FEEL WANTED."
GEE, HI! I'M DANNY D'ANGELO, AND THESE ARE MY FRIENDS CARLA AND SAYID!
THANK YOU FOR MAKING US FEEL SO... WELCOMED.
OH, IT WAS NOTHING!
KICK ME
WOW, KIND AND BEAUTIFUL! WHAT A COMBO!
9

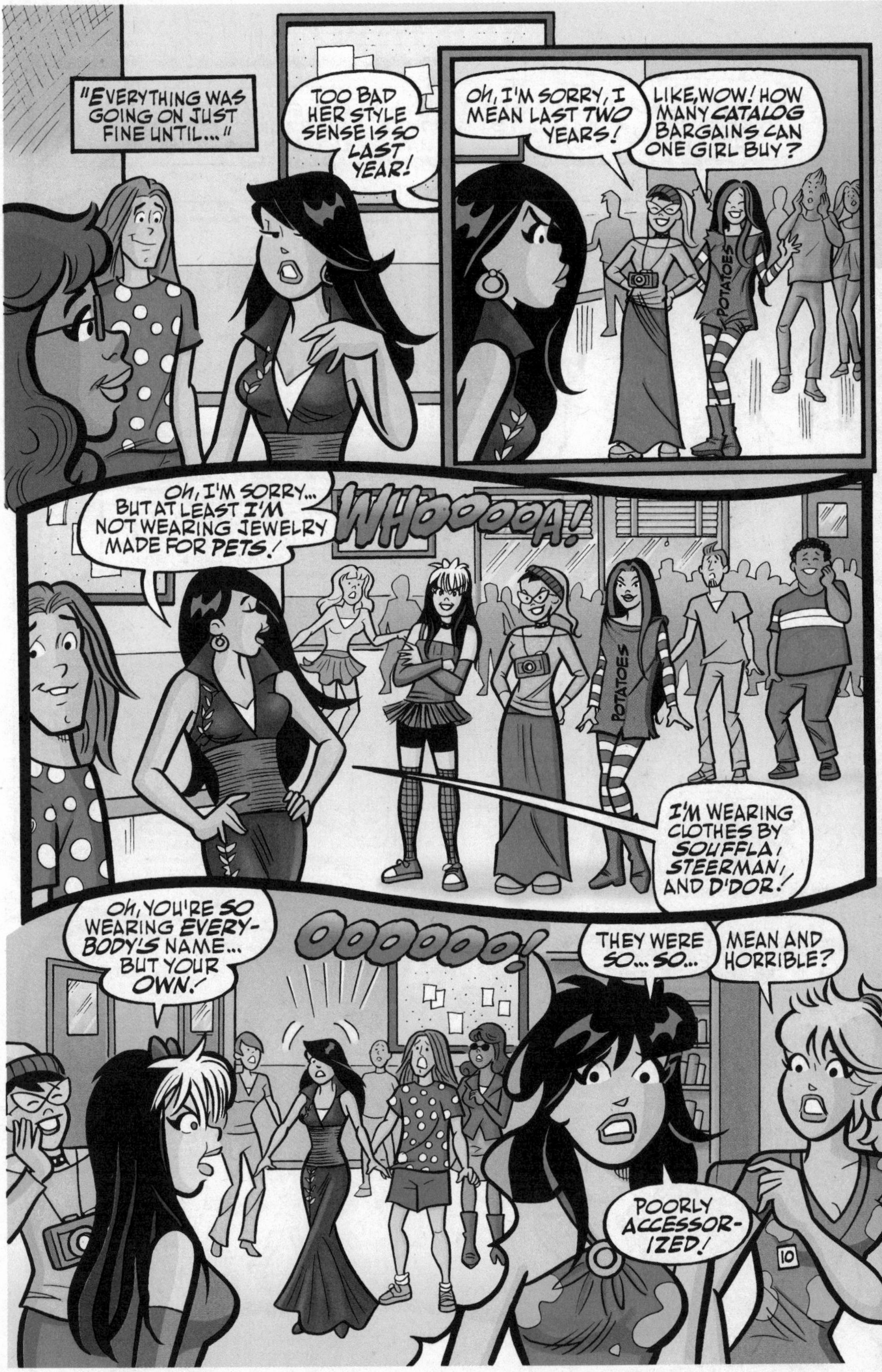
"EVERYTHING WAS GOING ON JUST FINE UNTIL..."
TOO BAD HER STYLE SENSE IS SO LAST YEAR!
OH, I'M SORRY, I MEAN LAST TWO YEARS!
LIKE, WOW! HOW MANY CATALOG BARGAINS CAN ONE GIRL BUY?
POTATOES
OH, I'M SORRY... BUT AT LEAST I'M NOT WEARING JEWELRY MADE FOR PETS!
WHOOOOOA!
POTATOES
I'M WEARING CLOTHES BY SOUFFLA, STEERMAN, AND D'DOR!
OH, YOU'RE SO WEARING EVERYBODY'S NAME... BUT YOUR OWN!
OOOOOOO!
THEY WERE SO... SO...
MEAN AND HORRIBLE?
POORLY ACCESSORIZED!
10

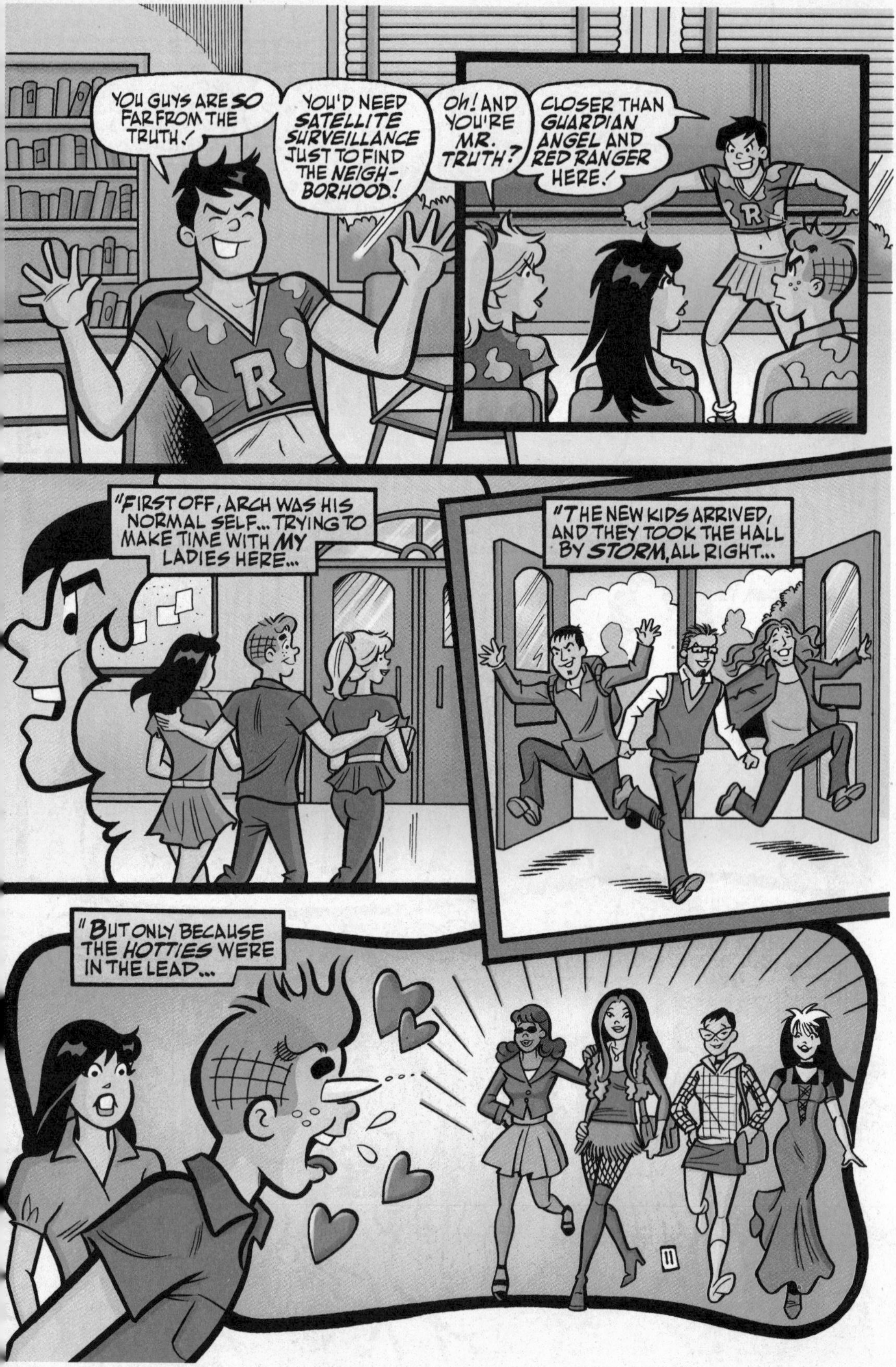
YOU GUYS ARE SO FAR FROM THE TRUTH!
YOU'D NEED SATELLITE SURVEILLANCE JUST TO FIND THE NEIGHBORHOOD!
Oh! AND YOU'RE MR. TRUTH?
CLOSER THAN GUARDIAN ANGEL AND RED RANGER HERE!
"FIRST OFF, ARCH WAS HIS NORMAL SELF... TRYING TO MAKE TIME WITH MY LADIES HERE...
"THE NEW KIDS ARRIVED, AND THEY TOOK THE HALL BY STORM, ALL RIGHT...
"BUT ONLY BECAUSE THE HOTTIES WERE IN THE LEAD...
11

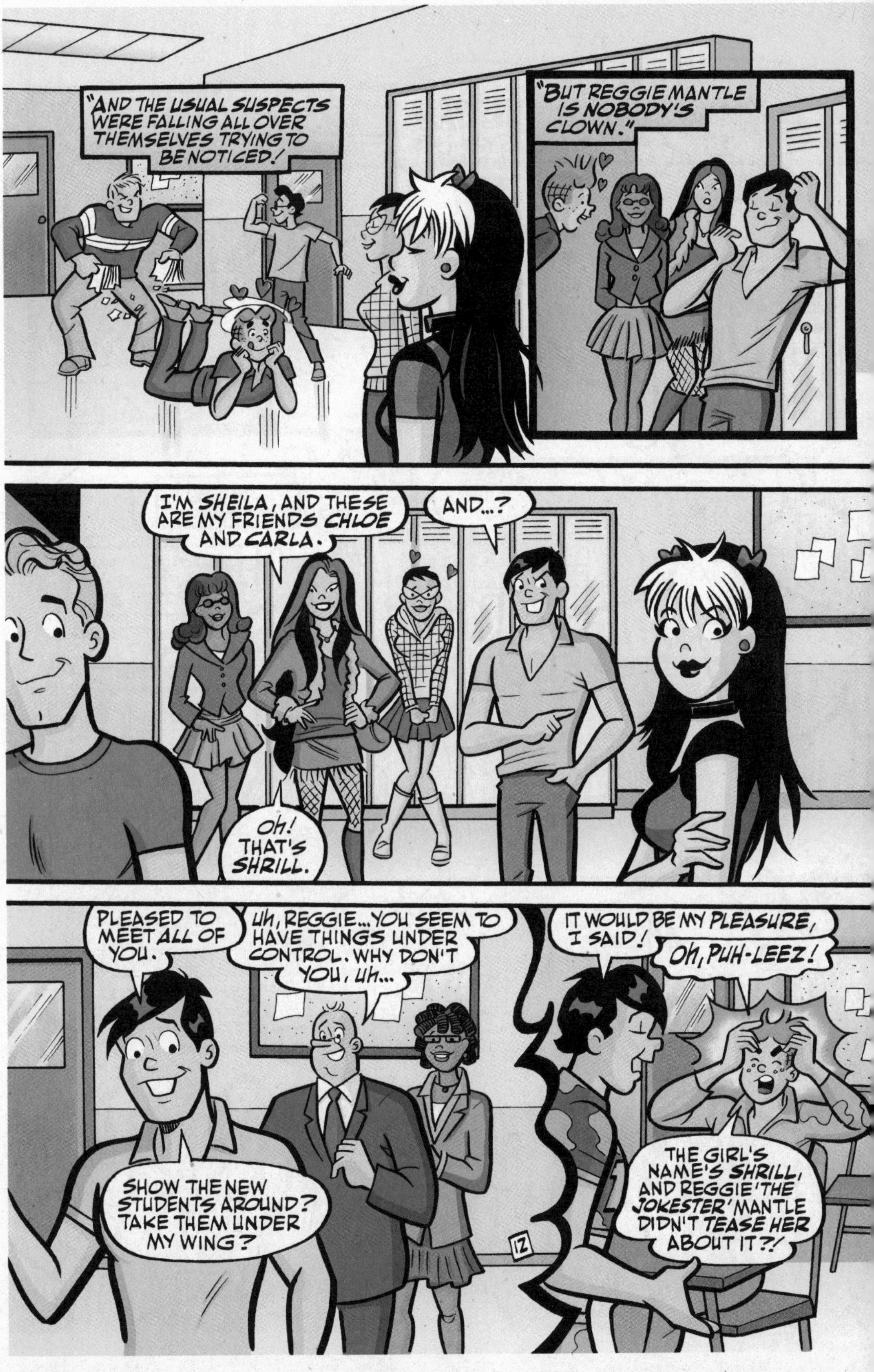
"AND THE USUAL SUSPECTS WERE FALLING ALL OVER THEMSELVES TRYING TO BE NOTICED!
"BUT REGGIE MANTLE IS NOBODY'S CLOWN."
I'M SHEILA, AND THESE ARE MY FRIENDS CHLOE AND CARLA.
AND...?
OH! THAT'S SHRILL.
PLEASED TO MEET ALL OF YOU.
UH, REGGIE...YOU SEEM TO HAVE THINGS UNDER CONTROL. WHY DON'T YOU, UH...
SHOW THE NEW STUDENTS AROUND? TAKE THEM UNDER MY WING?
IT WOULD BE MY PLEASURE, I SAID!
OH, PUH-LEEZ!
THE GIRL'S NAME'S SHRILL, AND REGGIE 'THE JOKESTER' MANTLE DIDN'T TEASE HER ABOUT IT?!
12

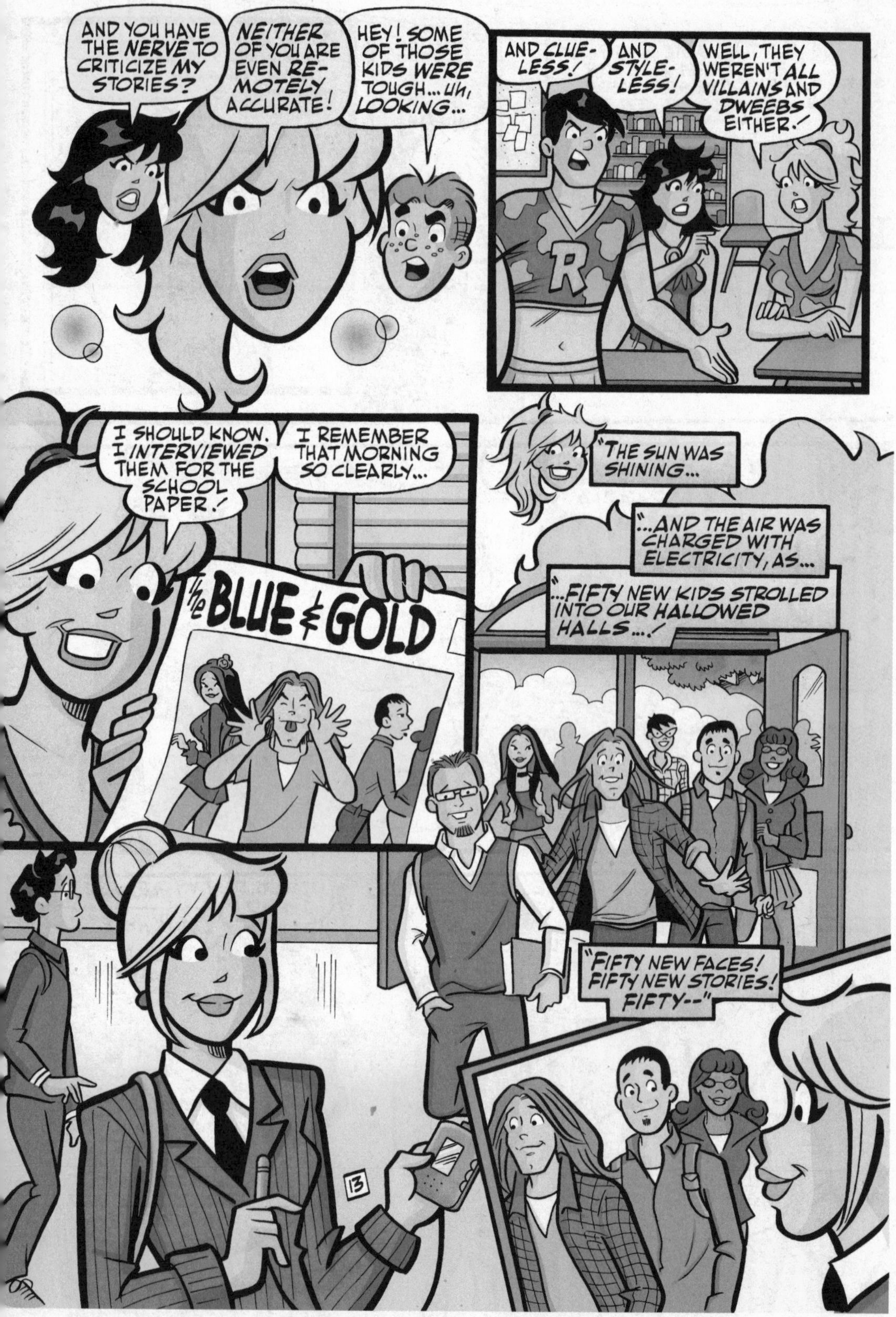
AND YOU HAVE THE NERVE TO CRITICIZE MY STORIES?
NEITHER OF YOU ARE EVEN REMOTELY ACCURATE!
HEY! SOME OF THOSE KIDS WERE TOUGH... UH, LOOKING...
AND CLUE-LESS!
AND STYLE-LESS!
WELL, THEY WEREN'T ALL VILLAINS AND DWEEBS EITHER.!
I SHOULD KNOW. I INTERVIEWED THEM FOR THE SCHOOL PAPER.!
I REMEMBER THAT MORNING SO CLEARLY...
THE BLUE & GOLD
"THE SUN WAS SHINING...
"...AND THE AIR WAS CHARGED WITH ELECTRICITY, AS...
"...FIFTY NEW KIDS STROLLED INTO OUR HALLOWED HALLS...!
"FIFTY NEW FACES! FIFTY NEW STORIES! FIFTY--"
13

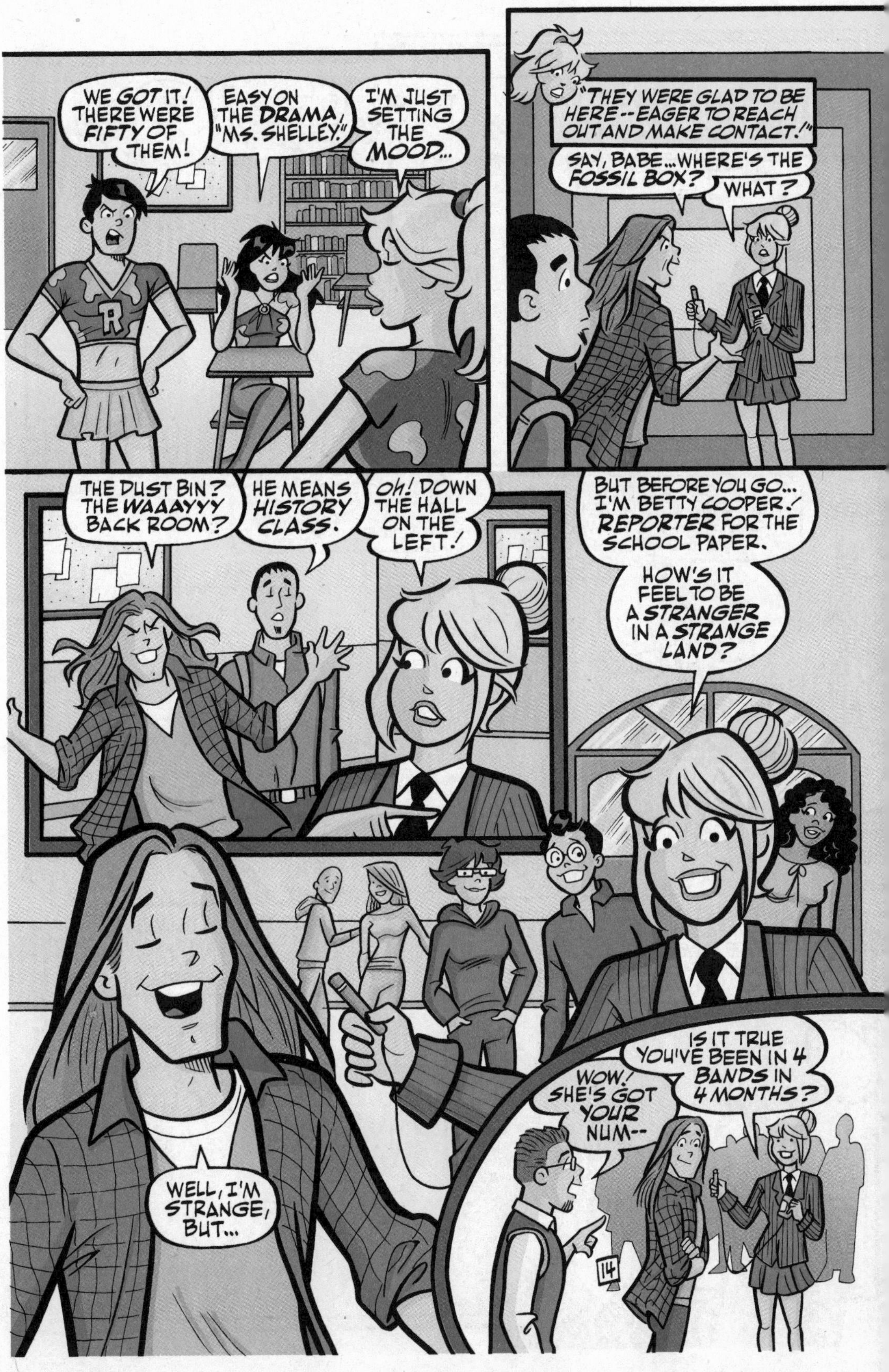
WE GOT IT! THERE WERE FIFTY OF THEM!
EASY ON THE DRAMA, "MS. SHELLEY."
I'M JUST SETTING THE MOOD...
"THEY WERE GLAD TO BE HERE--EAGER TO REACH OUT AND MAKE CONTACT!"
SAY, BABE...WHERE'S THE FOSSIL BOX?
WHAT?
THE DUST BIN? THE WAAAYYY BACK ROOM?
HE MEANS HISTORY CLASS.
OH! DOWN THE HALL ON THE LEFT!
BUT BEFORE YOU GO... I'M BETTY COOPER! REPORTER FOR THE SCHOOL PAPER.
HOW'S IT FEEL TO BE A STRANGER IN A STRANGE LAND?
WELL, I'M STRANGE, BUT...
IS IT TRUE YOU'VE BEEN IN 4 BANDS IN 4 MONTHS?
WOW! SHE'S GOT YOUR NUM--
14

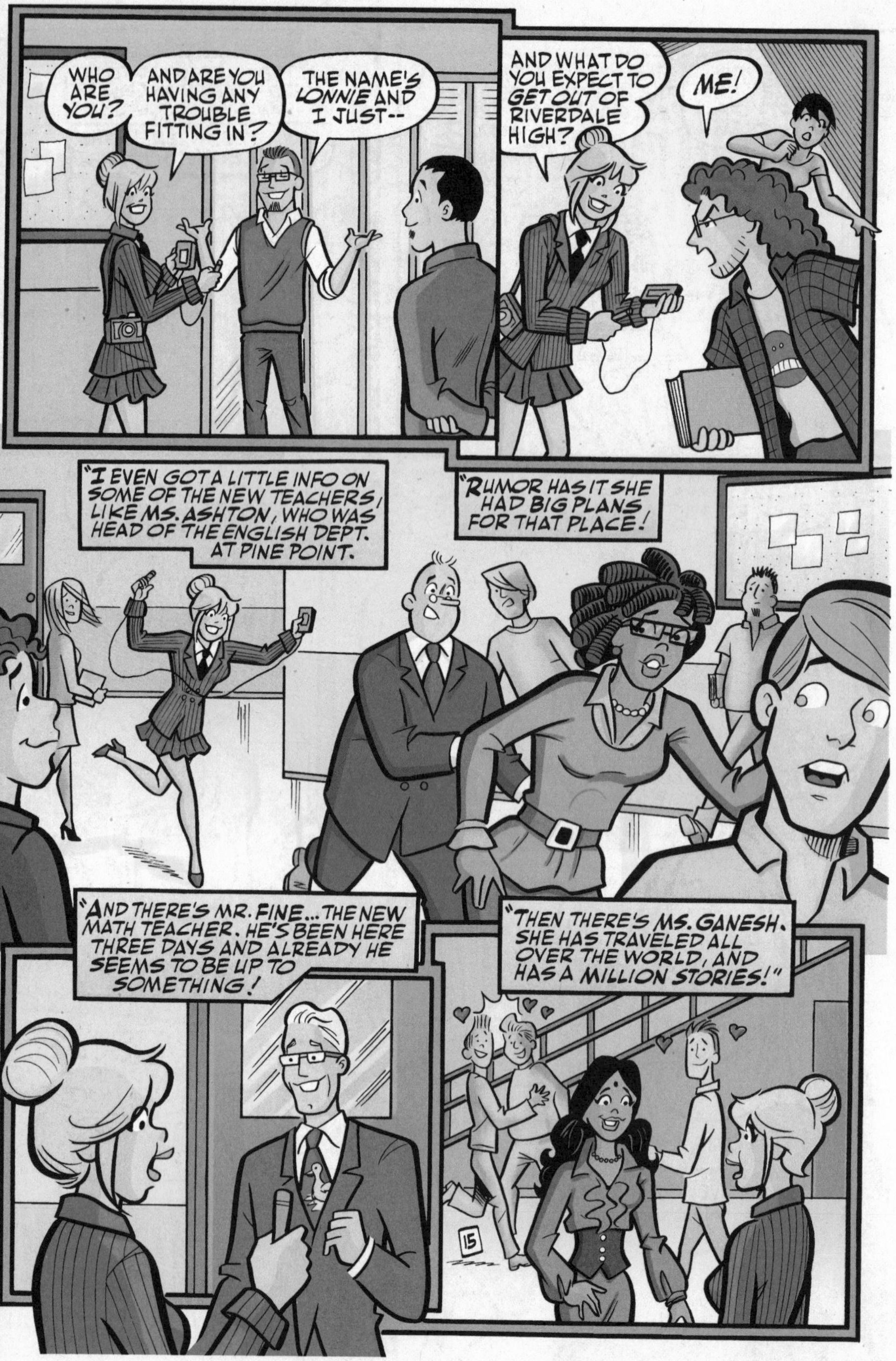
WHO ARE YOU?
AND ARE YOU HAVING ANY TROUBLE FITTING IN?
THE NAME'S LONNIE AND I JUST--
AND WHAT DO YOU EXPECT TO GET OUT OF RIVERDALE HIGH?
ME!
"I EVEN GOT A LITTLE INFO ON SOME OF THE NEW TEACHERS, LIKE MS. ASHTON, WHO WAS HEAD OF THE ENGLISH DEPT. AT PINE POINT.
"RUMOR HAS IT SHE HAD BIG PLANS FOR THAT PLACE!
"AND THERE'S MR. FINE... THE NEW MATH TEACHER. HE'S BEEN HERE THREE DAYS AND ALREADY HE SEEMS TO BE UP TO SOMETHING!
"THEN THERE'S MS. GANESH. SHE HAS TRAVELED ALL OVER THE WORLD, AND HAS A MILLION STORIES!"
15

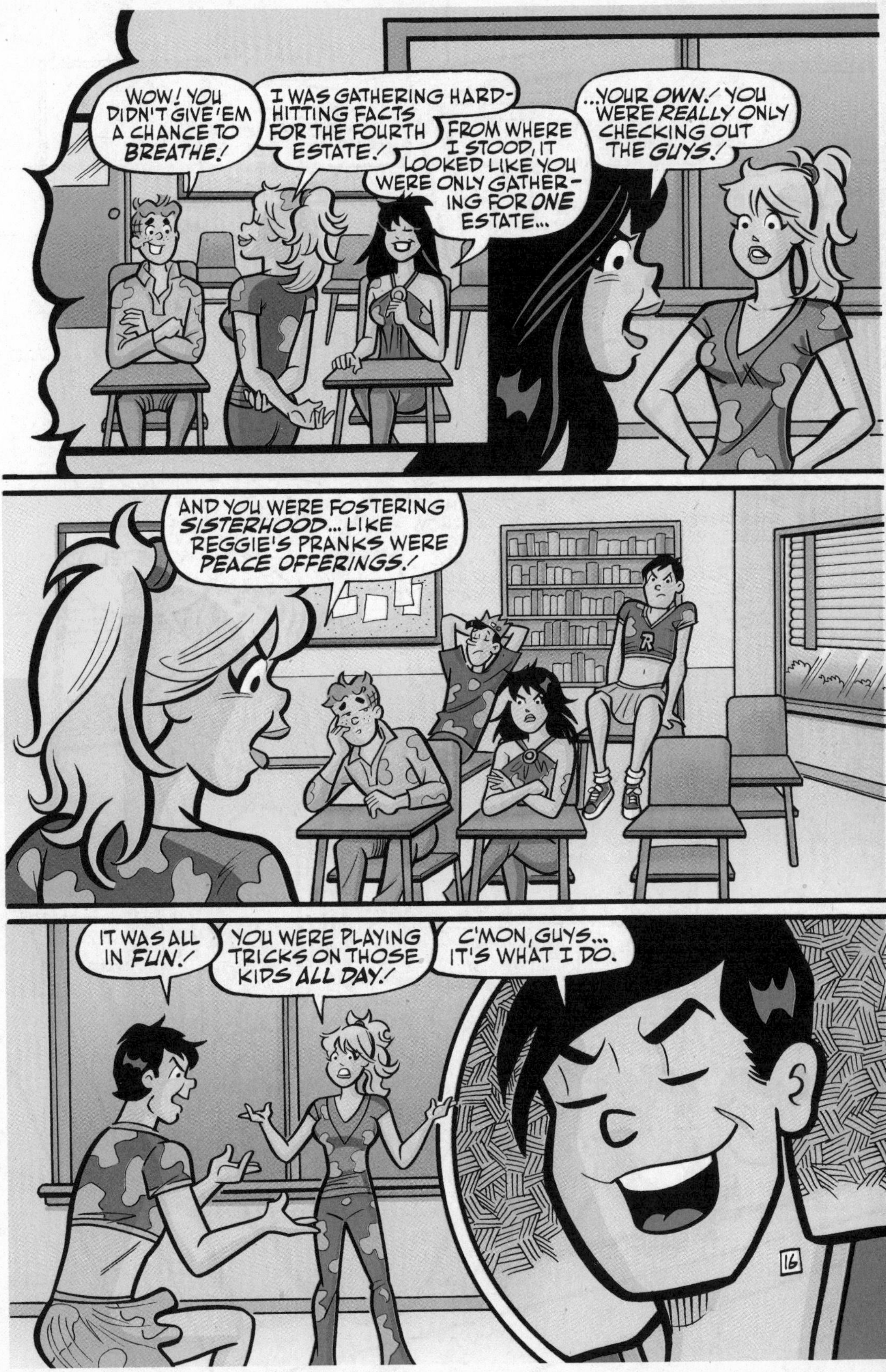
WOW! YOU DIDN'T GIVE 'EM A CHANCE TO BREATHE!
I WAS GATHERING HARD-HITTING FACTS FOR THE FOURTH ESTATE!
FROM WHERE I STOOD, IT LOOKED LIKE YOU WERE ONLY GATHERING FOR ONE ESTATE...
...YOUR OWN! YOU WERE REALLY ONLY CHECKING OUT THE GUYS!
AND YOU WERE FOSTERING SISTERHOOD... LIKE REGGIE'S PRANKS WERE PEACE OFFERINGS!
R
IT WAS ALL IN FUN!
YOU WERE PLAYING TRICKS ON THOSE KIDS ALL DAY!
C'MON, GUYS... IT'S WHAT I DO.
16

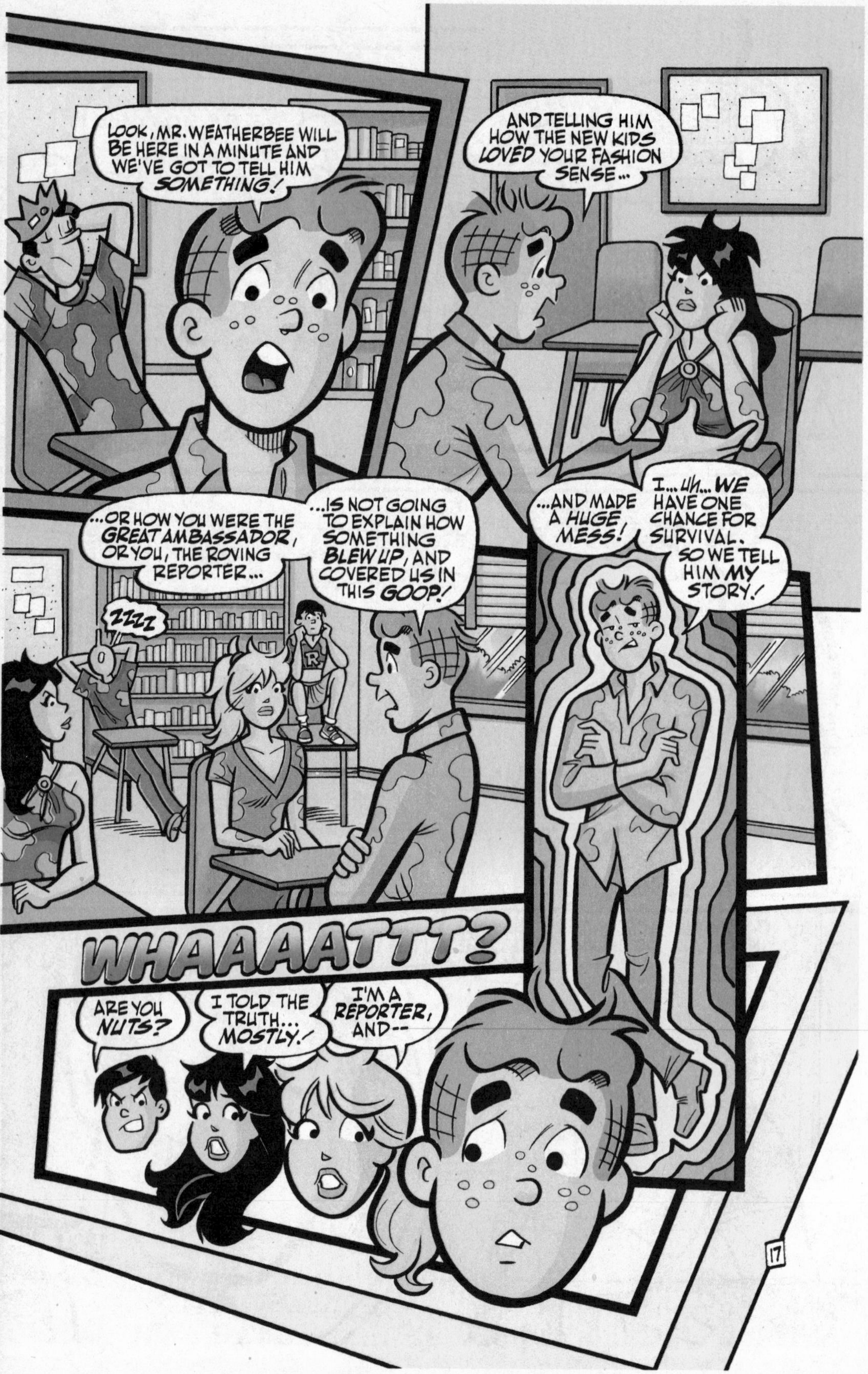
LOOK, MR. WEATHERBEE WILL BE HERE IN A MINUTE AND WE'VE GOT TO TELL HIM SOMETHING!
AND TELLING HIM HOW THE NEW KIDS LOVED YOUR FASHION SENSE...
...OR HOW YOU WERE THE GREAT AMBASSADOR, OR YOU, THE ROVING REPORTER...
...IS NOT GOING TO EXPLAIN HOW SOMETHING BLEW UP, AND COVERED US IN THIS GOOP!
ZZZZ
...AND MADE A HUGE MESS!
I... uh... WE HAVE ONE CHANCE FOR SURVIVAL.
SO WE TELL HIM MY STORY!
WHAAAAATTT?
ARE YOU NUTS?
I TOLD THE TRUTH... MOSTLY!
I'M A REPORTER, AND--
17

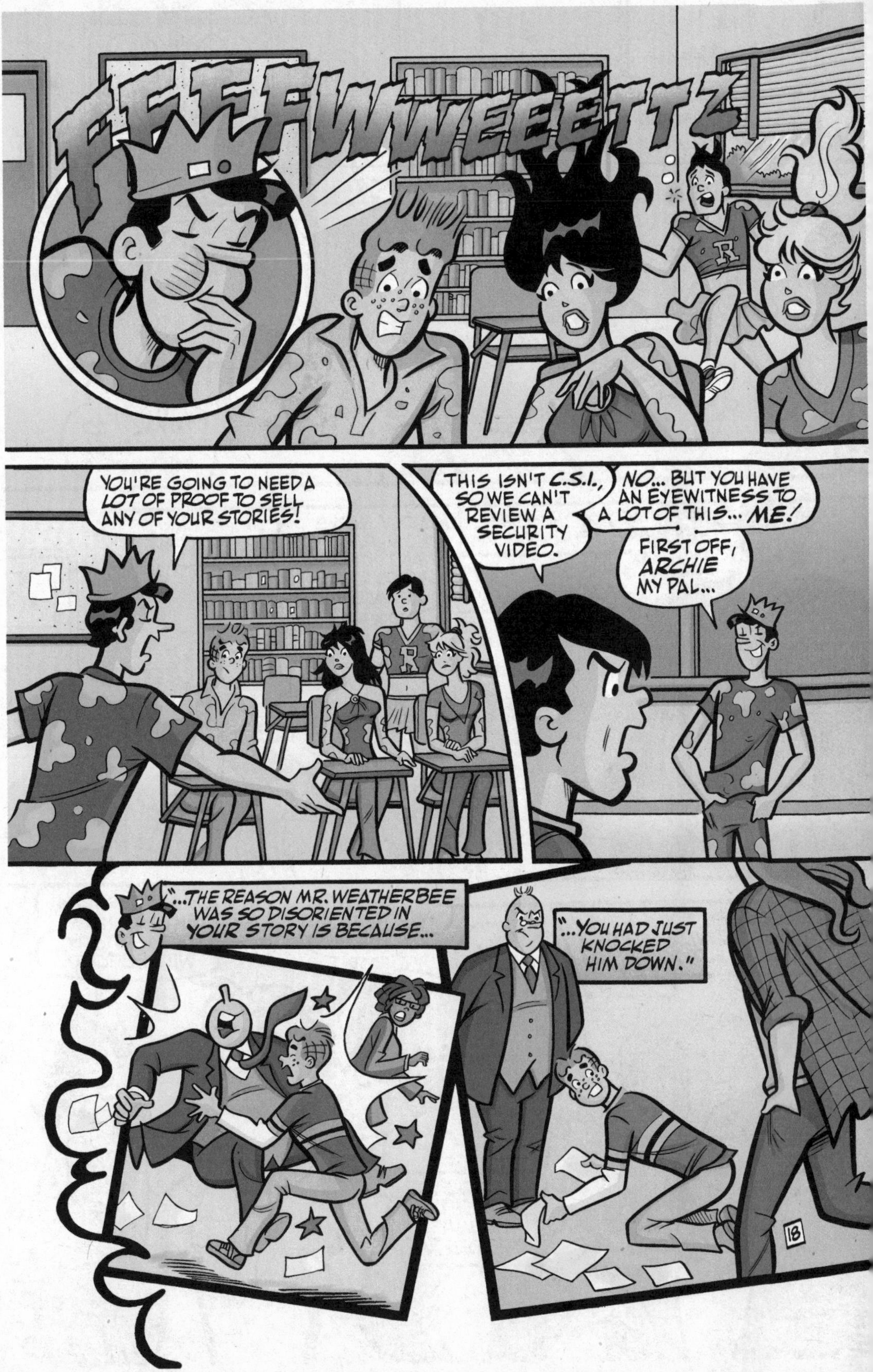
FFFFWWEEETTTZ
YOU'RE GOING TO NEED A LOT OF PROOF TO SELL ANY OF YOUR STORIES!
THIS ISN'T C.S.I., SO WE CAN'T REVIEW A SECURITY VIDEO.
NO... BUT YOU HAVE AN EYEWITNESS TO A LOT OF THIS... ME!
FIRST OFF, ARCHIE MY PAL...
"...THE REASON MR. WEATHERBEE WAS SO DISORIENTED IN YOUR STORY IS BECAUSE...
"...YOU HAD JUST KNOCKED HIM DOWN."
18

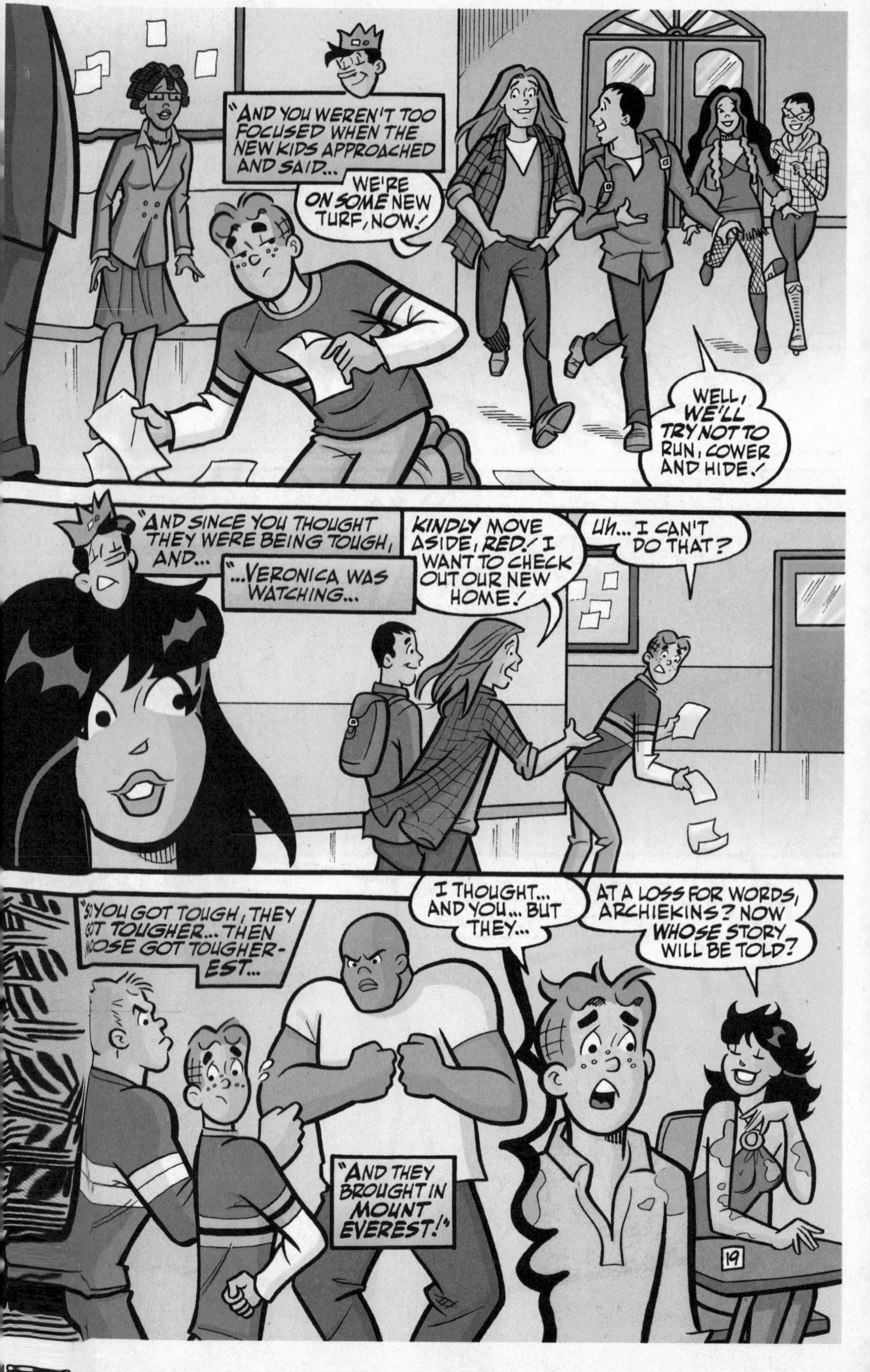
"AND YOU WEREN'T TOO FOCUSED WHEN THE NEW KIDS APPROACHED AND SAID...
WE'RE ON SOME NEW TURF, NOW!
WELL, WE'LL TRY NOT TO RUN, COWER AND HIDE!
"AND SINCE YOU THOUGHT THEY WERE BEING TOUGH, AND...
"...VERONICA WAS WATCHING...
KINDLY MOVE ASIDE, RED! I WANT TO CHECK OUT OUR NEW HOME!
UH... I CAN'T DO THAT?
"SO YOU GOT TOUGH, THEY GOT TOUGHER... THEN MOOSE GOT TOUGHER-EST...
"AND THEY BROUGHT IN MOUNT EVEREST!"
I THOUGHT... AND YOU... BUT THEY...
AT A LOSS FOR WORDS, ARCHIEKINS? NOW WHOSE STORY WILL BE TOLD?
19

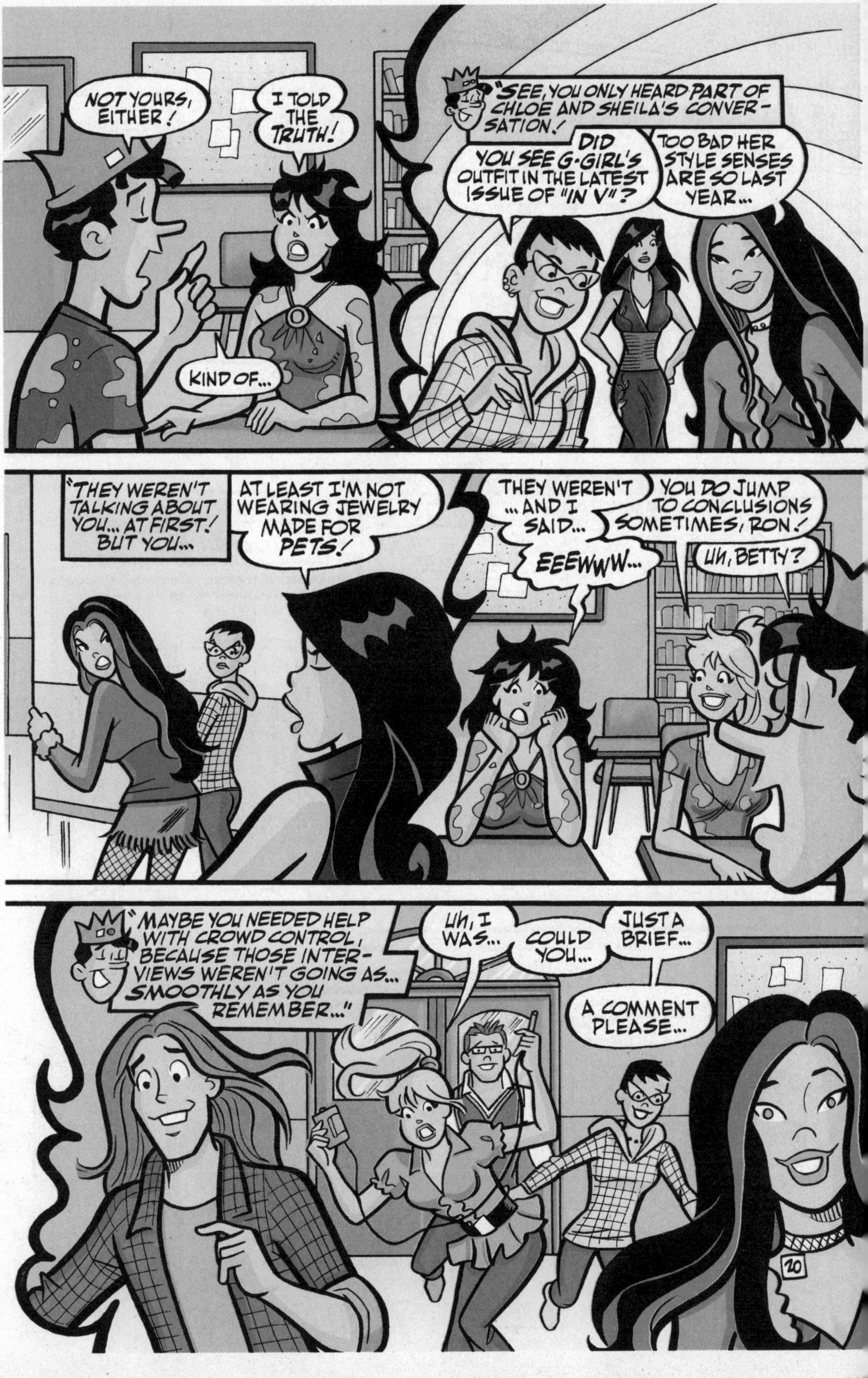
NOT YOURS, EITHER!
I TOLD THE TRUTH!
KIND OF...
"SEE, YOU ONLY HEARD PART OF CHLOE AND SHEILA'S CONVERSATION!
DID YOU SEE G-GIRL'S OUTFIT IN THE LATEST ISSUE OF "IN V"?
TOO BAD HER STYLE SENSES ARE SO LAST YEAR...
"THEY WEREN'T TALKING ABOUT YOU... AT FIRST! BUT YOU...
AT LEAST I'M NOT WEARING JEWELRY MADE FOR PETS!
THEY WEREN'T ...AND I SAID...
EEEWWW...
YOU DO JUMP TO CONCLUSIONS SOMETIMES, RON!
UH, BETTY?
"MAYBE YOU NEEDED HELP WITH CROWD CONTROL, BECAUSE THOSE INTERVIEWS WEREN'T GOING AS... SMOOTHLY AS YOU REMEMBER..."
UH, I WAS...
COULD YOU...
JUST A BRIEF...
A COMMENT PLEASE...
20

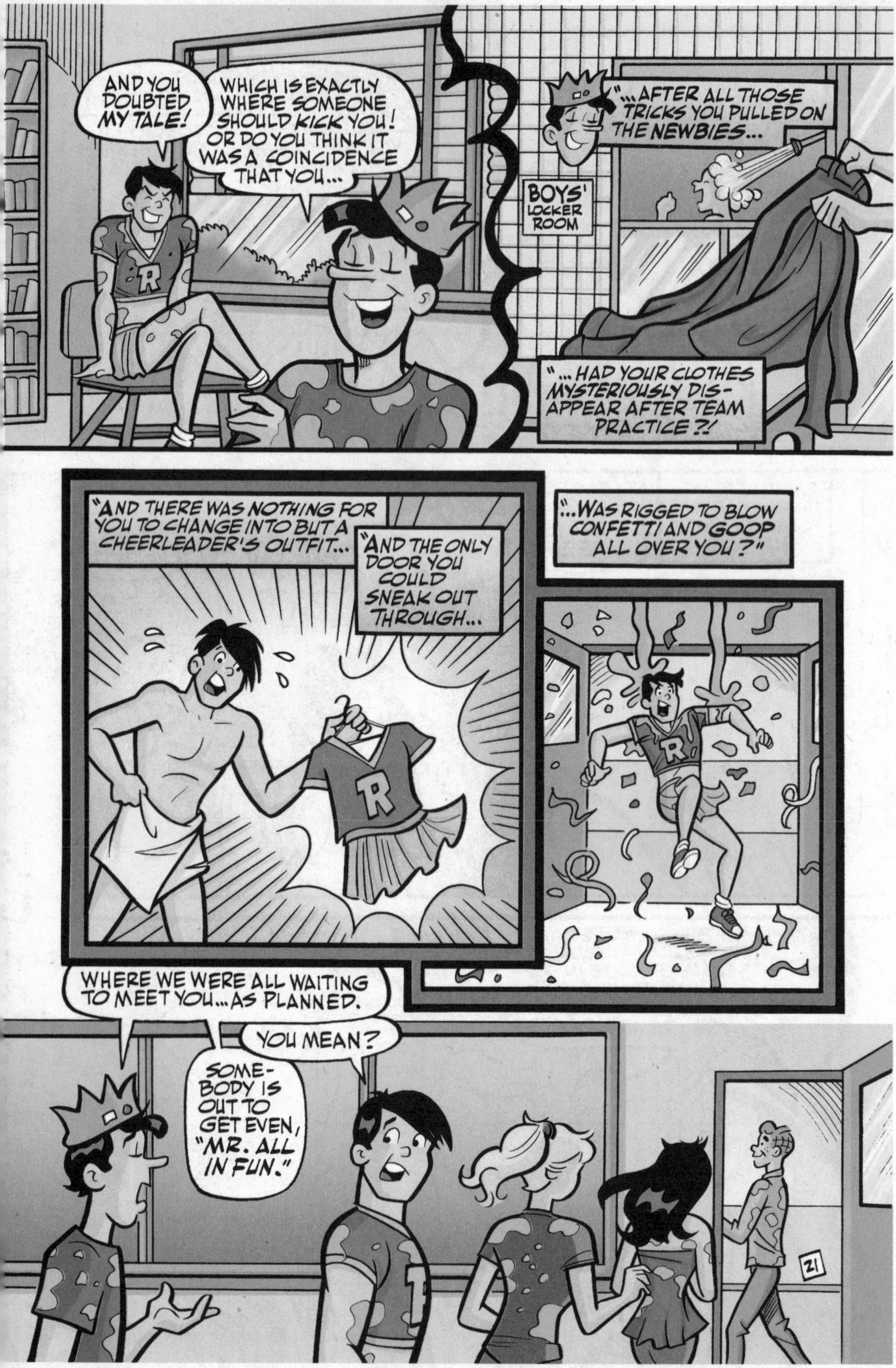
AND YOU DOUBTED MY TALE!
WHICH IS EXACTLY WHERE SOMEONE SHOULD KICK YOU! OR DO YOU THINK IT WAS A COINCIDENCE THAT YOU...
"...AFTER ALL THOSE TRICKS YOU PULLED ON THE NEWBIES...
BOYS' LOCKER ROOM
"...HAD YOUR CLOTHES MYSTERIOUSLY DIS-APPEAR AFTER TEAM PRACTICE?!
"AND THERE WAS NOTHING FOR YOU TO CHANGE INTO BUT A CHEERLEADER'S OUTFIT...
"AND THE ONLY DOOR YOU COULD SNEAK OUT THROUGH...
"...WAS RIGGED TO BLOW CONFETTI AND GOOP ALL OVER YOU?"
WHERE WE WERE ALL WAITING TO MEET YOU...AS PLANNED.
YOU MEAN?
SOME-BODY IS OUT TO GET EVEN, "MR. ALL IN FUN."
21

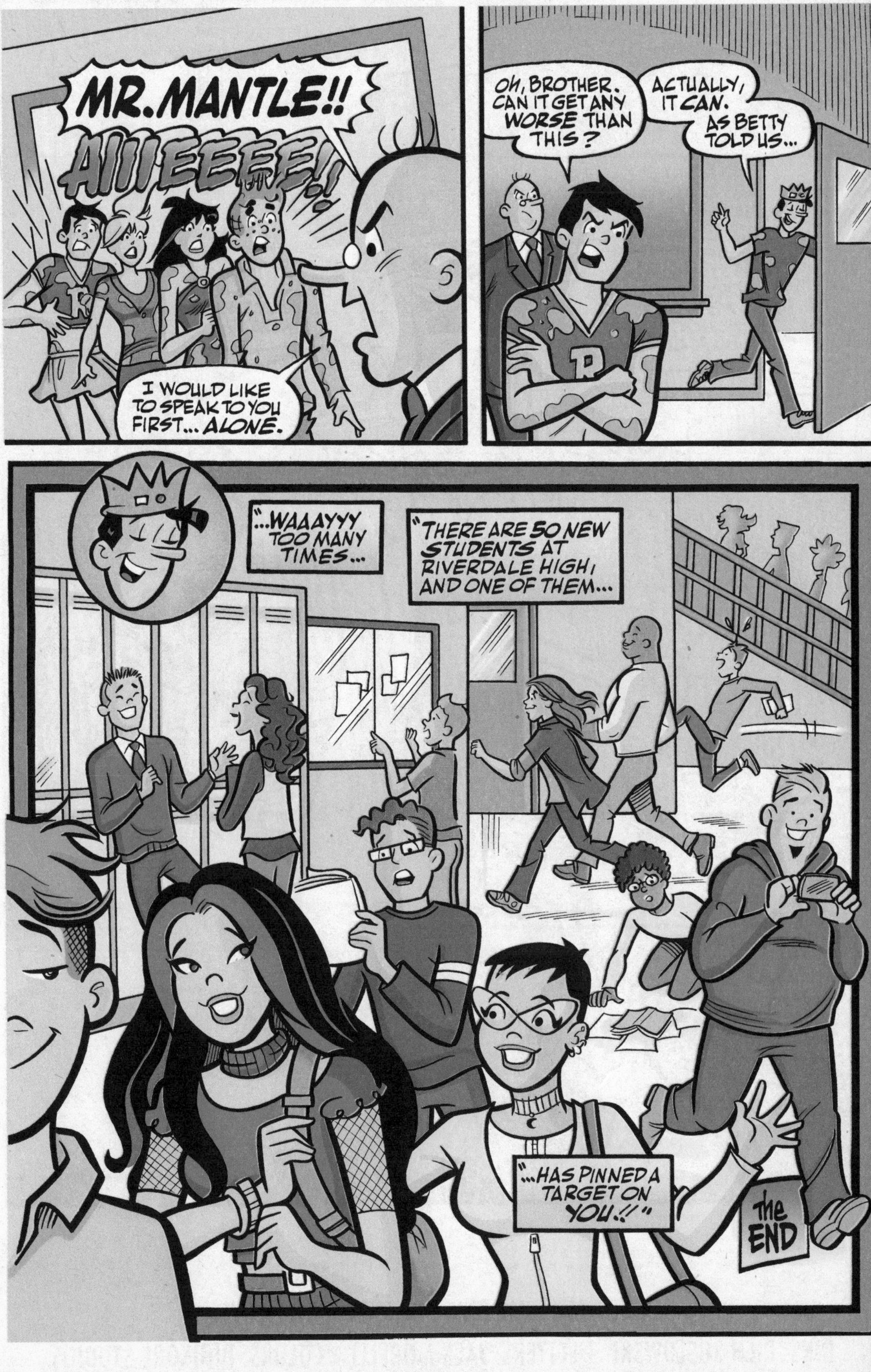
MR. MANTLE!!
AIIIEEEEE!!
I WOULD LIKE TO SPEAK TO YOU FIRST... ALONE.
OH, BROTHER. CAN IT GET ANY WORSE THAN THIS?
ACTUALLY, IT CAN.
AS BETTY TOLD US...
"...WAAAYYY TOO MANY TIMES...
"THERE ARE 50 NEW STUDENTS AT RIVERDALE HIGH, AND ONE OF THEM...
"...HAS PINNED A TARGET ON YOU!!"
the END

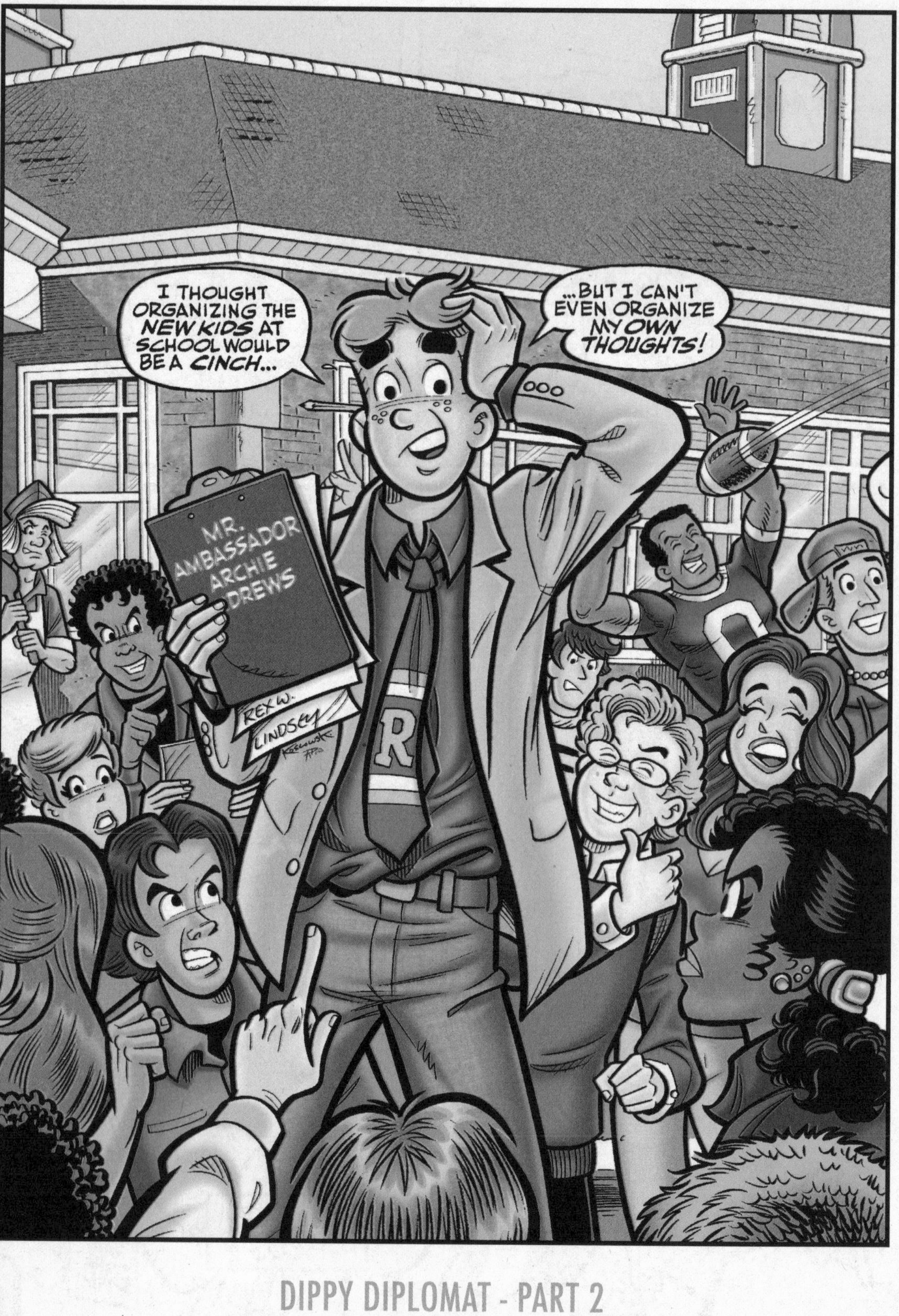
I THOUGHT ORGANIZING THE NEW KIDS AT SCHOOL WOULD BE A CINCH...
...BUT I CAN'T EVEN ORGANIZE MY OWN THOUGHTS!
MR. AMBASSADOR ARCHIE ANDREWS
REX W.
LINDSEY

DIPPY DIPLOMAT - PART 2

SCRIPT: ALEX SIMMONS PENCILS: DAN PARENT

INKS: RICH KOSLOWSKI LETTERS: JACK MORELLI COLORS: DIGIKORE STUDIOS

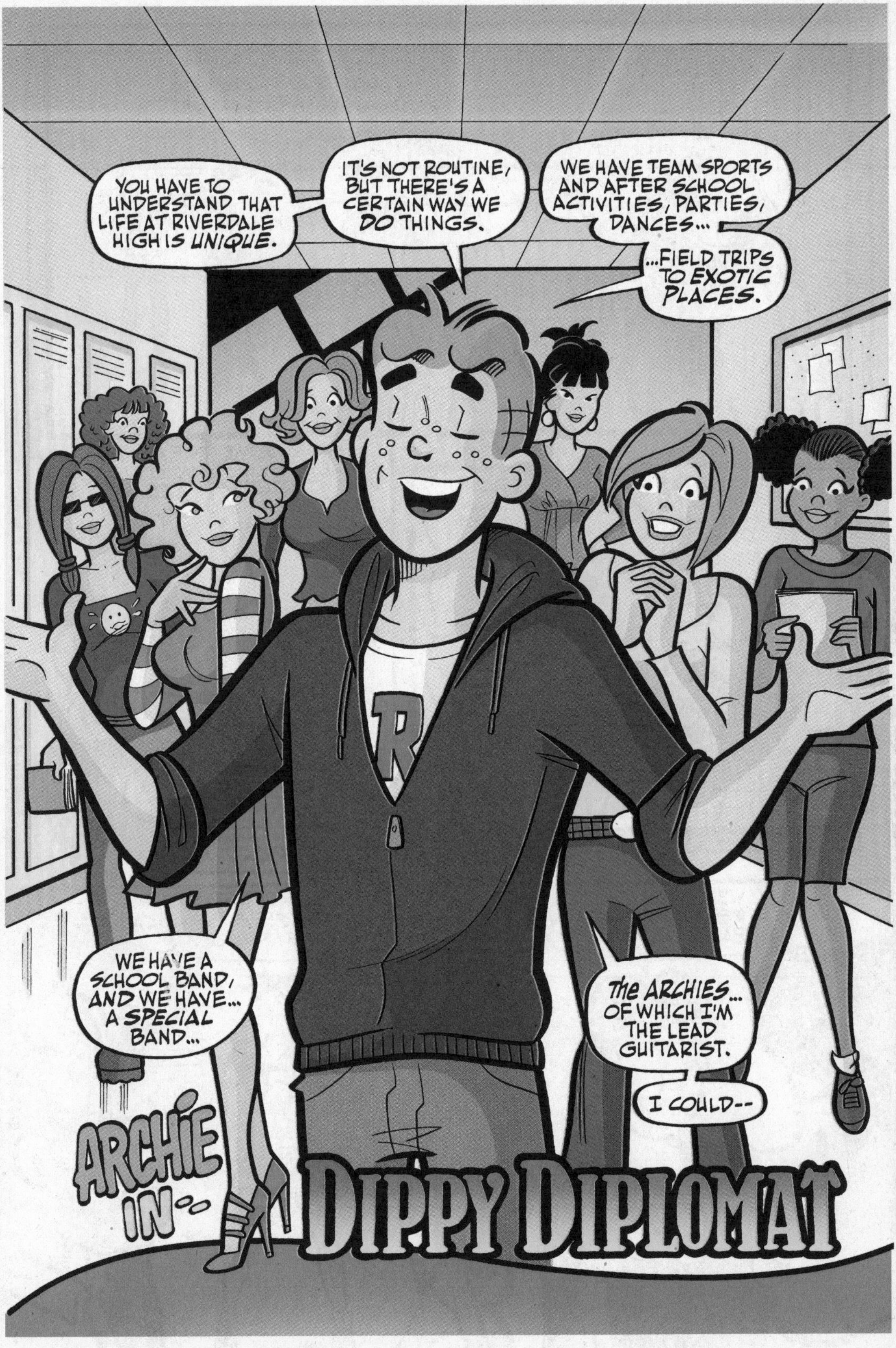
YOU HAVE TO UNDERSTAND THAT LIFE AT RIVERDALE HIGH IS *UNIQUE*.
IT'S NOT ROUTINE, BUT THERE'S A CERTAIN WAY WE *DO* THINGS.
WE HAVE TEAM SPORTS AND AFTER SCHOOL ACTIVITIES, PARTIES, DANCES...
...FIELD TRIPS TO *EXOTIC PLACES*.
WE HAVE A SCHOOL BAND, AND WE HAVE... A *SPECIAL* BAND...
The ARCHIES... OF WHICH I'M THE LEAD GUITARIST.
I COULD--
ARCHIE IN...
DIPPY DIPLOMAT

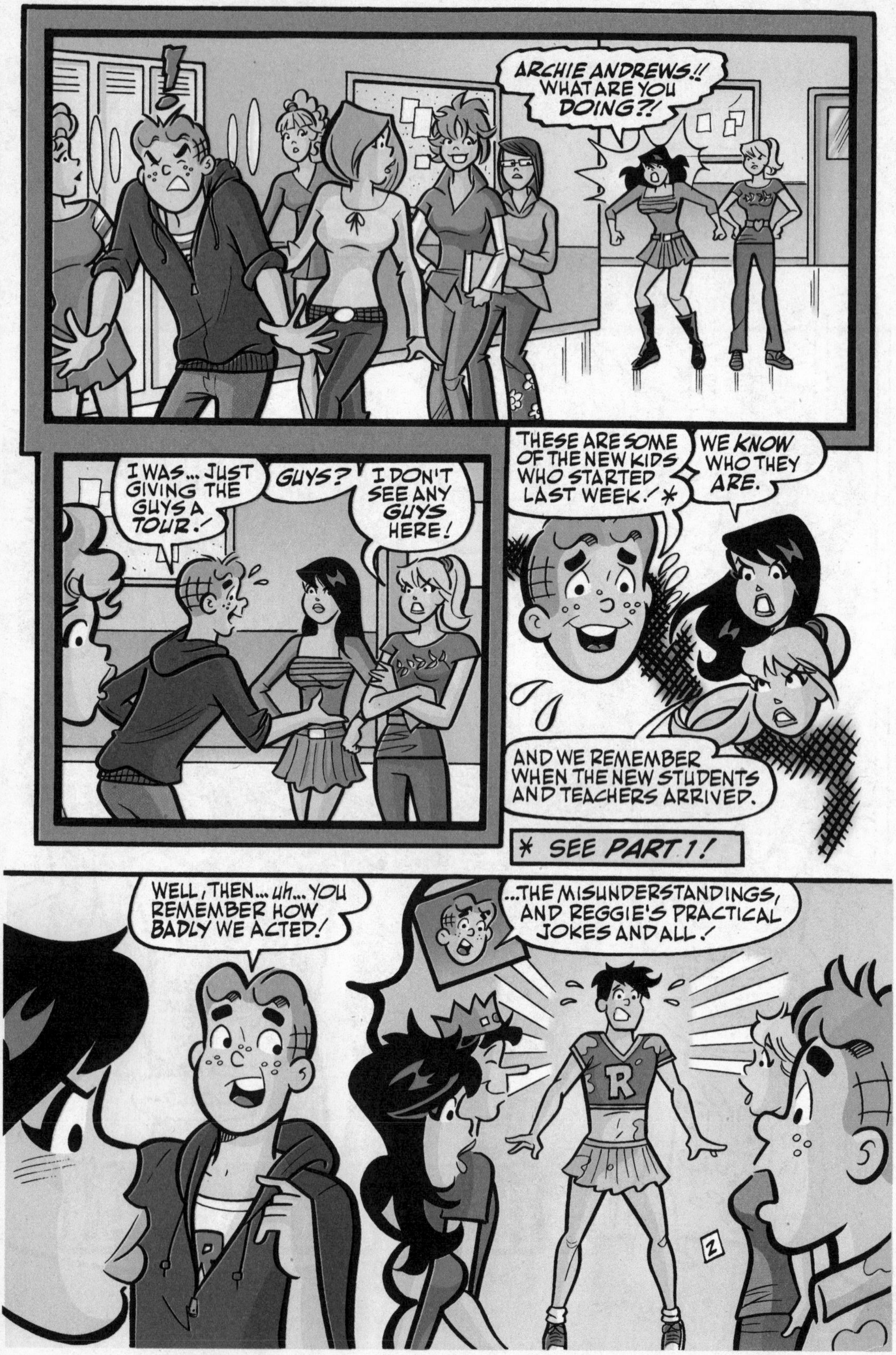

ARCHIE ANDREWS!! WHAT ARE YOU DOING?!
I WAS... JUST GIVING THE GUYS A TOUR!
GUYS?
I DON'T SEE ANY GUYS HERE!
THESE ARE SOME OF THE NEW KIDS WHO STARTED LAST WEEK! *
WE KNOW WHO THEY ARE.
AND WE REMEMBER WHEN THE NEW STUDENTS AND TEACHERS ARRIVED.
* SEE PART 1!
WELL, THEN... uh... YOU REMEMBER HOW BADLY WE ACTED!
...THE MISUNDERSTANDINGS, AND REGGIE'S PRACTICAL JOKES AND ALL!

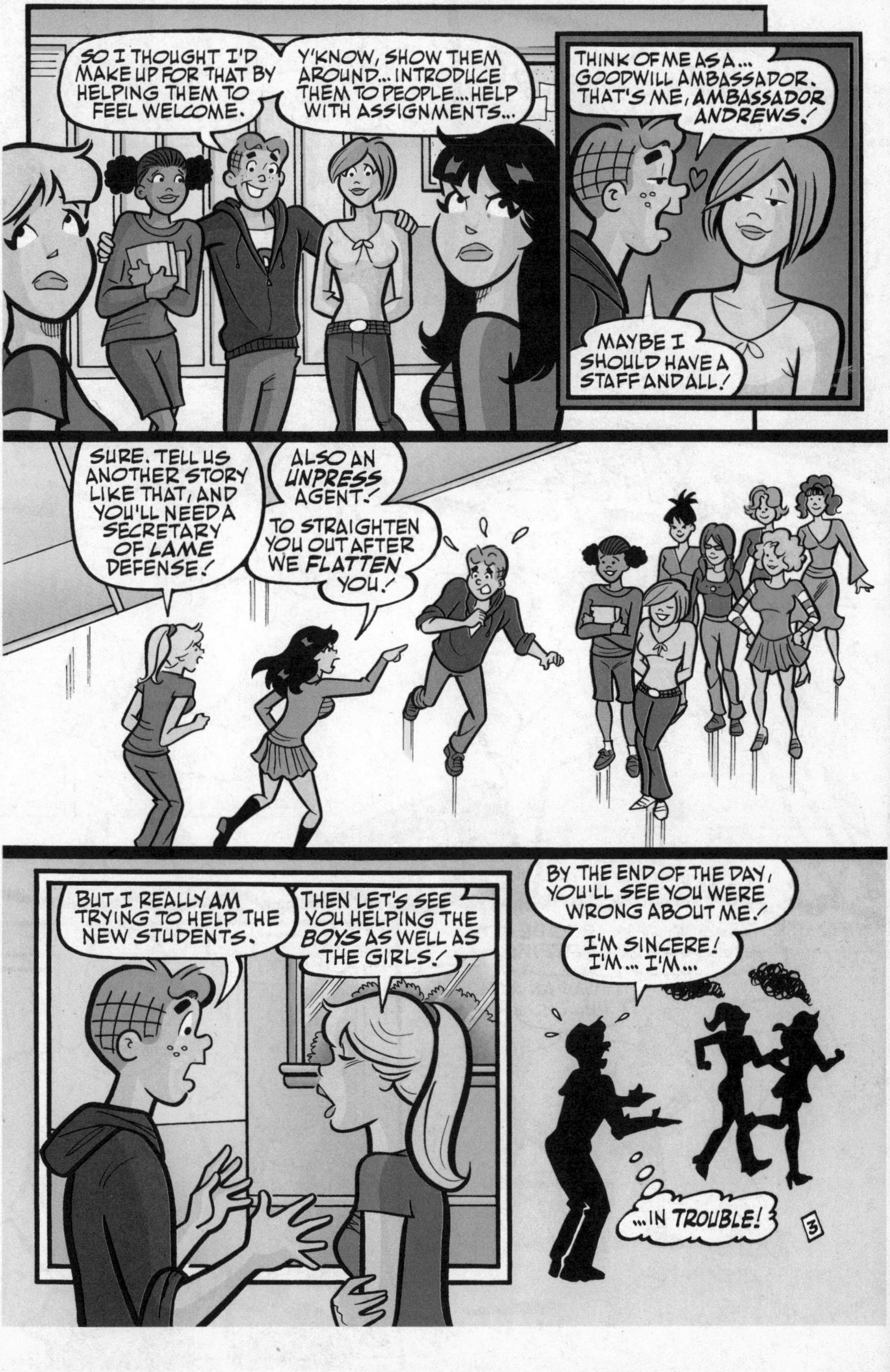
SO I THOUGHT I'D MAKE UP FOR THAT BY HELPING THEM TO FEEL WELCOME.
Y'KNOW, SHOW THEM AROUND... INTRODUCE THEM TO PEOPLE... HELP WITH ASSIGNMENTS...
THINK OF ME AS A... GOODWILL AMBASSADOR. THAT'S ME, AMBASSADOR ANDREWS!
MAYBE I SHOULD HAVE A STAFF AND ALL!
SURE. TELL US ANOTHER STORY LIKE THAT, AND YOU'LL NEED A SECRETARY OF LAME DEFENSE!
ALSO AN UNPRESS AGENT!
TO STRAIGHTEN YOU OUT AFTER WE FLATTEN YOU!
BUT I REALLY AM TRYING TO HELP THE NEW STUDENTS.
THEN LET'S SEE YOU HELPING THE BOYS AS WELL AS THE GIRLS!
BY THE END OF THE DAY, YOU'LL SEE YOU WERE WRONG ABOUT ME!
I'M SINCERE! I'M... I'M...
...IN TROUBLE!
3

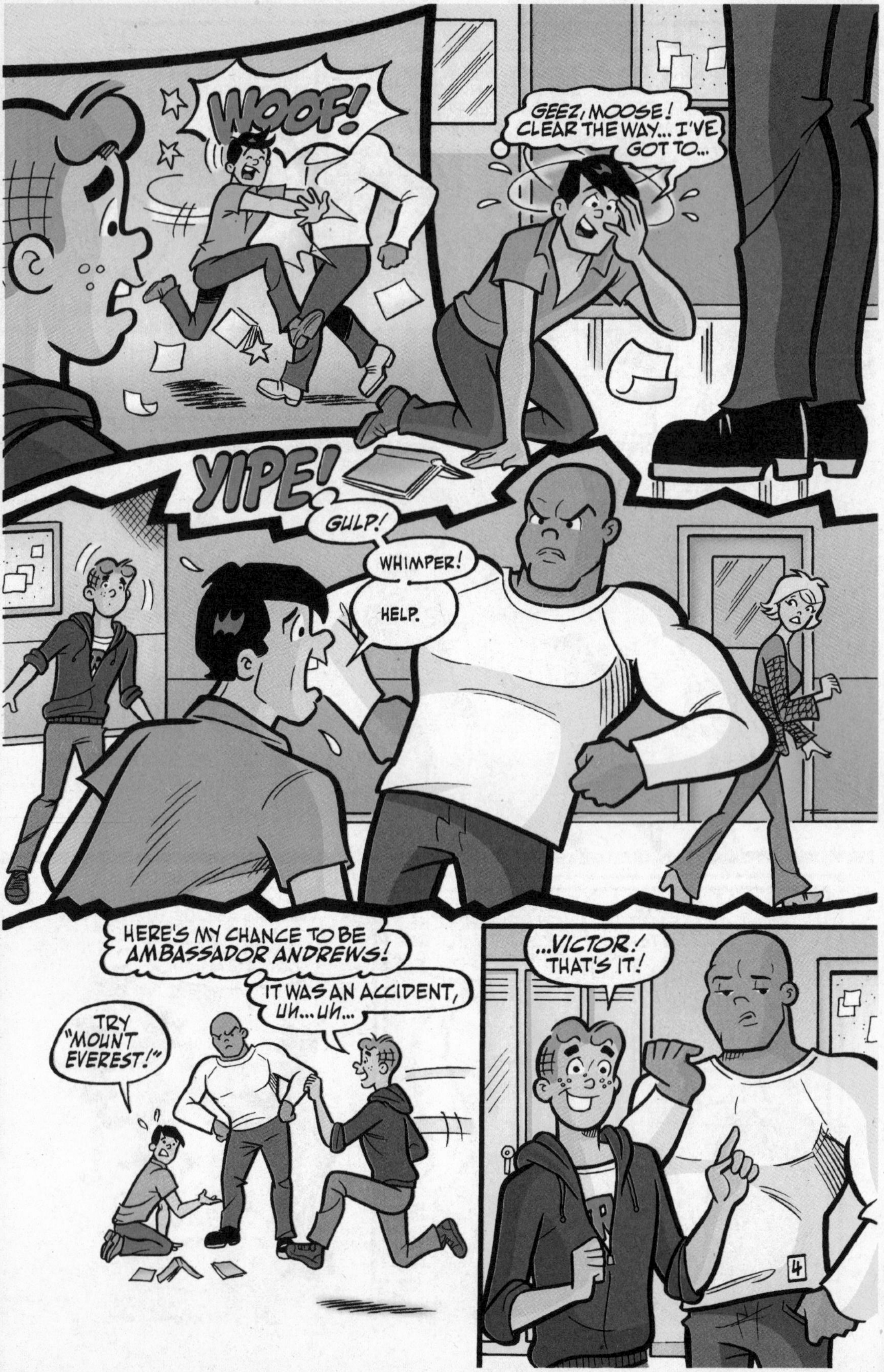
WOOF!
GEEZ, MOOSE! CLEAR THE WAY... I'VE GOT TO...
YIPE!
GULP!
WHIMPER!
HELP.
HERE'S MY CHANCE TO BE AMBASSADOR ANDREWS!
IT WAS AN ACCIDENT, UH... UH...
TRY "MOUNT EVEREST!"
...VICTOR! THAT'S IT!
4

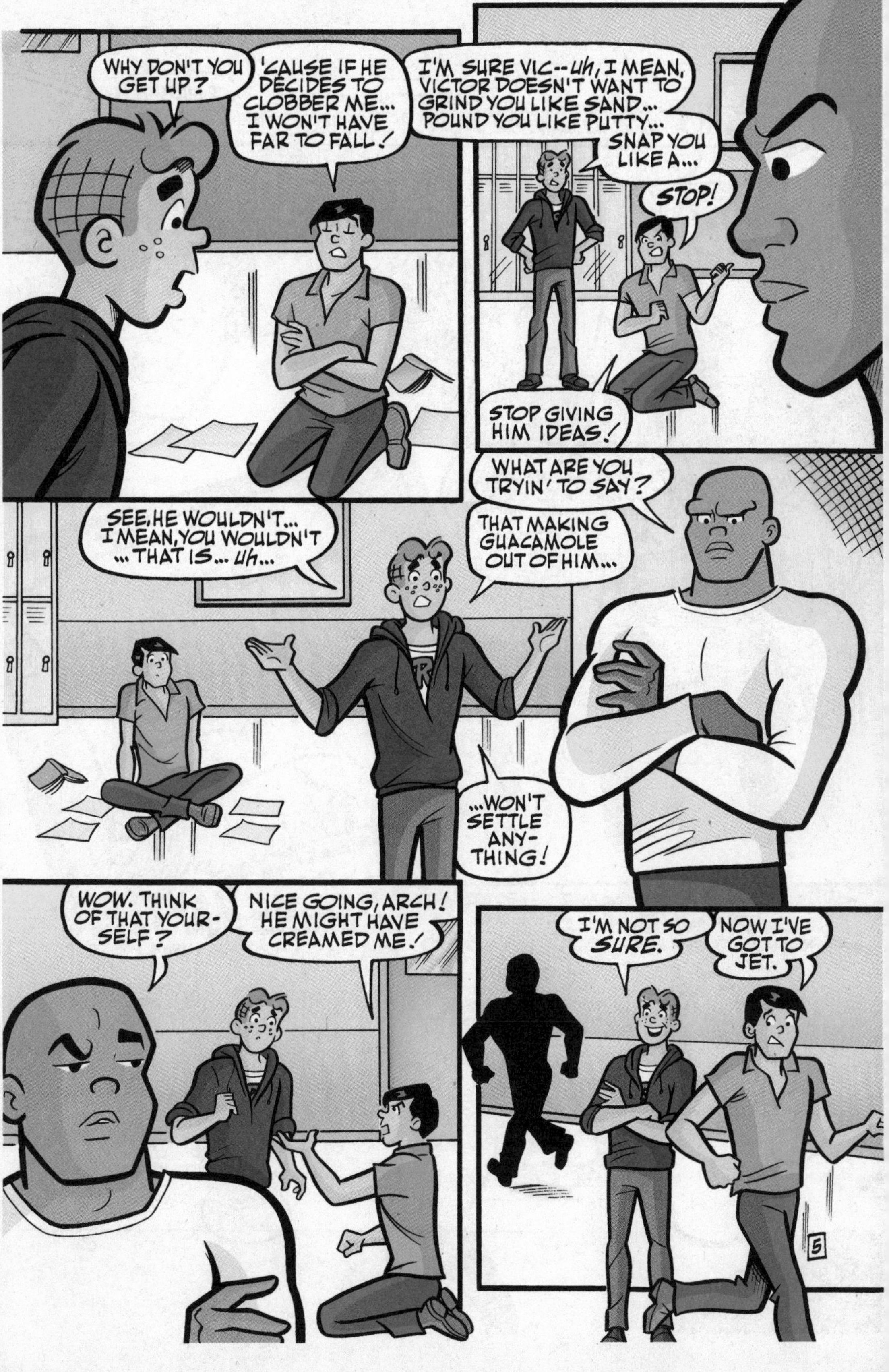
WHY DON'T YOU GET UP?
'CAUSE IF HE DECIDES TO CLOBBER ME... I WON'T HAVE FAR TO FALL!
I'M SURE VIC--uh, I MEAN, VICTOR DOESN'T WANT TO GRIND YOU LIKE SAND... POUND YOU LIKE PUTTY...
SNAP YOU LIKE A...
STOP!
STOP GIVING HIM IDEAS!
SEE, HE WOULDN'T... I MEAN, YOU WOULDN'T ...THAT IS... uh...
WHAT ARE YOU TRYIN' TO SAY?
THAT MAKING GUACAMOLE OUT OF HIM...
...WON'T SETTLE ANY-THING!
WOW. THINK OF THAT YOUR-SELF?
NICE GOING, ARCH! HE MIGHT HAVE CREAMED ME!
I'M NOT SO SURE.
NOW I'VE GOT TO JET.
5

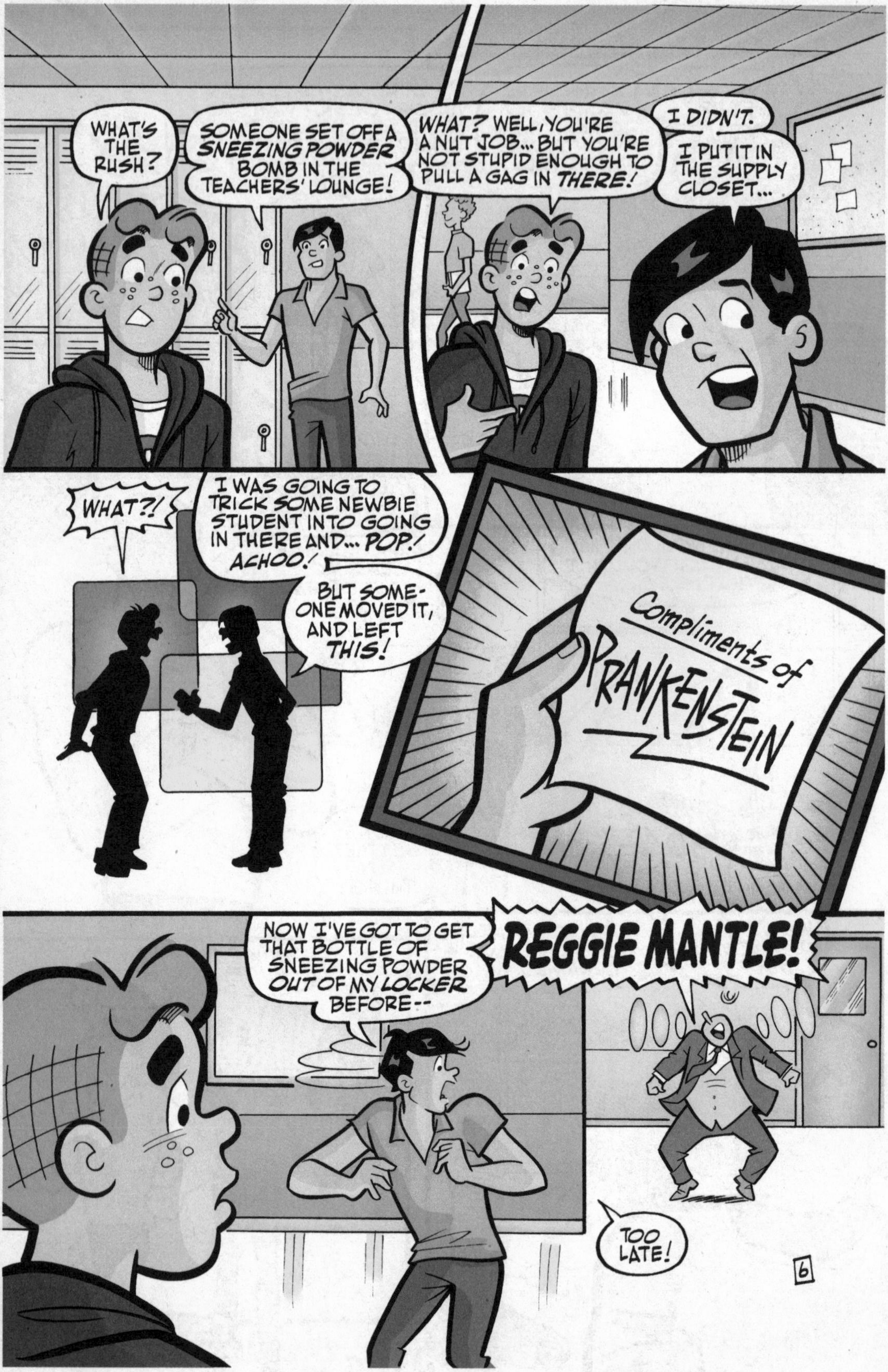
WHAT'S THE RUSH?
SOMEONE SET OFF A SNEEZING POWDER BOMB IN THE TEACHERS' LOUNGE!
WHAT? WELL, YOU'RE A NUT JOB... BUT YOU'RE NOT STUPID ENOUGH TO PULL A GAG IN THERE!
I DIDN'T.
I PUT IT IN THE SUPPLY CLOSET...
WHAT?!
I WAS GOING TO TRICK SOME NEWBIE STUDENT INTO GOING IN THERE AND... POP! ACHOO!
BUT SOME-ONE MOVED IT, AND LEFT THIS!
Compliments of PRANKENSTEIN
NOW I'VE GOT TO GET THAT BOTTLE OF SNEEZING POWDER OUT OF MY LOCKER BEFORE--
REGGIE MANTLE!
TOO LATE!
6

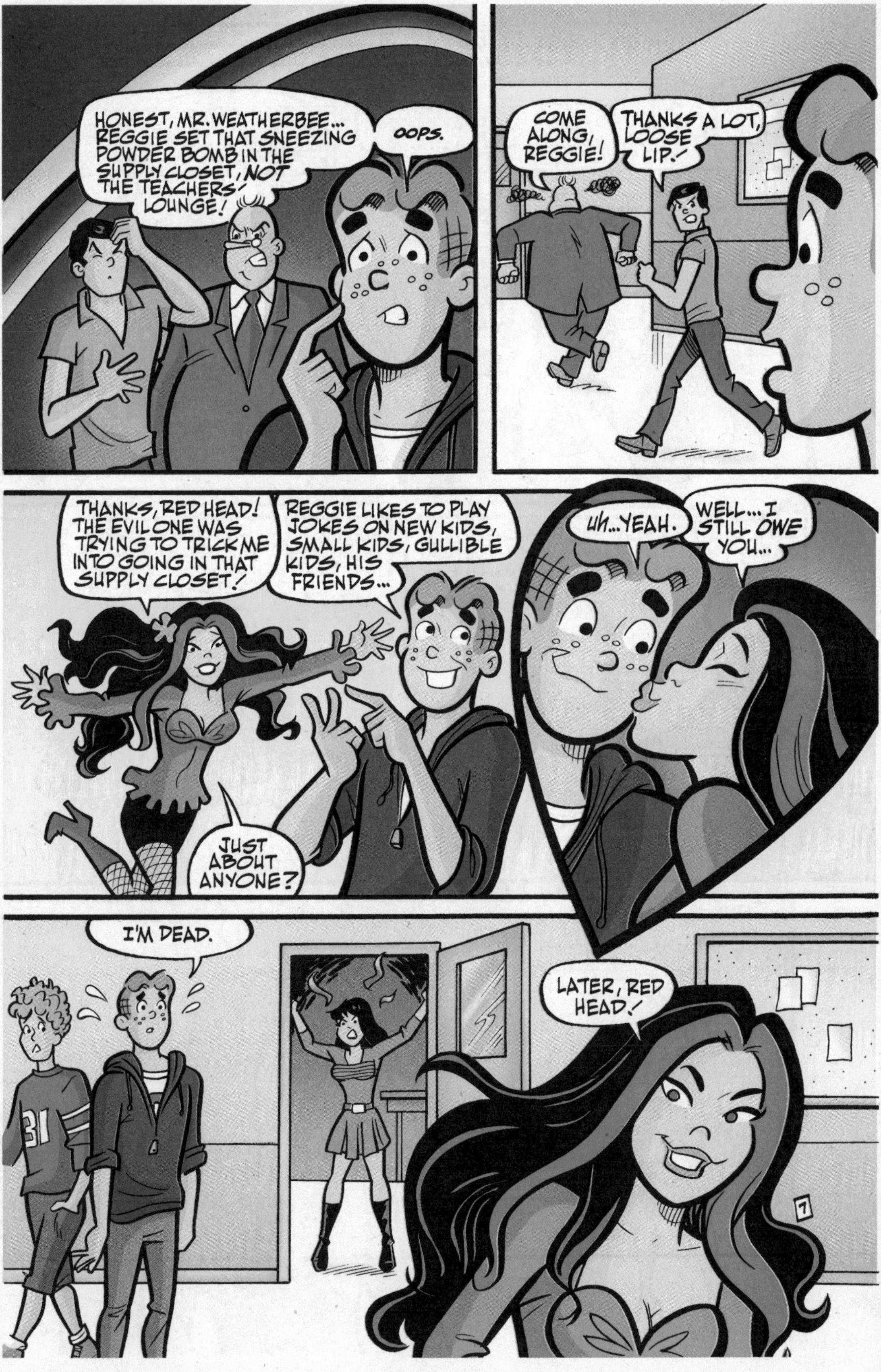
HONEST, MR. WEATHERBEE... REGGIE SET THAT SNEEZING POWDER BOMB IN THE SUPPLY CLOSET, NOT THE TEACHERS' LOUNGE!
OOPS.
COME ALONG, REGGIE!
THANKS A LOT, LOOSE LIP!
THANKS, RED HEAD! THE EVIL ONE WAS TRYING TO TRICK ME INTO GOING IN THAT SUPPLY CLOSET!
REGGIE LIKES TO PLAY JOKES ON NEW KIDS, SMALL KIDS, GULLIBLE KIDS, HIS FRIENDS...
JUST ABOUT ANYONE?
UH...YEAH.
WELL... I STILL OWE YOU...
I'M DEAD.
LATER, RED HEAD!
7

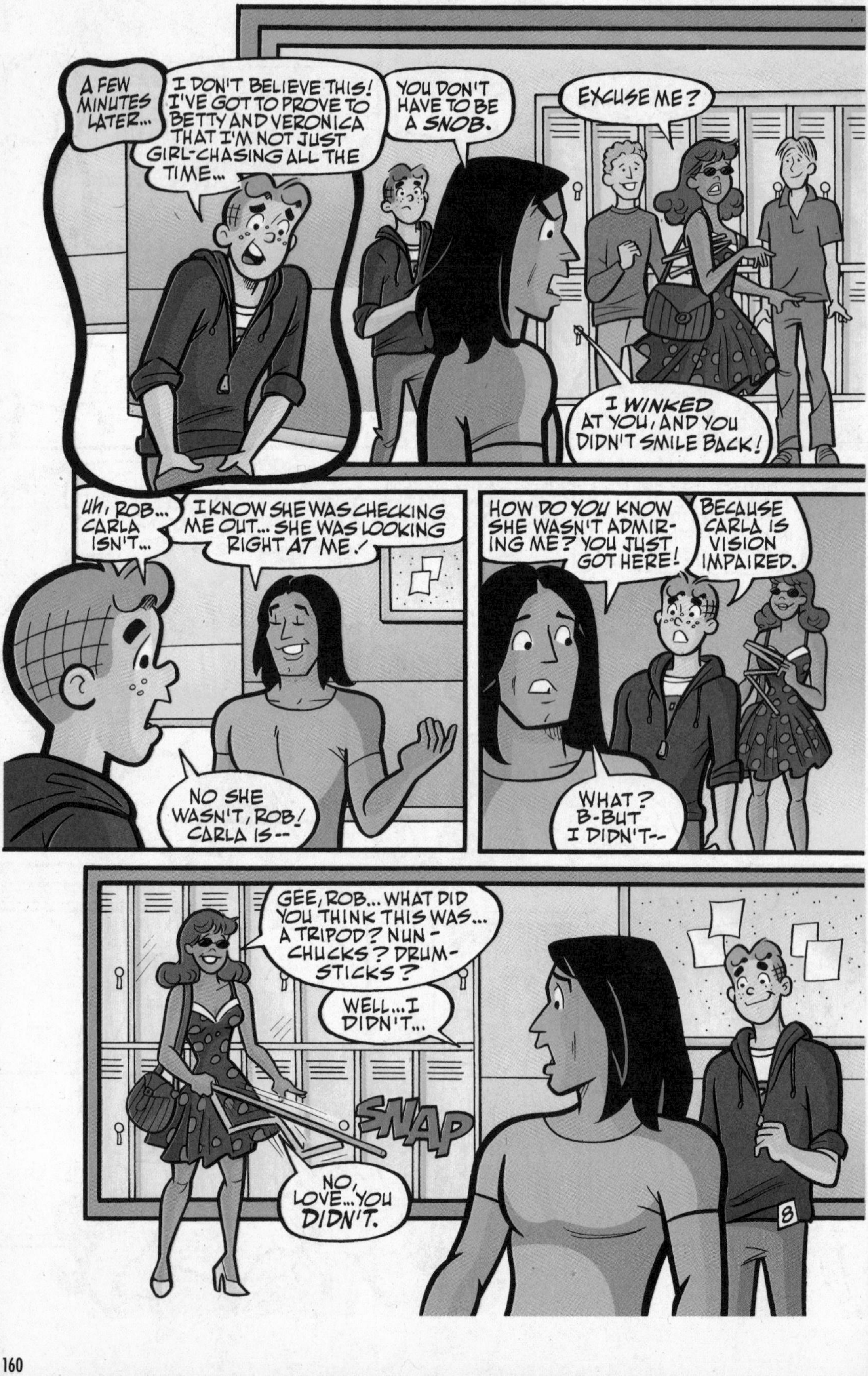
A FEW MINUTES LATER...
I DON'T BELIEVE THIS! I'VE GOT TO PROVE TO BETTY AND VERONICA THAT I'M NOT JUST GIRL-CHASING ALL THE TIME...
YOU DON'T HAVE TO BE A SNOB.
EXCUSE ME?
I WINKED AT YOU, AND YOU DIDN'T SMILE BACK!
UH, ROB... CARLA ISN'T...
I KNOW SHE WAS CHECKING ME OUT... SHE WAS LOOKING RIGHT AT ME!
NO SHE WASN'T, ROB! CARLA IS--
HOW DO YOU KNOW SHE WASN'T ADMIRING ME? YOU JUST GOT HERE!
BECAUSE CARLA IS VISION IMPAIRED.
WHAT? B-BUT I DIDN'T--
GEE, ROB... WHAT DID YOU THINK THIS WAS... A TRIPOD? NUN-CHUCKS? DRUM-STICKS?
WELL...I DIDN'T...
SNAP
NO, LOVE...YOU DIDN'T.
8

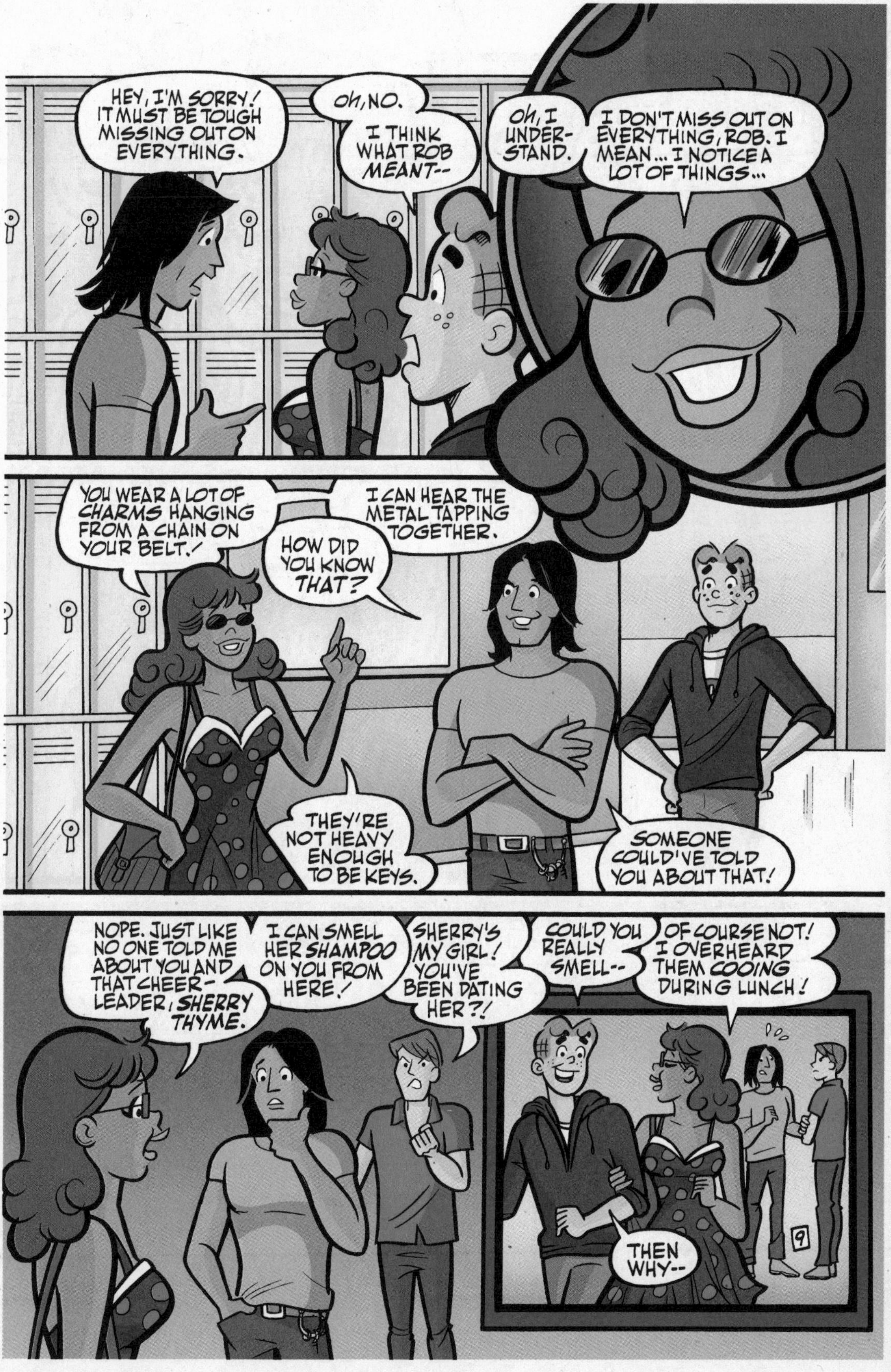
HEY, I'M SORRY! IT MUST BE TOUGH MISSING OUT ON EVERYTHING.
OH, NO.
I THINK WHAT ROB MEANT--
OH, I UNDER-STAND.
I DON'T MISS OUT ON EVERYTHING, ROB. I MEAN... I NOTICE A LOT OF THINGS...
YOU WEAR A LOT OF CHARMS HANGING FROM A CHAIN ON YOUR BELT.!
HOW DID YOU KNOW THAT?
I CAN HEAR THE METAL TAPPING TOGETHER.
THEY'RE NOT HEAVY ENOUGH TO BE KEYS.
SOMEONE COULD'VE TOLD YOU ABOUT THAT!
NOPE. JUST LIKE NO ONE TOLD ME ABOUT YOU AND THAT CHEER-LEADER, SHERRY THYME.
I CAN SMELL HER SHAMPOO ON YOU FROM HERE!
SHERRY'S MY GIRL! YOU'VE BEEN DATING HER?!
COULD YOU REALLY SMELL--
OF COURSE NOT! I OVERHEARD THEM COOING DURING LUNCH!
THEN WHY--
9

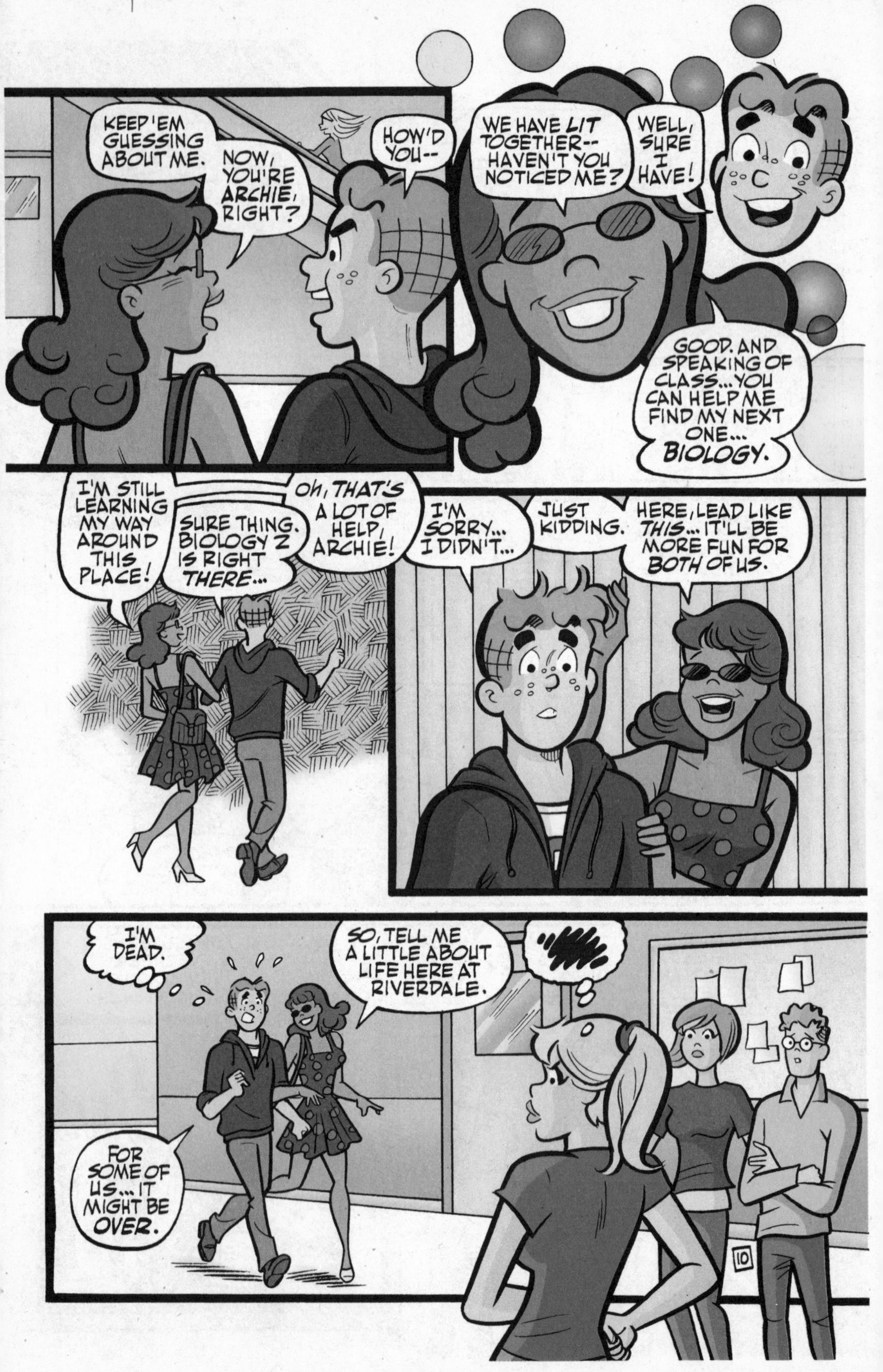
KEEP 'EM GUESSING ABOUT ME.
NOW, YOU'RE ARCHIE, RIGHT?
HOW'D YOU--
WE HAVE LIT TOGETHER-- HAVEN'T YOU NOTICED ME?
WELL, SURE I HAVE!
GOOD. AND SPEAKING OF CLASS... YOU CAN HELP ME FIND MY NEXT ONE... BIOLOGY.
I'M STILL LEARNING MY WAY AROUND THIS PLACE!
SURE THING. BIOLOGY 2 IS RIGHT THERE...
OH, THAT'S A LOT OF HELP, ARCHIE!
I'M SORRY... I DIDN'T...
JUST KIDDING.
HERE, LEAD LIKE THIS... IT'LL BE MORE FUN FOR BOTH OF US.
I'M DEAD.
SO, TELL ME A LITTLE ABOUT LIFE HERE AT RIVERDALE.
FOR SOME OF US... IT MIGHT BE OVER.
10

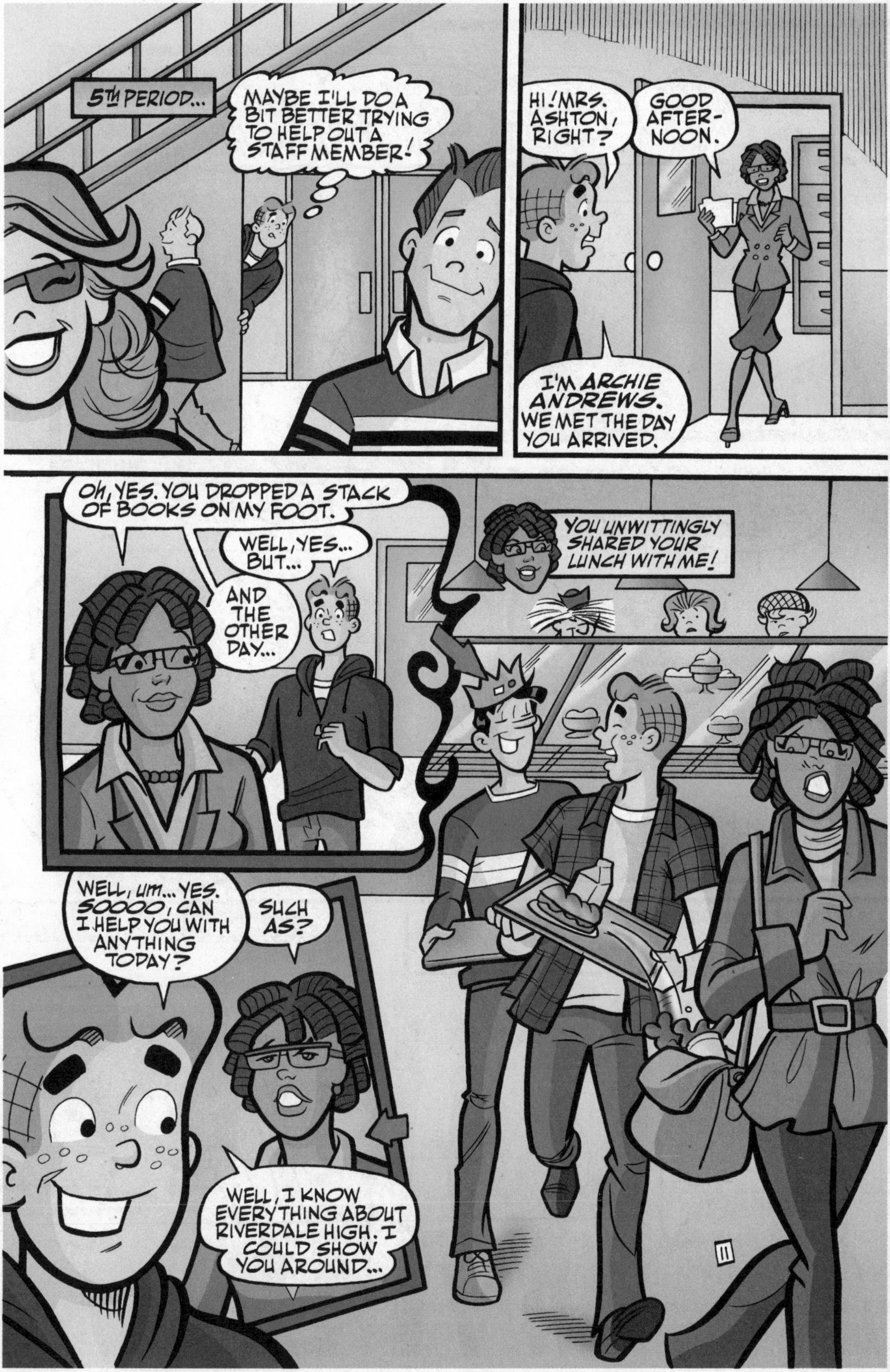
5th PERIOD...
MAYBE I'LL DO A BIT BETTER TRYING TO HELP OUT A STAFF MEMBER!
HI! MRS. ASHTON, RIGHT?
GOOD AFTER-NOON.
I'M ARCHIE ANDREWS. WE MET THE DAY YOU ARRIVED.
OH, YES. YOU DROPPED A STACK OF BOOKS ON MY FOOT.
WELL, YES... BUT...
AND THE OTHER DAY...
YOU UNWITTINGLY SHARED YOUR LUNCH WITH ME!
WELL, UM... YES. SOOOO, CAN I HELP YOU WITH ANYTHING TODAY?
SUCH AS?
WELL, I KNOW EVERYTHING ABOUT RIVERDALE HIGH. I COULD SHOW YOU AROUND...

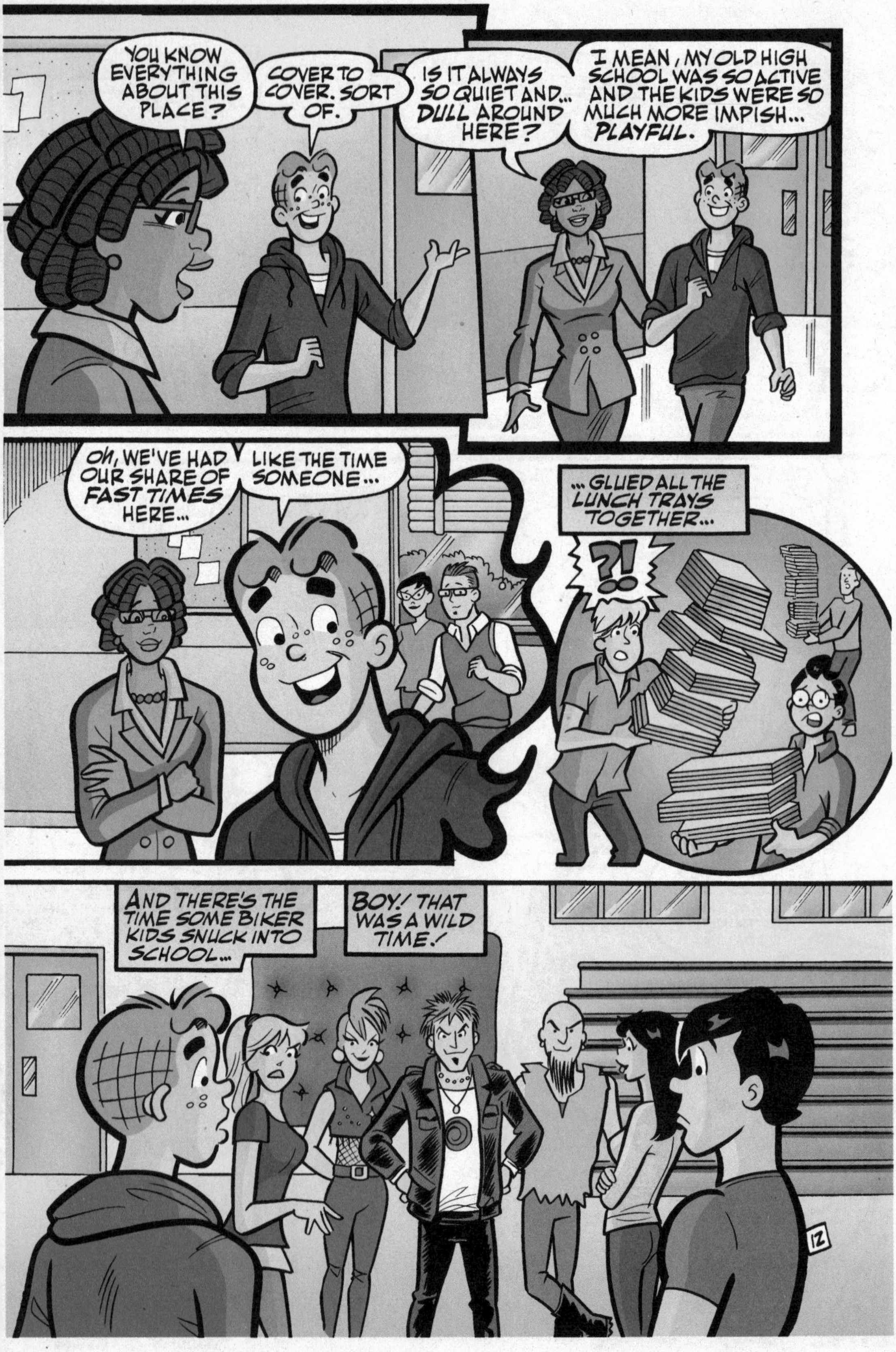

YOU KNOW EVERYTHING ABOUT THIS PLACE?
COVER TO COVER. SORT OF.
IS IT ALWAYS SO QUIET AND... DULL AROUND HERE?
I MEAN, MY OLD HIGH SCHOOL WAS SO ACTIVE AND THE KIDS WERE SO MUCH MORE IMPISH... PLAYFUL.
OH, WE'VE HAD OUR SHARE OF FAST TIMES HERE...
LIKE THE TIME SOMEONE...
...GLUED ALL THE LUNCH TRAYS TOGETHER...
?!
AND THERE'S THE TIME SOME BIKER KIDS SNUCK INTO SCHOOL...
BOY! THAT WAS A WILD TIME!
12

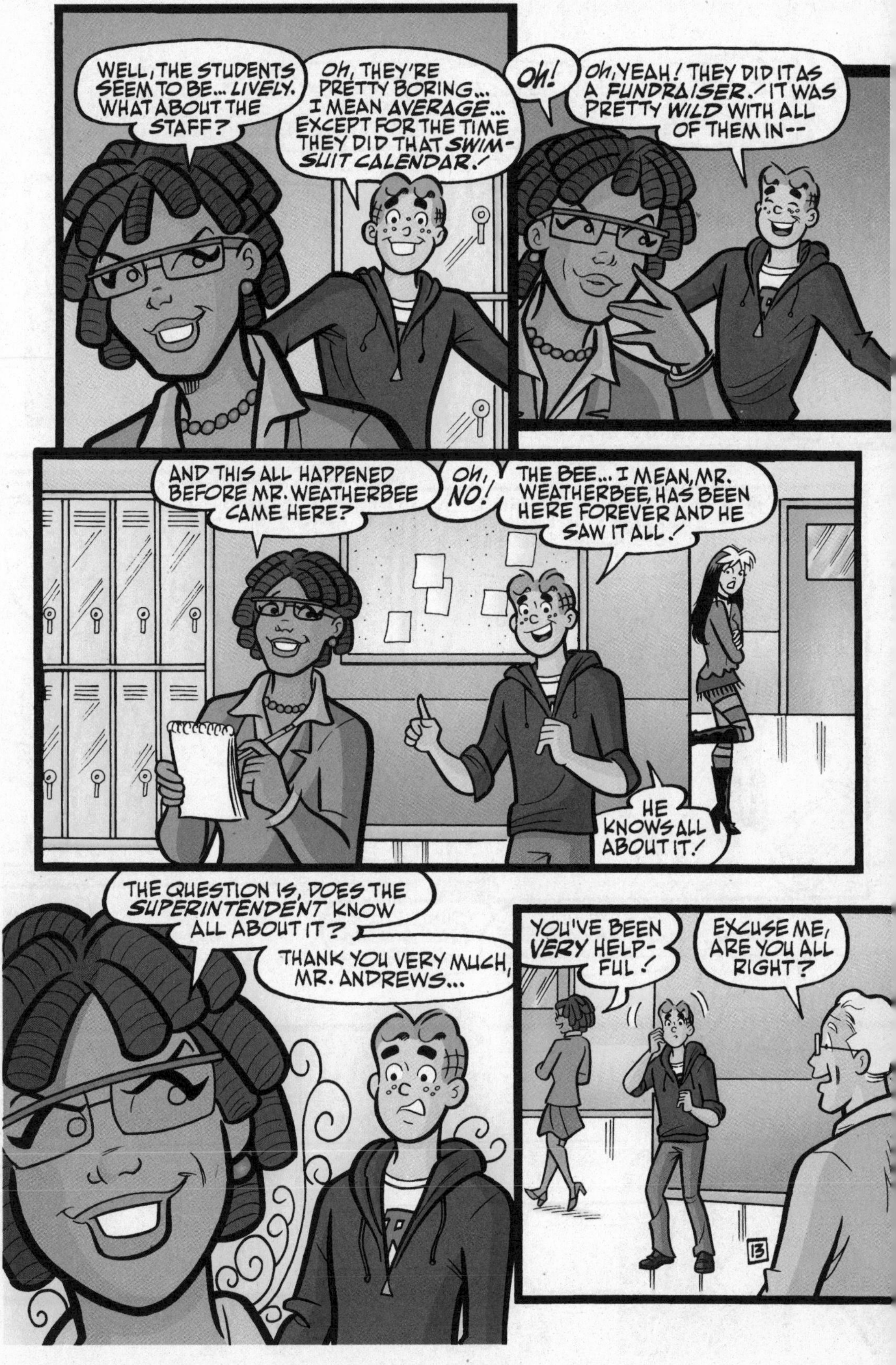
WELL, THE STUDENTS SEEM TO BE... LIVELY. WHAT ABOUT THE STAFF?
OH, THEY'RE PRETTY BORING... I MEAN AVERAGE... EXCEPT FOR THE TIME THEY DID THAT SWIM-SUIT CALENDAR!
OH!
OH, YEAH! THEY DID IT AS A FUNDRAISER! IT WAS PRETTY WILD WITH ALL OF THEM IN--
AND THIS ALL HAPPENED BEFORE MR. WEATHERBEE CAME HERE?
OH, NO!
THE BEE... I MEAN, MR. WEATHERBEE, HAS BEEN HERE FOREVER AND HE SAW IT ALL!
HE KNOWS ALL ABOUT IT!
THE QUESTION IS, DOES THE SUPERINTENDENT KNOW ALL ABOUT IT?
THANK YOU VERY MUCH, MR. ANDREWS...
YOU'VE BEEN VERY HELP-FUL!
EXCUSE ME, ARE YOU ALL RIGHT?
13

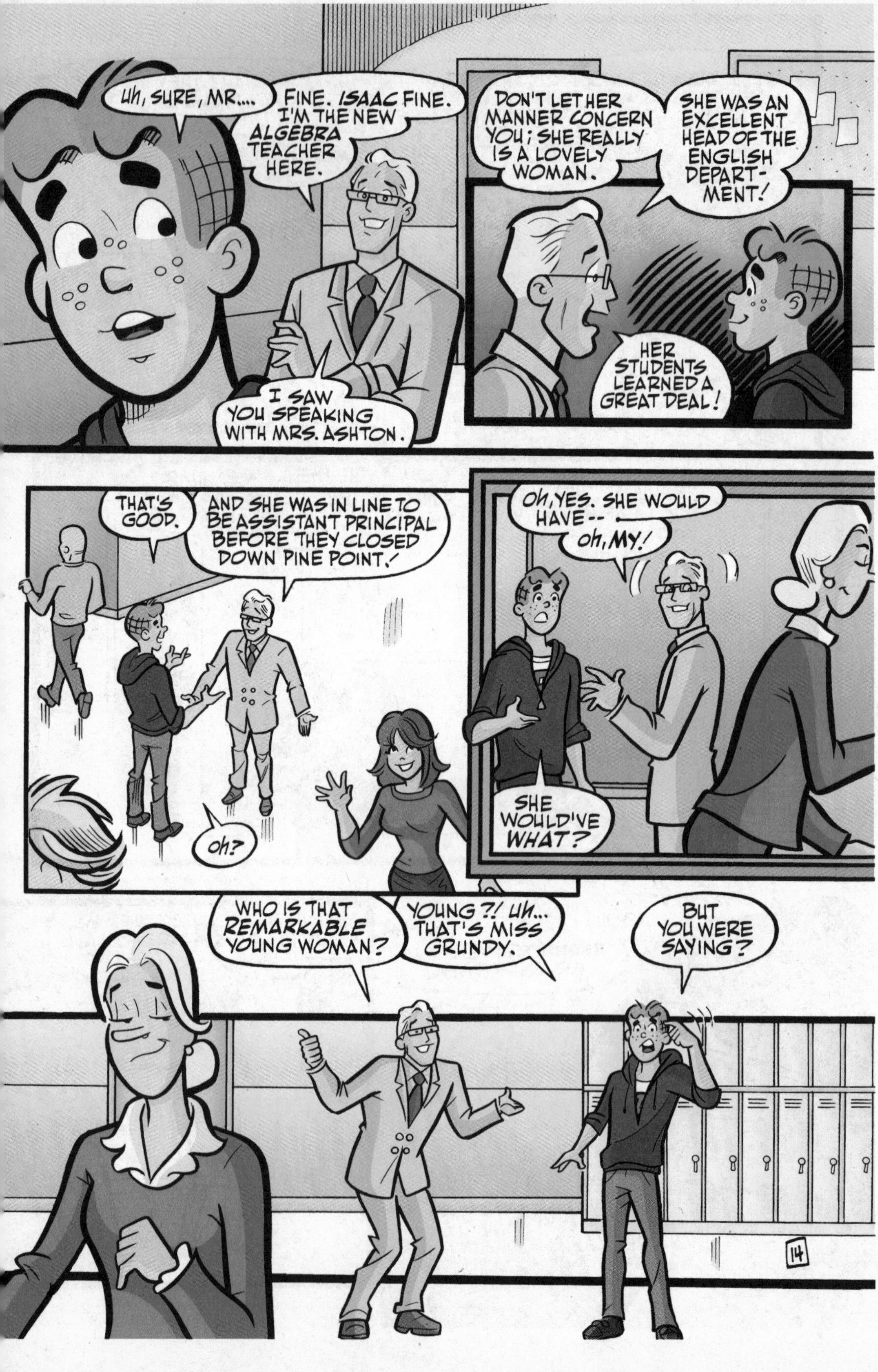

UH, SURE, MR....
FINE. ISAAC FINE. I'M THE NEW ALGEBRA TEACHER HERE.
I SAW YOU SPEAKING WITH MRS. ASHTON.
DON'T LET HER MANNER CONCERN YOU; SHE REALLY IS A LOVELY WOMAN.
SHE WAS AN EXCELLENT HEAD OF THE ENGLISH DEPARTMENT!
HER STUDENTS LEARNED A GREAT DEAL!
THAT'S GOOD.
AND SHE WAS IN LINE TO BE ASSISTANT PRINCIPAL BEFORE THEY CLOSED DOWN PINE POINT!
OH?
OH, YES. SHE WOULD HAVE --
OH, MY!
SHE WOULD'VE WHAT?
WHO IS THAT REMARKABLE YOUNG WOMAN?
YOUNG?! UH... THAT'S MISS GRUNDY.
BUT YOU WERE SAYING?
14

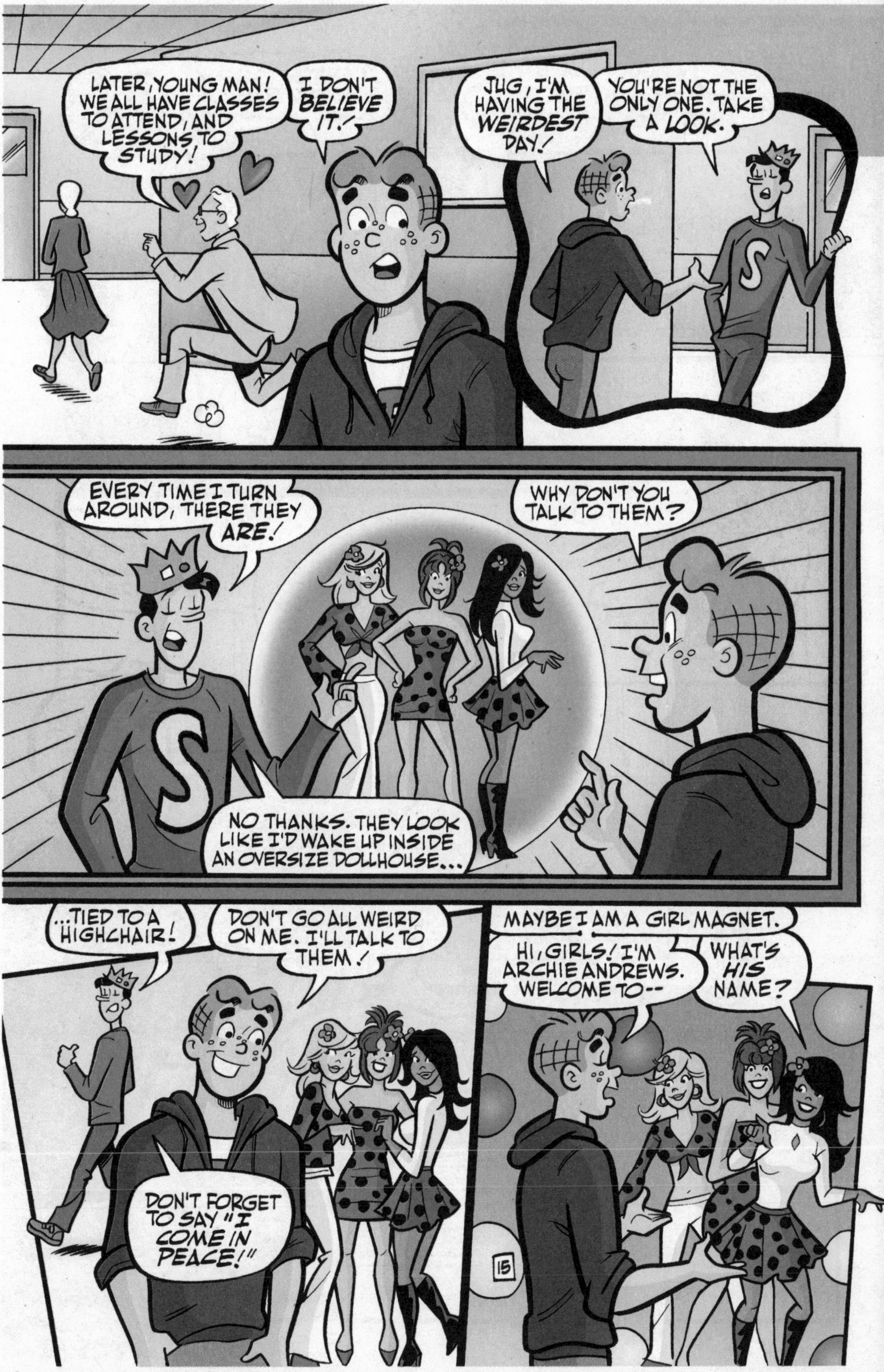
LATER, YOUNG MAN! WE ALL HAVE CLASSES TO ATTEND, AND LESSONS TO STUDY!
I DON'T BELIEVE IT!
JUG, I'M HAVING THE WEIRDEST DAY!
YOU'RE NOT THE ONLY ONE. TAKE A LOOK.
EVERY TIME I TURN AROUND, THERE THEY ARE!
WHY DON'T YOU TALK TO THEM?
NO THANKS. THEY LOOK LIKE I'D WAKE UP INSIDE AN OVERSIZE DOLLHOUSE...
...TIED TO A HIGHCHAIR!
DON'T GO ALL WEIRD ON ME. I'LL TALK TO THEM!
DON'T FORGET TO SAY "I COME IN PEACE!"
MAYBE I AM A GIRL MAGNET.
HI, GIRLS! I'M ARCHIE ANDREWS. WELCOME TO--
WHAT'S HIS NAME?
15

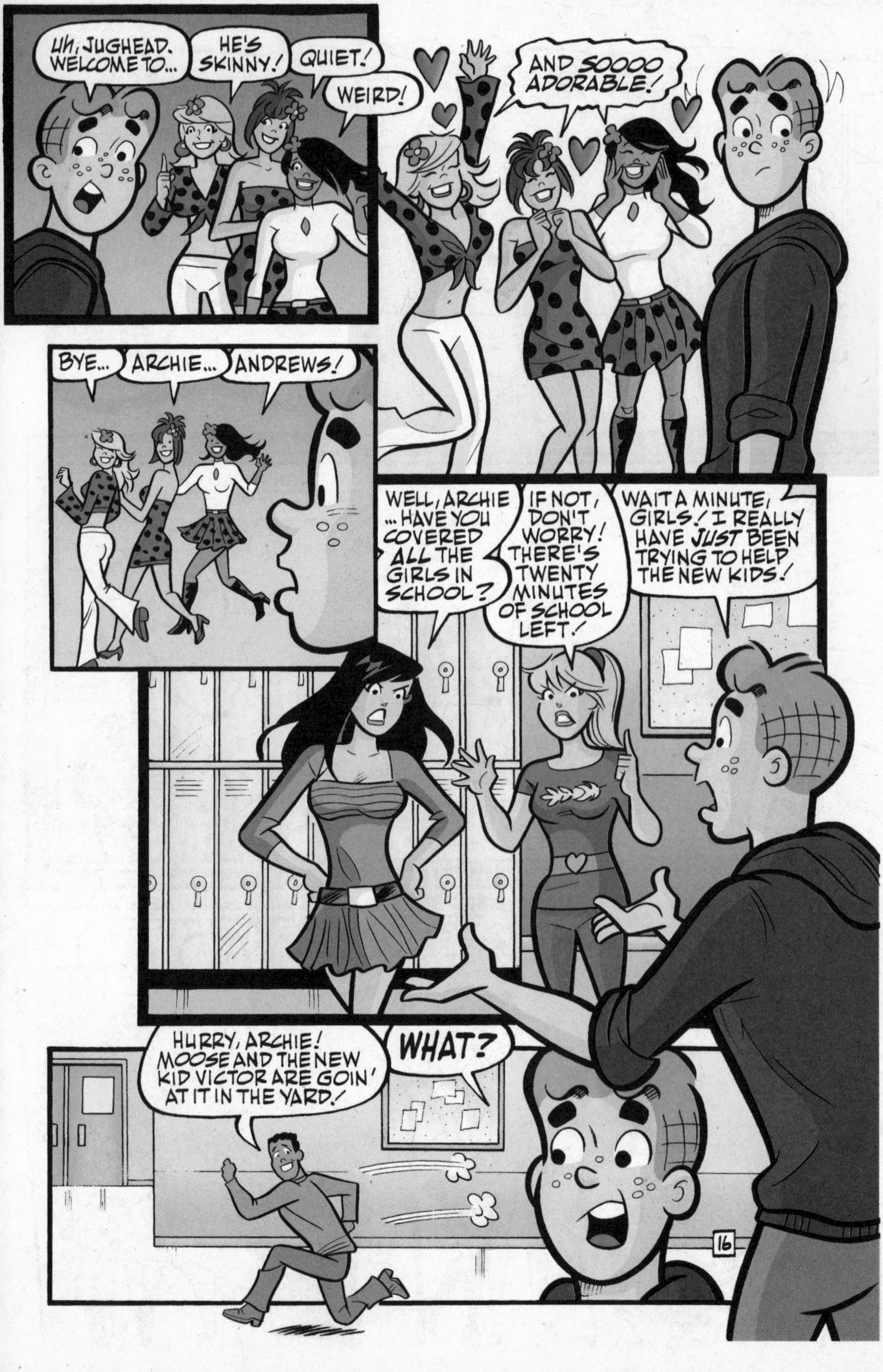
UH, JUGHEAD. WELCOME TO...
HE'S SKINNY!
QUIET!
WEIRD!
AND SOOOO ADORABLE!
BYE...
ARCHIE...
ANDREWS!
WELL, ARCHIE ...HAVE YOU COVERED ALL THE GIRLS IN SCHOOL?
IF NOT, DON'T WORRY! THERE'S TWENTY MINUTES OF SCHOOL LEFT!
WAIT A MINUTE, GIRLS! I REALLY HAVE JUST BEEN TRYING TO HELP THE NEW KIDS!
HURRY, ARCHIE! MOOSE AND THE NEW KID VICTOR ARE GOIN' AT IT IN THE YARD!
WHAT?
16

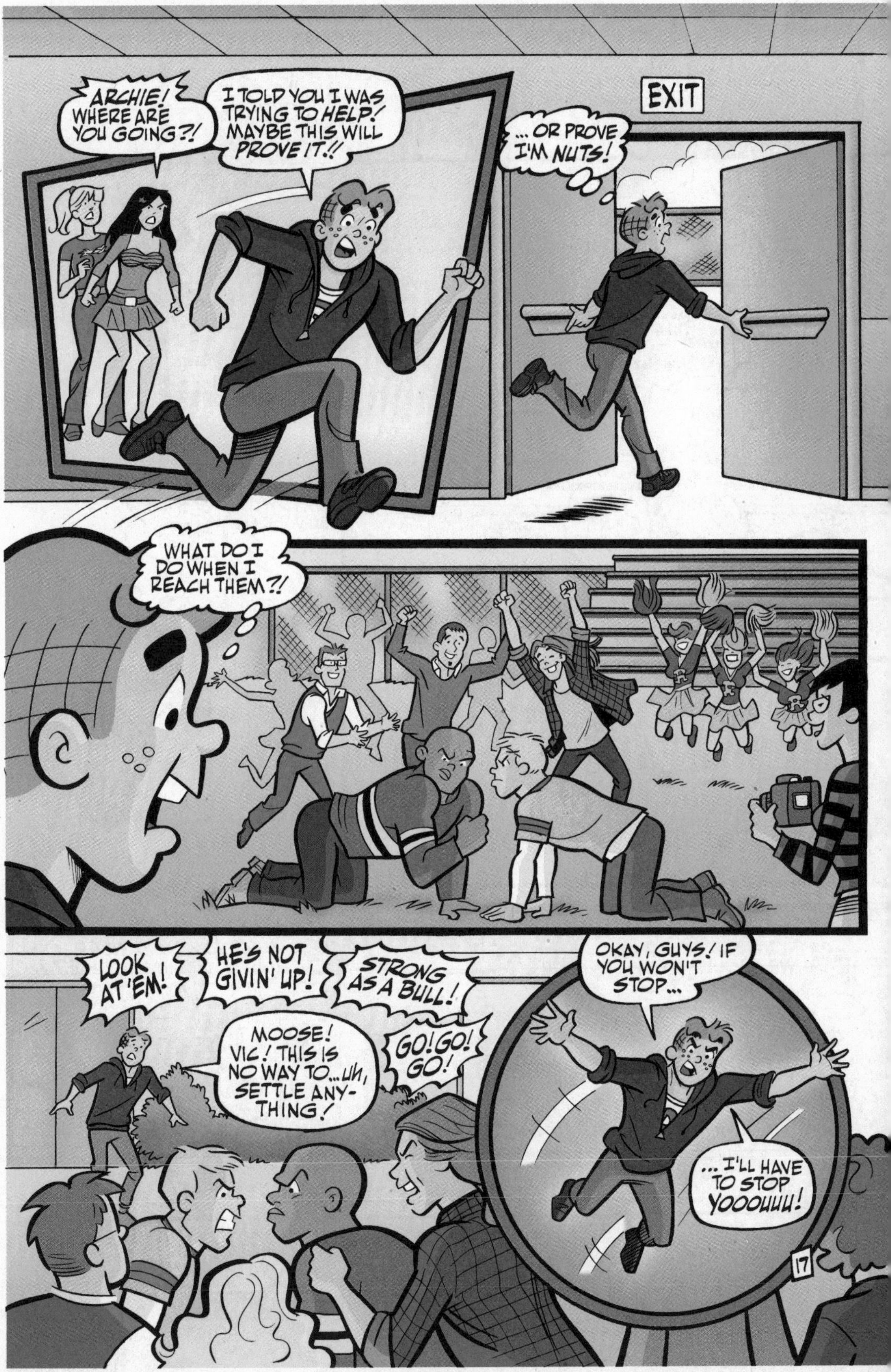
ARCHIE! WHERE ARE YOU GOING?!
I TOLD YOU I WAS TRYING TO HELP! MAYBE THIS WILL PROVE IT!!
EXIT
...OR PROVE I'M NUTS!
WHAT DO I DO WHEN I REACH THEM?!
LOOK AT 'EM!
HE'S NOT GIVIN' UP!
STRONG AS A BULL!
MOOSE! VIC! THIS IS NO WAY TO...UH, SETTLE ANY-THING!
GO! GO! GO!
OKAY, GUYS! IF YOU WON'T STOP...
...I'LL HAVE TO STOP YOOOUUU!
17

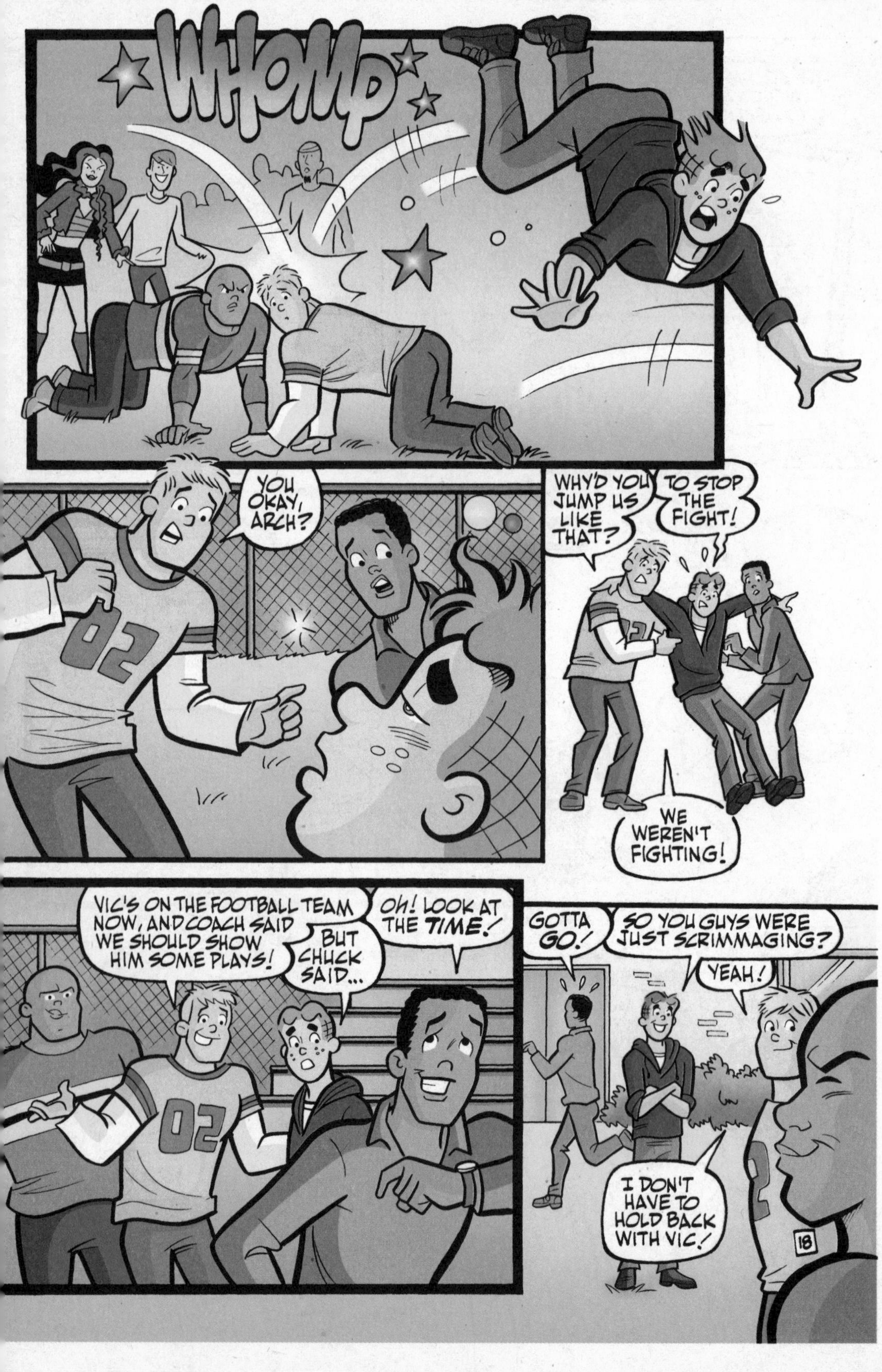
WHOMP
YOU OKAY, ARCH?
WHY'D YOU JUMP US LIKE THAT?
TO STOP THE FIGHT!
WE WEREN'T FIGHTING!
VIC'S ON THE FOOTBALL TEAM NOW, AND COACH SAID WE SHOULD SHOW HIM SOME PLAYS!
BUT CHUCK SAID...
OH! LOOK AT THE TIME!
GOTTA GO!
SO YOU GUYS WERE JUST SCRIMMAGING?
YEAH!
I DON'T HAVE TO HOLD BACK WITH VIC!
18

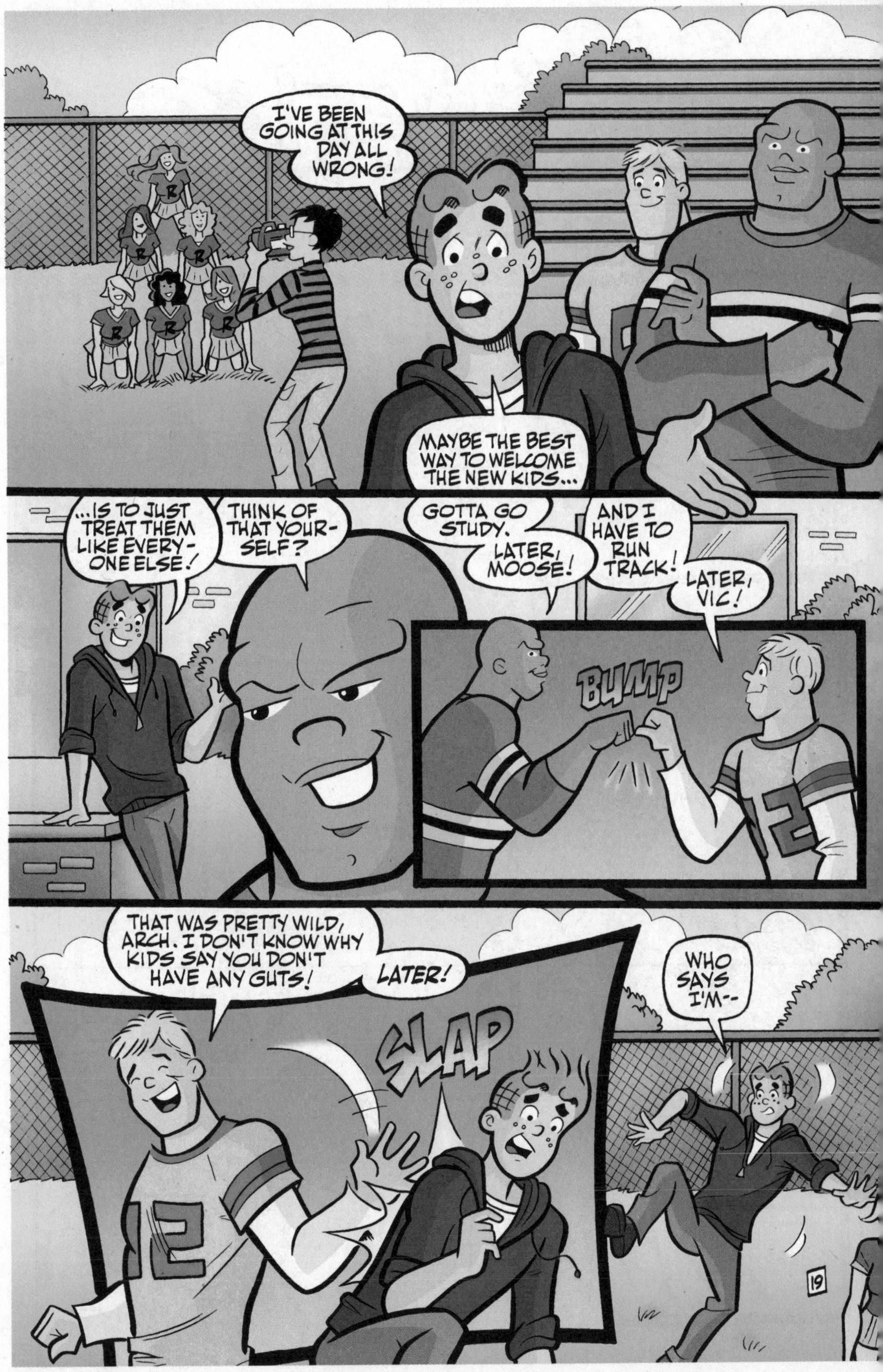
I'VE BEEN GOING AT THIS DAY ALL WRONG!
MAYBE THE BEST WAY TO WELCOME THE NEW KIDS...
...IS TO JUST TREAT THEM LIKE EVERY-ONE ELSE!
THINK OF THAT YOUR-SELF?
GOTTA GO STUDY.
LATER, MOOSE!
AND I HAVE TO RUN TRACK!
LATER, VIC!
BUMP
THAT WAS PRETTY WILD, ARCH. I DON'T KNOW WHY KIDS SAY YOU DON'T HAVE ANY GUTS!
LATER!
SLAP
WHO SAYS I'M--
19

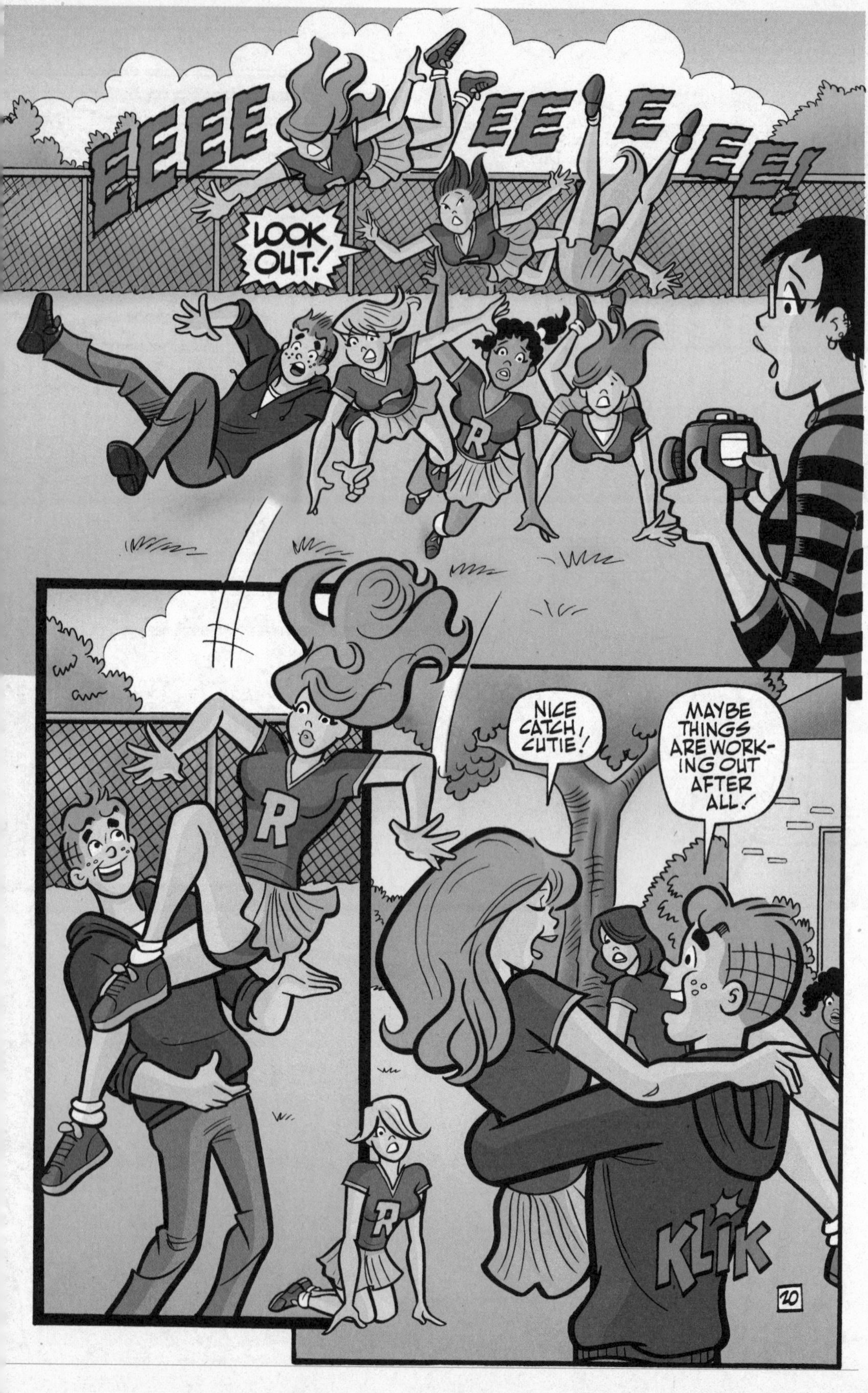
EEEE EE E EE!
LOOK OUT!
NICE CATCH, CUTIE!
MAYBE THINGS ARE WORKING OUT AFTER ALL!
KLIK
20

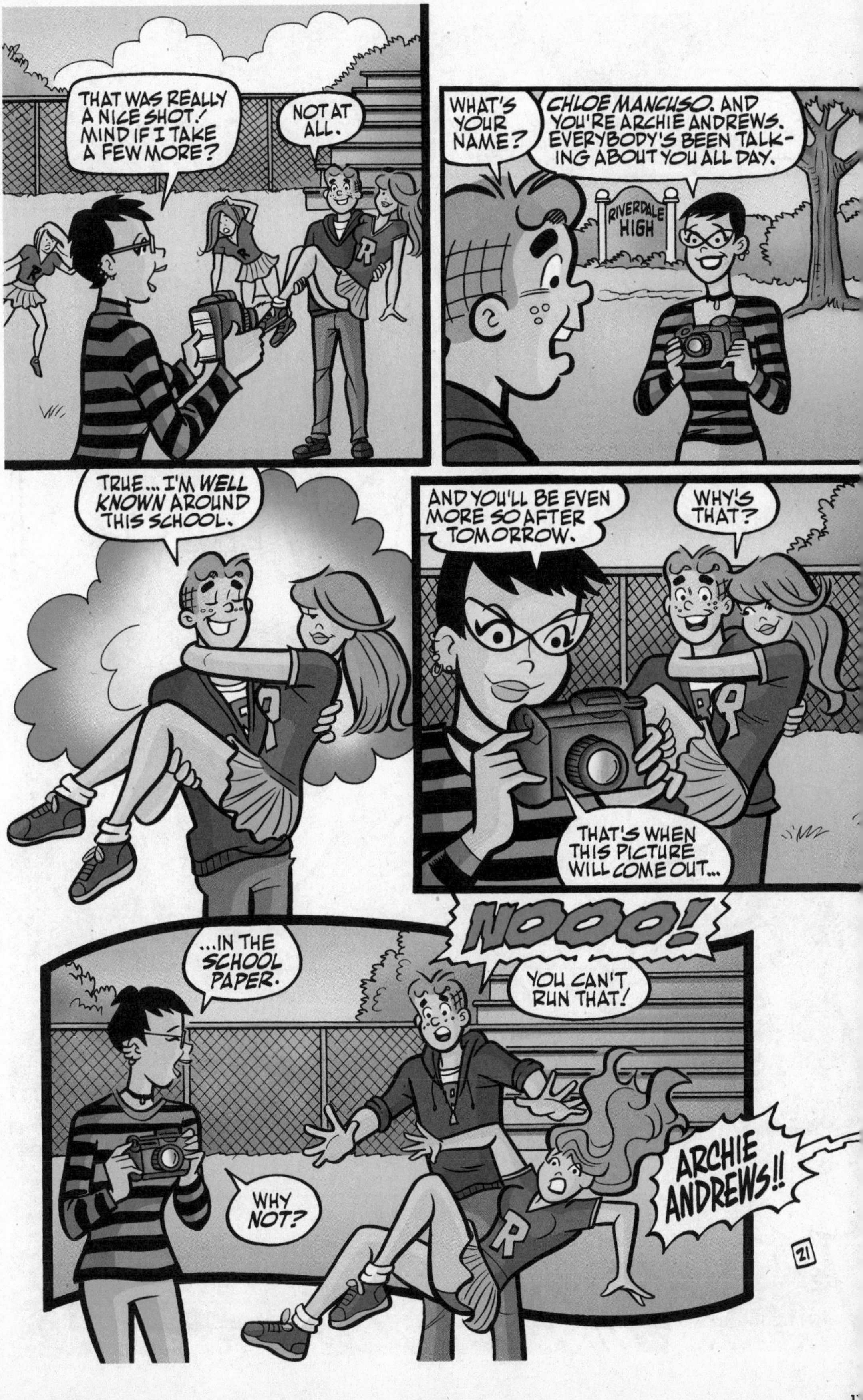
THAT WAS REALLY A NICE SHOT! MIND IF I TAKE A FEW MORE?
NOT AT ALL.
WHAT'S YOUR NAME?
CHLOE MANCUSO. AND YOU'RE ARCHIE ANDREWS. EVERYBODY'S BEEN TALKING ABOUT YOU ALL DAY.
RIVERDALE HIGH
TRUE... I'M WELL KNOWN AROUND THIS SCHOOL.
AND YOU'LL BE EVEN MORE SO AFTER TOMORROW.
WHY'S THAT?
THAT'S WHEN THIS PICTURE WILL COME OUT...
...IN THE SCHOOL PAPER.
NOOO!
YOU CAN'T RUN THAT!
WHY NOT?
ARCHIE ANDREWS!!
21

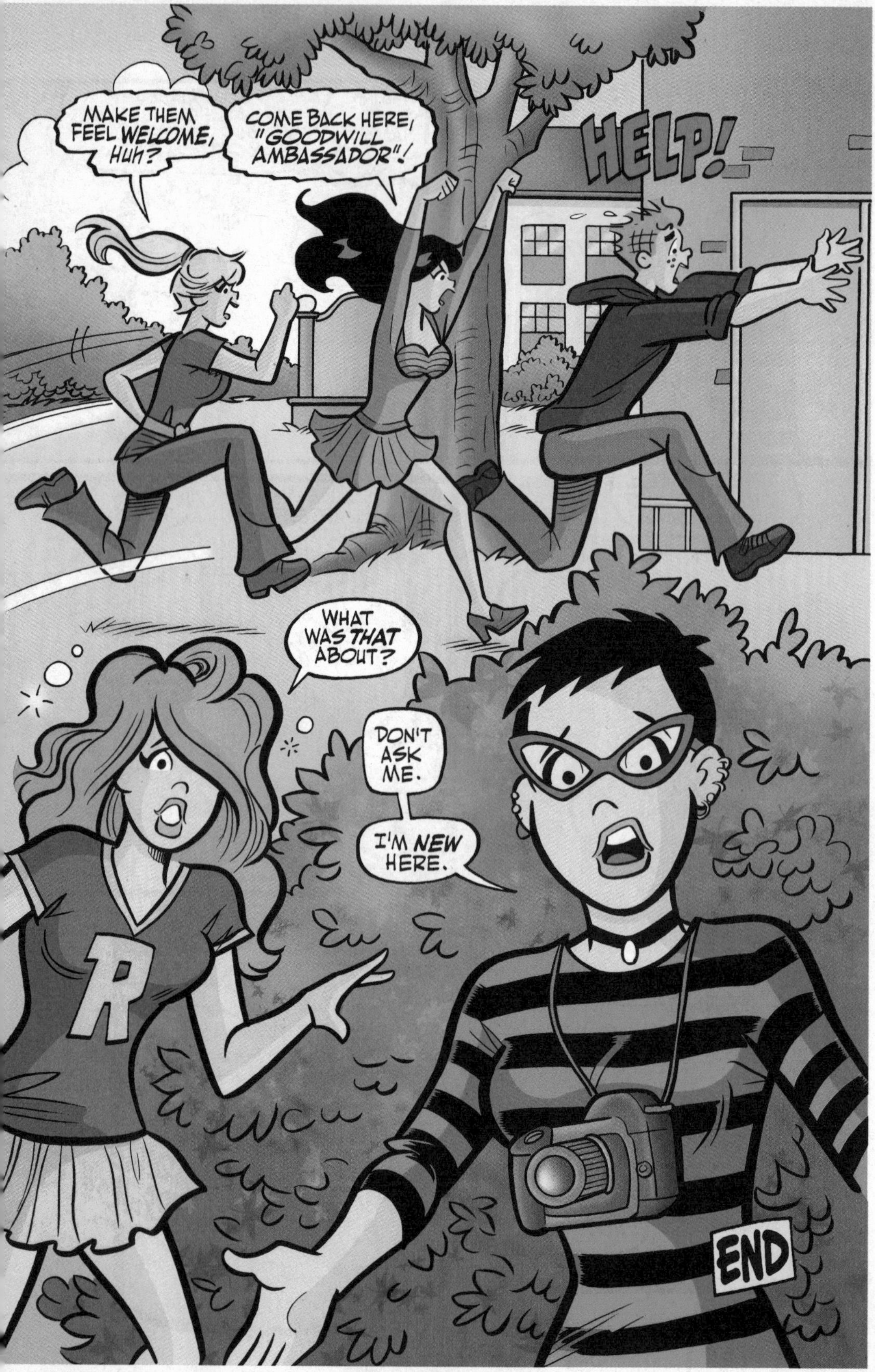
MAKE THEM FEEL WELCOME, Huh?
COME BACK HERE, "GOODWILL AMBASSADOR"!
HELP!
WHAT WAS THAT ABOUT?
DON'T ASK ME.
I'M NEW HERE.
END

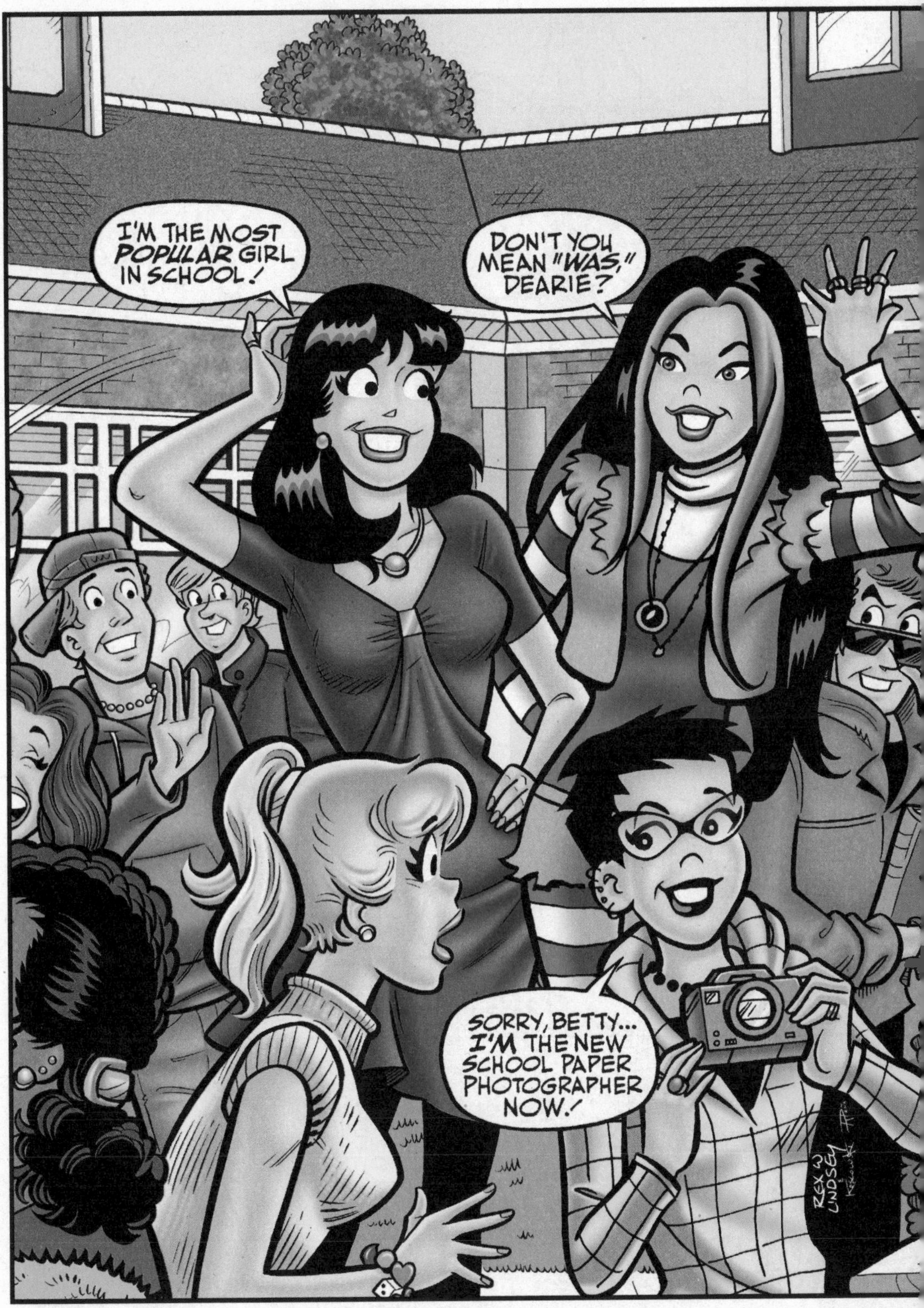
I'M THE MOST POPULAR GIRL IN SCHOOL!
DON'T YOU MEAN "WAS," DEARIE?
SORRY, BETTY... I'M THE NEW SCHOOL PAPER PHOTOGRAPHER NOW!
REX W LINDSEY & KOSLOWSKI

WHAT I LIKE ABOUT ME - PART 3

SCRIPT: ALEX SIMMONS PENCILS: DAN PARENT

INKS: RICH KOSLOWSKI LETTERS: JACK MORELLI COLORS: DIGIKORE STUDIOS

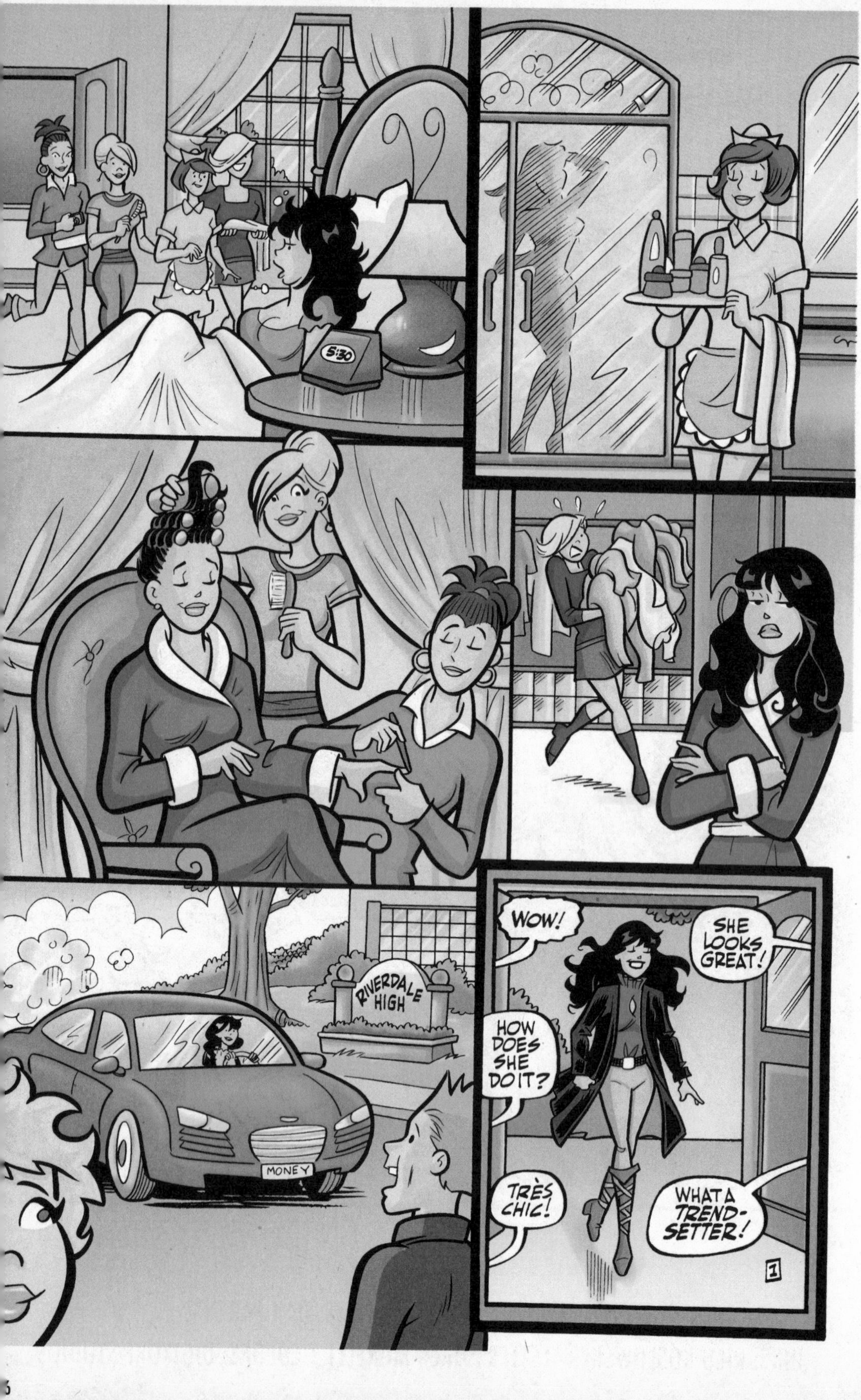
5:30
RIVERDALE HIGH
MONEY
WOW!
SHE LOOKS GREAT!
HOW DOES SHE DO IT?
TRÈS CHIC!
WHAT A TREND-SETTER!
1

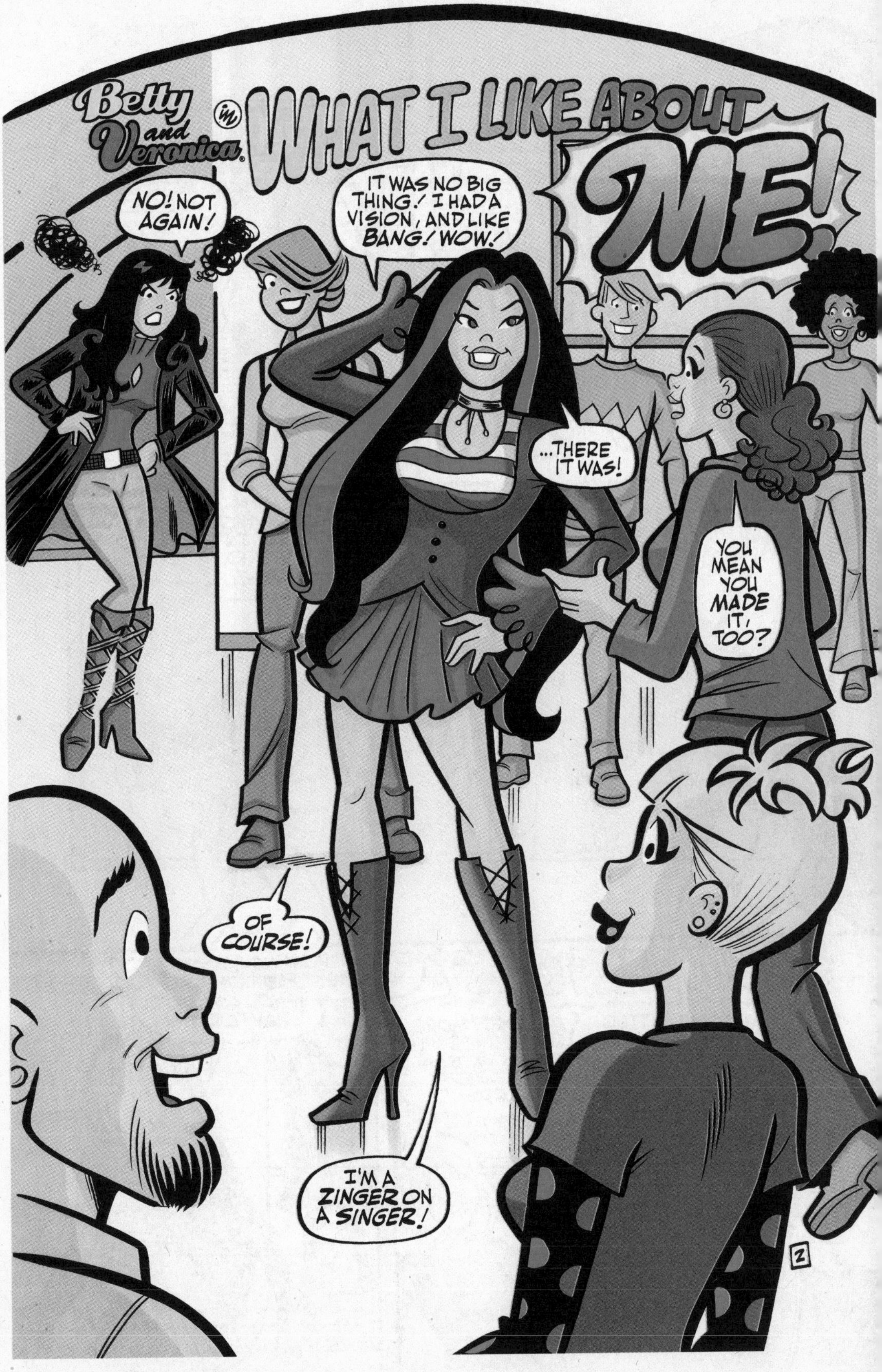
Betty and Veronica in
WHAT I LIKE ABOUT ME!
NO! NOT AGAIN!
IT WAS NO BIG THING! I HAD A VISION, AND LIKE BANG! WOW!
...THERE IT WAS!
YOU MEAN YOU MADE IT, TOO?
OF COURSE!
I'M A ZINGER ON A SINGER!
2

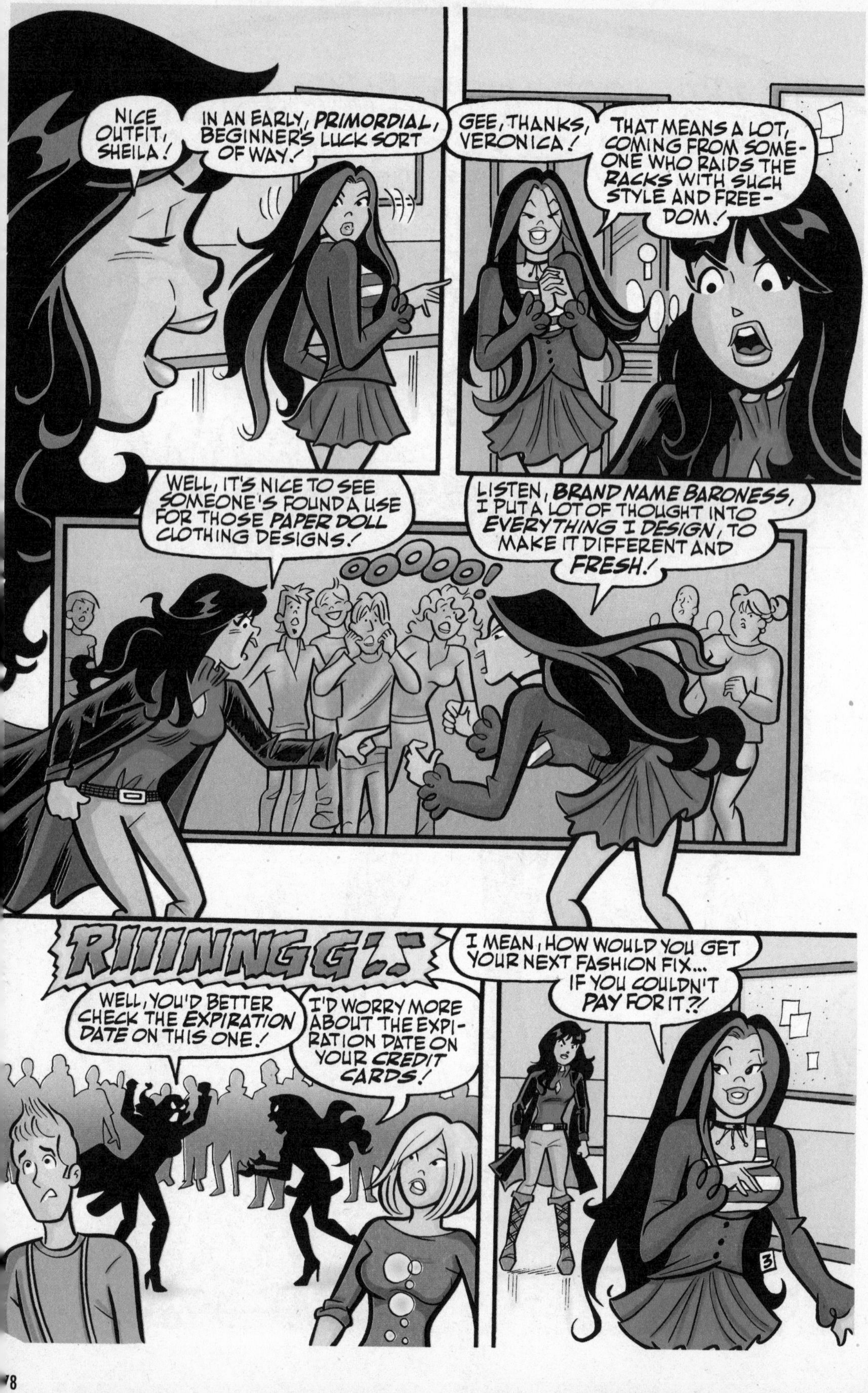
NICE OUTFIT, SHEILA!
IN AN EARLY, PRIMORDIAL, BEGINNER'S LUCK SORT OF WAY!
GEE, THANKS, VERONICA!
THAT MEANS A LOT, COMING FROM SOME-ONE WHO RAIDS THE RACKS WITH SUCH STYLE AND FREE-DOM!
WELL, IT'S NICE TO SEE SOMEONE'S FOUND A USE FOR THOSE PAPER DOLL CLOTHING DESIGNS!
LISTEN, BRAND NAME BARONESS, I PUT A LOT OF THOUGHT INTO EVERYTHING I DESIGN, TO MAKE IT DIFFERENT AND FRESH!
OOOOOO!
RIIINNGG!
WELL, YOU'D BETTER CHECK THE EXPIRATION DATE ON THIS ONE!
I'D WORRY MORE ABOUT THE EXPI-RATION DATE ON YOUR CREDIT CARDS!
I MEAN, HOW WOULD YOU GET YOUR NEXT FASHION FIX... IF YOU COULDN'T PAY FOR IT?!
3

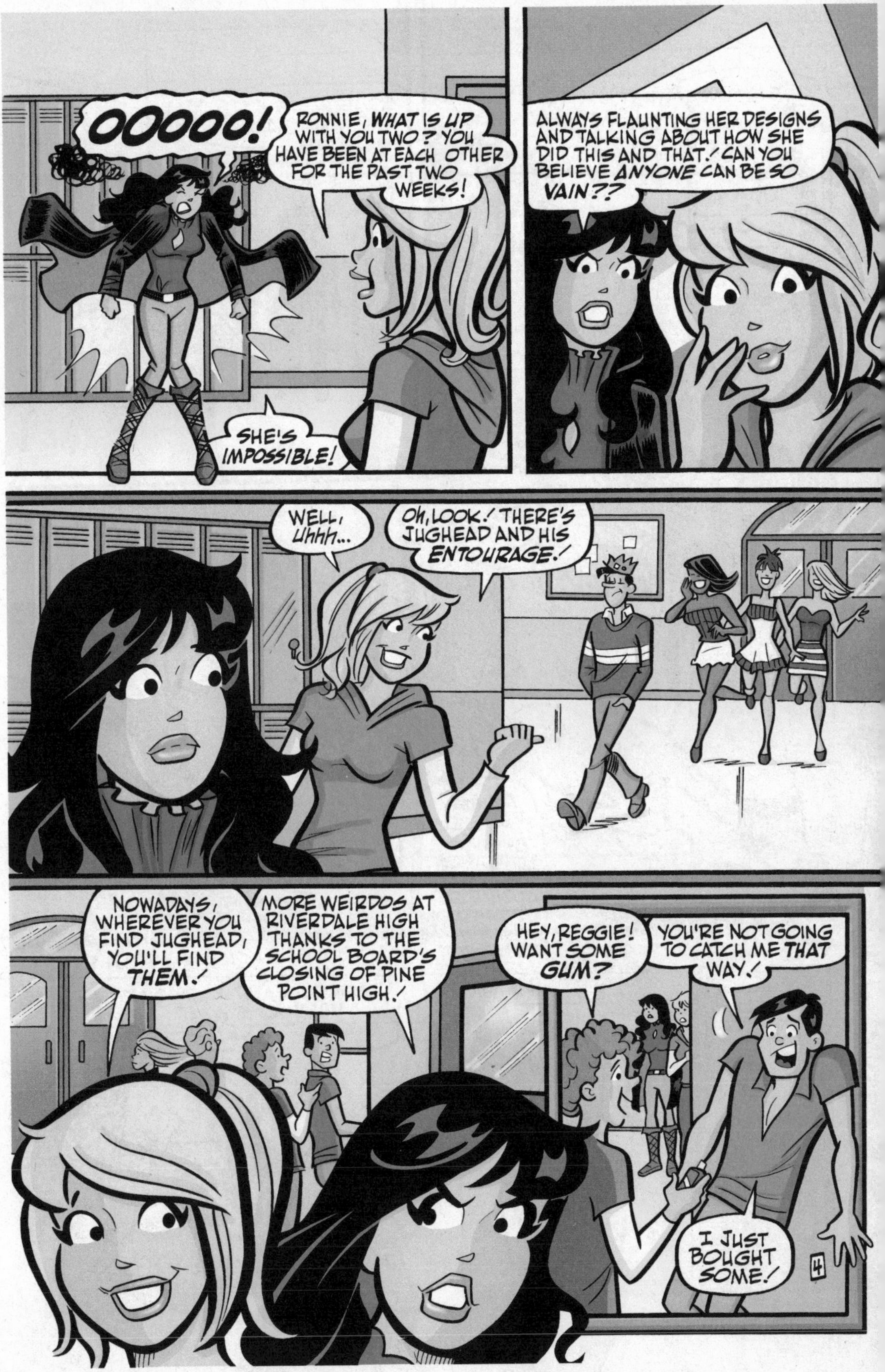
OOOOO!
RONNIE, WHAT IS UP WITH YOU TWO? YOU HAVE BEEN AT EACH OTHER FOR THE PAST TWO WEEKS!
SHE'S IMPOSSIBLE!
ALWAYS FLAUNTING HER DESIGNS AND TALKING ABOUT HOW SHE DID THIS AND THAT! CAN YOU BELIEVE ANYONE CAN BE SO VAIN??
WELL, UHHH...
OH, LOOK! THERE'S JUGHEAD AND HIS ENTOURAGE!
NOWADAYS, WHEREVER YOU FIND JUGHEAD, YOU'LL FIND THEM!
MORE WEIRDOS AT RIVERDALE HIGH THANKS TO THE SCHOOL BOARD'S CLOSING OF PINE POINT HIGH!
HEY, REGGIE! WANT SOME GUM?
YOU'RE NOT GOING TO CATCH ME THAT WAY!
I JUST BOUGHT SOME!
4

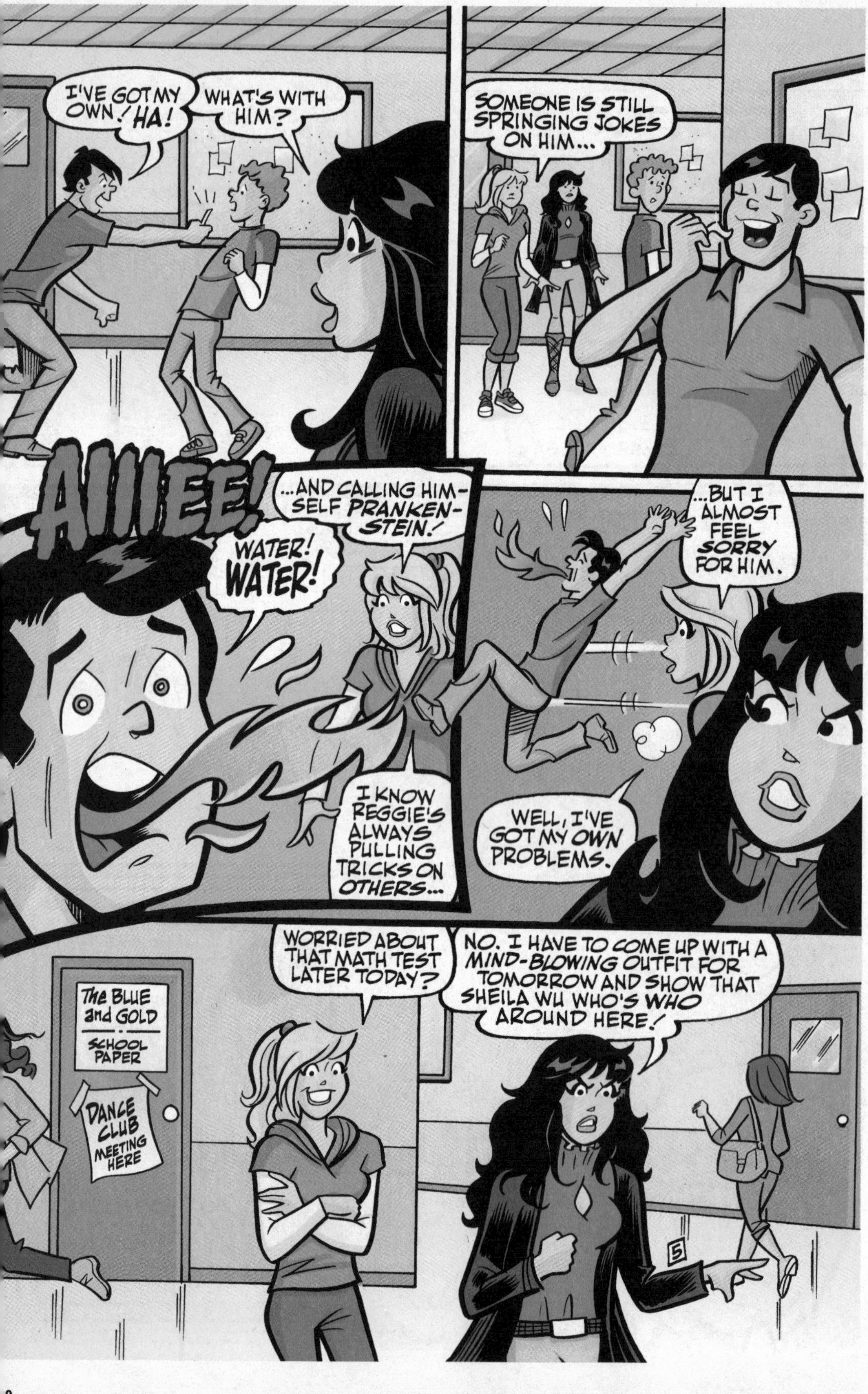
I'VE GOT MY OWN! HA!
WHAT'S WITH HIM?
SOMEONE IS STILL SPRINGING JOKES ON HIM...
AIIIEE!
WATER! WATER!
...AND CALLING HIMSELF PRANKENSTEIN!
I KNOW REGGIE'S ALWAYS PULLING TRICKS ON OTHERS...
...BUT I ALMOST FEEL SORRY FOR HIM.
WELL, I'VE GOT MY OWN PROBLEMS.
WORRIED ABOUT THAT MATH TEST LATER TODAY?
NO. I HAVE TO COME UP WITH A MIND-BLOWING OUTFIT FOR TOMORROW AND SHOW THAT SHEILA WU WHO'S WHO AROUND HERE!
The BLUE and GOLD
SCHOOL PAPER
DANCE CLUB MEETING HERE
5

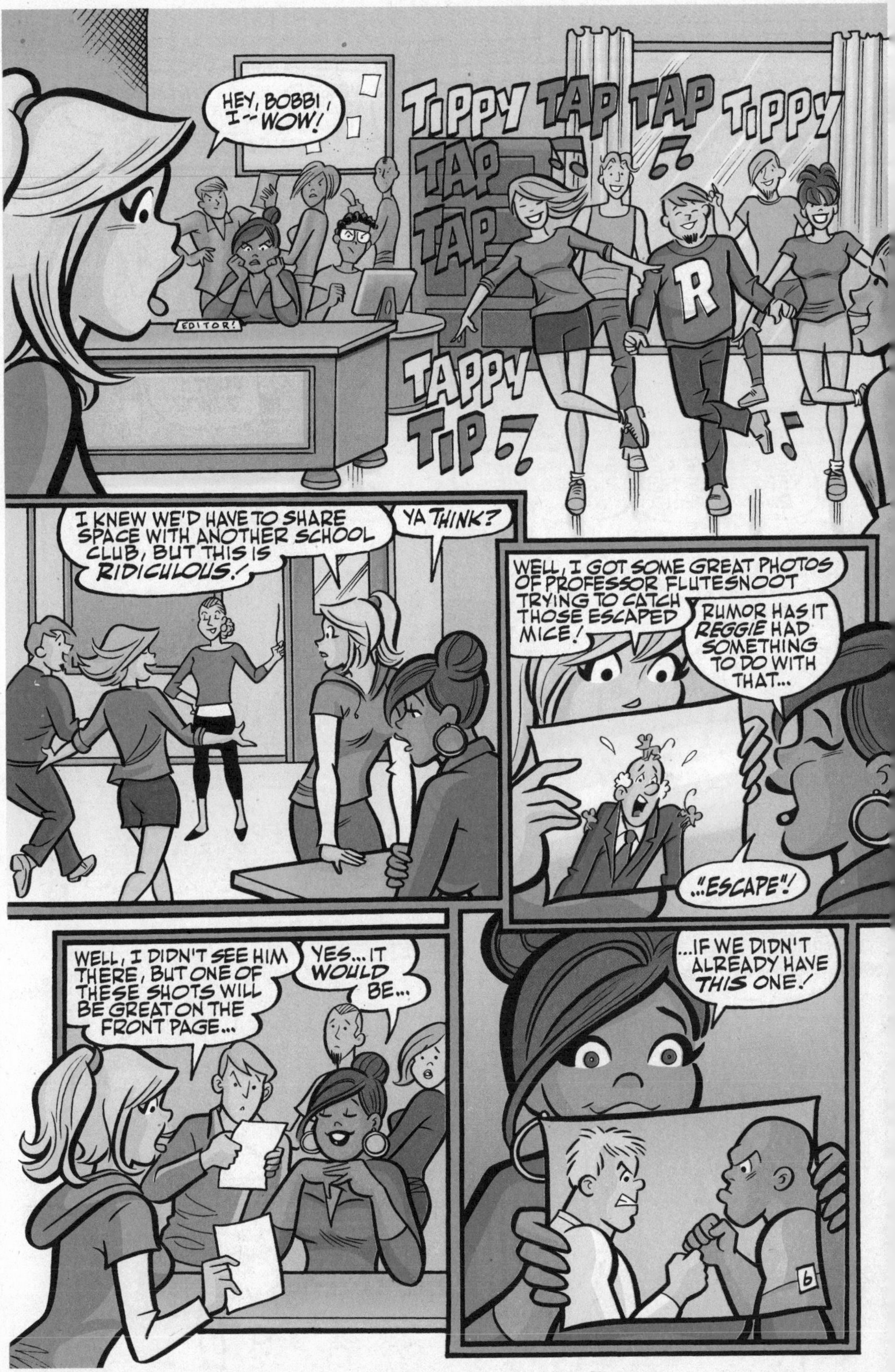
HEY, BOBBI, I-- WOW!
EDITOR
TIPPY TAP TAP TIPPY
TAP TAP
TAPPY TIP
I KNEW WE'D HAVE TO SHARE SPACE WITH ANOTHER SCHOOL CLUB, BUT THIS IS RIDICULOUS!
YA THINK?
WELL, I GOT SOME GREAT PHOTOS OF PROFESSOR FLUTESNOOT TRYING TO CATCH THOSE ESCAPED MICE!
RUMOR HAS IT REGGIE HAD SOMETHING TO DO WITH THAT...
..."ESCAPE"!
WELL, I DIDN'T SEE HIM THERE, BUT ONE OF THESE SHOTS WILL BE GREAT ON THE FRONT PAGE...
YES... IT WOULD BE...
...IF WE DIDN'T ALREADY HAVE THIS ONE!
6

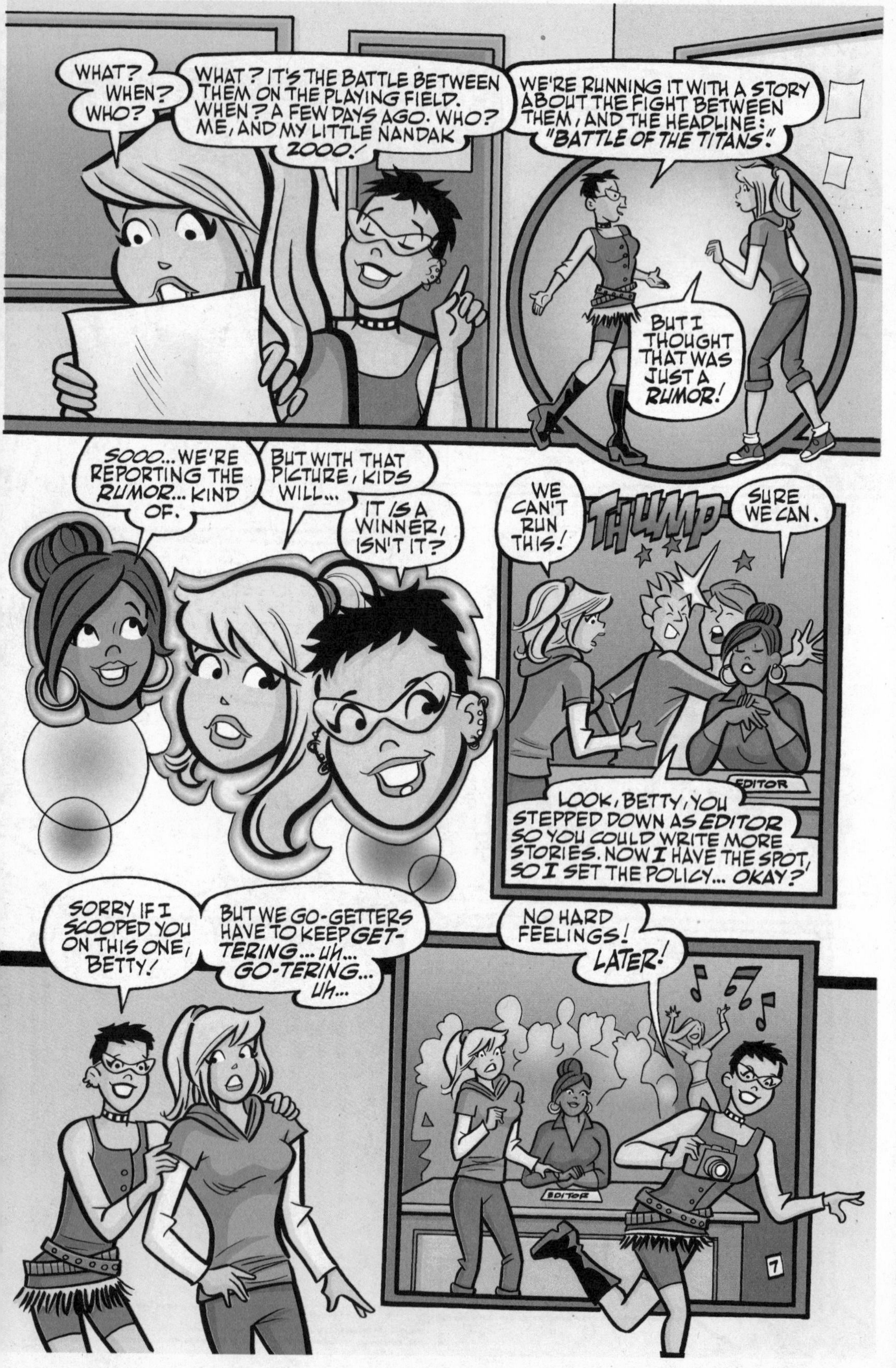
WHAT? WHEN? WHO?
WHAT? IT'S THE BATTLE BETWEEN THEM ON THE PLAYING FIELD. WHEN? A FEW DAYS AGO. WHO? ME, AND MY LITTLE NANDAK ZOOO!
WE'RE RUNNING IT WITH A STORY ABOUT THE FIGHT BETWEEN THEM, AND THE HEADLINE: "BATTLE OF THE TITANS"!
BUT I THOUGHT THAT WAS JUST A RUMOR!
SOOO... WE'RE REPORTING THE RUMOR... KIND OF.
BUT WITH THAT PICTURE, KIDS WILL...
IT IS A WINNER, ISN'T IT?
WE CAN'T RUN THIS!
THUMP
SURE WE CAN.
EDITOR
LOOK, BETTY, YOU STEPPED DOWN AS EDITOR SO YOU COULD WRITE MORE STORIES. NOW I HAVE THE SPOT, SO I SET THE POLICY... OKAY?
SORRY IF I SCOOPED YOU ON THIS ONE, BETTY!
BUT WE GO-GETTERS HAVE TO KEEP GET-TERING... UH... GO-TERING... UH...
NO HARD FEELINGS! LATER!
EDITOR
7

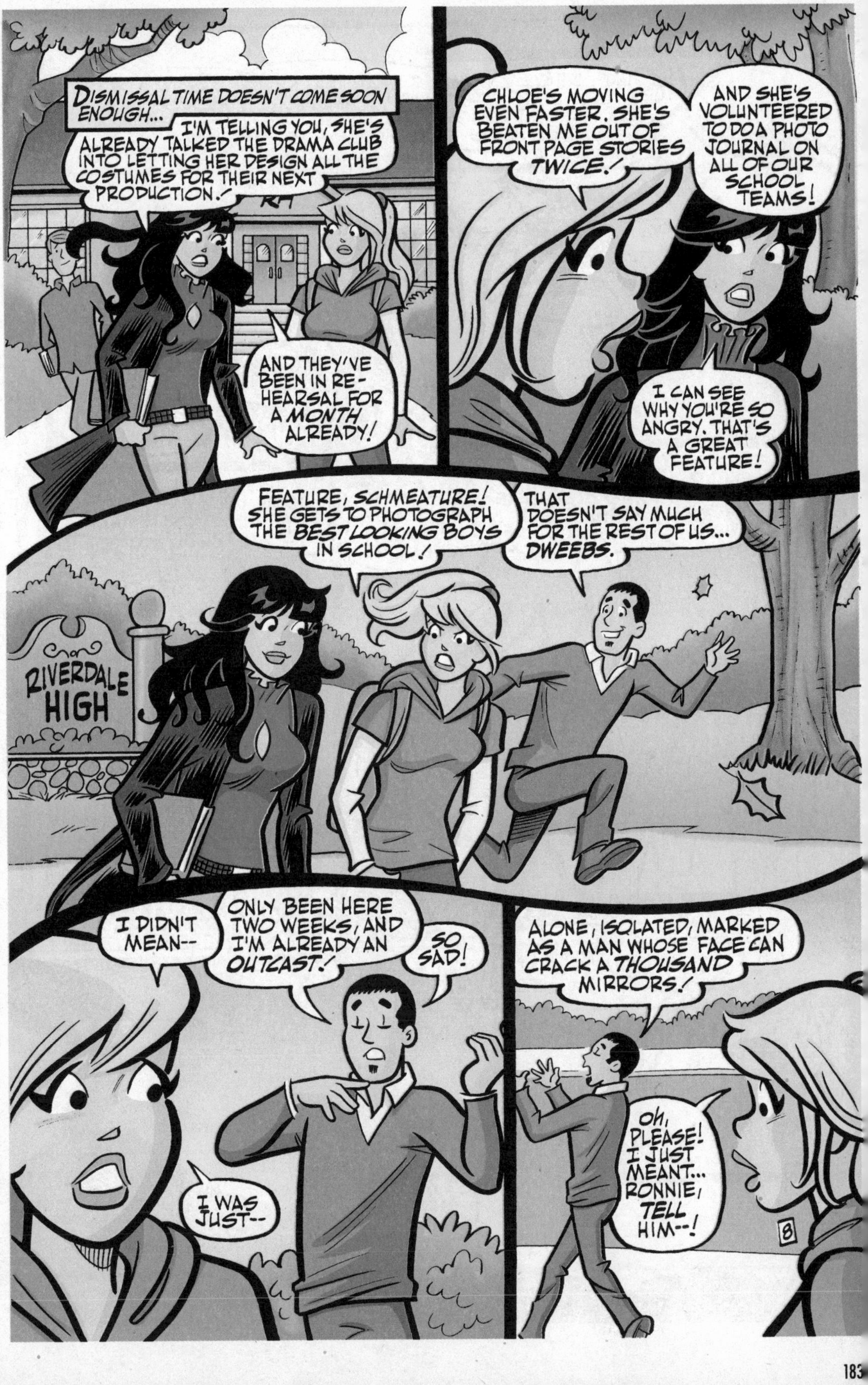
DISMISSAL TIME DOESN'T COME SOON ENOUGH...
I'M TELLING YOU, SHE'S ALREADY TALKED THE DRAMA CLUB INTO LETTING HER DESIGN ALL THE COSTUMES FOR THEIR NEXT PRODUCTION!
AND THEY'VE BEEN IN RE-HEARSAL FOR A MONTH ALREADY!
CHLOE'S MOVING EVEN FASTER. SHE'S BEATEN ME OUT OF FRONT PAGE STORIES TWICE!
AND SHE'S VOLUNTEERED TO DO A PHOTO JOURNAL ON ALL OF OUR SCHOOL TEAMS!
I CAN SEE WHY YOU'RE SO ANGRY. THAT'S A GREAT FEATURE!
FEATURE, SCHMEATURE! SHE GETS TO PHOTOGRAPH THE BEST LOOKING BOYS IN SCHOOL!
THAT DOESN'T SAY MUCH FOR THE REST OF US... DWEEBS.
RIVERDALE HIGH
I DIDN'T MEAN--
ONLY BEEN HERE TWO WEEKS, AND I'M ALREADY AN OUTCAST!
SO SAD!
I WAS JUST--
ALONE, ISOLATED, MARKED AS A MAN WHOSE FACE CAN CRACK A THOUSAND MIRRORS!
OH, PLEASE! I JUST MEANT... RONNIE, TELL HIM--!
8

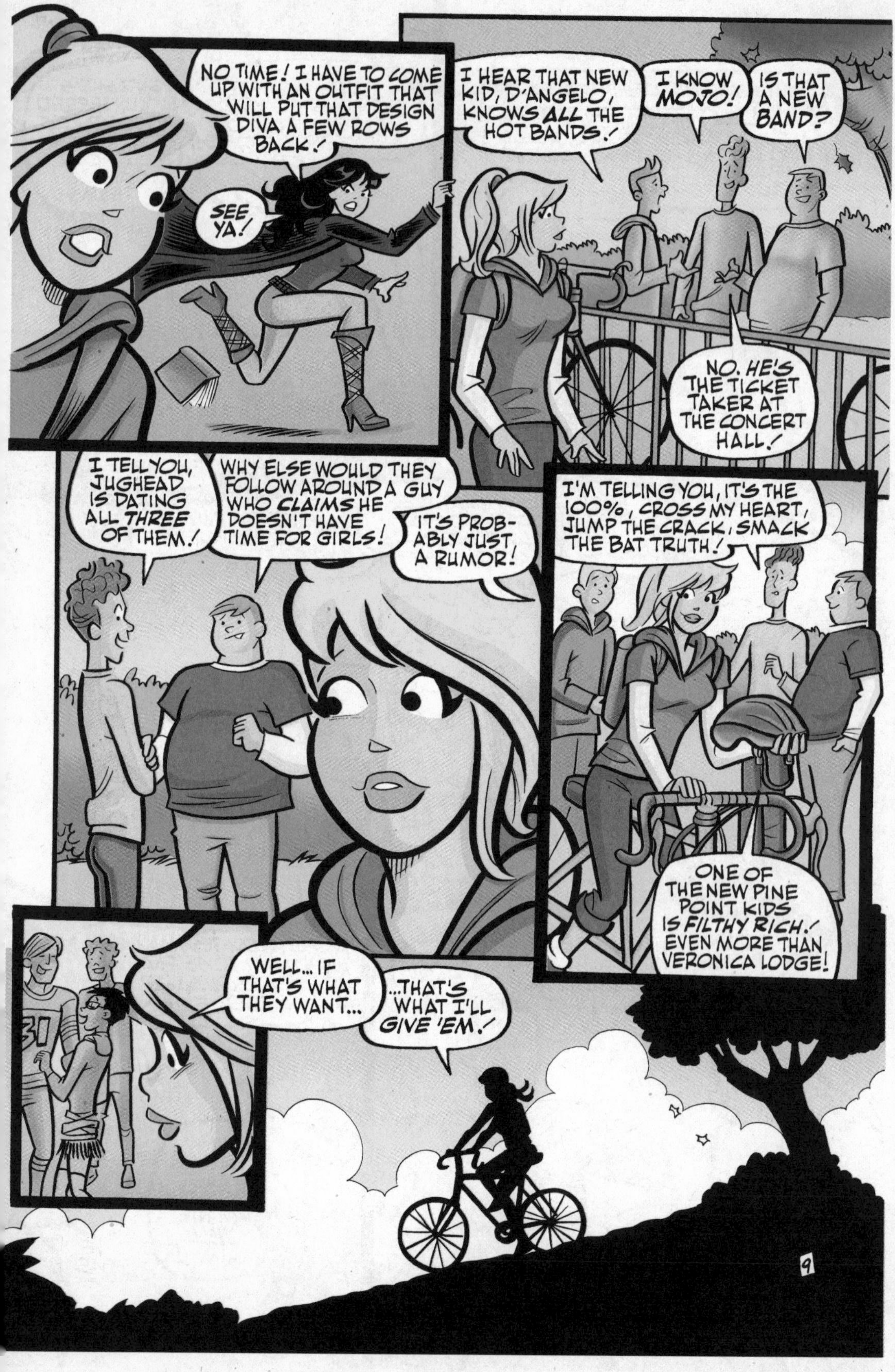
NO TIME! I HAVE TO COME UP WITH AN OUTFIT THAT WILL PUT THAT DESIGN DIVA A FEW ROWS BACK!
SEE YA!
I HEAR THAT NEW KID, D'ANGELO, KNOWS ALL THE HOT BANDS!
I KNOW MOJO!
IS THAT A NEW BAND?
NO. HE'S THE TICKET TAKER AT THE CONCERT HALL!
I TELL YOU, JUGHEAD IS DATING ALL THREE OF THEM!
WHY ELSE WOULD THEY FOLLOW AROUND A GUY WHO CLAIMS HE DOESN'T HAVE TIME FOR GIRLS!
IT'S PROBABLY JUST A RUMOR!
I'M TELLING YOU, IT'S THE 100%, CROSS MY HEART, JUMP THE CRACK, SMACK THE BAT TRUTH!
ONE OF THE NEW PINE POINT KIDS IS FILTHY RICH! EVEN MORE THAN VERONICA LODGE!
WELL... IF THAT'S WHAT THEY WANT...
...THAT'S WHAT I'LL GIVE 'EM!
9

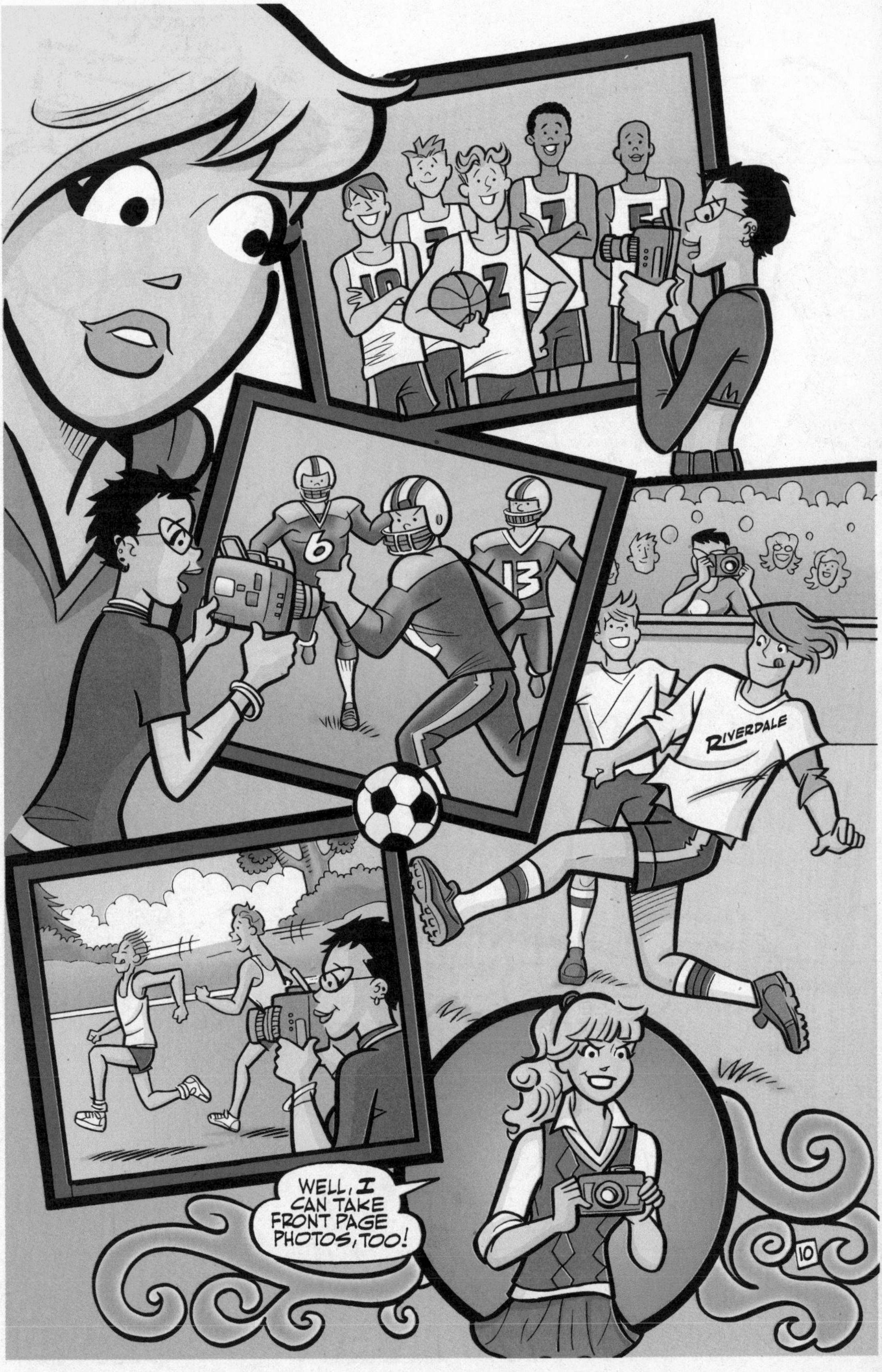
WELL, I CAN TAKE FRONT PAGE PHOTOS, TOO!
RIVERDALE
10

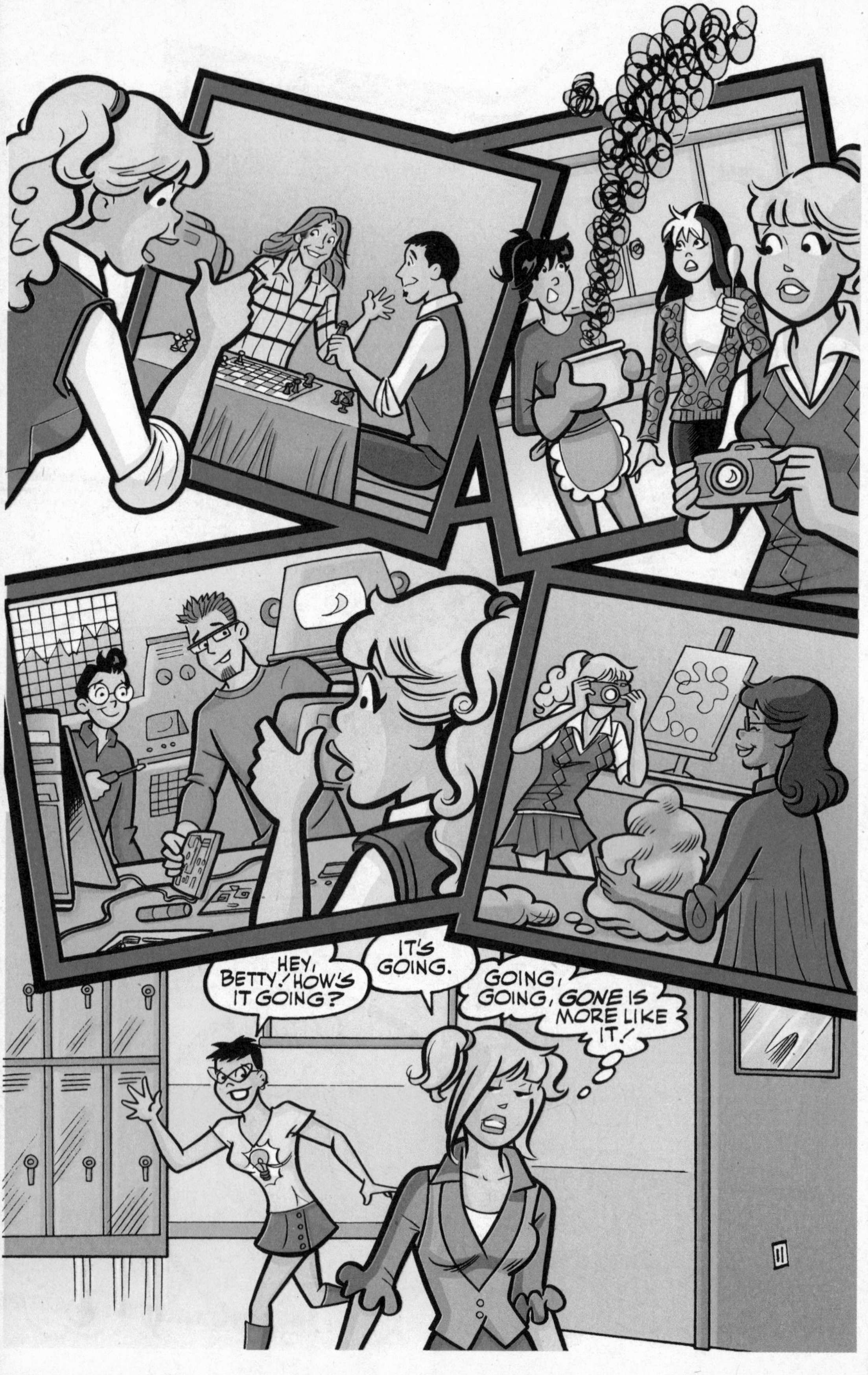
HEY, BETTY! HOW'S IT GOING?
IT'S GOING.
GOING, GOING, GONE IS MORE LIKE IT!

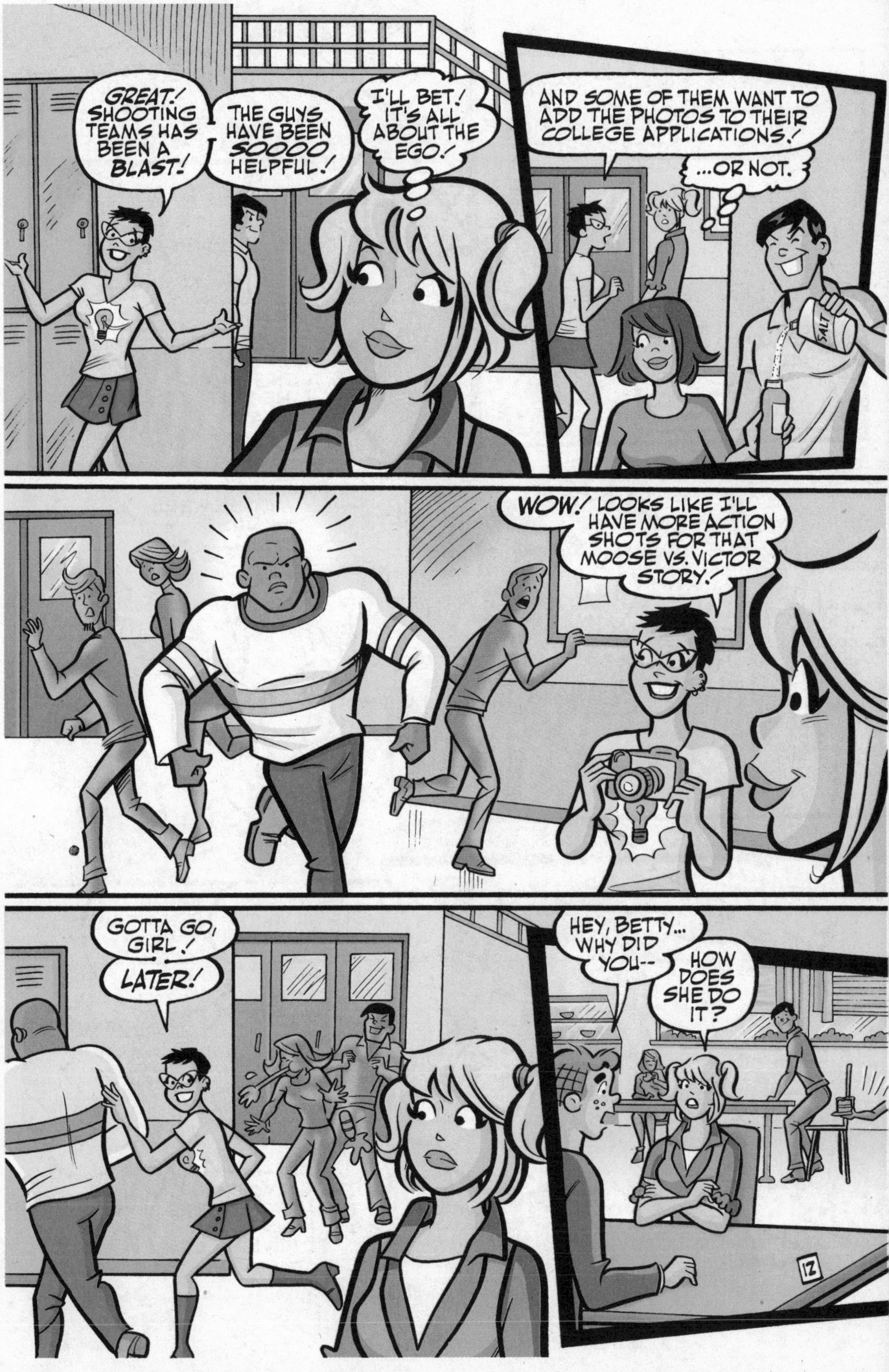
GREAT! SHOOTING TEAMS HAS BEEN A BLAST!
THE GUYS HAVE BEEN SOOOO HELPFUL!
I'LL BET! IT'S ALL ABOUT THE EGO!
AND SOME OF THEM WANT TO ADD THE PHOTOS TO THEIR COLLEGE APPLICATIONS!
...OR NOT.
SALT
WOW! LOOKS LIKE I'LL HAVE MORE ACTION SHOTS FOR THAT MOOSE VS. VICTOR STORY!
GOTTA GO, GIRL!
LATER!
HEY, BETTY... WHY DID YOU--
HOW DOES SHE DO IT?
12

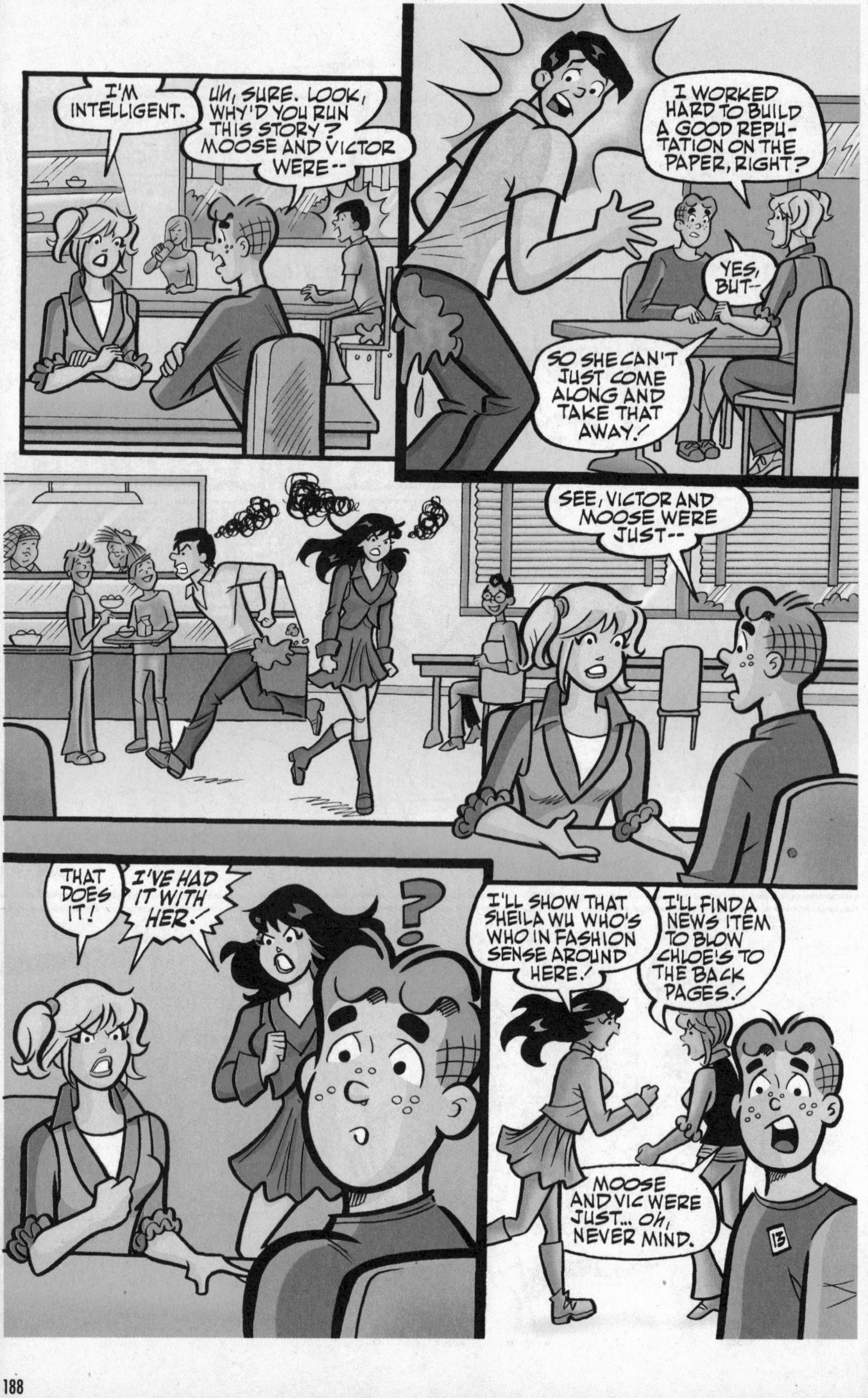
I'M INTELLIGENT.
UH, SURE. LOOK, WHY'D YOU RUN THIS STORY? MOOSE AND VICTOR WERE--
I WORKED HARD TO BUILD A GOOD REPUTATION ON THE PAPER, RIGHT?
YES, BUT--
SO SHE CAN'T JUST COME ALONG AND TAKE THAT AWAY!
SEE, VICTOR AND MOOSE WERE JUST--
THAT DOES IT!
I'VE HAD IT WITH HER!
?
I'LL SHOW THAT SHEILA WU WHO'S WHO IN FASHION SENSE AROUND HERE!
I'LL FIND A NEWS ITEM TO BLOW CHLOE'S TO THE BACK PAGES!
MOOSE AND VIC WERE JUST... OH, NEVER MIND.

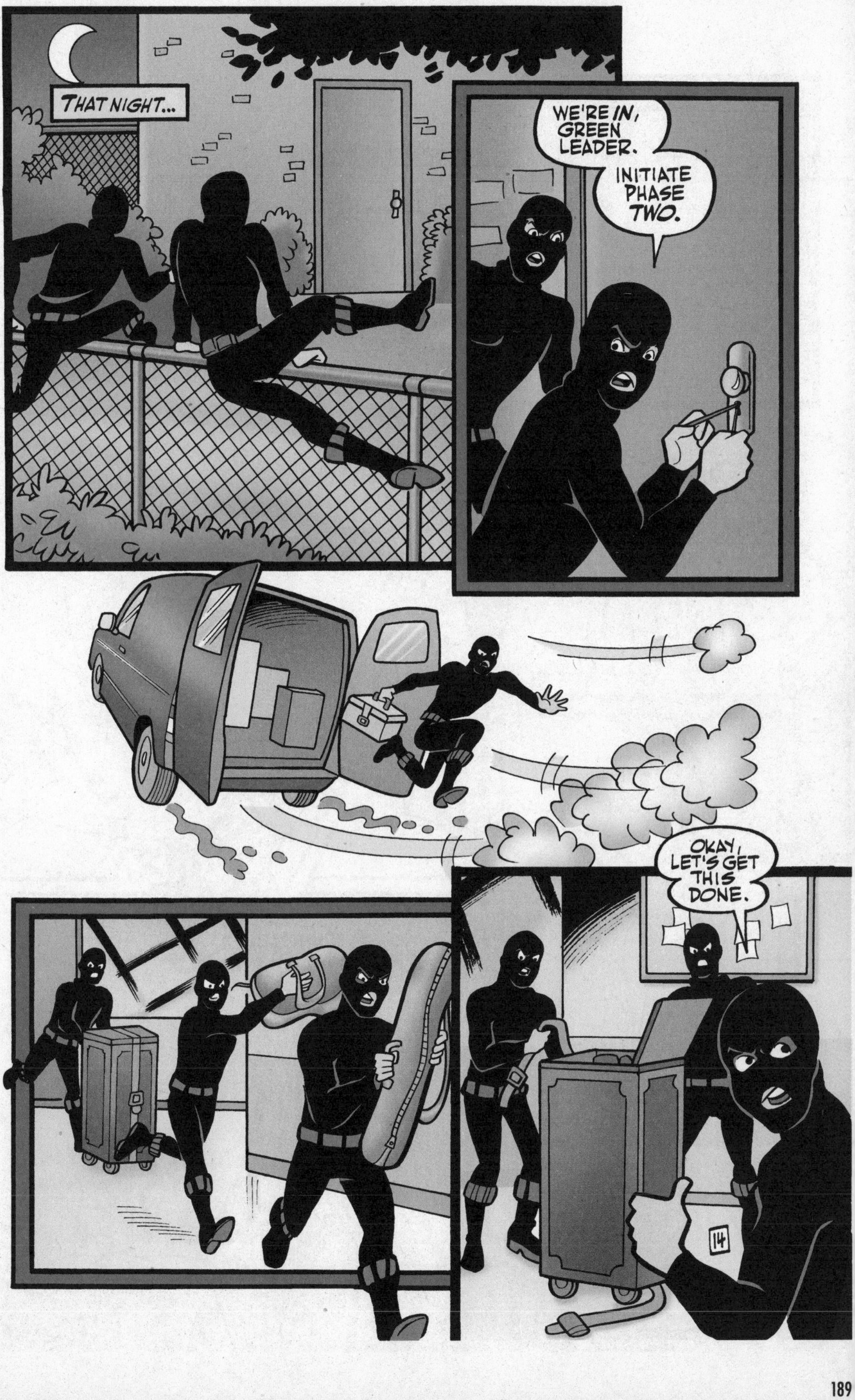
THAT NIGHT...
WE'RE IN, GREEN LEADER.
INITIATE PHASE TWO.
OKAY, LET'S GET THIS DONE.
14

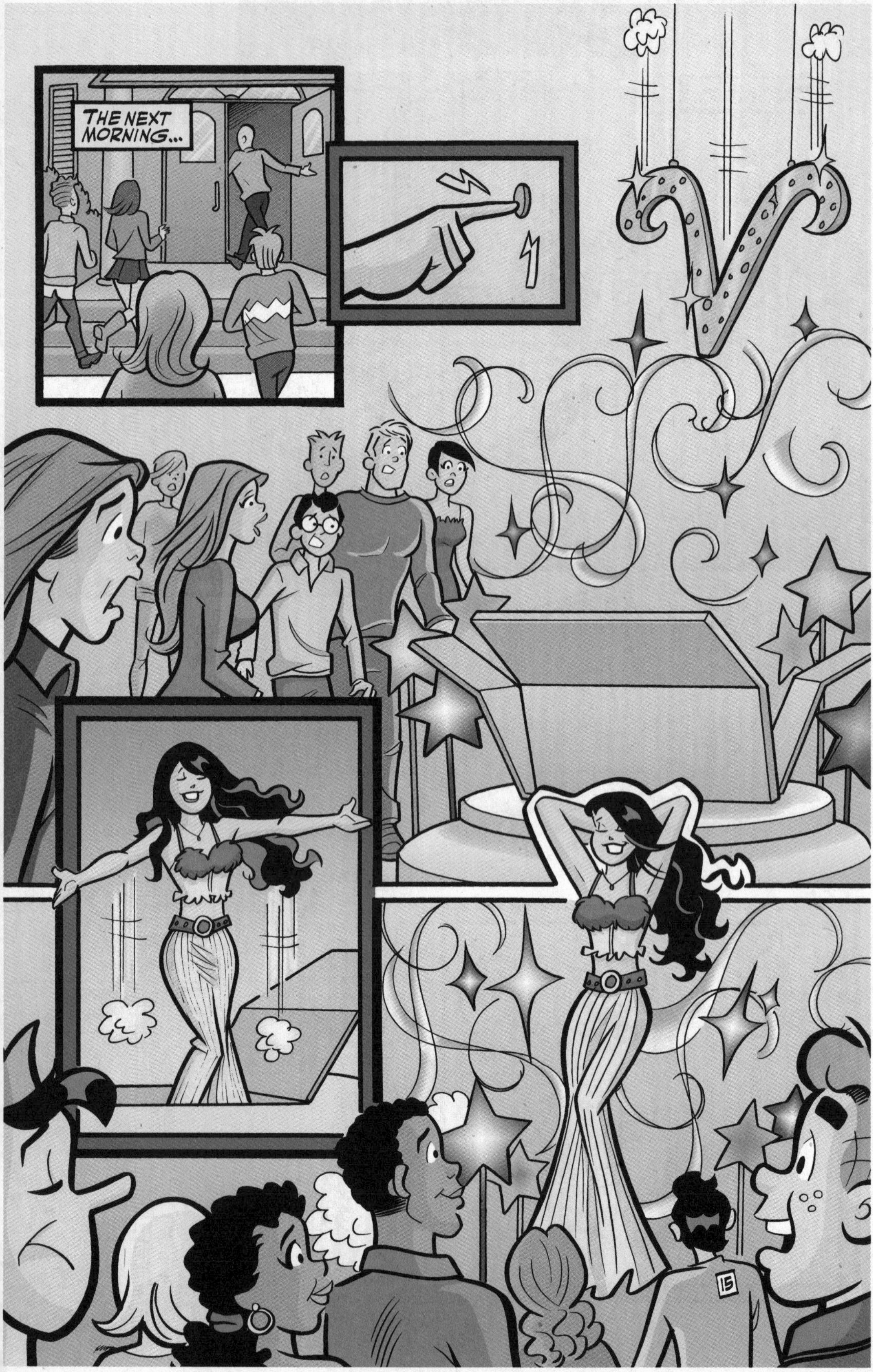
THE NEXT MORNING...

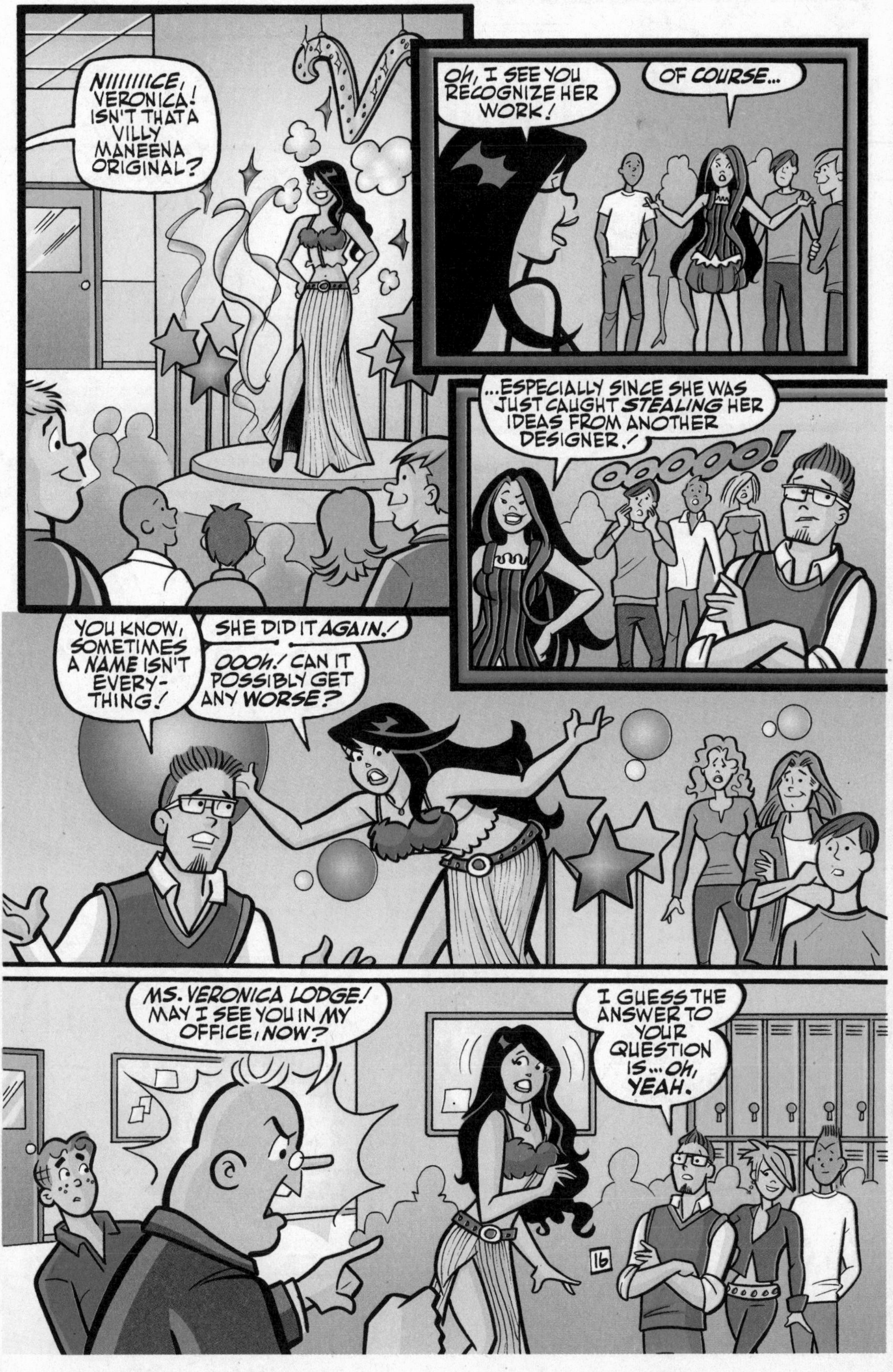
NIIIIIIICE, VERONICA! ISN'T THAT A VILLY MANEENA ORIGINAL?
OH, I SEE YOU RECOGNIZE HER WORK!
OF COURSE...
...ESPECIALLY SINCE SHE WAS JUST CAUGHT STEALING HER IDEAS FROM ANOTHER DESIGNER!
OOOOO!
YOU KNOW, SOMETIMES A NAME ISN'T EVERY-THING!
SHE DID IT AGAIN!
OOOH! CAN IT POSSIBLY GET ANY WORSE?
MS. VERONICA LODGE! MAY I SEE YOU IN MY OFFICE, NOW?
I GUESS THE ANSWER TO YOUR QUESTION IS... OH, YEAH.
16

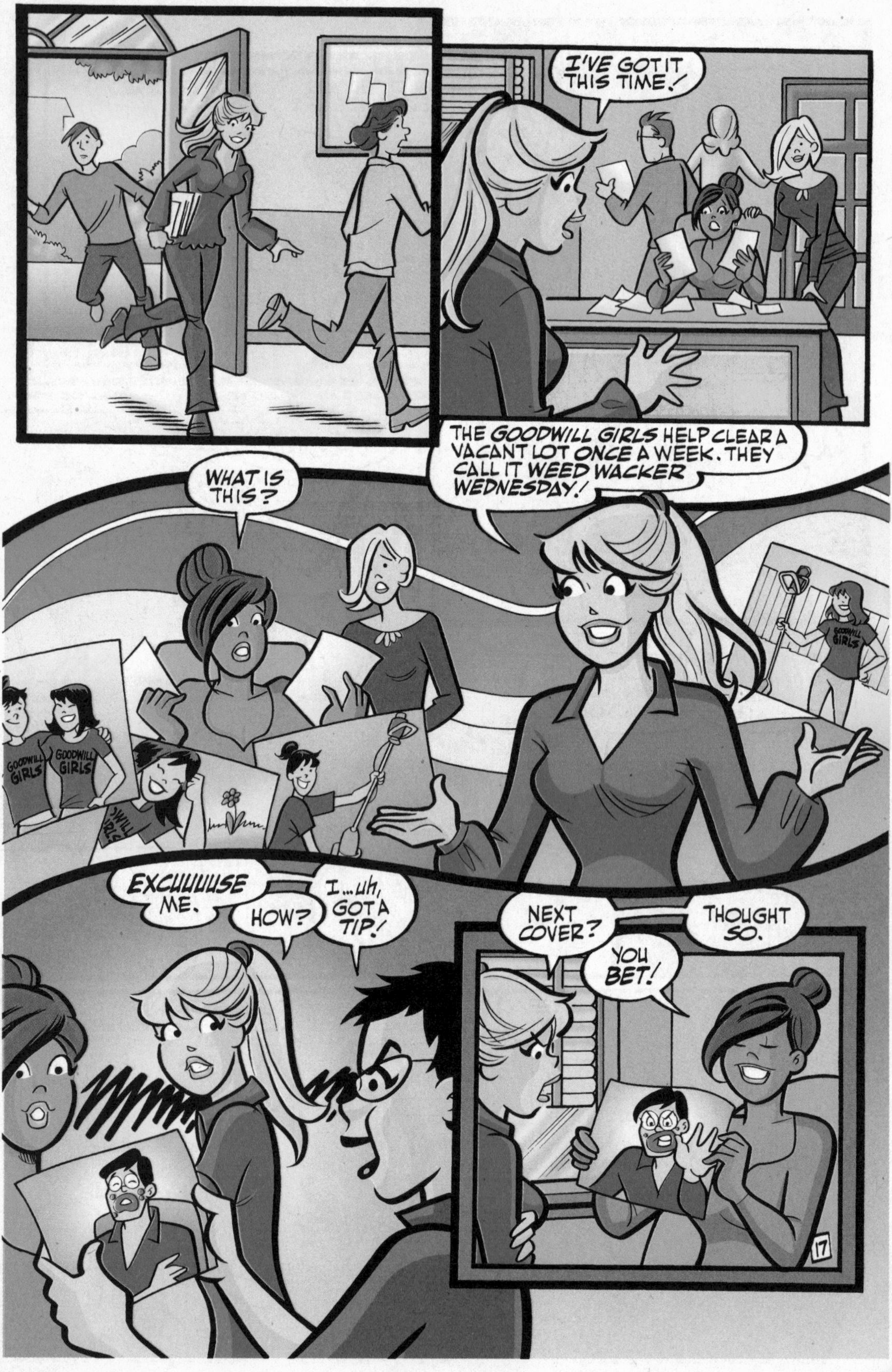
I'VE GOT IT THIS TIME!
WHAT IS THIS?
THE GOODWILL GIRLS HELP CLEAR A VACANT LOT ONCE A WEEK. THEY CALL IT WEED WACKER WEDNESDAY!
GOODWILL GIRLS
GOODWILL GIRLS
GOODWILL GIRLS
EXCUUUUSE ME.
HOW?
I...uh, GOT A TIP!
NEXT COVER?
YOU BET!
THOUGHT SO.
17

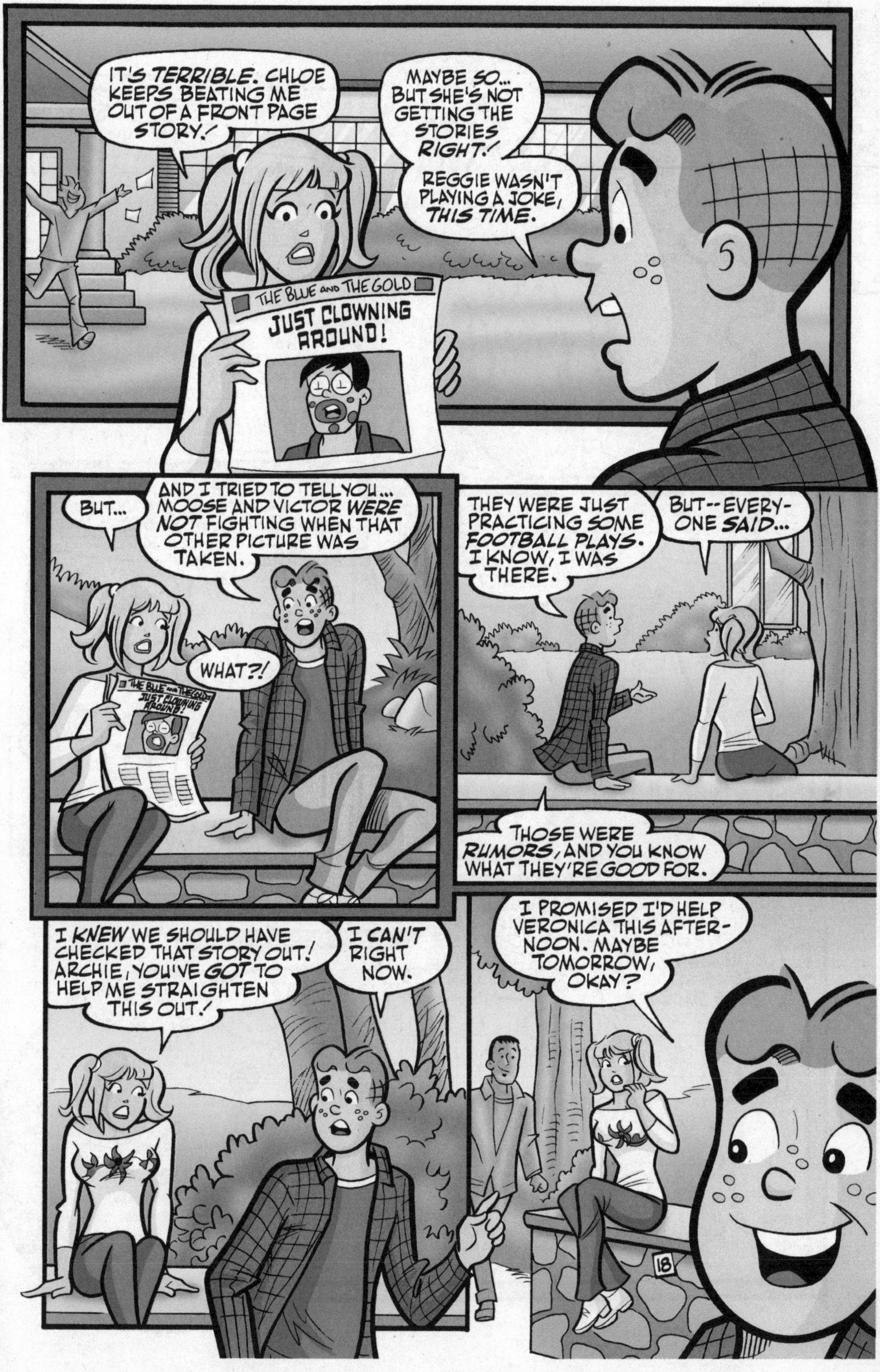
IT'S TERRIBLE. CHLOE KEEPS BEATING ME OUT OF A FRONT PAGE STORY!
MAYBE SO... BUT SHE'S NOT GETTING THE STORIES RIGHT!
REGGIE WASN'T PLAYING A JOKE, THIS TIME.
THE BLUE AND THE GOLD
JUST CLOWNING AROUND!
BUT...
AND I TRIED TO TELL YOU... MOOSE AND VICTOR WERE NOT FIGHTING WHEN THAT OTHER PICTURE WAS TAKEN.
WHAT?!
THEY WERE JUST PRACTICING SOME FOOTBALL PLAYS. I KNOW, I WAS THERE.
BUT--EVERY-ONE SAID...
THOSE WERE RUMORS, AND YOU KNOW WHAT THEY'RE GOOD FOR.
I KNEW WE SHOULD HAVE CHECKED THAT STORY OUT! ARCHIE, YOU'VE GOT TO HELP ME STRAIGHTEN THIS OUT!
I CAN'T RIGHT NOW.
I PROMISED I'D HELP VERONICA THIS AFTER-NOON. MAYBE TOMORROW, OKAY?
18

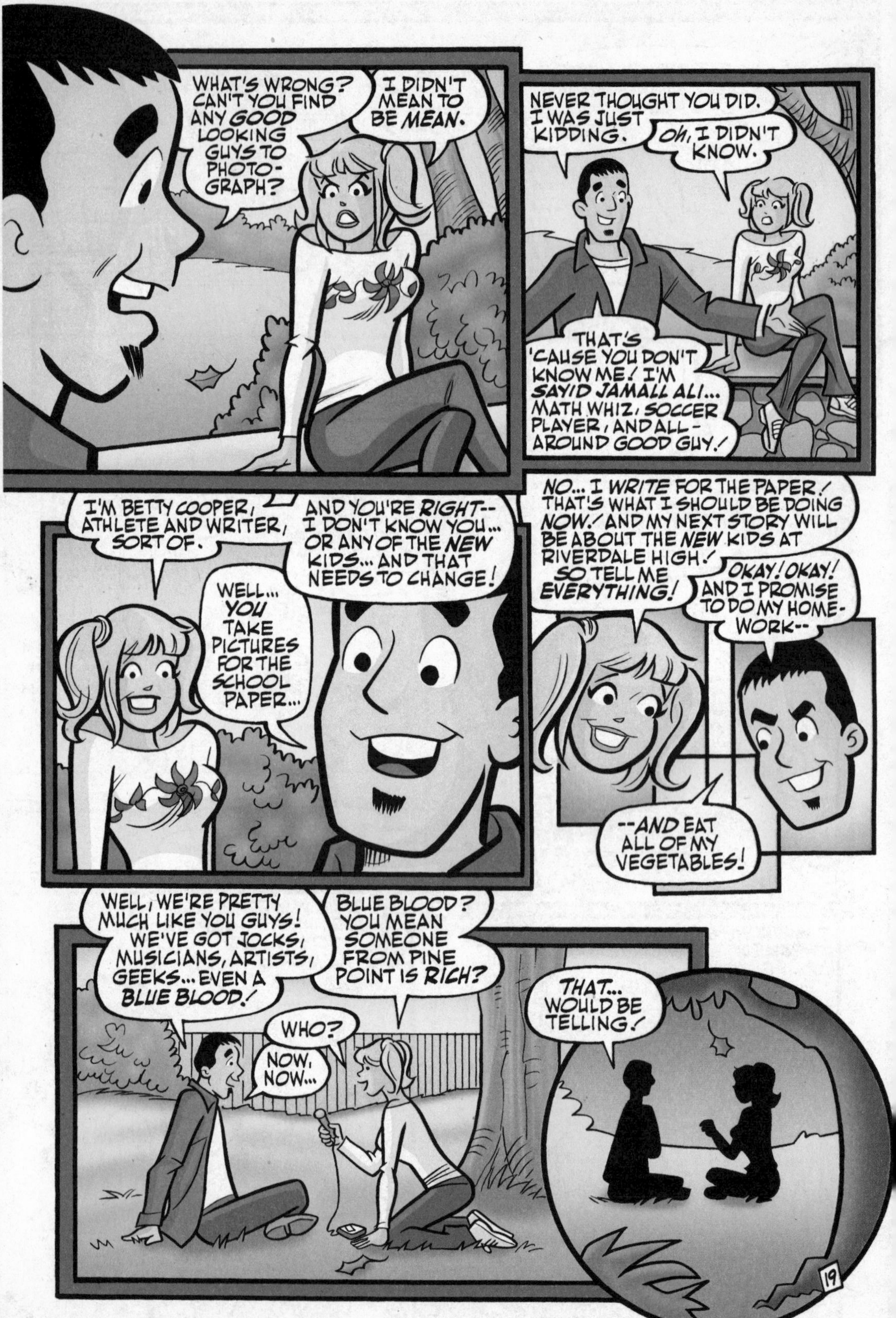
WHAT'S WRONG? CAN'T YOU FIND ANY GOOD LOOKING GUYS TO PHOTO-GRAPH?
I DIDN'T MEAN TO BE MEAN.
NEVER THOUGHT YOU DID. I WAS JUST KIDDING.
Oh, I DIDN'T KNOW.
THAT'S 'CAUSE YOU DON'T KNOW ME! I'M SAYID JAMALL ALI... MATH WHIZ, SOCCER PLAYER, AND ALL-AROUND GOOD GUY!
I'M BETTY COOPER, ATHLETE AND WRITER, SORT OF.
AND YOU'RE RIGHT-- I DON'T KNOW YOU... OR ANY OF THE NEW KIDS... AND THAT NEEDS TO CHANGE!
WELL... YOU TAKE PICTURES FOR THE SCHOOL PAPER...
NO... I WRITE FOR THE PAPER! THAT'S WHAT I SHOULD BE DOING NOW! AND MY NEXT STORY WILL BE ABOUT THE NEW KIDS AT RIVERDALE HIGH! SO TELL ME EVERYTHING!
OKAY! OKAY! AND I PROMISE TO DO MY HOME-WORK--
--AND EAT ALL OF MY VEGETABLES!
WELL, WE'RE PRETTY MUCH LIKE YOU GUYS! WE'VE GOT JOCKS, MUSICIANS, ARTISTS, GEEKS... EVEN A BLUE BLOOD!
BLUE BLOOD? YOU MEAN SOMEONE FROM PINE POINT IS RICH?
WHO?
NOW, NOW...
THAT... WOULD BE TELLING!
19

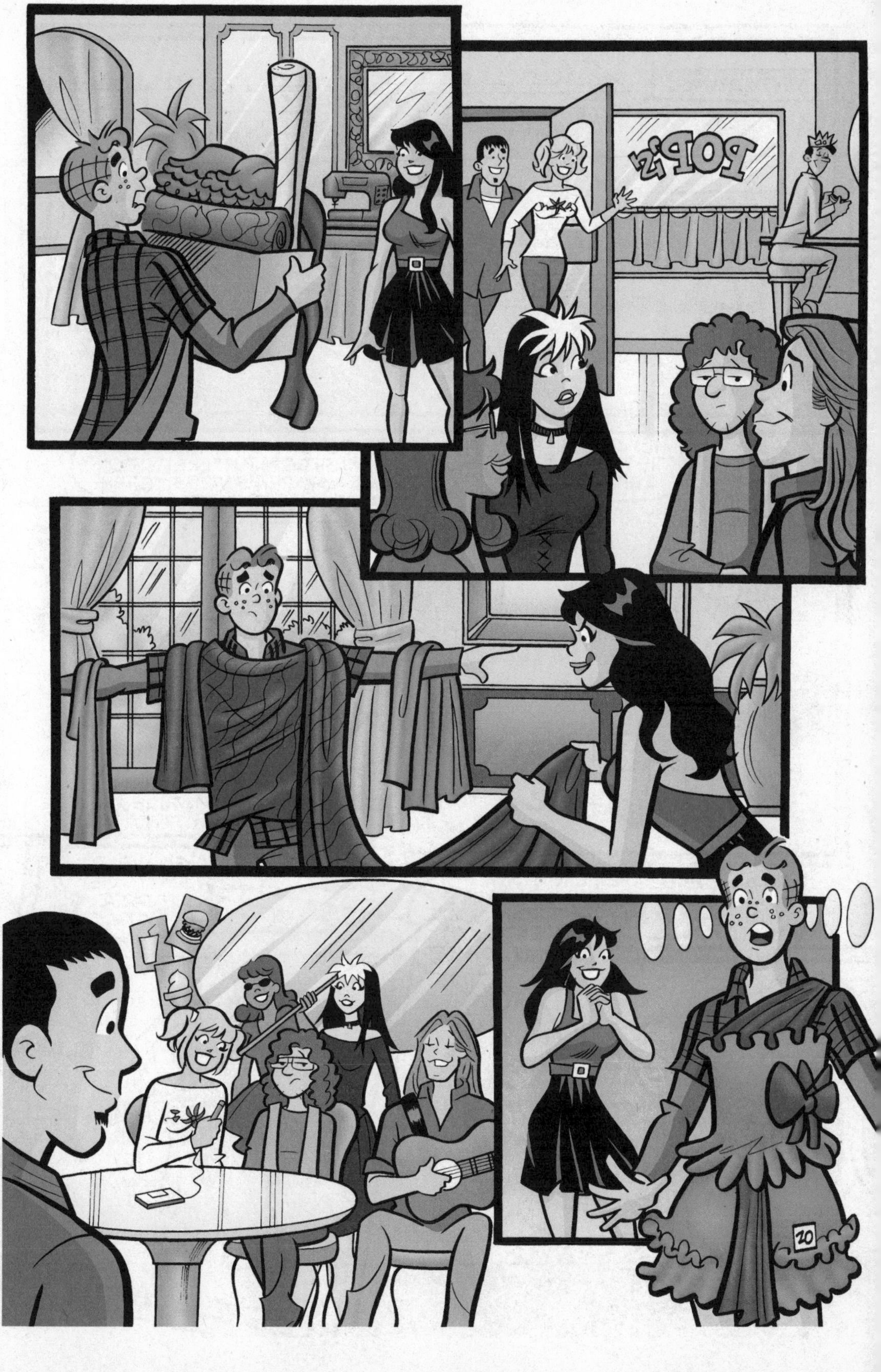
POP'S

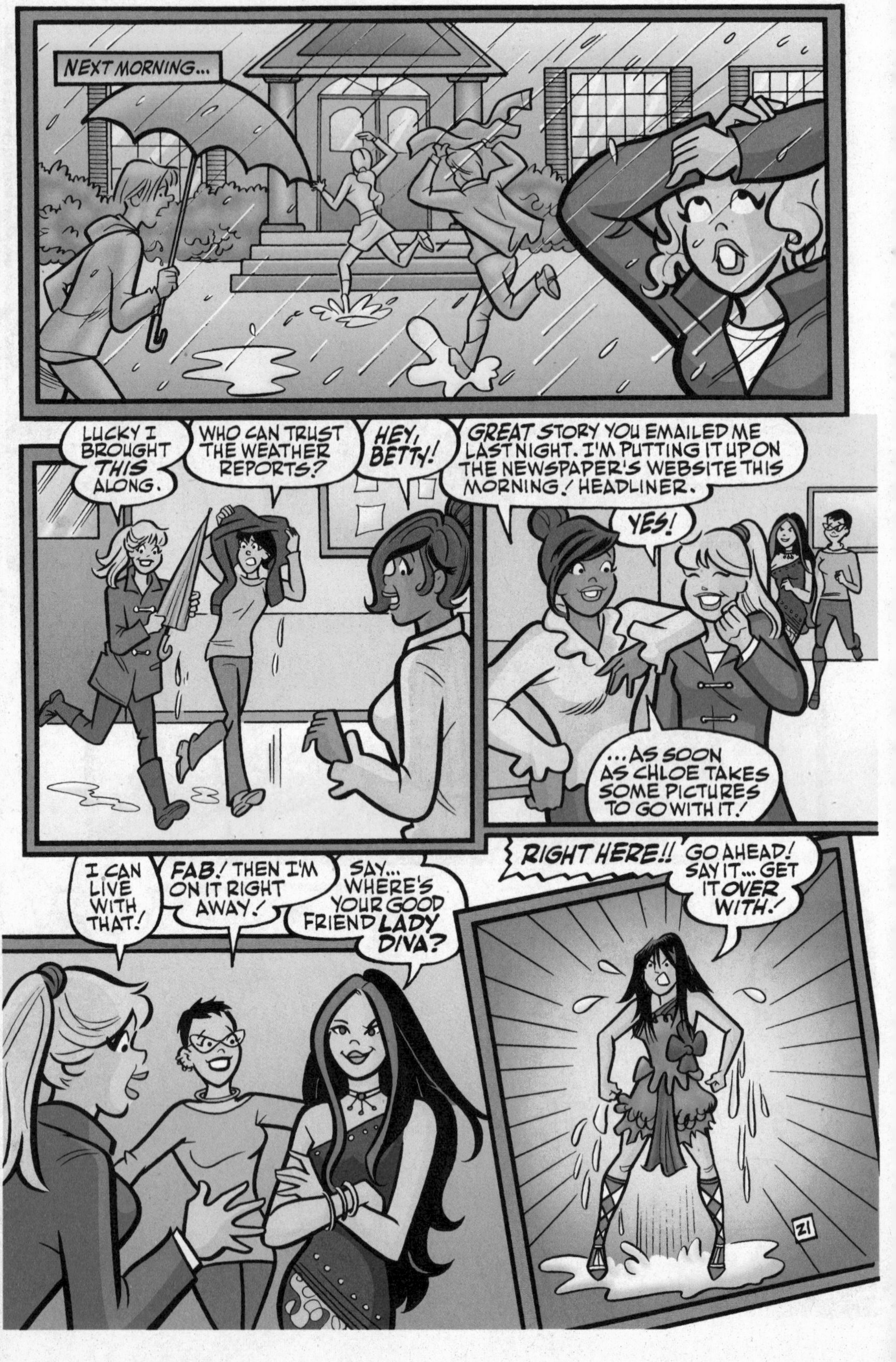
NEXT MORNING...
LUCKY I BROUGHT THIS ALONG.
WHO CAN TRUST THE WEATHER REPORTS?
HEY, BETTY!
GREAT STORY YOU EMAILED ME LAST NIGHT. I'M PUTTING IT UP ON THE NEWSPAPER'S WEBSITE THIS MORNING! HEADLINER.
YES!
...AS SOON AS CHLOE TAKES SOME PICTURES TO GO WITH IT!
I CAN LIVE WITH THAT!
FAB! THEN I'M ON IT RIGHT AWAY!
SAY... WHERE'S YOUR GOOD FRIEND LADY DIVA?
RIGHT HERE!!
GO AHEAD! SAY IT... GET IT OVER WITH!
21

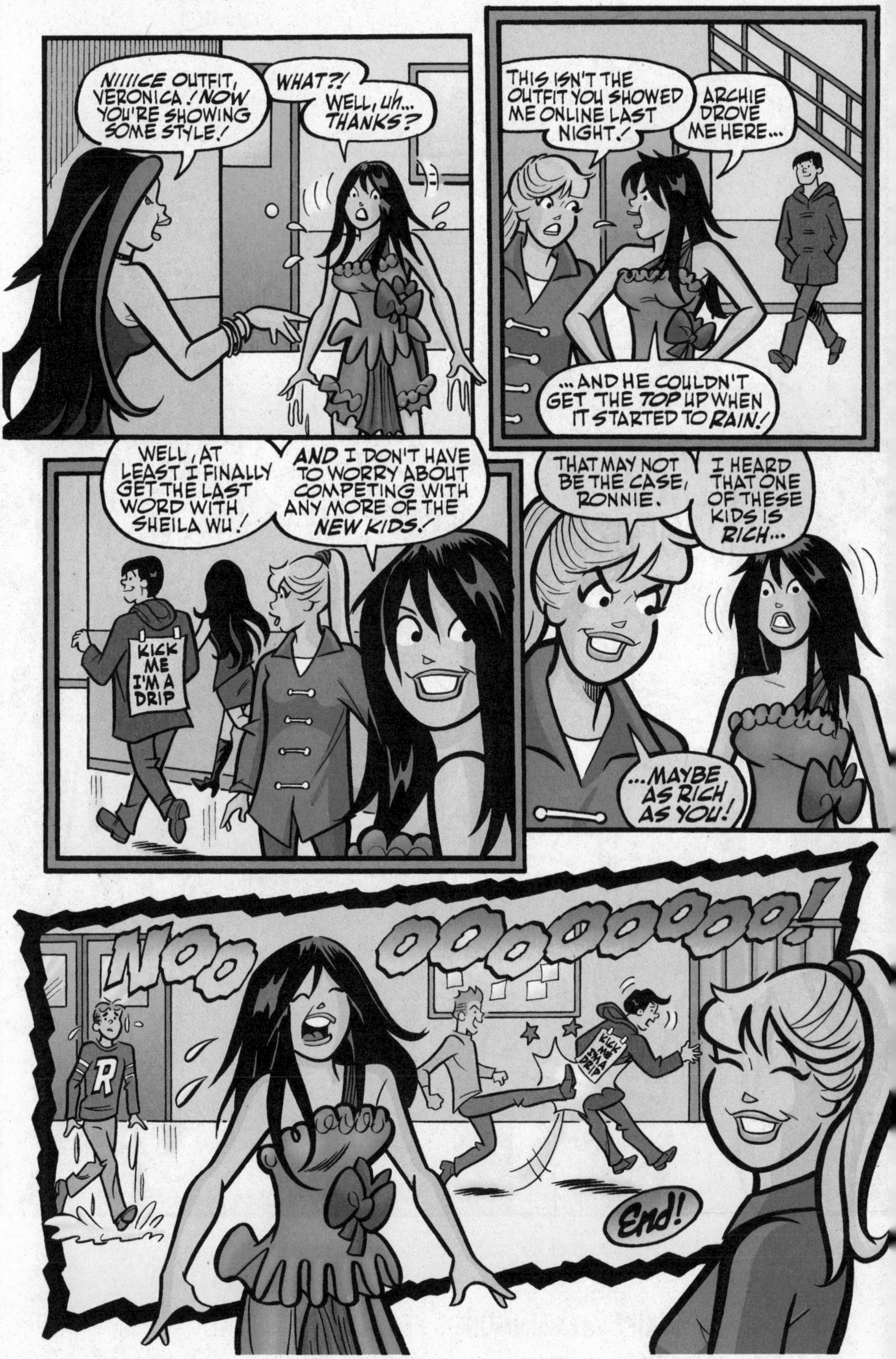
NIIIICE OUTFIT, VERONICA! NOW YOU'RE SHOWING SOME STYLE!
WHAT?!
WELL, uh... THANKS?
THIS ISN'T THE OUTFIT YOU SHOWED ME ONLINE LAST NIGHT!
ARCHIE DROVE ME HERE...
...AND HE COULDN'T GET THE TOP UP WHEN IT STARTED TO RAIN!
WELL, AT LEAST I FINALLY GET THE LAST WORD WITH SHEILA WU!
AND I DON'T HAVE TO WORRY ABOUT COMPETING WITH ANY MORE OF THE NEW KIDS!
KICK ME I'M A DRIP
THAT MAY NOT BE THE CASE, RONNIE.
I HEARD THAT ONE OF THESE KIDS IS RICH...
...MAYBE AS RICH AS YOU!
NOOOOOOOOOOO!
R
End!

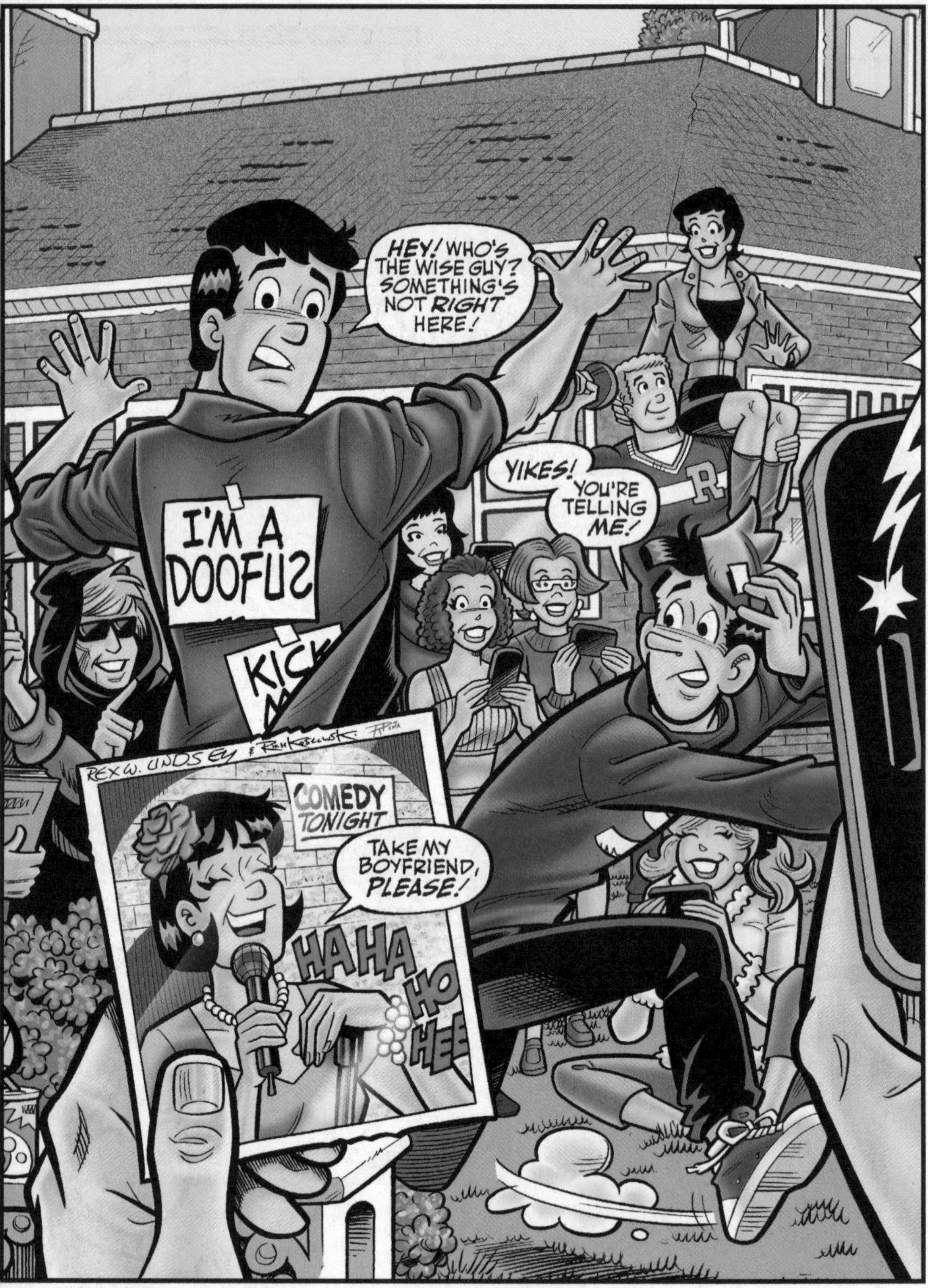
HEY! WHO'S THE WISE GUY? SOMETHING'S NOT RIGHT HERE!
I'M A DOOFUS
YIKES! YOU'RE TELLING ME!
COMEDY TONIGHT
TAKE MY BOYFRIEND, PLEASE!
HAHA

PRANKENSTEIN AND THE TWITTERS - PART 4

SCRIPT: ALEX SIMMONS PENCILS: DAN PARENT
INKS: RICH KOSLOWSKI LETTERS: JACK MORELLI COLORS: DIGIKORE STUDIOS

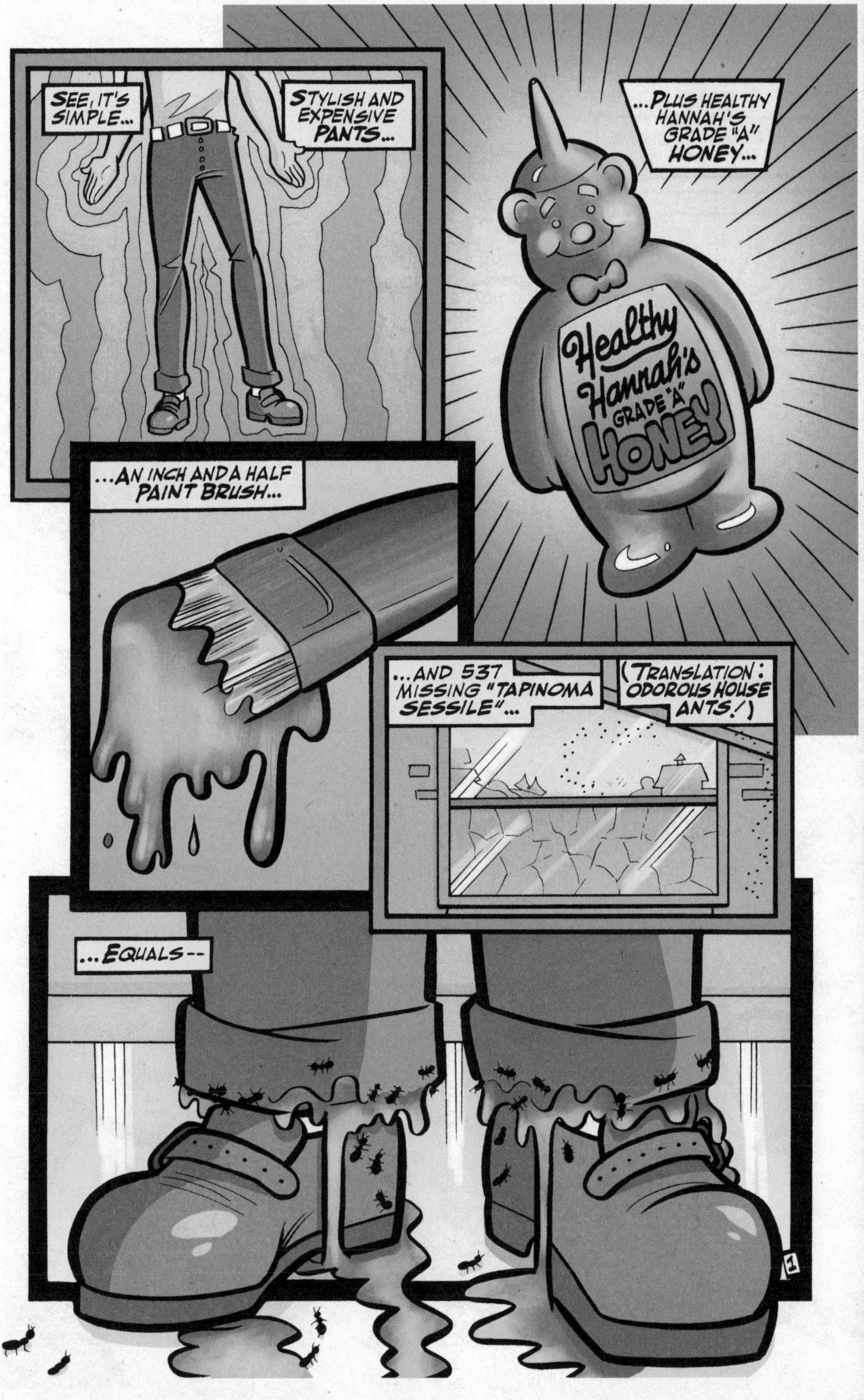
SEE, IT'S SIMPLE...
STYLISH AND EXPENSIVE PANTS...
...PLUS HEALTHY HANNAH'S GRADE "A" HONEY...
Healthy Hannah's GRADE "A" HONEY
...AN INCH AND A HALF PAINT BRUSH...
...AND 537 MISSING "TAPINOMA SESSILE"...
(TRANSLATION: ODOROUS HOUSE ANTS!)
...EQUALS--
1

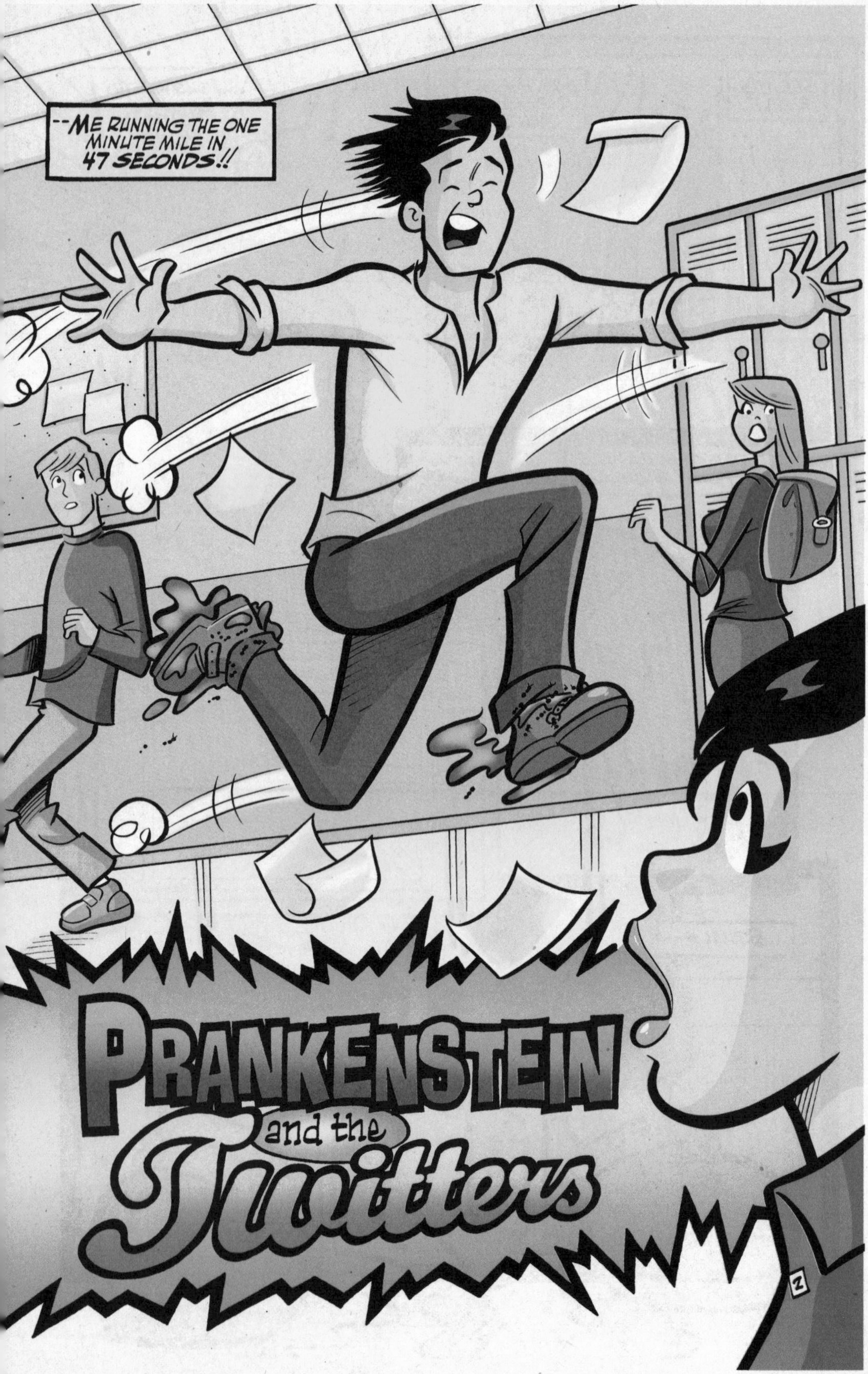
--ME RUNNING THE ONE MINUTE MILE IN 47 SECONDS!!
PRANKENSTEIN and the Twitters

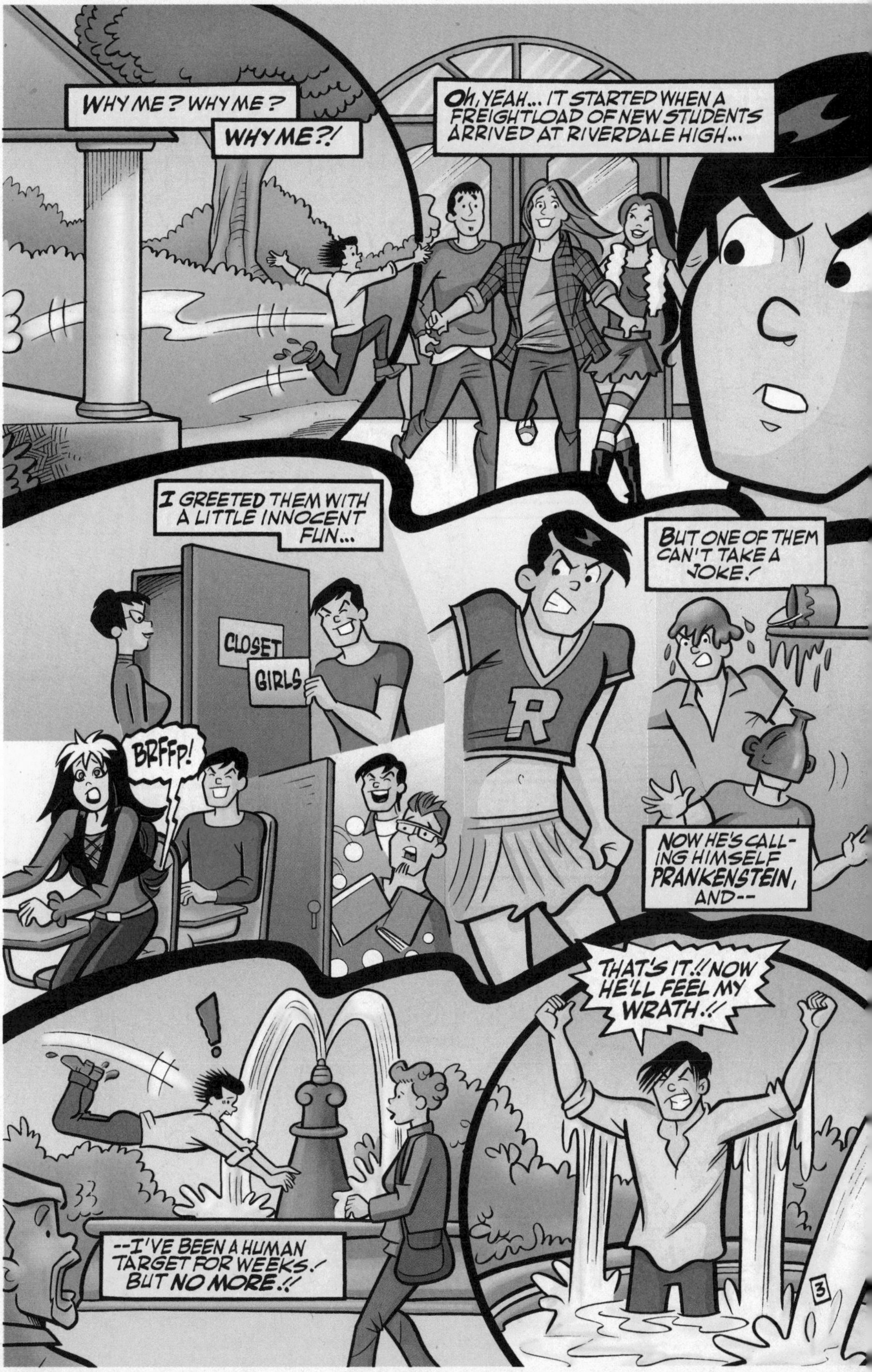
WHY ME? WHY ME?
WHY ME?!
OH, YEAH... IT STARTED WHEN A FREIGHTLOAD OF NEW STUDENTS ARRIVED AT RIVERDALE HIGH...
I GREETED THEM WITH A LITTLE INNOCENT FUN...
CLOSET
GIRLS
BRFFP!
BUT ONE OF THEM CAN'T TAKE A JOKE!
NOW HE'S CALLING HIMSELF PRANKENSTEIN, AND--
THAT'S IT!! NOW HE'LL FEEL MY WRATH!!
--I'VE BEEN A HUMAN TARGET FOR WEEKS! BUT NO MORE!!
3

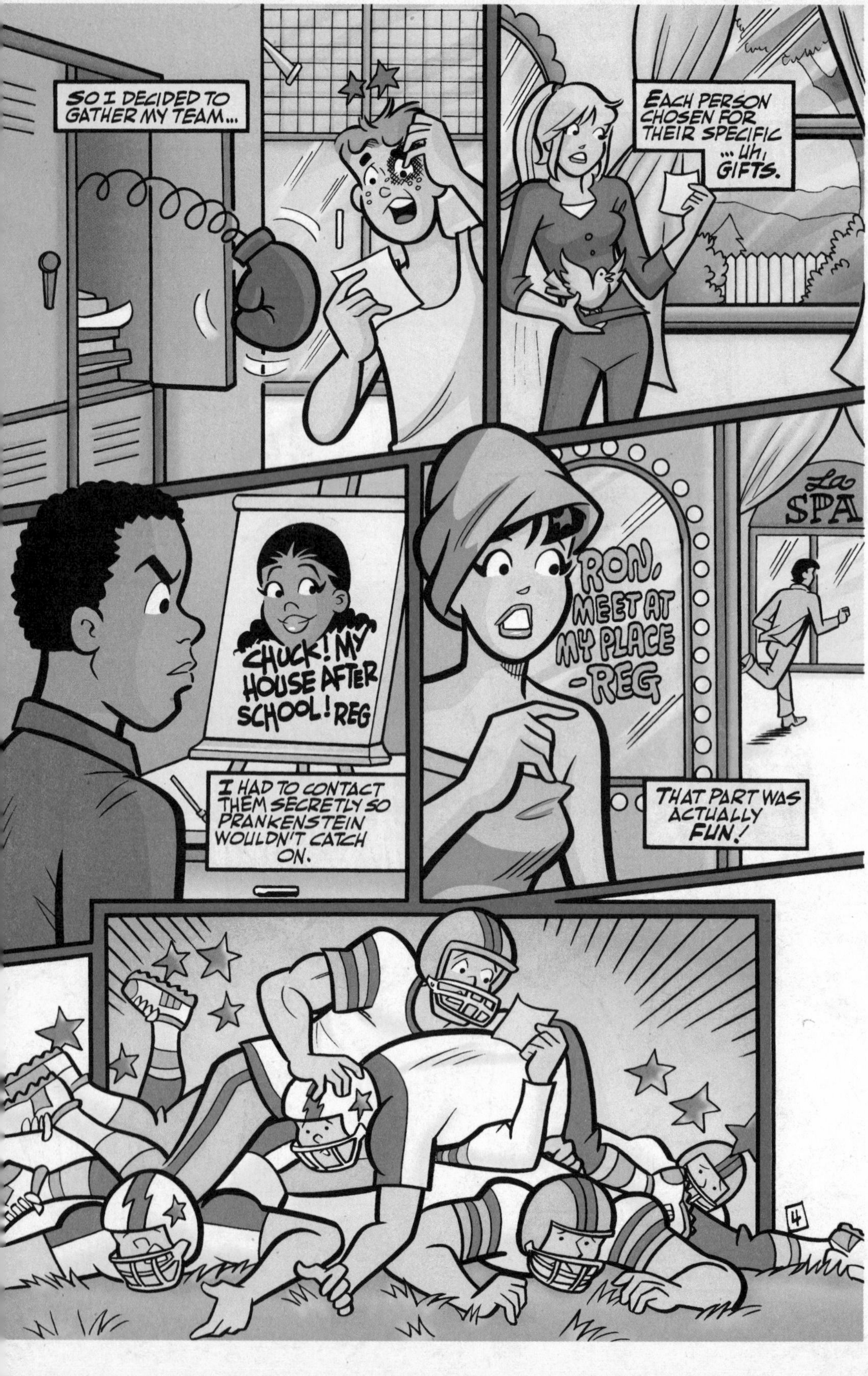
SO I DECIDED TO GATHER MY TEAM...
EACH PERSON CHOSEN FOR THEIR SPECIFIC ...UH, GIFTS.
CHUCK! MY HOUSE AFTER SCHOOL! REG
I HAD TO CONTACT THEM SECRETLY SO PRANKENSTEIN WOULDN'T CATCH ON.
RON, MEET AT MY PLACE -REG
La SPA
THAT PART WAS ACTUALLY FUN!
4

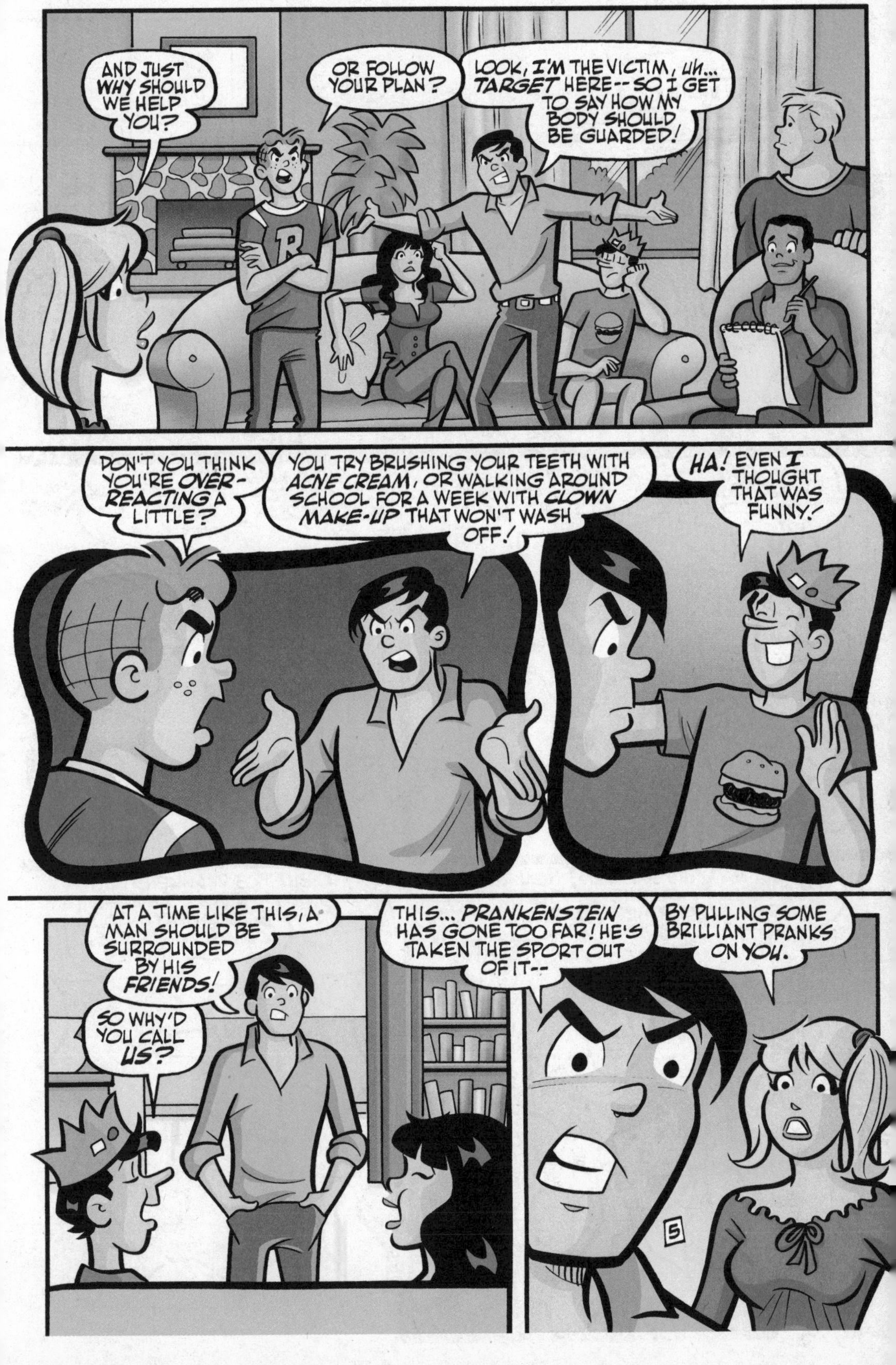
AND JUST WHY SHOULD WE HELP YOU?
OR FOLLOW YOUR PLAN?
LOOK, I'M THE VICTIM, UH... TARGET HERE-- SO I GET TO SAY HOW MY BODY SHOULD BE GUARDED!
DON'T YOU THINK YOU'RE OVER-REACTING A LITTLE?
YOU TRY BRUSHING YOUR TEETH WITH ACNE CREAM, OR WALKING AROUND SCHOOL FOR A WEEK WITH CLOWN MAKE-UP THAT WON'T WASH OFF!
HA! EVEN I THOUGHT THAT WAS FUNNY!
AT A TIME LIKE THIS, A MAN SHOULD BE SURROUNDED BY HIS FRIENDS!
SO WHY'D YOU CALL US?
THIS... PRANKENSTEIN HAS GONE TOO FAR! HE'S TAKEN THE SPORT OUT OF IT--
BY PULLING SOME BRILLIANT PRANKS ON YOU.
5

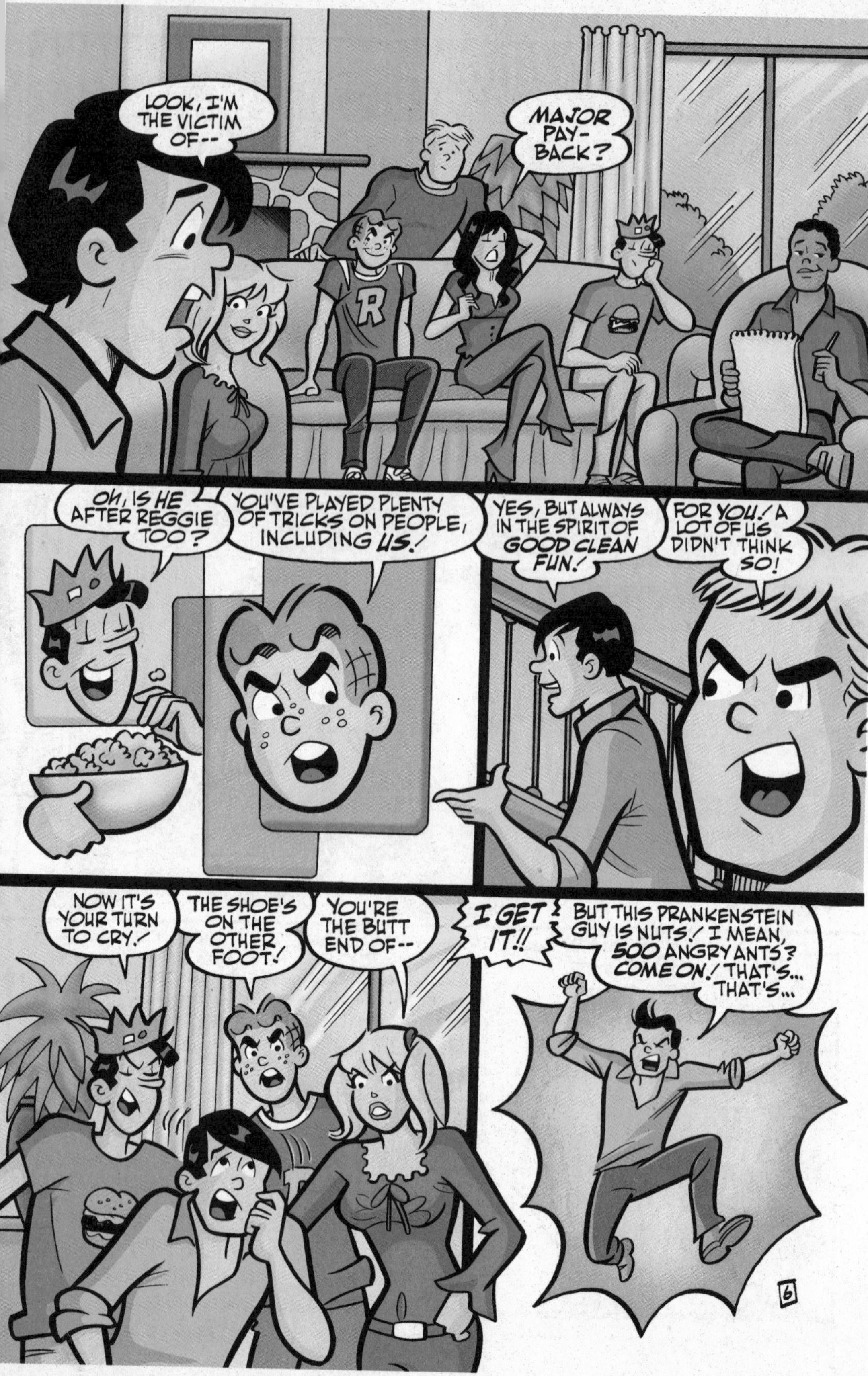
LOOK, I'M THE VICTIM OF--
MAJOR PAY-BACK?
OH, IS HE AFTER REGGIE TOO?
YOU'VE PLAYED PLENTY OF TRICKS ON PEOPLE, INCLUDING US!
YES, BUT ALWAYS IN THE SPIRIT OF GOOD CLEAN FUN!
FOR YOU! A LOT OF US DIDN'T THINK SO!
NOW IT'S YOUR TURN TO CRY!
THE SHOE'S ON THE OTHER FOOT!
YOU'RE THE BUTT END OF--
I GET IT!!
BUT THIS PRANKENSTEIN GUY IS NUTS! I MEAN, 500 ANGRY ANTS? COME ON! THAT'S... THAT'S...
6

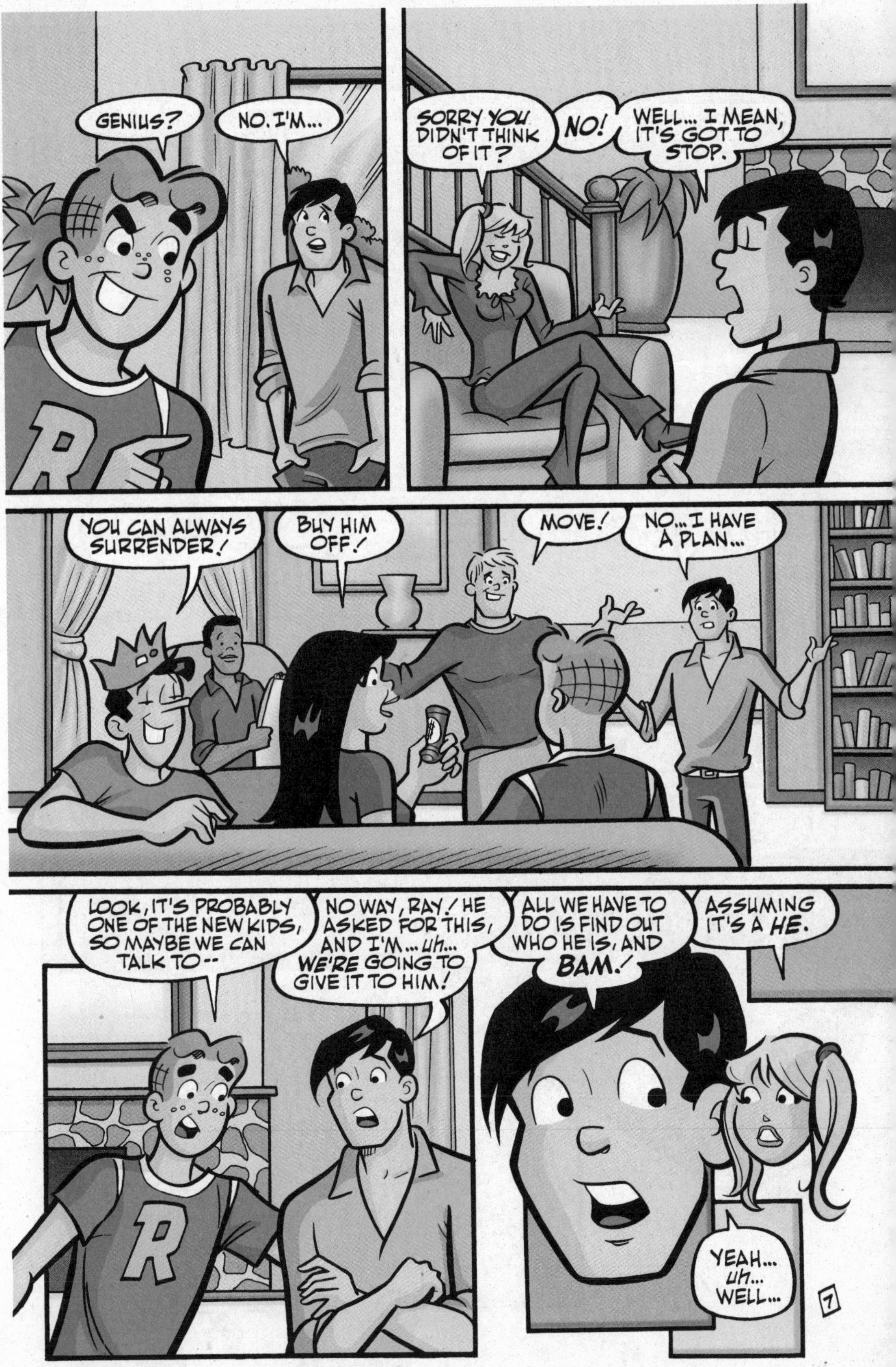
GENIUS?
NO. I'M...
SORRY YOU DIDN'T THINK OF IT?
NO!
WELL... I MEAN, IT'S GOT TO STOP.
YOU CAN ALWAYS SURRENDER!
BUY HIM OFF!
MOVE!
NO... I HAVE A PLAN...
LOOK, IT'S PROBABLY ONE OF THE NEW KIDS, SO MAYBE WE CAN TALK TO--
NO WAY, RAY! HE ASKED FOR THIS, AND I'M... uh... WE'RE GOING TO GIVE IT TO HIM!
ALL WE HAVE TO DO IS FIND OUT WHO HE IS, AND BAM!
ASSUMING IT'S A HE.
YEAH... uh... WELL...
7

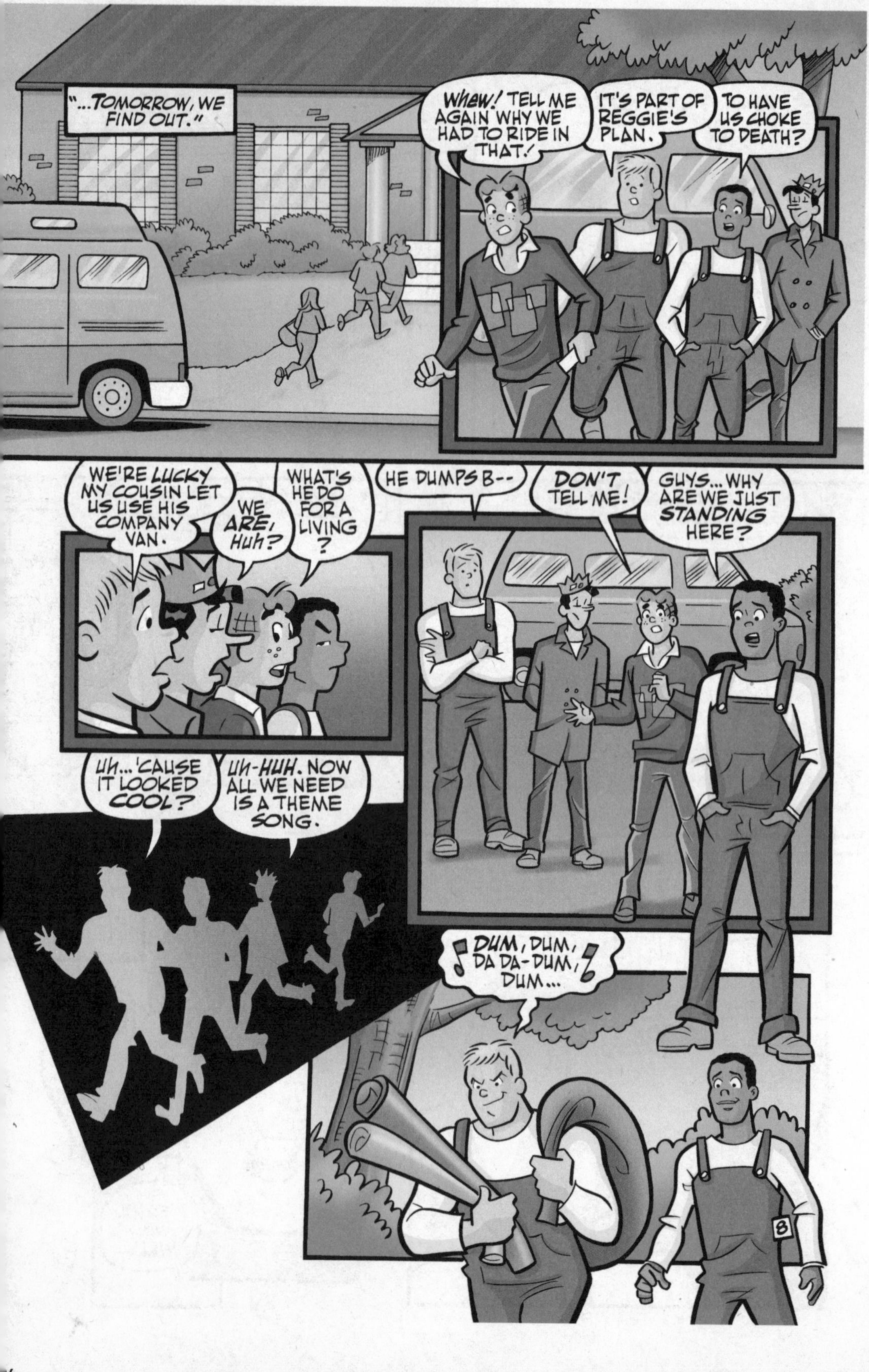
"...TOMORROW, WE FIND OUT."
WHEW! TELL ME AGAIN WHY WE HAD TO RIDE IN THAT.!
IT'S PART OF REGGIE'S PLAN.
TO HAVE US CHOKE TO DEATH?
WE'RE LUCKY MY COUSIN LET US USE HIS COMPANY VAN.
WE ARE, HUH?
WHAT'S HE DO FOR A LIVING ?
HE DUMPS B--
DON'T TELL ME!
GUYS... WHY ARE WE JUST STANDING HERE?
UH... 'CAUSE IT LOOKED COOL?
UH-HUH. NOW ALL WE NEED IS A THEME SONG.
DUM, DUM, DA DA-DUM, DUM...
8

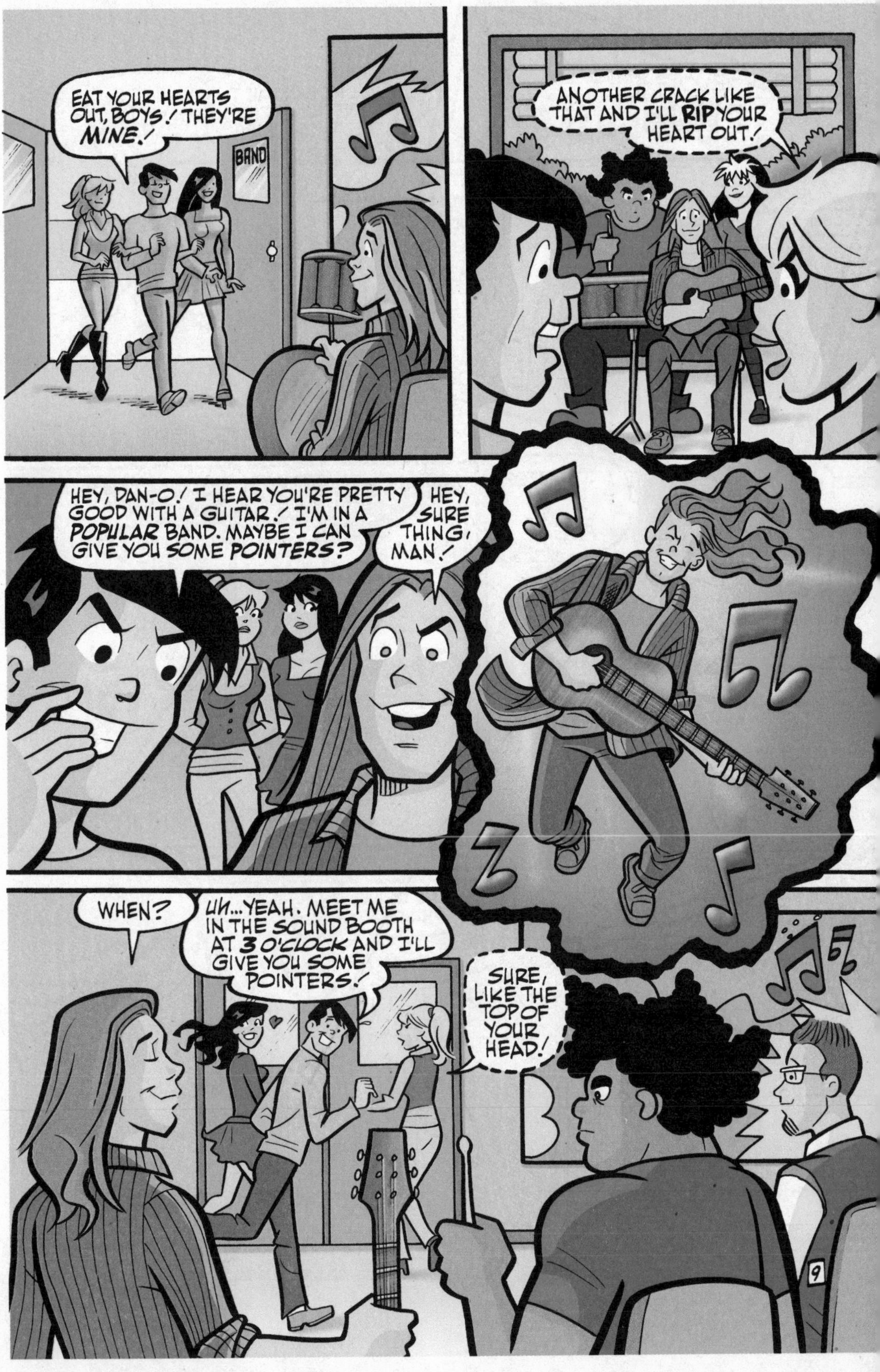
EAT YOUR HEARTS OUT, BOYS! THEY'RE MINE!
BAND
ANOTHER CRACK LIKE THAT AND I'LL RIP YOUR HEART OUT!
HEY, DAN-O! I HEAR YOU'RE PRETTY GOOD WITH A GUITAR! I'M IN A POPULAR BAND. MAYBE I CAN GIVE YOU SOME POINTERS?
HEY, SURE THING, MAN!
WHEN?
UH...YEAH. MEET ME IN THE SOUND BOOTH AT 3 O'CLOCK AND I'LL GIVE YOU SOME POINTERS!
SURE, LIKE THE TOP OF YOUR HEAD!
9

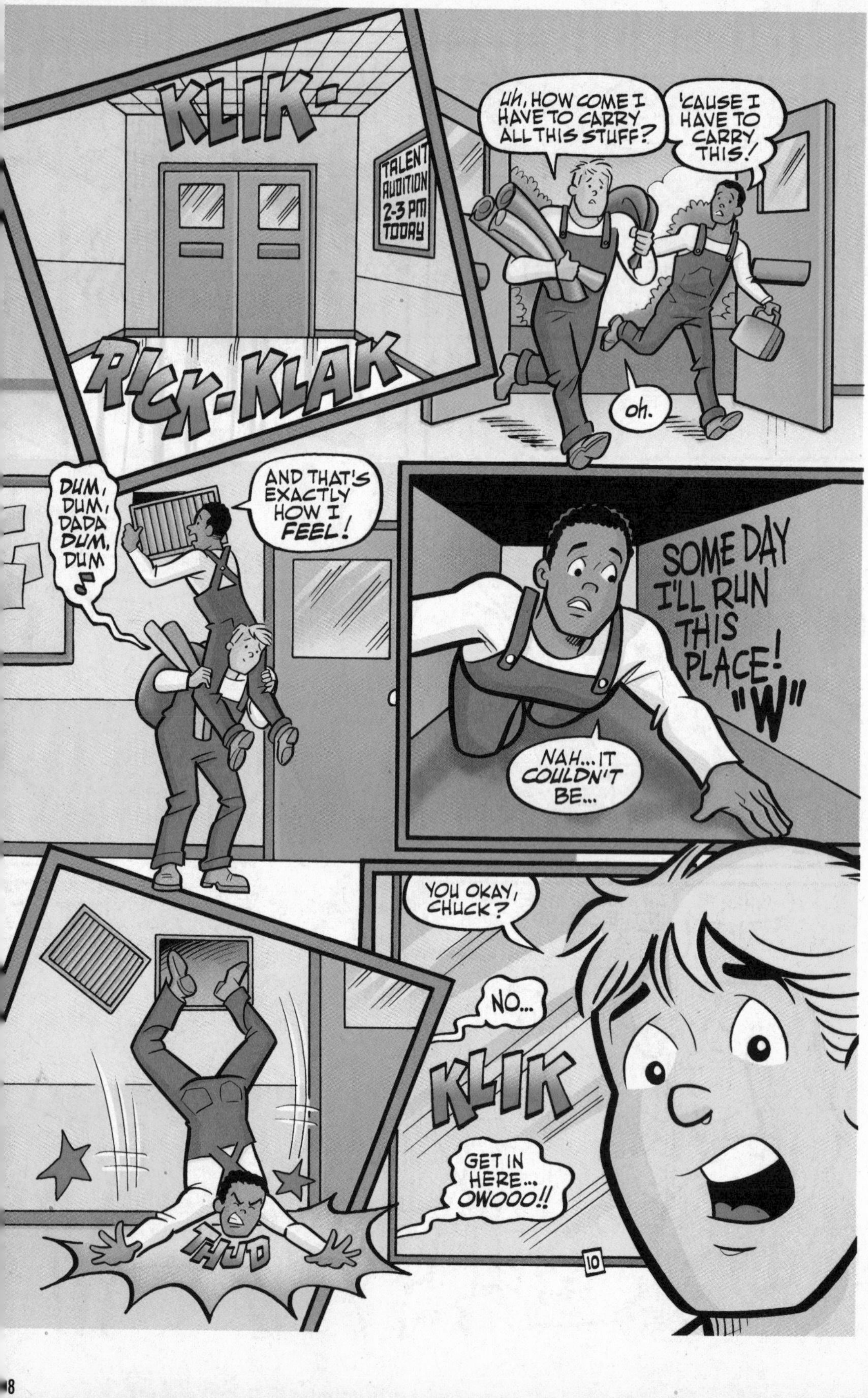
KLIK-
TALENT AUDITION 2-3 PM TODAY
RICK-KLAK
UH, HOW COME I HAVE TO CARRY ALL THIS STUFF?
'CAUSE I HAVE TO CARRY THIS!
oh.
DUM, DUM, DADA DUM, DUM
AND THAT'S EXACTLY HOW I FEEL!
SOME DAY I'LL RUN THIS PLACE! "W"
NAH... IT COULDN'T BE...
THUD
YOU OKAY, CHUCK?
NO...
KLIK
GET IN HERE... OWOOO!!
10

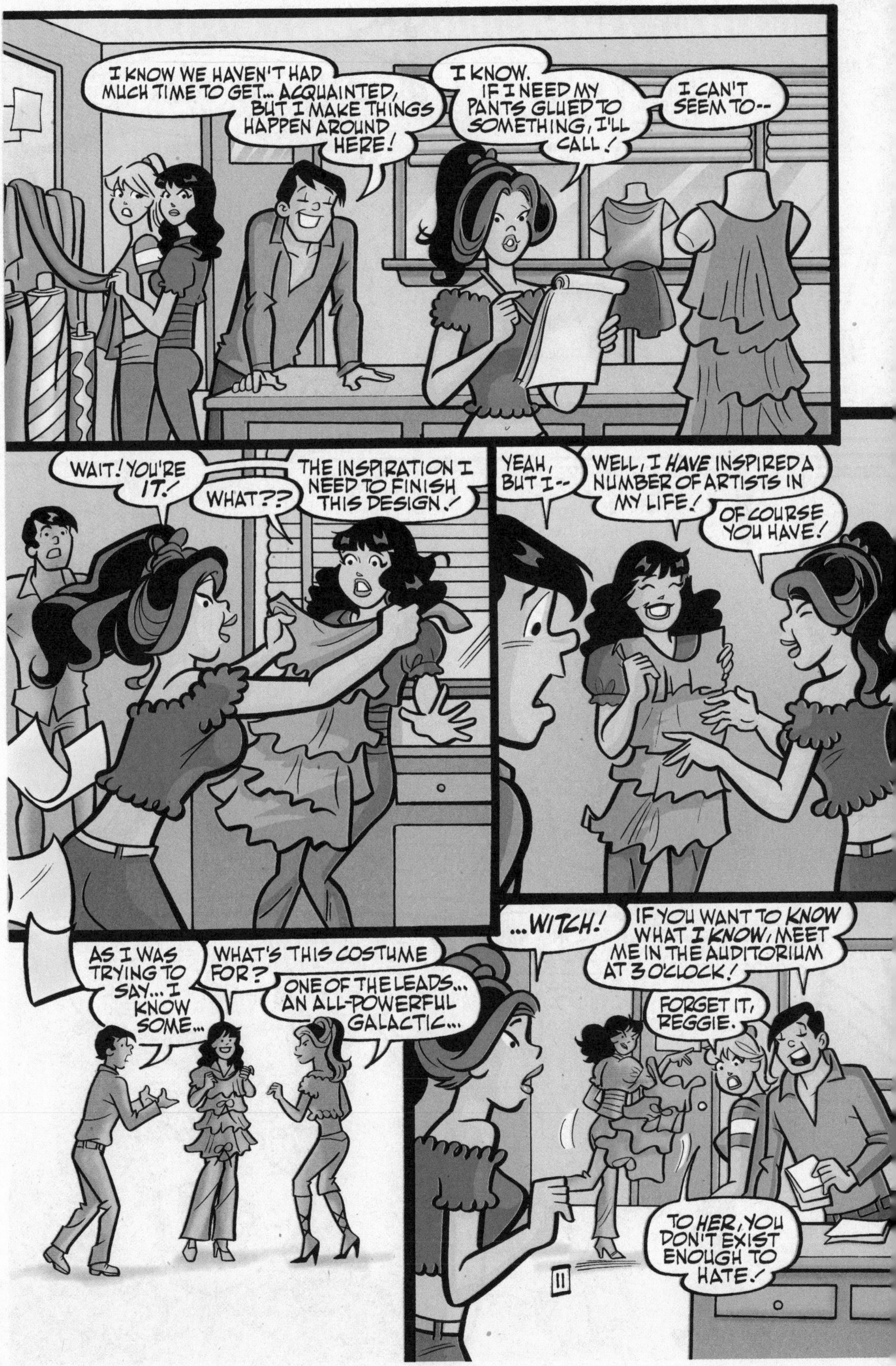
I KNOW WE HAVEN'T HAD MUCH TIME TO GET... ACQUAINTED, BUT I MAKE THINGS HAPPEN AROUND HERE!
I KNOW. IF I NEED MY PANTS GLUED TO SOMETHING, I'LL CALL!
I CAN'T SEEM TO--
WAIT! YOU'RE IT!
WHAT??
THE INSPIRATION I NEED TO FINISH THIS DESIGN!
YEAH, BUT I--
WELL, I HAVE INSPIRED A NUMBER OF ARTISTS IN MY LIFE!
OF COURSE YOU HAVE!
AS I WAS TRYING TO SAY... I KNOW SOME...
WHAT'S THIS COSTUME FOR?
ONE OF THE LEADS... AN ALL-POWERFUL GALACTIC...
...WITCH!
IF YOU WANT TO KNOW WHAT I KNOW, MEET ME IN THE AUDITORIUM AT 3 O'CLOCK!
FORGET IT, REGGIE.
TO HER, YOU DON'T EXIST ENOUGH TO HATE!
11

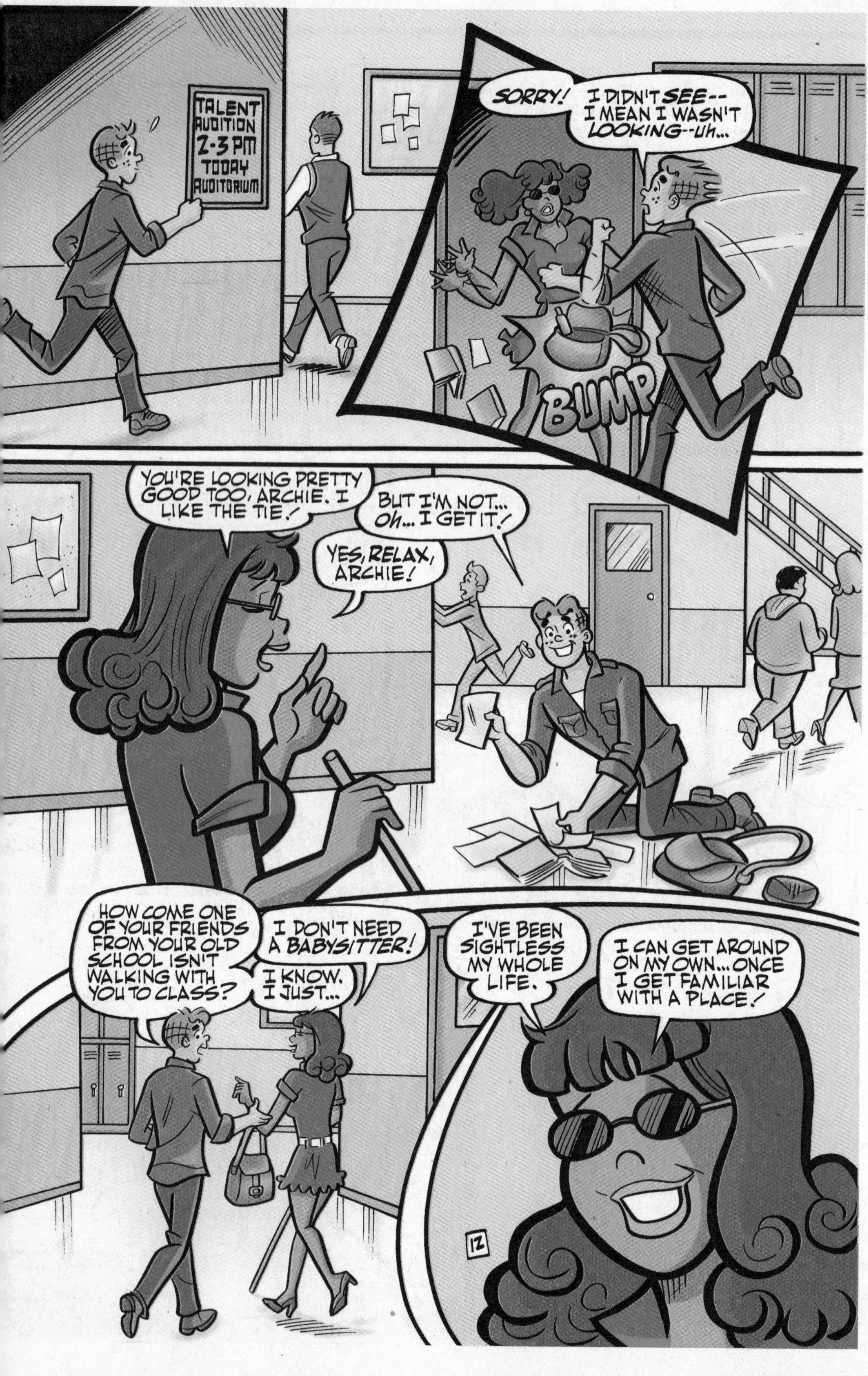
TALENT AUDITION 2-3 PM TODAY AUDITORIUM
SORRY!
I DIDN'T SEE-- I MEAN I WASN'T LOOKING--uh...
BUMP
YOU'RE LOOKING PRETTY GOOD TOO, ARCHIE. I LIKE THE TIE!
BUT I'M NOT... Oh... I GET IT!
YES, RELAX, ARCHIE!
HOW COME ONE OF YOUR FRIENDS FROM YOUR OLD SCHOOL ISN'T WALKING WITH YOU TO CLASS?
I DON'T NEED A BABYSITTER!
I KNOW. I JUST...
I'VE BEEN SIGHTLESS MY WHOLE LIFE.
I CAN GET AROUND ON MY OWN... ONCE I GET FAMILIAR WITH A PLACE!
12

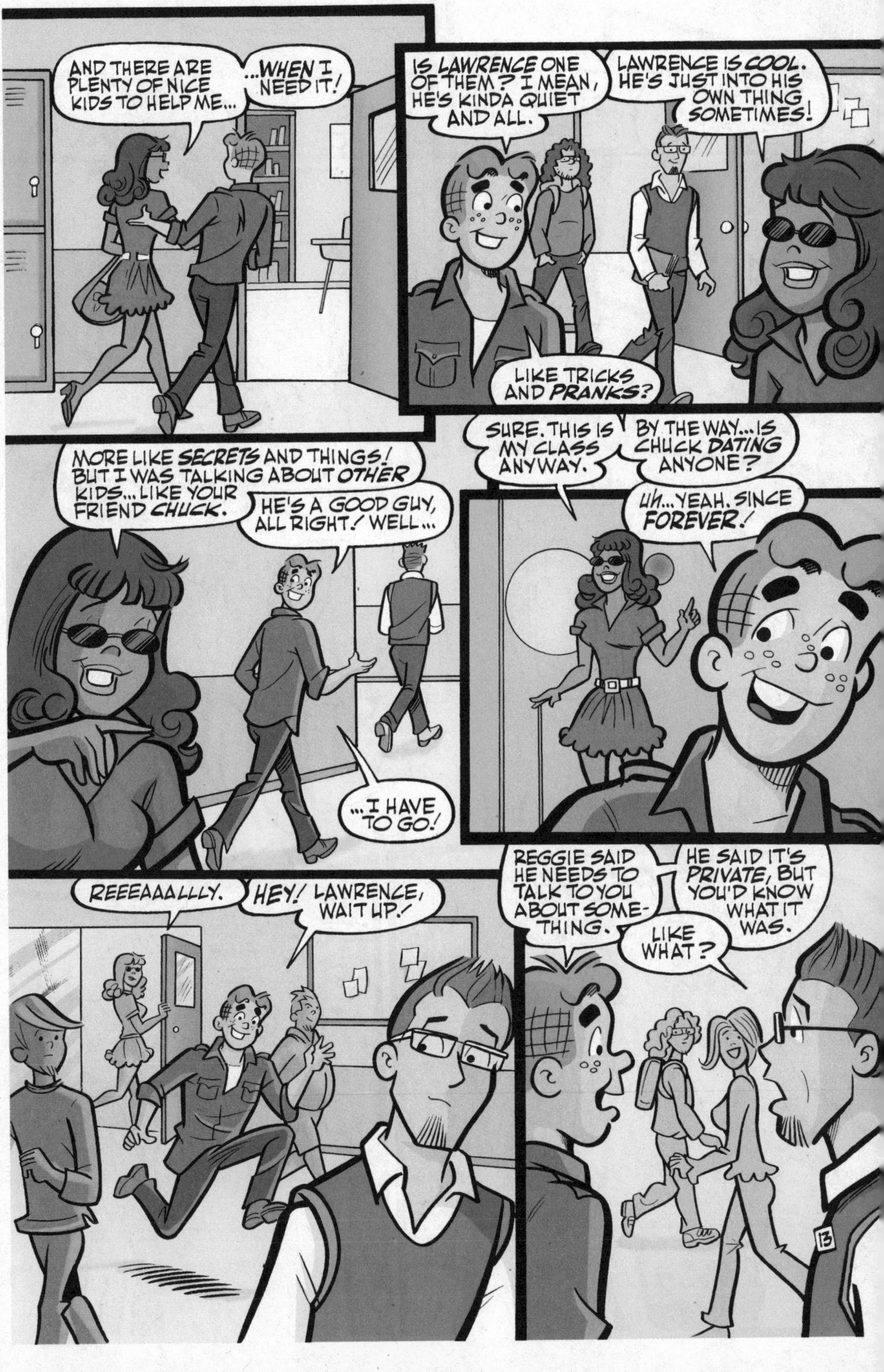
AND THERE ARE PLENTY OF NICE KIDS TO HELP ME...
...WHEN I NEED IT!
IS LAWRENCE ONE OF THEM? I MEAN, HE'S KINDA QUIET AND ALL.
LAWRENCE IS COOL. HE'S JUST INTO HIS OWN THING SOMETIMES!
LIKE TRICKS AND PRANKS?
MORE LIKE SECRETS AND THINGS! BUT I WAS TALKING ABOUT OTHER KIDS... LIKE YOUR FRIEND CHUCK.
HE'S A GOOD GUY, ALL RIGHT! WELL...
...I HAVE TO GO!
SURE. THIS IS MY CLASS ANYWAY.
BY THE WAY... IS CHUCK DATING ANYONE?
UH... YEAH. SINCE FOREVER!
REEEAAALLLY.
HEY! LAWRENCE, WAIT UP!
REGGIE SAID HE NEEDS TO TALK TO YOU ABOUT SOMETHING.
LIKE WHAT?
HE SAID IT'S PRIVATE, BUT YOU'D KNOW WHAT IT WAS.
13

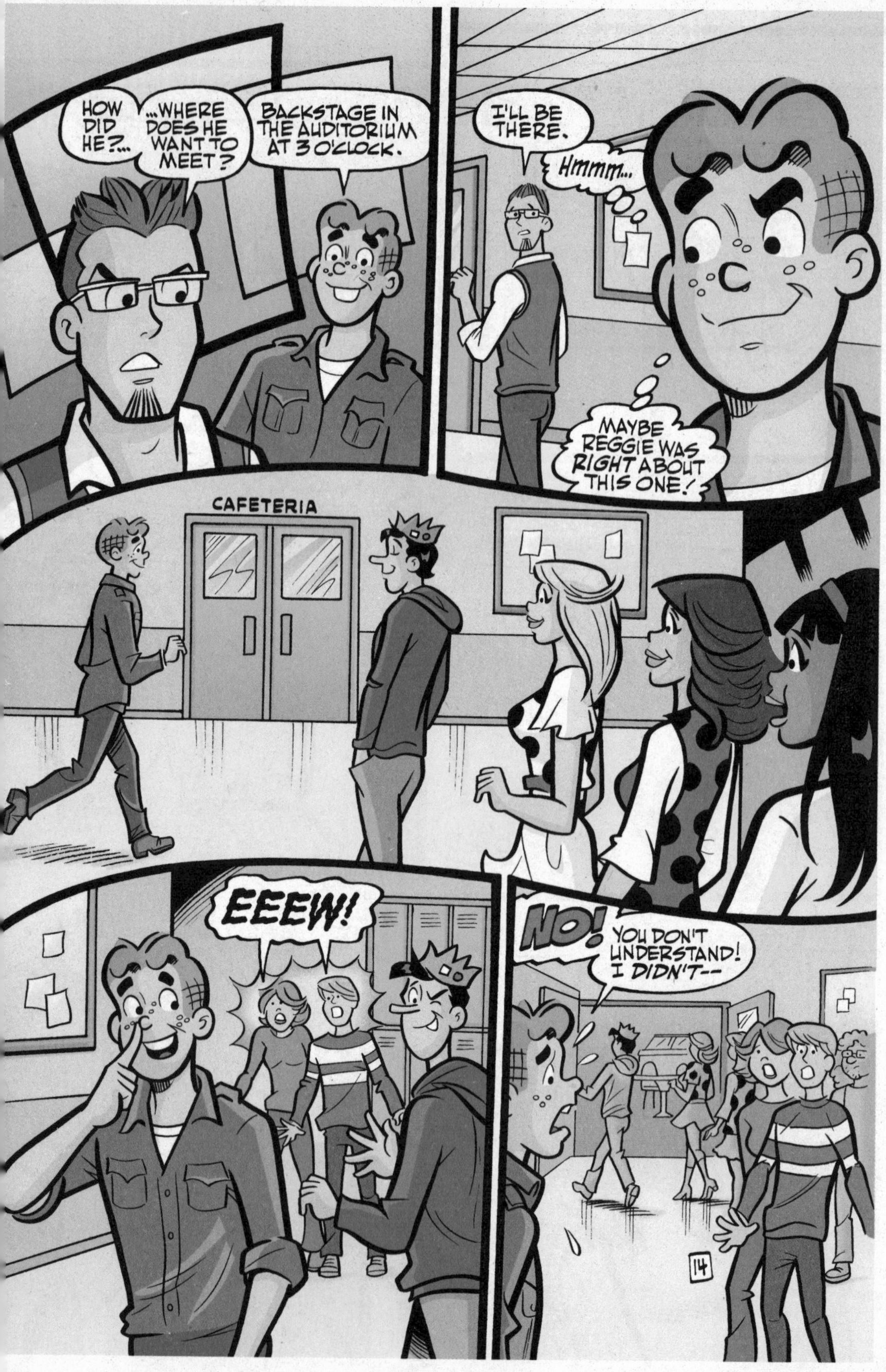
HOW DID HE?...
...WHERE DOES HE WANT TO MEET?
BACKSTAGE IN THE AUDITORIUM AT 3 O'CLOCK.
I'LL BE THERE.
Hmmm...
MAYBE REGGIE WAS RIGHT ABOUT THIS ONE!
CAFETERIA
EEEW!
NO!
YOU DON'T UNDERSTAND! I DIDN'T--
14

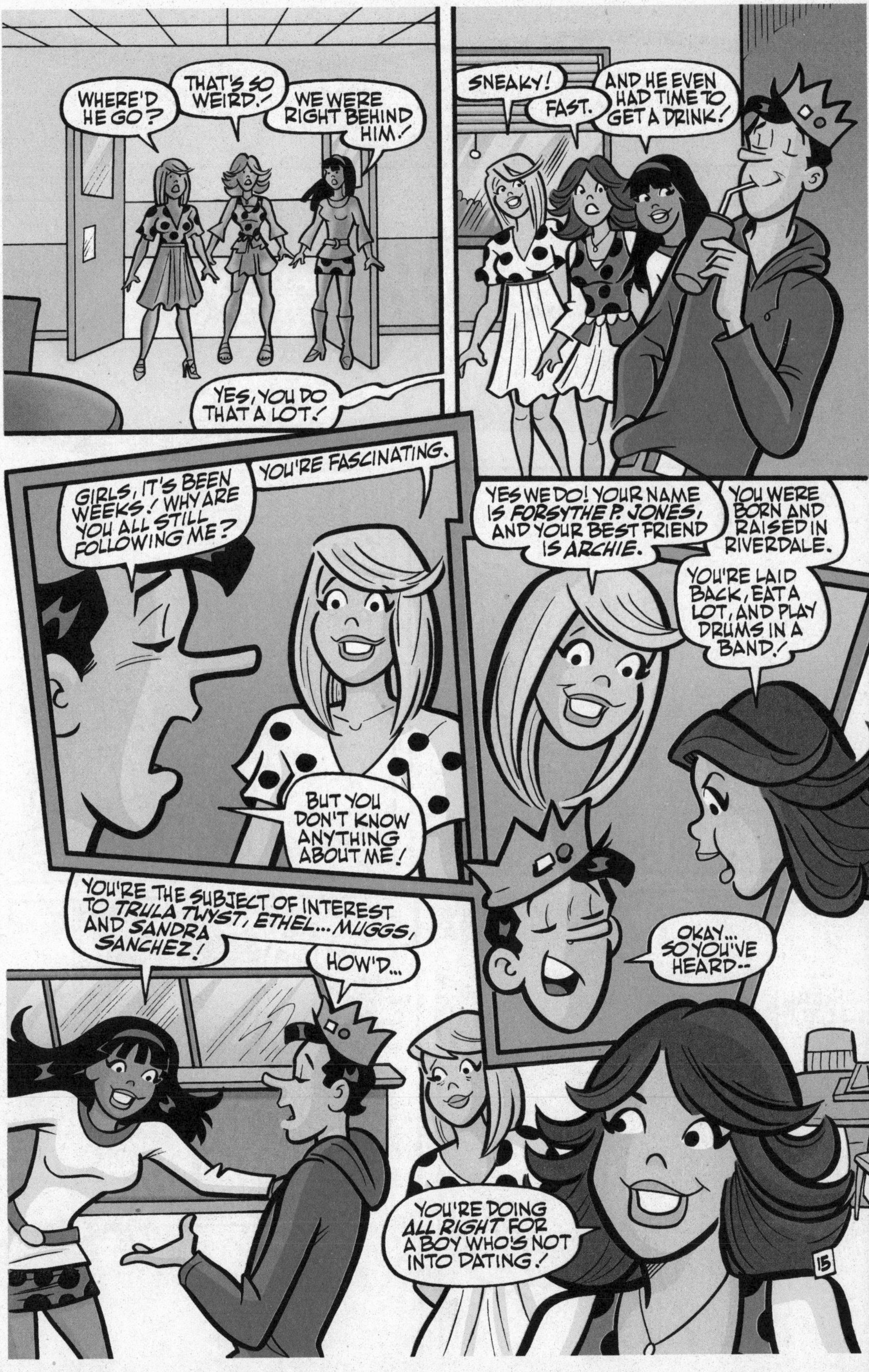
WHERE'D HE GO?
THAT'S SO WEIRD.
WE WERE RIGHT BEHIND HIM.
YES, YOU DO THAT A LOT.
SNEAKY!
FAST.
AND HE EVEN HAD TIME TO GET A DRINK!
GIRLS, IT'S BEEN WEEKS! WHY ARE YOU ALL STILL FOLLOWING ME?
YOU'RE FASCINATING.
BUT YOU DON'T KNOW ANYTHING ABOUT ME!
YES WE DO! YOUR NAME IS FORSYTHE P. JONES, AND YOUR BEST FRIEND IS ARCHIE.
YOU WERE BORN AND RAISED IN RIVERDALE.
YOU'RE LAID BACK, EAT A LOT, AND PLAY DRUMS IN A BAND.
OKAY... SO YOU'VE HEARD--
YOU'RE THE SUBJECT OF INTEREST TO TRULA TWYST, ETHEL... MUGGS, AND SANDRA SANCHEZ!
HOW'D...
YOU'RE DOING ALL RIGHT FOR A BOY WHO'S NOT INTO DATING!
15

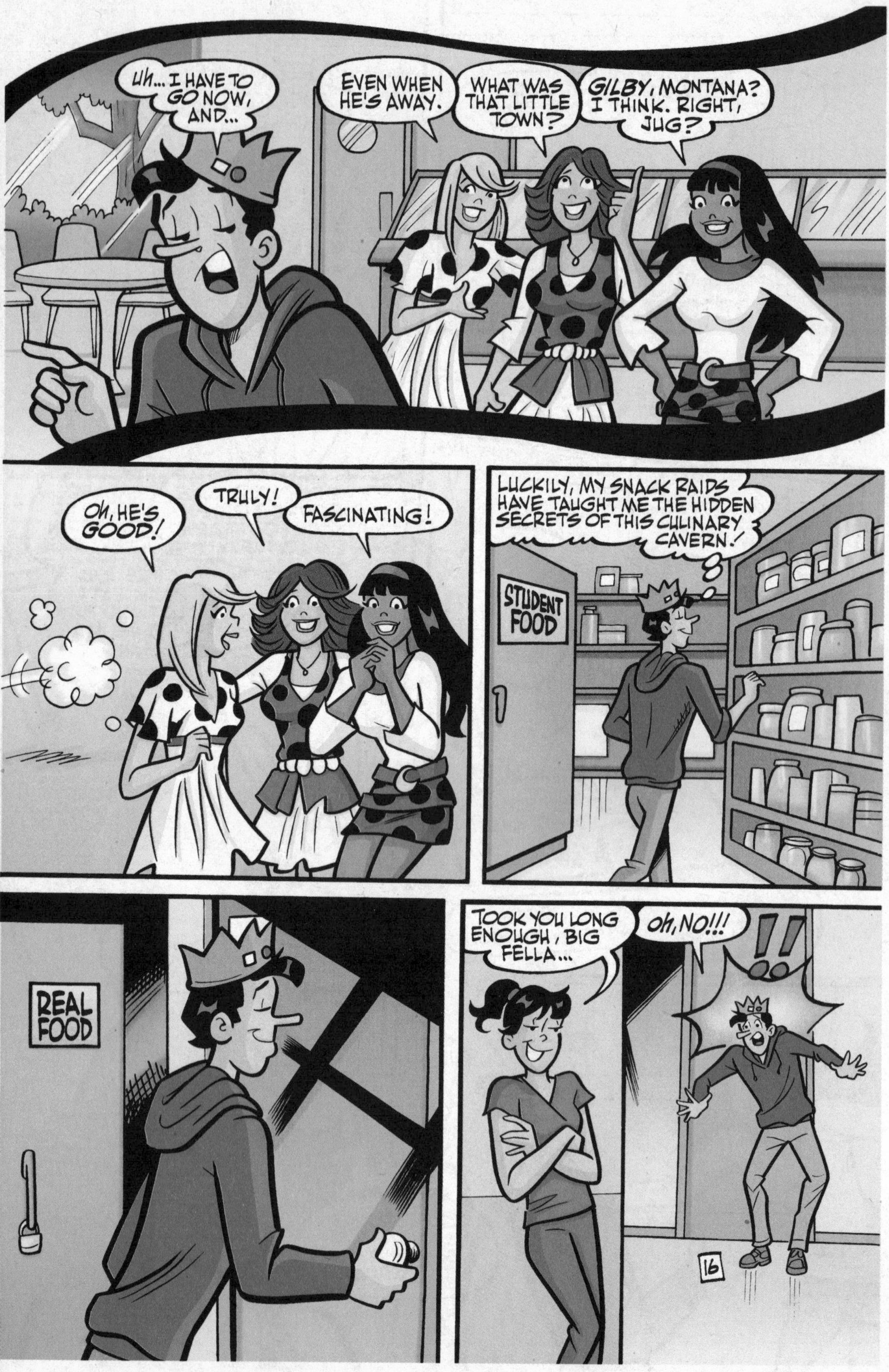

UH... I HAVE TO GO NOW, AND...
EVEN WHEN HE'S AWAY.
WHAT WAS THAT LITTLE TOWN?
GILBY, MONTANA? I THINK. RIGHT, JUG?
OH, HE'S GOOD!
TRULY!
FASCINATING!
LUCKILY, MY SNACK RAIDS HAVE TAUGHT ME THE HIDDEN SECRETS OF THIS CULINARY CAVERN!
STUDENT FOOD
REAL FOOD
TOOK YOU LONG ENOUGH, BIG FELLA...
OH, NO!!!
!!
16

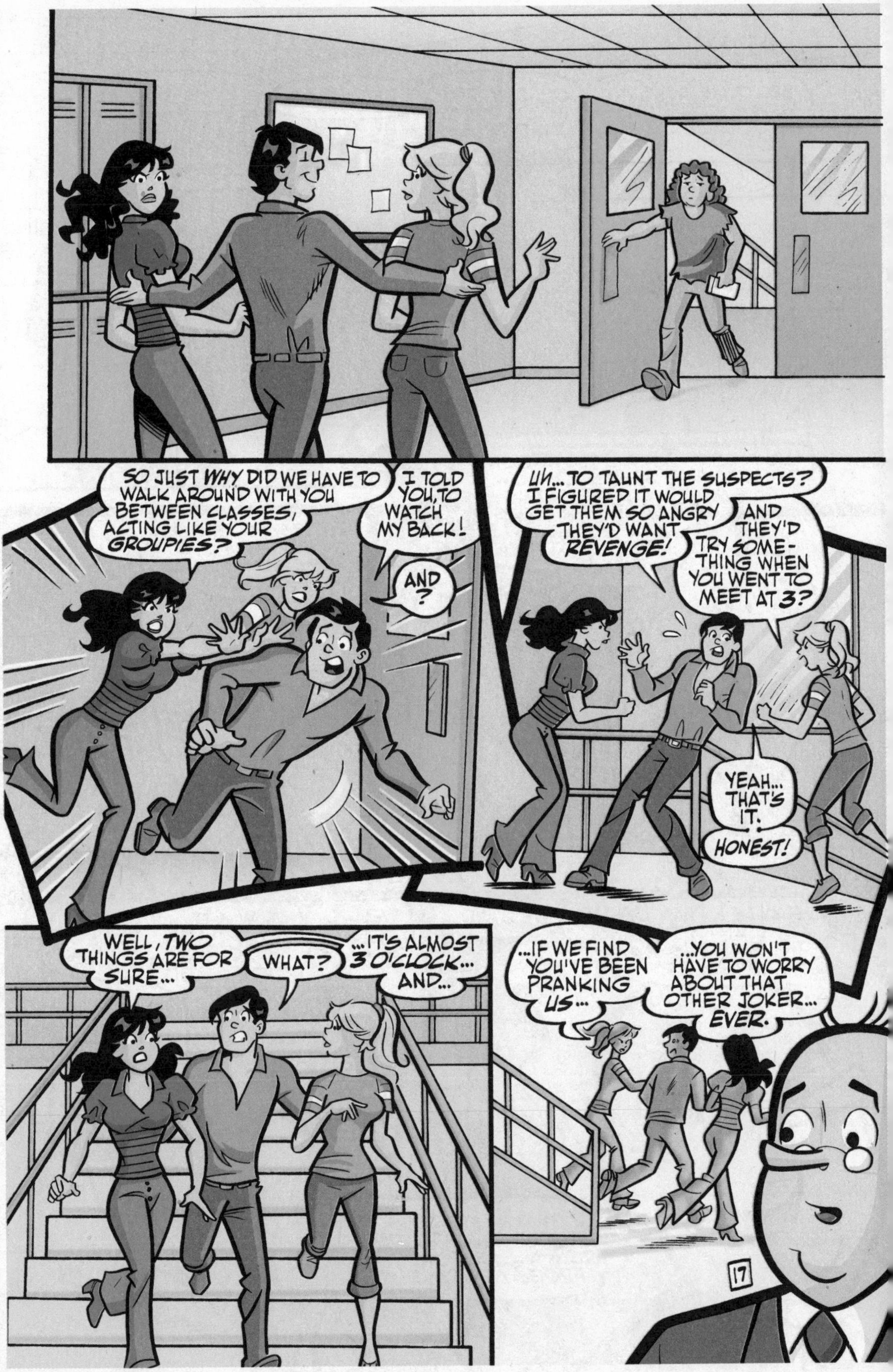
SO JUST WHY DID WE HAVE TO WALK AROUND WITH YOU BETWEEN CLASSES, ACTING LIKE YOUR GROUPIES?
I TOLD YOU, TO WATCH MY BACK!
AND ?
UH... TO TAUNT THE SUSPECTS? I FIGURED IT WOULD GET THEM SO ANGRY THEY'D WANT REVENGE!
AND THEY'D TRY SOME-THING WHEN YOU WENT TO MEET AT 3?
YEAH... THAT'S IT.
HONEST!
WELL, TWO THINGS ARE FOR SURE...
WHAT?
...IT'S ALMOST 3 O'CLOCK... AND...
...IF WE FIND YOU'VE BEEN PRANKING US...
...YOU WON'T HAVE TO WORRY ABOUT THAT OTHER JOKER... EVER.
17

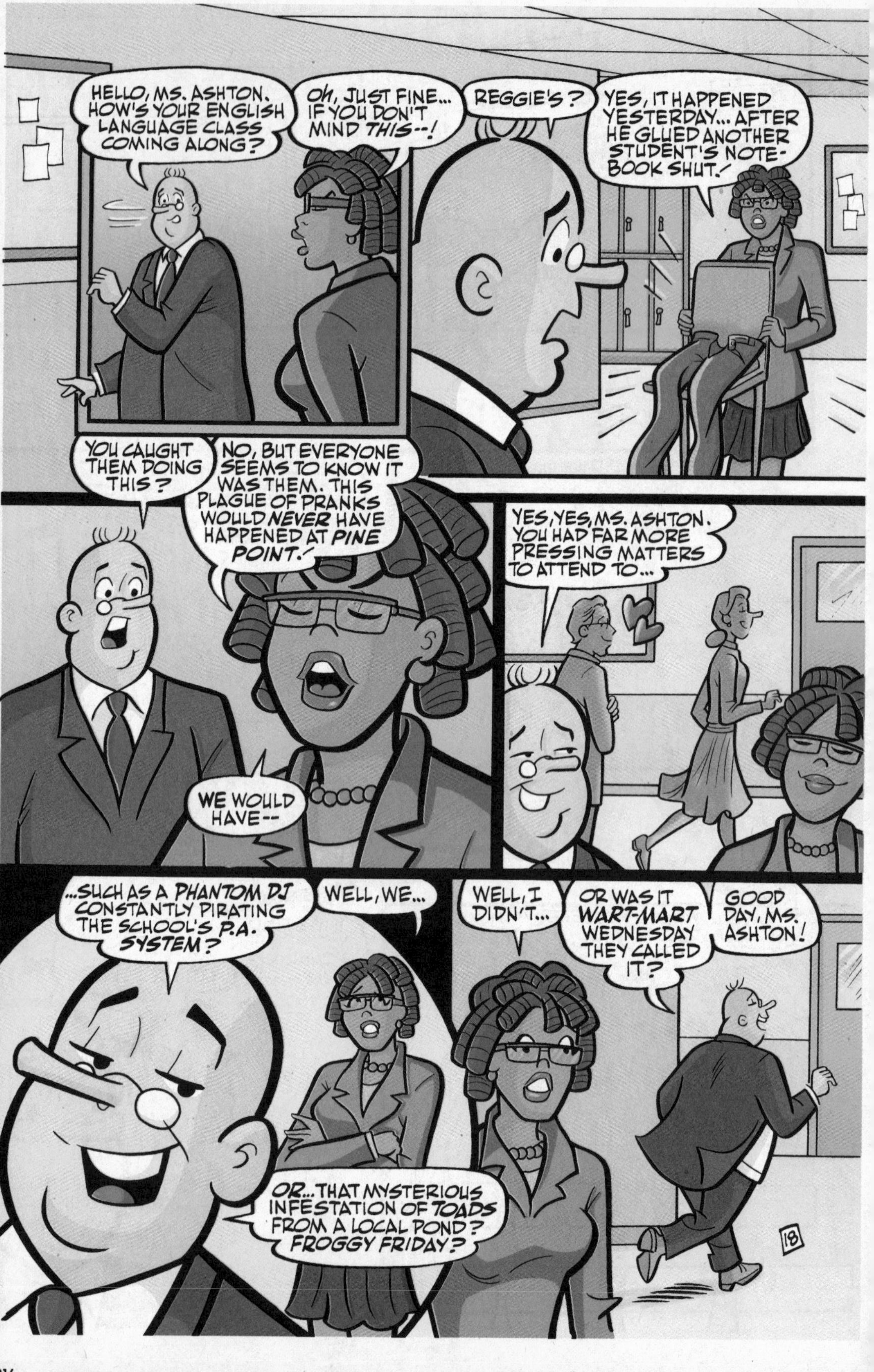
HELLO, MS. ASHTON. HOW'S YOUR ENGLISH LANGUAGE CLASS COMING ALONG?
OH, JUST FINE... IF YOU DON'T MIND THIS--!
REGGIE'S?
YES, IT HAPPENED YESTERDAY... AFTER HE GLUED ANOTHER STUDENT'S NOTE-BOOK SHUT.!
YOU CAUGHT THEM DOING THIS?
NO, BUT EVERYONE SEEMS TO KNOW IT WAS THEM. THIS PLAGUE OF PRANKS WOULD NEVER HAVE HAPPENED AT PINE POINT.!
WE WOULD HAVE--
YES, YES, MS. ASHTON. YOU HAD FAR MORE PRESSING MATTERS TO ATTEND TO...
...SUCH AS A PHANTOM DJ CONSTANTLY PIRATING THE SCHOOL'S P.A. SYSTEM?
WELL, WE...
OR... THAT MYSTERIOUS INFESTATION OF TOADS FROM A LOCAL POND? FROGGY FRIDAY?
WELL, I DIDN'T...
OR WAS IT WART-MART WEDNESDAY THEY CALLED IT?
GOOD DAY, MS. ASHTON!
18

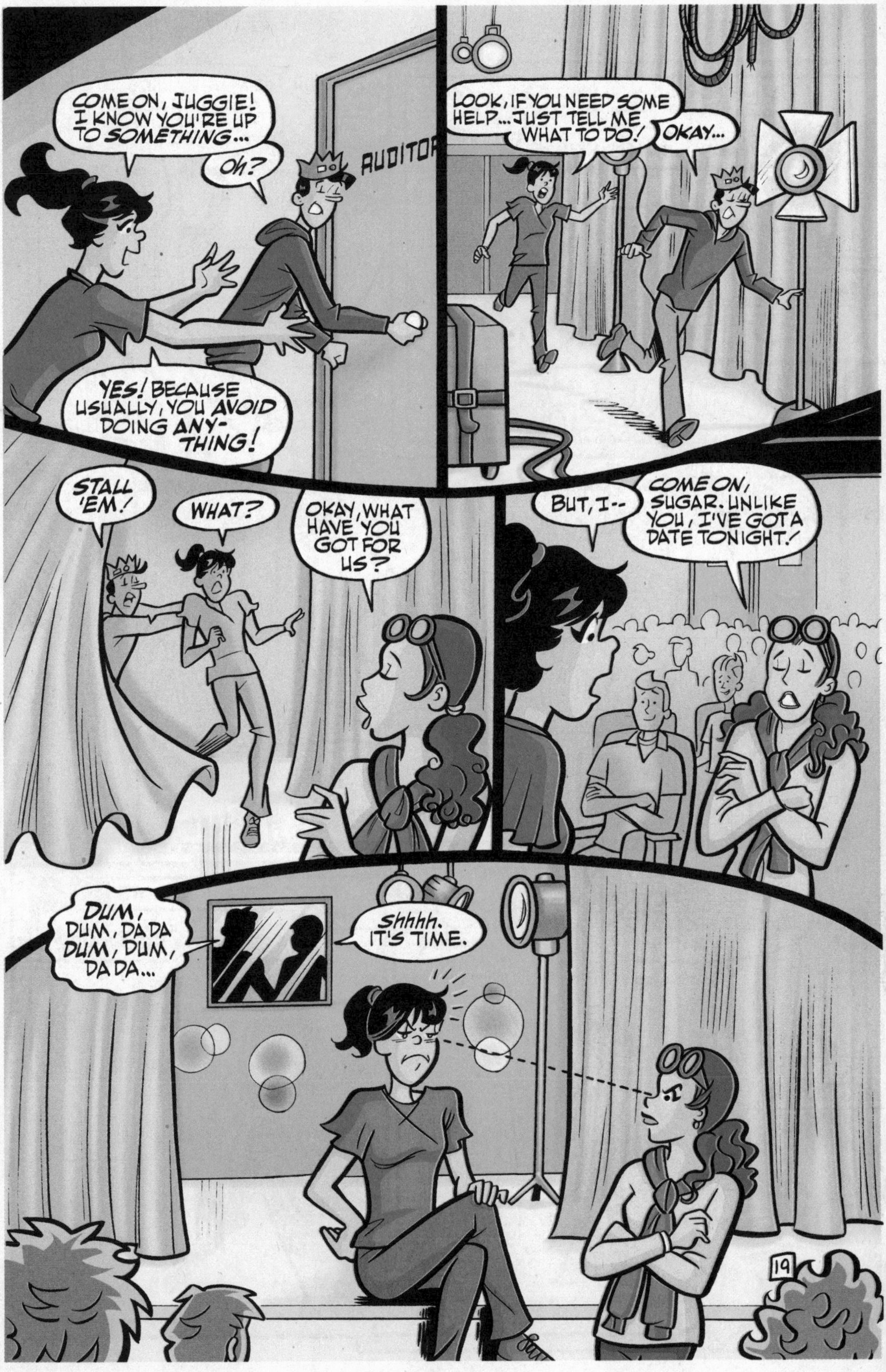
COME ON, JUGGIE! I KNOW YOU'RE UP TO SOMETHING...
Oh?
AUDITOR
YES! BECAUSE USUALLY, YOU AVOID DOING ANY-THING!
LOOK, IF YOU NEED SOME HELP... JUST TELL ME WHAT TO DO!
OKAY...
STALL 'EM!
WHAT?
OKAY, WHAT HAVE YOU GOT FOR US?
BUT, I--
COME ON, SUGAR. UNLIKE YOU, I'VE GOT A DATE TONIGHT!
DUM, DUM, DA DA DUM, DUM, DA DA...
Shhhh. IT'S TIME.
19

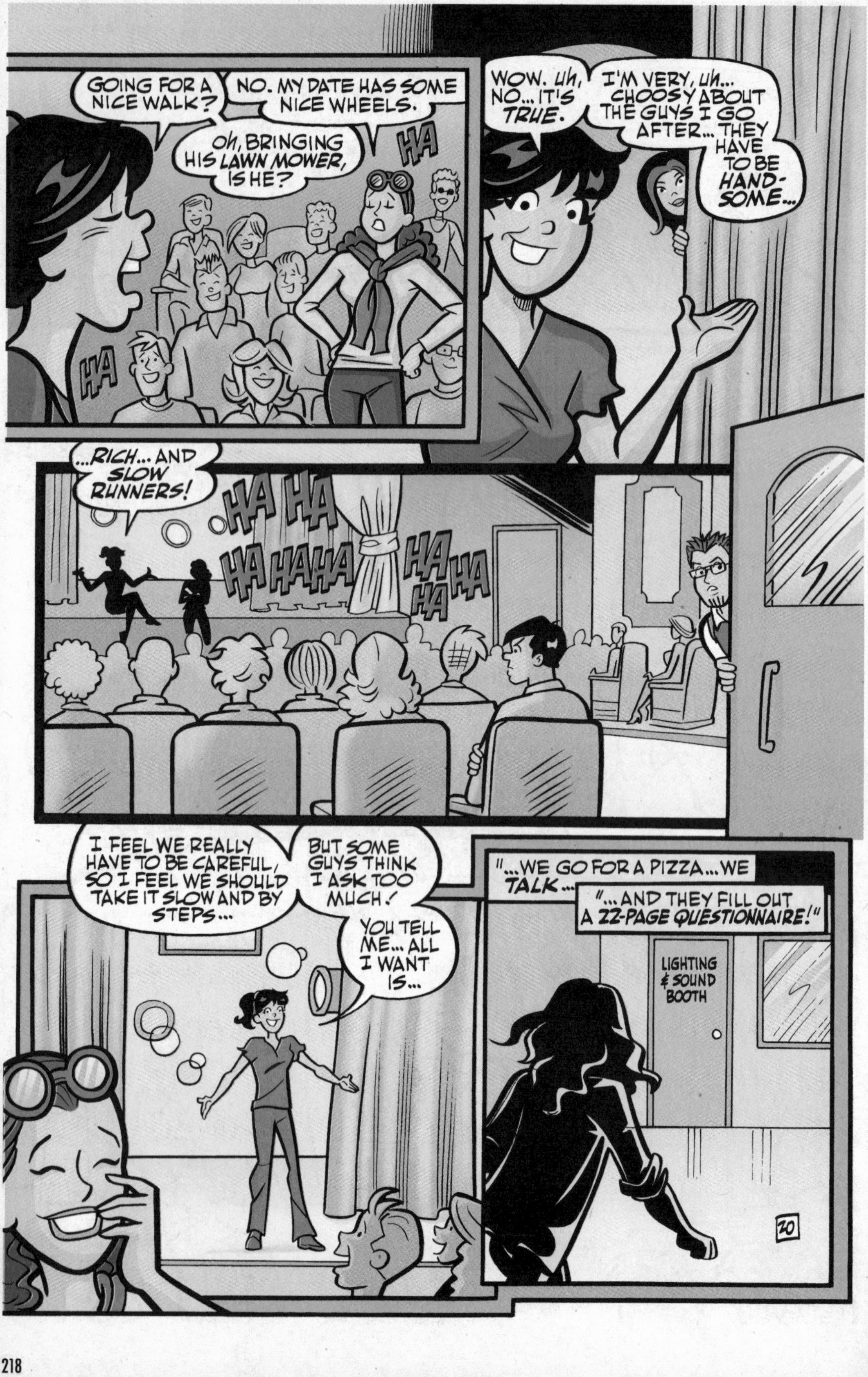
GOING FOR A NICE WALK?
NO. MY DATE HAS SOME NICE WHEELS.
Oh, BRINGING HIS LAWN MOWER, IS HE?
HA
HA
WOW. uh, NO... IT'S TRUE.
I'M VERY, uh... CHOOSY ABOUT THE GUYS I GO AFTER... THEY HAVE TO BE HAND-SOME...
...RICH... AND SLOW RUNNERS!
HA HA
HA HAHA
HA HA HA
I FEEL WE REALLY HAVE TO BE CAREFUL, SO I FEEL WE SHOULD TAKE IT SLOW AND BY STEPS...
BUT SOME GUYS THINK I ASK TOO MUCH!
YOU TELL ME... ALL I WANT IS...
"...WE GO FOR A PIZZA... WE TALK...
"...AND THEY FILL OUT A 22-PAGE QUESTIONNAIRE!"
LIGHTING & SOUND BOOTH
20

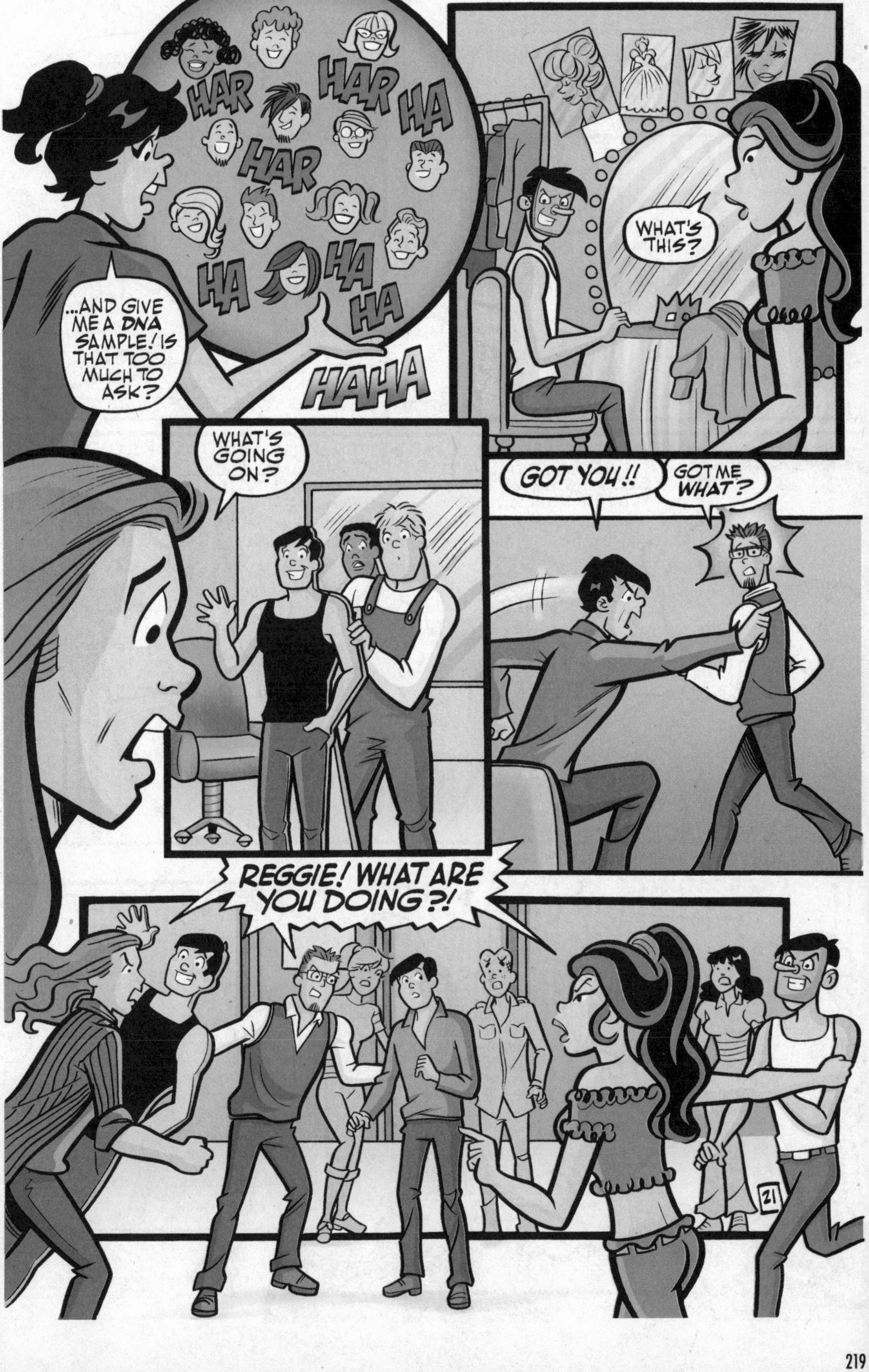

...AND GIVE ME A DNA SAMPLE! IS THAT TOO MUCH TO ASK?
HAR HAR HA HAR HA HA HA HAHA
WHAT'S THIS?
WHAT'S GOING ON?
GOT YOU!!
GOT ME WHAT?
REGGIE! WHAT ARE YOU DOING?!
21

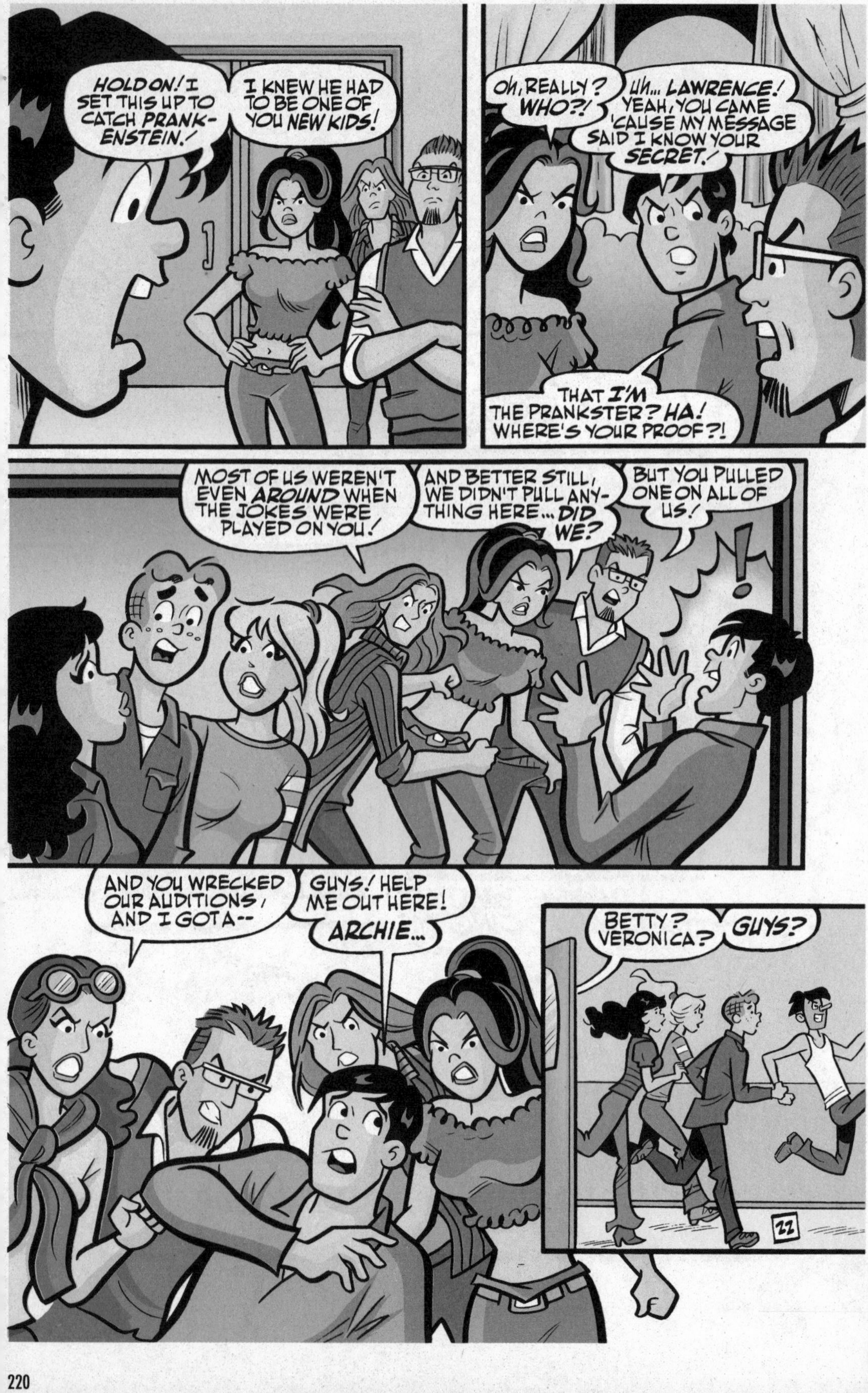

HOLD ON! I SET THIS UP TO CATCH PRANK-ENSTEIN!
I KNEW HE HAD TO BE ONE OF YOU NEW KIDS!
Oh, REALLY? WHO?!
Uh... LAWRENCE! YEAH, YOU CAME 'CAUSE MY MESSAGE SAID I KNOW YOUR SECRET!
THAT I'M THE PRANKSTER? HA! WHERE'S YOUR PROOF?!
MOST OF US WEREN'T EVEN AROUND WHEN THE JOKES WERE PLAYED ON YOU!
AND BETTER STILL, WE DIDN'T PULL ANY-THING HERE... DID WE?
BUT YOU PULLED ONE ON ALL OF US!
!
AND YOU WRECKED OUR AUDITIONS, AND I GOT A--
GUYS! HELP ME OUT HERE! ARCHIE...
BETTY? VERONICA?
GUYS?
22

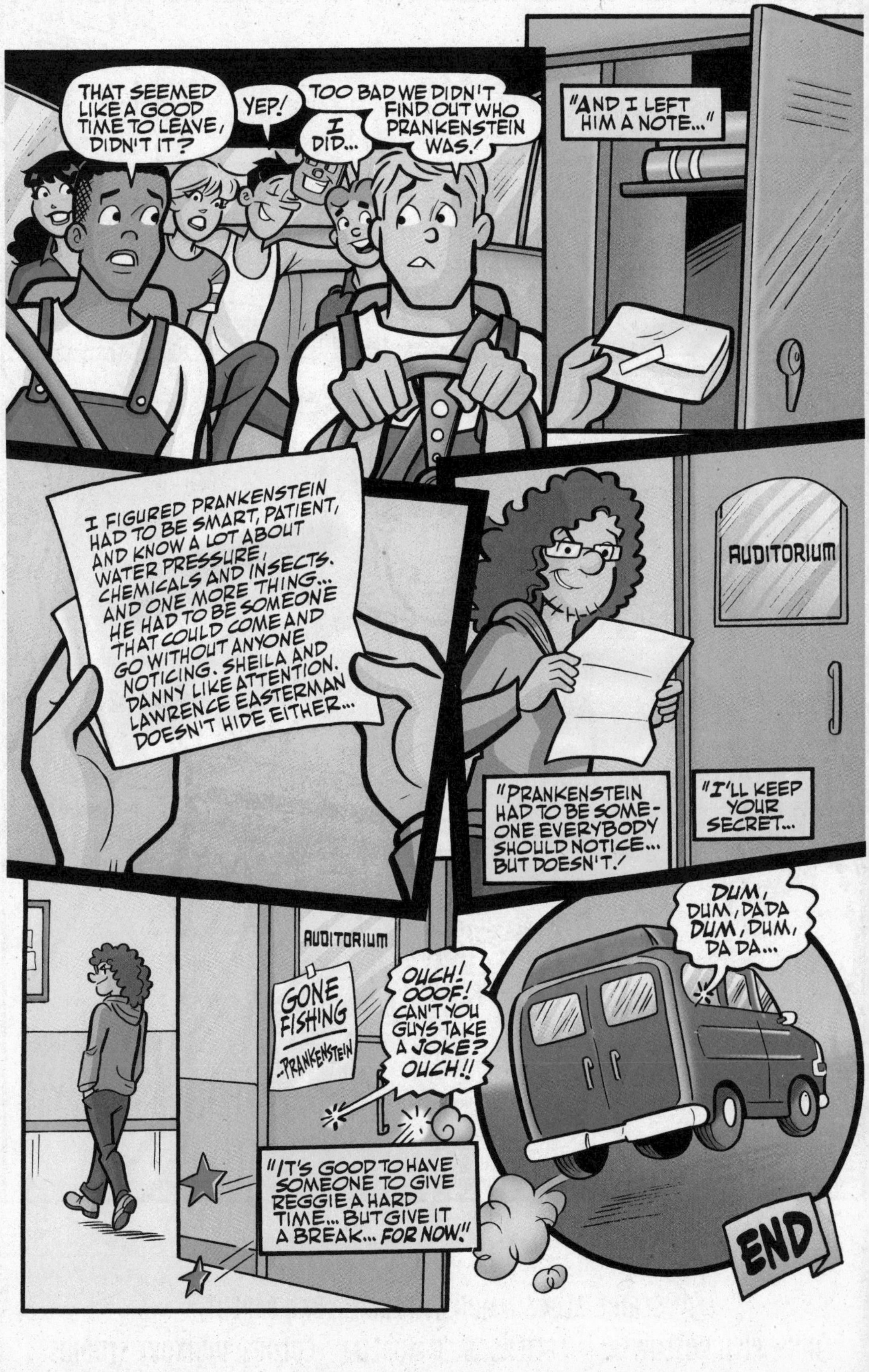
THAT SEEMED LIKE A GOOD TIME TO LEAVE, DIDN'T IT?
YEP!
TOO BAD WE DIDN'T FIND OUT WHO PRANKENSTEIN WAS!
I DID...
"AND I LEFT HIM A NOTE..."
I FIGURED PRANKENSTEIN HAD TO BE SMART, PATIENT, AND KNOW A LOT ABOUT WATER PRESSURE, CHEMICALS AND INSECTS. AND ONE MORE THING... HE HAD TO BE SOMEONE THAT COULD COME AND GO WITHOUT ANYONE NOTICING. SHEILA AND DANNY LIKE ATTENTION. LAWRENCE EASTERMAN DOESN'T HIDE EITHER...
AUDITORIUM
"PRANKENSTEIN HAD TO BE SOMEONE EVERYBODY SHOULD NOTICE... BUT DOESN'T!
"I'LL KEEP YOUR SECRET...
AUDITORIUM
GONE FISHING
-PRANKENSTEIN
OUCH! OOOF! CAN'T YOU GUYS TAKE A JOKE? OUCH!!
"IT'S GOOD TO HAVE SOMEONE TO GIVE REGGIE A HARD TIME... BUT GIVE IT A BREAK... FOR NOW!"
DUM, DUM, DA DA DUM, DUM, DA DA...
END

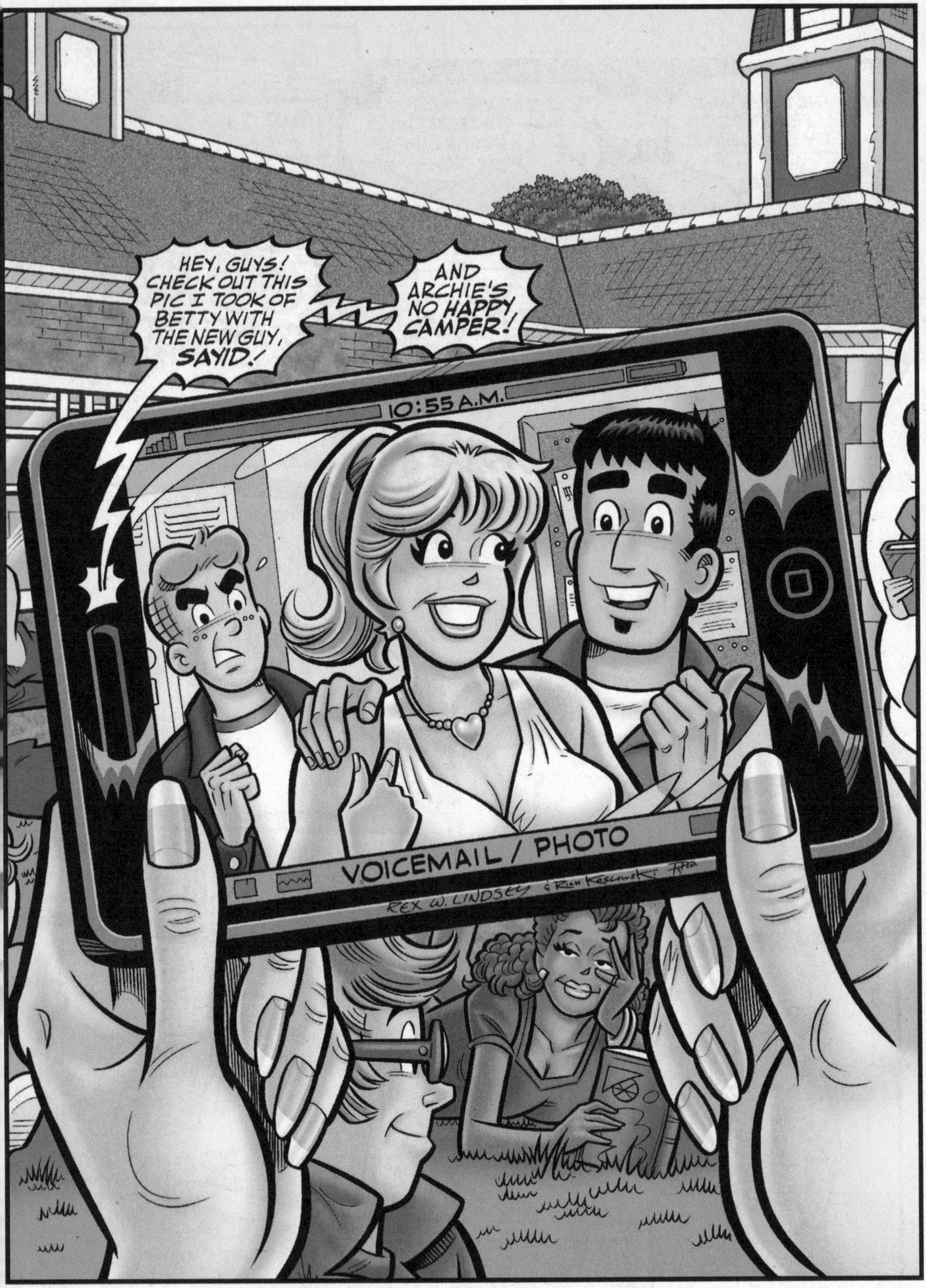
HEY, GUYS! CHECK OUT THIS PIC I TOOK OF BETTY WITH THE NEW GUY, SAYID!
AND ARCHIE'S NO HAPPY CAMPER!
10:55 A.M.
VOICEMAIL / PHOTO
REX W. LINDSEY

WHAT'S OLD IS NEW AGAIN - PART 5

SCRIPT: ALEX SIMMONS PENCILS: DAN PARENT

INKS: RICH KOSLOWSKI LETTERS: JACK MORELLI COLORS: DIGIKORE STUDIOS

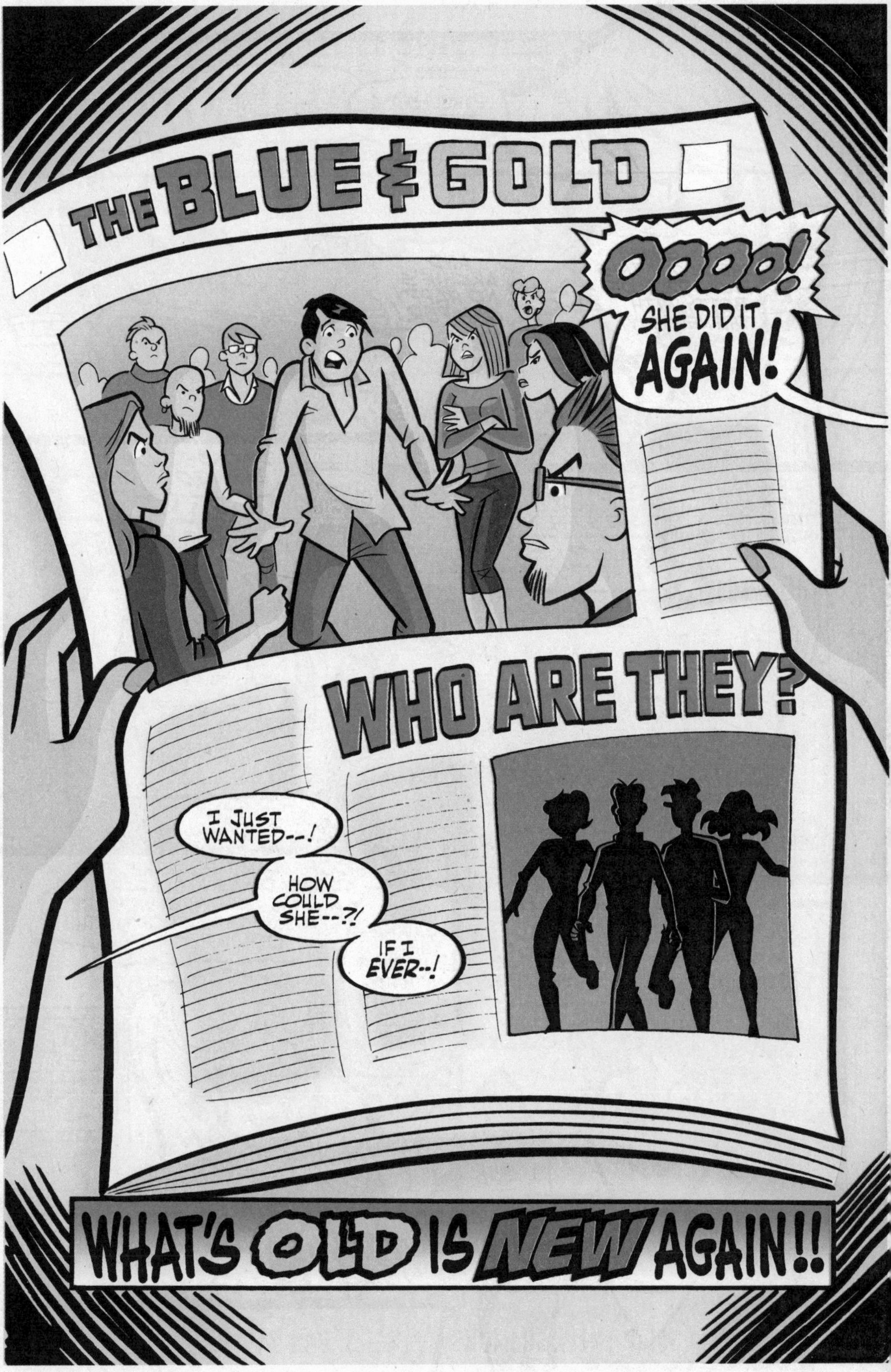
THE BLUE & GOLD
OOOO! SHE DID IT AGAIN!
WHO ARE THEY?
I JUST WANTED--!
HOW COULD SHE--?!
IF I EVER--!
WHAT'S OLD IS NEW AGAIN!!

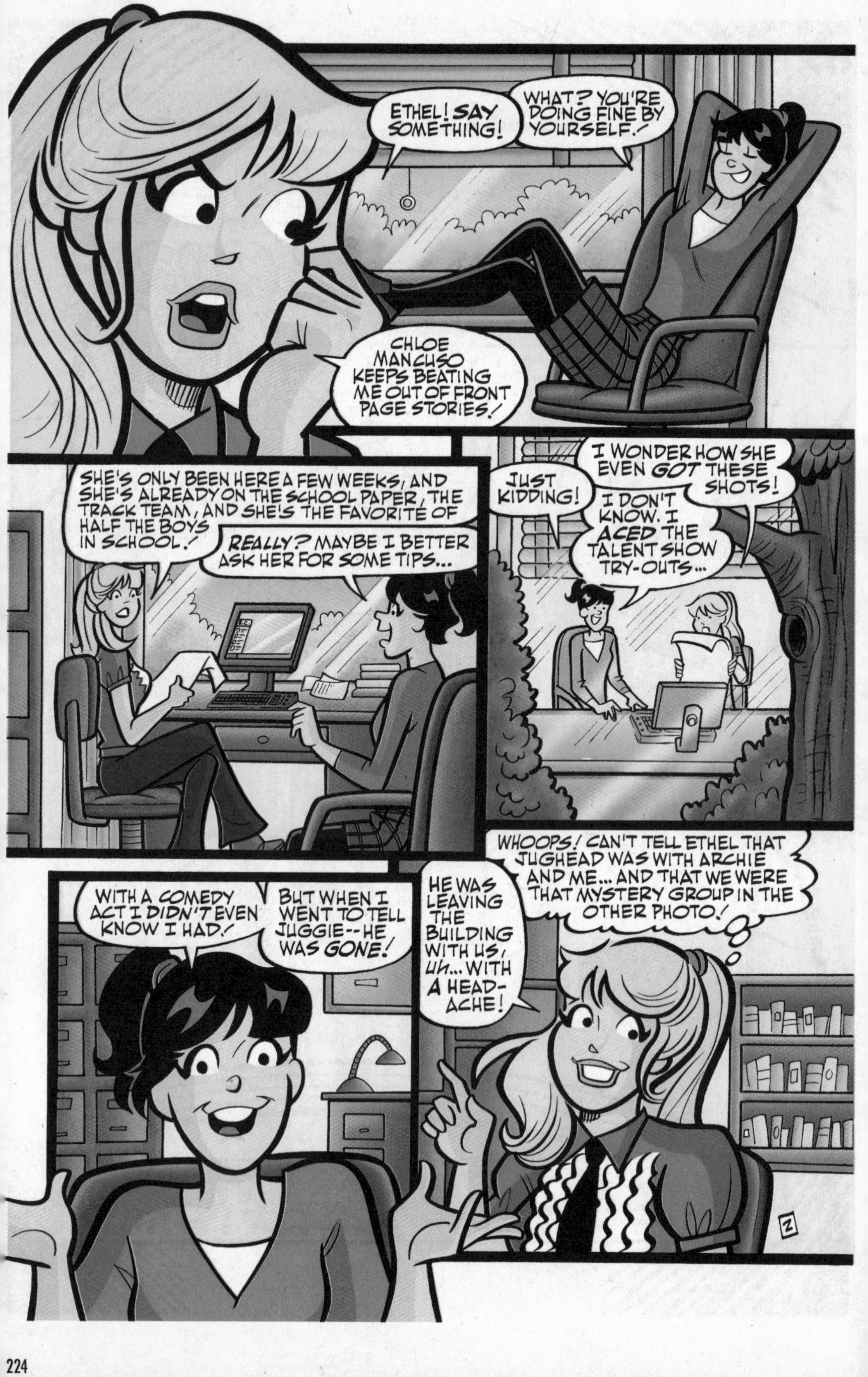

ETHEL! SAY SOMETHING!
WHAT? YOU'RE DOING FINE BY YOURSELF.!
CHLOE MANCUSO KEEPS BEATING ME OUT OF FRONT PAGE STORIES!
SHE'S ONLY BEEN HERE A FEW WEEKS, AND SHE'S ALREADY ON THE SCHOOL PAPER, THE TRACK TEAM, AND SHE'S THE FAVORITE OF HALF THE BOYS IN SCHOOL!
REALLY? MAYBE I BETTER ASK HER FOR SOME TIPS...
JUST KIDDING!
I WONDER HOW SHE EVEN GOT THESE SHOTS!
I DON'T KNOW. I ACED THE TALENT SHOW TRY-OUTS...
WITH A COMEDY ACT I DIDN'T EVEN KNOW I HAD!
BUT WHEN I WENT TO TELL JUGGIE--HE WAS GONE!
HE WAS LEAVING THE BUILDING WITH US, UH... WITH A HEAD-ACHE!
WHOOPS! CAN'T TELL ETHEL THAT JUGHEAD WAS WITH ARCHIE AND ME... AND THAT WE WERE THAT MYSTERY GROUP IN THE OTHER PHOTO!
2

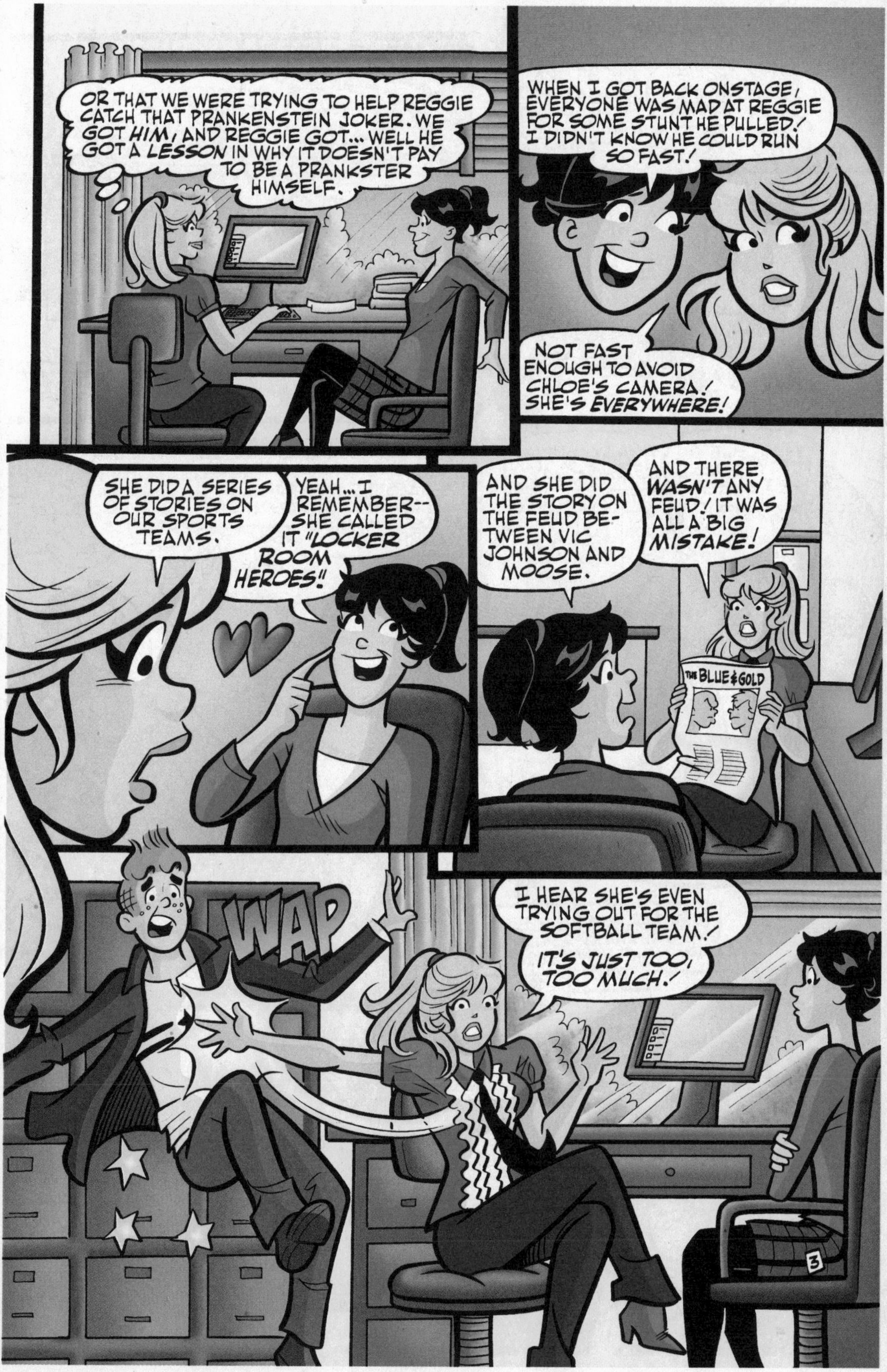

OR THAT WE WERE TRYING TO HELP REGGIE CATCH THAT PRANKENSTEIN JOKER. WE GOT HIM, AND REGGIE GOT... WELL HE GOT A LESSON IN WHY IT DOESN'T PAY TO BE A PRANKSTER HIMSELF.
WHEN I GOT BACK ONSTAGE, EVERYONE WAS MAD AT REGGIE FOR SOME STUNT HE PULLED! I DIDN'T KNOW HE COULD RUN SO FAST!
NOT FAST ENOUGH TO AVOID CHLOE'S CAMERA! SHE'S EVERYWHERE!
SHE DID A SERIES OF STORIES ON OUR SPORTS TEAMS.
YEAH... I REMEMBER-- SHE CALLED IT "LOCKER ROOM HEROES!"
AND SHE DID THE STORY ON THE FEUD BE-TWEEN VIC JOHNSON AND MOOSE.
AND THERE WASN'T ANY FEUD! IT WAS ALL A BIG MISTAKE!
THE BLUE & GOLD
WAP
I HEAR SHE'S EVEN TRYING OUT FOR THE SOFTBALL TEAM!
IT'S JUST TOO, TOO MUCH!
3

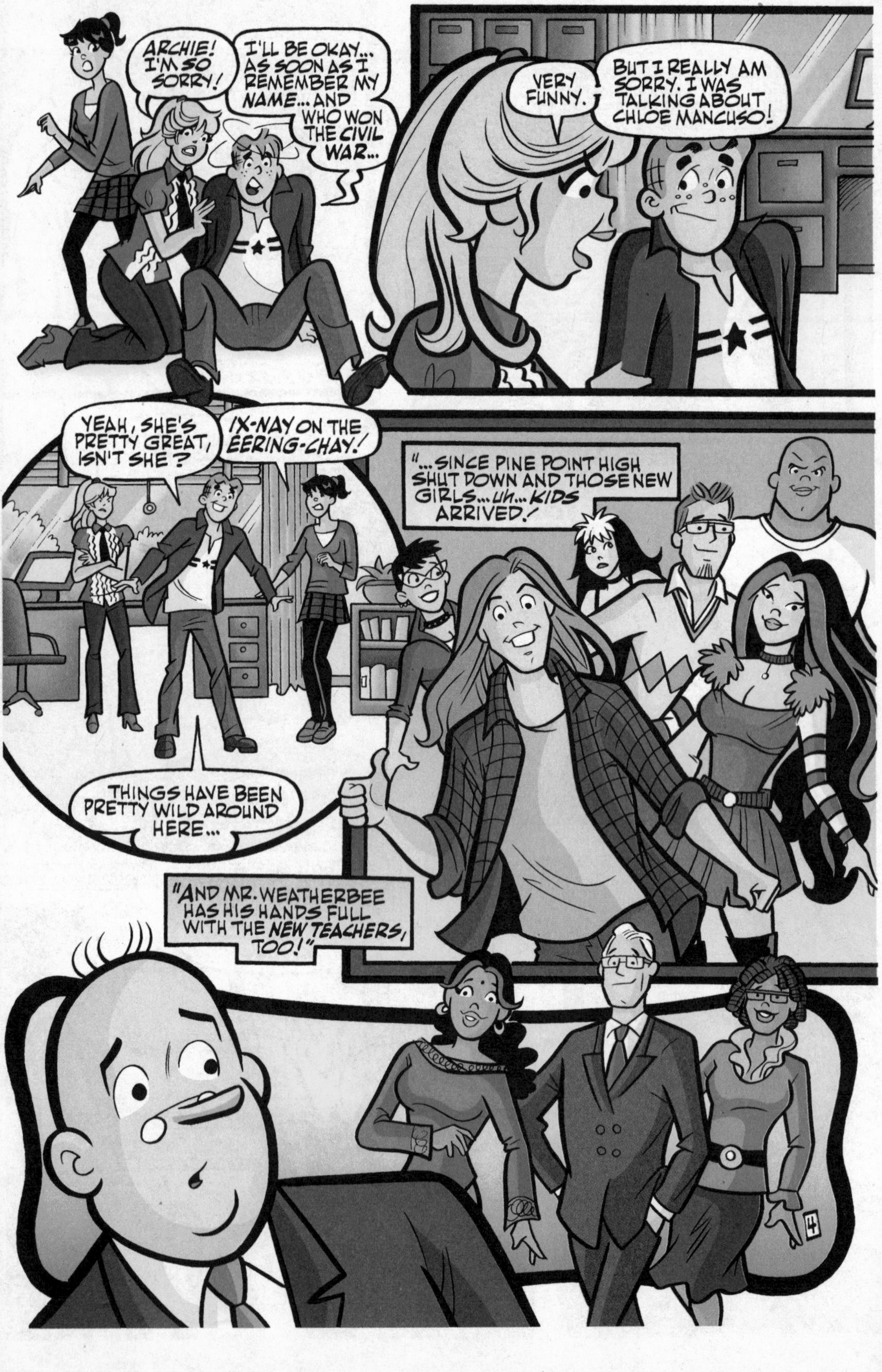
ARCHIE! I'M SO SORRY!
I'LL BE OKAY... AS SOON AS I REMEMBER MY NAME... AND WHO WON THE CIVIL WAR...
VERY FUNNY.
BUT I REALLY AM SORRY. I WAS TALKING ABOUT CHLOE MANCUSO!
YEAH, SHE'S PRETTY GREAT, ISN'T SHE?
IX-NAY ON THE EERING-CHAY!
THINGS HAVE BEEN PRETTY WILD AROUND HERE...
"...SINCE PINE POINT HIGH SHUT DOWN AND THOSE NEW GIRLS... uh... KIDS ARRIVED!
"AND MR. WEATHERBEE HAS HIS HANDS FULL WITH THE NEW TEACHERS, TOO!"
4

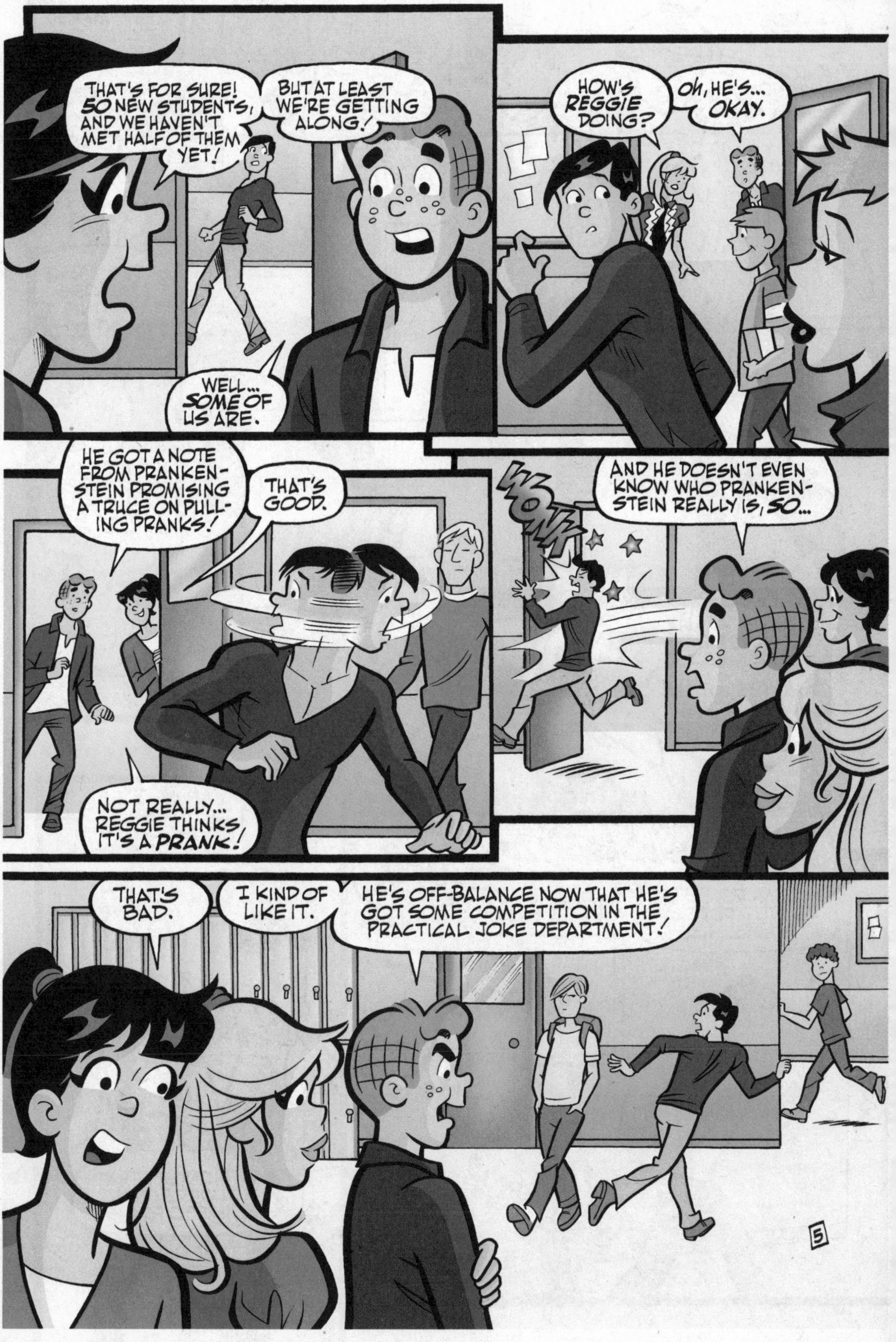
THAT'S FOR SURE! 50 NEW STUDENTS, AND WE HAVEN'T MET HALF OF THEM YET!
BUT AT LEAST WE'RE GETTING ALONG!
WELL... SOME OF US ARE.
HOW'S REGGIE DOING?
OH, HE'S... OKAY.
HE GOT A NOTE FROM PRANKENSTEIN PROMISING A TRUCE ON PULLING PRANKS!
THAT'S GOOD.
NOT REALLY... REGGIE THINKS IT'S A PRANK!
WONK
AND HE DOESN'T EVEN KNOW WHO PRANKENSTEIN REALLY IS, SO...
THAT'S BAD.
I KIND OF LIKE IT.
HE'S OFF-BALANCE NOW THAT HE'S GOT SOME COMPETITION IN THE PRACTICAL JOKE DEPARTMENT!
5

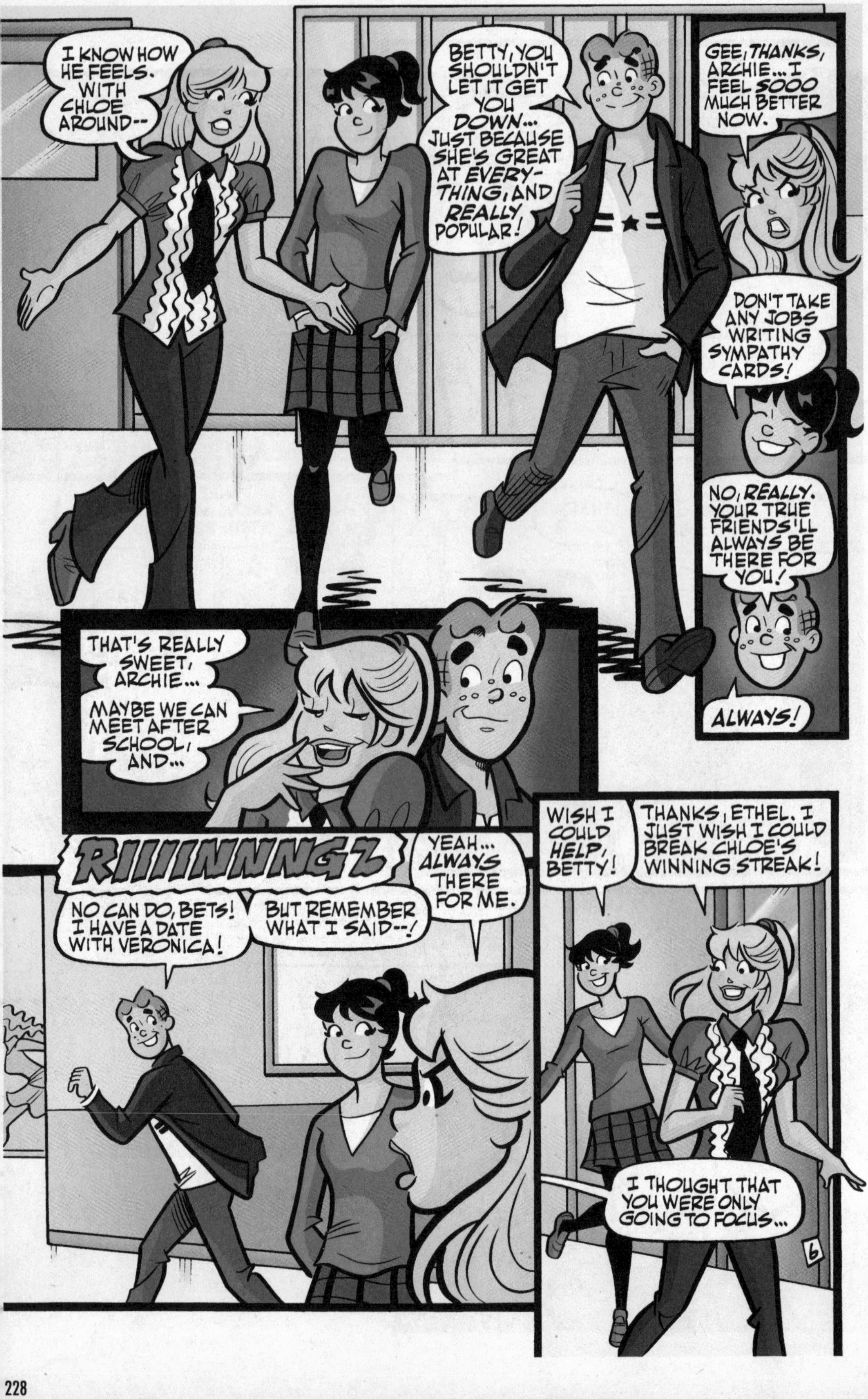
I KNOW HOW HE FEELS. WITH CHLOE AROUND--
BETTY, YOU SHOULDN'T LET IT GET YOU DOWN... JUST BECAUSE SHE'S GREAT AT EVERY-THING, AND REALLY POPULAR!
GEE, THANKS, ARCHIE... I FEEL SOOO MUCH BETTER NOW.
DON'T TAKE ANY JOBS WRITING SYMPATHY CARDS!
NO, REALLY. YOUR TRUE FRIENDS'LL ALWAYS BE THERE FOR YOU!
ALWAYS!
THAT'S REALLY SWEET, ARCHIE...
MAYBE WE CAN MEET AFTER SCHOOL, AND...
RIIIINNNGZ
NO CAN DO, BETS! I HAVE A DATE WITH VERONICA!
BUT REMEMBER WHAT I SAID--!
YEAH... ALWAYS THERE FOR ME.
WISH I COULD HELP, BETTY!
THANKS, ETHEL. I JUST WISH I COULD BREAK CHLOE'S WINNING STREAK!
I THOUGHT THAT YOU WERE ONLY GOING TO FOCUS...
6

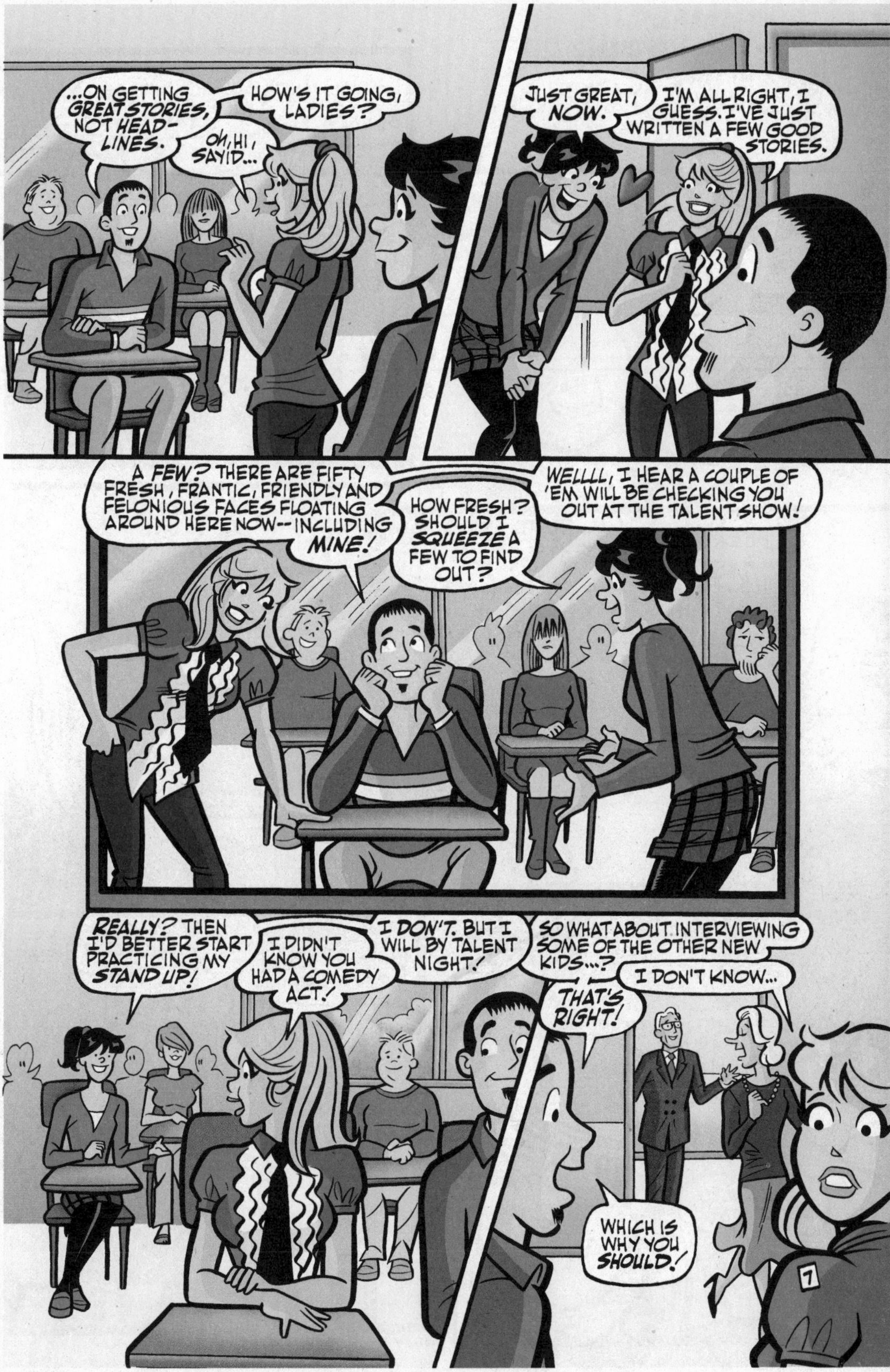
...ON GETTING GREAT STORIES, NOT HEAD-LINES.
HOW'S IT GOING, LADIES?
OH, HI, SAYID...
JUST GREAT, NOW.
I'M ALL RIGHT, I GUESS. I'VE JUST WRITTEN A FEW GOOD STORIES.
A FEW? THERE ARE FIFTY FRESH, FRANTIC, FRIENDLY AND FELONIOUS FACES FLOATING AROUND HERE NOW-- INCLUDING MINE!
HOW FRESH? SHOULD I SQUEEZE A FEW TO FIND OUT?
WELLLL, I HEAR A COUPLE OF 'EM WILL BE CHECKING YOU OUT AT THE TALENT SHOW!
REALLY? THEN I'D BETTER START PRACTICING MY STAND UP!
I DIDN'T KNOW YOU HAD A COMEDY ACT!
I DON'T. BUT I WILL BY TALENT NIGHT!
SO WHAT ABOUT INTERVIEWING SOME OF THE OTHER NEW KIDS...?
I DON'T KNOW...
THAT'S RIGHT!
WHICH IS WHY YOU SHOULD!

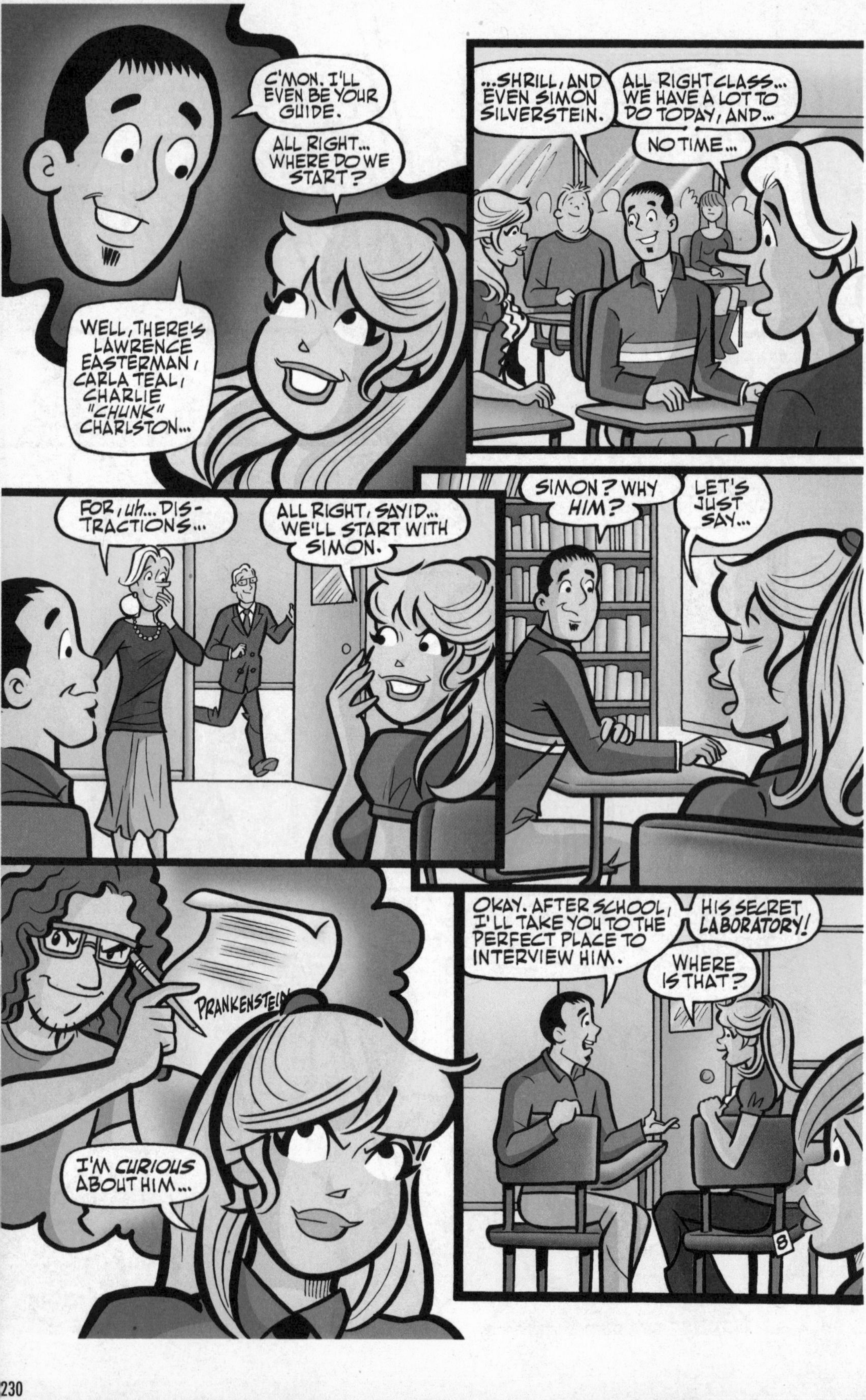
C'MON. I'LL EVEN BE YOUR GUIDE.
ALL RIGHT... WHERE DO WE START?
WELL, THERE'S LAWRENCE EASTERMAN, CARLA TEAL, CHARLIE "CHUNK" CHARLSTON...
...SHRILL, AND EVEN SIMON SILVERSTEIN.
ALL RIGHT CLASS... WE HAVE A LOT TO DO TODAY, AND...
NO TIME...
FOR, uh... DIS-TRACTIONS...
ALL RIGHT, SAYID... WE'LL START WITH SIMON.
SIMON? WHY HIM?
LET'S JUST SAY...
PRANKENSTEIN
I'M CURIOUS ABOUT HIM...
OKAY. AFTER SCHOOL, I'LL TAKE YOU TO THE PERFECT PLACE TO INTERVIEW HIM.
HIS SECRET LABORATORY!
WHERE IS THAT?
8

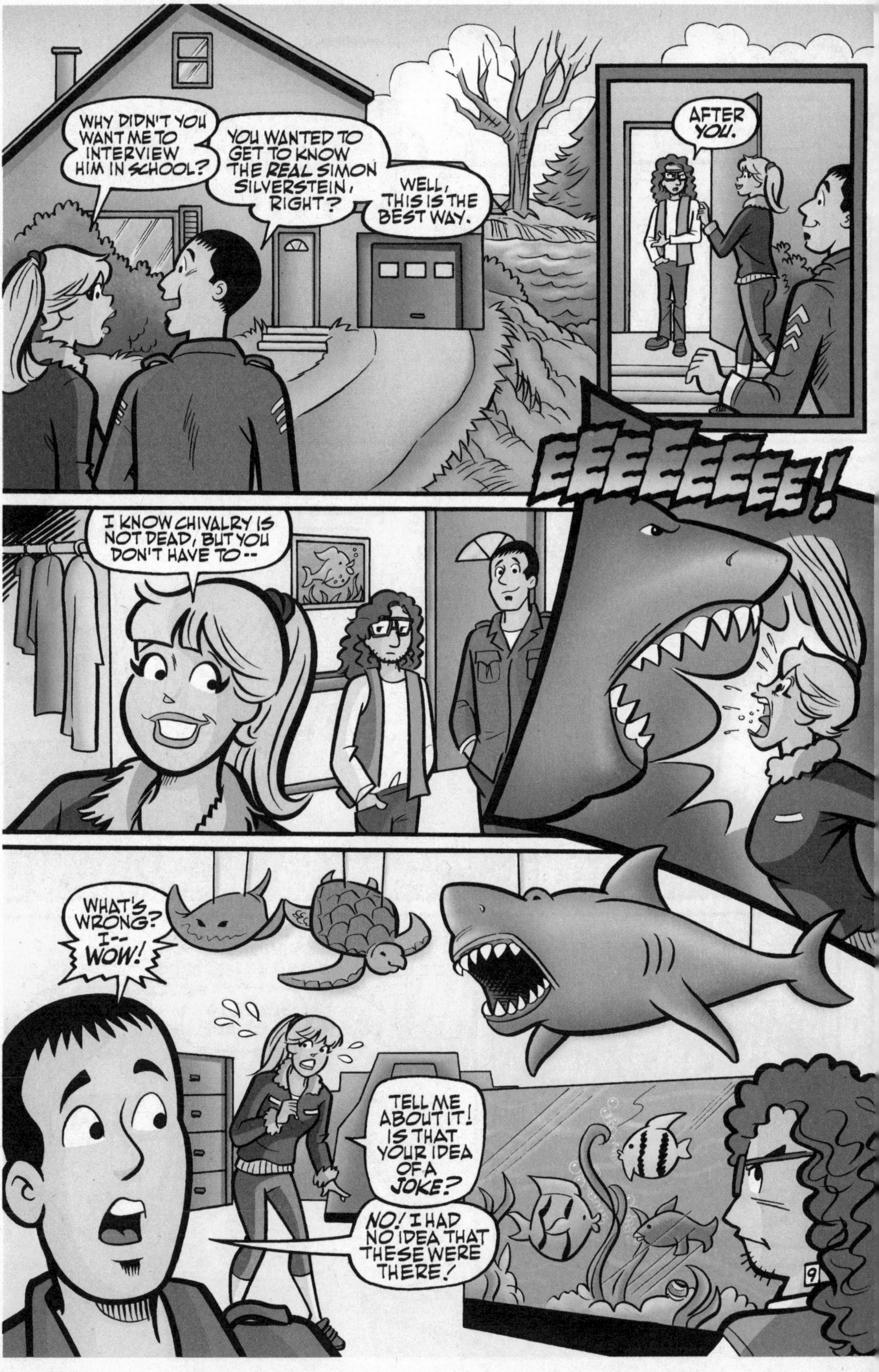
WHY DIDN'T YOU WANT ME TO INTERVIEW HIM IN SCHOOL?
YOU WANTED TO GET TO KNOW THE REAL SIMON SILVERSTEIN, RIGHT?
WELL, THIS IS THE BEST WAY.
AFTER YOU.
I KNOW CHIVALRY IS NOT DEAD, BUT YOU DON'T HAVE TO--
EEEEEEEEE!
WHAT'S WRONG? I-- WOW!
TELL ME ABOUT IT! IS THAT YOUR IDEA OF A JOKE?
NO! I HAD NO IDEA THAT THESE WERE THERE!

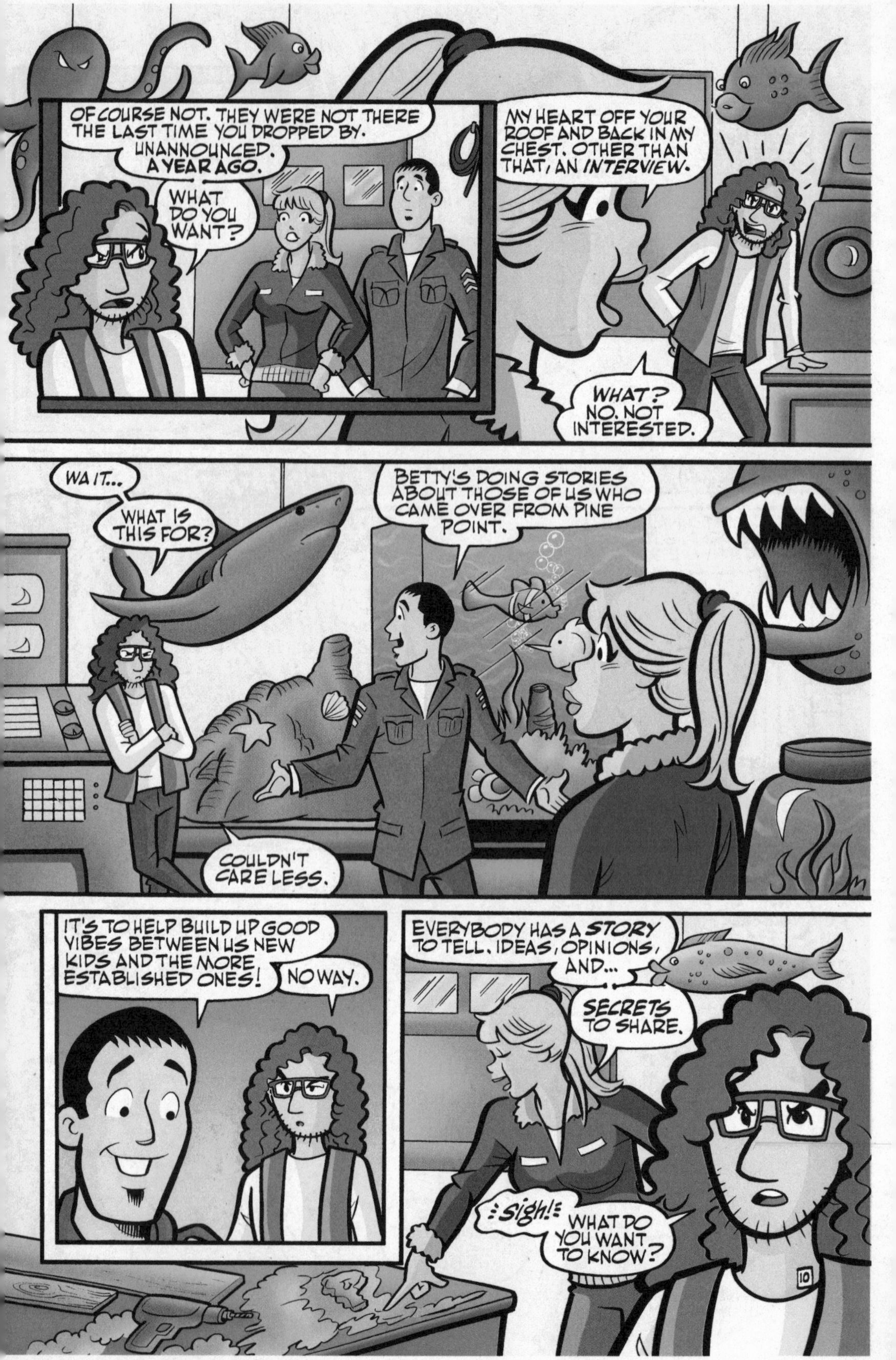
OF COURSE NOT. THEY WERE NOT THERE THE LAST TIME YOU DROPPED BY. UNANNOUNCED. A YEAR AGO.
WHAT DO YOU WANT?
MY HEART OFF YOUR ROOF AND BACK IN MY CHEST. OTHER THAN THAT, AN INTERVIEW.
WHAT? NO. NOT INTERESTED.
WAIT...
WHAT IS THIS FOR?
BETTY'S DOING STORIES ABOUT THOSE OF US WHO CAME OVER FROM PINE POINT.
COULDN'T CARE LESS.
IT'S TO HELP BUILD UP GOOD VIBES BETWEEN US NEW KIDS AND THE MORE ESTABLISHED ONES!
NO WAY.
EVERYBODY HAS A STORY TO TELL. IDEAS, OPINIONS, AND...
SECRETS TO SHARE.
SIGH!
WHAT DO YOU WANT TO KNOW?
10

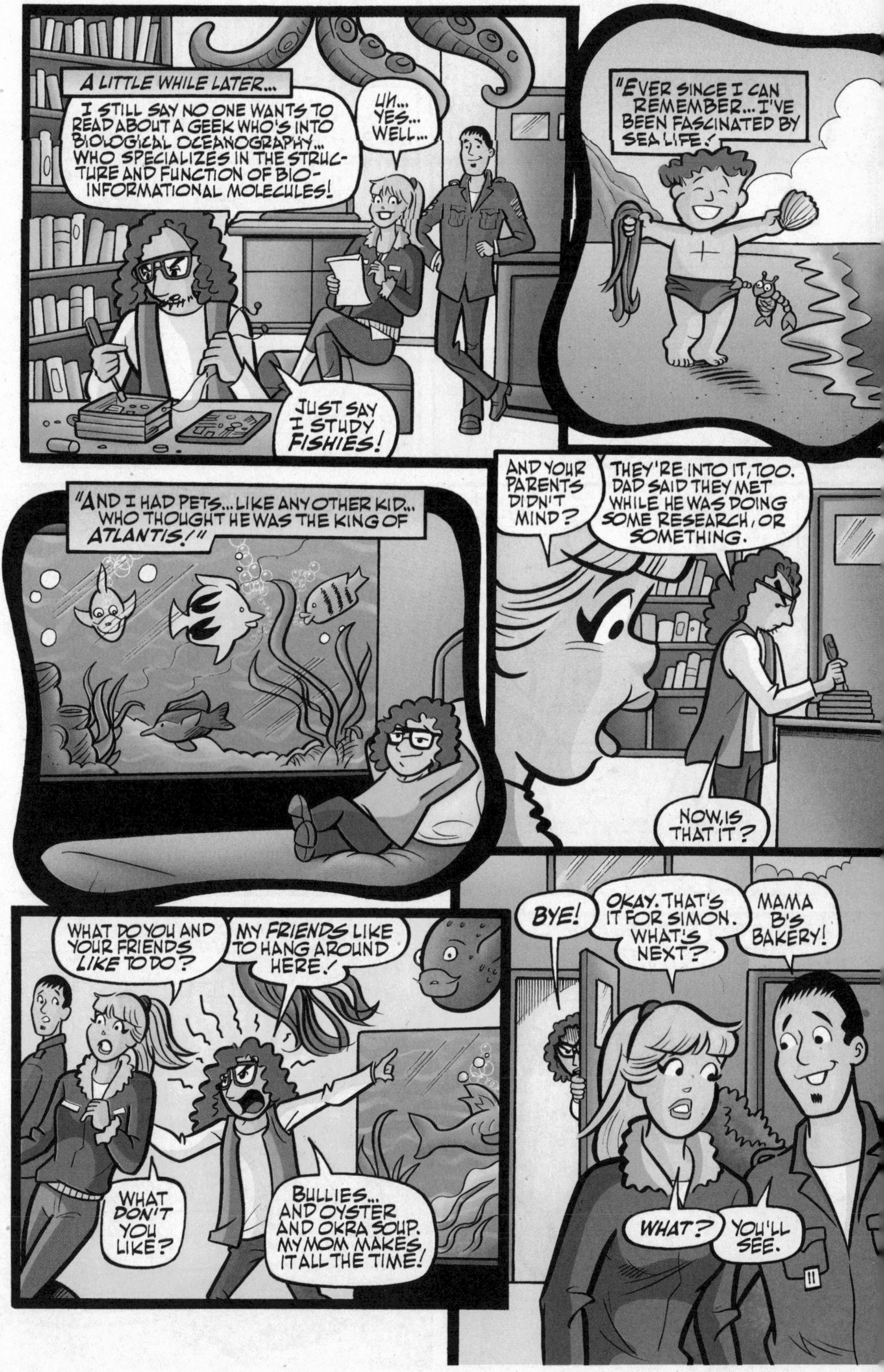
A LITTLE WHILE LATER...
I STILL SAY NO ONE WANTS TO READ ABOUT A GEEK WHO'S INTO BIOLOGICAL OCEANOGRAPHY... WHO SPECIALIZES IN THE STRUCTURE AND FUNCTION OF BIO-INFORMATIONAL MOLECULES!
UH... YES... WELL...
JUST SAY I STUDY FISHIES!
"EVER SINCE I CAN REMEMBER... I'VE BEEN FASCINATED BY SEA LIFE!
"AND I HAD PETS... LIKE ANY OTHER KID... WHO THOUGHT HE WAS THE KING OF ATLANTIS!"
AND YOUR PARENTS DIDN'T MIND?
THEY'RE INTO IT, TOO. DAD SAID THEY MET WHILE HE WAS DOING SOME RESEARCH, OR SOMETHING.
NOW, IS THAT IT?
WHAT DO YOU AND YOUR FRIENDS LIKE TO DO?
MY FRIENDS LIKE TO HANG AROUND HERE!
WHAT DON'T YOU LIKE?
BULLIES... AND OYSTER AND OKRA SOUP. MY MOM MAKES IT ALL THE TIME!
BYE!
OKAY. THAT'S IT FOR SIMON. WHAT'S NEXT?
MAMA B'S BAKERY!
WHAT?
YOU'LL SEE.

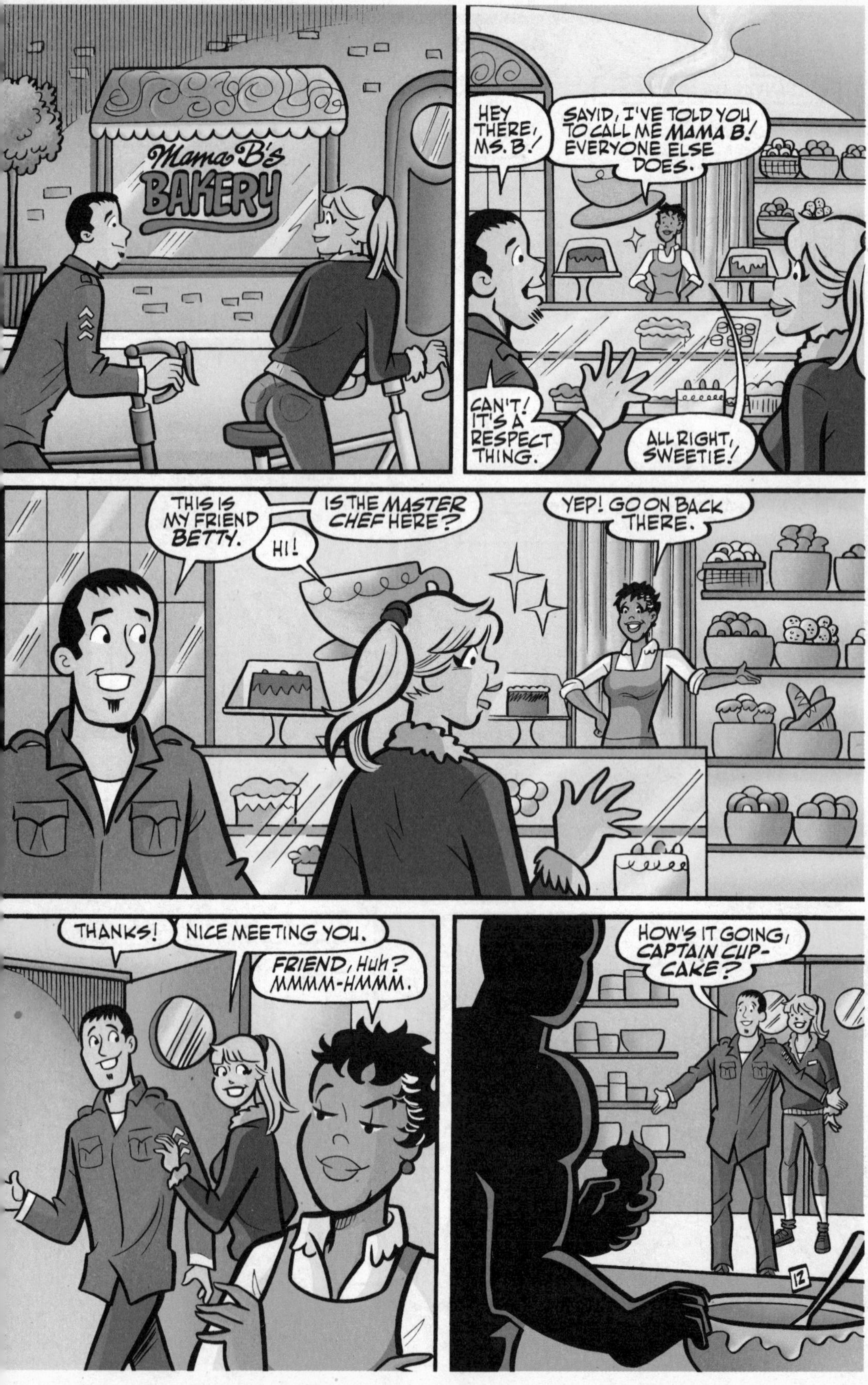
Mama B's BAKERY
HEY THERE, MS. B.!
SAYID, I'VE TOLD YOU TO CALL ME MAMA B! EVERYONE ELSE DOES.
CAN'T! IT'S A RESPECT THING.
ALL RIGHT, SWEETIE!
THIS IS MY FRIEND BETTY.
HI!
IS THE MASTER CHEF HERE?
YEP! GO ON BACK THERE.
THANKS!
NICE MEETING YOU.
FRIEND, Huh? MMMM-HMMM.
HOW'S IT GOING, CAPTAIN CUP-CAKE?
12

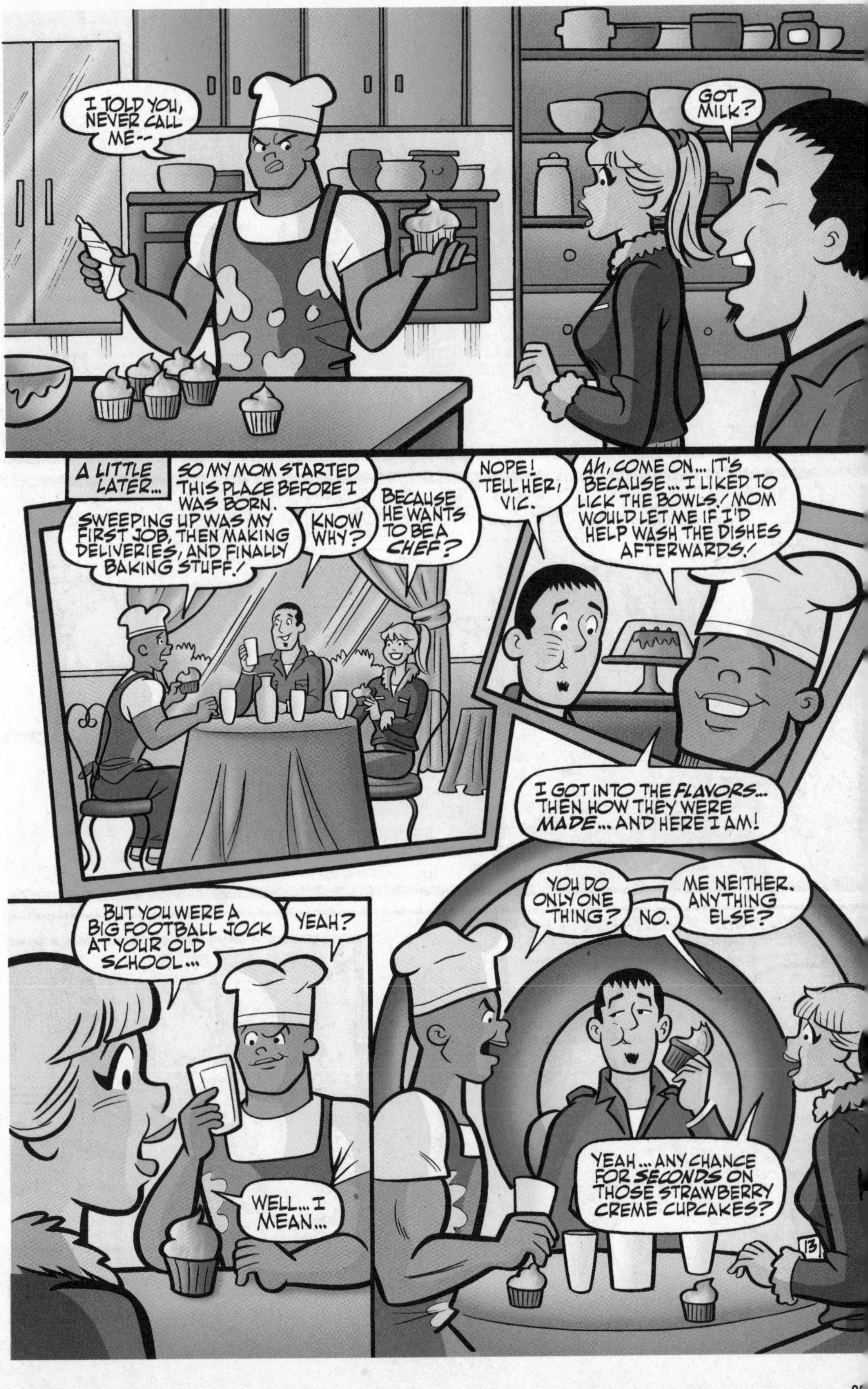
I TOLD YOU, NEVER CALL ME--
GOT MILK?
A LITTLE LATER...
SO MY MOM STARTED THIS PLACE BEFORE I WAS BORN.
SWEEPING UP WAS MY FIRST JOB, THEN MAKING DELIVERIES, AND FINALLY BAKING STUFF!
KNOW WHY?
BECAUSE HE WANTS TO BE A CHEF?
NOPE! TELL HER, VIC.
AH, COME ON... IT'S BECAUSE... I LIKED TO LICK THE BOWLS! MOM WOULD LET ME IF I'D HELP WASH THE DISHES AFTERWARDS!
I GOT INTO THE FLAVORS... THEN HOW THEY WERE MADE... AND HERE I AM!
BUT YOU WERE A BIG FOOTBALL JOCK AT YOUR OLD SCHOOL...
YEAH?
WELL... I MEAN...
YOU DO ONLY ONE THING?
NO.
ME NEITHER. ANYTHING ELSE?
YEAH... ANY CHANCE FOR SECONDS ON THOSE STRAWBERRY CREME CUPCAKES?
13

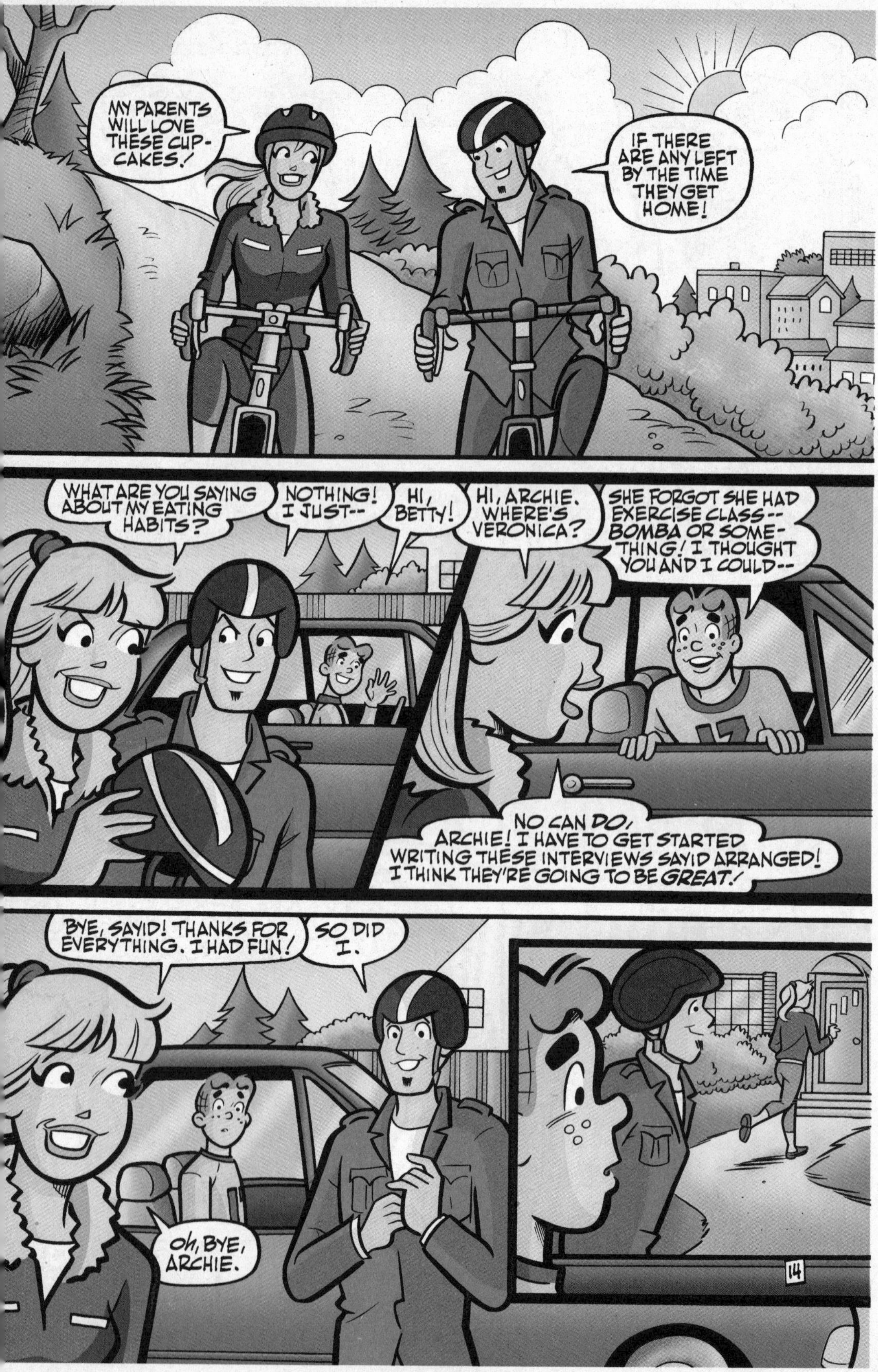
MY PARENTS WILL LOVE THESE CUP-CAKES!
IF THERE ARE ANY LEFT BY THE TIME THEY GET HOME!
WHAT ARE YOU SAYING ABOUT MY EATING HABITS?
NOTHING! I JUST--
HI, BETTY!
HI, ARCHIE. WHERE'S VERONICA?
SHE FORGOT SHE HAD EXERCISE CLASS-- BOMBA OR SOME-THING! I THOUGHT YOU AND I COULD--
NO CAN DO, ARCHIE! I HAVE TO GET STARTED WRITING THESE INTERVIEWS SAYID ARRANGED! I THINK THEY'RE GOING TO BE GREAT!
BYE, SAYID! THANKS FOR EVERYTHING. I HAD FUN!
SO DID I.
oh, BYE, ARCHIE.
14

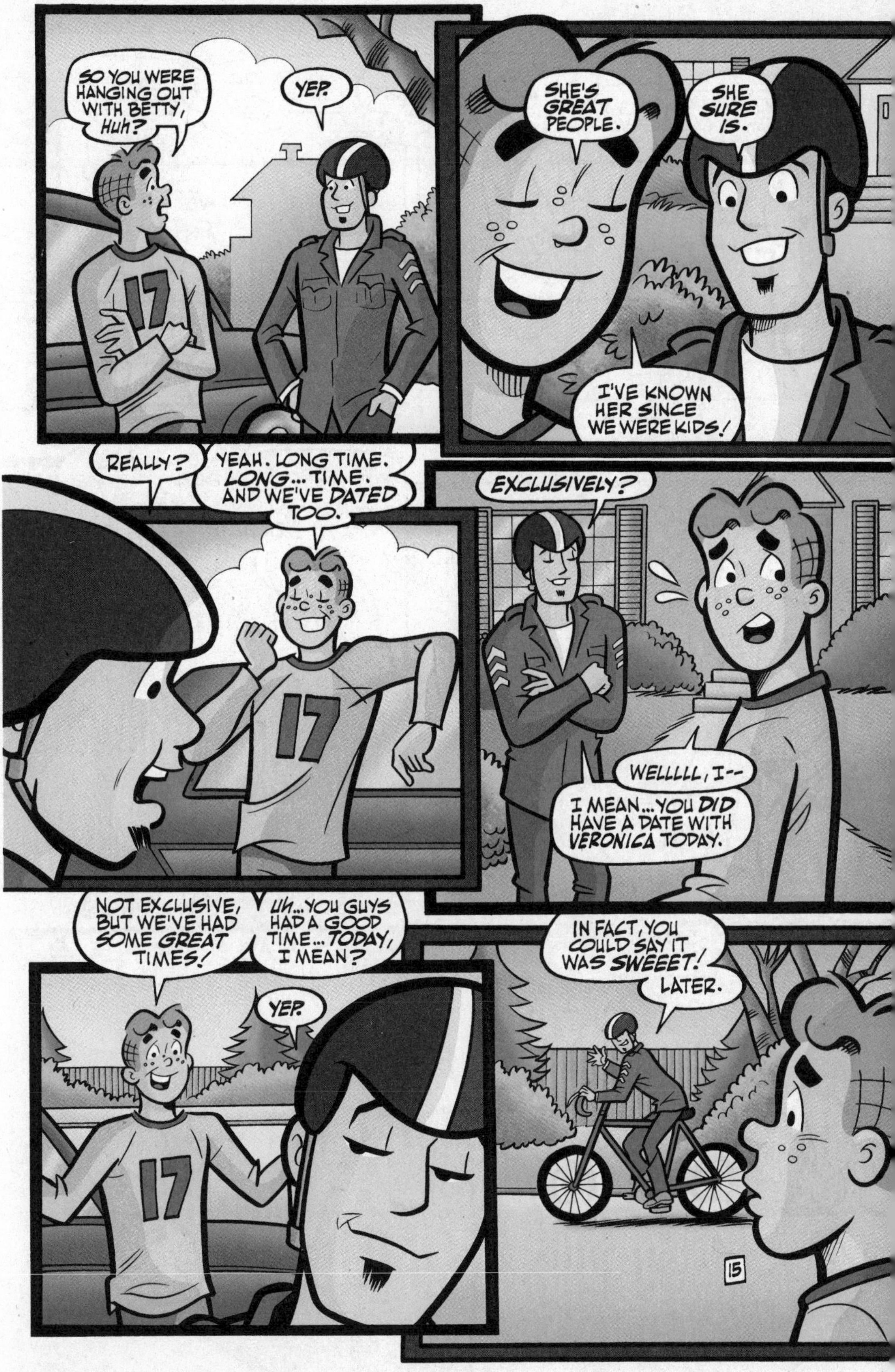
SO YOU WERE HANGING OUT WITH BETTY, HUH?
YEP.
SHE'S GREAT PEOPLE.
SHE SURE IS.
I'VE KNOWN HER SINCE WE WERE KIDS!
REALLY?
YEAH. LONG TIME. LONG... TIME. AND WE'VE DATED TOO.
EXCLUSIVELY?
WELLLLL, I--
I MEAN... YOU DID HAVE A DATE WITH VERONICA TODAY.
NOT EXCLUSIVE, BUT WE'VE HAD SOME GREAT TIMES!
UH... YOU GUYS HAD A GOOD TIME... TODAY, I MEAN?
YEP.
IN FACT, YOU COULD SAY IT WAS SWEEET!
LATER.
15

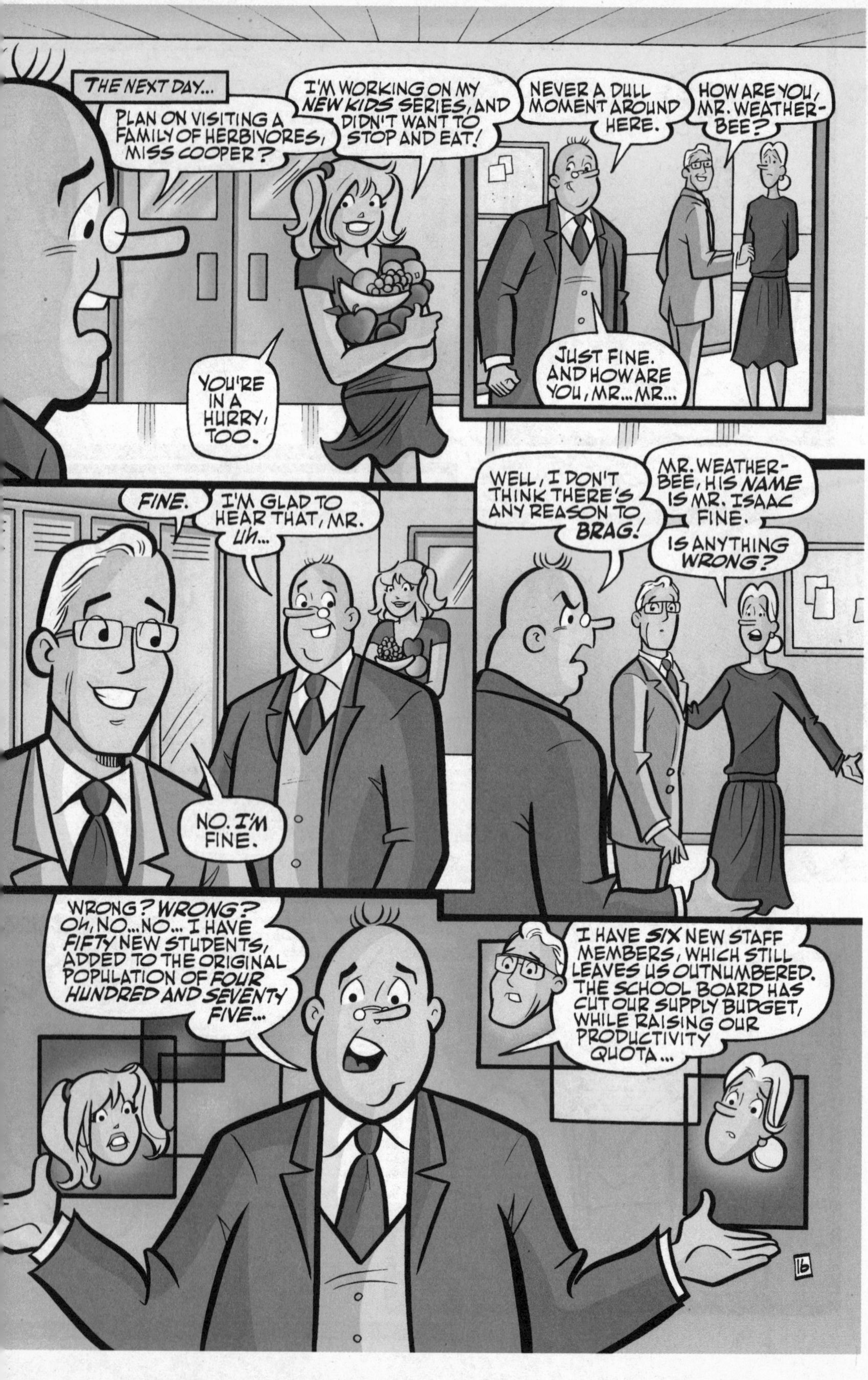
THE NEXT DAY...
PLAN ON VISITING A FAMILY OF HERBIVORES, MISS COOPER?
I'M WORKING ON MY NEW KIDS SERIES, AND DIDN'T WANT TO STOP AND EAT!
YOU'RE IN A HURRY, TOO.
NEVER A DULL MOMENT AROUND HERE.
HOW ARE YOU, MR. WEATHER-BEE?
JUST FINE. AND HOW ARE YOU, MR... MR...
FINE.
I'M GLAD TO HEAR THAT, MR. UH...
NO. I'M FINE.
WELL, I DON'T THINK THERE'S ANY REASON TO BRAG!
MR. WEATHER-BEE, HIS NAME IS MR. ISAAC FINE.
IS ANYTHING WRONG?
WRONG? WRONG? OH, NO...NO... I HAVE FIFTY NEW STUDENTS, ADDED TO THE ORIGINAL POPULATION OF FOUR HUNDRED AND SEVENTY FIVE...
I HAVE SIX NEW STAFF MEMBERS, WHICH STILL LEAVES US OUTNUMBERED. THE SCHOOL BOARD HAS CUT OUR SUPPLY BUDGET, WHILE RAISING OUR PRODUCTIVITY QUOTA...
16

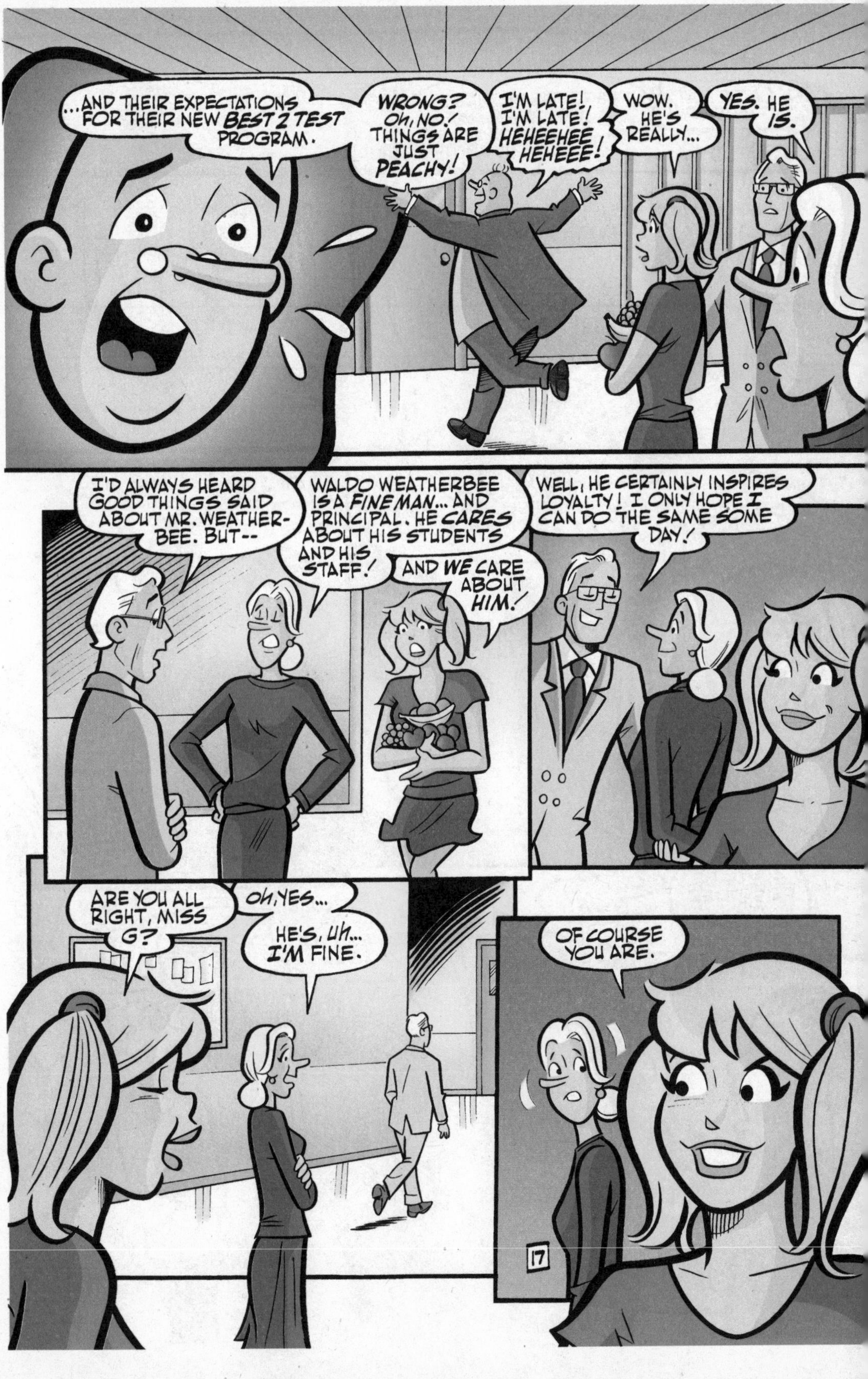
...AND THEIR EXPECTATIONS FOR THEIR NEW BEST 2 TEST PROGRAM.
WRONG? OH, NO! THINGS ARE JUST PEACHY!
I'M LATE! I'M LATE! HEHEEHEE HEHEEE!
WOW. HE'S REALLY...
YES. HE IS.
I'D ALWAYS HEARD GOOD THINGS SAID ABOUT MR. WEATHER-BEE. BUT--
WALDO WEATHERBEE IS A FINE MAN... AND PRINCIPAL. HE CARES ABOUT HIS STUDENTS AND HIS STAFF!
AND WE CARE ABOUT HIM!
WELL, HE CERTAINLY INSPIRES LOYALTY! I ONLY HOPE I CAN DO THE SAME SOME DAY!
ARE YOU ALL RIGHT, MISS G?
OH, YES...
HE'S, UH... I'M FINE.
OF COURSE YOU ARE.
17

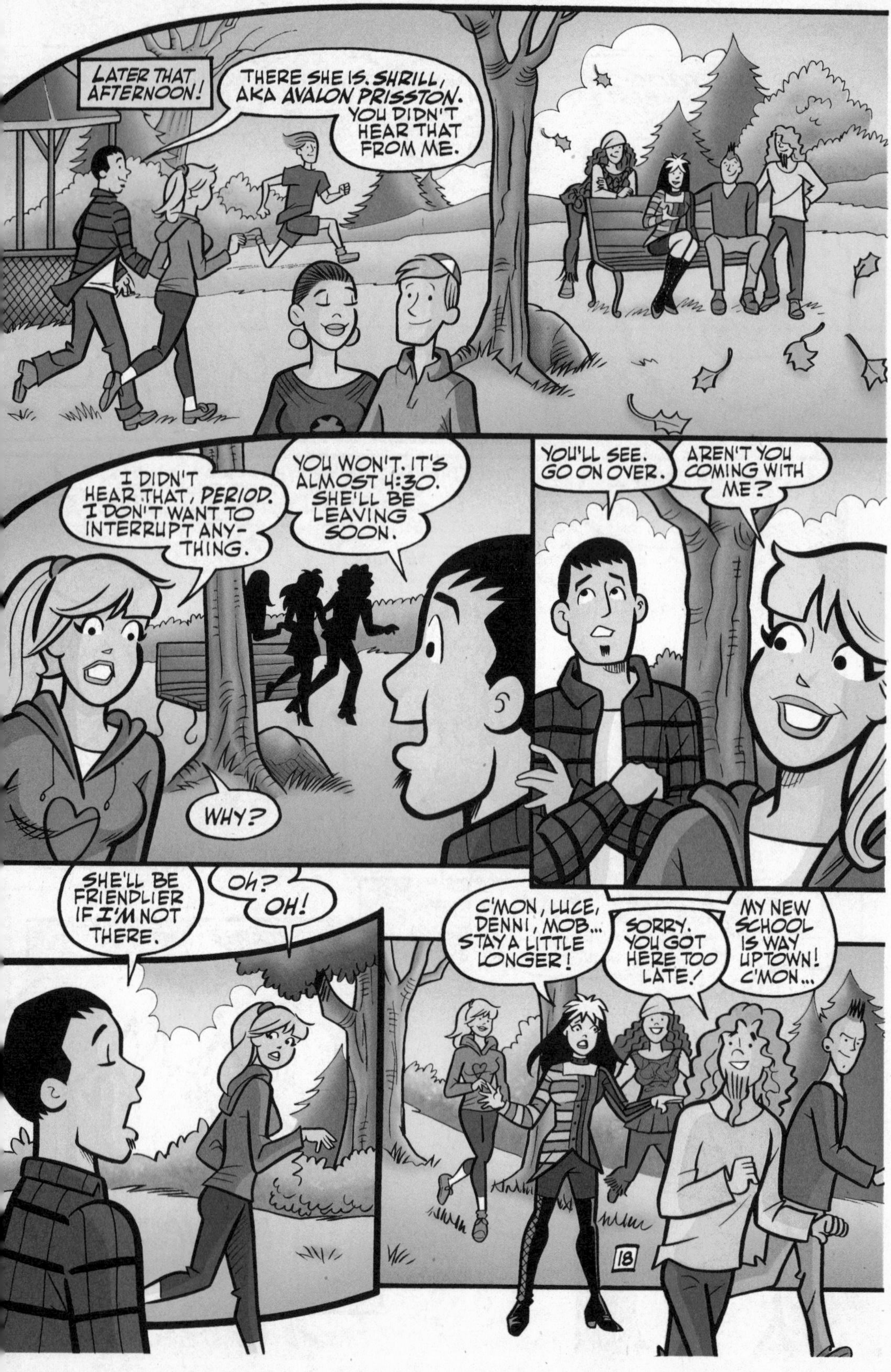
LATER THAT AFTERNOON!
THERE SHE IS. SHRILL, AKA AVALON PRISSTON. YOU DIDN'T HEAR THAT FROM ME.
I DIDN'T HEAR THAT, PERIOD. I DON'T WANT TO INTERRUPT ANY-THING.
YOU WON'T. IT'S ALMOST 4:30. SHE'LL BE LEAVING SOON.
WHY?
YOU'LL SEE. GO ON OVER.
AREN'T YOU COMING WITH ME?
SHE'LL BE FRIENDLIER IF I'M NOT THERE.
Oh? OH!
C'MON, LUCE, DENNI, MOB... STAY A LITTLE LONGER!
SORRY. YOU GOT HERE TOO LATE!
MY NEW SCHOOL IS WAY UPTOWN! C'MON...
18

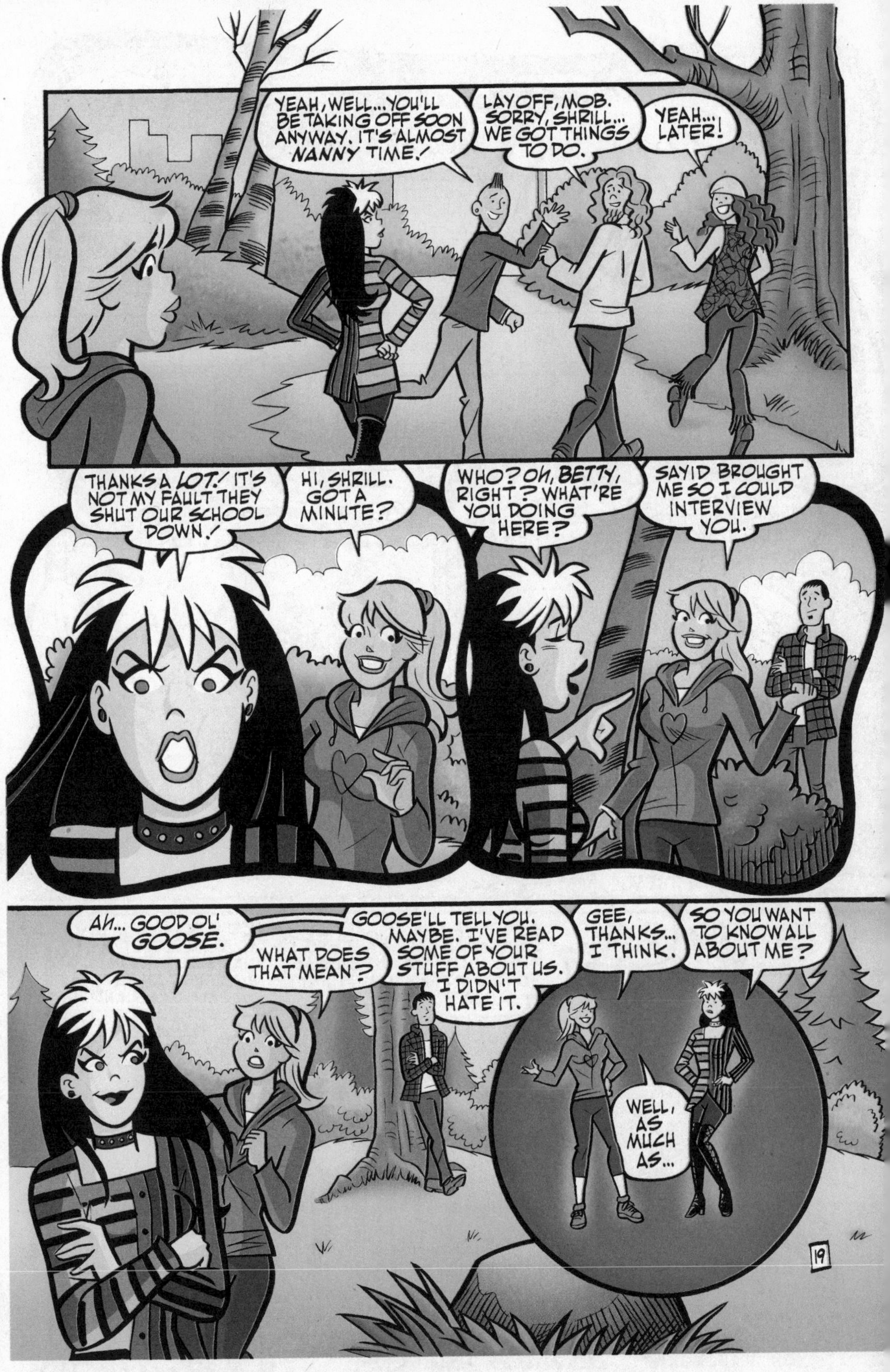
YEAH, WELL...YOU'LL BE TAKING OFF SOON ANYWAY. IT'S ALMOST NANNY TIME!
LAYOFF, MOB. SORRY, SHRILL... WE GOT THINGS TO DO.
YEAH... LATER!
THANKS A LOT! IT'S NOT MY FAULT THEY SHUT OUR SCHOOL DOWN!
HI, SHRILL. GOT A MINUTE?
WHO? OH, BETTY, RIGHT? WHAT'RE YOU DOING HERE?
SAYID BROUGHT ME SO I COULD INTERVIEW YOU.
AH... GOOD OL' GOOSE.
WHAT DOES THAT MEAN?
GOOSE'LL TELL YOU. MAYBE. I'VE READ SOME OF YOUR STUFF ABOUT US. I DIDN'T HATE IT.
GEE, THANKS... I THINK.
SO YOU WANT TO KNOW ALL ABOUT ME?
WELL, AS MUCH AS...
19

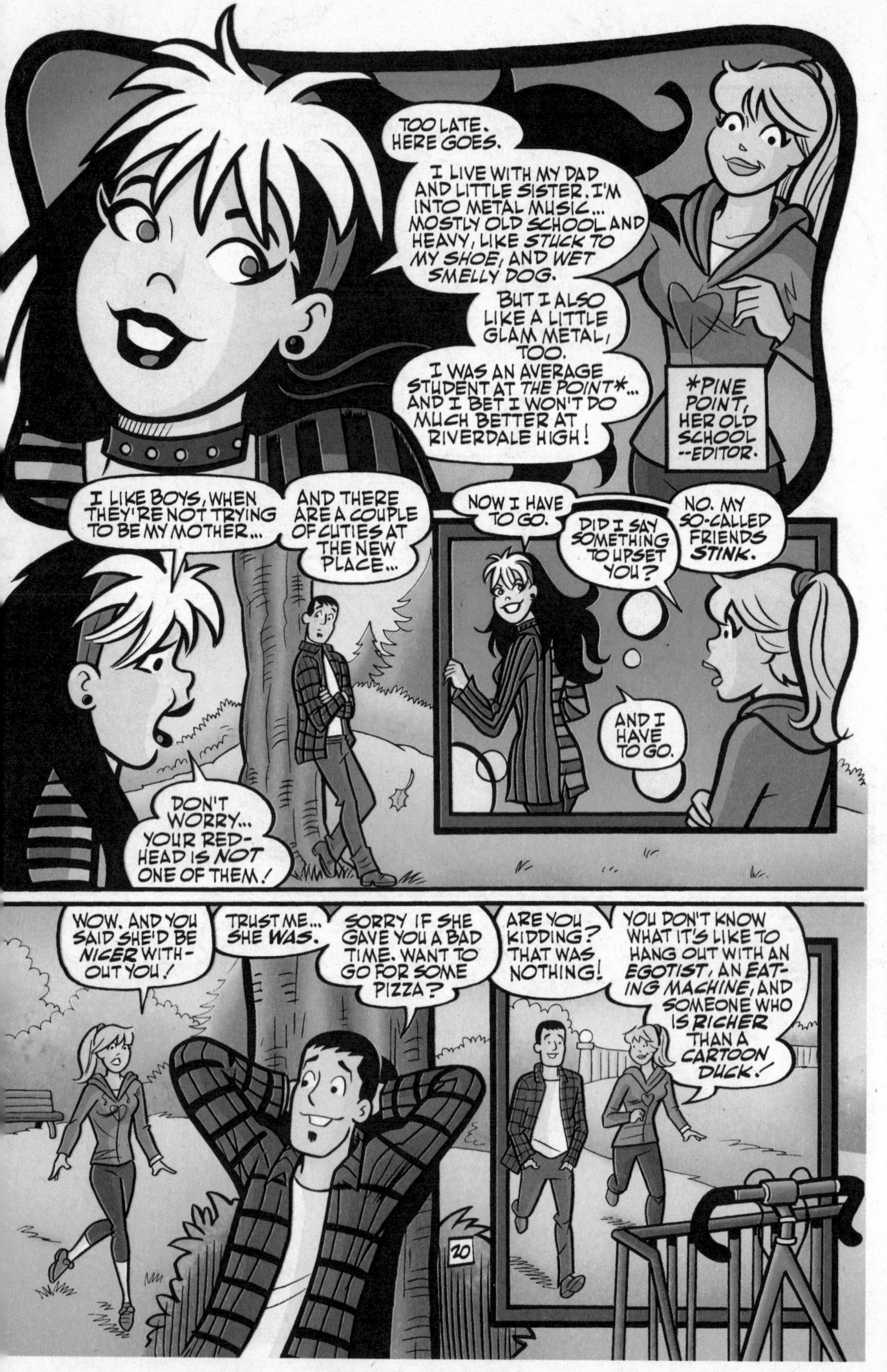
TOO LATE. HERE GOES.
I LIVE WITH MY DAD AND LITTLE SISTER. I'M INTO METAL MUSIC... MOSTLY OLD SCHOOL AND HEAVY, LIKE STUCK TO MY SHOE, AND WET SMELLY DOG.
BUT I ALSO LIKE A LITTLE GLAM METAL, TOO.
I WAS AN AVERAGE STUDENT AT THE POINT*... AND I BET I WON'T DO MUCH BETTER AT RIVERDALE HIGH!
*PINE POINT, HER OLD SCHOOL --EDITOR.
I LIKE BOYS, WHEN THEY'RE NOT TRYING TO BE MY MOTHER...
AND THERE ARE A COUPLE OF CUTIES AT THE NEW PLACE...
DON'T WORRY... YOUR RED-HEAD IS NOT ONE OF THEM!
NOW I HAVE TO GO.
DID I SAY SOMETHING TO UPSET YOU?
NO. MY SO-CALLED FRIENDS STINK.
AND I HAVE TO GO.
WOW. AND YOU SAID SHE'D BE NICER WITH-OUT YOU!
TRUST ME... SHE WAS.
SORRY IF SHE GAVE YOU A BAD TIME. WANT TO GO FOR SOME PIZZA?
ARE YOU KIDDING? THAT WAS NOTHING!
YOU DON'T KNOW WHAT IT'S LIKE TO HANG OUT WITH AN EGOTIST, AN EAT-ING MACHINE, AND SOMEONE WHO IS RICHER THAN A CARTOON DUCK!
20

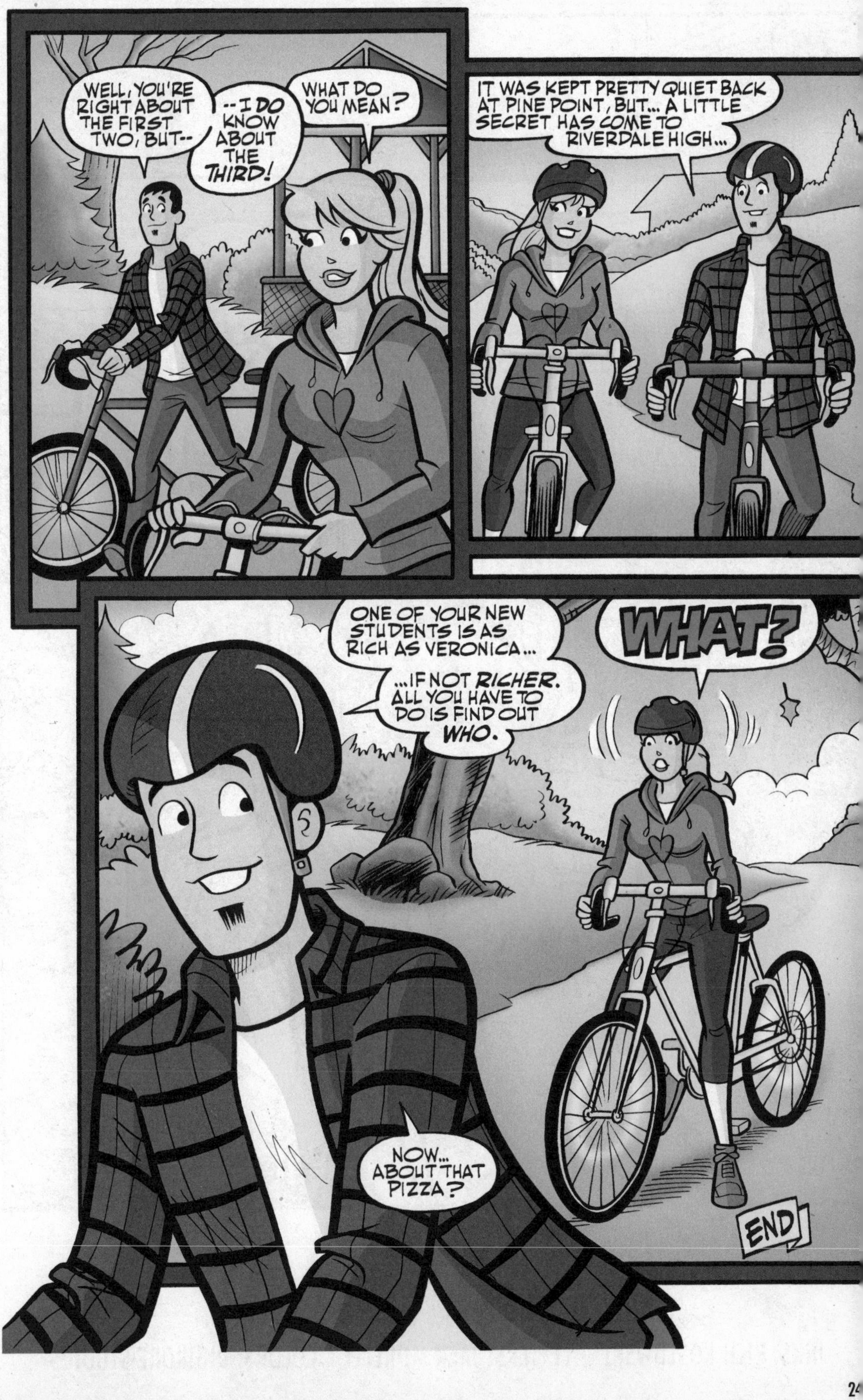
WELL, YOU'RE RIGHT ABOUT THE FIRST TWO, BUT--
--I DO KNOW ABOUT THE THIRD!
WHAT DO YOU MEAN?
IT WAS KEPT PRETTY QUIET BACK AT PINE POINT, BUT... A LITTLE SECRET HAS COME TO RIVERDALE HIGH...
ONE OF YOUR NEW STUDENTS IS AS RICH AS VERONICA...
...IF NOT RICHER. ALL YOU HAVE TO DO IS FIND OUT WHO.
WHAT?
NOW... ABOUT THAT PIZZA?
END

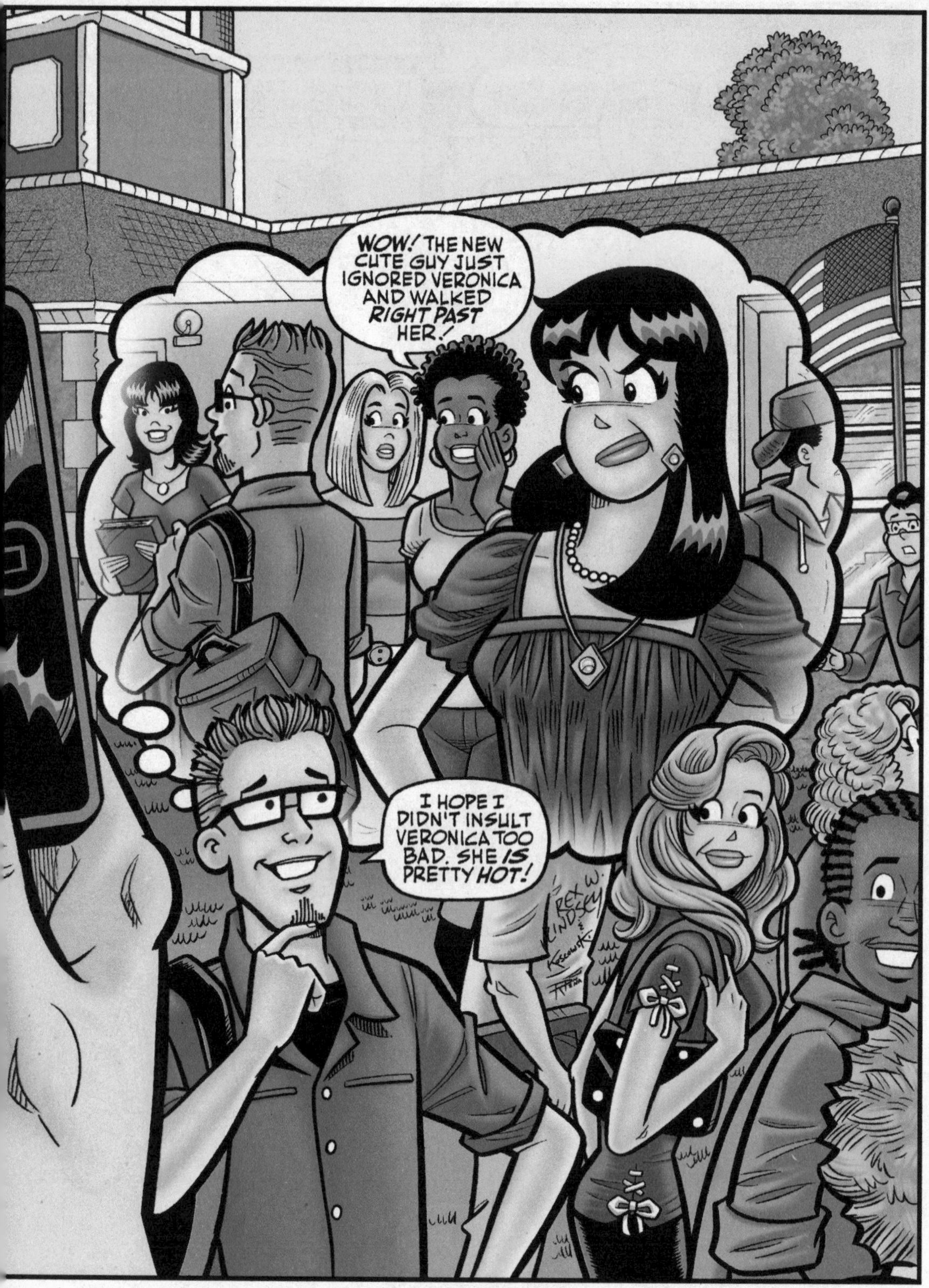
WOW! THE NEW CUTE GUY JUST IGNORED VERONICA AND WALKED RIGHT PAST HER!
I HOPE I DIDN'T INSULT VERONICA TOO BAD. SHE IS PRETTY HOT!
REX W. LINDSEY & KOSLOWSKI

ALL THAT AND A BAG OF CHIPS - PART 6

SCRIPT: ALEX SIMMONS PENCILS: DAN PARENT
INKS: RICH KOSLOWSKI LETTERS: JACK MORELLI COLORS: DIGIKORE STUDIOS

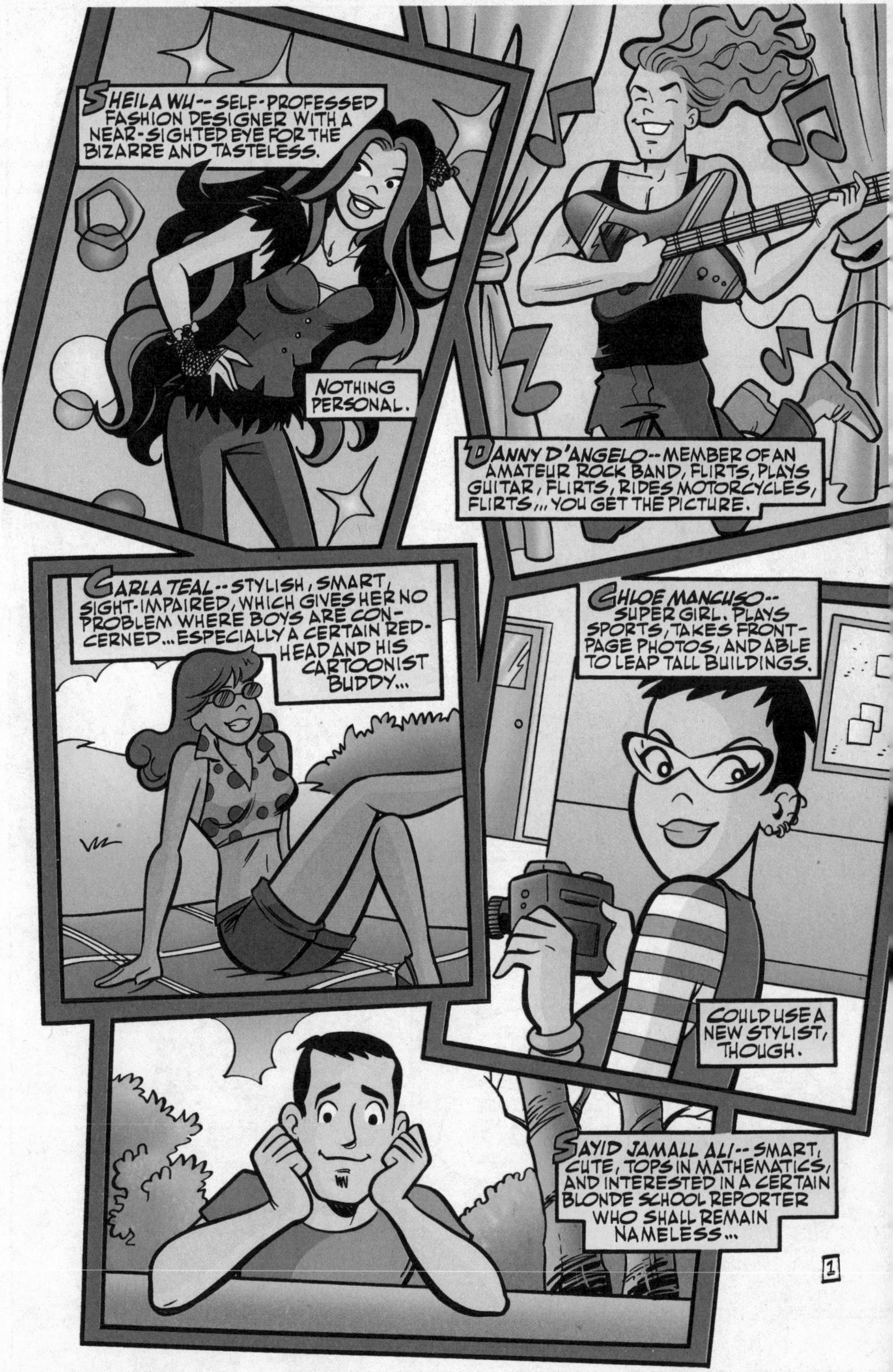
SHEILA WU-- SELF-PROFESSED FASHION DESIGNER WITH A NEAR-SIGHTED EYE FOR THE BIZARRE AND TASTELESS.
NOTHING PERSONAL.
DANNY D'ANGELO-- MEMBER OF AN AMATEUR ROCK BAND, FLIRTS, PLAYS GUITAR, FLIRTS, RIDES MOTORCYCLES, FLIRTS... YOU GET THE PICTURE.
CARLA TEAL-- STYLISH, SMART, SIGHT-IMPAIRED, WHICH GIVES HER NO PROBLEM WHERE BOYS ARE CONCERNED... ESPECIALLY A CERTAIN RED-HEAD AND HIS CARTOONIST BUDDY...
CHLOE MANCUSO-- SUPER GIRL. PLAYS SPORTS, TAKES FRONT-PAGE PHOTOS, AND ABLE TO LEAP TALL BUILDINGS.
COULD USE A NEW STYLIST, THOUGH.
SAYID JAMALL ALI-- SMART, CUTE, TOPS IN MATHEMATICS, AND INTERESTED IN A CERTAIN BLONDE SCHOOL REPORTER WHO SHALL REMAIN NAMELESS...
1

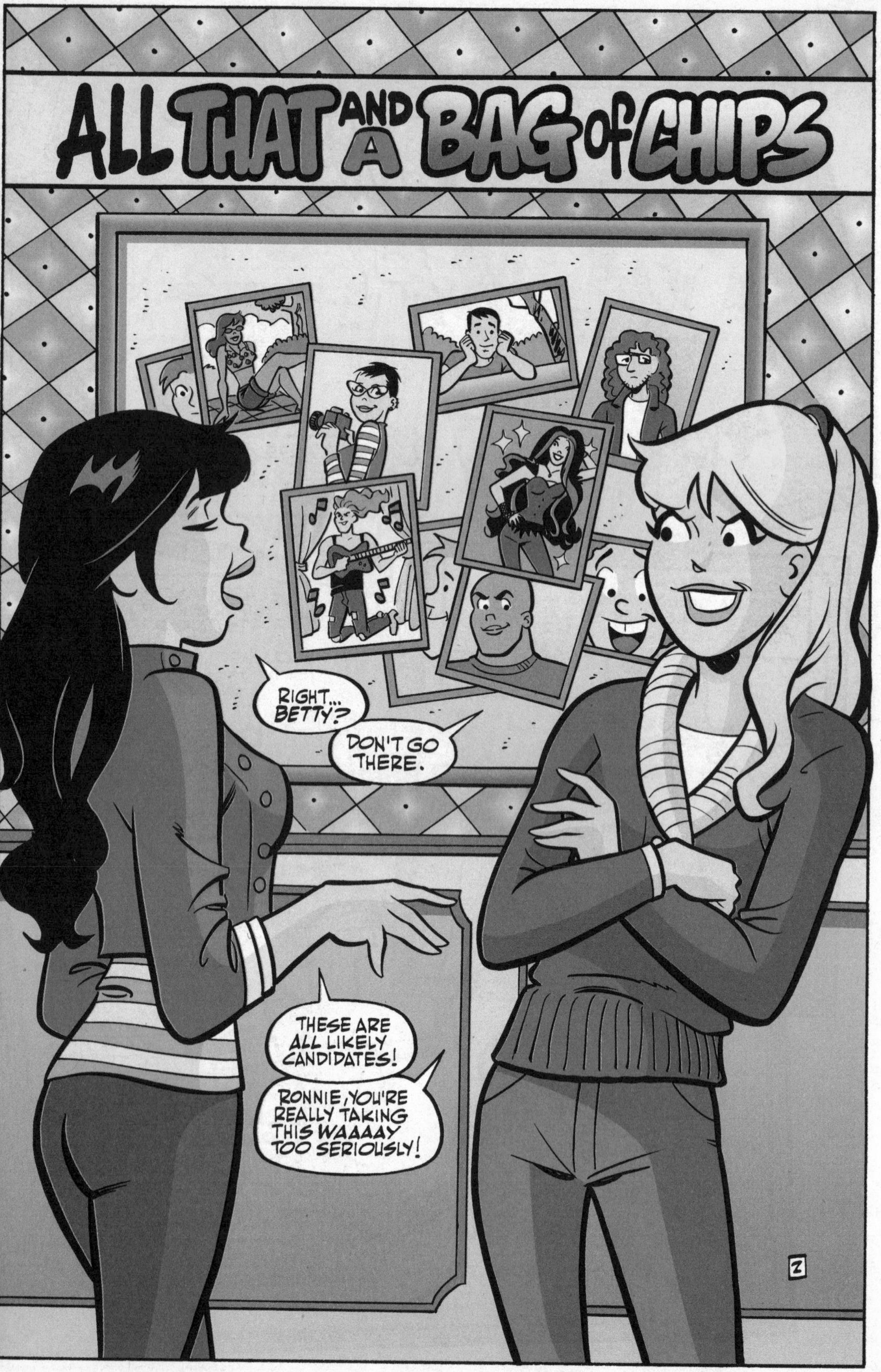
ALL THAT AND A BAG of CHIPS
RIGHT... BETTY?
DON'T GO THERE.
THESE ARE ALL LIKELY CANDIDATES!
RONNIE, YOU'RE REALLY TAKING THIS WAAAAY TOO SERIOUSLY!

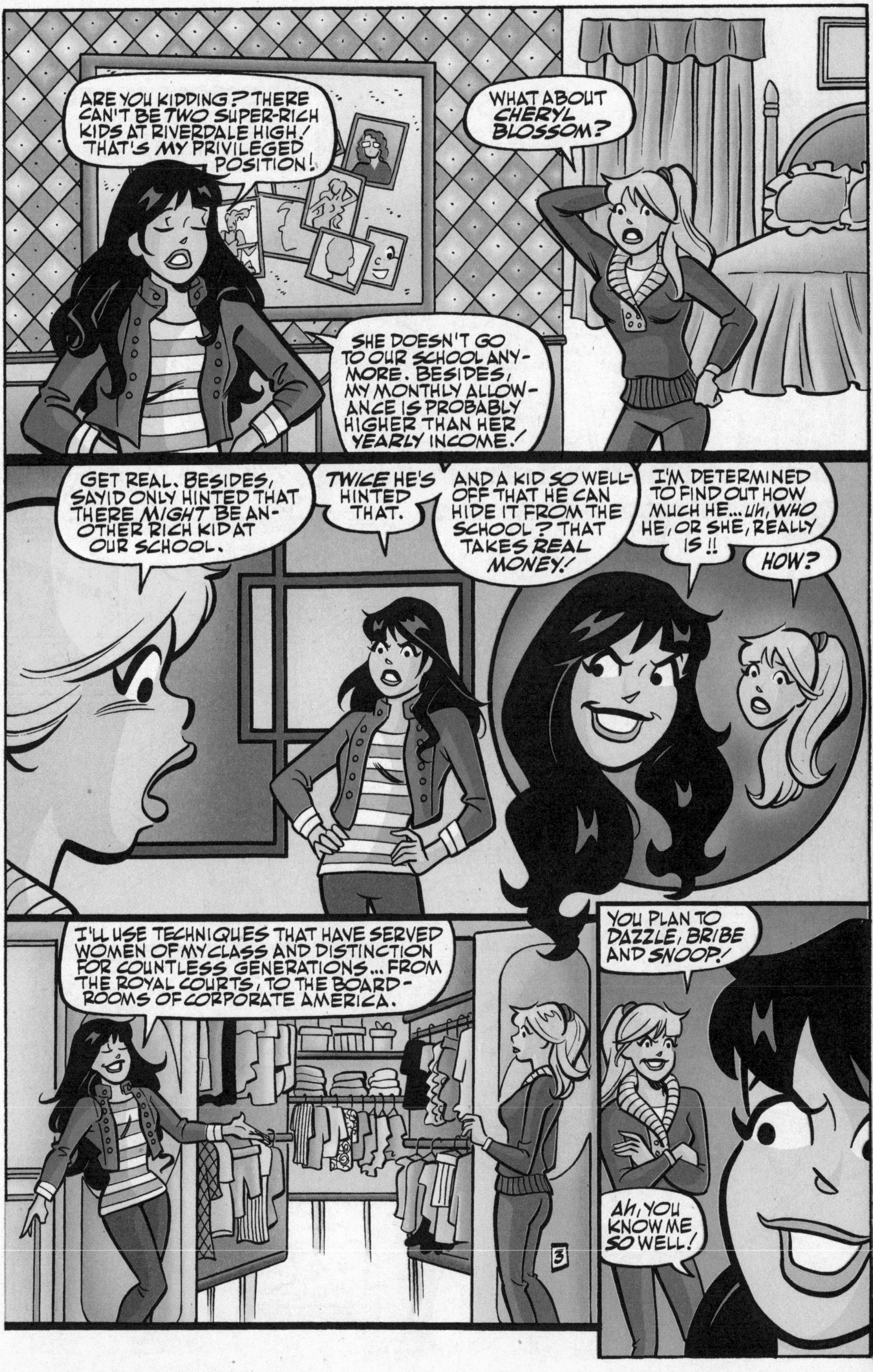

ARE YOU KIDDING? THERE CAN'T BE TWO SUPER-RICH KIDS AT RIVERDALE HIGH! THAT'S MY PRIVILEGED POSITION!
WHAT ABOUT CHERYL BLOSSOM?
SHE DOESN'T GO TO OUR SCHOOL ANY-MORE. BESIDES, MY MONTHLY ALLOW-ANCE IS PROBABLY HIGHER THAN HER YEARLY INCOME!
GET REAL. BESIDES, SAYID ONLY HINTED THAT THERE MIGHT BE AN-OTHER RICH KID AT OUR SCHOOL.
TWICE HE'S HINTED THAT.
AND A KID SO WELL-OFF THAT HE CAN HIDE IT FROM THE SCHOOL? THAT TAKES REAL MONEY!
I'M DETERMINED TO FIND OUT HOW MUCH HE... uh, WHO HE, OR SHE, REALLY IS!!
HOW?
I'LL USE TECHNIQUES THAT HAVE SERVED WOMEN OF MY CLASS AND DISTINCTION FOR COUNTLESS GENERATIONS... FROM THE ROYAL COURTS, TO THE BOARD-ROOMS OF CORPORATE AMERICA.
3
YOU PLAN TO DAZZLE, BRIBE AND SNOOP!
Ah, YOU KNOW ME SO WELL!

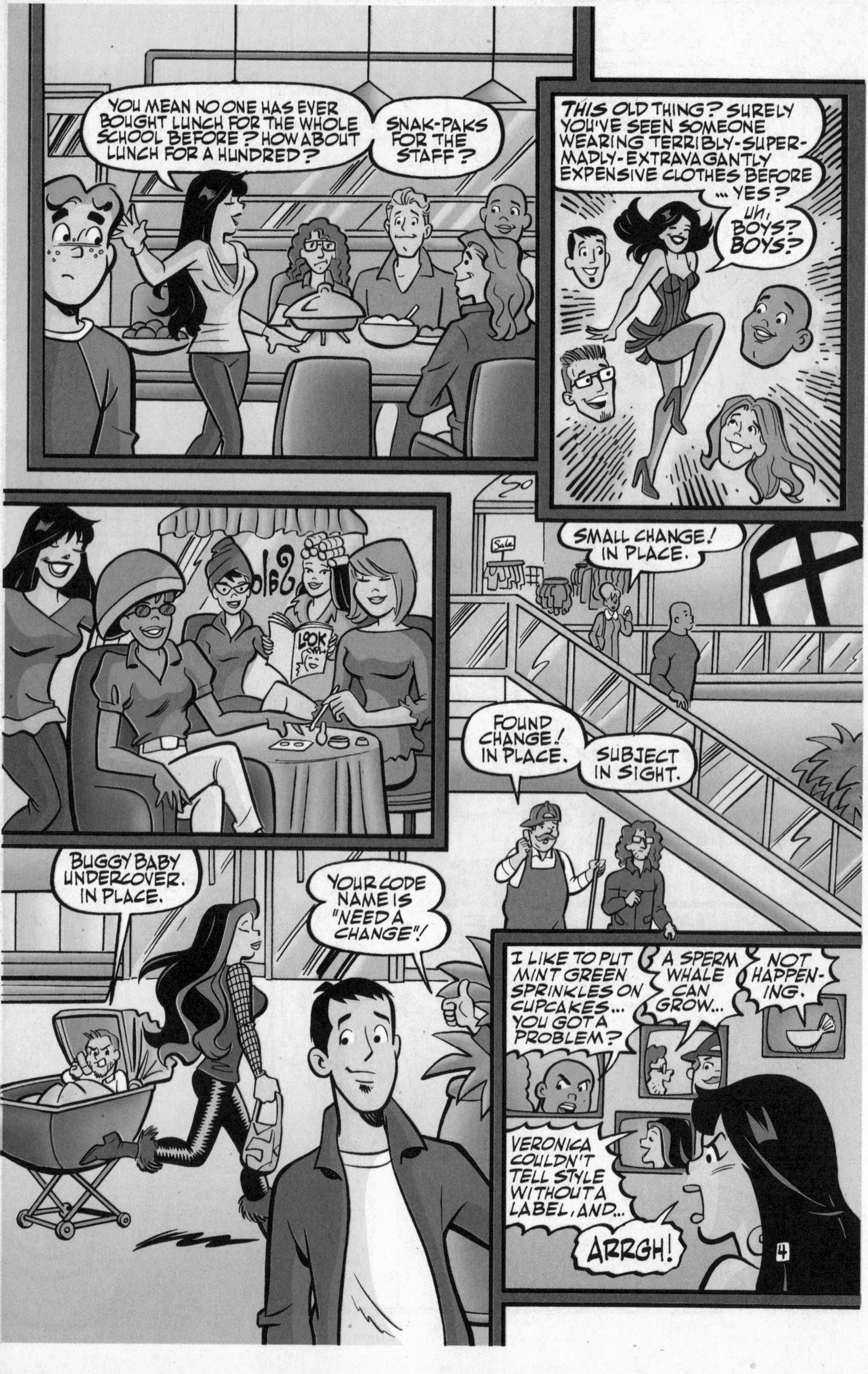
YOU MEAN NO ONE HAS EVER BOUGHT LUNCH FOR THE WHOLE SCHOOL BEFORE? HOW ABOUT LUNCH FOR A HUNDRED?
SNAK-PAKS FOR THE STAFF?
THIS OLD THING? SURELY YOU'VE SEEN SOMEONE WEARING TERRIBLY-SUPER-MADLY-EXTRAVAGANTLY EXPENSIVE CLOTHES BEFORE ... YES?
UH, BOYS? BOYS?
LOOK
SMALL CHANGE! IN PLACE.
FOUND CHANGE! IN PLACE.
SUBJECT IN SIGHT.
BUGGY BABY UNDERCOVER. IN PLACE.
YOUR CODE NAME IS "NEED A CHANGE"!
I LIKE TO PUT MINT GREEN SPRINKLES ON CUPCAKES... YOU GOT A PROBLEM?
A SPERM WHALE CAN GROW...
NOT HAPPEN-ING.
VERONICA COULDN'T TELL STYLE WITHOUT A LABEL, AND...
ARRGH!
4

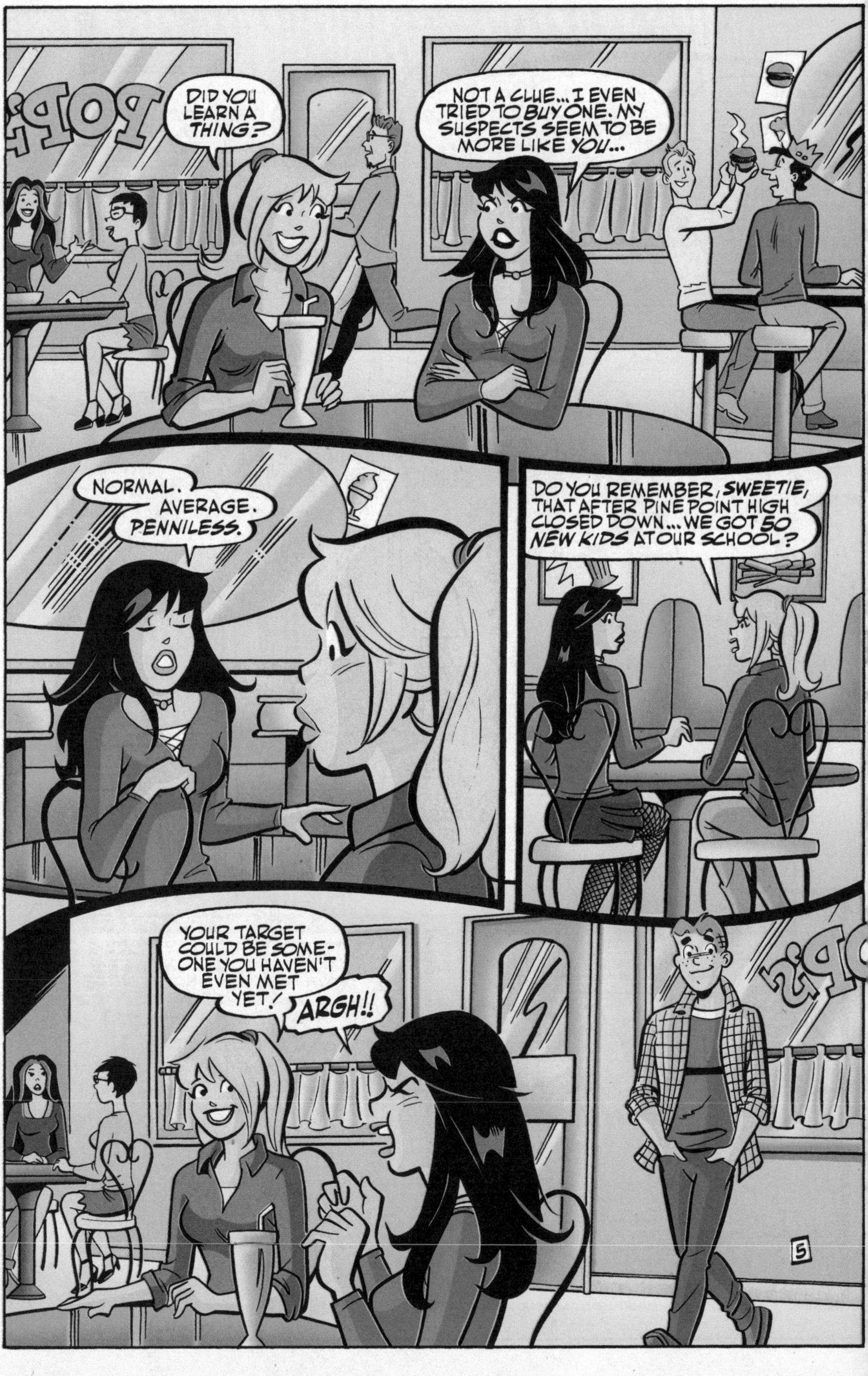
POP'S
DID YOU LEARN A THING?
NOT A CLUE... I EVEN TRIED TO BUY ONE. MY SUSPECTS SEEM TO BE MORE LIKE YOU...
NORMAL. AVERAGE. PENNILESS.
DO YOU REMEMBER, SWEETIE, THAT AFTER PINE POINT HIGH CLOSED DOWN... WE GOT 50 NEW KIDS AT OUR SCHOOL?
YOUR TARGET COULD BE SOME-ONE YOU HAVEN'T EVEN MET YET!
ARGH!!
POP'S
5

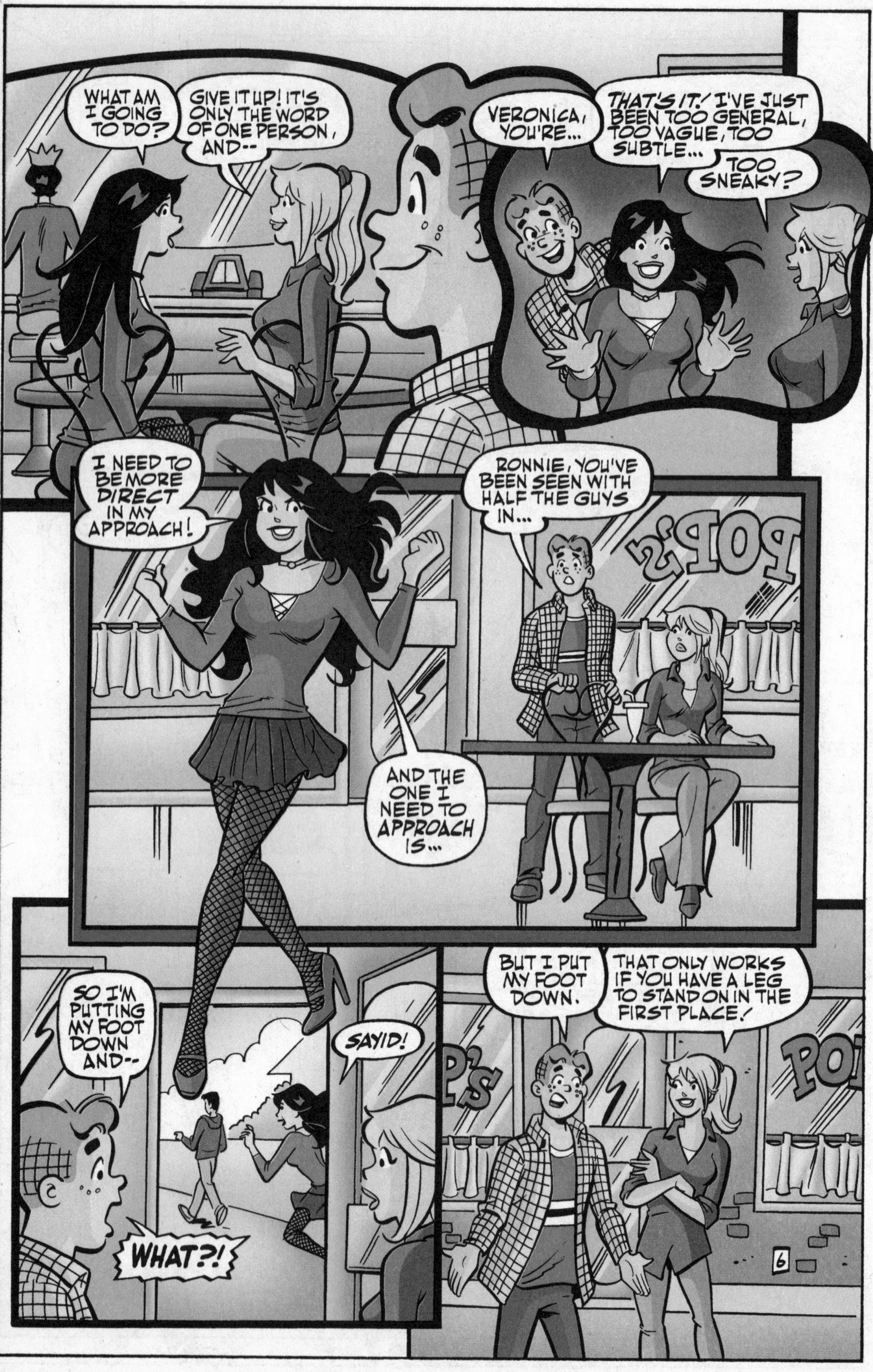
WHAT AM I GOING TO DO?
GIVE IT UP! IT'S ONLY THE WORD OF ONE PERSON, AND--
VERONICA, YOU'RE...
THAT'S IT! I'VE JUST BEEN TOO GENERAL, TOO VAGUE, TOO SUBTLE...
TOO SNEAKY?
I NEED TO BE MORE DIRECT IN MY APPROACH!
RONNIE, YOU'VE BEEN SEEN WITH HALF THE GUYS IN...
POP'S
AND THE ONE I NEED TO APPROACH IS...
SO I'M PUTTING MY FOOT DOWN AND--
SAYID!
WHAT?!
BUT I PUT MY FOOT DOWN.
THAT ONLY WORKS IF YOU HAVE A LEG TO STAND ON IN THE FIRST PLACE!
6

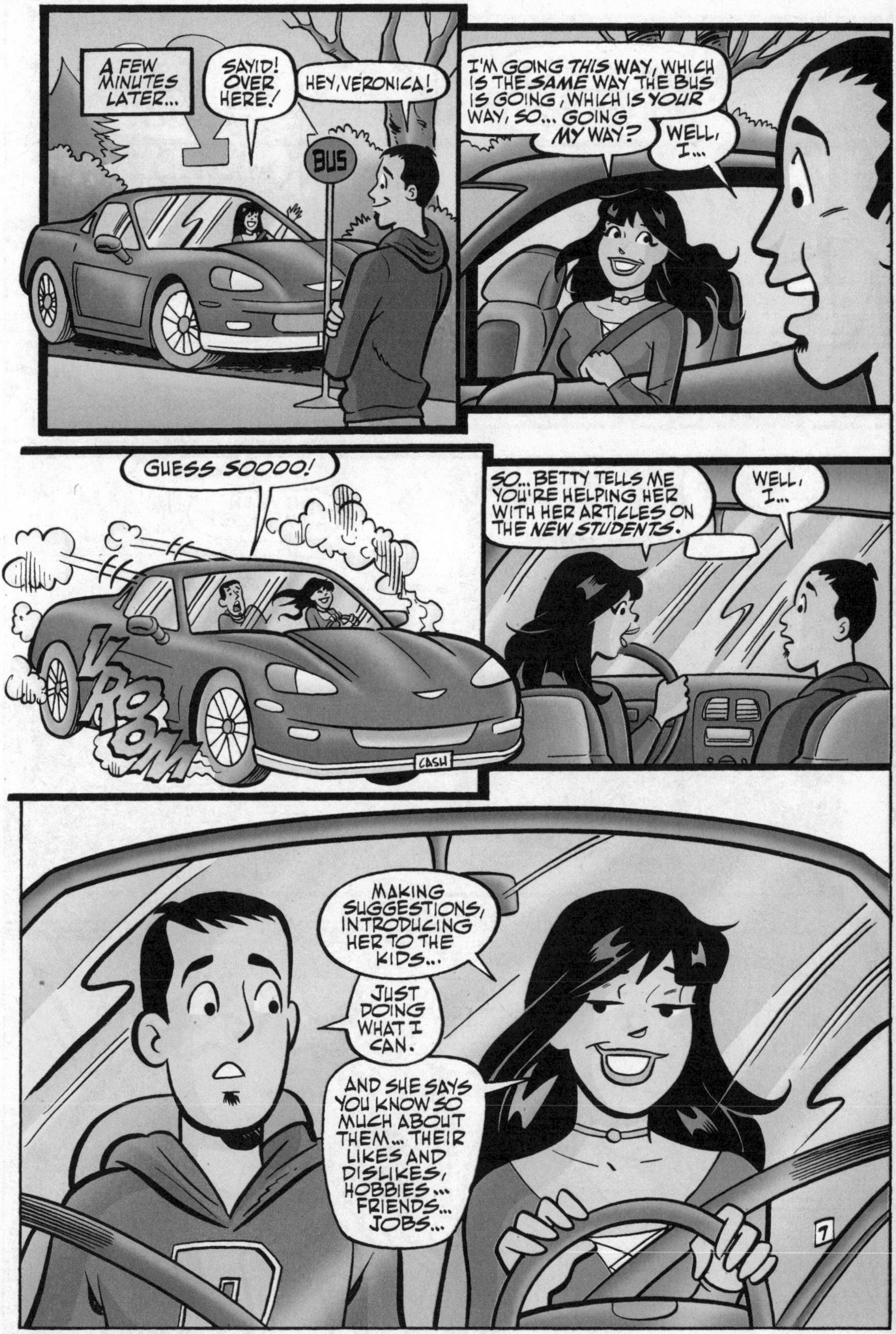
A FEW MINUTES LATER...
SAYID! OVER HERE!
HEY, VERONICA!
BUS
I'M GOING THIS WAY, WHICH IS THE SAME WAY THE BUS IS GOING, WHICH IS YOUR WAY, SO... GOING MY WAY?
WELL, I...
GUESS SOOOO!
VROOM
CASH
SO... BETTY TELLS ME YOU'RE HELPING HER WITH HER ARTICLES ON THE NEW STUDENTS.
WELL, I...
MAKING SUGGESTIONS, INTRODUCING HER TO THE KIDS...
JUST DOING WHAT I CAN.
AND SHE SAYS YOU KNOW SO MUCH ABOUT THEM... THEIR LIKES AND DISLIKES, HOBBIES... FRIENDS... JOBS...
7

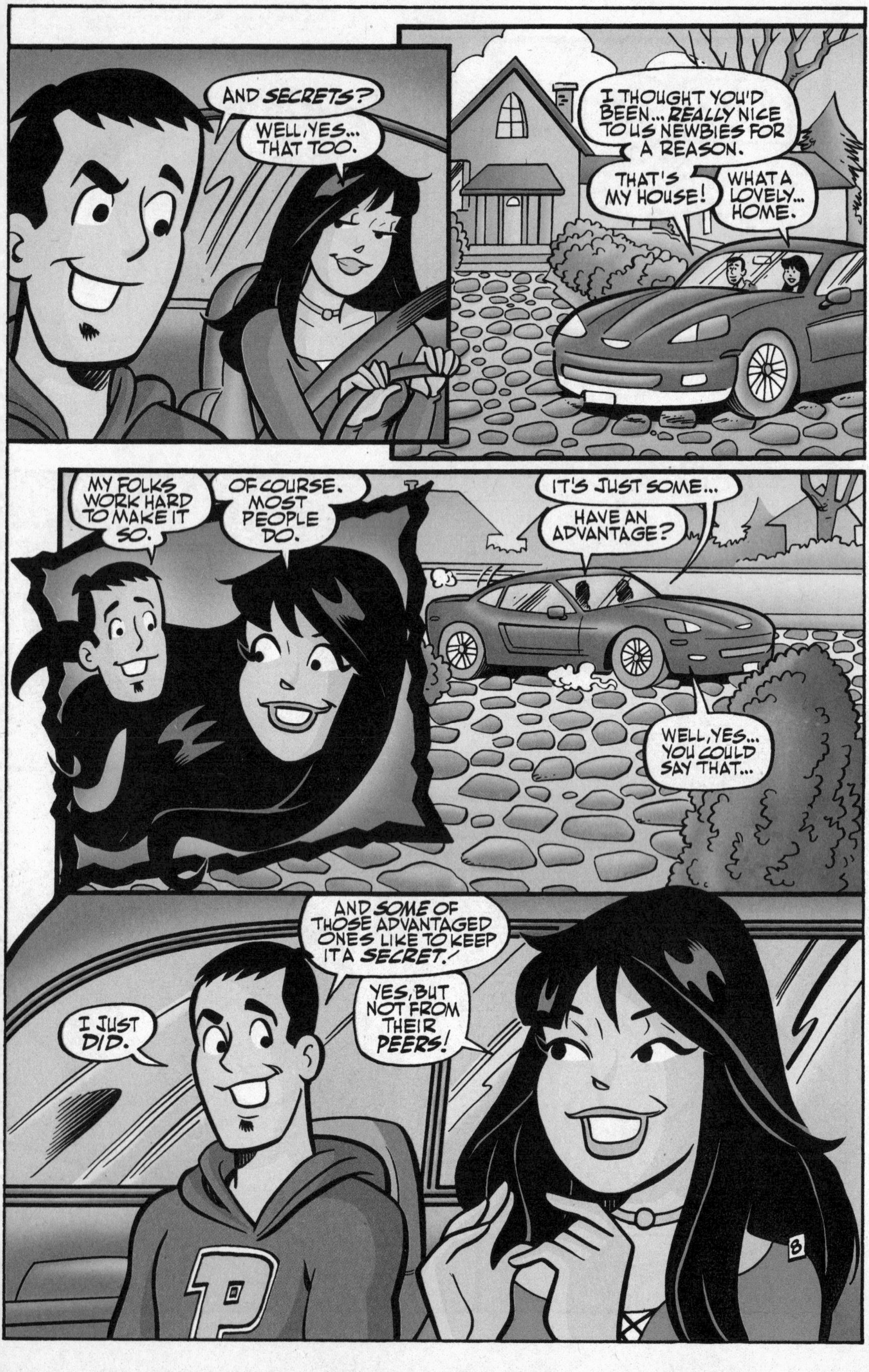
AND SECRETS?
WELL, YES... THAT TOO.
I THOUGHT YOU'D BEEN... REALLY NICE TO US NEWBIES FOR A REASON.
THAT'S MY HOUSE!
WHAT A LOVELY... HOME.
MY FOLKS WORK HARD TO MAKE IT SO.
OF COURSE. MOST PEOPLE DO.
IT'S JUST SOME...
HAVE AN ADVANTAGE?
WELL, YES... YOU COULD SAY THAT...
AND SOME OF THOSE ADVANTAGED ONES LIKE TO KEEP IT A SECRET!
YES, BUT NOT FROM THEIR PEERS!
I JUST DID.
8

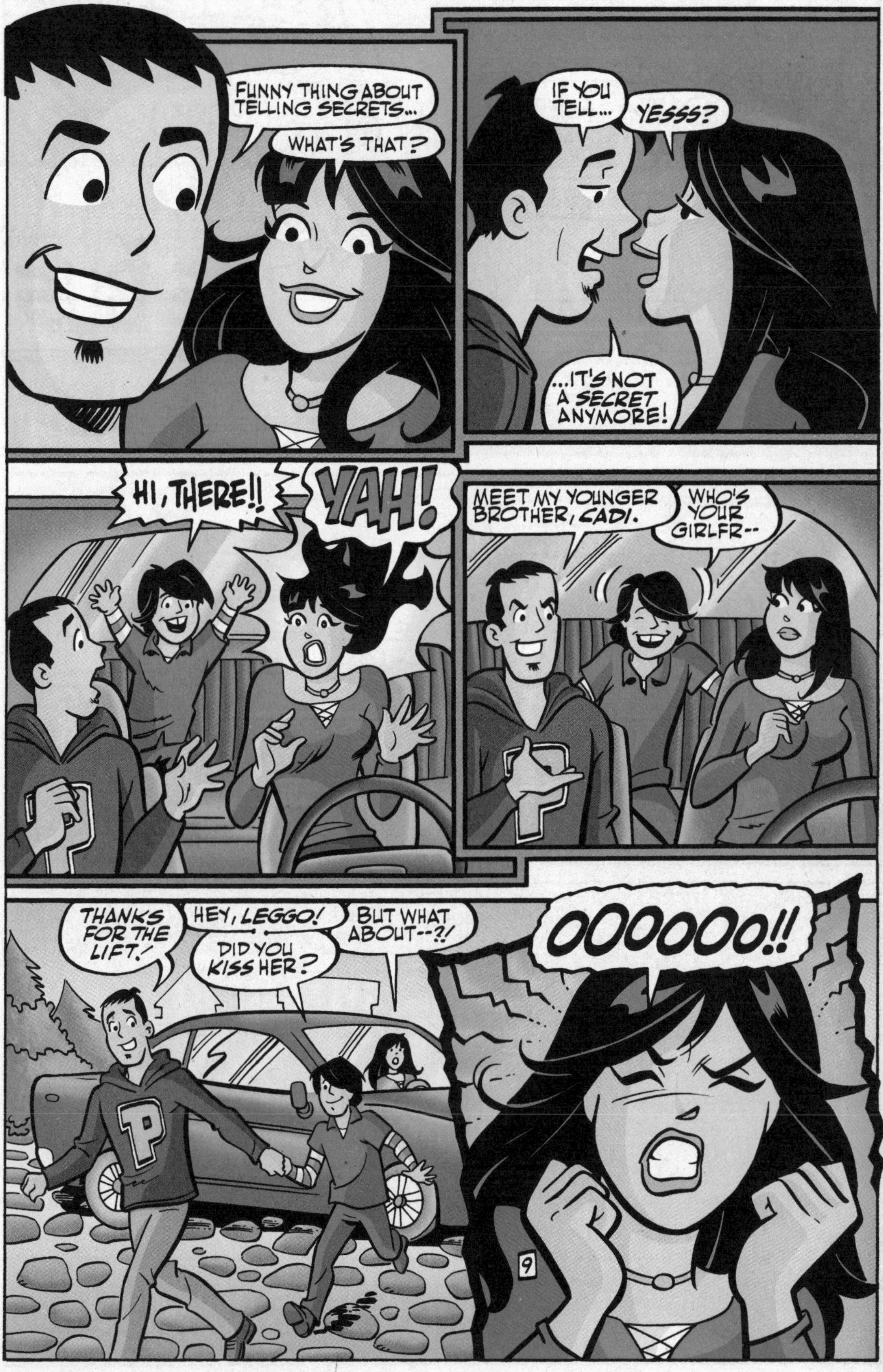
FUNNY THING ABOUT TELLING SECRETS...
WHAT'S THAT?
IF YOU TELL...
YESSS?
...IT'S NOT A SECRET ANYMORE!
HI, THERE!!
YAH!
MEET MY YOUNGER BROTHER, CADI.
WHO'S YOUR GIRLFR--
THANKS FOR THE LIFT!
HEY, LEGGO!
DID YOU KISS HER?
BUT WHAT ABOUT--?!
OOOOOO!!
9

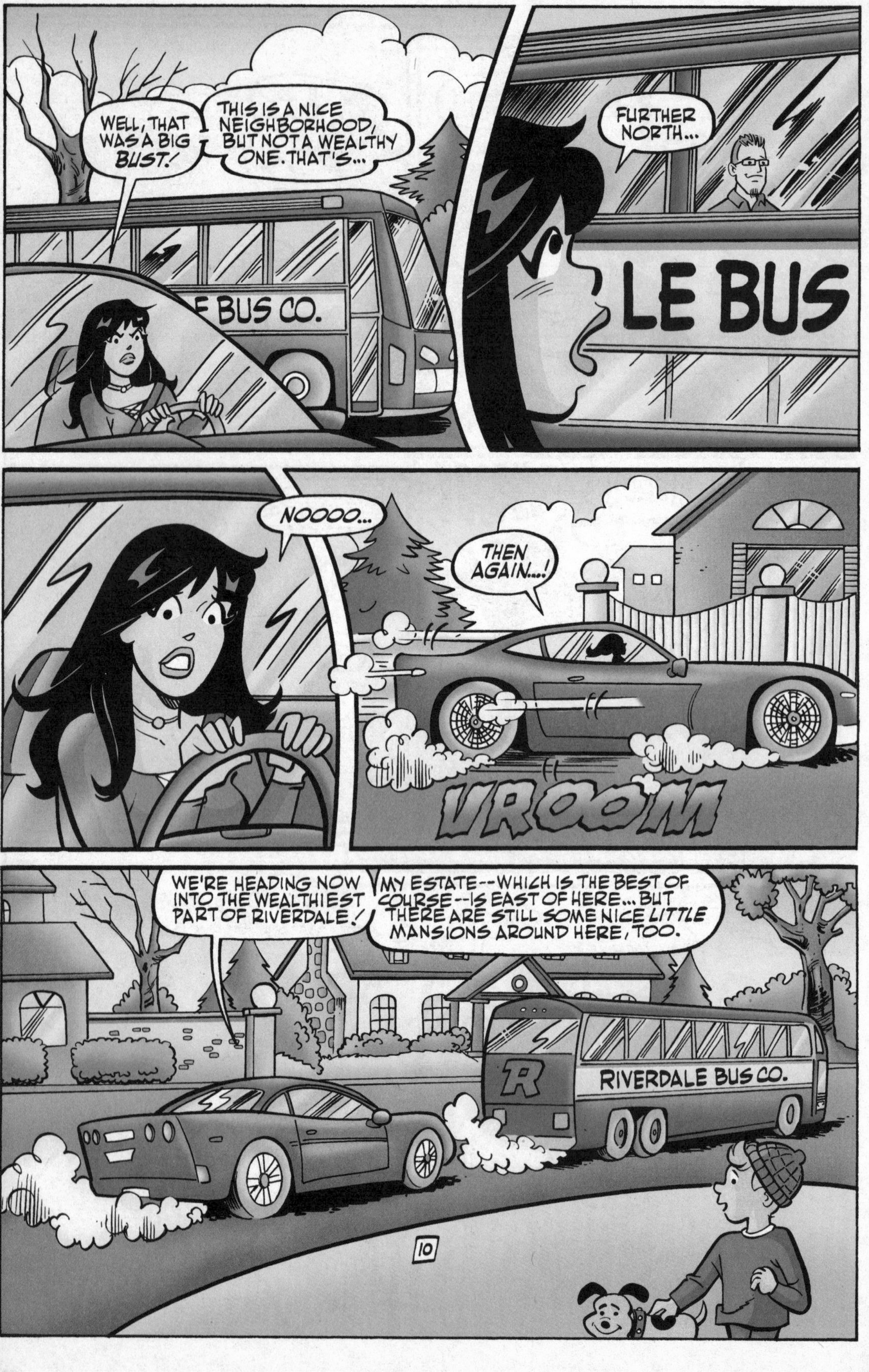
WELL, THAT WAS A BIG BUST!
THIS IS A NICE NEIGHBORHOOD, BUT NOT A WEALTHY ONE. THAT'S...
E BUS CO.
FURTHER NORTH...
LE BUS
NOOOO...
THEN AGAIN...!
VROOM
WE'RE HEADING NOW INTO THE WEALTHIEST PART OF RIVERDALE!
MY ESTATE--WHICH IS THE BEST OF COURSE--IS EAST OF HERE... BUT THERE ARE STILL SOME NICE LITTLE MANSIONS AROUND HERE, TOO.
RIVERDALE BUS CO.
10

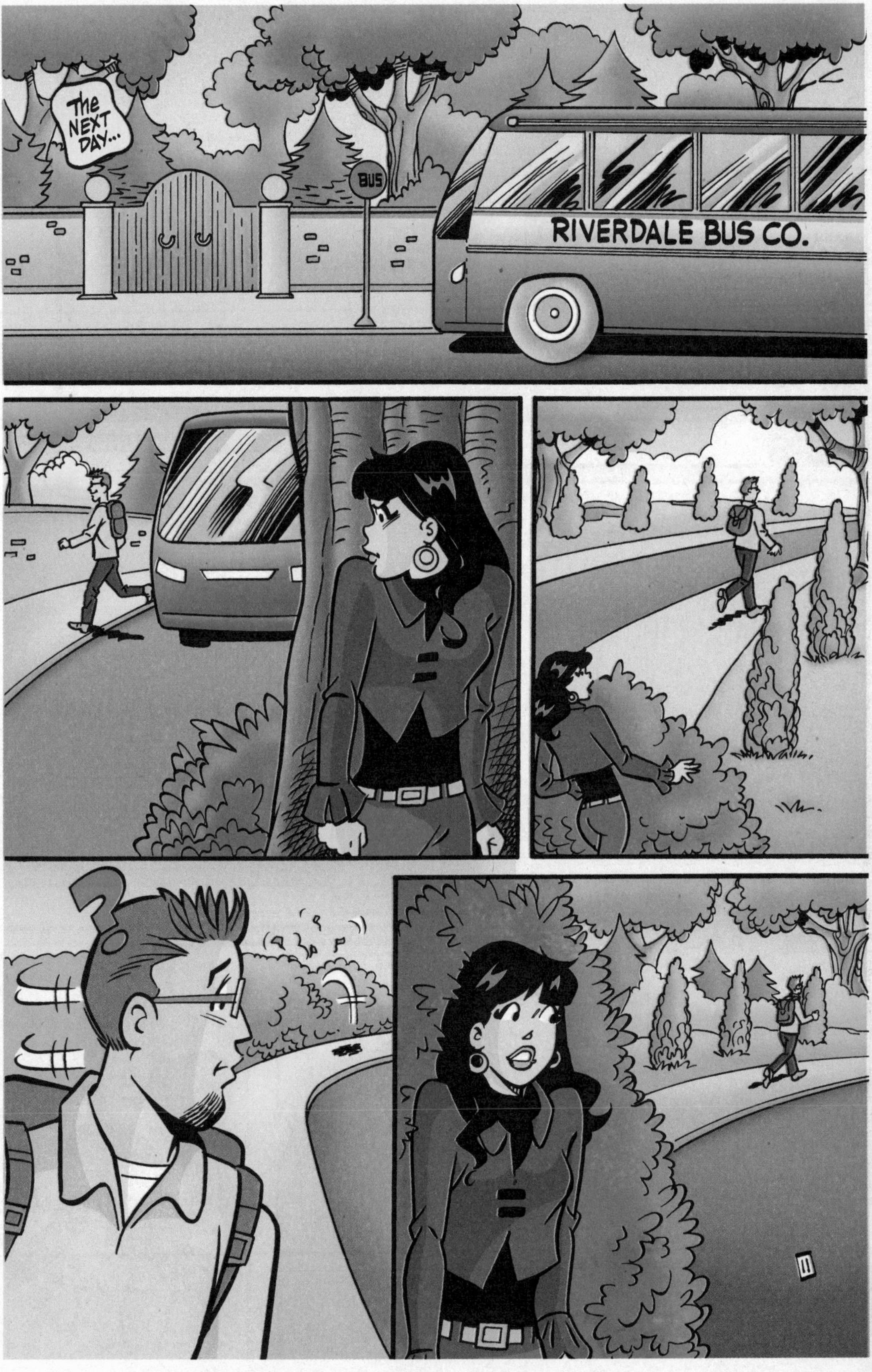
The NEXT DAY...
BUS
RIVERDALE BUS CO.

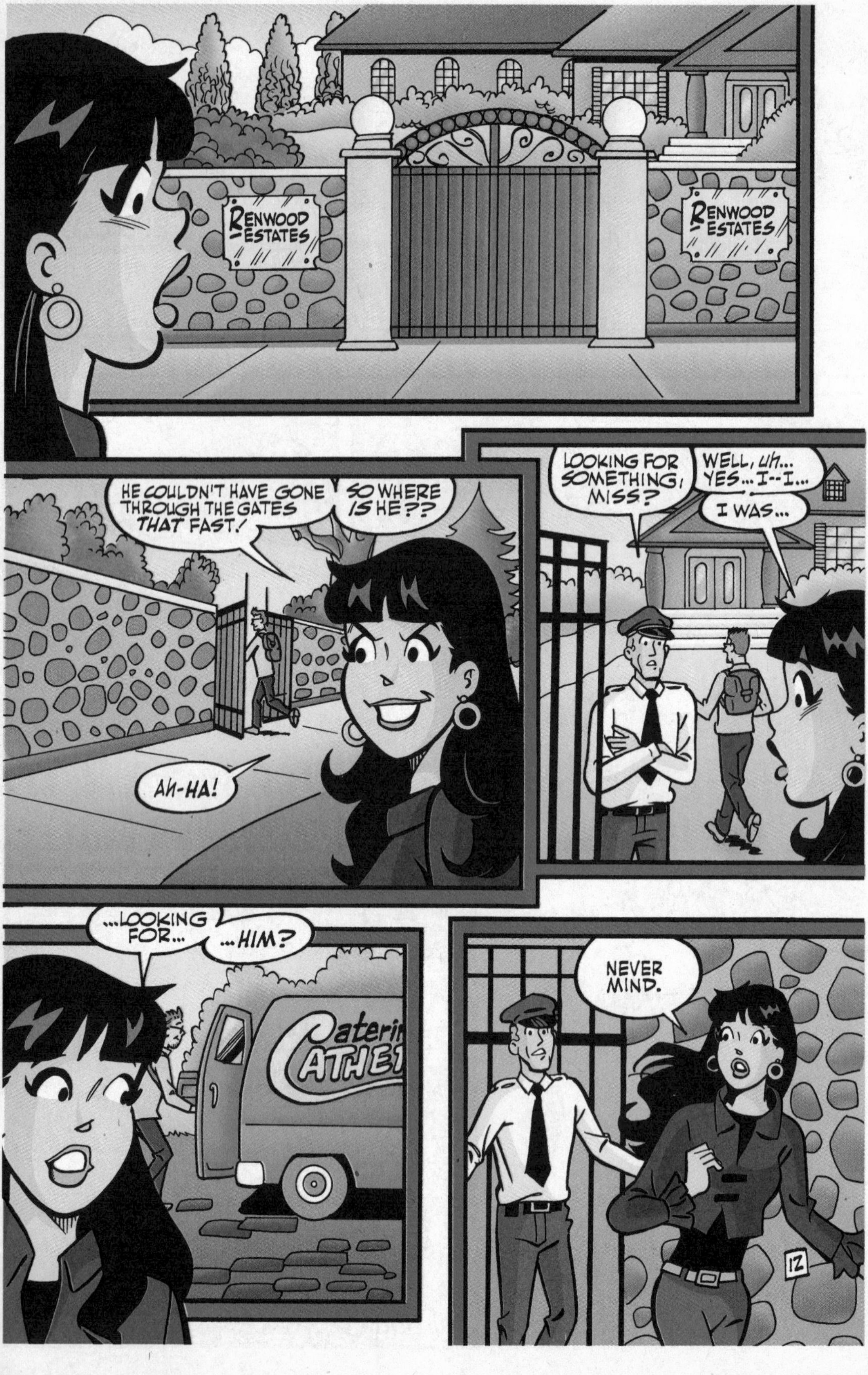
RENWOOD ESTATES
RENWOOD ESTATES
HE COULDN'T HAVE GONE THROUGH THE GATES THAT FAST!
SO WHERE IS HE??
AH-HA!
LOOKING FOR SOMETHING, MISS?
WELL, uh... YES... I--I...
I WAS...
...LOOKING FOR...
...HIM?
NEVER MIND.
12

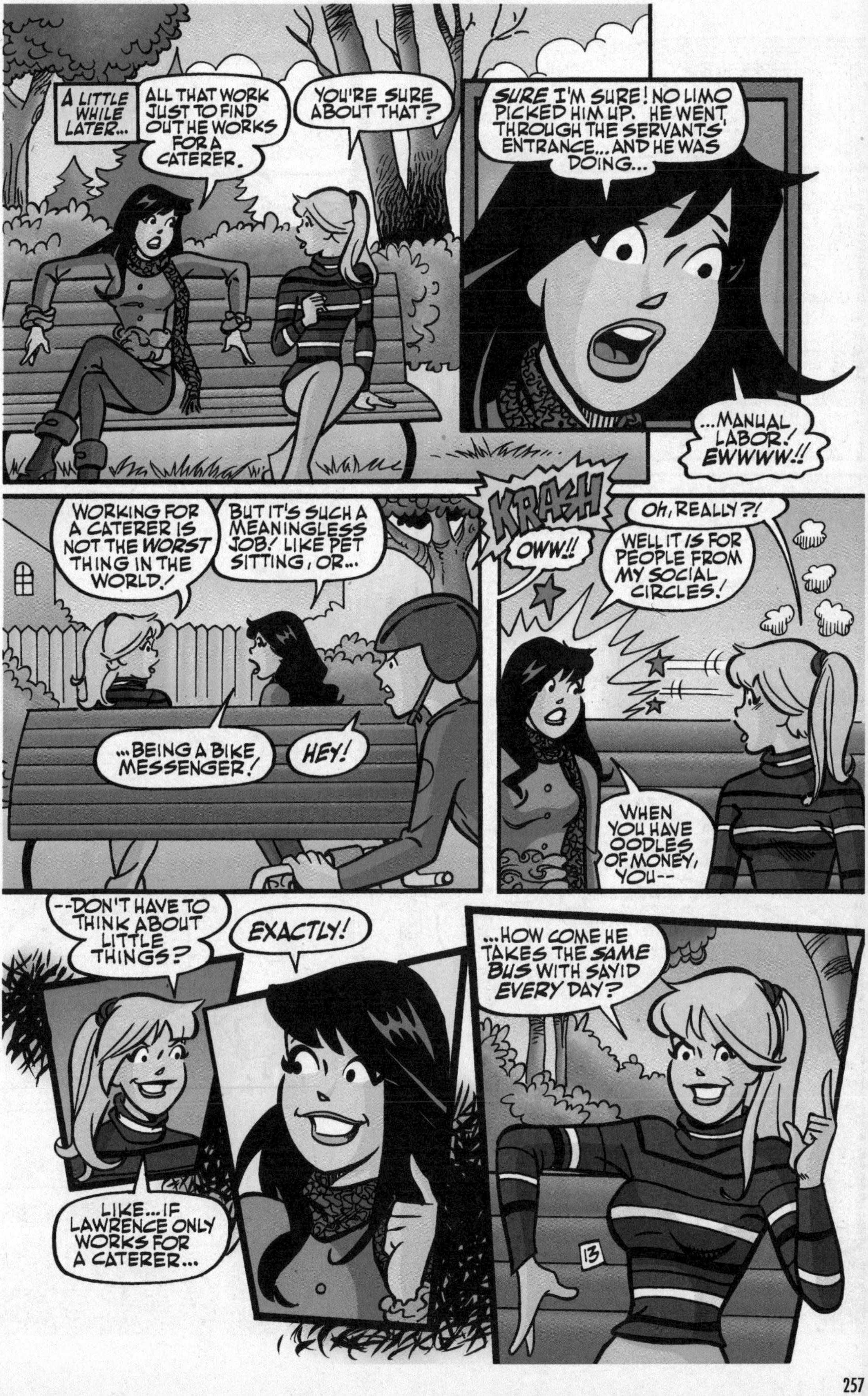
A LITTLE WHILE LATER...
ALL THAT WORK JUST TO FIND OUT HE WORKS FOR A CATERER.
YOU'RE SURE ABOUT THAT?
SURE I'M SURE! NO LIMO PICKED HIM UP. HE WENT THROUGH THE SERVANTS' ENTRANCE... AND HE WAS DOING...
...MANUAL LABOR! EWWWW!!
WORKING FOR A CATERER IS NOT THE WORST THING IN THE WORLD!
BUT IT'S SUCH A MEANINGLESS JOB! LIKE PET SITTING, OR...
...BEING A BIKE MESSENGER!
HEY!
KRASH
OWW!!
OH, REALLY?!
WELL IT IS FOR PEOPLE FROM MY SOCIAL CIRCLES!
WHEN YOU HAVE OODLES OF MONEY, YOU--
--DON'T HAVE TO THINK ABOUT LITTLE THINGS?
EXACTLY!
LIKE... IF LAWRENCE ONLY WORKS FOR A CATERER...
...HOW COME HE TAKES THE SAME BUS WITH SAYID EVERY DAY?
13

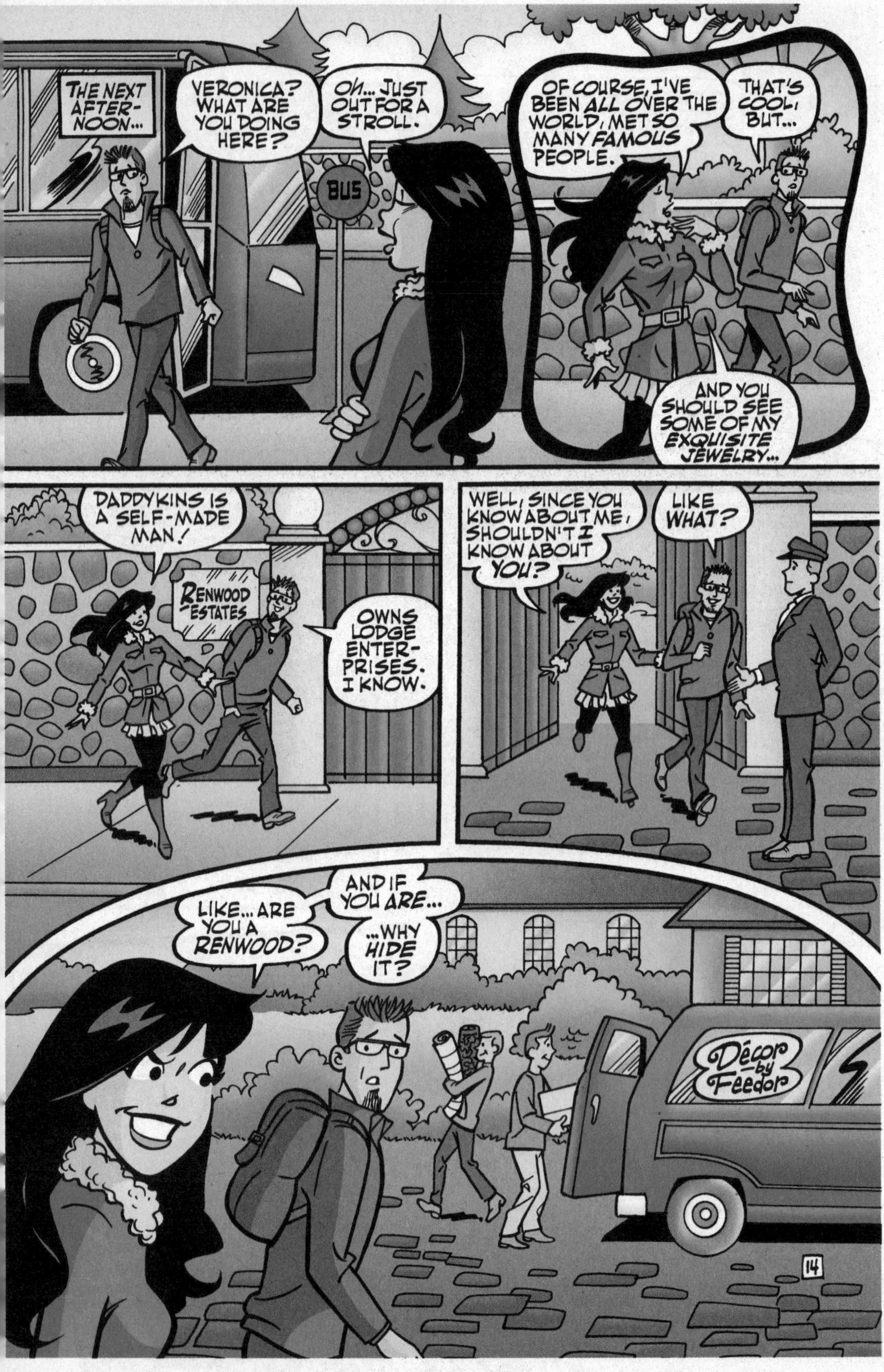
THE NEXT AFTERNOON...
VERONICA? WHAT ARE YOU DOING HERE?
OH... JUST OUT FOR A STROLL.
BUS
OF COURSE, I'VE BEEN ALL OVER THE WORLD, MET SO MANY FAMOUS PEOPLE.
THAT'S COOL, BUT...
AND YOU SHOULD SEE SOME OF MY EXQUISITE JEWELRY...
DADDYKINS IS A SELF-MADE MAN!
RENWOOD ESTATES
OWNS LODGE ENTERPRISES. I KNOW.
WELL, SINCE YOU KNOW ABOUT ME, SHOULDN'T I KNOW ABOUT YOU?
LIKE WHAT?
LIKE... ARE YOU A RENWOOD?
AND IF YOU ARE...
...WHY HIDE IT?
Décor by Feedor
14

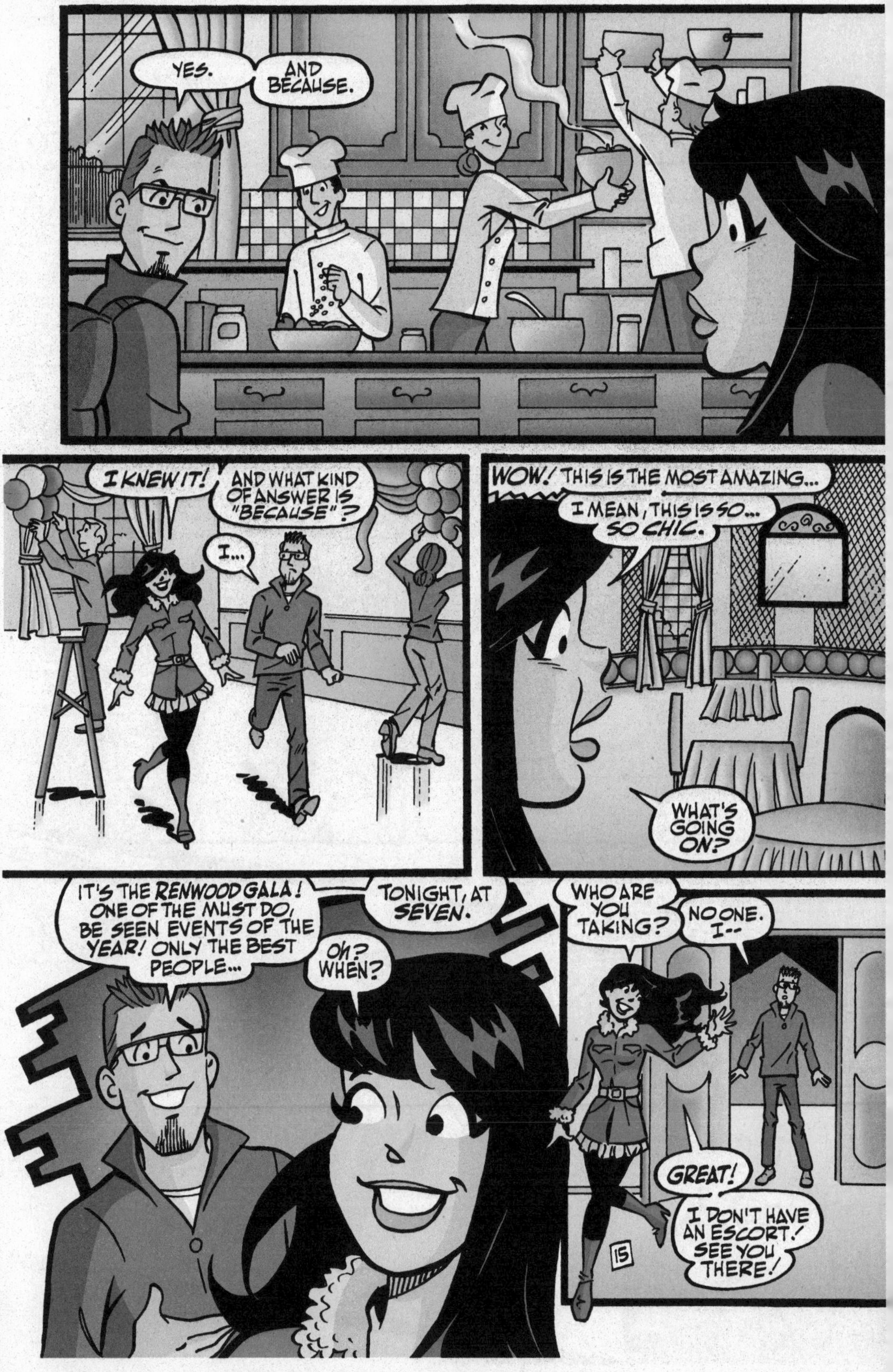
YES.
AND BECAUSE.
I KNEW IT!
AND WHAT KIND OF ANSWER IS "BECAUSE"?
I...
WOW! THIS IS THE MOST AMAZING...
I MEAN, THIS IS SO... SO CHIC.
WHAT'S GOING ON?
IT'S THE RENWOOD GALA! ONE OF THE MUST DO, BE SEEN EVENTS OF THE YEAR! ONLY THE BEST PEOPLE...
OH? WHEN?
TONIGHT, AT SEVEN.
WHO ARE YOU TAKING?
NO ONE. I--
GREAT!
I DON'T HAVE AN ESCORT! SEE YOU THERE!
15

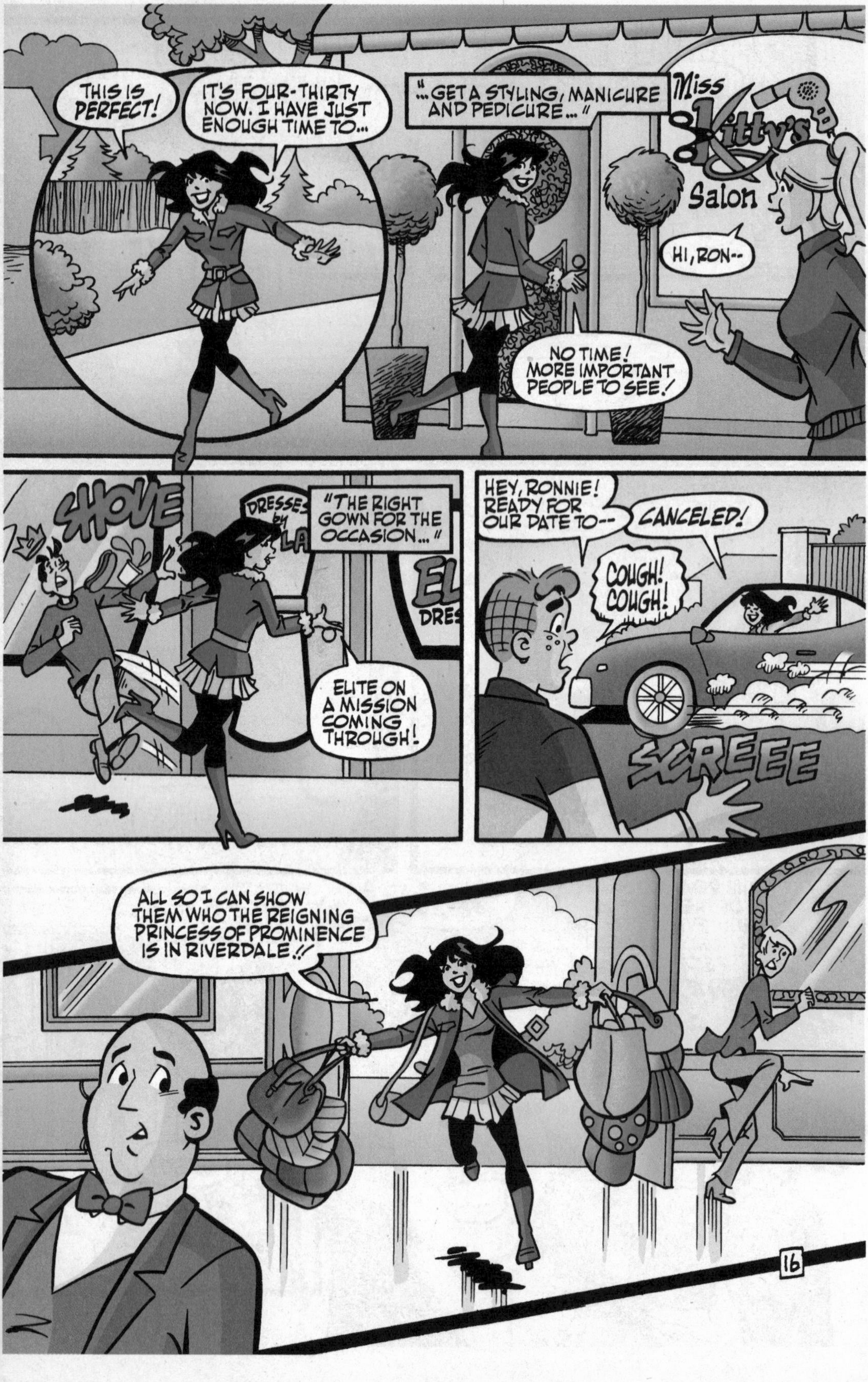
THIS IS PERFECT!
IT'S FOUR-THIRTY NOW. I HAVE JUST ENOUGH TIME TO...
"...GET A STYLING, MANICURE AND PEDICURE..."
Miss Kitty's Salon
HI, RON--
NO TIME! MORE IMPORTANT PEOPLE TO SEE!
SHOVE
DRESSES by LA
"THE RIGHT GOWN FOR THE OCCASION..."
ELITE ON A MISSION COMING THROUGH!
HEY, RONNIE! READY FOR OUR DATE TO--
CANCELED!
COUGH! COUGH!
SCREEE
ALL SO I CAN SHOW THEM WHO THE REIGNING PRINCESS OF PROMINENCE IS IN RIVERDALE!!
16

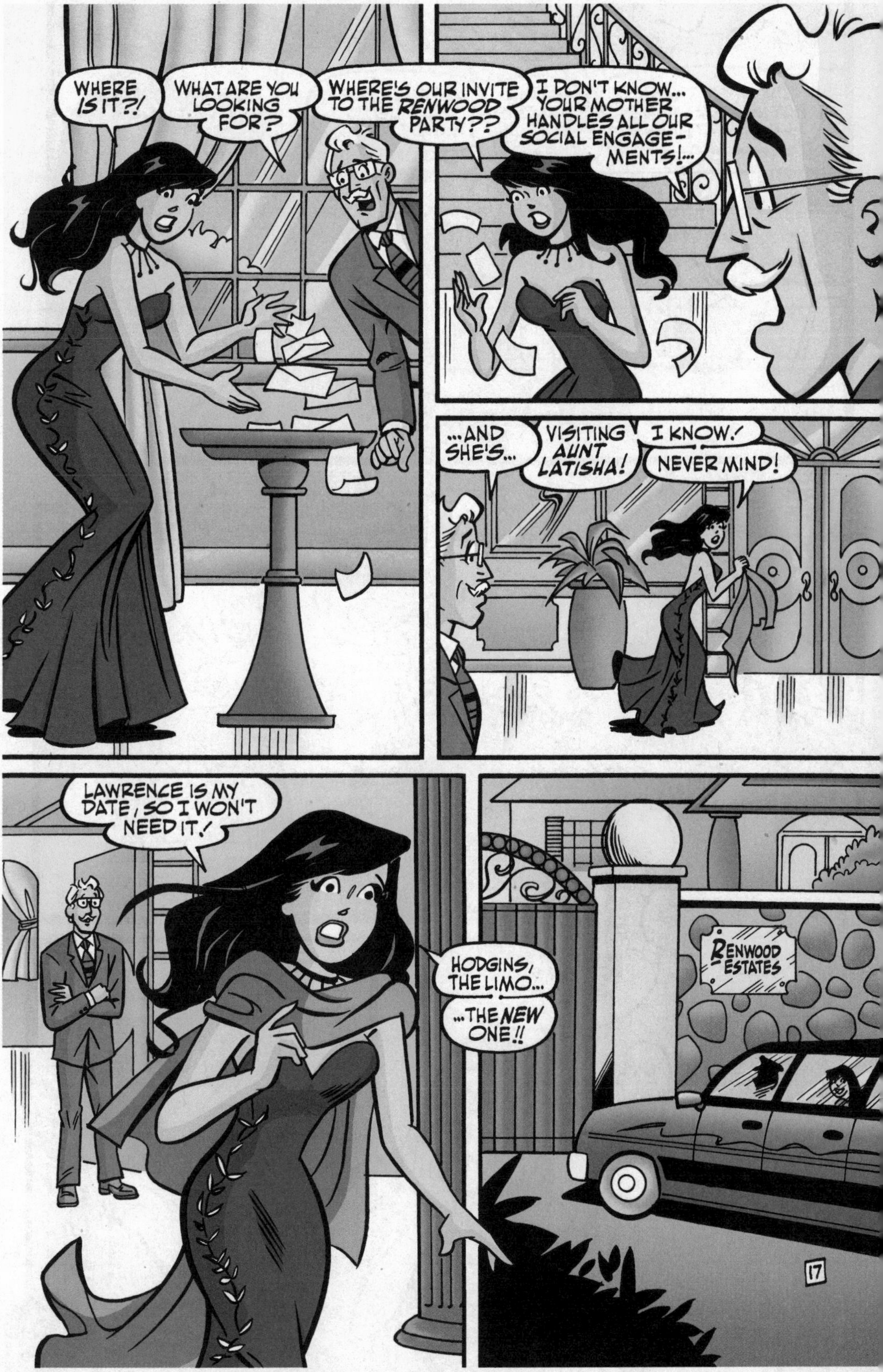
WHERE IS IT?!
WHAT ARE YOU LOOKING FOR?
WHERE'S OUR INVITE TO THE RENWOOD PARTY??
I DON'T KNOW... YOUR MOTHER HANDLES ALL OUR SOCIAL ENGAGE-MENTS!...
...AND SHE'S...
VISITING AUNT LATISHA!
I KNOW!
NEVER MIND!
LAWRENCE IS MY DATE, SO I WON'T NEED IT!
HODGINS, THE LIMO...
...THE NEW ONE!!
RENWOOD ESTATES
17

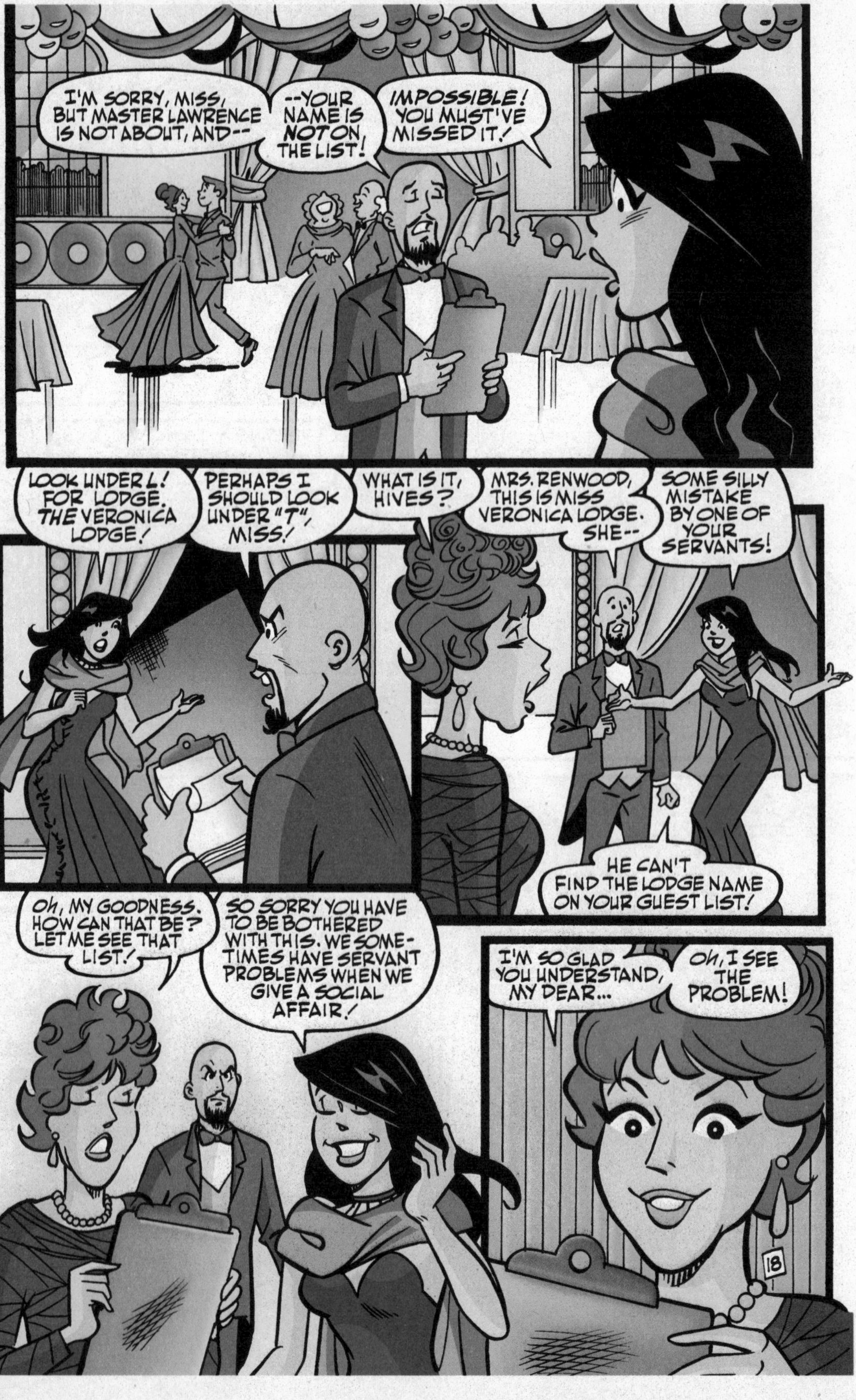
I'M SORRY, MISS, BUT MASTER LAWRENCE IS NOT ABOUT, AND--
--YOUR NAME IS NOT ON THE LIST!
IMPOSSIBLE! YOU MUST'VE MISSED IT!
LOOK UNDER L! FOR LODGE. THE VERONICA LODGE!
PERHAPS I SHOULD LOOK UNDER "T", MISS!
WHAT IS IT, HIVES?
MRS. RENWOOD, THIS IS MISS VERONICA LODGE. SHE--
SOME SILLY MISTAKE BY ONE OF YOUR SERVANTS!
HE CAN'T FIND THE LODGE NAME ON YOUR GUEST LIST!
OH, MY GOODNESS. HOW CAN THAT BE? LET ME SEE THAT LIST!
SO SORRY YOU HAVE TO BE BOTHERED WITH THIS. WE SOMETIMES HAVE SERVANT PROBLEMS WHEN WE GIVE A SOCIAL AFFAIR!
I'M SO GLAD YOU UNDERSTAND, MY DEAR...
OH, I SEE THE PROBLEM!
18

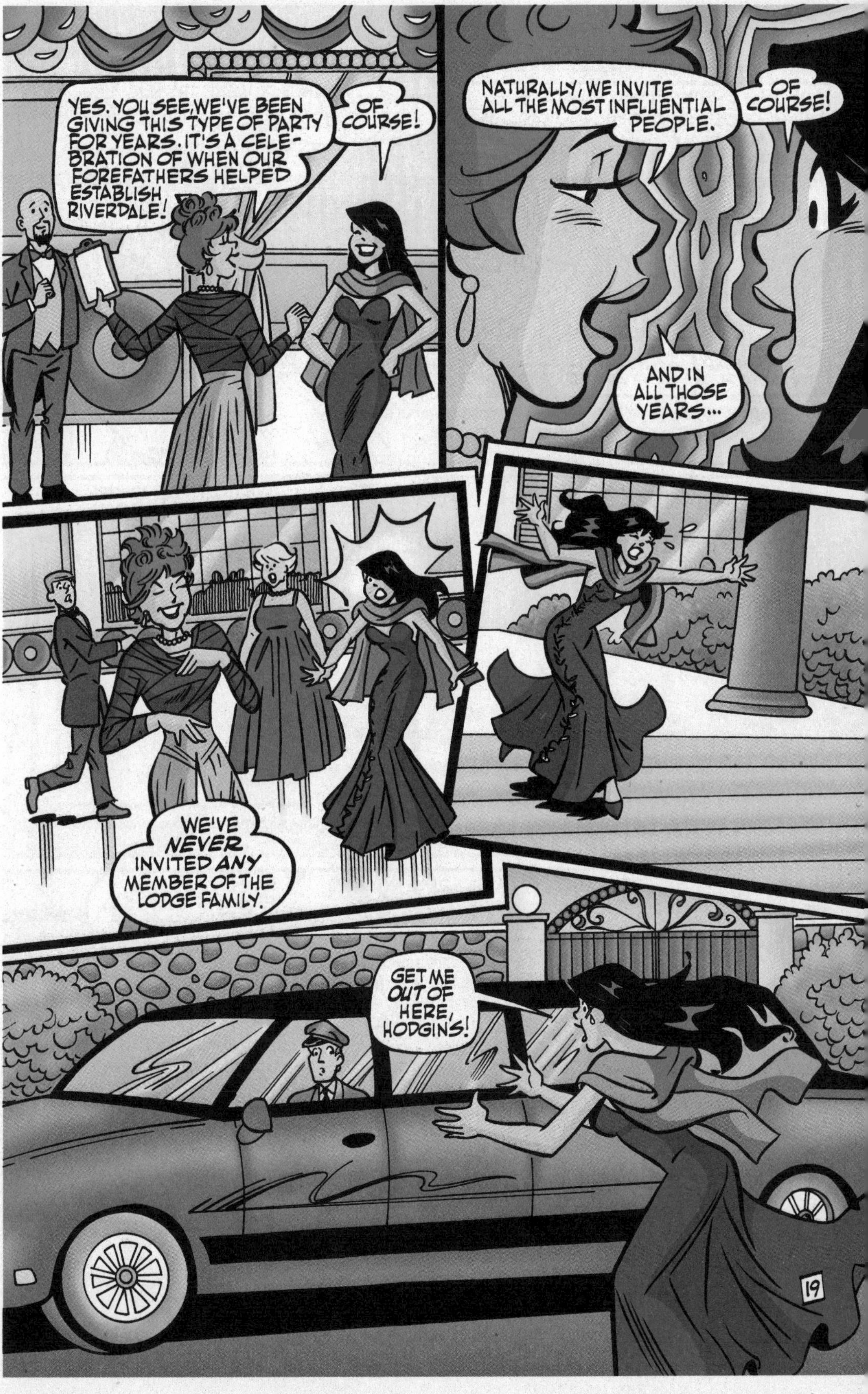

YES. YOU SEE, WE'VE BEEN GIVING THIS TYPE OF PARTY FOR YEARS. IT'S A CELEBRATION OF WHEN OUR FOREFATHERS HELPED ESTABLISH RIVERDALE!
OF COURSE!
NATURALLY, WE INVITE ALL THE MOST INFLUENTIAL PEOPLE.
OF COURSE!
AND IN ALL THOSE YEARS...
WE'VE NEVER INVITED ANY MEMBER OF THE LODGE FAMILY.
GET ME OUT OF HERE, HODGINS!
19

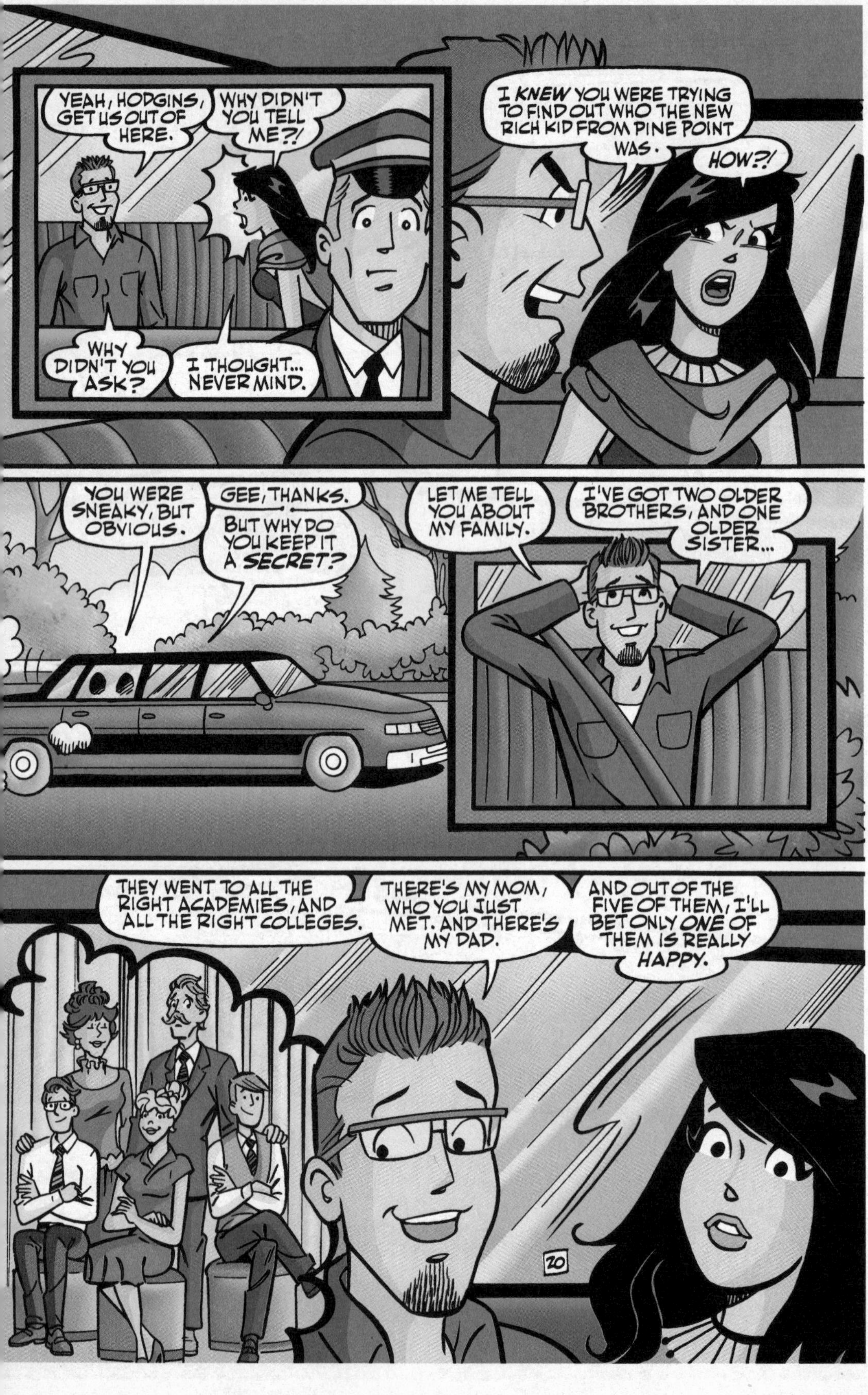
YEAH, HODGINS, GET US OUT OF HERE.
WHY DIDN'T YOU TELL ME?!
WHY DIDN'T YOU ASK?
I THOUGHT... NEVER MIND.
I KNEW YOU WERE TRYING TO FIND OUT WHO THE NEW RICH KID FROM PINE POINT WAS.
HOW?!
YOU WERE SNEAKY, BUT OBVIOUS.
GEE, THANKS.
BUT WHY DO YOU KEEP IT A SECRET?
LET ME TELL YOU ABOUT MY FAMILY.
I'VE GOT TWO OLDER BROTHERS, AND ONE OLDER SISTER...
THEY WENT TO ALL THE RIGHT ACADEMIES, AND ALL THE RIGHT COLLEGES.
THERE'S MY MOM, WHO YOU JUST MET. AND THERE'S MY DAD.
AND OUT OF THE FIVE OF THEM, I'LL BET ONLY ONE OF THEM IS REALLY HAPPY.
20

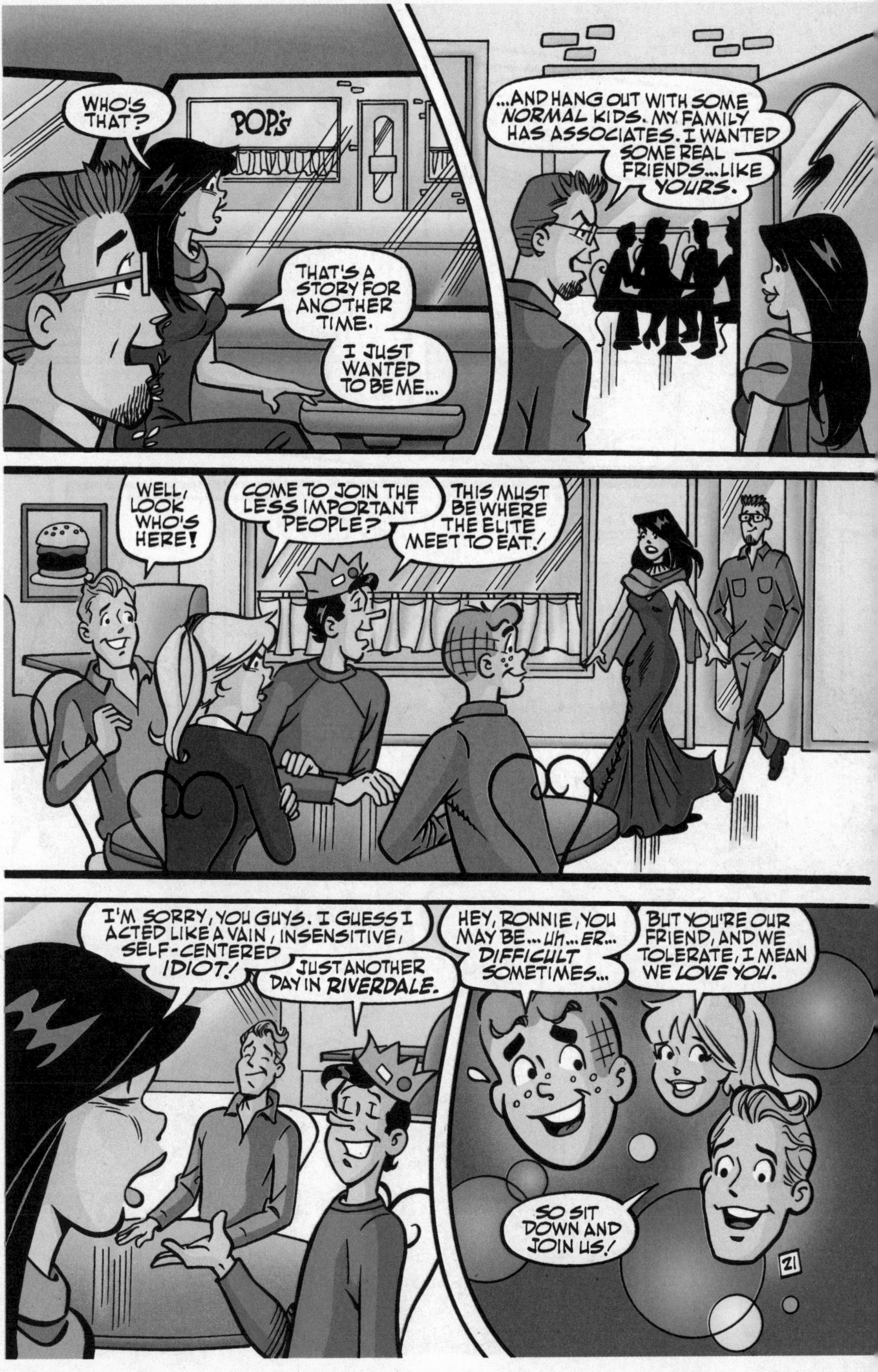
WHO'S THAT?
POP'S
THAT'S A STORY FOR ANOTHER TIME.
I JUST WANTED TO BE ME...
...AND HANG OUT WITH SOME NORMAL KIDS. MY FAMILY HAS ASSOCIATES. I WANTED SOME REAL FRIENDS...LIKE YOURS.
WELL, LOOK WHO'S HERE!
COME TO JOIN THE LESS IMPORTANT PEOPLE?
THIS MUST BE WHERE THE ELITE MEET TO EAT!
I'M SORRY, YOU GUYS. I GUESS I ACTED LIKE A VAIN, INSENSITIVE, SELF-CENTERED IDIOT!
JUST ANOTHER DAY IN RIVERDALE.
HEY, RONNIE, YOU MAY BE... UH... ER... DIFFICULT SOMETIMES...
BUT YOU'RE OUR FRIEND, AND WE TOLERATE, I MEAN WE LOVE YOU.
SO SIT DOWN AND JOIN US!
21

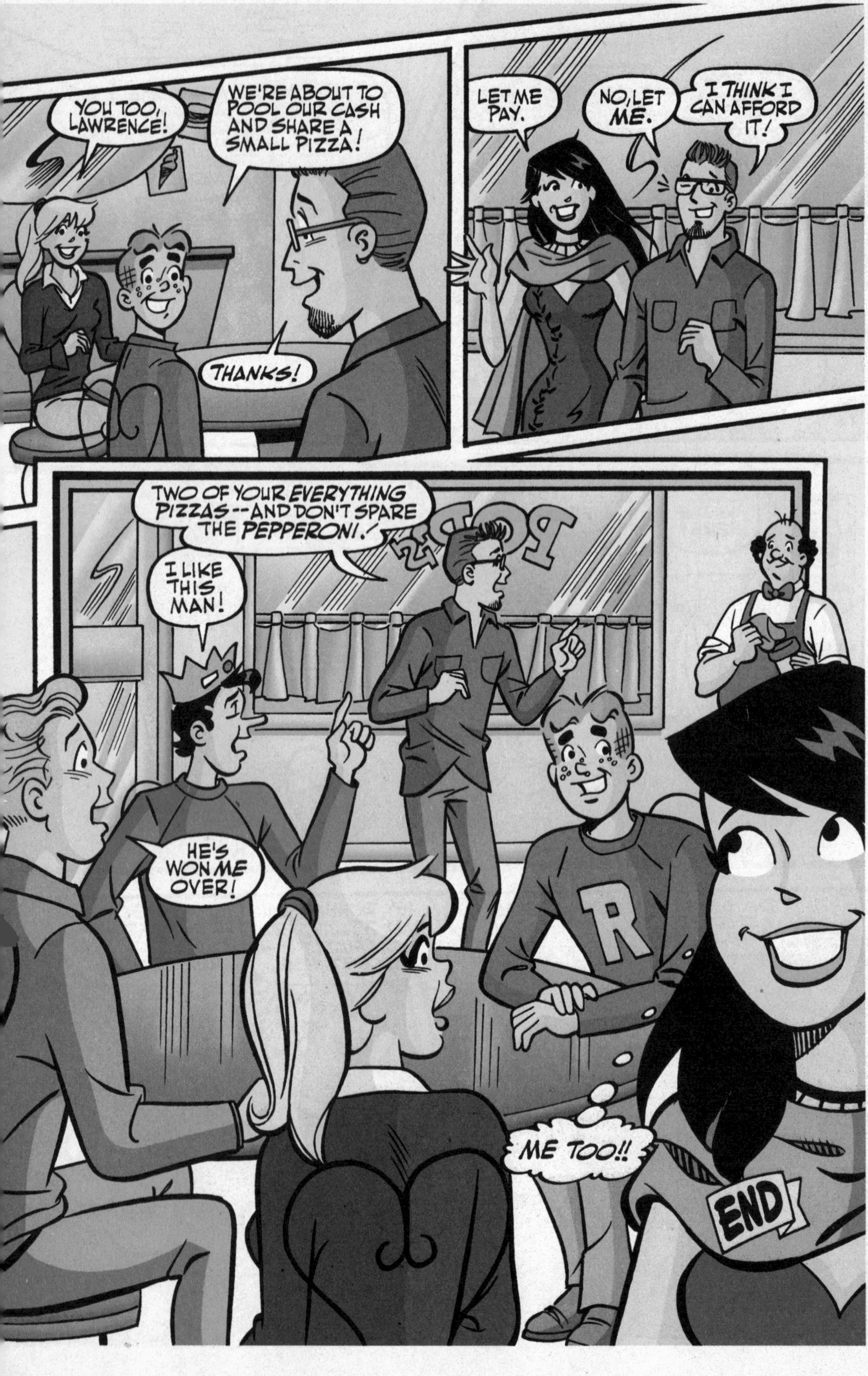
YOU TOO, LAWRENCE!
WE'RE ABOUT TO POOL OUR CASH AND SHARE A SMALL PIZZA!
THANKS!
LET ME PAY.
NO, LET ME.
I THINK I CAN AFFORD IT!
TWO OF YOUR EVERYTHING PIZZAS--AND DON'T SPARE THE PEPPERONI!
POP'S
I LIKE THIS MAN!
HE'S WON ME OVER!
ME TOO!!
END

CHAPTER THREE

High School Hijinks

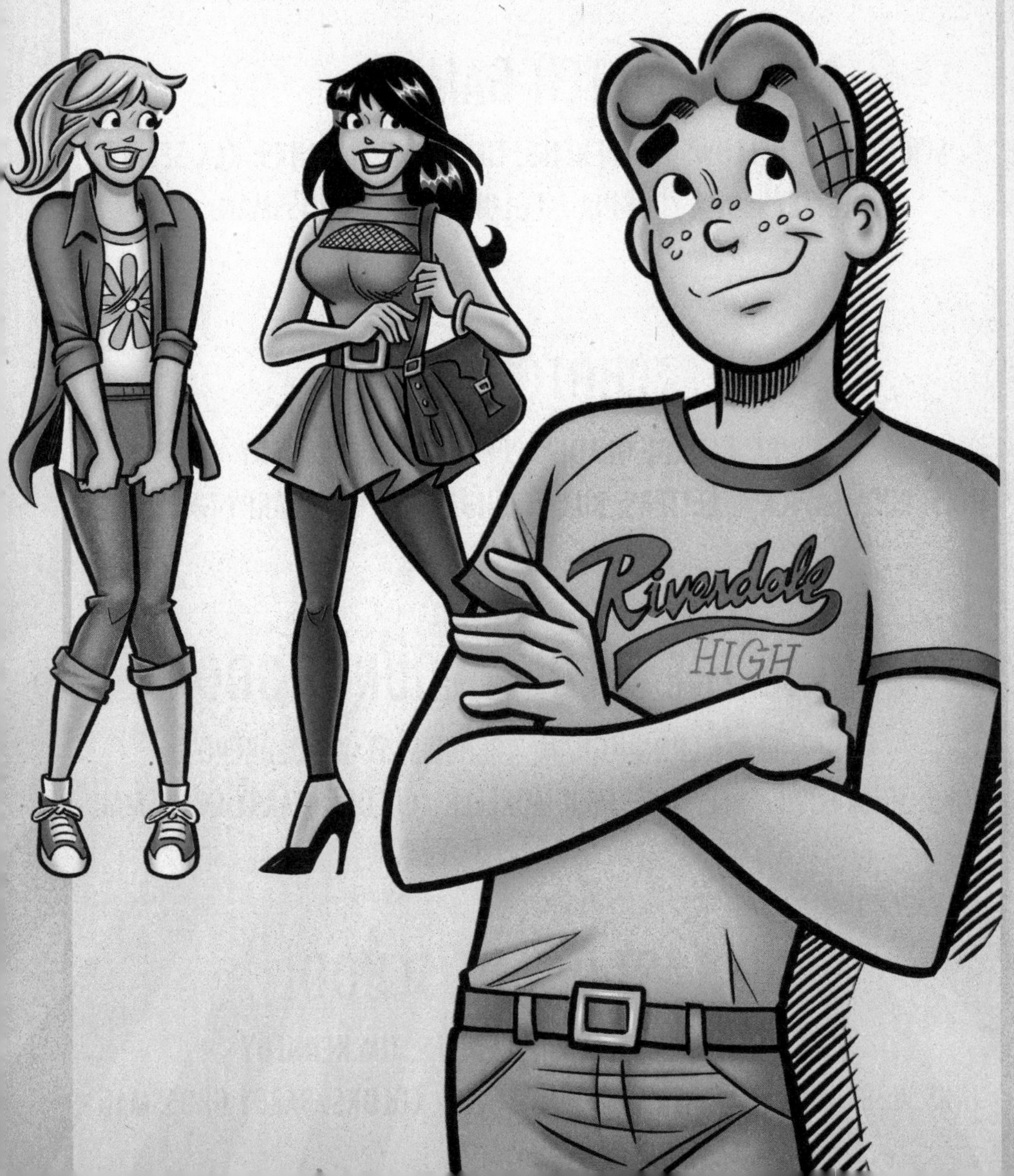
Riverdale
HIGH

ARCHIE & FRIENDS IN
NOT TO BE BEE

SCRIPT: MIKE PELLOWSKI   PENCILS: STAN GOLDBERG   INKS: JON D'AGOSTINO
LETTERS: VICKIE WILLIAMS   COLORS: BARRY GROSSMAN

ARCHIE & FRIENDS IN
IN A FOOD MOOD

SCRIPT: GEORGE GLADIR   PENCILS: REX LINDSEY
LETTERS: BILL YOSHIDA   COLORS: BARRY GROSSMAN

ARCHIE IN
MATCH GAME

SCRIPT: MIKE PELLOWSKI   PENCILS: TIM KENNEDY   INKS: KEN SELIG
LETTERS: BILL YOSHIDA   COLORS: BARRY GROSSMAN

ARCHIE IN
PHOTO FUN

SCRIPT: GEORGE GLADIR   PENCILS: TIM KENNEDY
INKS: RUDY LAPICK   LETTERS: BILL YOSHIDA   COLORS: BARRY GROSSMAN

ARCHIE & FRIENDS IN
BEHIND THE FACULTY LOUNGE DOOR

SCRIPT: SCOTT CUNNINGHAM   PENCILS: STAN GOLDBERG
INKS: JOHN LOWE   LETTERS: JACK MORELLI   COLORS: BARRY GROSSMAN

ARCHIE IN
THE LAST DAY OF SCHOOL

SCRIPT: GEORGE GLADIR   PENCILS: TIM KENNEDY
INKS: BOB SMITH   LETTERS: JACK MORELLI   COLORS: BARRY GROSSMAN

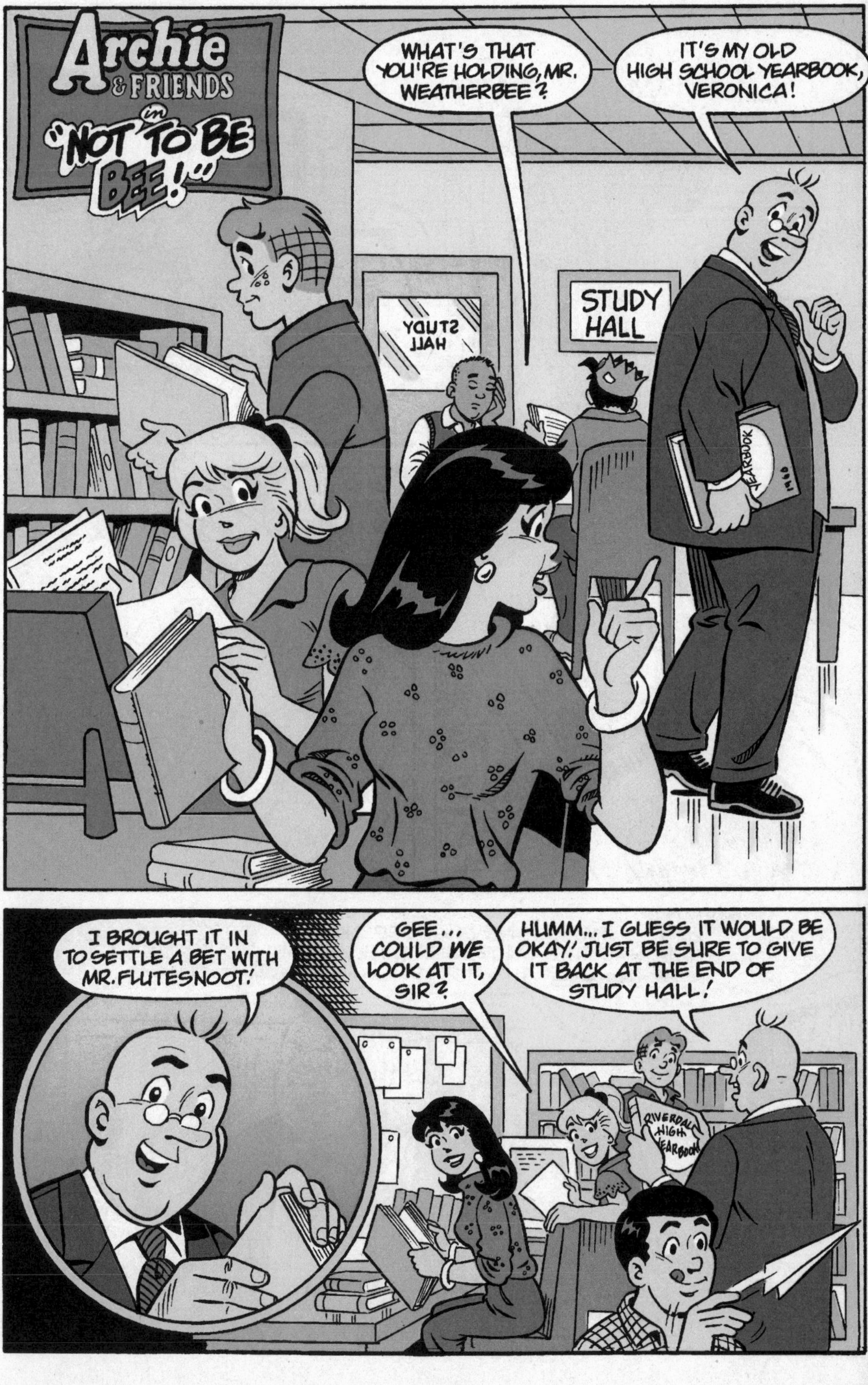
Archie & FRIENDS in "NOT TO BE BEE!"
WHAT'S THAT YOU'RE HOLDING, MR. WEATHERBEE?
IT'S MY OLD HIGH SCHOOL YEARBOOK, VERONICA!
STUDY HALL
YEARBOOK 1960
I BROUGHT IT IN TO SETTLE A BET WITH MR. FLUTESNOOT!
GEE... COULD WE LOOK AT IT, SIR?
HUMM... I GUESS IT WOULD BE OKAY! JUST BE SURE TO GIVE IT BACK AT THE END OF STUDY HALL!
RIVERDALE HIGH YEARBOOK

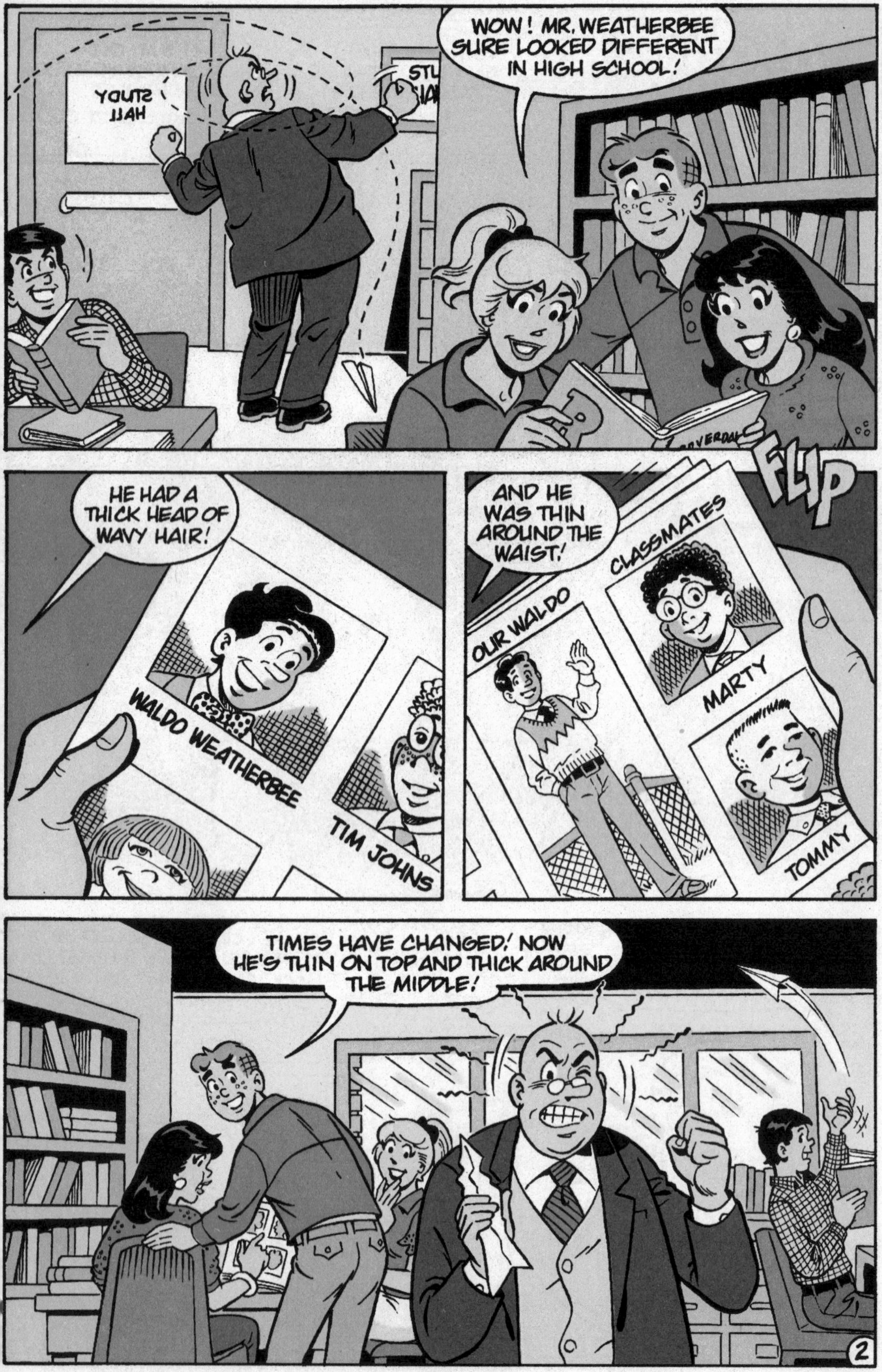
STUDY HALL
WOW! MR. WEATHERBEE SURE LOOKED DIFFERENT IN HIGH SCHOOL!
HE HAD A THICK HEAD OF WAVY HAIR!
WALDO WEATHERBEE
TIM JOHNS
FLIP
AND HE WAS THIN AROUND THE WAIST!
CLASSMATES
OUR WALDO
MARTY
TOMMY
TIMES HAVE CHANGED! NOW HE'S THIN ON TOP AND THICK AROUND THE MIDDLE!
2

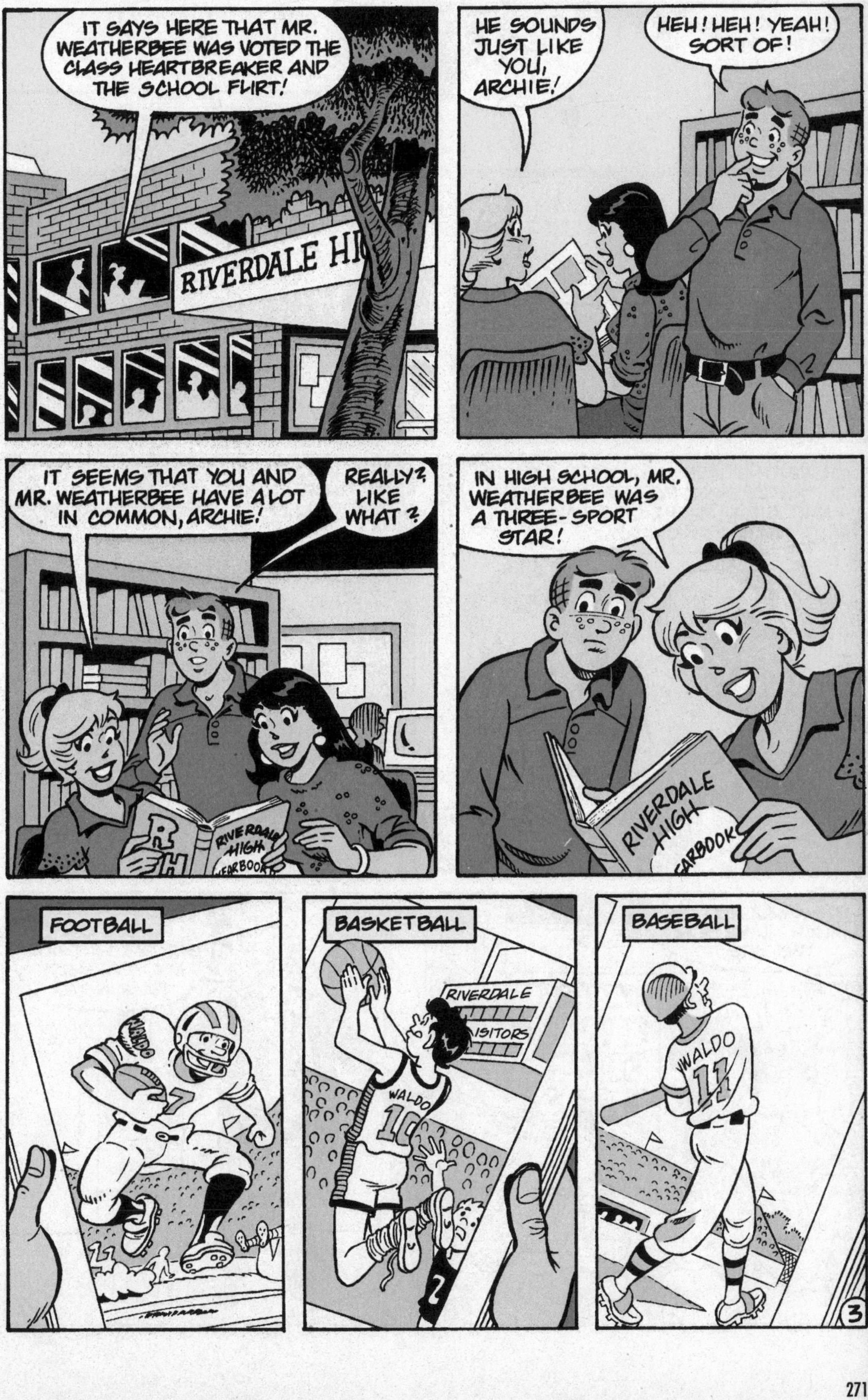
IT SAYS HERE THAT MR. WEATHERBEE WAS VOTED THE CLASS HEARTBREAKER AND THE SCHOOL FLIRT!
RIVERDALE HI
HE SOUNDS JUST LIKE YOU, ARCHIE!
HEH! HEH! YEAH! SORT OF!
IT SEEMS THAT YOU AND MR. WEATHERBEE HAVE A LOT IN COMMON, ARCHIE!
REALLY? LIKE WHAT?
RH
RIVERDALE HIGH
IN HIGH SCHOOL, MR. WEATHERBEE WAS A THREE-SPORT STAR!
RIVERDALE HIGH
FOOTBALL
BASKETBALL
RIVERDALE
WALDO
10
BASEBALL
WALDO
11
3

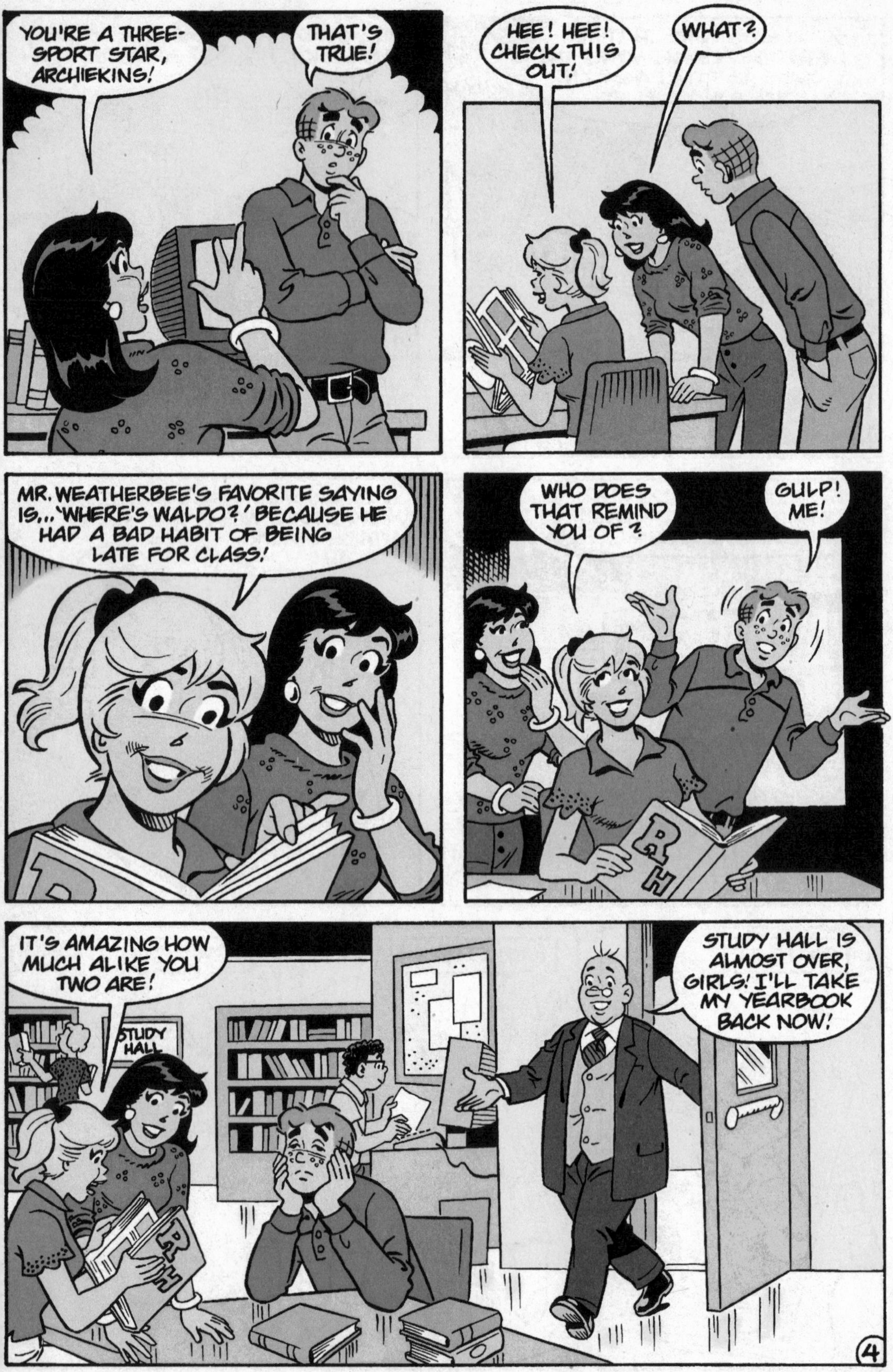
YOU'RE A THREE-SPORT STAR, ARCHIEKINS!
THAT'S TRUE!
HEE! HEE! CHECK THIS OUT!
WHAT?
MR. WEATHERBEE'S FAVORITE SAYING IS... 'WHERE'S WALDO?' BECAUSE HE HAD A BAD HABIT OF BEING LATE FOR CLASS!
WHO DOES THAT REMIND YOU OF?
GULP! ME!
IT'S AMAZING HOW MUCH ALIKE YOU TWO ARE!
STUDY HALL
STUDY HALL IS ALMOST OVER, GIRLS! I'LL TAKE MY YEARBOOK BACK NOW!
4

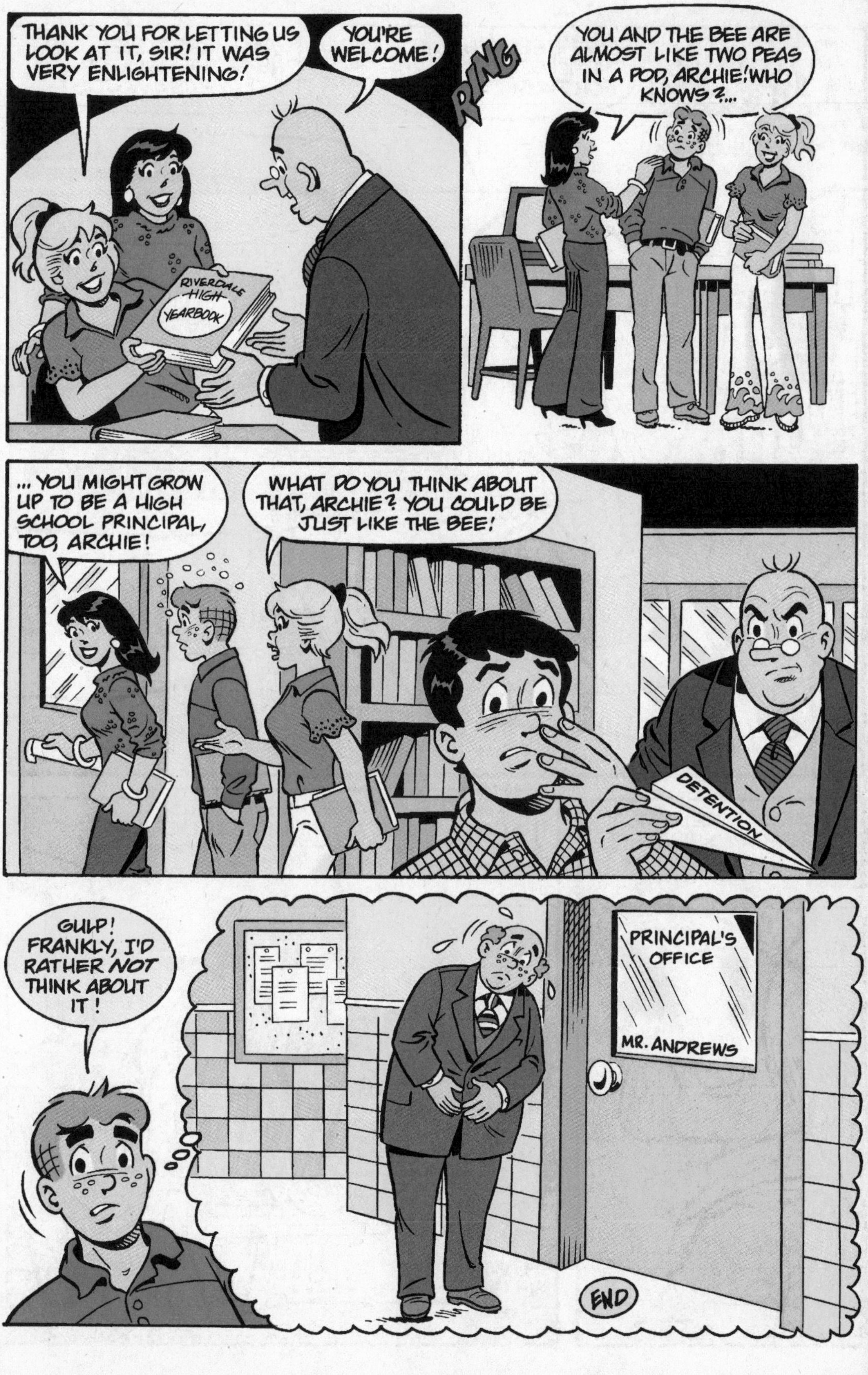
THANK YOU FOR LETTING US LOOK AT IT, SIR! IT WAS VERY ENLIGHTENING!
YOU'RE WELCOME!
RIVERDALE HIGH YEARBOOK
RING
YOU AND THE BEE ARE ALMOST LIKE TWO PEAS IN A POD, ARCHIE! WHO KNOWS?...
... YOU MIGHT GROW UP TO BE A HIGH SCHOOL PRINCIPAL, TOO, ARCHIE!
WHAT DO YOU THINK ABOUT THAT, ARCHIE? YOU COULD BE JUST LIKE THE BEE!
DETENTION
GULP! FRANKLY, I'D RATHER NOT THINK ABOUT IT!
PRINCIPAL'S OFFICE
MR. ANDREWS
END

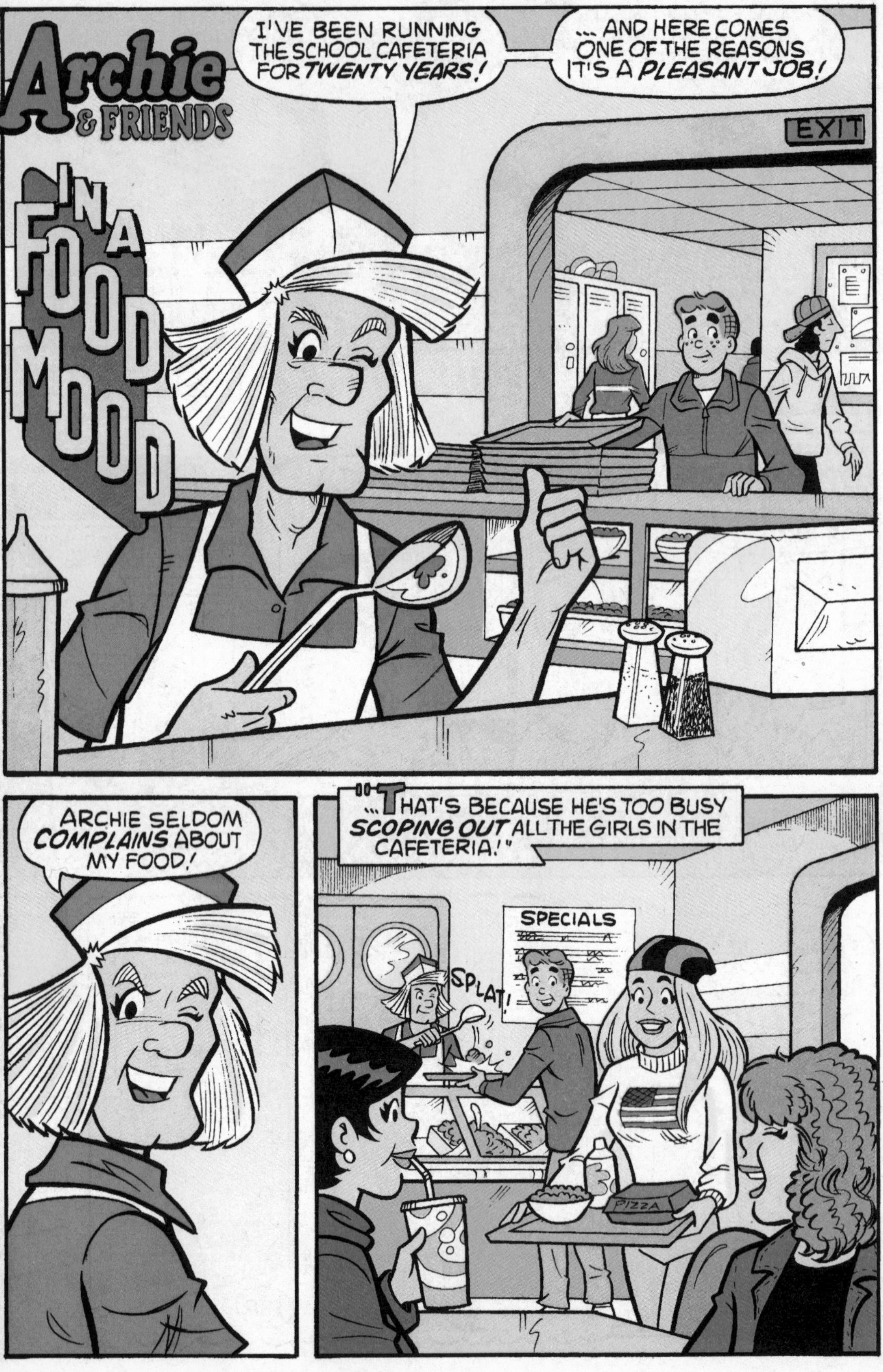
Archie & FRIENDS
IN A FOOD MOOD
I'VE BEEN RUNNING THE SCHOOL CAFETERIA FOR TWENTY YEARS!
... AND HERE COMES ONE OF THE REASONS IT'S A PLEASANT JOB!
EXIT
ARCHIE SELDOM COMPLAINS ABOUT MY FOOD!
"...THAT'S BECAUSE HE'S TOO BUSY SCOPING OUT ALL THE GIRLS IN THE CAFETERIA!"
SPECIALS
SPLAT!
PIZZA

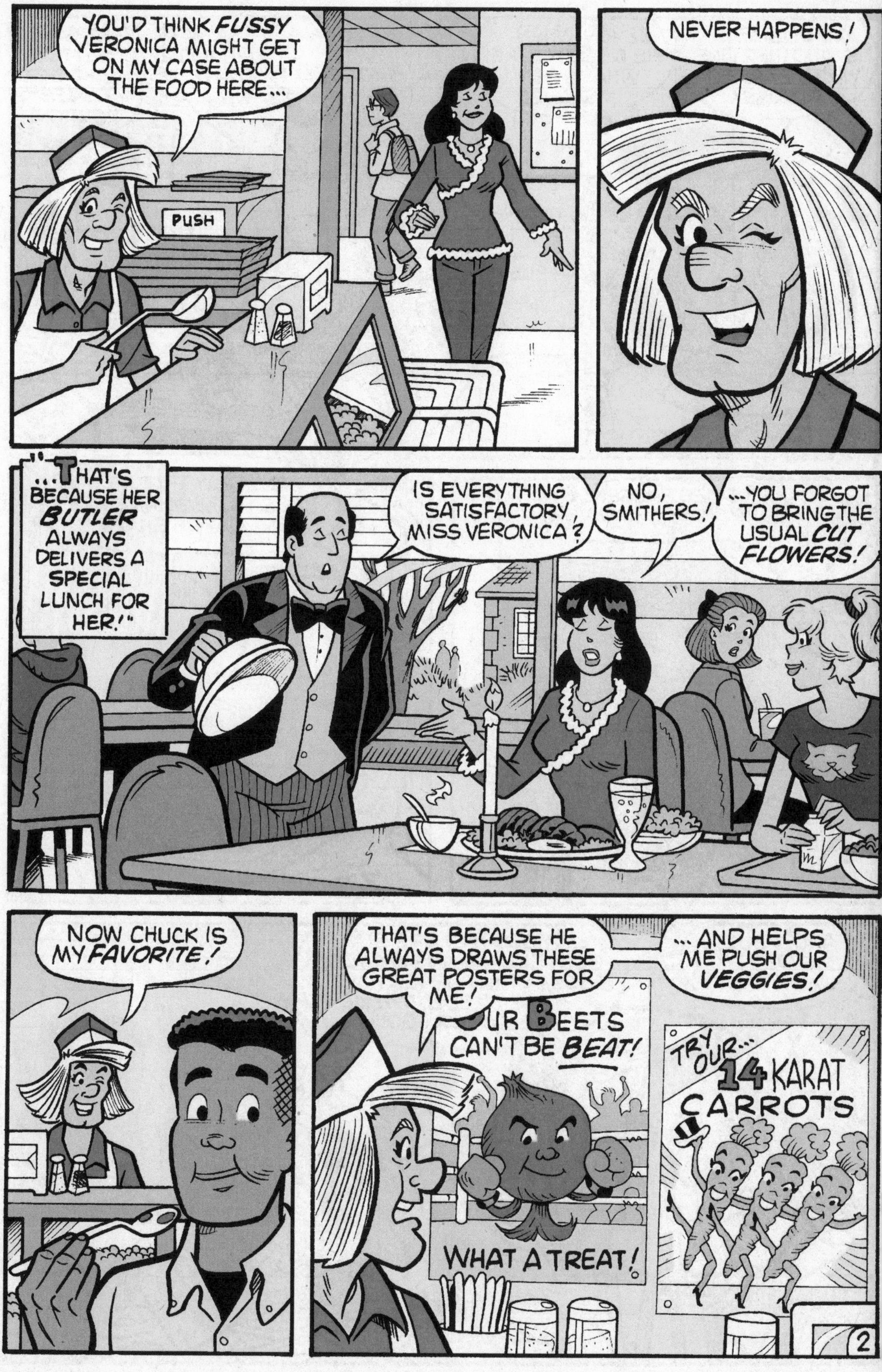
YOU'D THINK FUSSY VERONICA MIGHT GET ON MY CASE ABOUT THE FOOD HERE...
PUSH
NEVER HAPPENS!
"...THAT'S BECAUSE HER BUTLER ALWAYS DELIVERS A SPECIAL LUNCH FOR HER!"
IS EVERYTHING SATISFACTORY, MISS VERONICA?
NO, SMITHERS!
...YOU FORGOT TO BRING THE USUAL CUT FLOWERS!
NOW CHUCK IS MY FAVORITE!
THAT'S BECAUSE HE ALWAYS DRAWS THESE GREAT POSTERS FOR ME!
...AND HELPS ME PUSH OUR VEGGIES!
OUR BEETS CAN'T BE BEAT!
WHAT A TREAT!
TRY OUR... 14 KARAT CARROTS
2

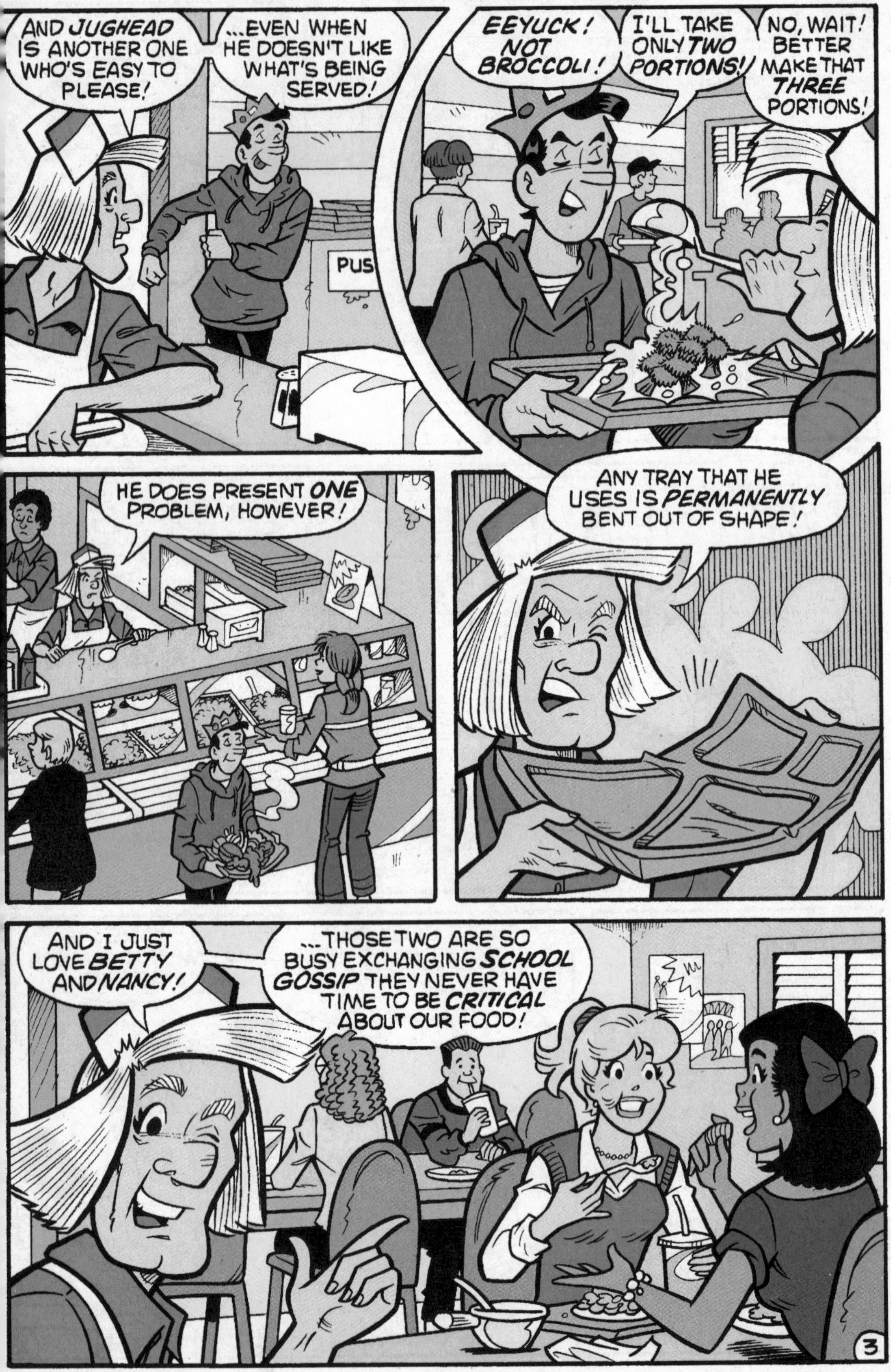
AND JUGHEAD IS ANOTHER ONE WHO'S EASY TO PLEASE!
...EVEN WHEN HE DOESN'T LIKE WHAT'S BEING SERVED!
PUS
EEYUCK! NOT BROCCOLI!
I'LL TAKE ONLY TWO PORTIONS!
NO, WAIT! BETTER MAKE THAT THREE PORTIONS!
HE DOES PRESENT ONE PROBLEM, HOWEVER!
ANY TRAY THAT HE USES IS PERMANENTLY BENT OUT OF SHAPE!
AND I JUST LOVE BETTY AND NANCY!
...THOSE TWO ARE SO BUSY EXCHANGING SCHOOL GOSSIP THEY NEVER HAVE TIME TO BE CRITICAL ABOUT OUR FOOD!
3

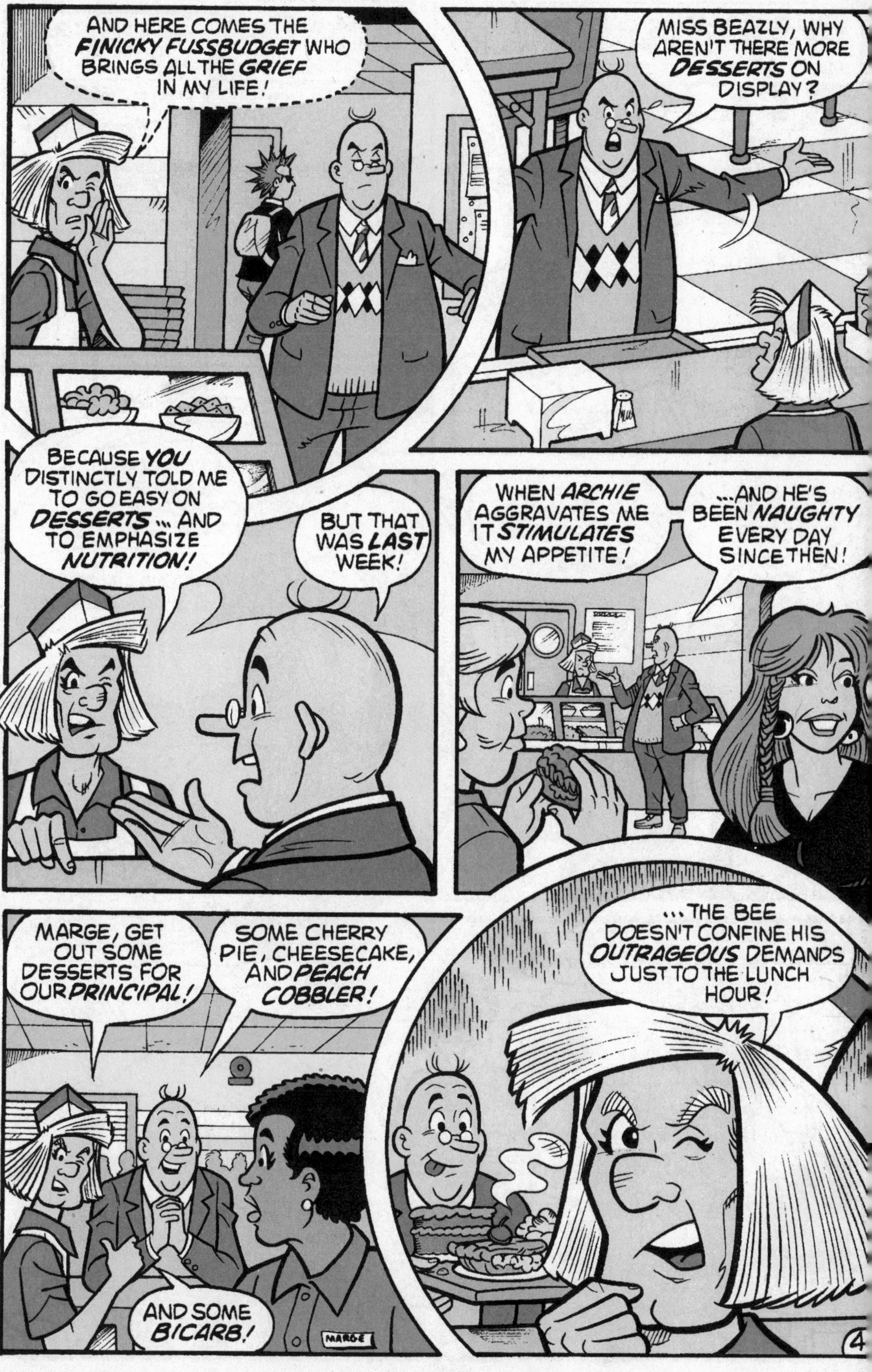
AND HERE COMES THE FINICKY FUSSBUDGET WHO BRINGS ALL THE GRIEF IN MY LIFE!
MISS BEAZLY, WHY AREN'T THERE MORE DESSERTS ON DISPLAY?
BECAUSE YOU DISTINCTLY TOLD ME TO GO EASY ON DESSERTS ... AND TO EMPHASIZE NUTRITION!
BUT THAT WAS LAST WEEK!
WHEN ARCHIE AGGRAVATES ME IT STIMULATES MY APPETITE!
...AND HE'S BEEN NAUGHTY EVERY DAY SINCE THEN!
MARGE, GET OUT SOME DESSERTS FOR OUR PRINCIPAL!
SOME CHERRY PIE, CHEESECAKE, AND PEACH COBBLER!
AND SOME BICARB!
MARGE
... THE BEE DOESN'T CONFINE HIS OUTRAGEOUS DEMANDS JUST TO THE LUNCH HOUR!
4

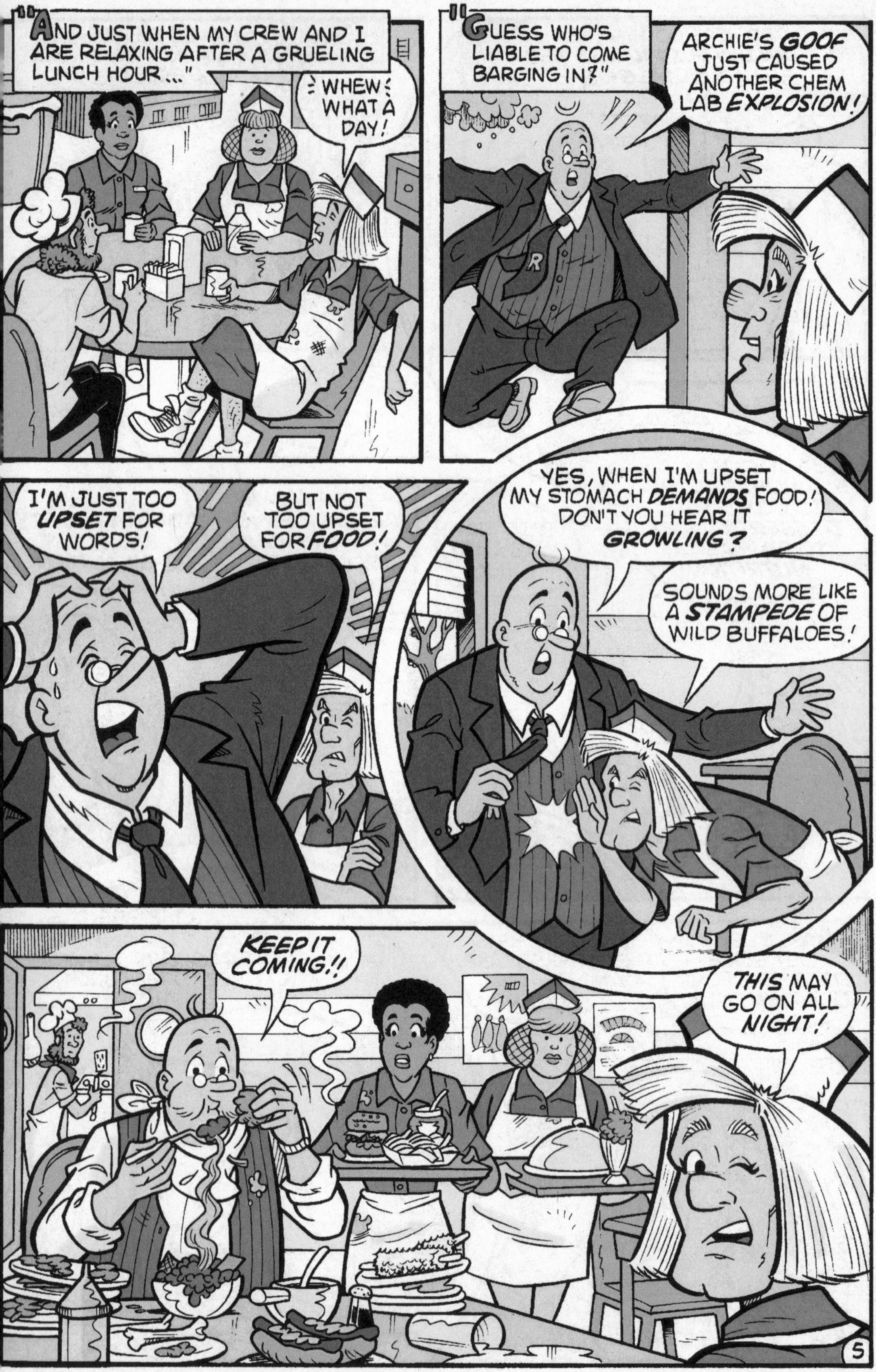
"AND JUST WHEN MY CREW AND I ARE RELAXING AFTER A GRUELING LUNCH HOUR..."
WHEW WHAT A DAY!
"GUESS WHO'S LIABLE TO COME BARGING IN?"
ARCHIE'S GOOF JUST CAUSED ANOTHER CHEM LAB EXPLOSION!
I'M JUST TOO UPSET FOR WORDS!
BUT NOT TOO UPSET FOR FOOD!
YES, WHEN I'M UPSET MY STOMACH DEMANDS FOOD! DON'T YOU HEAR IT GROWLING?
SOUNDS MORE LIKE A STAMPEDE OF WILD BUFFALOES!
KEEP IT COMING!!
THIS MAY GO ON ALL NIGHT!
5

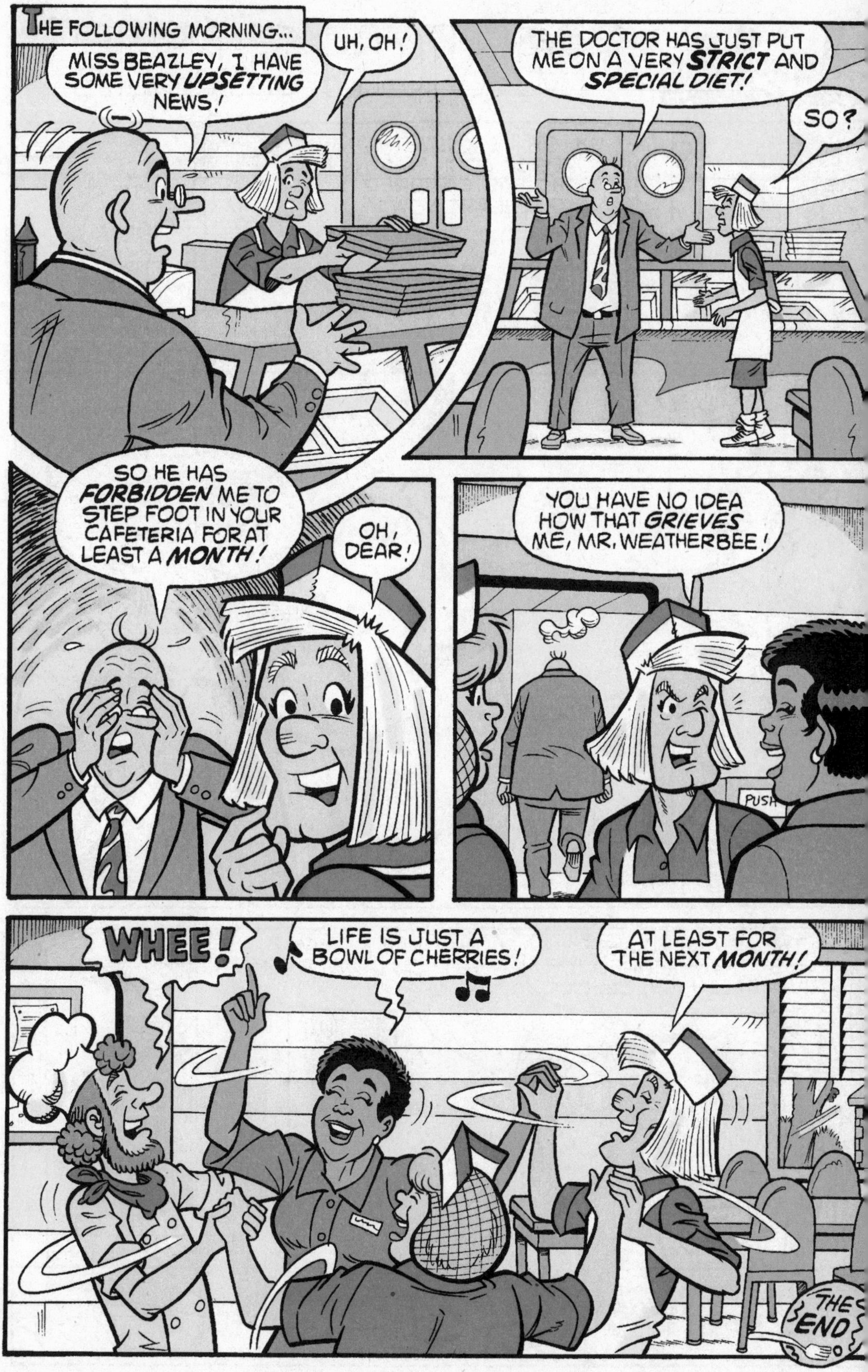
THE FOLLOWING MORNING...
MISS BEAZLEY, I HAVE SOME VERY UPSETTING NEWS!
UH, OH!
THE DOCTOR HAS JUST PUT ME ON A VERY STRICT AND SPECIAL DIET!
SO?
SO HE HAS FORBIDDEN ME TO STEP FOOT IN YOUR CAFETERIA FOR AT LEAST A MONTH!
OH, DEAR!
YOU HAVE NO IDEA HOW THAT GRIEVES ME, MR. WEATHERBEE!
PUSH
WHEE!
LIFE IS JUST A BOWL OF CHERRIES!
AT LEAST FOR THE NEXT MONTH!
THE END

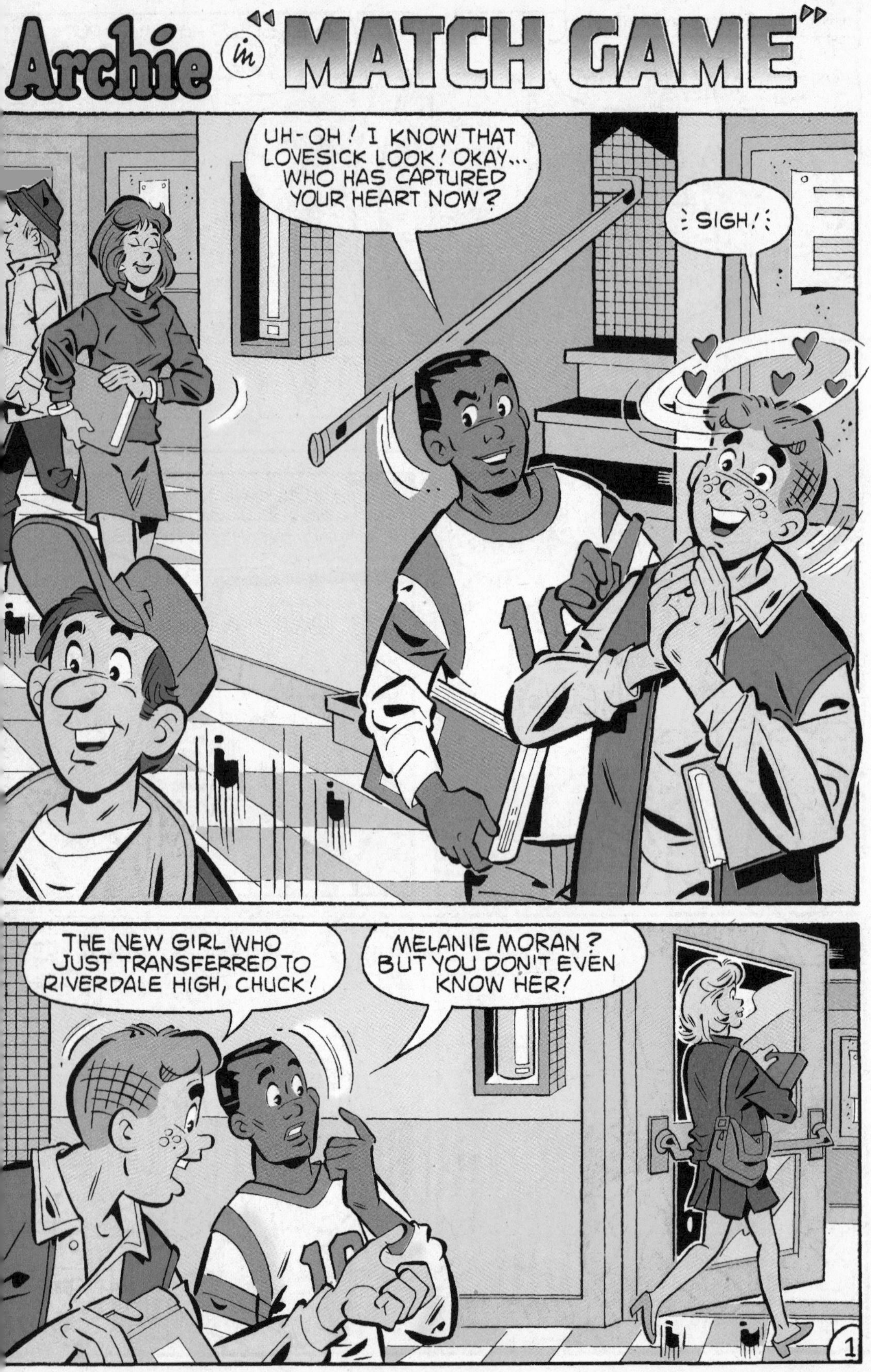
Archie in "MATCH GAME"
UH-OH! I KNOW THAT LOVESICK LOOK! OKAY... WHO HAS CAPTURED YOUR HEART NOW?
SIGH!
THE NEW GIRL WHO JUST TRANSFERRED TO RIVERDALE HIGH, CHUCK!
MELANIE MORAN? BUT YOU DON'T EVEN KNOW HER!
1

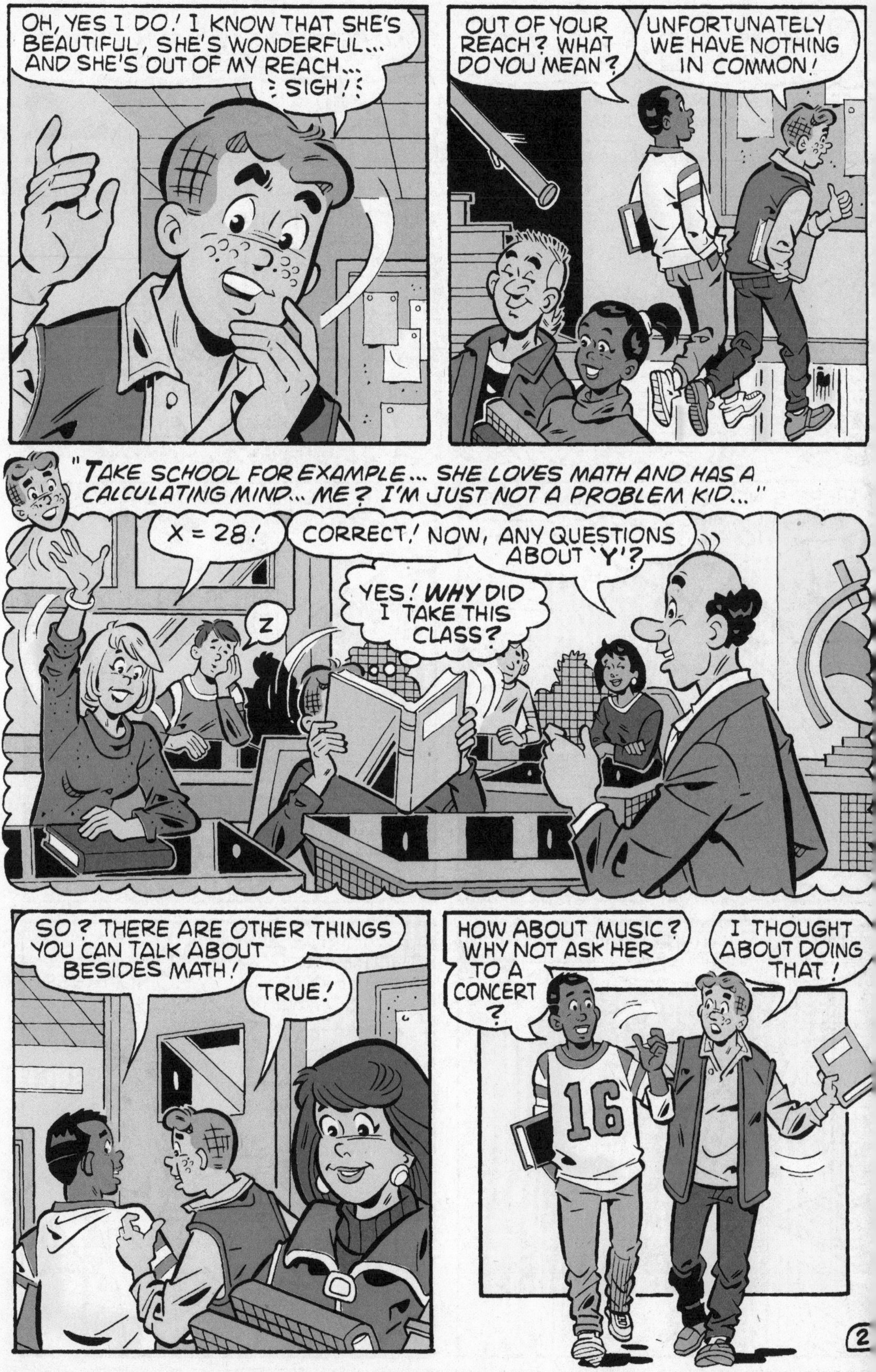
OH, YES I DO! I KNOW THAT SHE'S BEAUTIFUL, SHE'S WONDERFUL... AND SHE'S OUT OF MY REACH...
SIGH!
OUT OF YOUR REACH? WHAT DO YOU MEAN?
UNFORTUNATELY WE HAVE NOTHING IN COMMON!
"TAKE SCHOOL FOR EXAMPLE... SHE LOVES MATH AND HAS A CALCULATING MIND... ME? I'M JUST NOT A PROBLEM KID..."
X = 28!
CORRECT! NOW, ANY QUESTIONS ABOUT 'Y'?
Z
YES! WHY DID I TAKE THIS CLASS?
SO? THERE ARE OTHER THINGS YOU CAN TALK ABOUT BESIDES MATH!
TRUE!
HOW ABOUT MUSIC? WHY NOT ASK HER TO A CONCERT?
I THOUGHT ABOUT DOING THAT!
16
2

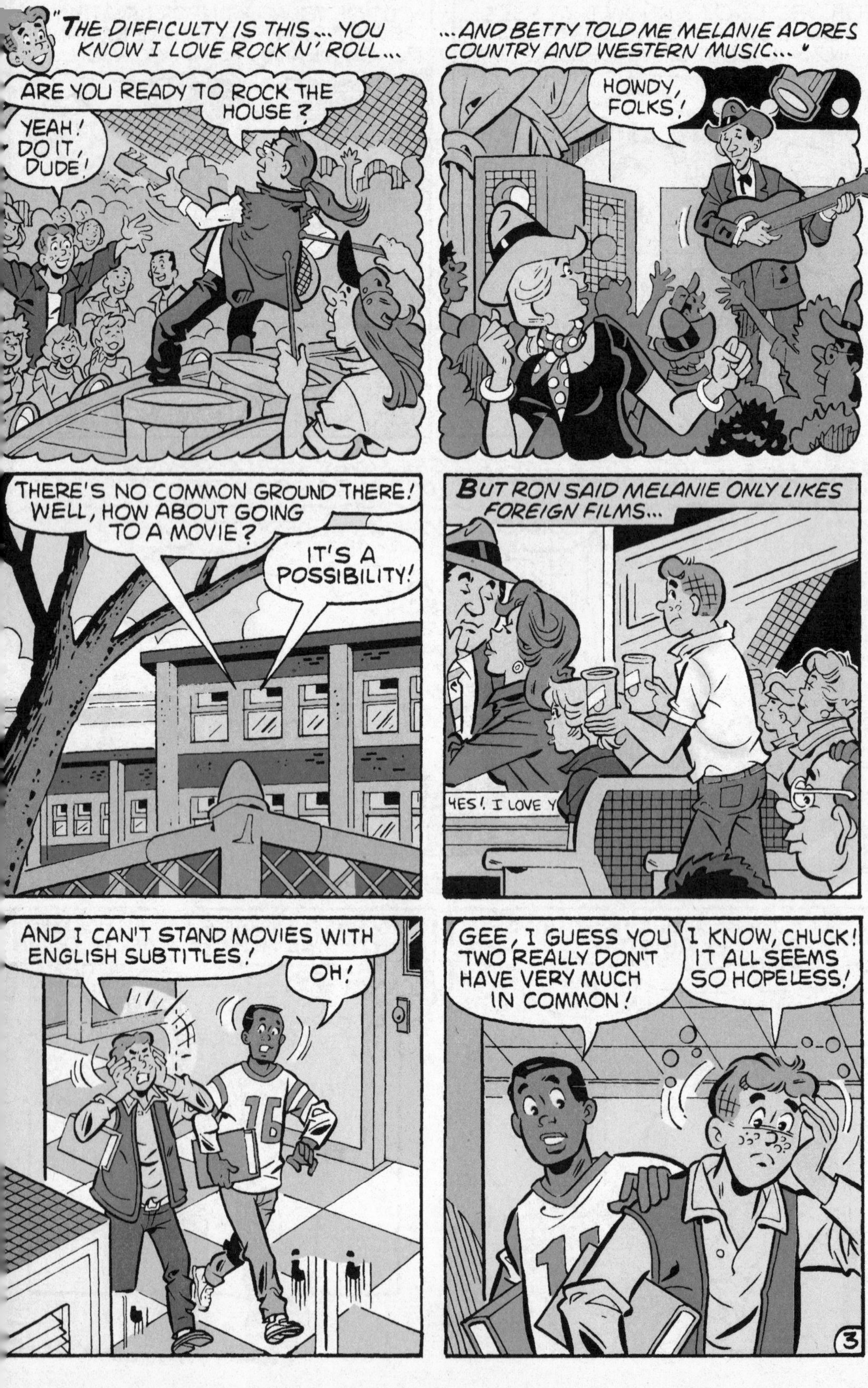
"THE DIFFICULTY IS THIS... YOU KNOW I LOVE ROCK N' ROLL...
ARE YOU READY TO ROCK THE HOUSE?
YEAH! DO IT, DUDE!
...AND BETTY TOLD ME MELANIE ADORES COUNTRY AND WESTERN MUSIC..."
HOWDY, FOLKS!
THERE'S NO COMMON GROUND THERE! WELL, HOW ABOUT GOING TO A MOVIE?
IT'S A POSSIBILITY!
BUT RON SAID MELANIE ONLY LIKES FOREIGN FILMS...
YES! I LOVE Y
AND I CAN'T STAND MOVIES WITH ENGLISH SUBTITLES!
OH!
GEE, I GUESS YOU TWO REALLY DON'T HAVE VERY MUCH IN COMMON!
I KNOW, CHUCK! IT ALL SEEMS SO HOPELESS!
3

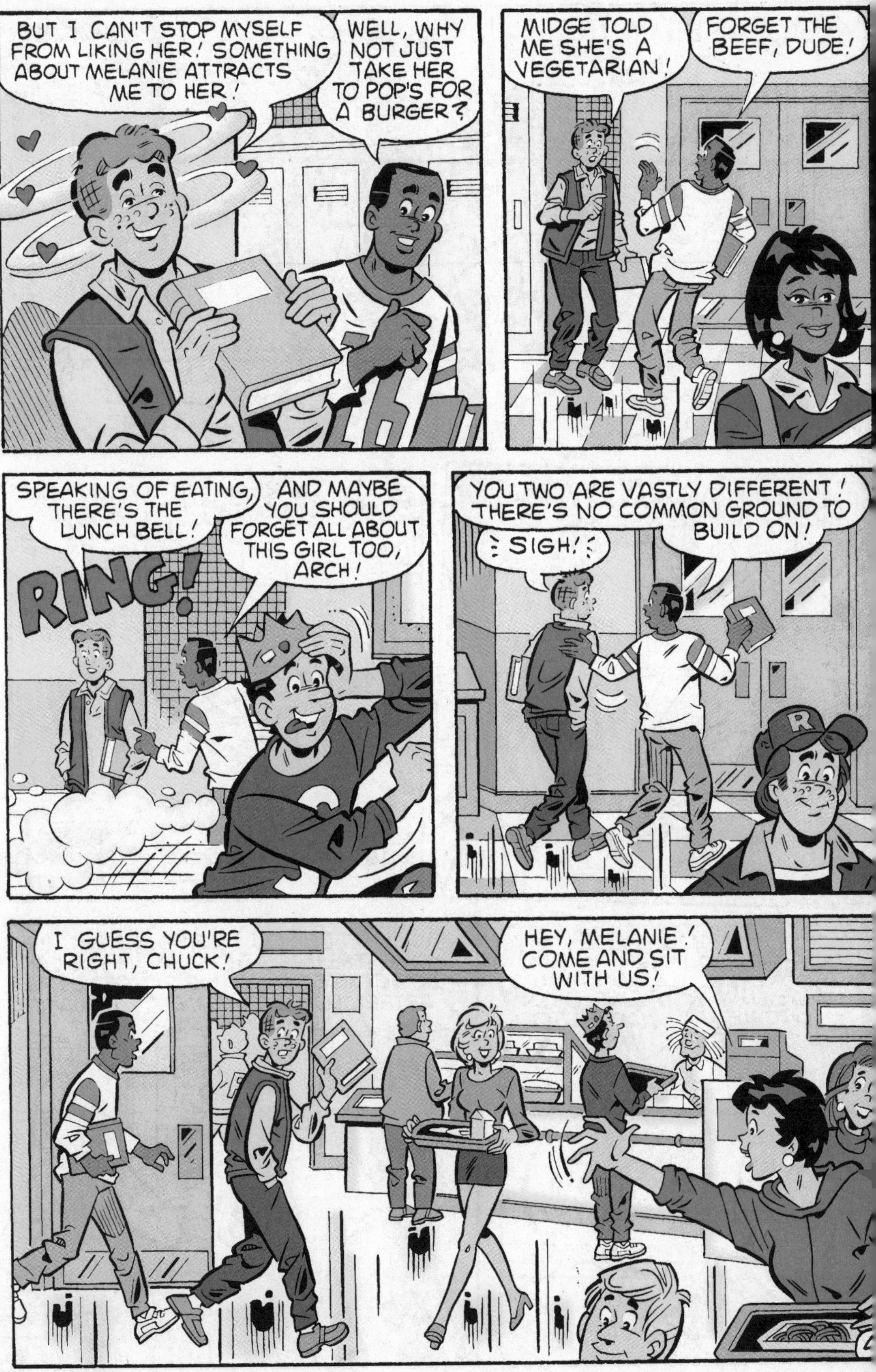
BUT I CAN'T STOP MYSELF FROM LIKING HER! SOMETHING ABOUT MELANIE ATTRACTS ME TO HER!
WELL, WHY NOT JUST TAKE HER TO POP'S FOR A BURGER?
MIDGE TOLD ME SHE'S A VEGETARIAN!
FORGET THE BEEF, DUDE!
SPEAKING OF EATING, THERE'S THE LUNCH BELL!
RING!
AND MAYBE YOU SHOULD FORGET ALL ABOUT THIS GIRL TOO, ARCH!
YOU TWO ARE VASTLY DIFFERENT! THERE'S NO COMMON GROUND TO BUILD ON!
SIGH!
I GUESS YOU'RE RIGHT, CHUCK!
HEY, MELANIE! COME AND SIT WITH US!

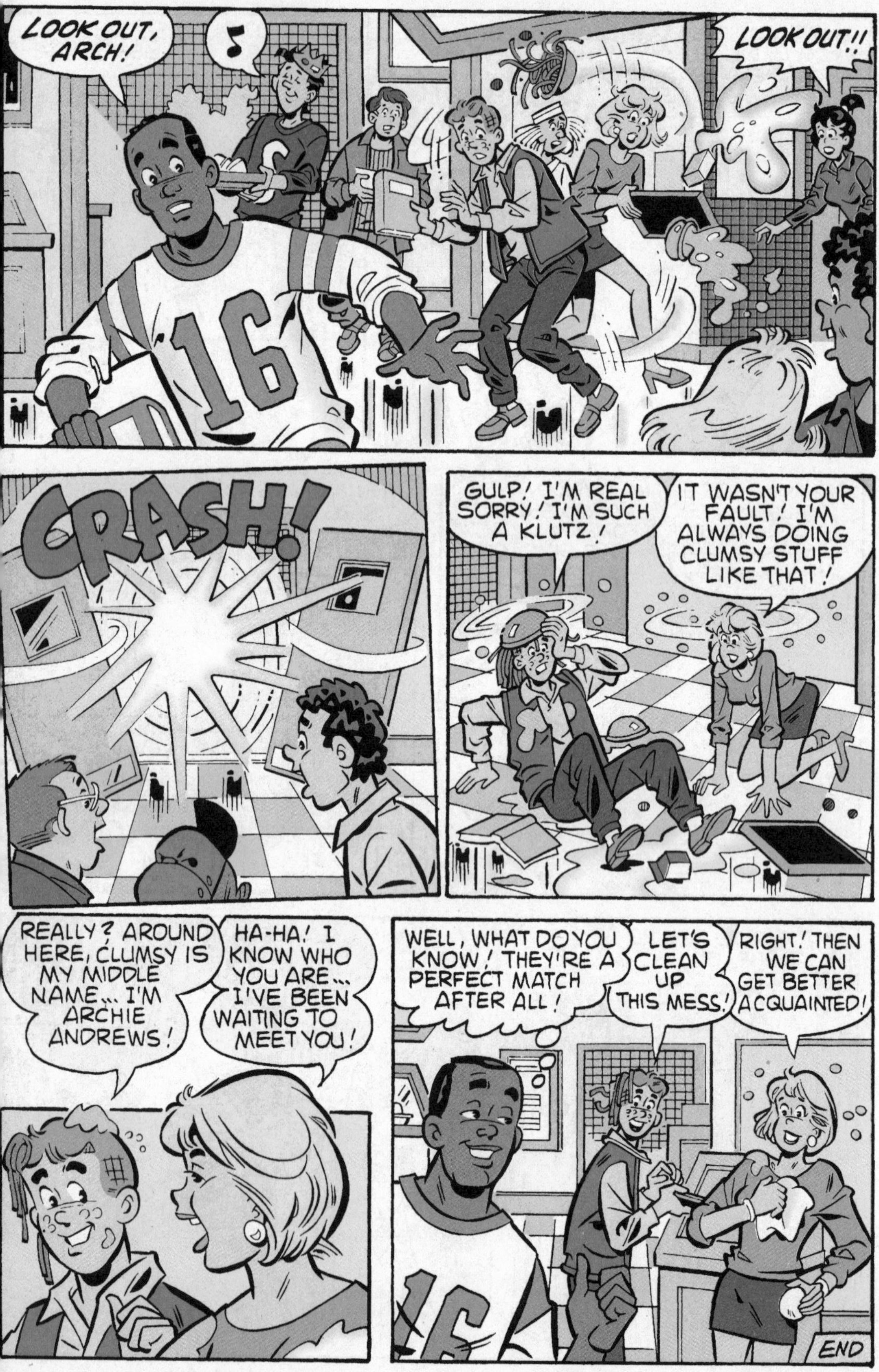
LOOK OUT, ARCH!
♪
LOOK OUT!!
CRASH!
GULP! I'M REAL SORRY! I'M SUCH A KLUTZ!
IT WASN'T YOUR FAULT! I'M ALWAYS DOING CLUMSY STUFF LIKE THAT!
REALLY? AROUND HERE, CLUMSY IS MY MIDDLE NAME... I'M ARCHIE ANDREWS!
HA-HA! I KNOW WHO YOU ARE... I'VE BEEN WAITING TO MEET YOU!
WELL, WHAT DO YOU KNOW! THEY'RE A PERFECT MATCH AFTER ALL!
LET'S CLEAN UP THIS MESS!
RIGHT! THEN WE CAN GET BETTER ACQUAINTED!
END

LOOK, ARCHIE! EVERYONE IS EXCITED ABOUT OUR NEW YEARBOOK!
THAT'S BECAUSE I TOOK THOSE SHOTS FOR THE BOOK!
Archie in "PHOTO FUN
WHERE'S THAT ARCHIE?!!
? SOUNDS LIKE SOMEONE WITH A BEEF!
ARCHIE'S PHOTO WILL MAKE ME THE LAUGHING STOCK OF THE SCHOOL!!
BUT IT'S A NICE PHOTO OF YOU, MISS BEAZLY!

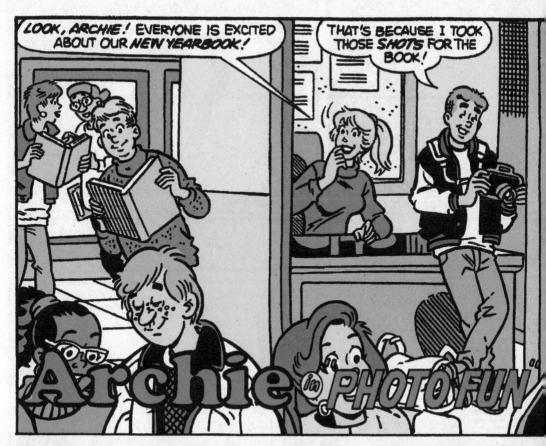

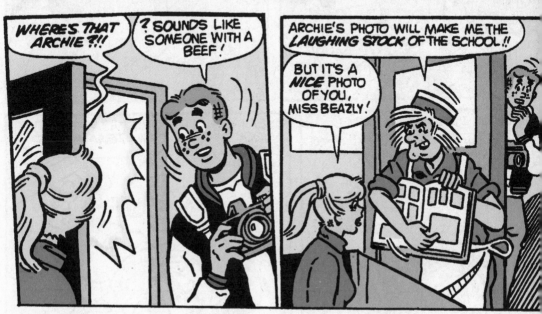

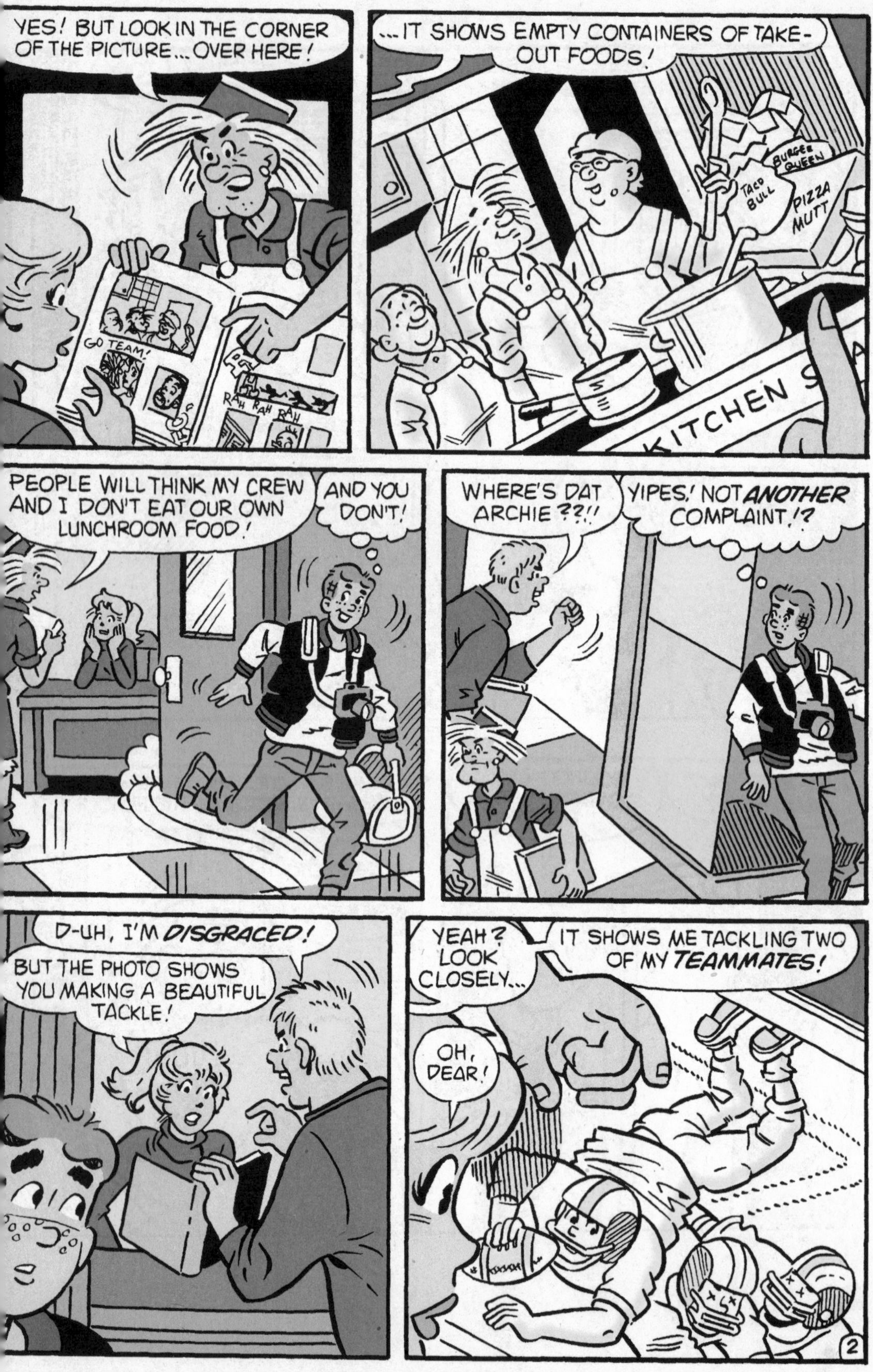
YES! BUT LOOK IN THE CORNER OF THE PICTURE... OVER HERE!
GO TEAM!
RAH RAH RAH
...IT SHOWS EMPTY CONTAINERS OF TAKE-OUT FOODS!
TACO BULL
BURGER QUEEN
PIZZA MUTT
KITCHEN S
PEOPLE WILL THINK MY CREW AND I DON'T EAT OUR OWN LUNCHROOM FOOD!
AND YOU DON'T!
WHERE'S DAT ARCHIE??!!
YIPES! NOT ANOTHER COMPLAINT!?
D-UH, I'M DISGRACED!
BUT THE PHOTO SHOWS YOU MAKING A BEAUTIFUL TACKLE!
YEAH? LOOK CLOSELY...
IT SHOWS ME TACKLING TWO OF MY TEAMMATES!
OH, DEAR!
2

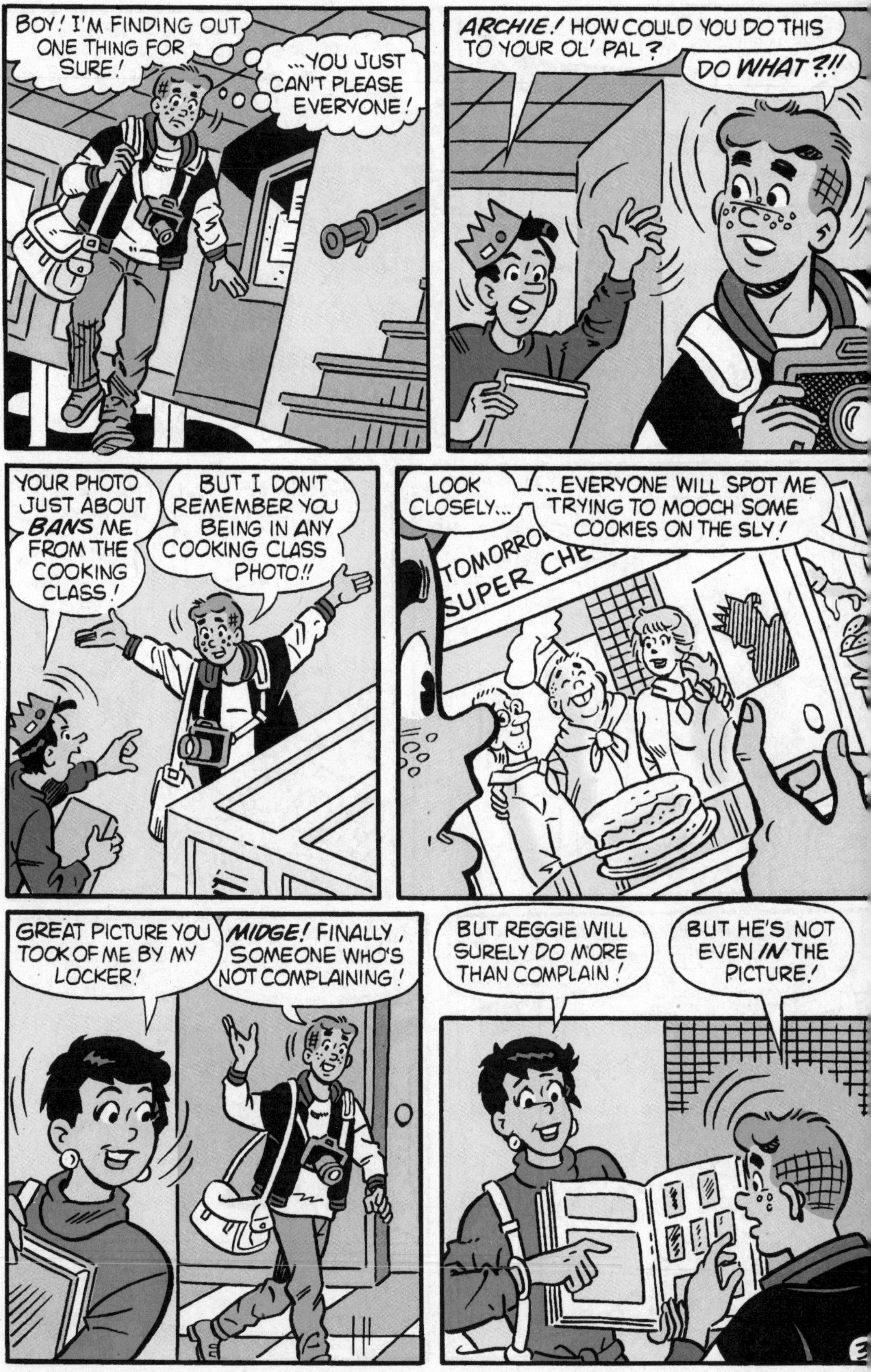
BOY! I'M FINDING OUT ONE THING FOR SURE!
...YOU JUST CAN'T PLEASE EVERYONE!
ARCHIE! HOW COULD YOU DO THIS TO YOUR OL' PAL?
DO WHAT?!!
YOUR PHOTO JUST ABOUT BANS ME FROM THE COOKING CLASS!
BUT I DON'T REMEMBER YOU BEING IN ANY COOKING CLASS PHOTO!!
LOOK CLOSELY...
...EVERYONE WILL SPOT ME TRYING TO MOOCH SOME COOKIES ON THE SLY!
TOMORRO
SUPER CHE
GREAT PICTURE YOU TOOK OF ME BY MY LOCKER!
MIDGE! FINALLY, SOMEONE WHO'S NOT COMPLAINING!
BUT REGGIE WILL SURELY DO MORE THAN COMPLAIN!
BUT HE'S NOT EVEN IN THE PICTURE!

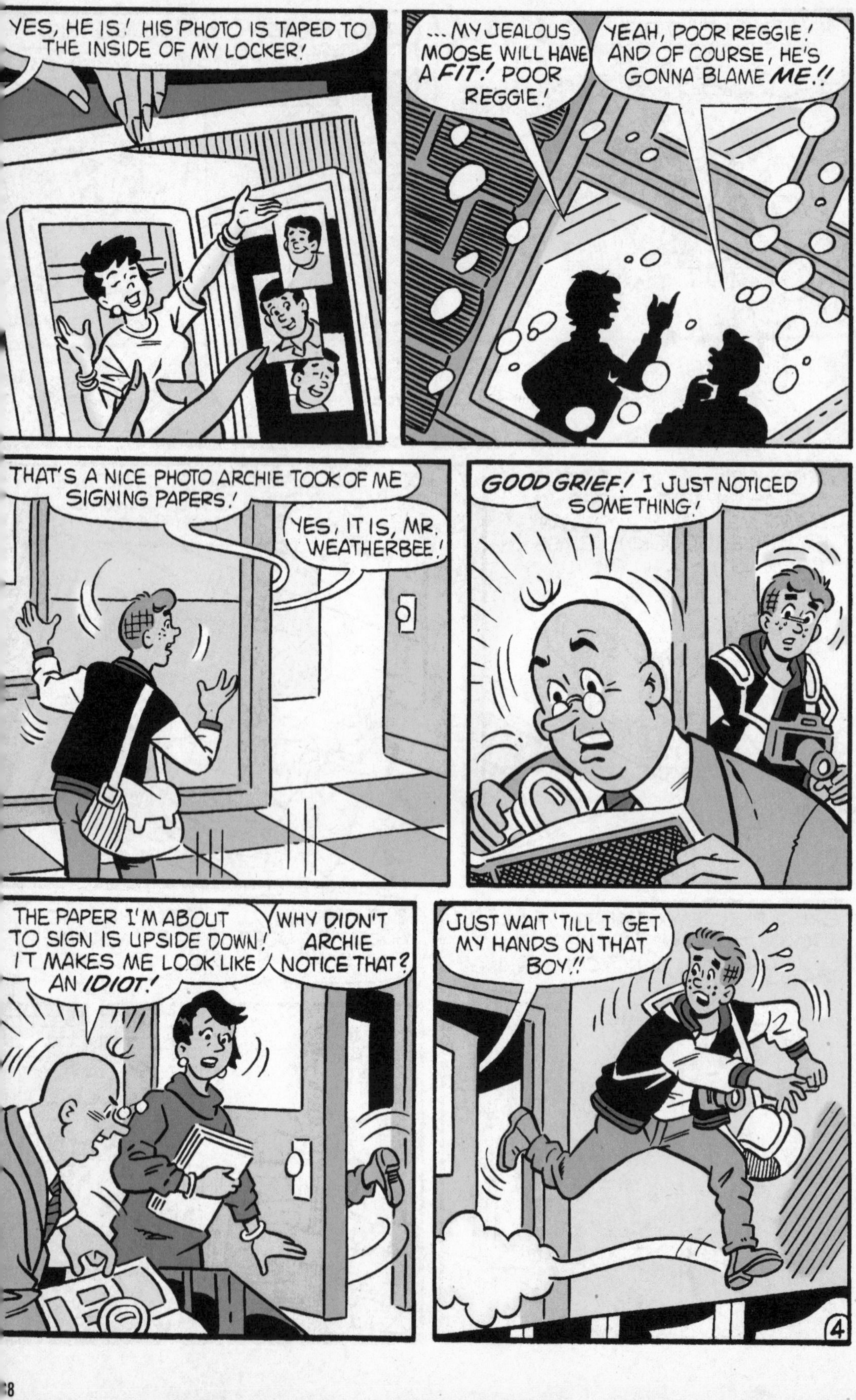
YES, HE IS! HIS PHOTO IS TAPED TO THE INSIDE OF MY LOCKER!
...MY JEALOUS MOOSE WILL HAVE A FIT! POOR REGGIE!
YEAH, POOR REGGIE! AND OF COURSE, HE'S GONNA BLAME ME!!
THAT'S A NICE PHOTO ARCHIE TOOK OF ME SIGNING PAPERS!
YES, IT IS, MR. WEATHERBEE!
GOOD GRIEF! I JUST NOTICED SOMETHING!
THE PAPER I'M ABOUT TO SIGN IS UPSIDE DOWN! IT MAKES ME LOOK LIKE AN IDIOT!
WHY DIDN'T ARCHIE NOTICE THAT?
JUST WAIT 'TILL I GET MY HANDS ON THAT BOY!!
4

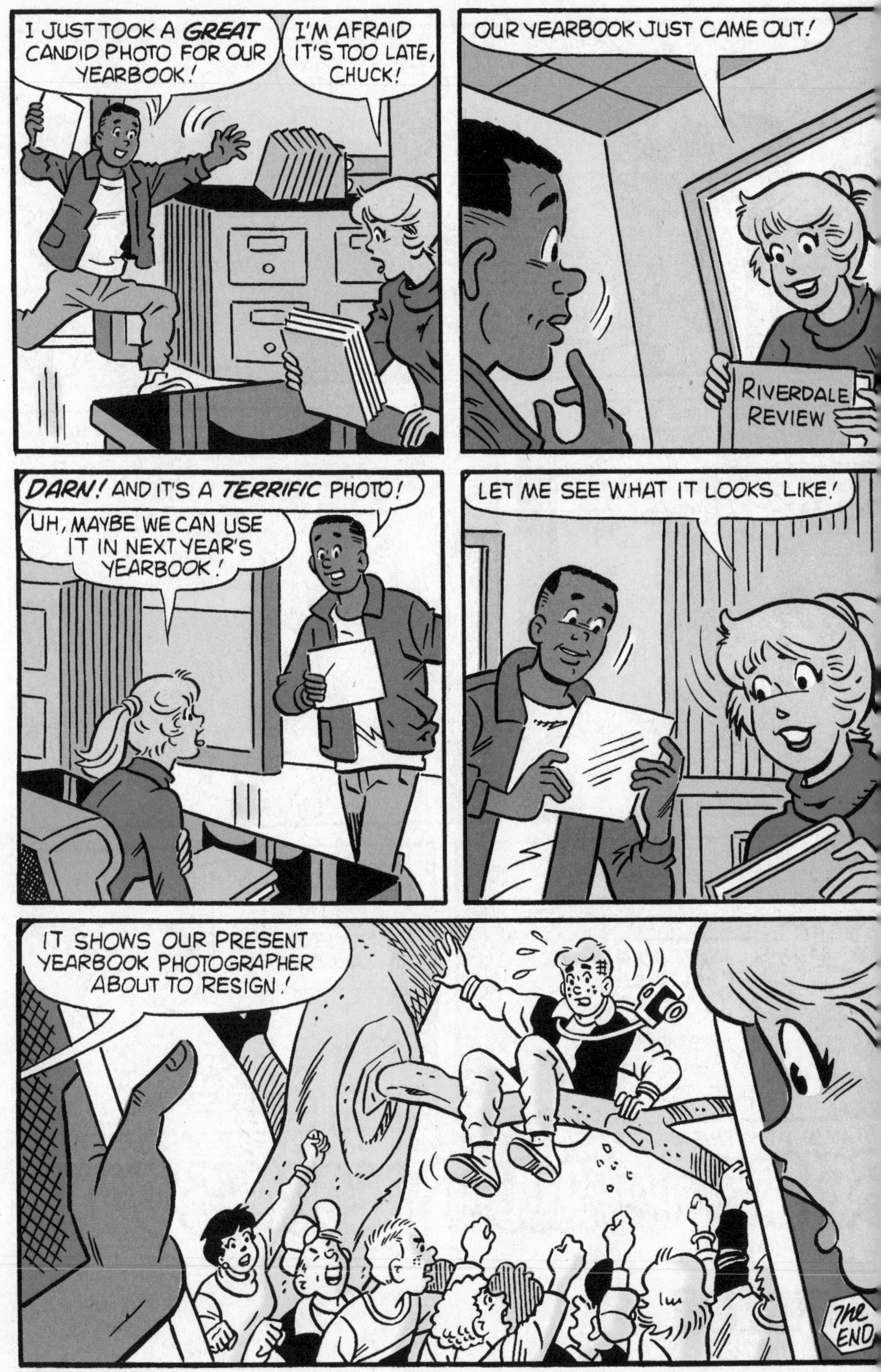
I JUST TOOK A GREAT CANDID PHOTO FOR OUR YEARBOOK!
I'M AFRAID IT'S TOO LATE, CHUCK!
OUR YEARBOOK JUST CAME OUT!
RIVERDALE REVIEW
DARN! AND IT'S A TERRIFIC PHOTO!
UH, MAYBE WE CAN USE IT IN NEXT YEAR'S YEARBOOK!
LET ME SEE WHAT IT LOOKS LIKE!
IT SHOWS OUR PRESENT YEARBOOK PHOTOGRAPHER ABOUT TO RESIGN!
THE END

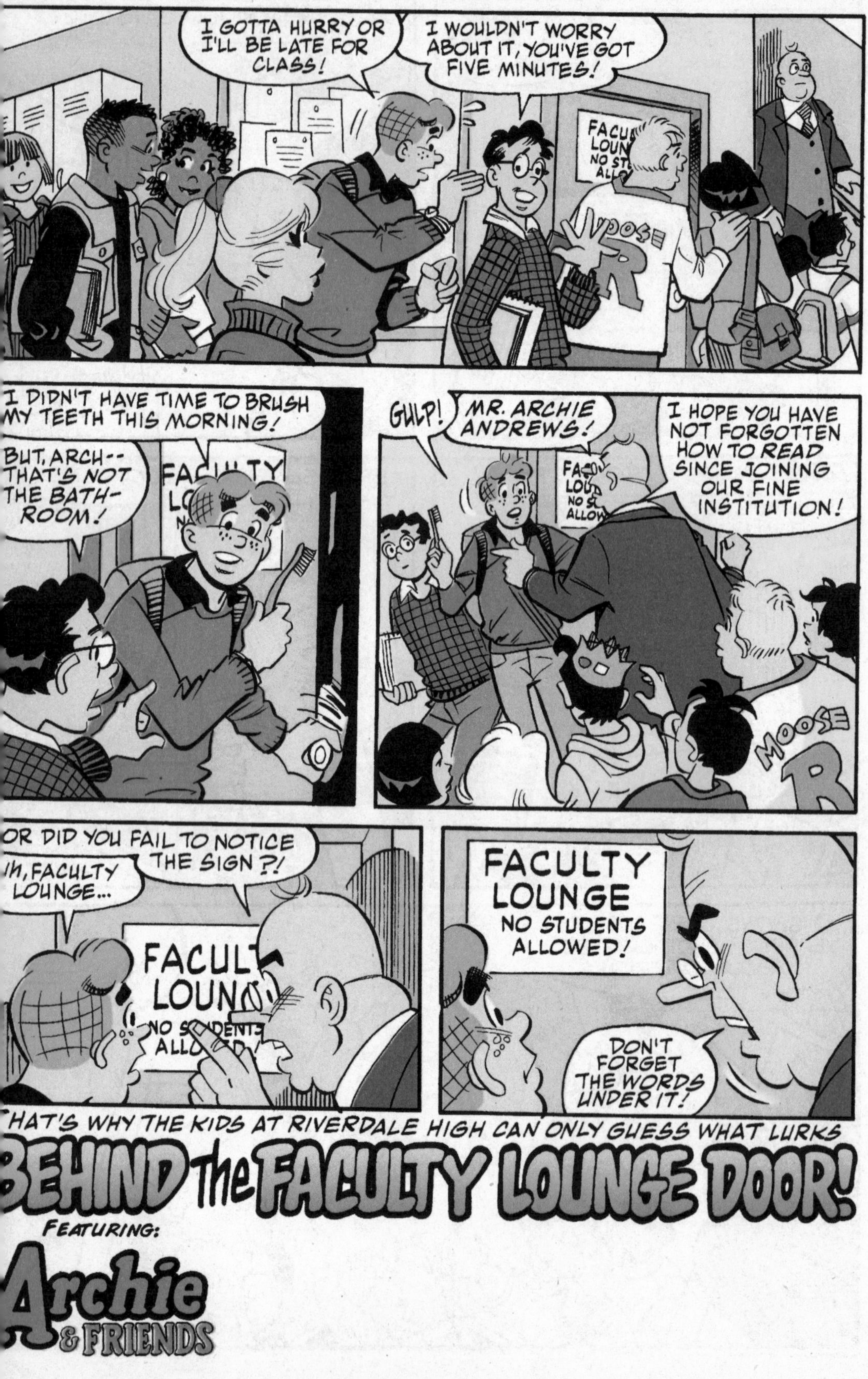
I GOTTA HURRY OR I'LL BE LATE FOR CLASS!
I WOULDN'T WORRY ABOUT IT, YOU'VE GOT FIVE MINUTES!
I DIDN'T HAVE TIME TO BRUSH MY TEETH THIS MORNING!
BUT, ARCH-- THAT'S NOT THE BATH-ROOM!
GULP!
MR. ARCHIE ANDREWS!
I HOPE YOU HAVE NOT FORGOTTEN HOW TO READ SINCE JOINING OUR FINE INSTITUTION!
OR DID YOU FAIL TO NOTICE THE SIGN?!
'H, FACULTY LOUNGE...
FACULTY LOUNGE NO STUDENTS ALLOWED!
DON'T FORGET THE WORDS UNDER IT!
THAT'S WHY THE KIDS AT RIVERDALE HIGH CAN ONLY GUESS WHAT LURKS
BEHIND the FACULTY LOUNGE DOOR!
FEATURING:
Archie & FRIENDS

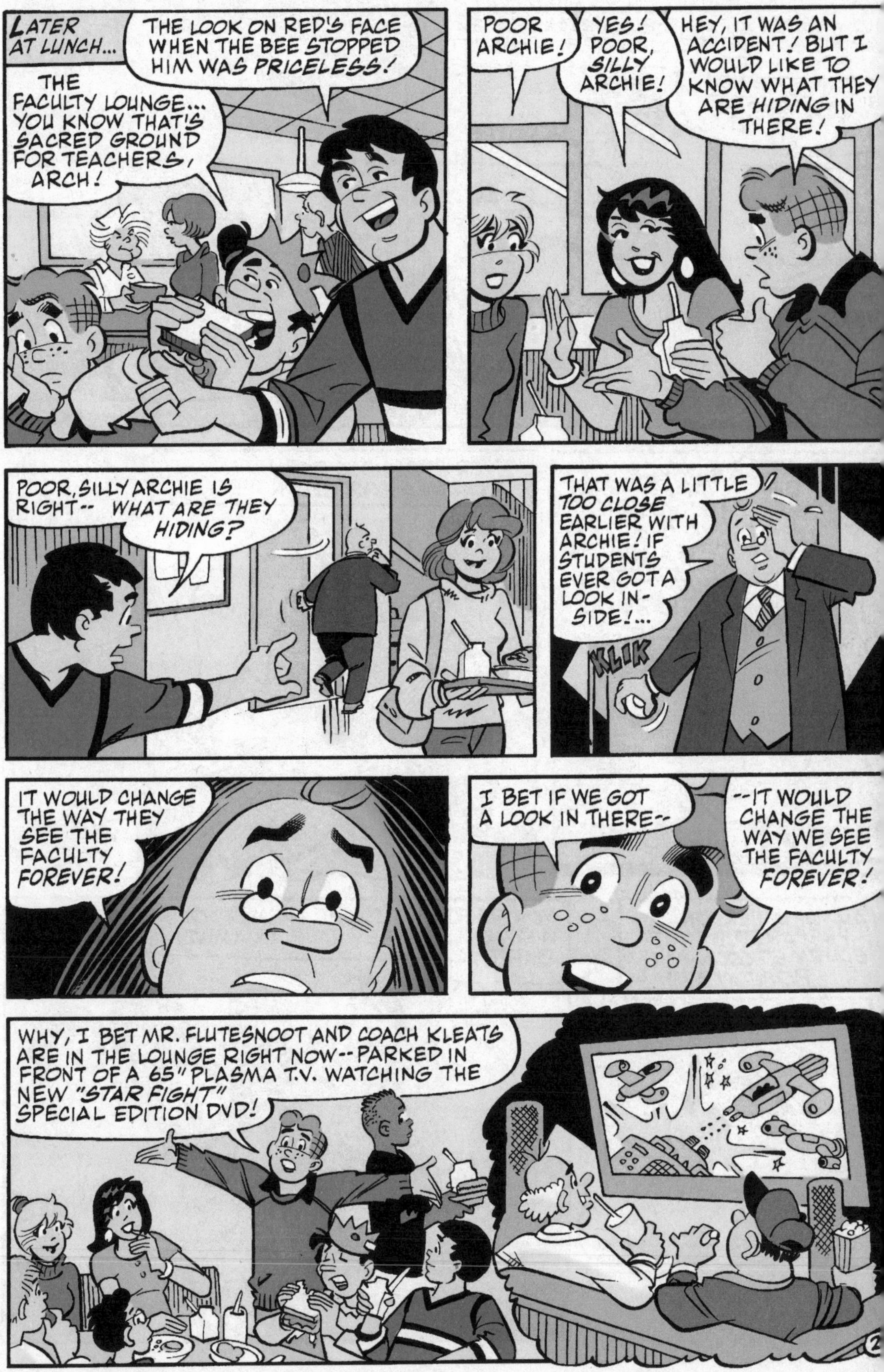
LATER AT LUNCH...
THE LOOK ON RED'S FACE WHEN THE BEE STOPPED HIM WAS PRICELESS!
THE FACULTY LOUNGE... YOU KNOW THAT'S SACRED GROUND FOR TEACHERS, ARCH!
POOR ARCHIE!
YES! POOR, SILLY ARCHIE!
HEY, IT WAS AN ACCIDENT! BUT I WOULD LIKE TO KNOW WHAT THEY ARE HIDING IN THERE!
POOR, SILLY ARCHIE IS RIGHT-- WHAT ARE THEY HIDING?
THAT WAS A LITTLE TOO CLOSE EARLIER WITH ARCHIE! IF STUDENTS EVER GOT A LOOK IN-SIDE!...
KLIK
IT WOULD CHANGE THE WAY THEY SEE THE FACULTY FOREVER!
I BET IF WE GOT A LOOK IN THERE--
--IT WOULD CHANGE THE WAY WE SEE THE FACULTY FOREVER!
WHY, I BET MR. FLUTESNOOT AND COACH KLEATS ARE IN THE LOUNGE RIGHT NOW--PARKED IN FRONT OF A 65" PLASMA T.V. WATCHING THE NEW "STAR FIGHT" SPECIAL EDITION DVD!

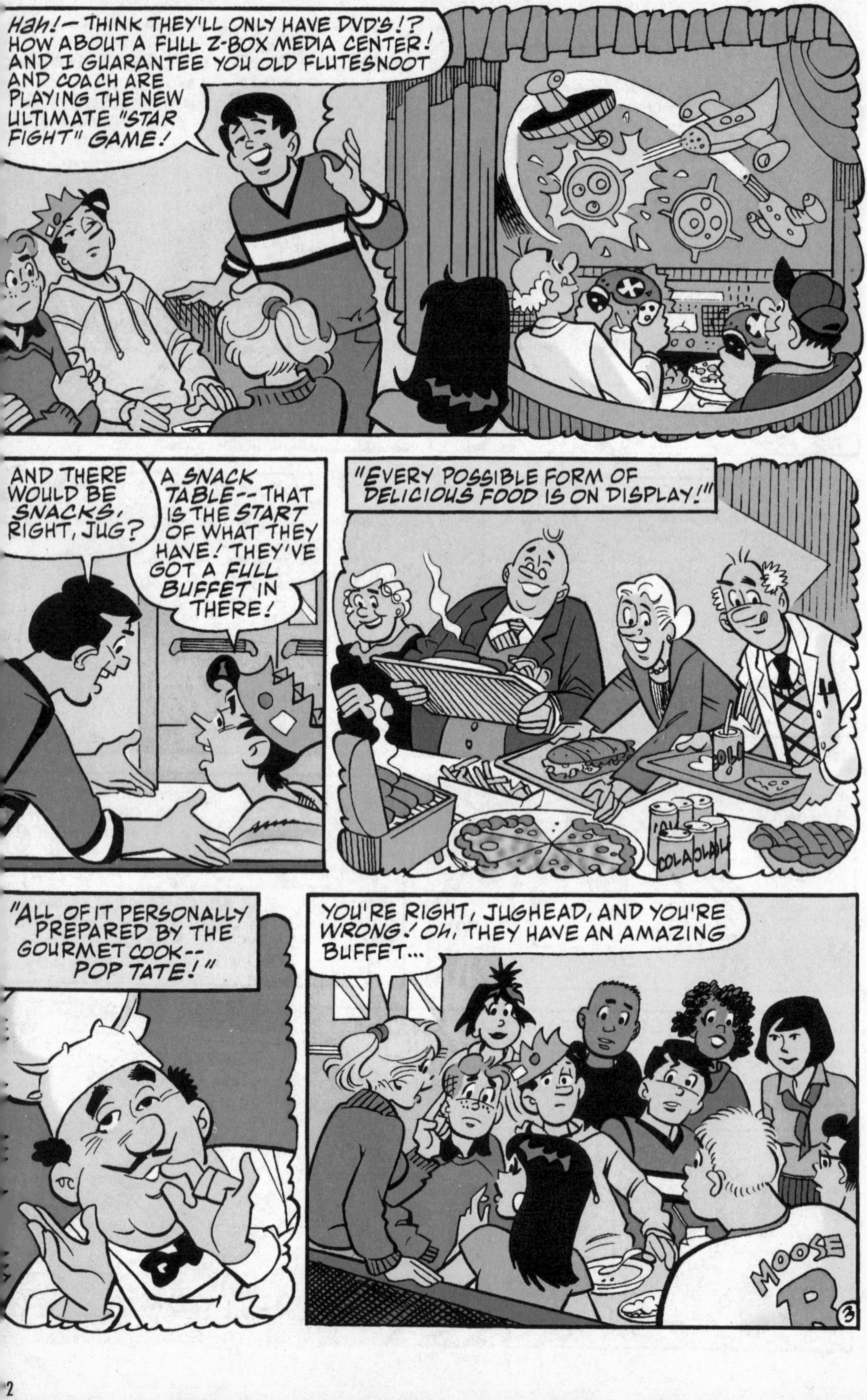
Hah! — THINK THEY'LL ONLY HAVE DVD'S!? HOW ABOUT A FULL Z-BOX MEDIA CENTER! AND I GUARANTEE YOU OLD FLUTESNOOT AND COACH ARE PLAYING THE NEW ULTIMATE "STAR FIGHT" GAME!
AND THERE WOULD BE SNACKS, RIGHT, JUG?
A SNACK TABLE-- THAT IS THE START OF WHAT THEY HAVE! THEY'VE GOT A FULL BUFFET IN THERE!
"EVERY POSSIBLE FORM OF DELICIOUS FOOD IS ON DISPLAY!"
COLA
"ALL OF IT PERSONALLY PREPARED BY THE GOURMET COOK-- POP TATE!"
YOU'RE RIGHT, JUGHEAD, AND YOU'RE WRONG! Oh, THEY HAVE AN AMAZING BUFFET...
MOOSE
3

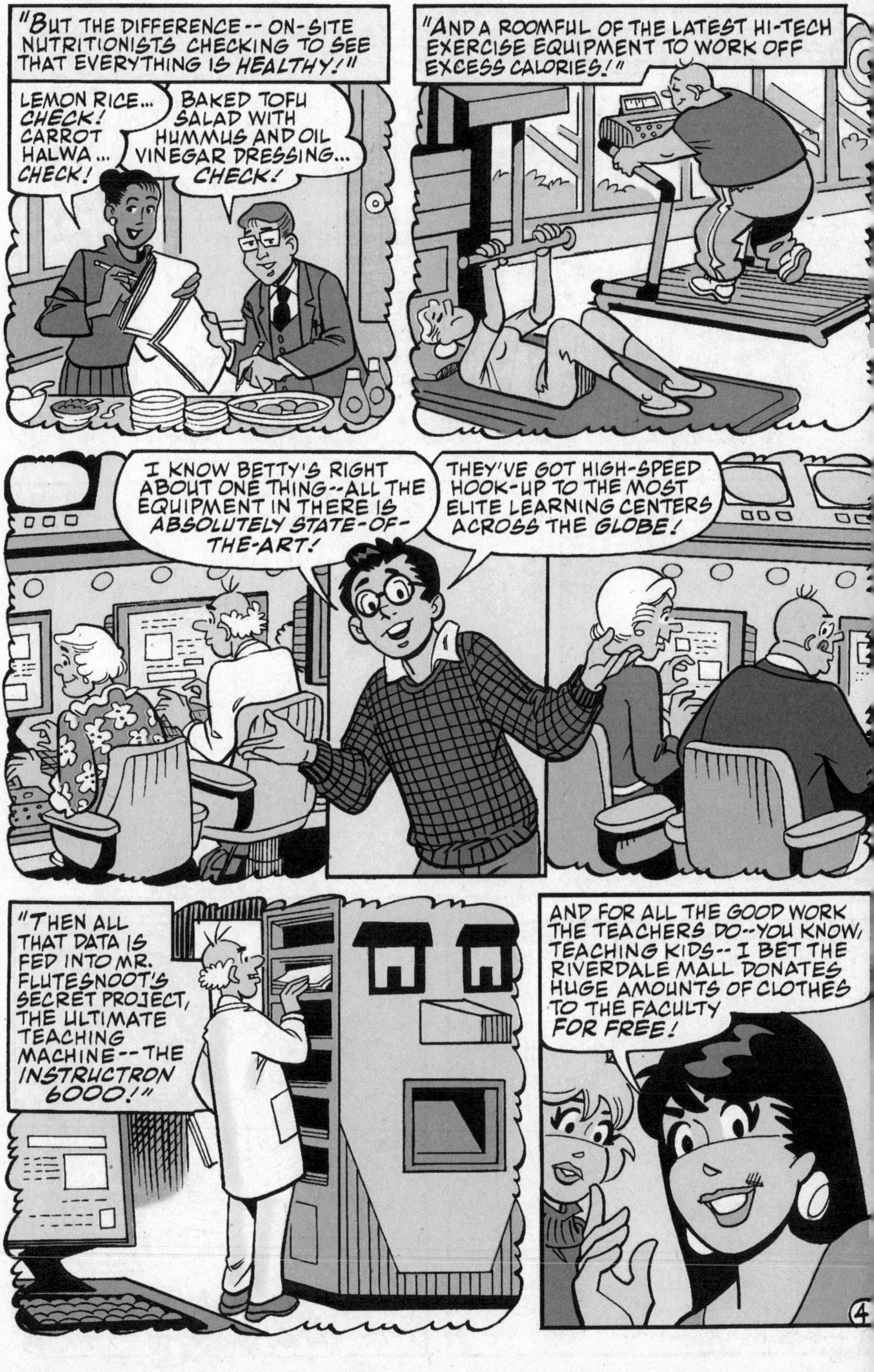
"BUT THE DIFFERENCE -- ON-SITE NUTRITIONISTS CHECKING TO SEE THAT EVERYTHING IS HEALTHY!"
LEMON RICE... CHECK! CARROT HALWA... CHECK!
BAKED TOFU SALAD WITH HUMMUS AND OIL VINEGAR DRESSING... CHECK!
"AND A ROOMFUL OF THE LATEST HI-TECH EXERCISE EQUIPMENT TO WORK OFF EXCESS CALORIES!"
I KNOW BETTY'S RIGHT ABOUT ONE THING--ALL THE EQUIPMENT IN THERE IS ABSOLUTELY STATE-OF-THE-ART!
THEY'VE GOT HIGH-SPEED HOOK-UP TO THE MOST ELITE LEARNING CENTERS ACROSS THE GLOBE!
"THEN ALL THAT DATA IS FED INTO MR. FLUTESNOOT'S SECRET PROJECT, THE ULTIMATE TEACHING MACHINE--THE INSTRUCTRON 6000!"
AND FOR ALL THE GOOD WORK THE TEACHERS DO--YOU KNOW, TEACHING KIDS-- I BET THE RIVERDALE MALL DONATES HUGE AMOUNTS OF CLOTHES TO THE FACULTY FOR FREE!
4

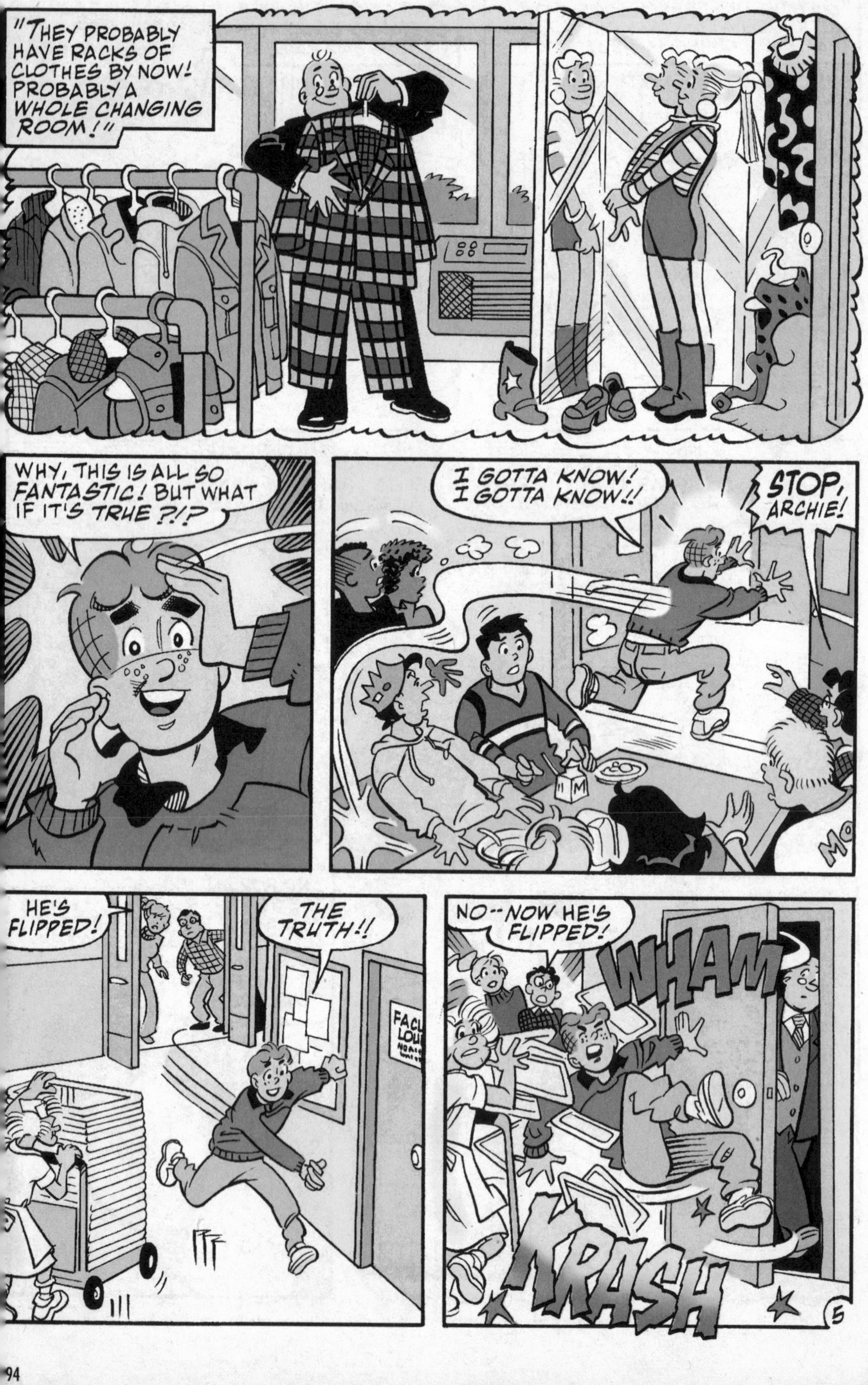
"THEY PROBABLY HAVE RACKS OF CLOTHES BY NOW! PROBABLY A WHOLE CHANGING ROOM!"
WHY, THIS IS ALL SO FANTASTIC! BUT WHAT IF IT'S TRUE?!?
I GOTTA KNOW! I GOTTA KNOW!!
STOP, ARCHIE!
HE'S FLIPPED!
THE TRUTH!!
NO--NOW HE'S FLIPPED!
WHAM
KRASH
5

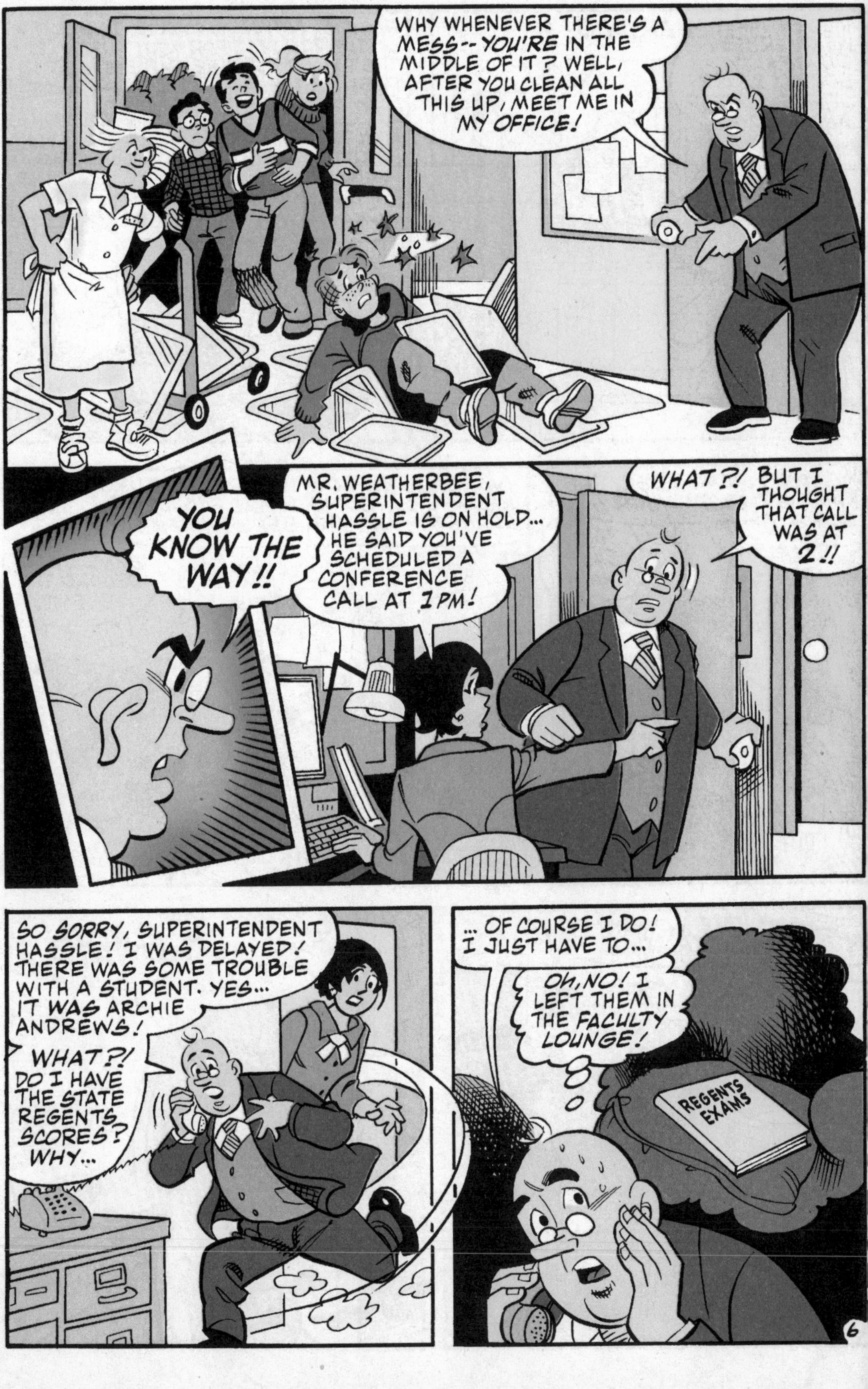
WHY WHENEVER THERE'S A MESS-- YOU'RE IN THE MIDDLE OF IT? WELL, AFTER YOU CLEAN ALL THIS UP, MEET ME IN MY OFFICE!
YOU KNOW THE WAY!!
MR. WEATHERBEE, SUPERINTENDENT HASSLE IS ON HOLD... HE SAID YOU'VE SCHEDULED A CONFERENCE CALL AT 1 PM!
WHAT?! BUT I THOUGHT THAT CALL WAS AT 2!!
SO SORRY, SUPERINTENDENT HASSLE! I WAS DELAYED! THERE WAS SOME TROUBLE WITH A STUDENT. YES... IT WAS ARCHIE ANDREWS!
WHAT?! DO I HAVE THE STATE REGENTS SCORES? WHY...
... OF COURSE I DO! I JUST HAVE TO...
OH, NO! I LEFT THEM IN THE FACULTY LOUNGE!
REGENTS EXAMS
6

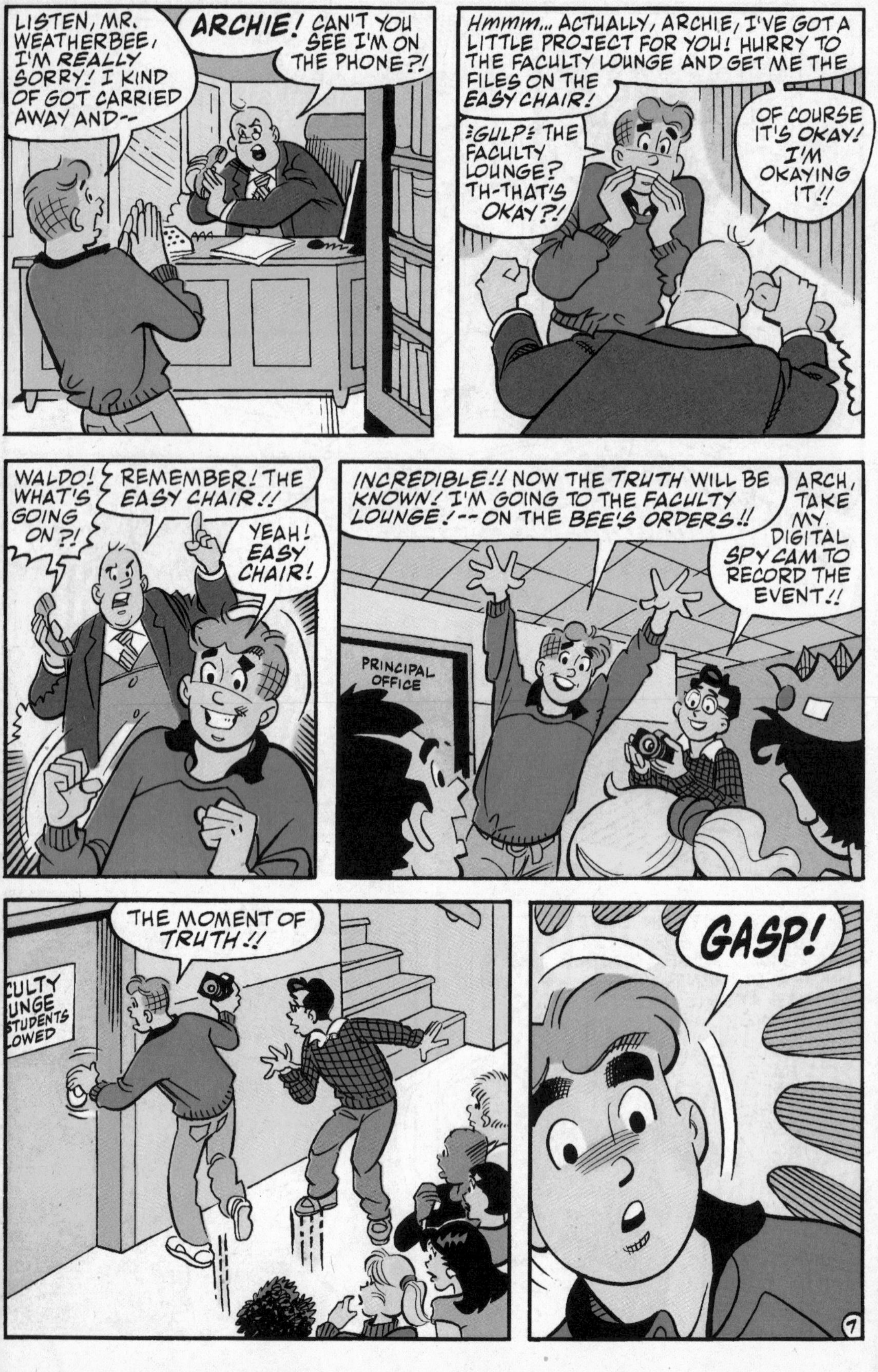
LISTEN, MR. WEATHERBEE, I'M REALLY SORRY! I KIND OF GOT CARRIED AWAY AND--
ARCHIE! CAN'T YOU SEE I'M ON THE PHONE?!
Hmmm... ACTUALLY, ARCHIE, I'VE GOT A LITTLE PROJECT FOR YOU! HURRY TO THE FACULTY LOUNGE AND GET ME THE FILES ON THE EASY CHAIR!
:GULP: THE FACULTY LOUNGE? TH-THAT'S OKAY?!
OF COURSE IT'S OKAY! I'M OKAYING IT!!
WALDO! WHAT'S GOING ON?!
REMEMBER! THE EASY CHAIR!!
YEAH! EASY CHAIR!
INCREDIBLE!! NOW THE TRUTH WILL BE KNOWN! I'M GOING TO THE FACULTY LOUNGE! -- ON THE BEE'S ORDERS!!
ARCH, TAKE MY DIGITAL SPY CAM TO RECORD THE EVENT!!
PRINCIPAL OFFICE
THE MOMENT OF TRUTH!!
CULTY UNGE STUDENTS LOWED
GASP!
7

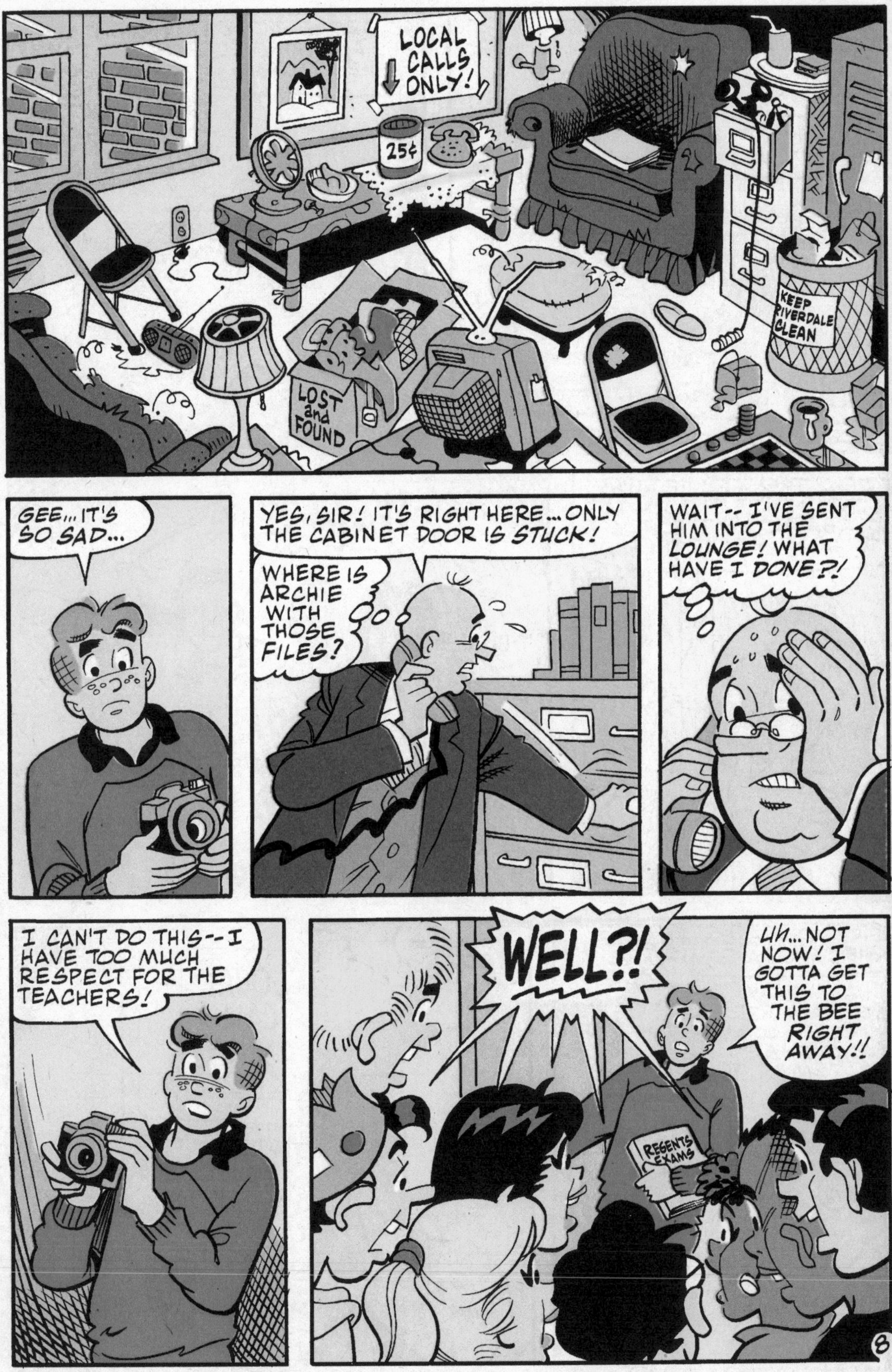
LOCAL CALLS ONLY!
25¢
LOST and FOUND
KEEP RIVERDALE CLEAN
GEE... IT'S SO SAD...
YES, SIR! IT'S RIGHT HERE... ONLY THE CABINET DOOR IS STUCK!
WHERE IS ARCHIE WITH THOSE FILES?
WAIT-- I'VE SENT HIM INTO THE LOUNGE! WHAT HAVE I DONE?!
I CAN'T DO THIS-- I HAVE TOO MUCH RESPECT FOR THE TEACHERS!
WELL?!
UH... NOT NOW! I GOTTA GET THIS TO THE BEE RIGHT AWAY!!
REGENTS EXAMS
8

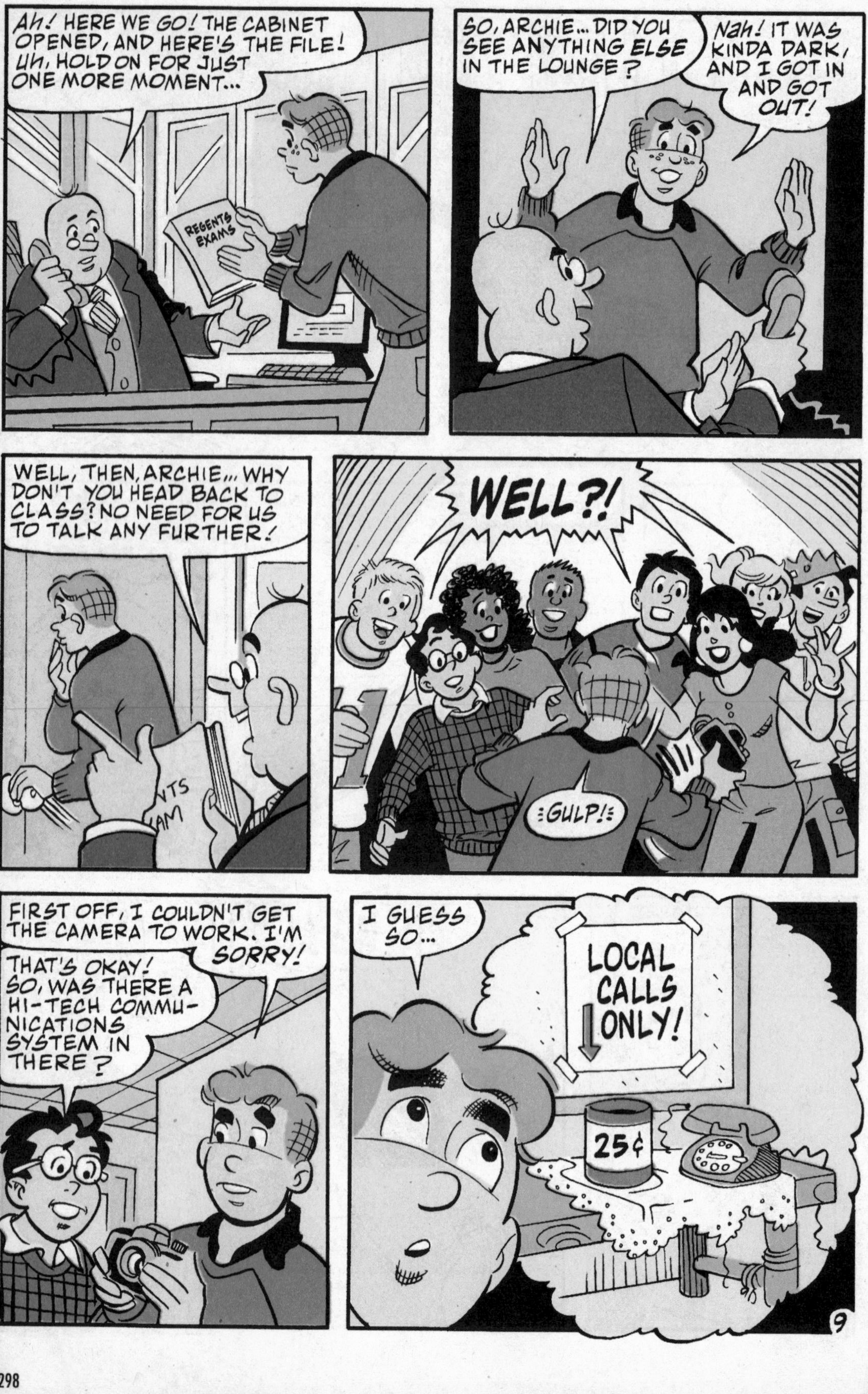
Ah! HERE WE GO! THE CABINET OPENED, AND HERE'S THE FILE! Uh, HOLD ON FOR JUST ONE MORE MOMENT...
REGENTS EXAMS
SO, ARCHIE... DID YOU SEE ANYTHING ELSE IN THE LOUNGE?
Nah! IT WAS KINDA DARK, AND I GOT IN AND GOT OUT!
WELL, THEN, ARCHIE... WHY DON'T YOU HEAD BACK TO CLASS? NO NEED FOR US TO TALK ANY FURTHER!
WELL?!
GULP!
FIRST OFF, I COULDN'T GET THE CAMERA TO WORK. I'M SORRY!
THAT'S OKAY! SO, WAS THERE A HI-TECH COMMUNICATIONS SYSTEM IN THERE?
I GUESS SO...
LOCAL CALLS ONLY!
25¢
9

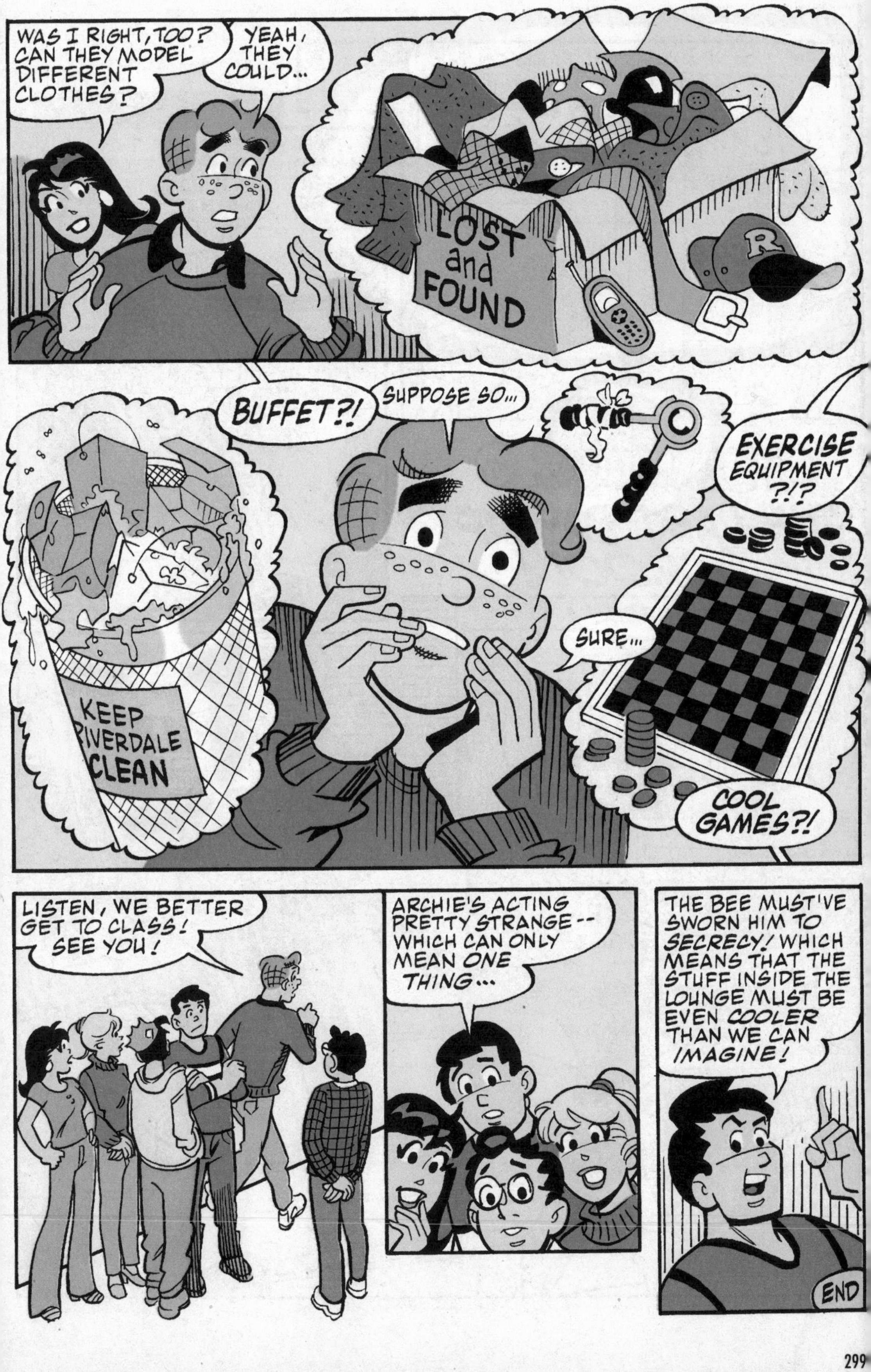
WAS I RIGHT, TOO? CAN THEY MODEL DIFFERENT CLOTHES?
YEAH, THEY COULD...
LOST and FOUND
R
BUFFET?!
SUPPOSE SO...
EXERCISE EQUIPMENT ?!?
SURE...
KEEP RIVERDALE CLEAN
COOL GAMES?!
LISTEN, WE BETTER GET TO CLASS! SEE YOU!
ARCHIE'S ACTING PRETTY STRANGE -- WHICH CAN ONLY MEAN ONE THING...
THE BEE MUST'VE SWORN HIM TO SECRECY! WHICH MEANS THAT THE STUFF INSIDE THE LOUNGE MUST BE EVEN COOLER THAN WE CAN IMAGINE!
END

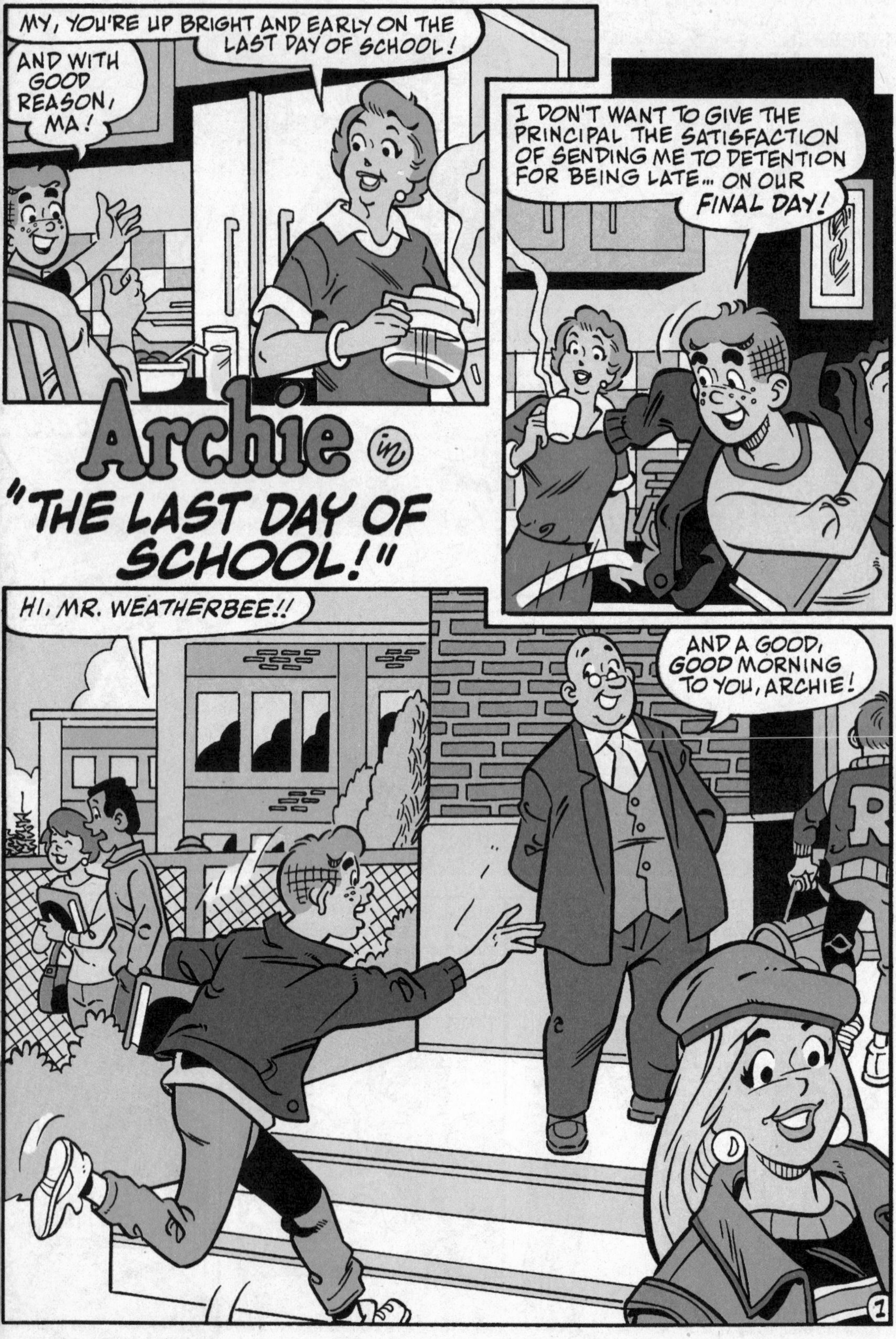
MY, YOU'RE UP BRIGHT AND EARLY ON THE LAST DAY OF SCHOOL!
AND WITH GOOD REASON, MA!
I DON'T WANT TO GIVE THE PRINCIPAL THE SATISFACTION OF SENDING ME TO DETENTION FOR BEING LATE... ON OUR FINAL DAY!
Archie in
"THE LAST DAY OF SCHOOL!"
HI, MR. WEATHERBEE!!
AND A GOOD, GOOD MORNING TO YOU, ARCHIE!
R
1

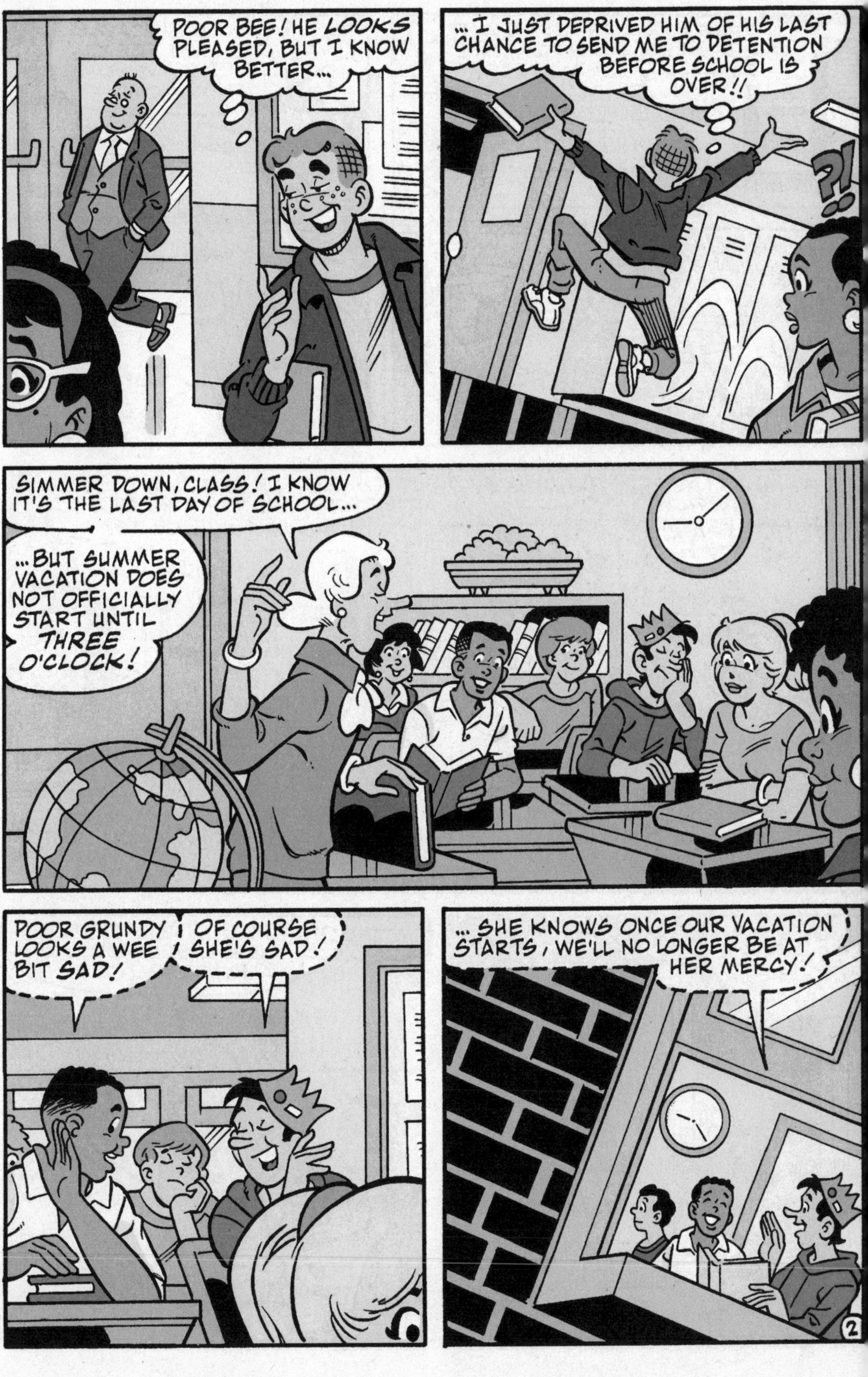
POOR BEE! HE LOOKS PLEASED, BUT I KNOW BETTER...
... I JUST DEPRIVED HIM OF HIS LAST CHANCE TO SEND ME TO DETENTION BEFORE SCHOOL IS OVER!!
?!
SIMMER DOWN, CLASS! I KNOW IT'S THE LAST DAY OF SCHOOL...
...BUT SUMMER VACATION DOES NOT OFFICIALLY START UNTIL THREE O'CLOCK!
POOR GRUNDY LOOKS A WEE BIT SAD!
OF COURSE SHE'S SAD!
... SHE KNOWS ONCE OUR VACATION STARTS, WE'LL NO LONGER BE AT HER MERCY!
2

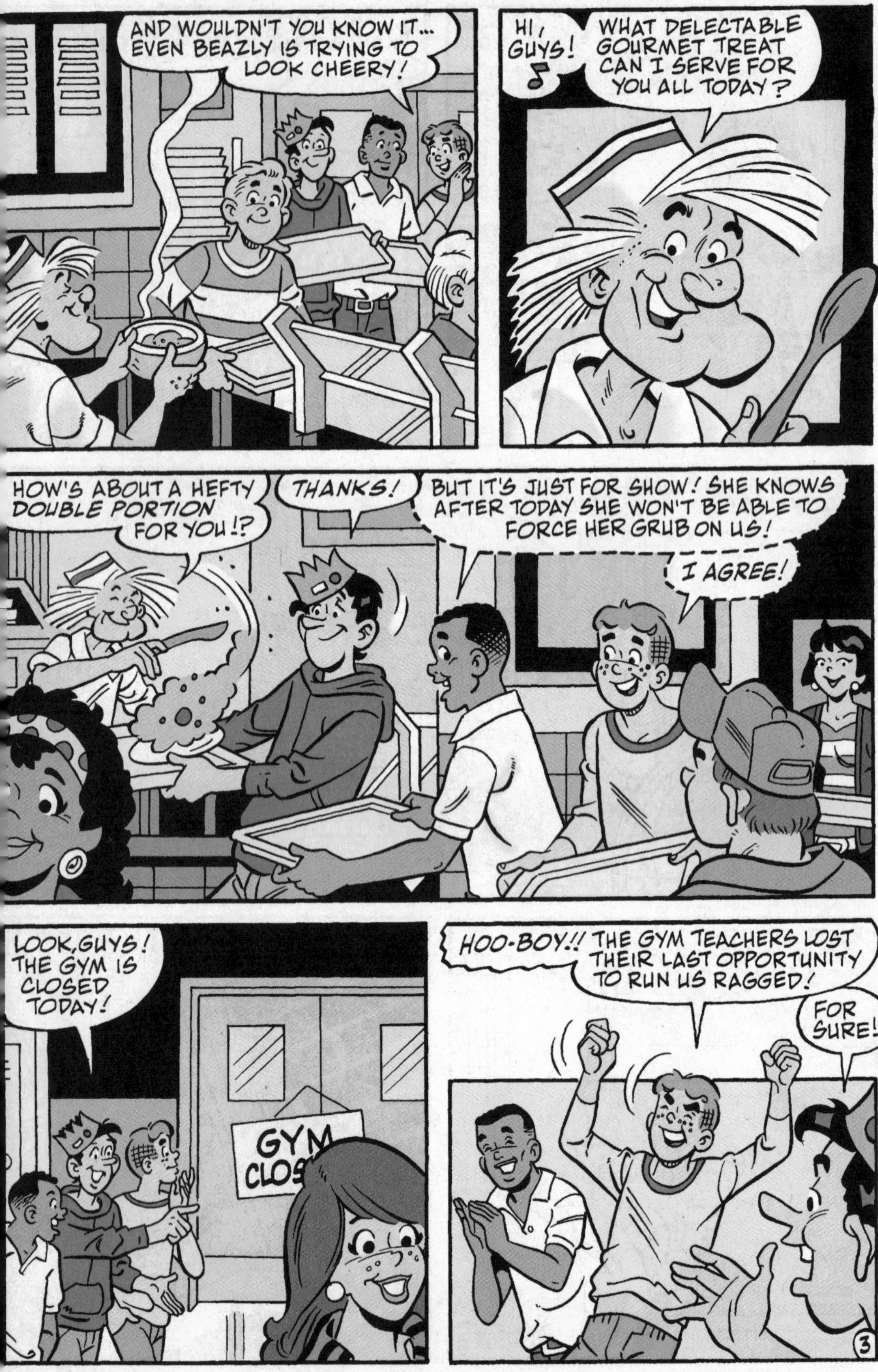
AND WOULDN'T YOU KNOW IT... EVEN BEAZLY IS TRYING TO LOOK CHEERY!
HI, GUYS!
WHAT DELECTABLE GOURMET TREAT CAN I SERVE FOR YOU ALL TODAY?
HOW'S ABOUT A HEFTY DOUBLE PORTION FOR YOU!?
THANKS!
BUT IT'S JUST FOR SHOW! SHE KNOWS AFTER TODAY SHE WON'T BE ABLE TO FORCE HER GRUB ON US!
I AGREE!
LOOK, GUYS! THE GYM IS CLOSED TODAY!
GYM CLOS
HOO-BOY!! THE GYM TEACHERS LOST THEIR LAST OPPORTUNITY TO RUN US RAGGED!
FOR SURE!
3

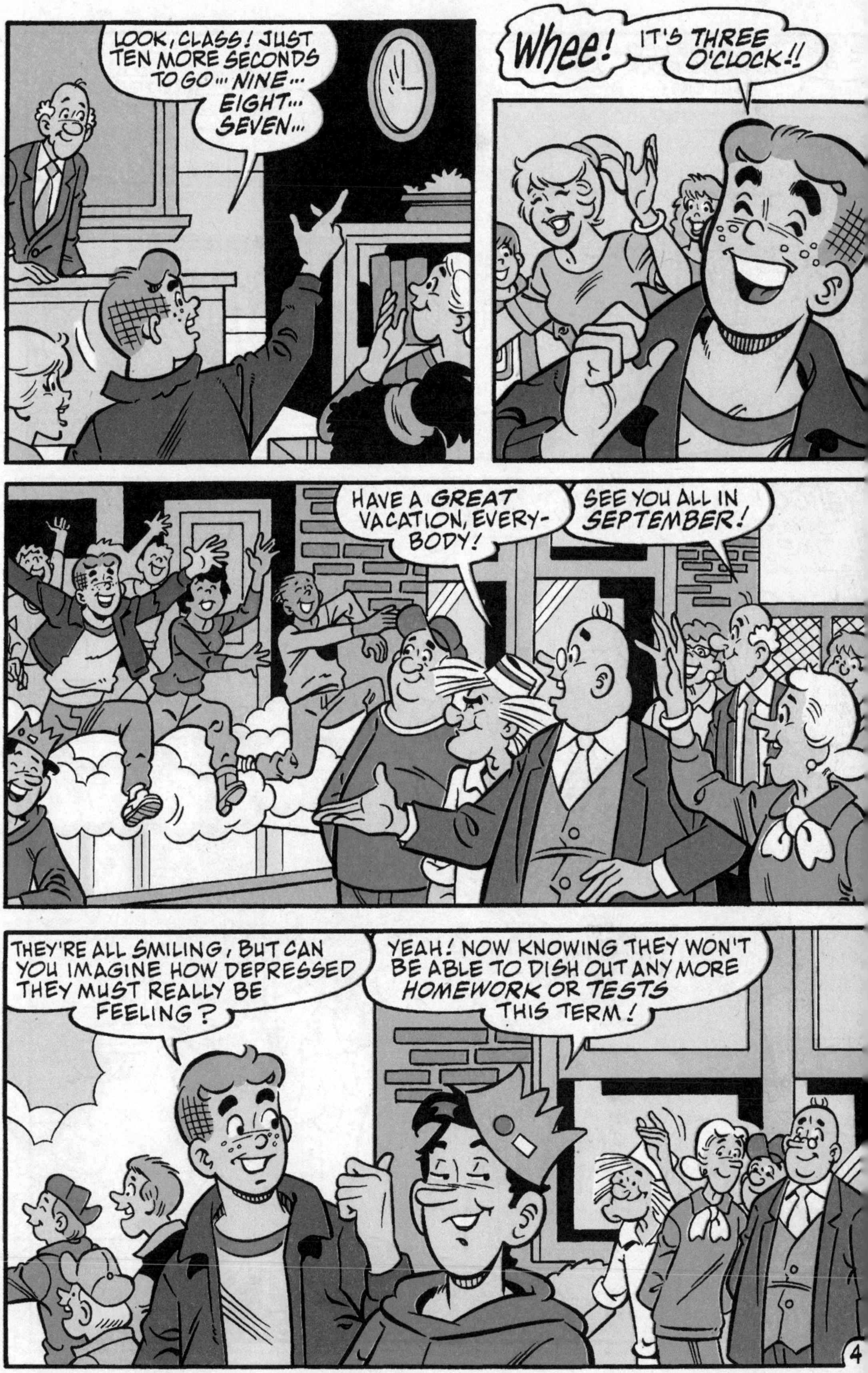
LOOK, CLASS! JUST TEN MORE SECONDS TO GO... NINE... EIGHT... SEVEN...
Whee!
IT'S THREE O'CLOCK!!
HAVE A GREAT VACATION, EVERY-BODY!
SEE YOU ALL IN SEPTEMBER!
THEY'RE ALL SMILING, BUT CAN YOU IMAGINE HOW DEPRESSED THEY MUST REALLY BE FEELING?
YEAH! NOW KNOWING THEY WON'T BE ABLE TO DISH OUT ANY MORE HOMEWORK OR TESTS THIS TERM!
4

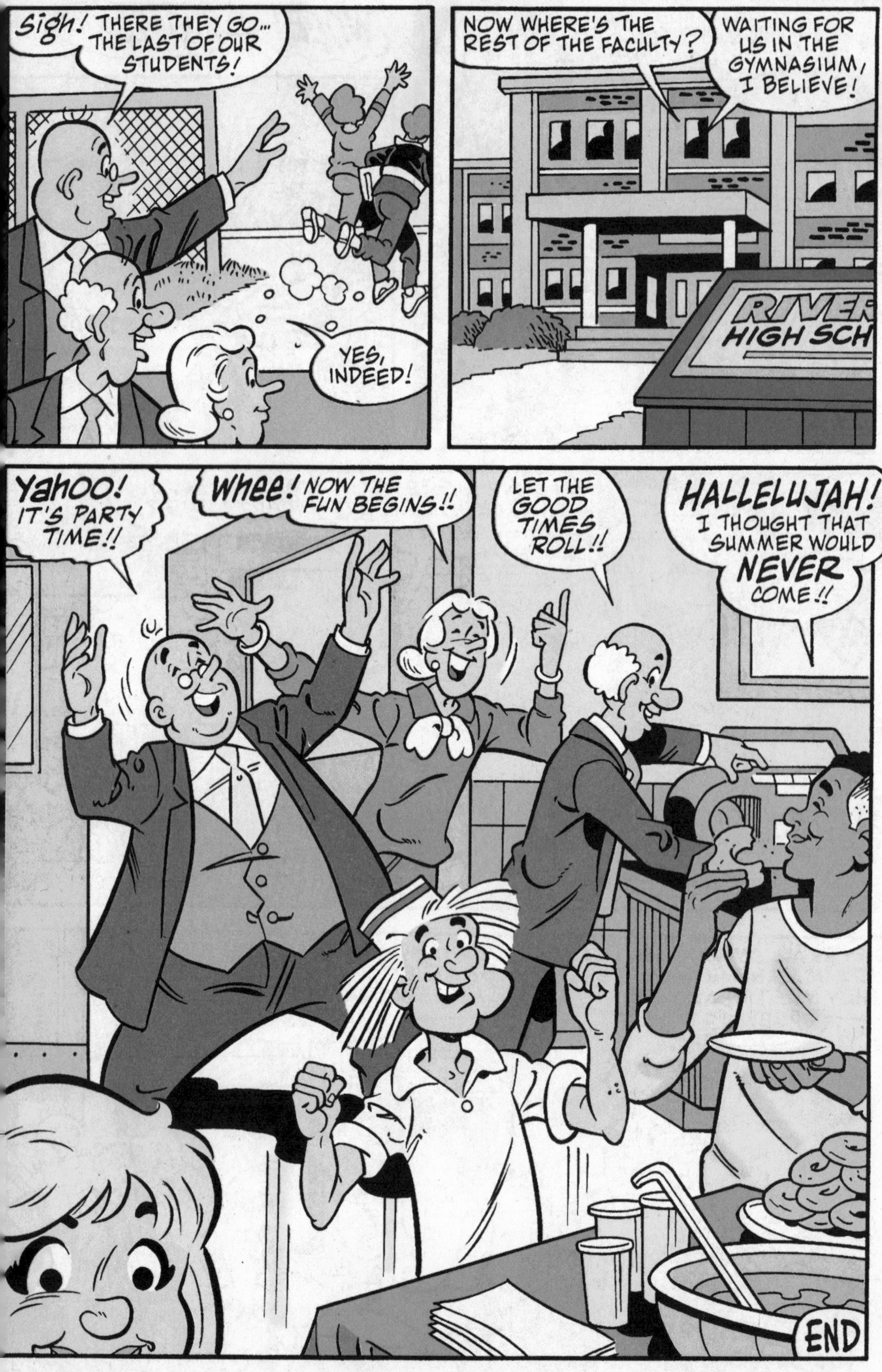
Sigh! THERE THEY GO... THE LAST OF OUR STUDENTS!
YES, INDEED!
NOW WHERE'S THE REST OF THE FACULTY?
WAITING FOR US IN THE GYMNASIUM, I BELIEVE!
RIVER
HIGH SCH
Yahoo! IT'S PARTY TIME!!
Whee! NOW THE FUN BEGINS!!
LET THE GOOD TIMES ROLL!!
HALLELUJAH! I THOUGHT THAT SUMMER WOULD NEVER COME!!
END